A of Thread GOLD

A Three Century Search for a Colorado Gold Bonanza

BY R. REED JOHNSON

D0957291

WESTERN REFLECTIONS PUBLISHING COMPANY®
Montrose, CO

© 2005 R. Reed Johnson
All rights reserved in whole or in part.

ISBN-13: 978-1-932738-12-4
ISBN-10: 1-932738-12-6

Library of Congress Control Number: 2005932421

First Edition
Printed in the United States of America

Cover illustration: *Harper's New Monthly Magazine*
No. CXIX, April, 1860, p. 599
Published by Harper & Brothers, Franklin Square, New York.

Western Reflections Publishing Company®
219 Main Street
Montrose, CO 81401
www.westernreflectionspub.com

PREFACE

At the onset of my writing, in compliance with the wishes of my lovely wife, Tee, I fully intended this to be an autobiography, and for a short period of time that is what it was. However, I soon became bored by the humdrum happenings of my own life. At that same time, I was reading a book entitled *Bayou Salado*, written by Virginia McConnell Simmons and containing a fascinating account of the early history of Colorado's South Park region. A number of factual events recounted by Ms. Simmons stimulated my interest, and after I finished reading it, I resolved to change course somewhat and write a novel in which I combine some of my personal experiences on a farm south of Littleton, Colorado, in the 1930s with several lesser-known events that span parts of three centuries of Colorado, New Mexico, and Texas history. These I hoped to weave into a novel, the fabric of which is stitched together by a fabulously rich bonanza, hence the title, *A Thread of Gold*.

By writing it I hoped also to ignite in the reader's mind an avid interest in the remarkable early day history of this part of the American West as well as an appreciation of the hardships our forebears endured with such great fortitude. The result of my effort is what you will read in this book. If, after reading it, you are interested further you might enjoy reading the "Fact or Fiction" section that follows the epilogue. In it, I differentiate some of the facts in the story from fiction. Also included is a list of references from which I gleaned a great deal of fascinating information.

I sincerely hope that all those who read this novel will enjoy reading it even half as much as I have enjoyed writing it.

R. Reed Johnson

ACKNOWLEDGEMENTS

Before relating my story, I wish to thank a number of individuals and institutions for their help in writing it. First and foremost of these is my patient and long-suffering wife, Tee. It has taken me well over twelve years to research, write, and edit this novel, interspersed with innumerable delays for deletions, corrections, and hunt-and-peck revisions. A much longer pause would come with the onset of spring each year, when I would stop writing and go to work in our garden until the winter cold drove me back to my computer. Through all of this, Tee has been remarkably tolerant and helpful, although I fear that the many hours she spent in proofreading may have strained her patience at times — if not our marriage.

My elder son, Randy, a true computer expert, has equipped me with updated computers and patiently instructed me in how to use them, and then straightening out the many messes I'd get myself in. I'm grateful to him and also to his wife, Carol, who has helped me by proofreading and editing my novel, and by acquainting me with the complexities of publishing and marketing my novel. My two other children, Pamela Hay and Brad Johnson and their spouses, Trey and Patti, as well as my five grandchildren have also provided much appreciated support and encouragement, as has my brother, Julius, the "J. J." of my story.

I'm very grateful also to the following friends for their help and support — and for reading an earlier and much longer version of my story. The late Doctor Richard Hawes, besides urging me to read *Bayou Salado*, also persistently encouraged me to persevere in my writing. And Doctor Seymour Wheelock has helped me immensely by giving freely of his advice and editing skills as well as by creating the fine sketches that are used throughout the book. An old high school friend, Murray Thomas, a retired dean of education at the University of California at Santa Barbara and a writer himself, has provided ongoing support as well as valuable advice on the complexities of writing and publishing. He also revised Colonel Anza's campaign map, making it much easier to interpret. My sincere thanks to Doctor Keith McDonald for his advice and editing suggestions; and to Wayne and Mardie Van Arsdale; Doctor Homer and Mary Cowen; Doctor Bill Ziegler, his daughter Retta, and her husband, Mark Dunn; Doctor Prather Ashe; Doctor Tom Mahoney; Doctor Howard Kelsall; Reverend Howard Childers; and Eunice Ogier for their ongoing encouragement and support after reading the early version of my novel. Doctor Henry Toll also helped me by reading and critiquing the earlier draft of the book and by obtaining permission from the Denver Westerners, allowing me to use and to alter the Colorado map found at the beginning of Part 3. Two editors, Karen Nicholson and Bonnie Beach, have helped me greatly in the final edit of my novel, as has Barbara Munson, an excellent editor and publisher — I thank them all.

I am especially indebted to Becky Lintz, the director of the Stephen H. Hart Library of the Colorado Historic Society in Denver, for providing many of the pictures and historical maps in the novel. She has helped me immensely. I am equally indebted to Lorena Donohue, the curator and deputy director of the Littleton Historical Museum, for her ongoing support and for providing pictures of early day Littleton. Nancy Fagan and the other librarians of the Bemis Library in Littleton have been very helpful in locating the many reference books and maps that I have consulted. I thank them and I thank all the librarians at the Western History Division of the Denver Public Library for their kind help in finding some of the photographs used in the novel.

I'm also indebted to Mr. Dan Miller, the owner of the Signal Graphics franchise in southwest Englewood, for his expert help in printing the preliminary version of my story. And finally I thank Luther Wilson, director of the University of New Mexico Press, and Sandra Bond, a Denver literary agent, for their sound advice on editing. I also thank Sandra for suggesting that I submit my novel to Western Reflections Publishing Company in Montrose, Colorado. The publisher, Mr. P. David Smith, and his associate, Carole London, are experts in their field and very knowledgeable and pleasant people with whom to work.

I apologize if I have inadvertently overlooked anyone.
R. Reed Johnson

AUTHOR'S NOTE

This is the story of three pairs of brothers and how their lives intertwine, even though each pair lives in a different century — eighteenth, nineteenth and twentieth — and comes from a different territory or province of the western United States — namely Texas, Colorado, and the Spanish province of New Mexico. The thread of gold that binds these six lives together is their search for a fabulously rich bonanza that lay hidden in the rugged Lost Creek Canyon in the Tarryall Mountains of Colorado. Their experiences are set within historical conditions and events that the brothers encounter — each in their own time and place.

Parts of the story are written in a narrative fashion, and some of the language is spoken in a dialect as it might have been used by an unschooled back-country rancher, farmer, or miner. Much of PARTS TWO AND FOUR of the novel is related from the perspective of an eleven-year-old boy and written in a manner more or less compatible with his age. Other parts, however — particularly the descriptive passages — are expressed more by words as they might be spoken by an adult in order to better portray the image or feeling the author wishes to convey. If the reader doesn't realize this to begin with, he or she might be confused as to who it is doing the talking.

R. Reed Johnson

❧ PART ONE ❧

NORTHERN NEW MEXICO AND LOWER SOUTHEASTERN COLORADO AUGUST 1779 TO THE SPRING OF 1780

Juan Bautista de Anza. A picture drawn from a portrait in oil by Fray Orsi in 1774 on page 316 volume 1, History of California, *by Zoeth Skinner Eldredge. New York, The Century History Company, 1915. The authenticity of the picture is being questioned because the beard and plumed hat were not in vogue at the time it was drawn. It is currently under investigation.*
(Courtesy of The Center for Advanced Technology in Education, The University of Oregon, Eugene, OR)

CHAPTER 1

Silent and still as the rocks that surrounded them, the two brothers stood on the summit of a high sierra in the northern reaches of the Spanish province of New Mexico. The hot midday sun blazed down upon them as they carefully inspected the surrounding hills and valleys for any sign of movement. Except for the silent flight of two majestic eagles soaring in the thermals high above their heads and the occasional flick of their horses' tails as they whisked away an annoying fly, everything was quiet. Far below and miles to the south of them, a yellow haze of dust hovered above the valley floor, marking the advance of a ragtag army led by Lieutenant Colonel Don Juan Bautista de Anza, the current governor and commandant of the Province of New Mexico. The vast region was so named in the 1500s after the Spanish had captured the territory and declared it to be a possession of Spain.

Juan and Pedro Vasquez were scouts for the army. Juan, the older of the two, was a man in his late twenties, of medium height, stocky, and powerfully built. His jet-black hair with matching eyes accented his swarthy, sunburned countenance. He appeared to be a man of great strength and dependability, an impression enhanced by his firm, squared jaw, now covered by a week's growth of beard. Pedro presented a sharp contrast. Indeed, upon seeing them side by side, no one would have suspected that they were related, let alone brothers. Although two years younger than Juan, Pedro was fully six inches taller and as slender as a sapling. His skin was fair, reflecting the Castilian ancestry of their mother. He was deeply tanned, his eyes blue, and his hair the color of gold. He moved with the grace of a dancer that concealed the surprising strength of his lean muscles.

Scouting was what Juan and Pedro liked to do best, and they were good at it. They both could read animal and Indian signs better than most folks could read books. Rarely did anything escape their attention.

Five days ago on Sunday, August the fifteenth, Juan and Pedro had accompanied Governor Anza and eighty-five Spanish soldiers as they marched twelve leagues northward along the Camino Real from

Santa Fe to an encampment in the Wood of San Juan de los Caballeros. There, the colonel ordered a halt in order to assemble the balance of his troops before proceeding on his campaign. Immediately upon their arrival, he dispatched Juan and Pedro with orders to scout along his intended route for any sign of the Comanche renegades that had been wreaking havoc in the northern reaches of the Province of New Mexico. They were to rejoin the army four days hence — sooner if they had something to report.

Several attempts to quell the Comanche attacks had been made by Don Pedro Fermin de Mendinueta, the prior governor of New Mexico, and by his predecessors, but all had met with failure. In the fall of 1778, Anza was appointed governor, replacing de Mendinueta, and now, almost a year later, he was setting forth on a determined effort to rid the country of the Comanche scourge.

Comanche Warchief
(A pen and ink drawing by Doctor Seymour Wheelock)

For many years, the warlike Comanche had ravaged the Spanish settlements and farms throughout the vast Province of New Mexico. Most recently, however, their attacks had concentrated on the valley of the Rio Grande del Norte. Leaving their well-guarded families in rancherias hidden in the coulees and draws of the grass-covered plains east of the Sangre de Cristo Mountains, the fierce Comanche warriors ranged far and wide, pillaging and killing with a barbarity that cast terror into the hearts of the settlers. Nor were members of other Indian tribes spared their savagery. The Ute, Apache, and Navajo were avowed enemies of the Comanche, as their many bloody battles attested.

One Comanche leader stood out above all the others in daring and bravery as well as ferocity. His name was Cuerno Verde (Greenhorn), the celebrated war chief of the Comanche. He was so named by the old men of the Comanche council because he was bold, daring, and fearless, like a young buck deer whose antlers were still green with velvet. Cuerno Verde's consuming hatred of the Spaniards was born the moment they had killed his father in battle. Seeking revenge, he had destroyed many pueblos and farms, massacring hundreds with a cold fury.

Governor Mendinueta had made a valiant but unsuccessful attempt to curb this cunning enemy, and the lot now fell to his successor. Don Juan de Anza willingly picked up the gauntlet. Both his father and grandfather had campaigned against the Indians in years past, and some of the governor's own family had been brutally killed in a Comanche raid. So not surprisingly, hatred of the Comanche burned as deeply in his heart as did hatred of the Spanish in Cuerno Verde's, and for much the same reason.

Early in the morning on the twentieth day of August, Colonel Anza, along with 573 variously equipped soldiers, settlers, and Indians left the encampment and crossed over to the west side of the Rio Grande del Norte. From there they intended to proceed in a north-northwesterly direction, staying well to the west of the Rio Grande del Norte and taking precautions to avoid being discovered. All previous campaigns had gone north up the Rio Grande del Norte valley and then eastward over a pass in the Taos Mountains into the Great Plains — the home of the Comanche. Without exception, their quarry, having been forewarned, escaped.

This was the day Juan and Pedro were to report to Colonel Anza, and they had little to relate, for they had found no evidence of Indian activity, either friendly or hostile. But that would soon change. It was midafternoon when Pedro called Juan's attention to a cloud of dust rising from the valley of the Rio de los Conejos valley several leagues to the north. But what was causing it? From where they were standing they couldn't be sure. It might only be a herd of buffalo milling about in the valley, but, what was just as likely and far more worrisome, it might be a Comanche war party on their way to attack Colonel Anza's army. Fearing the latter, the brothers mounted their horses and rode

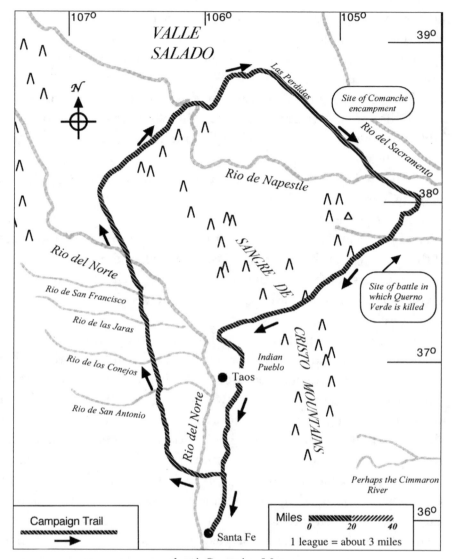

Anza's Campaign Map

(Modified and redrawn by Murray Thomas Ph.D., a retired dean of Educational Psychology from Stanford University.)

northward as rapidly as they dared without stirring up a telltale dust cloud of their own.

Shortly before sundown, Juan and Pedro approached a ridge overlooking the Rio de los Conejos. Dismounting, they cautiously led their horses to a vantage point where they looked down upon a startling sight. An Indian war party, numbering in the hundreds, was hurrying to set up camp before they were overtaken by darkness. But who were they? And to what nation did they belong? Were they Ute, Apache, Navaho, or the dreaded Comanche? From this distance they couldn't be sure.

Tying their mounts to a nearby tree, the brothers slowly crept closer until the Indians were no more than three hundred feet below them. After studying them carefully for a few moments, Juan heaved a great sigh of relief.

"They're Utes," he whispered. "The tall fellow standing by that big rock is Moara, the war chief of the Mouache. His son, Pinto, is standing on his right, and the powerfully built Indian next to him is the war chief of the Jicarilla Apaches. I'm sure you remember, Pedro, you met all three of them at that meeting in Santa Fe when the Ute and Jicarilla Apache leaders came to ask the governor for his help in putting an end to Cuerno Verde's raids. They must be on their way to join the colonel right now."

Remounting their horses, the brothers slowly worked their way down to the valley floor with their muskets held high above their heads in a gesture of peace. As they drew near to the Indian encampment, Juan called out to them in their own language, assuring them that he and Pedro had come in peace and asking that they be taken to Chief Moara. As they approached, the chiefs recognized them and welcomed them by clasping their arms in a gesture of friendship. Chief Moara was a tall, muscular man in the prime of his life. His handsome face and brow were accentuated by an aquiline nose set between two piercing black eyes, framed by jet-black hair that fell to his shoulders in two long braids. Pinto was the same age as Juan, and, while he wasn't as striking in appearance as his father, he was nonetheless handsome. His hair was black like Moara's, but his skin was much lighter and, surprisingly, his eyes were blue.

After their initial greetings, Juan explained to the chiefs that their war party need go no farther for Colonel Anza and his army would be joining them on the following day. That evening the brothers enjoyed the food and hospitality of their Indian hosts, and the following morning at daybreak they left to inform Colonel Anza that his Ute and Apache allies were awaiting his arrival in the Rio de los Conejos valley.

It was midafternoon on the following day when Anza's army arrived at the Indian encampment, and, within minutes of their arrival, the colonel, Chief Moara, and the Apache war chiefs met to discuss and decide how best to proceed from there in order to catch Cuerno Verde by surprise. With Juan acting as interpreter, the colonel outlined the route he proposed they take on the campaign. After listening carefully to his suggestions and adding some of their own, the chiefs agreed. Following that, the colonel explained to the Indians that they and their warriors were to be subject to his orders — a stipulation to which they also readily agreed.

Early the next morning, the army resumed its advance, marching north-northeast over very rough terrain until they reached the Rio de las Jaras. Following Chief Moara's advice, for the next four days they marched only at night to avoid being seen by an enemy scout from atop an overlooking mountain. Two nights later they entered a wide valley bordered by lofty mountains on either side, and on the morning of the twenty-fifth of August, eleven days out of Santa Fe, they arrived at an arroyo the colonel named Santa Xines. Immediately upon their arrival, Colonel Anza, Chief Moara, and the Apache chiefs met to discuss and decide how best to proceed from there. Chief Moara advised that they continue going north past the Rio de Napestle and over a small mountain range into a vast, open valley called "The Valle Salado" — so named by the early Spanish explorers because of a large salt deposit near its west side. Upon reaching the park, the army should then head eastward to the foot of the Sierra Almagre and, from there, proceed in a southeasterly direction, skirting the south side of a lofty, snow-capped mountain and entering into the great plains — the homeland of the Comanche.

Considering it good advice, Colonel Anza ordered Juan and Pedro to scout out a good route for the army to follow. Should they see any sign of the Comanche, they were to return at once and report to the colonel; otherwise they were to rejoin the army while it was en route on the following day.

Accordingly, after a short rest, the brothers left on their assignment. Riding rapidly to the northern end of the valley, they ascended to the summit of a pass where they sat in their saddles and looked with awe at a range of mighty mountains — one lofty peak after another, stretching into the north, seemingly without end. The Rio de Napestle bordered it on the east. After a brief pause to eat and rest, the brothers descended a narrow ravine into the valley and, after fording the river, continued to ride northward over a low range of mountains and into the southern end of the vast Valle Salado. From there they headed eastward in the direction of the Sierra del Almagre.

As they drew near to the mountains, they came upon a small, sheltered valley where there was abundant grass and water. It was a pleasant spot, and because it would soon be dark they set up camp for the night. By leaving early the following morning, they could easily rejoin the army and report to Colonel Anza before he reached the Valle Salado. That evening, as Juan and Pedro were setting up camp, they were startled to hear a deep raspy voice utter a gruff greeting.

"Buenos dias, amigos."

Taken completely by surprise, both brothers grabbed for their muskets, searching at the same time for the source of the gravel-throated greeting. There, no more than twenty feet away, stood a small, bearded man dressed in dirty buckskins and wearing a disreputable looking fur hat. Two observant blue eyes peered from beneath the cap and above a craggy nose, which was largely engulfed by a magnificent gray beard that covered his entire upper chest — matched by an even longer mane of white hair extending down his back.

"Buenos dias." The old man said a second time as he stood cradling his musket in his arms. The brothers were astounded. How long had this old man been standing there, and how had he come so close to them without warning? It was as though he had sprung from out of the earth. After drawing near to their campfire, the old man apologized for giving them such a start.

"Sorry I snuck up on you boys like that, but my eyesight ain't what it used to be, and I had to be shore you fellas was friendly afore I let you know I was here. My name's Silas Smith, and I's camped in the bottom of an arroyo no more than thirty yards to the east of here. But what in God's green earth are you two hombres doing in these parts? I never expected to run into a white man 'til I got down 'round Taos way."

"My brother and I are scouts for Colonel Juan Bautista de Anza," Juan explained. "He's the commander of an army of soldiers, settlers, and Indians that is trying to find Cuerno Verde and his warriors so he can put and end to their killing."

"Wal, I wish you luck. I's heard plenty of stories about that miserable varmit and I reckon they's all bad. So far I ain't never met up with him, and I hope and pray I never do. By the way, where do you boys hail from?"

"We're from Santa Fe," Pedro answered.

"Wal now, that's damned peculiar. Me and my family have been livin' there for the past ten years. So how come I've never run into you two fellas afore now? 'Course, most fall, winter, and springs I's off huntin' or trappin', but I spend most all my summers in Santa Fe, so it's funny we haven't met up with each other 'til now."

"Probably it's because Pedro and I scout for the military during the summers, and we're away a lot of the time. But how does it happen that you and your family are living in Santa Fe? There aren't many Anglos in these parts. I've only met two or three in my entire life."

Smith smiled, "Wal, I reckon I makes it either three or four. My daddy was a merchant in Nouvelle Orleans when it was a French settlement back in the early 1700s. That's where I growed up. But when the French sold Nouvelle Orleans to Spain in 1762, my folks decided to go back to England. But I stayed, and later on me and some of my Spanish buddies moved to Mexico City. That's where I met and married my pretty Spanish wife. Then, back in '69, when the governor asked for volunteers to help settle the Province of New Mexico, me and my family moved to Santa Fe, and we's been livin' there ever since. I's kept busy takin' care of my wife and eight kids, 'long with hunting and trapping. It's been a good life, I reckon, but it's been a hard one, too.

"You know, if'n I was you boys, I reckon I'd move yore camp over closer to mine. That way you'll have some shelter from the storm what's acomin' this way."

"What makes you think a storm's coming, Smith?" Pedro asked.

"Take a gander up yonder, boys." And he waved his arm towards the north. "See them black cloud banks buildin' up over the upper end of the valley? They's chock full of snow and they's headin' our way."

After thanking him for the warning, Juan and Pedro moved into the arroyo and tethered their horses near the three burros belonging to Smith. Then they joined the old man by his campfire.

"You know, it shore pleasures me to talk to you boys. I ain't had nobody to talk to for going on ten months now, 'ceptin' my burros, and they ain't too good at palaverin'. 'Course, I reckon you boys already knows I's a trapper," and he pointed to the stacks of dried animal pelts bordering his camp. "It's been close to a year since I left Santa Fe. Most all of last fall, winter, and spring I spent trappin' — mainly for beaver pelts but some bear and cougar, too. I's pretty much been all over these here parts — mainly workin' up the streams and river valleys. Now I's headin' back to Santa Fe afore the winter snows shut down the mountain passes.

"The reason I's so late goin' back this year is on account of my findin' gold in a little crick t'other side of them mountains." He nodded in the direction of the Sierra del Almagre. "I spent the last two months pannin' in a little stream I calls 'Lost Crick' — found some pretty damned good nuggets too."

To prove his point, the old man removed a small leather bag hanging by a thong around his neck and poured five gold nuggets into the palm of his hand, each one the size of a pigeon egg or larger. The brothers gaped in wonder as they watched him put the nuggets back into the bag and carefully tuck it under his beard. When it was securely in place, Smith continued his narrative.

"I figured all them nuggets must be comin' from a mother lode somewheres further on up the crick, but damned if I could ever find it. I wasted a passel of time lookin' for it. It must be a big one, though, judging from all the gold what's in the crick.

"Why, I's heard tell of some lodes what's nothin' but solid gold, ten feet or more wide and goin' back hundreds of feet into the mountain. I wouldn't be a bit surprised but what this here lode is one of them big ones — maybe real big."

The more the old man talked, the more excited the brothers became. All of their lives, Juan and Pedro had heard stories of fabulous deposits of gold called bonanzas, but they had never actually met anyone who had found one or, as in this case, was sure that he knew where one was.

So they plied the old trapper with questions until finally he laughed and said, "You know, seein' as how you boys are so damned interested, I reckon I'd be happy to tell you how to get to the crick where I found the gold. I shore as hell ain't never goin' back there again, that's for damned shore. I's too old, and besides, I jest ain't cut out for muckin' around in the dirt like a damned mole or freezin' my legs off in hip-deep, icy cold water. It makes my bones hurt somethin' awful, and I's gettin' bad rheumatiz in my knees. Besides that, I shore ain't a greedy man. I's already got all the gold I need."

Juan and Pedro could scarcely believe all that the old trapper had told them, or that he had so freely shown them his nuggets — even where he kept them hidden. But they were even more surprised by his offer to tell them how to find the stream where he'd found the nuggets. As he was talking, the same idea struck them both. If, as they hoped, the campaign against Cuerno Verde ended soon, they might be able to explore the region where Smith found the gold and get the lay of the land before going back to Santa Fe. Then, if it looked promising, they could return the following spring and look for the bonanza.

After a brief discussion, Juan told the old man, "Silas, Pedro and I would like to take you up on your offer, but are you sure you or someone in your family won't want to go there and look for the lode someday?"

"I's damned shore," the old man said firmly. "Like I told you, I shore as hell ain't goin' there no more, and I don't want nobody in my family goin' there neither. It's jest too damn dangerous. In fact, come to think of it, you boys best think twice about goin' there yoreselves — 'specially this late in the year." But Juan and Pedro were not to be dissuaded; they assured Smith that they really wanted to go and that they would be very careful when they did.

"Wal, I reckon I'll tell how to find it then, but I shore hope you don't regret it. Now this is how you get there. First off, you head north to the upper end of the Valle Salado, then turn east and climb to a pass at the far end of the Sierra del Amalgre. From there, turn south and go down the divide 'til you come to a little lake what's got a crick runnin' out of it. That's the headwaters of 'Lost Crick,' and if you follow it down, you'll come to the pretty meadow I calls 'Lost Park.' After the crick leaves the meadow, it runs into a narrow canyon chock-full of monstrous big rocks what's fallen off'n a cliff higher up on the mountain. That's the roughest damned country I's ever had the misfortune of bein' in. Some of them rocks is ten times bigger than my house back in Santa Fe, and that damned crick keeps goin' in and out from under them. That's how come I calls it Lost Crick.

"I was lookin' for beaver sign, but half the time I couldn't even find the crick, let alone any beaver. But I shore seen more'n my share of bear and cougar. They was bent on makin' a meal out of my burros — most likely out of me, too. The stretch of the crick where I found the gold is no more'n three, maybe four miles downstream from the meadow, give or take a half mile — 'cept'n it seemed like a hundred. The first nuggets I found was in a stretch of quiet water a little downstream from a place where the crick comes out of a cave-like opening between the rocks into the upper end of a big open valley. After that, I kept pannin' the crick in the upper end of the meadow, and by late afternoon I'd found bet-ter'n two ounces of flakes and a whole bunch more nuggets.

"Then, I spent three more weeks tryin' to find the mother lode, and I reckon I might have found it if'n it warn't for seven or eight Comanche braves checkin' out my last night's campsite. And it was a damned good thing I seen them before they spotted me. If'n I hadn't, I reckon I wouldn't be here talkin' to you fellas now. But it was almost dark when I seen them, so I hid out amongst the rocks all the rest of that night. Next morning, right at first light, I lit out and, like I said, I ain't never goin' back."

As they were talking, it had grown much colder. The wind had risen and a few snowflakes stung their faces, announcing the arrival of the storm the old trapper had predicted. Rolling up in their bedrolls, they quickly fell asleep.

The morning of August the twenty-eighth, all three awakened and brushed the light coating of snow from their bedrolls before climbing out into the frigid air. Speaking only when necessary, they set about building a fire and preparing a meager breakfast.

After they'd eaten, Juan and Pedro were preparing to leave when the old trapper announced, "You know boys, I's been thinkin'. If'n it's all right with you, I reckon I'll stay here and wait 'til the army shows up. I figure I can be of some help in roundin' up that old renegade, Cuerno Verde. And, besides that, I reckon I'll be a damned site safer if'n I was to ride with the army on my way back to Santa Fe. I'm shore the colonel won't mind none 'cause a few years back I was the sutler for one of his campaigns, and before that I was a scout for Governor Mendinueta."

After assuring Smith that the colonel would be pleased to have him join his army, the brothers mounted their horses, said goodbye to the old man, and rode toward the south end of the Valle Salado and their appointed rendezvous.

CHAPTER 2

It was the middle of the afternoon when they rejoined the army and made their report to Colonel Anza. Upon hearing it, he ordered the army to press on to the sheltered valley. It was evening when they arrived, and darkness overtook them as they were setting up camp. That night, the fog and snow grew in intensity, as did the discomfort of the troops. The army was ninety-five leagues from Santa Fe, the most northern point of their march, and the colonel called it "Las Lomas Perdidas" because of all the problems they had encountered there.

The following day the weather was miserable and so were the men. Nevertheless, on the colonel's orders, at eight in the morning they resumed their march and for the first time headed in a southeasterly direction, skirting the western flank of the Sierra Almagre. It was the fifteenth day of the campaign, and they had yet to discover any sign of Cuerno Verde. Five days later, on the second of September, that would change.

Following Chief Moara's instructions, Colonel Anza and his army headed east over the Sierra Almagre and around the south flank of a massive snow-covered peak to a high vantage point overlooking the vast, grass-covered prairie east of the mountains. Directly below them, nestled amongst the trees bordering a stream was a large Comanche rancheria. Hoping to catch them by surprise, the colonel ordered an immediate attack and in the action that followed, several Comanche warriors were taken prisoner. While Cuerno Verde was not one of them, Colonel Anza was nevertheless pleased, for the captured warriors had told him that Cuerno Verde and his renegade warriors would be returning to the great grasslands sometime within the next two or three days. The pass in the Sangre de Cristo Mountains and the valley down which they'd be coming was a two-day ride so they must hurry if they wished to intercept him.

Colonel Anza felt sure that the Comanche warriors had been telling him the truth, for Cuerno Verde had used the same brutal tactics on them as he had on the Spanish in order to force them to do his bidding. As a result, their hatred of Cuerno Verde was as great as his own.

(A pen and ink drawing by Doctor Seymour Wheelock)

Early the next morning, Colonel Anza and his army advanced seven leagues to the confluence of the Rio del Sacramento where they bivouacked for the night. The following day, hoping that they could give prior warning of the oncoming Comanche, Juan, Pedro, and Silas Smith were ordered to scout far in advance of the army. Following rapidly, Colonel Anza and the remainder of his forces forded the Rio de Napestle and marched for nine more leagues toward the southwest, at which point the advance scouts returned and reported that a large number of Comanche warriors were approaching and that, so far at least, they were unaware of the army's presence.

Reacting quickly, the colonel deployed his entire army and baggage train in a wooded area overlooking the narrow valley and quietly waited for the Indians to appear. Shortly before sundown, their patience was rewarded as a horde of Indians appeared on the opposite side of the valley. Hoping to cut off their escape, the colonel ordered an attack, but the wily Comanche soon realized what was happening and vanished into the gathering darkness.

The next morning, believing that his mission had failed, the colonel ordered his army to make ready to return to Santa Fe. But even as he issued the order, a horde of Comanche warriors, brandishing weapons and shouting their defiance, appeared on the opposite side of the valley. Colonel Anza responded rapidly. But even as he was deploying his troops, a number of enemy warriors made a dash forward while at the same time firing their muskets. Stopping a little out of musket range, they whirled their horses about in a dizzying fashion. At the head of the group with his musket held high above his head rode a formidable-appearing Indian astride a huge snow-white horse. His handsome eagle feather headdress and proud and contemptuous manner announced to all who saw him that this was indeed Cuerno Verde, the dreaded war chief of the Comanche.

In the action that followed, the colonel feigned a retreat with a portion of his army, hoping to entrap the main body of the Comanche in a boggy area bordering the stream, thereby enabling the main body of his troops to encircle the Indians and attack them from the rear. But the wily Cuerno Verde, realizing what was happening, ordered his men to retreat. The colonel, in turn, ordered an all-out attack that succeeded in cutting off Cuerno Verde and his closest followers from the main body of his warriors. Relentlessly, the Comanche war chief and his men were driven into the bog in the gully, and there, as Colonel Anza was to write later, "They made a defense as brave as it was glorious." Springing to the ground, they entrenched themselves behind their horses, where they fought valiantly until the last one of them was dead. Cuerno Verde perished along with his first-born son, the heir to his command, four of his most famous captains, and ten other warriors as well as a medicine man, who believed himself to be immortal. The rest of the warriors scattered in all directions like dust before the wind.

Colonel Anza was pleased. Even though most of the Indians had escaped, he felt sure that this would put an end to the attacks, for it was very unlikely that any other Comanche leader would be able to match Cuerno Verde in cunning and daring. "One could not but admire the courage of this man," the colonel said. "He was truly a great leader, and I declare this valley to be named "Green Horn Valley" in his honor.

Soon after the battle ended, the colonel dispatched scouts to be sure that the remaining Comanche warriors were not organizing a counterattack. While waiting for their return, Juan and Pedro met with the colonel and asked if they might speak to him about a personal matter. He agreed and listened with interest as they outlined all that Smith had told them about the gold in Lost Creek and their proposed plan of action. Now that the campaign was over and their services were no longer needed, they were hoping the colonel would release them from the army so that they might go to Lost Creek and see if there was any truth in what Smith had said. If it turned out there was, they'd return to Santa Fe for the winter and come back in the spring with the equipment they needed to look for the bonanza.

Colonel Anza liked these men. They had served him well on many occasions, and he wanted to oblige them; so, though it was against his better judgment, he told them that they were free to go, but that he thought it very unwise for them to be going so late in the year. It would be better and far safer if they waited until the following spring. But neither Juan nor Pedro would listen to the colonel's good advice. They just thanked him and assured him that he needn't worry, for they'd be sure to get back to Santa Fe long before there was any danger of becoming snowbound. Realizing that it was useless to try to change their minds, the colonel told them good-bye, good luck, and Godspeed.

After thanking the colonel, the brothers began making preparations to leave. They found Silas Smith comfortably reclining in the shade of a large scrub oak. He seemed pleased to see them and asked them to sit a spell. But when they told him what it was they were planning to do, they were shocked by his explosive response.

"You two must be plumb crazy to be goin' there this late in the year! It's too damned dangerous. Heavy snow's likely to fall most any day now, and if'n you don't get snowed in and starved or froze to death, you'll most likely get et by cougars, kilt by hostiles, or break yore damn fool necks. You boys best wait 'til next year." But nothing Smith could say made the slightest impression on either Juan or Pedro, and the old trapper finally gave in.

"I jest cain't believe you two are so damned stupid, but if yo're really set on goin', yo're gonna need a good outfit, and I jest might be willin' to sell you a couple of my burros, 'long with two pair of leather panniers and most all my minin' gear and supplies, includin' picks and shovels, axes and gold pans. I'll even throw in some blastin' powder, rope, and most all my grub jest for good measure 'cause I shore as hell ain't gonna be needin' them. From here on I's gonna stick to trappin' like I should of done in the first place."

It was midmorning when the scouts returned and reported that the Indians had vanished. The only sign of them was the dust of their retreat rising above the eastern plain. Soon after that, at eleven o'clock on the third day of September 1779 and the twentieth day of the campaign, amidst loud cheers from the soldiers and settlers, Colonel Anza ordered his army to begin the march back to their homes in the San Luis Valley and Santa Fe. Before leaving, Smith embraced the brothers warmly and wished them a safe and successful journey. He made no further mention of the risks they were taking.

As Juan and Pedro were making final preparations to leave, Chief Moara paid them a visit. He had heard of their plans from Silas Smith and was well acquainted with the region they intended to explore. He too, warned them of the dangers that they might encounter but did not persist in his warnings when he saw how determined they both were to go. Instead, he wished them well and as a token of his high regard for them, he gave each of them a fine stallion that was far superior to the mounts they had been riding. Juan and Pedro were delighted. They thanked him and told him that someday they would repay him for his kindness. As the chief clasped their arms in farewell, he told them there was no need for repayment, for they were his brothers.

CHAPTER 3

As the army moved off to the south, the two brothers traveled in the opposite direction and returned to the south bank of the Rio de Napestle, riding upstream to where they had forded the river eight days earlier. After crossing to the north side of the river, they climbed to the summit of the small mountain range at the southern end of the Valle Salado, where they bivouacked for the night.

The following morning, after a hurried breakfast, the brothers rode as rapidly as the terrain would permit, down to the foot of the mountain and north to the upper end of the valley. From there, following Silas Smith's instructions, they rode east to the summit of a pass over the Sierra del Almagre and then in a southwesterly direction until they came to a small lake. A crystal clear stream was running out of it. Believing it to be the headwaters of Lost Creek, the brothers followed it down the mountainside, and, on the evening of the fourth day since leaving the Greenhorn Valley, they rode into the lovely little meadow the old trapper had called "Lost Park."

Lost Creek Canyon
(Picture taken by Julius E. Johnson Sr. in 1915)

Next morning, after an unrewarding check for gold in the meadow, they followed Lost Creek downstream and entered the upper end of what Silas Smith had called the "Cañon Diablo." And it was every bit as rugged as the old trapper had said it would be. Massive rocks had fallen from high up on the canyon walls down to the valley floor where they lay in a chaotic jumble, stacked one upon another, creating what appeared to be an impassable maze that stretched far down the valley. Lost Creek was well named, for much of the time it was flowing beneath the rocks. The game trail Smith had described had been easy to find, but following it was not, as it wound its way up and down the canyon side through narrow passageways between the rocks in search of the open stretches of water. At times, when the stream emerged from beneath the boulders, the rushing waters would tumble and splash over rocks and downed timber as though desperate to leave that gloomy, godforsaken place. At other times, it slowed and ran quietly through deep, tranquil pools as though resting before resuming its frantic downhill race.

Sometimes, the sands on the bottom of a pool would sparkle seductively in the reflected light of the sun, and Juan and Pedro would rush out into the water thinking it was gold — only to discover that it was nothing but bright, shiny fool's gold and not worth a single centavo. Disappointed, they would continue to work their way down the stream, always following the game trail as it led them on a fruitless game of hide-and-seek.

It was late afternoon, and the September sun was setting behind the Sierra del Almagre when Juan and Pedro rode onto the crest of a small hill at the lower end of the canyon. At that very same moment, the entire western sky exploded in a burst of glorious color, and the forested mountain slopes glowed gold with the reflected light of the setting sun. But the brothers had no eyes for beauty as they stood and looked down into a large, open valley. They could scarcely contain their excitement: Surely this was the valley where Silas Smith had found his gold nuggets! He'd said it was about a league and a half below Lost Park, and they felt sure that they had come at least that far — it seemed like a lot more. The valley was bordered on either side by dark forests of pine and large aspen groves, while on the floor of the valley, the sinuous channel of Lost Creek was ablaze with reflected colors of the sunset as it wove its lazy way down the center of a grass-covered meadow.

Their hopes and spirits soared as they rode down the hill and set up camp in an aspen grove on the banks of Lost Creek. As the last sliver of the setting sun slipped behind the Sierra del Almagre, Pedro went down to the creek for coffee water. As he stooped to fill the pot, a bright golden glitter caught his eye. Shouting for his brother to join him, Pedro jumped into the hip-deep water and began to grope about on the sandy bottom, and by the time his brother arrived, he was holding up a nugget in each hand. While neither was as large as the ones the old mountain man had shown them, they were, nonetheless, both pure gold.

The next morning, just as the first gray light of dawn lit the eastern sky, the brothers hurried down to the creek and began to pan for gold. By noon, each of them had collected well over an ounce of gold dust and an occasional nugget, but nothing to equal the size of the ones Silas had found. But, even so, they were convinced that this was the meadow in which Silas Smith had found his nuggets. To add to their conviction, they discovered a cave-like opening in the rocks at the upper end of the meadow with Lost Creek flowing from it. Everything was just like the old trapper had said it would be, and if he was right about the mother lode as well, they'd be richer than they could ever have imagined — even in their wildest dreams. The rest of that day, they panned for gold in Lost Creek while discussing how and where to begin their search for the mother lode on the following day.

Juan spoke first. "You know, Pedro, I wonder where all the gold in the meadow is coming from? We've already checked all the open water for gold between here and Lost Park, but we didn't find a trace until we got to the meadow. And something else puzzles me. Why is it that the flow of water in Lost Creek is noticeably greater when it comes out of the cave than it was when we last saw it disappear? Do you suppose a tributary is coming down the west slope of the Sierra Almagre and running into Lost Creek somewhere under the rocks? If that is so, the mother lode might be on that tributary and not on Lost Creek at all. It's unlikely, I guess, but it's a possibility we should explore."

Pedro agreed, and the following morning, after tethering both horses and one of their burros in the meadow, Juan and Pedro loaded their mining equipment on their other burro and started up the steep slopes on the west side of Lost Creek. Upon reaching a rock-covered bench at the base of a towering cliff halfway up the mountainside, they sat down on a boulder near the edge of the bench to rest and survey the surrounding countryside. Shortly, they noticed a soft, whispering sound coming from behind and above them. Turning about, they carefully studied the face of the cliff. A moment later Pedro cried out excitedly, as he pointed to a waterfall that fell precipitously over the edge of the cliff and vanished among the huge boulders below.

"Hey, Juan, you were right! There is another stream coming down this side of the mountain. Let's follow it and see where it goes."

Hurriedly, Juan and Pedro worked their way across the outer edge of the bench until they intercepted the stream where it spilled from the bench and into a deep ravine. They were elated. Surely this was the creek where they'd find the mother lode of their dreams.

After skidding down the steep side of the ravine, the brothers carefully examined the streambed for signs of gold. Finding none, they continued checking as they worked their way down the creek. The ravine was steep, the creek bed rugged, and the going very difficult, but in their excitement they didn't notice, for at any moment they expected to find the bonanza. As they drew near to the lower end of the stream and its confluence with Lost Creek, however, and had found but scant traces of gold, the brothers' dreams of wealth faded with each fruitless pan of sand and gravel.

Though it seemed pointless, they continued to follow the stream as it flowed around the base of a gravel-covered knoll, across a flat expanse of sand, and into a small pond at the base of a massive boulder. Juan was discouraged and ready to go back to camp, but Pedro insisted on taking a closer look. And it was well that they did, for instead of one huge boulder as it had appeared, there were actually two with the stream flowing between them. At first glance the opening between the rocks appeared to be little more than a crack, but as they drew closer, they discovered that it was considerably wider than they had at first thought — easily large enough for a man to pass through and possibly even a burro. Pedro's hopes soared. Perhaps there was still a chance that they would find the bonanza.

After tying their burro to a small pine tree near the entrance of the passageway, the brothers waded out into the hip-deep water and made their way along the narrow corridor. The current was strong, the water cold and deep, and the farther they went down the channel the darker it became. They were becoming frightened, and even Pedro was beginning to question the wisdom of this venture. But a little farther along the passageway, a ghostly light began to filter through the cracks between the rocks above their heads. They heard the muted sound of a waterfall from farther down the channel, and their spirits revived. A few moments later, they stepped out into a large, rock-enclosed chamber nearly thirty feet wide and over twice that in length. They could scarcely believe their eyes. Soft rays of sunlight streamed though narrow openings between the rocks in the granite ceiling, lighting the interior of the chamber with a rich golden glow that nourished a lush growth of grass on its loamy floor.

After entering, the stream tarried briefly in a quiet pool near one side of the chamber before resuming its serpentine flow across the floor until it vanished from sight as it plunged over the edge of a cliff. Rushing forward, the brothers stood and looked down in wonder at an enchanted grotto fully twelve feet below. It was smaller than the upper chamber and had a misty, magical appearance, as though it was the dwelling place of fairies or pixies or other strange, mythical creatures. A noisy, tumultuous waterfall splashed into a crystal clear pool at the foot of the cliff, filling the chamber with a fine mist that nourished the thick layer of moss covering the granite walls of the grotto. After pausing briefly in the pool, the stream resumed its flow across the white sandy floor of the grotto until it joined with the waters of Lost Creek.

Juan and Pedro stared in disbelief at the floor of the grotto. Surely their eyes were playing tricks on them! Hundreds of bright yellow objects that glittered like stars in the firmament were scattered about in the sand. Some were small, but many appeared to be the size of a large apple. Though they feared that it was only fool's gold, they still had difficulty in curbing their expectations.

"How are we going to get down there, Juan? There's no way we can climb down these steep, moss-covered rock walls."

"You're right," Juan answered, "But we can use the manila rope that Silas Smith insisted we take with us. He said it might come in handy, and he was right. It's in one of the panniers on our burro. It might be a tight squeeze, but why don't we see if we can bring the burro into the upper chamber."

This they accomplished without any difficulty. After Juan had secured the rope to a large rock in the upper chamber, he lowered it to the floor of the grotto. Then Pedro, the more agile of the two, slid rapidly down it and began to examine the sandy floor of the grotto, while Juan held his breath as he anxiously awaited his brother's verdict. Moments later, a loud shout of triumph echoed throughout the rocky chamber as Pedro jumped to his feet and shouted "Quick, come on down, Juan! There's gold all over the place! Lots of the nuggets are even bigger than these!" And he held aloft several large nuggets in both of his hands.

In his haste, Juan almost fell down the rope. After confirming that it was indeed gold, he and Pedro examined the bottom of the pool at the foot of the waterfall and found it literally carpeted with large nuggets. Hoping to locate the source of the gold, the brothers stripped away the moss from the rock wall behind the waterfall. They stared in wonder at what they found. It was their wildest dream come true. The entire face of the cliff was composed of white and rose-colored quartz with large veins of what appeared to be pure gold scattered throughout it. One vein was fully seven or eight feet wide. It was a fabulous bonanza, and they were very, very rich men. After the initial shock had worn off, the brothers began to collect nuggets from the bottom of the pool and grotto floor and haul them to the upper chamber by means of the rope and a bucket. They alternated the tasks of filling the bucket and hauling it up the cliff, and by late afternoon they were both stiff and cold from the spray of the waterfall.

Daylight was fading rapidly as they led the burro out of the cavern and hurried back to the meadow. When they arrived there, a terrible sight met their eyes. Pedro's horse lay dead, and the other horse and burro were nowhere to be seen. Judging from tracks in the soft earth surrounding the carcass, their horse had been killed by a cougar, just as Silas Smith warned them might happen. After eating its fill, it had dragged the remnants of the carcass under some nearby bushes in order to hide it from other predators. They found Juan's horse grazing quietly farther down the valley, and for that they were grateful. But, though they searched frantically until dark overtook them, the brothers could find no sign of their burro. That night they set up camp at a spot well away from the scene of the killing and staked out their animals close beside them. After eating, they rolled up in their blankets near the fire

— muskets close at hand. But neither of them could sleep — especially after the chilling scream of a cougar echoed eerily back and forth between the canyon walls.

At first light on the following morning, they resumed their search for the burro, but again it was a futile effort, so they packed up their gear, broke camp, and returned to the bonanza. After bringing their two remaining animals inside the cavern and staking them out to graze, the brothers took stock of their situation. Juan was the first to speak.

"Pedro, I hate to say it, but now that we're short on animals, we're going to have to pack up and head back to Santa Fe. We'll be needing our horse and burro to pack out our gear along with as much gold as they can carry, so we'll have to walk, and it's going to take us a lot longer to get home than we had originally planned. But, actually, it's time we were leaving anyway. It's late September, and we could be caught in a blizzard most any time now. Not only that, we're real low on food."

"You're crazy, Juan," Pedro almost shouted as he vigorously shook his head back and forth. "I don't know why you always worry so much. The weather's been fine up to now, and as far as I can see, it shows no sign of changing. But even if it does, we'd be warm and snug inside the cavern. It'd take a mighty big storm to keep us from going back to Santa Fe, and ..."

"We can't take any chances, Pedro," Juan broke in. "You know as well as I do that the weather in these parts can change within the space of an hour. You're probably right about our being able to weather a storm in this cavern, but what if we are caught by a blizzard when we're out in the middle of the Valle Salado? We'd be lucky to make it back alive. No, we have to play it safe and leave now, while we still can. Maybe you've forgotten it, Pedro, but before we came on this trip, you and I both agreed that all we'd do this time was check out the country around Lost Creek to see what it was like and to make sure Silas Smith was telling us the truth. Then, if it turned out he was, we'd come back in the spring to look for the mother lode. Well, we've done all that and a lot more — we even found the bonanza, and now it's time for us to go home while we still can." But Pedro still stubbornly refused to give in, and after arguing heatedly for well over an hour, Juan reluctantly agreed to stay.

CHAPTER 4

Their disagreement temporarily settled, the brothers set about assembling the equipment they needed to mine and process the ore. They cut down tall pine trees with which to build a crude ladder so they could get in and out of the grotto. More timbers served to deflect the waterfall so that it would spill on the far side of the grotto, enabling them to stay relatively dry while they worked. Next, they built a sturdy windlass with which to pull up bucket loads of ore to be processed in the upper chamber, and lastly they built an arrastra. Years ago, while visiting their grandparents, the brothers had seen one being used in the mountains near Mexico City. It was a simple device that would enable them to free the gold from the gold ore, and Juan felt they could build one quite easily by using two rocks, called "mullers," to crush up the ore on the large flat rock in the cavern.

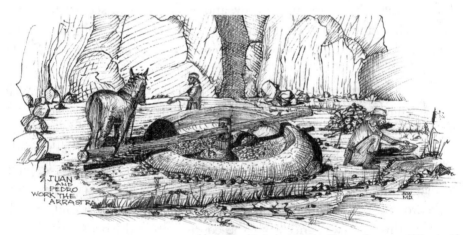

(A pen and ink drawing by Doctor Seymour Wheelock)

After four full days spent making the necessary preparations, they set to work mining the ore. Pedro stayed down in the grotto, breaking up the ore with his pickax and loading it into a bucket. Juan then would crank the windlass and hoist the bucket to the upper chamber and dump the ore in a pile. After grinding it in the arrastra and panning it to collect the gold, he put it in their panniers, making sure that they would balance each other when placed on the pack animals. By the end of the eighth day, they had amassed a large quantity of gold, and Juan once again confronted his brother.

"Pedro, it's time to leave. We'd be foolish to stay any longer. A big blizzard might hit us most any day now, and if it does, it'll make our trip home a whole lot harder — if not impossible." But Pedro still stubbornly refused to listen to his brother's good advice.

"Like I told you before, Juan, you worry too much. A few more days won't make a bit of difference, and we still need more gold. Our burro can carry all that we've already collected, and in a few more days, we'll have enough for our horse to carry. Besides that, I can carry some in my backpack."

Juan was becoming more and more irritated by Pedro's obstinacy and lack of common sense, so he once again attempted to persuade his brother to leave. But then Pedro became angry.

"If you're so hell-bent on leaving, Juan, why don't you just take the burro and go? I'll come later with the horse when I have enough gold."

That, in turn, angered Juan. "Pedro, all this gold has robbed you of your senses. I doubt you'll ever think you have enough — and there's no way I'll leave without you — so just forget about that. If we don't stay together, neither of us is likely to make it home safely."

Time and time again, over and over, Juan argued, but Pedro stubbornly refused to listen to reason. Finally, despite his anger and frustration, Juan agreed to stay for three more days, but only if Pedro promised in the name of the Blessed Virgin Mary that they both would leave together on the morning of the fourth day, regardless of how much gold they had accumulated. Eventually and reluctantly, Pedro promised to comply with his brother's demand, and they returned to work.

Two days later, they had amassed so much gold that even Pedro seemed to be satisfied, and a large pile of ore was yet to be processed. On the morning of the third day, Pedro left the rocky chamber intending to replenish their depleted meat supply before they began the long trip home. Realizing that he had angered Juan and hoping to make amends, Pedro asked his brother to go along with him on the hunt. But Juan was still angry and curtly turned him down, saying that he would prefer to stay in the cavern and make ready for their departure on the following morning. Visibly hurt, Pedro shouldered his musket and led the burro out of the chamber and into the upper end of the meadow.

As a rule, there were deer grazing in the meadow, and today was no exception, as a fat spike buck raised his head upon hearing his approach and died instantly with a bullet through the heart. As Pedro was hanging the buck from the limb of a tree in order to gut it, he failed to notice the terrified behavior of his burro as she jerked on her tether in a frantic effort to escape. Not until she broke free and raced down the meadow did he realize what was happening. At that very moment, a threatening snarl erupted from the top of a nearby rock. Looking up with alarm, Pedro's blood turned to ice. A huge cougar was crouching on the rock above him, its long, yellow fangs bared as it snarled and tensed its powerful muscles in preparation for its attack. Pedro, paralyzed by fear, realized with horror that his unloaded musket was leaning uselessly against a nearby tree. His only hope now was his knife, and it was on the ground several feet away from where he was standing.

Mustering his courage and uttering a silent prayer, he dove to where his knife was lying and grasped it just as the cougar's full weight crashed down upon him, pinning him to the ground. Pedro felt the massive cat's murderous fangs tear deeply into the muscles of his right leg. Then its mighty jaws seized his left arm above the elbow, ripping his flesh from the bone. Incredibly, Pedro felt no pain as he rolled from beneath the big cat and plunged the long blade of his knife deep into the cougar's side. As he pulled it forth to strike again the terrible jaws closed upon his neck, and a sudden darkness enveloped him as the cat struggled to rise to its feet in order to complete its kill. Then abruptly, with a great shudder, it collapsed and lay lifeless on the ground. Unaware that his desperate prayer had been answered, Pedro lay bleeding and unconscious beside the tawny body of the cougar. The one thrust of his knife had pierced the cougar's heart.

After several minutes, Pedro slowly regained consciousness. He was terribly weak — his vision blurred. As it slowly cleared and he saw the body of the cougar lying by his side, he realized what a miracle it was that he was still alive. After whispering a fervent prayer of thanks, Pedro attempted to sit up. Instantly, a terrible pain shot though his mutilated left arm and right upper leg, as well as his neck. At the same time, blood spurted from all of his wounds. Realizing that he most certainly would bleed to death if he didn't do something to check the loss of blood, Pedro used his teeth, along with his knife and good right arm, to rip strips of cloth from one of his pant legs. Using them as tourniquets, he succeeded in checking the flow of blood from his leg and arm. Then he controlled the bleeding vessels in his neck by pressing on them with his bandanna.

Exhausted by his efforts and loss of blood, Pedro lay back on the ground and forced himself to focus his pain-clouded mind on what he could do next. Fearing an attack by another cougar or bear, he wiped the blood from his knife and put it back in its sheath — praying that he would not have to use it. Though his gun was near at hand, there seemed no point in trying to load it, for even if he should succeed, he didn't have the strength to lift it — let alone aim and shoot it. He knew that his brother would come to look for him if he was too long in returning, but by that time he might be long dead.

At length he decided that, if he could manage to load his musket, despite the effort it would require, and fire it several times in succession at fairly regular intervals, Juan would hear the reports, realize that something was wrong, and come looking for him. At least it was worth a try — if only he had the strength to do it. Slowly and painfully, Pedro inched his way over to where his musket was leaning against a tree. He poured a charge of black powder into the muzzle, followed by the ball and wadding. After tamping it down with the ramrod, he primed it, fired the first shot, and then laboriously repeated the procedure three more times as close together as he could manage. Having succeeded in that, he loaded it one more time and lay back on the grass exhausted, praying that his brother would correctly interpret the shots and come quickly to his aid.

Juan was busily making preparations to leave when he heard the first shot. When he heard the one following he assumed that his brother had wounded the buck with his first shot and dispatched it with the second. But upon hearing two more shots in slow succession, he realized that his brother must be in serious trouble, and he quickly saddled his mare, picked up his musket, and, beset with anxiety and guilt, hurried to the meadow.

He could never forgive himself if something bad had happened to his brother. He should never have let his anger keep him from accompanying Pedro on the hunt as he had asked him to do. But, what troubled him far more, he had allowed Pedro to persuade him to stay longer. If only he had insisted on their leaving, they would be halfway to Santa Fe by now. Raising his eyes towards heaven, Juan cried aloud to Almighty God, beseeching Him and the Blessed Virgin Mary that nothing serious had happened to Pedro.

As he entered the upper end of the meadow, Juan called Pedro's name, praying for a response. After the third call, a barely audible cry came from farther down the valley. Spurring his horse to a gallop, Juan rushed over and around fallen timber and rocks until he arrived at the spot where his brother lay injured beside the body of the dead cougar. Praying that Pedro was still alive, he dismounted and knelt beside his mangled body. Holding his breath in suspense, he pressed his ear against his brother's chest. Pedro stirred at his touch and opened his eyes. He was still alive! His prayers had been answered. Praise be to God!

After loosening the tourniquets to restore the circulation in Pedro's arm and leg, Juan promptly tightened them again when the bleeding resumed. Pedro was barely conscious as Juan lifted him onto the horse, which was a blessing, for otherwise the pain would have been unbearable. After tying his brother onto the saddle with a short piece of rope, Juan led them to the upper end of the meadow, stopping at intervals to loosen the tourniquets and ropes to restore the circulation in Pedro's arm and leg. Each time they stopped, Juan carefully inspected the surrounding coun- tryside, praying that he might find their missing burro. But he saw no sign of it, and his heart filled with fear as he contemplated the seeming- ly impossible task that lay before him. Somehow, someway, with the con- tinued blessing and help of Almighty God, he and the little horse must take his beloved brother from this vale of sorrow to a place of safety, where Pedro could recover from his terrible wounds.

As they were entering the cavern, Pedro began to shake uncontrol- lably and his pale skin felt icy cold to the touch. Juan hurriedly built up the fire, and as soon as it was warmer and Pedro had stopped shivering, he set to work cleansing and bandaging his wounds. Fortunately, the bleeding had stopped. After he'd finished, Juan sat beside his sleeping brother and struggled to muster his thoughts. By all rights, Pedro should stay in the cavern until his wounds were healing and his strength had returned but, of course, that was not possible. Their food supply was almost exhausted, and while he could easily replenish it with wild game, they couldn't survive on meat alone. When their staples were gone, they would slowly starve to death. But what was equally worrisome, winter was close at hand and should a heavy snowfall close the passes out of the Valle Salado, neither he nor his brother would leave Lost Creek alive. This cold, icy cavern would become their tomb forever.

Juan had no other choice. As soon as Pedro regained consciousness and was a little stronger, they must leave. In the meantime, he would make the necessary preparations. Leaving Pedro in the cavern, Juan returned to the meadow and brought the carcass of the buck that Pedro had killed back to the cavern where he butchered it and laid thin slices of the meat to dry on rocks by the fire. Then he packed the remaining food and clothing they would take with them into his backpack. After hefting it to determine its weight, Juan filled a leather bag with nuggets and placed it in the backpack. He hefted it again and added a few more nuggets.

As night approached and the light in the cavern faded, Juan checked once more on his brother. Finding him peacefully sleeping, he built up the fire with pine logs that were heavy with pitch, hoping that they would provide warmth throughout the night. By the light of the blazing fire, he cut a piece from the deerskin and, using the tip of his skinning knife, drew a crude map on it showing the location of the bonanza. After rubbing gunpowder into the cuts to make them more readable, he put it in his backpack. Then he rolled up in his blankets and instantly fell asleep — to awaken just as the first light of dawn spread its ghostly glow throughout the interior of the cavern.

Juan put more wood on the embers of last night's fire. It was cold — a thick layer of ice covered the pool, and the strips of venison were frozen solid. As Juan was building up the fire, Pedro stirred and opened his eyes. They were clear and his voice was surprisingly strong as he greeted his brother and asked what had happened. All he could remember was seeing the cougar as it leapt upon him. Beyond that, all was a merciful blank. Juan quickly filled him in on all that had happened to him since he lost consciousness, as well as his proposed plan of departure. As they were talking, he checked his brother's bandages and was relieved to find that there had been no more bleeding.

As Pedro watched his brother make preparations for their long trip back to civilization, he became more and more agitated. Struggling to push up on an elbow, he whispered in a weak, raspy voice,

"Juan, we just can't go off and leave all this gold in the cavern. What if somebody finds it and steals it? You've got to figure out some way to hide it."

"That's not going to happen, Pedro. Nobody's going to come to this godforsaken spot except us. We're the only ones that know about the gold. Except for Silas Smith, of course, and he swore he'd never come here again. You heard him say that."

"But what if he's changed his mind?" Pedro persisted. "Or what if he told somebody else how to find it? You've got to hide it Juan. You've just got to. I won't leave 'til you do. I'll do it myself if I can," and with that he made another futile attempt to get up.

Fearful that Pedro might further hurt himself in his agitated state of mind, Juan reluctantly agreed to comply with his brother's request. He began by placing all four of their leather panniers and two saddle-bags filled with gold nuggets and the highest grade ore into the crevices between the massive boulders that formed the walls of the cavern. After putting Pedro's helmet, musket, and armored coat on top of them, he spread the fresh deerskin on the floor of yet another crevice, piled more ore on it, and put their tools and other equipment on top of that. Following that, he secreted all of the remaining gold ore in other crevices and carefully stacked boulders from the cavern floor in front of them to make it appear like a natural rock fall. After dismantling the arrastra, Juan rolled the mullers over the edge of the cliff onto the sandy floor of the grotto. Finally, he burned the ladder, windlass, and pine logs that were too large to hide. Then he surveyed his work. He was pleased. Now, if by chance a stranger should happen to find the cavern, it would be very unlikely that he would suspect their earlier presence or that a fortune in gold was hidden there.

But Pedro had yet another request. To be absolutely sure that no one could enter the cavern after they'd left, he wanted Juan to set off a charge of black powder just outside the entrance of the passageway to hide the entryway. Again Juan agreed to his brother's request — in part to keep Pedro from becoming upset but also to allay his own feelings of guilt for refusing to accompany him on the deer hunt. Had he done so, Pedro would not have been so grievously injured.

Before leaving the cavern, they ate a meager meal of boiled beans along with a little meat broth. After packing the remnants of their meal into his backpack, Juan scattered the ashes of their campfire in among the rocks at the edge of the chamber, covered the blackened fire pit with small rocks and grass, then carried the remnants of the firewood outside the cavern. And finally, after a brief but fervent prayer to Almighty God asking Him to grant them a safe return to Santa Fe, Juan lifted Pedro onto the saddle and strapped their bedrolls and greatcoats behind the cantle. Then he shouldered his knapsack and led the little horse through the passageway and out into the warm, autumn sunlight.

Leaving Pedro and his horse in the shelter of a large rock, Juan skidded back down the slope and placed several packets of black powder under the front edges of the rocks on either side of the passageway. After attaching a long fuse to each charge, he lit them and hurried up the hill to join his brother. The horse shied at the sound of the blast and again as small pieces of rock showered down about them, prompting Juan to keep a firm grip on the reins. After the dust had begun to settle, Juan led Pedro and the little horse back down the hill to see if the blast was successful in blocking the passageway. And it was — unfortunately, far more than he had wanted.

Even as they watched, dirt and small rocks continued to fall from the boulders on either side of the passageway, and the muddy water from the pool at their base was beginning to flow down the valley in a southeasterly direction, seeking a new route to Lost Creek. Surprisingly, two smaller boulders that were perched on top of one of the massive rocks flanking the passageway had been reshaped by the blast, so that they now had an uncanny resemblance to two big owls.

After carefully marking the location of the owls on his crude map and labeling them "lechusas doble," Juan picked up the lead rope to his horse, and the two brothers began their long journey back to Santa Fe. Surprisingly, Pedro tolerated the ride up the rocky canyon remarkably well, and that evening, the brothers bivouacked in a grove of aspen trees at the upper end of Lost Park. Early the following morning, they set out again, hoping to reach the Valle Salado by nightfall.

CHAPTER 5

It was the sixteenth of October when the brothers wound their way down the western slope of the Sierra Almagre into the upper reaches of the Valle Salado. Pedro had not fared well this day. Twice he had almost fallen from the horse, forcing Juan to tie him into the saddle. By midafternoon it was obvious that he could go no farther. He was exhausted and becoming incoherent. That evening, Juan heated water over the campfire with which to wash and redress his brother's wounds, but when he removed the dressings and saw them, he sobbed uncontrollably. All of Pedro's wounds were swollen, inflamed, and draining pus, and Juan had no medicines with which to treat them. All he could do was bandage them with strips of material torn from a none-too-clean blanket and pray to Almighty God that He would, by some great miracle, spare his brother's life.

So far the weather had been perfect. The days were crystal clear, cool and crisp in the shadows, pleasantly warm in the sun. The intensely blue sky was strewn with gossamer clouds like those of a midsummer's day. The illusion of summer vanished, however, the moment the last golden rays of the sun disappeared behind the dark mountain peaks in the west, and a blanket of penetrating cold descended over the valley. Then, as night spread over the land, the velvety black canopy above their heads sparkled with a myriad of brilliant stars. In better times, they both would have marveled at the sight, but now the heavenly glory went unnoticed as they shivered by the fire. That night, as he lay in his bedroll looking up at the heavens, Juan prayed over and over again, asking — begging — the Blessed Virgin Mary and Almighty God to save his brother's life.

The next morning when they awoke, their bedrolls were heavily coated with frost and their breath hung in lingering clouds before their faces. Pedro was much weaker than the day before and obviously unable to ride the horse, so Juan built a travois using the trunks and branches from aspen trees and tied the front end of it to either side of the saddle. Then he laid his brother on the crude sled, covering him with all their blankets, as well as Pedro's greatcoat.

By midmorning they were under way again. Juan was surprised and pleased at how well the travois traveled. His valiant little horse seemed to have no trouble in dragging it along, pulling it up the slopes with almost as much ease as down. At one point they crossed a fair-sized stream without any difficulty. As they rode, they would occasionally startle small bands of antelope or deer that were feeding in the hidden swales. On one occasion, a large herd of buffalo stopped grazing and briefly raised their heads to watch as the brothers passed by.

Late in the afternoon, when they were about two thirds of the way down the valley, Pedro began to moan and cry out as though in great terror. Babbling unintelligibly, he struggled to free himself from his covers while flailing about wildly with his arms, as though fending off some unseen attacker. He would have fallen from the travois had it not been for Juan's strenuous efforts to restrain him. Pedro seemed possessed of superhuman powers as he fought with every ounce of his remaining strength to overcome whatever nightmare horror was tormenting him. Finally, at the very peak of his struggles, he collapsed and lay quietly, sobbing and shaking while cradled in his brother's arms.

Greatly distraught, Juan realized that Pedro was desperately ill. Sweat poured from his brother's face, and he could feel the heat radiating through the multiple layers of his clothing. Feeling sick from fear and anxiety himself, he removed as much of Pedro's clothing as he felt advisable to allow the mountain air to cool him, after which he sponged his forehead and chest with frigid water from a nearby pond. As Pedro's fever dropped he became more rational, and in a weak, quavering voice, he asked Juan if he had seen the cougar that had been attacking him. As he talked, his gaze shifted about frantically as though he expected it to return. Juan did his best to reassure him that he was safe and that there was no cougar except in his dreams. After several more anxious minutes, Pedro drifted into a deep sleep, or perhaps unconsciousness. Juan couldn't be sure.

Juan knew he should reexamine Pedro's wounds, even though he had no way of treating them, and indeed, no more materials with which to re-bandage them. He approached the task with great apprehension, fearful of what he might find, and it was far worse than he had imagined. The neck and shoulder injuries were both about the same, but the leg was much worse. The tissues that surrounded it were swollen and red streaks extended upward towards Pedro's groin. But what frightened Juan the most was the dark purple discoloration of the lower leg. He knew at a glance that the leg was gangrenous and there was nothing he could do for it — nothing that is, except pray. And pray he did, with all his might, asking Almighty God over and over again to spare Pedro's life.

Words couldn't begin to describe Juan's feelings of horror and disbelief. His brother, in whom he had so much pride and joy, the brother he loved so dearly, was going to die, for despite his prayers to the contrary, he knew there was no conceivable way that Pedro could survive. Juan had seen too many others with similar injuries and infections to believe otherwise. Grief stricken, he sat by the side of his unconscious brother for what seemed like hours, stroking his yellow hair and wiping the beads of perspiration from his forehead with a cool, soft cloth. Over and over again he repeated his desperate entreaty that God might spare Pedro's life.

As Juan sat immersed in his own thoughts and sorrows, he failed to notice the sudden onset of a cold north wind. The temperature had dropped precipitously in just the last few minutes. Eventually, he shivered as the cold finally intruded upon his thoughts, and he looked up to see a towering mass of black clouds looming over the northern end of the valley. A massive storm was approaching rapidly and would soon be upon them. Juan instantly scrambled to his feet, fully aware of the gravity of their situation. To be caught by a blizzard in the middle of this great open valley without shelter from the cold wind and driving snow would mean certain death — not only for Pedro, but for himself as well.

Quickly, Juan restored Pedro's blankets and tucked his greatcoat about him. After shrugging on his own greatcoat, he hastened to resume their trek, leading his horse and travois towards the southern end of the valley as rapidly as the terrain would permit. After traveling no more than a mile, the blizzard encompassed them as the sky grew dark and the temperature plummeted further. Blown by the furious wind, the snow began to accumulate in drifts on the windward side of the hills and in the depths of the draws and coulees. Juan soon lost all sense of direction as he stumbled through the blinding snow. But even as he struggled he continued to pray, begging God to guide them to a sheltered haven where they might safely wait out the storm.

Time seemed suspended as Juan stubbornly fought to make headway through the storm — half blinded by the blowing snow, fearful and lost, yet stubbornly determined that the violent wind and bitter cold should not overcome them. Howling like an infuriated creature, with ever-increasing force, the blizzard seemed equally determined to blow them into eternity, and it would have succeeded had it not been for the support of the sturdy little horse.

But for the moment, at least, death was not to be the victor, for at last — spent by his struggles and disoriented by the intense cold — Juan felt the ground beneath his feet give way as they unexpectedly tobogganed into a deep ravine. As they slid down the steep embankment on loose gravel and snow, the travois acted as a drag, slowing their descent so that they reached the bottom of the ravine without mishap. Shielded from the icy blast of the wind, Juan's vision improved rapidly, enabling him to find shelter from the storm in a hollow beneath the roots of a large alder tree, toppled by the wind during a previous storm. Spring floods had undercut the bank beneath its roots, creating a small cavern large enough to accommodate the two of them.

Pedro seemed completely unaware of Juan's valiant efforts to get him into the shelter and make him comfortable. With eyes wide open and a faint smile fixed upon his pallid face, he appeared to gaze unseeingly towards some distant place. Juan shivered as he looked at his beloved brother, but from apprehension rather than cold. Was Pedro dead or only unconscious? He couldn't be sure as he continued his efforts to get him settled in the cavern and make him as warm as possible before examining him.

Once sheltered from the worst of the wind and snow, Juan attempted to light a fire with his flint and steel, but he had no dry tinder with which to start the blaze, so his efforts were for naught. Reluctantly, fearful of what he would find, Juan shook his brother by his good shoulder — gently at first and then more vigorously. Eliciting no response, he removed some of the blankets and robes that covered his brother's body and felt for his heartbeat. Failing in that, he gently placed his ear on Pedro's icy cold chest. During lulls in the wailing wind he listened breathlessly, praying that he might hear some sound. But none was forthcoming. All was silent. His brother was dead.

Sobbing uncontrollably, Juan tenderly closed Pedro's eyelids and replaced the covers over his beloved brother. He had known all along that it was inevitable Pedro would die, but only now did he realize the full extent of his loss. Here in the dark of the night in the middle of nowhere he felt utterly alone — completely abandoned — by Pedro, by Almighty God, by the Blessed Virgin Mary, and by everything and everyone he cared about or who cared about him. In the depths of his despair, Juan even cursed God for failing to save Pedro's life, and he swore that never again would he place his trust and faith in the God who had allowed his brother to die. Juan wished desperately that he might have been the one who had died instead of Pedro. He especially berated himself for not insisting that they leave Lost Creek in time to avoid this terrible storm. Or — and this pained him far more — for peevishly refusing to accompany Pedro on the deer hunt as he had asked. Either way, his brother would still be alive.

But now it was too late. The one he loved most in this world was gone, and he would never see him again. He had believed his mother when she told him on the day she died that one day she and his dead father would meet him again in Paradise. But how could that be true in a world where God allowed such terrible things to happen? Surely she couldn't have been right. They were dead and gone for good and so was Pedro, and without realizing it, in the depths of his confusion and despair, Juan prayed to the God in whom he no longer believed that he too might not survive this night. Huddled next to Pedro's cold, lifeless body, he prayed over and over for death to take him as well, but it was not to be as he drew his heavy blankets close about him and, exhausted by grief, fell into a deep and dreamless sleep.

Hours later, Juan was awakened with a start by a soft whinny from his horse. Having stayed close by throughout the night, the faithful little animal was hungry, thirsty, and impatient to leave. The wind had completely subsided, replaced by an unnerving silence. Sometime during the night the storm had ended, leaving a lingering legacy of cold and snow. In the east, the first blush of the approaching dawn slowly spread over the Sierra del Almagre. As the sun rose higher in the sky, the somber gray clouds changed to dazzling shades of red, then faded to hues of crimson and rose, which in turn yielded to brilliant pink, yellow, and orange as the sun rose above the black mass of mountains. High overhead, two great eagles floated in the thermals, majestically silhouetted against the azure blue backdrop.

But the fleeting beauty went unnoticed. Juan's grief was unremitting, though now he no longer wished to die. He would go on, but to what end he did not know. His first task was to safeguard Pedro's body from scavengers. He could not abide the thought of vultures or coyotes ravaging his brother's mortal remains. The numerous rocks that covered the bottom of the arroyo provided ample material to enclose his body in a stony crypt beneath the roots of the uprooted alder. It seemed fitting to Juan that the skeletal remains of this stately tree should stand watch over his brother. The rocky tomb completed, Juan covered it deeply with soft earth from the banks of the cavern and added yet more rock on top of that. The hard labor was, in some ways, therapeutic for him, but it did little to alleviate his overwhelming sense of guilt.

His task concluded, he turned his attention to other pressing needs. He was both hungry and thirsty. After eating sparingly of what little remained of the dried venison, he ate some snow, hoping that it would alleviate his thirst, but it did little to satisfy his need. After his sparse meal, Juan loaded his backpack and the rest of his equipment onto the back of his trusty little horse and led it out of the arroyo. Then he stopped and surveyed the surrounding landscape, hoping he would see a familiar landmark, but he saw none. Apparently, the storm had driven him far off course, for he found himself at the lower end of an unfamiliar valley that ascended to a saddle in the mountains over a league to the southwest. An ice-edged stream tumbled down the valley and, hoping to save precious time, Juan decided to see what lay beyond the saddle instead of backtracking in search of his former route. Hopefully, it would take him to the Rio de Napestle, and from there to Santa Fe.

Upon reaching the stream, Juan and his horse paused briefly to slake their thirst before resuming their uphill struggles through the deep, wind-crusted snow. Late in the afternoon, they finally reached the saddle at the head of the valley, and a welcome sight met his eyes. Miles to the west, a massive mountain range loomed on the horizon and a large river valley bordered it on the east. Juan's spirits soared. Surely it was the valley of the Rio de Napestle — the river he was seeking.

That evening he camped in a draw sheltered by tall pines where there was ample grass for his horse and dry fuel for a fire. After eating the last bit of dried venison and beans, Juan spread his bedroll by the fire. Then he rested and remembered his brother. There had been little time for reflection since leaving the arroyo, but now as he lay and watched the sparks and smoke of his campfire spiral upward into the night, all of his self-recrimination returned along with his feelings of guilt and remorse. But mercifully, his misery was short lived as the warmth of the campfire soon lulled him to sleep.

Early the next morning, Juan and his horse started down the steep piñon-covered slope on the west side of the saddle. After laboring through deep snow for almost a league, the slope leveled off in the bottom of a narrow valley. From there, a game trail followed along the side of a small stream that flowed towards the southwest. Both elk and deer had traveled the trail earlier this morning — their fresh tracks in the snow clearly marking their passage. Recalling his need for meat, Juan proceeded quietly down the trail, hoping to surprise an unwary animal while it was still within range of his musket.

After a short distance, the trail climbed up and over an ancient rockslide that had swept down the steep slope and onto the floor of the valley. Peering cautiously over the summit of the slide, Juan saw a large buck and several does grazing in a grove of aspen trees a little farther down the valley. Leaving his horse on the far side of the slide, Juan carefully worked his way along the trail. As yet unaware of his presence, the deer continued to munch on the lower branches of the trees, but as he grew within range and cocked his musket, they instantly became alert and began to move off in the opposite direction. Fearing they would soon be out of range of his musket, Juan hastened his shot at the buck at the rear of the herd. But at the moment he fired, the buck bounded off after his harem, leaving Juan to watch his spent bullet plunge harmlessly into the snow.

As he was turning to retrieve his horse, Juan heard a muted rumbling sound coming from the slope directly above his head. Looking up, he was overcome by terror as he saw a huge mass of turbulent snow and rock plummeting down the mountainside, coming straight at him with incredible speed. Frantically, he struggled to regain the summit of the rock slide, praying that he might reach safety on the far side of the ridge. But his efforts were for naught. After going but a few steps, he felt himself picked up by the leading edge of the raging mass of ice, rocks, and snow — his body buffeted back and forth like a feather caught in a tempest as it swept across the valley floor. He felt no pain, only a frantic desire to escape from the icy clutches of the slide and an overwhelming fear of being buried alive.

As the churning snow and rock crashed to the bottom of the hill, it slowed, then stopped, leaving a massive drift that spread halfway across the valley floor. While the loud roar of the snowslide had been terrifying, the complete silence that hung over the valley after the icy rubble had come to rest was far more so. Except for the occasional sound of a lone boulder tumbling down the mountain in the wake of the avalanche, all was silent.

For many minutes Juan lay unconscious, entombed beneath the snow. The fact that he was still alive was due in part to the fortuitous trunk of a pine tree that lay directly above his head, creating a small pocket in the debris that enabled him to breathe. It was well past mid-day when he finally regained consciousness. From his waist up, he hurt in every muscle, bone, and joint in his body; from the waist down, he could feel nothing. A pale yellow light filtering through the overlying mantle of snow enabled him to look about his icy crypt. Below the waist he was firmly encased in snow but, thanks to the sheltering pine tree, his chest, shoulders, arms, and head were relatively free.

Hoping to determine the depth of the snow covering his frigid cell, Juan tentatively stretched his right arm high above his head. A sharp pain, accompanied by a grating sensation, left little doubt that the arm was broken. Ignoring a sharp pain in his chest, Juan attempted to reach the overlying mantle of snow with his left arm, but no matter how high he stretched, it remained just beyond his reach. Unwilling to accept failure, Juan broke a small branch from the tree to use as a probe. After a few upward thrusts, followed by a cascade of ice and snow, he found himself looking into a dark blue sky.

"At least I won't suffocate," he thought. On the other hand, freezing to death was a distinct possibility, and with this thought for motivation, he attempted to free himself. Using the tree branch to break the hard-packed snow below his waist into chunks, he threw them through the opening above his head. After he had removed as much of the crusted snow and debris as he could, he took a firm hold of a sturdy branch of the tree above his head and pulled upward with all his might.

As Juan's legs suddenly broke free from the icy grasp of the snow, an agonizing pain exploded in his lower body, and he realized with horror that both of his legs were badly broken. Now it was pointless for him to try to free himself from his snowy cell, for even if he succeeded, he was still going to die. With two legs and an arm broken, it would be impossible for him to find food or protect himself from the elements and wild animals. Certainly he would never be able to travel. So what could he possibly do? Nothing, he thought — nothing at all, except pray.

But Juan no longer believed in prayer. Nor did he believe in miracles, for if there were such things, Pedro would still be alive. He had prayed over and over that his brother might live, but God had let him die anyway. And now it was his turn to die, and perhaps it was for the best. He knew that he deserved to die, if only to atone for his brother's death, but even more so because he had cursed Almighty God for failing to spare his brother's life. Surely God had abandoned him. Had He not allowed this disaster to befall him? Perhaps He had even caused it. But still, even though he was faced with certain death and overcome with self-recrimination, Juan prayed with all his heart and soul, asking God to forgive him for his sins and by some great miracle spare his life.

As the cold gradually lowered his body temperature, Juan's mind became numb as did his entire body, and he no longer felt the pain that had tormented him earlier. Huddled in his icy crypt, he seemed suspended in time. Had he been there an hour? — a day? He didn't know — nor did he really care. Nevertheless, Juan still fought to stay awake, for to go to sleep would be to die, and as yet he couldn't bring himself to accept the inevitable.

As Juan's cold benumbed mind struggled to stay awake, he slowly became aware of a faint murmuring sound coming from somewhere close by his icy burial crypt. As it grew louder and seemed to resemble the babble of human voices, he became convinced that he was hallucinating and that his mind was playing tricks on him. He became even more convinced when he thought he could understand some of the words being said. But it was not until a sprinkle of snow fell on him from above, and he looked up to see two concerned eyes peering down at him, that he realized that this was actually happening and not some figment of his disordered mind.

Miraculously, though buried alive in the midst of the wilderness, he had been found, and he was going to live. Never again would he doubt the never-ending love and power of Almighty God. And indeed, it was a far greater miracle than Juan could ever have imagined. Not only had he been rescued from what had appeared to be certain death, he actually knew the man who was peering down at him. It was Pinto, Chief Moara's only son, whom he had met in Santa Fe earlier and again on the campaign against Cuerno Verde.

Following Pinto's directions, several Ute braves set about freeing Juan from his place of imprisonment. After Juan had explained to them about his broken arm and legs, two of the braves carefully got down into the crypt on either side of him. Then, using tree limbs to loosen the packed snow encasing his legs, they piled it on a deerskin. Two other braves lifted it from outside the crypt. This done, the four braves carefully began to lift him to the surface. The instant they lifted, a thunderbolt of excruciating pain shot through Juan's legs and right arm, but it was nothing when compared to the agony from the broken ribs in his chest. Mercifully, he lost consciousness as he was taken from the crypt and carefully placed on a buffalo hide in the warmth of a blazing fire.

While Juan was yet unconscious, Pinto and his companions carefully examined his injuries. His broken right arm was expertly straightened and held fast between two pieces of a tree branch they had shaped into splints with their hunting knives. They splinted his left leg as well, though they could find no definite sign of a break. But there was no doubt that Juan's right leg was broken and broken very badly, for it bent outward at an alarming angle, and a splinter of bone protruded from the skin. Pinto shook his head in dismay. The others looked equally grim. Far too often they had seen comrades with similar injuries, and they knew too well what the final outcome would be. In the unlikely event that Juan survived, he would be a cripple for the rest of his life.

Fearing that he would soon regain consciousness, the Utes hastened to straighten the leg as much as possible. Earlier, they had discovered Juan's faithful horse patiently awaiting his return on the far side of the avalanche. After retrieving a blanket from its pack, they tore it into strips with which to bandage the injured leg before splinting it securely as they had the other leg. Next, with more strips torn from the blanket, they tightly wrapped Juan's chest, hoping that it might ease the pain of his broken ribs. And finally, having done all they knew how to do, they gently laid him on the buffalo robe by the fire.

Weak and exhausted, Juan slept fitfully the whole night through and awoke at daybreak to a world filled with pain. There wasn't an inch of his body that didn't hurt, but he was grateful just to be alive. Seeing him stir, Pinto came to stand by his side. His tall, lithe frame was clad in buckskin, and he was wearing a heavy coat made of buffalo hide. While the other members of the party were busily engaged in constructing a travois similar to the one Juan had built for Pedro, Pinto explained to Juan how it was that they had found him.

"We were on our way back to camp from a hunt in the Valle Salado when we came across your tracks in the snow and followed them to the place where you camped night before last. When we heard your musket shot and the roar of the avalanche, we got here as quickly as we could. We were afraid one of our own people was buried in the slide. But when we found one of the horses my father, Chief Moara, gave you and your brother, we knew it was you instead. We looked for a long time and were about to give up when I spotted the opening in the snow and looked in to find you. After that, some of the braves kept on looking for Pedro. I'm very sorry, but they never found him."

Though he was loath to talk about it, Juan explained what had happened to Pedro and, as he related the story, all of his terrible feelings of guilt and self-recrimination returned. In one sense, however, it helped allay some of Juan's own pain as he recalled all that his brother had endured. Perhaps it was only fair that now it was his turn to suffer. It might in some way atone for his brother's death. Pinto, realizing how painful it was for Juan to recall his experiences, did not question him further.

Pinto confirmed that the Rio de Napestle did indeed flow through the large valley to the west of them, as Juan had suspected. Their camp, he said, was at the foot of a great white cliff where a sacred spring of warm water bubbled from out of the ground. Pinto assured Juan that the hot, medicinal water of the spring was magical and could cure all manner of ills. Perhaps it would help him, for it was there that they were taking him.

The journey down the mountain was very difficult, not only for Juan, but for his Indian escorts as well. The travois was of limited help, and for much of the time, they were forced to carry him. For them it was an arduous ordeal. For Juan it was a living hell. After what seemed like an eternity, he became unconscious and remained so until they arrived at a cluster of wickiups and rock huts at the foot of a large chalk cliff. Just as Pinto had described, a steamy, odiferous spring of hot water bubbled from a crevice in the rocks below the cliff and flowed into a crystal-clear stream that ran past the camp on its way to join the Rio de Napestle. The largest of the huts was the one in which Chief Moara was staying along with his wife, Quana, and Tsashin, their seventeen-year-old daughter. There were two rooms within the hut, separated by a deerskin curtain. One of the rooms had a fire pit with a vent in the ceiling to allow the smoke to escape. A pallet of buffalo robes lay on the dirt floor on one side of the room, and it was on it that his weary rescuers placed the unconscious Juan.

Chief Moara was greatly distressed when he saw Juan in such a desperate condition, for he considered both Juan and Pedro to be good friends. He was even more disturbed when he learned of Pedro's death. Even though he had given them the horses, he had nevertheless had many misgivings when they left on their ill-fated venture. Now he regretted that he hadn't advised them against it more strongly and was determined to make every effort to save Juan's life and nurse him back to health with the help of Quana and Tsashin. But above all, he would pray to the Manitou, the great he-she spirit that lived alone in the sky and was the ruler of all that was, for, as Chief Moara knew, there were no other powers or gods — Manitou alone was God — only He could save Juan.

CHAPTER 6

And so began a long and painful period in Juan's life, a time of suffering and despair. Initially, when Quana and Tsashin had cleansed and redressed his wounds, they discovered numerous other cuts and abrasions that had been hidden by his torn and tattered clothing. These, along with his other open wounds, they sealed with heated resin from the piñon tree in order that the air might be excluded. During the final days of October and the first two weeks of November, Juan clung desperately to life. The third day after arriving at the encampment, his right leg had become infected at the site of the break, and red streaks extended up his leg towards his groin. His fever rose to an alarming degree and refused to come down, despite the best efforts of Quana, and especially Tsashin, to lower it.

This was not the first time she'd seen Juan. Although he had been unaware of it, she had observed him when he was acting as interpreter during a meeting between her father and Colonel Anza. She knew that both Pinto and her father liked and admired him, and she asked her brother, Pinto, who he was, for she thought him very handsome. Since that moment, she had not been able to stop thinking about him, and now, by some miracle, the Great Manitou had brought him to her, and she was determined that he would live. To that end, she spent many hours sponging his fevered body with cool cloths, as well as administering frequent portions of a liquid concoction she had made by boiling willow bark in water from the hot spring. These measures seemed to help briefly, and his fever would drop only to rise again — sometimes to even higher levels.

Devotedly, Tsashin either knelt or sat by Juan's side both day and night, never flagging in her determination to save his life. Reluctantly, at Quana's insistence, she would occasionally let Quana assume his care while she rested. But, more often than not, instead of resting, she would search the woods for herbs with which to make healing poultices she could apply to his infected wounds. At other times, she would try to persuade Juan to sip a little venison broth, take a few bites of dried raspberry or currants, or drink some of the medicinal water that flowed through his sick room.

On two occasions, Chief Moara enlisted the aid of Acari, the medicine man. He was a squat, heavy-set man with a barrel chest and muscular legs and forearms. His round face was crowned with black oily hair and his forehead encircled with a band of cloth. With his body draped with colorful blankets and an eagle claw necklace encircling his neck, he made a strange and striking impression as he knelt beside his patient and took a number of intriguing whistles, rattles, beads, and eagle feathers decorated with porcupine quills and bird claws from his medicine bag.

Ute Medicine Man.
(Courtesy of the Colorado Historical Society.)

After carefully arranging the objects, Acari would place his lips against Juan's chest and suck, while at the same time uttering low gurgling sounds. Sometimes this would continue throughout the night. At other times he knelt beside Juan and sang in a series of high-pitched grunts, gradually fading to a lower and more solemn tone. And sometimes, usually as a grand finale, he would dance about the room while vigorously shaking a rattle and giving forth frightful screams and howls that seemed to shake the rock walls of the house. But despite his best efforts, Juan's fever persisted.

It was nearing mid-October and Chief Moara was becoming concerned. They must leave soon and rejoin the other members of the Mouache tribe at their encampment many miles to the south. If they didn't, he and his people might be trapped here by the winter snows that were often heavy in late November and December — or even worse, they might be caught in a blizzard while en route. But the chief was reluctant to leave until Juan was strong enough to endure the rigors of the trip, and, after two more worrisome weeks, he finally was. His fever left him, his wounds and fractures appeared to be healing, and he was recovering, or so it appeared. Unfortunately it was only an illusion, for though his fractures and infection were healing, his mind and spirit were not.

As Juan's mind slowly cleared and he realized that he would never again walk in a normal fashion, he came to believe that it would have been far better for him to have died rather than be a useless cripple for the remainder of his life. Pinto, Quana, Chief Moara, and especially Tsashin did their best to convince him otherwise. They assured him that the best days of his life were yet to come, for though he might always need a crutch to help him get around, there were all sorts of rewarding ways in which he could work and enjoy the future. But despite all their efforts to encourage him, nothing they said or did seemed to help. Juan became even more convinced that Pedro's death was due to his negligence and that God was punishing him and would continue to punish him for the rest of his life and probably for all eternity. So what did it really matter if he lived or died? Either way, he was doomed to eternal misery.

Immersed in the realm of his own dark thoughts, Juan was scarcely aware of being placed on the travois as the Indians began the long, arduous trek to their southern encampment. All during the difficult journey, he seemed oblivious of Tsashin's constant attendance and of the valiant efforts of the Ute braves as they carried his travois over the rough passages where his little horse could not safely pull him. Not once did he thank them or Tsashin for all that they had done for him.

Fortunately, and to Chief Moara's great relief, they arrived safely at the site of their winter encampment without any mishap. There, in the midst of a large clearing in the forest, a cloud of odoriferous steam rose from a pool of hot, bubbling water and from the rivulet that flowed from the pool into to a nearby stream. Bordering the pool was a multi-layered rim of dried sediment, stained red, yellow, orange, and brown by the medicinal minerals in the water. This was the dwelling place of the "Gitche Manitou"— the spirit of good medicine.

As related by the ancient ones, the hot spring had been a gift from the Great Manitou. Many years ago, a terrible sickness had befallen a number of Utes while their tribe was encamped on this very spot. The sickness had spread rapidly, many had died, and the tribe was dwindling at an alarming rate. Finally, in desperation, a council was held by those who still survived and, following it, they chanted and danced for hours around a blazing fire, beseeching the Great Manitou to help them. The next morning the Indians awoke to discover that where the fire had been, there was now a "Pagosah," a spring of healing waters. The ailing Utes bathed in the spring, drank of its healing waters, and were restored to good health. From that day on, this had been a sacred spot to all those belonging to the Ute Nation and to other Indian nations as well.

As was the custom of the Utes, the women rapidly set about establishing their winter camp, while the men of the tribe sat idly by, talking and laughing as they watched the women construct their snug huts. Each one was positioned with its entrance facing the east in order to greet the morning sun. When all were completed, over fifty newly erected dwellings stood in the meadow at Pagosah. In addition to these, there were fifty or sixty more that belonged to members of other Mouache and Capote tribes. Chief Moara breathed a sigh of relief. Now that his tribe was safely housed for the oncoming winter, his troubles were over — except, of course, for Juan's lingering depression.

At Tsashin's insistence, her parents had erected Juan's hut next to their own so that she might continue in her efforts to nurse him back to health. She was determined to succeed in this endeavor. Her parents, however, were becoming discouraged. No matter what they did or how hard they tried to cheer him up, Juan's depression showed no sign of improvement. Though they knew it wasn't intentional, Chief Moara and Quana became annoyed by Juan's lack of response. Never once had he thanked them or shown any sign of appreciation for all of the help they had given him. He seemed completely unaware of their concern for him. Nor did he seem to have any interest in his surroundings or in the activities of the tribe. It troubled Chief Moara greatly, for though he wanted to help his friend recover, there was nothing more he could do. From now on, whether Juan recovered or remained an invalid depended entirely on the will of the Great Manitou.

Tsashin, however, would not give up. She was determined that Juan would recover — not just physically but emotionally as well. And so it was that she continued to spend her days in caring for him. Using the sharpened blade of his hunting knife, she carefully trimmed his hair and beard and washed them with soap made from the root of yucca plants. And she fed him delicacies, including dried and roasted yucca blossoms and pudding made from roasted piñon nuts mixed with a pulp made from the yucca fruit. She encouraged him to walk with the improvised crutch she had made with Pinto's help.

The many young braves of the tribe could not understand why a young woman as lovely as Tsashin would care for this sick, bearded Spaniard. And, though Juan was completely unaware of it, his devoted attendant was very beautiful, indeed. Though only seventeen, she was of moderate height, full bodied, slender, and long of limb. Her narrow waist was accented by the curves of her breasts and hips as they rounded enticingly against the restraint of her soft deerskin garments. Her raven black hair fell past her shoulders almost to her waist and gleamed with the luster of polished obsidian whenever the sun shone on it. Her unusually delicate features lacked the high cheekbones of some of her tribe. Her face was a lovely oval with a high, intelligent brow, a perky little nose, and an exquisitely formed, though resolute, chin. Her sensuous lips, when parted, revealed white, even teeth that sparkled in sharp contrast to the tawny color of her skin. But her most striking feature was her eyes. Unlike the piercing black eyes of her father, hers were as blue as the skies of summer and alight with a soft radiance that made her expressive face seem alive with joy and anticipation.

Tsashin was the granddaughter of a Spanish woman and a Ute warrior named Aguila, the eagle. When her grandmother was a young child she was taken prisoner by an Apache war party during a raid on a Spanish settlement near Taos and traded to the Utes in exchange for two horses. The little girl had been adopted into the family of one of the sub-chiefs of the Mouache tribe and raised as one of their own children — with love and tenderness. As she grew older, she became a beautiful woman and married a chieftain in the same tribe. And, while Tsashin's mother, Quana, was a child of that union, it was her grandmother that Tsashin resembled most, although her Indian blood had greatly enhanced her beauty far beyond that of her Spanish forebearers.

As December yielded to January, followed in turn by February and March, Tsashin's zeal and determination never slackened. Day after day, she remained faithful to her self-assigned task. Occasionally she felt encouraged when Juan would answer her questions or respond to her requests. Now and then he would even volunteer to say or do something on his own, but most of the time he remained locked in the grip of a paralyzing melancholy. And never once did he mention Pedro's death, nor did he seem to appreciate Tsashin's loving care.

When his flesh wounds had healed and he could hobble about to some extent, Tsashin persuaded him to commence bathing in the hot spring waters of Pagosah, explaining that they had magical curative powers. As Juan soaked, she would sit beside him while stretching and massaging the joints of his broken arm and misshapen leg until eventually, even though he was unaware of it, his strength gradually began to return, and he could walk somewhat better.

When Tsashin was not occupied in caring for Juan, she was kept busy by the many chores assigned to her by her mother. Perhaps her least favorite of these was fetching drinking and cooking water from the nearby stream. To do this, she would go to a small pool above their encampment and the place where water from the hot spring flowed into the stream. While others of the tribe were not so particular and got their water closer to the camp, Tsashin thought the mineral water added a peculiar taste to that of the stream, and drinking water in which people had bathed was even less appealing.

Late in the afternoon on a cold day in mid-March, Tsashin carefully seated Juan on a bench in front of his tent. After covering him with a heavy robe and assuring him that she would be back soon, she shouldered a wooden pole with a leather bucket suspended from either end and reluctantly set forth to haul the evening's supply of water. The pool from which she drew the water was a long stone's throw above the camp and would have been within sight of the bench where Juan was seated had it not been for the evergreen trees that surrounded it. Although Tsashin had not been aware of it, during the last few weeks whenever she was nearby, Juan never let her out of his sight. She had become such a vital part of his life that whenever she was away from him he felt far more depressed.

So it was that on this particular day he was watching her closely as she entered the woods.

As Tsashin was engaged in breaking a thin layer of ice from the surface of the pool with a small hatchet, she heard a low, ominous growl coming from somewhere nearby. Looking up, she was terrified to see an enormous, silvery-gray, humpbacked bear standing about thirty feet away on the far side of the stream. Even as she watched, the bear reared up on its hind legs and, baring its long, yellowed teeth, snarled a fearful warning while making threatening motions with its massive forelegs and clawed paws. Having but recently awakened from hibernation, the old bear was very grumpy and irritable from the pangs of a long empty stomach. He had been fishing, so far unsuccessfully, in a large pool on the other side of the stream when Tsashin had so unwittingly interrupted him.

Initially, Tsashin was immobilized by fear, but when the bear continued to stand and sway back and forth, she began to back away slowly in the direction of the camp. She would have screamed for help but didn't, for fear it would enrage the bear. As she slowly and carefully backed out of the woods and into the clearing, Tsashin prayed fervently that the Great Manitou would send the great bear away and not let it attack her. But even as she prayed, the huge animal dropped down on all four legs and started to cross the stream in her direction. Throwing all caution to the wind, she turned to run to the encampment, knowing full well that it was at least three hundred feet to the closest tent and that she would never be able to outrun the bear — but she had no other recourse.

As Tsashin turned to run, she was startled to see a man pass by her and confront the oncoming bear. After going several paces past Tsashin, he stopped and stood his ground, shouting ferociously in a loud voice at the bear and brandishing a stick above his head. Tsashin was astonished when she realized that the stick was a crutch and that the man was Juan. When Juan had seen her backing out of the woods as though in fear of something he couldn't see, he had become alarmed. Without waiting to see what it was that threatened her, or even stopping to consider whether or not he could walk, he had rushed to her rescue, all the while offering a silent prayer to Almighty God that He would let nothing bad happen to Tsashin.

Up to that point the old bear had not been seriously charging, but it was on the point of doing so when this insolent upstart confronted him. He stopped, reared up on his hind legs again, and, standing fully ten feet tall, roared back at Juan with equal ferocity. After perhaps a minute or two of this threatening interchange, the grizzled old bear apparently decided it was just too early in the season to have to deal with such a noisy nuisance as this, especially on an empty stomach. Whereupon he dropped back down on all four legs and plodded slowly back into the forest, now and then turning and looking back over his shoulder and giving forth a low, throaty growl in case this bothersome creature should have the temerity to follow him.

The crisis past, Juan almost collapsed on the ground, and would have if it hadn't been for the supporting arms of Tsashin. For just a moment they stood embraced in one another's arms, neither one able to say a thing. Juan was overwhelmed with relief to know that Tsashin was safe, and, as he looked into her lovely blue eyes, for the very first time he became aware of her astonishing beauty. Too soon, however, the magical moment was broken as the entire tribe gathered about them, chattering excitedly. Everyone, even the jealous braves, congratulated Juan on his quick action and courage. They were all amazed that he had been able to come to Tsashin's defense so quickly — or at all, for that matter. Though he hadn't realized it at the time, Juan had actually run to her rescue without the use of his crutch for support. And now that the crisis was past, he was delighted to discover that he was able to bear much of his weight on his crippled leg — although he still needed his crutch when he walked.

As the excitement subsided, Juan and Tsashin walked hand in hand back to the encampment escorted by Chief Moara, Quana, Pinto, and other members of the tribe. Later, while the men were all seated about the fire in front of Chief Moara's tepee discussing this remarkable event, the chief told them that it must be that the Great Manitou looked with much favor upon Juan and Tsashin, for he had ordered the great bear not to harm them.

Then he told Juan and the others how many years ago Manitou had created this earth and all the creatures on it, and for a long time they all lived together in peace. But then the coyote got bad and caused a lot of mischief and they began to fight. The strong killed the weak, and there was blood all over everything. The He-She, looking down on all this, was disgusted and decided to create the great grizzly bear and make him chief over all the rest of the animals. He was to rule them with wisdom and strength. The great bear explained to the rest of the animals that they should stop fighting and live in peace, for those were the orders of the great He-She, and if they did not do it he would punish them. After that most of them obeyed him, except for the coyote — he's still a troublemaker and the great He-She went back to the heavens to rest and left the bear to rule for him. And so it was that ever since that time, the Utes have treated the grizzly bear with great respect, for he is their brother and protector and the representative of the Great Manitou on this earth. Chief Moara said that it was a miracle that the great bear had spared Juan and Tsashin's lives, and that he was sure it was Manitou who had ordered it. But Juan didn't entirely agree. It was truly a miracle all right, but it was Almighty God who had spared their lives, not Manitou — of that he was sure.

At that moment, it was as though a great light had entered his mind and restored his spirit as Juan realized that God never had truly abandoned him. He had always been with him — even during those dark days when Pedro was so terribly ill and died, and when he was entombed by the avalanche. Though Juan had done nothing to warrant it, God had granted him two great gifts: He'd restored him to life, and he had given him Tsashin. And as he came to understand the wonder of it all, the dark curtain of his depression lifted and his world was filled with light again.

CHAPTER 7

The spring of 1780 came early to the pine-covered hills and open mead-ows that surrounded Pagosah. The winter snows had largely melted, lin-gering only on the northern slopes of the mountains and in the shaded depths of the coulees and canyons. Flowers in brilliant hues of blue and yellow thrust their heads above the greening grasses of the sun-dappled meadows, lovely harbingers of the rebirth of yet another spring.

But for Juan it was far from being just another spring. His life was beginning anew. Freed from the shackles of overwhelming guilt and despondency, it was as though he had emerged from the black cell of his depression into the bright sunshine of a new day, and he began to look forward with hopeful anticipation to what the future might bring. From that time on, Juan was able to tell Tsashin the many things he had been unable to talk about before — about his wonderful memories of Pedro and of the terrible ordeal that led to his death. When he told her about the bonanza and the troubles they had encountered after finding it, Tsashin asked him to promise that he would never again return to Lost Creek. No amount of gold was worth the risk of his life. Juan promised willingly, for he had no desire whatsoever to go back to that place of dreadful memories.

All through the month of April, Juan and Tsashin were insepara-ble, and with each passing day they fell more deeply in love. They spent their happiest hours riding through the fragrant forests and climbing to high mountain overlooks, from whence they watched the great eagles as they soared high above the seemingly endless panorama of peaks and valleys. Tsashin explained that her people loved their mountain domain and called them the "Shining Mountains" because of the way the sun shone on the lofty snow-covered peaks. And then, on the first day of May 1780, as they were sitting on the summit of a hill overlooking a lovely flower covered meadow, Juan proposed.

"Tsashin, I'm sure you must know by now how very much I love you. After Pedro died, a great emptiness came into my life, and I no longer cared whether I lived or died. But then you came and filled the emptiness with your love and caring. You restored me to my normal self. I know that I can never pay you or thank you enough for all that you've done for me, and now I'm going to ask even more of you. I want you to be my wife, so that we can spend the rest of our lives together. If you marry me, I'll be the happiest and luckiest man on this earth."

"Of course I'll marry you, Juan," Tsashin said smiling. "I've been in love with you ever since I first saw you at that meeting with my father and Colonel Anza in Santa Fe. Ever since that time, I've been praying that the Great Manitou would bring us together, and he did. I'll be forever grateful to him."

"I'm grateful, too, Tsashin, but I'm sure it was the Almighty God of the Christians — not Manitou — who was guiding us. I didn't realize it until now, but He's been directing my footsteps and yours ever since I left Santa Fe last year, and He's brought me through all sorts of trials and troubles in order to bring us together. And I'm sure He'll continue to do so if we put our faith and trust in Him."

Then Juan explained to Tsashin why it was important to him that she accept Jesus Christ as her Lord and Savior, put her trust in the one true God, and be baptized by Father Zarte at the Church of our Seraphic Father Saint Francis in Santa Fe, for in that way their marriage would be acceptable to the church. After that, he explained to Tsashin the reasons for his belief in Jesus. Tsashin listened carefully to all that Juan had said and after asking him many questions, she told him she was sure what he'd said was true, and that she would like to be baptized and married by Father Zarte. She did have one request, however. To honor both her parents and her people, she would also like to be married in accordance with the customs of the Utes. Juan willingly agreed to her request, feeling that it would be an ideal way for him to demonstrate his respect for Tsashin's parents and to thank them for their help in overcoming his injuries and illness.

Following this, Juan began to teach Tsashin how to speak and to understand his native tongue, and in a surprisingly short time she was speaking fluent Spanish. Then he described what he believed their lives together would be like after they were married. He felt sure that she would be welcomed by his family and friends as well as by the townspeople of Santa Fe. Although Juan's parents were no longer living, his two sisters, Maria and Dona, and their families were living there, as were his Uncle Bartolome Felipe Vasquez and his lovely young wife, Estrella. His uncle ran a profitable trading business that he and Juan's father had started twenty years ago, and Juan was hoping that he would ask him to join him in the business. But even if he didn't, he was sure that he could start a business of his own with the help of the gold in his backpack.

Tsashin's parents were pleased when they heard of Juan and Tsashin's wedding plans, for they were both very fond of Juan. Pinto was also pleased, and he promptly volunteered to instruct Juan in the various ways in which an amorous Ute brave might go about seeking his intended's parents' approval of marriage to their daughter.

"The simplest approach," Pinto said, "is for the brave to go to his intended's parents' tepee and lie down beside their daughter throughout the night, while her mother stays awake and watches them like a hawk to be sure that he doesn't touch her. At dawn he must leave. After that, if he wishes, he can return each night and repeat the procedure until eventually one of two things happens — either her mother gives her approval by going to sleep or she rejects him by throwing dirt in his face." After this Pinto smiled and added, "This isn't a particularly popular approach among the Ute braves."

"And I can certainly see why," Juan agreed.

"A second method of courting," Pinto continued, "is for the suitor to kill a fat buck or elk and hang it from the branch of a tree in front of his intended's tepee. She, having been forewarned, will then dress in her finest garments and rush outside, squealing in delight and pretending that it comes as a complete surprise. After butchering the animal, she will take some of the meat inside her parents' tepee and make a stew. And then, after a short wait, the brave, dressed in his finest buckskins, goes into the tepee and asks her parents for her hand in marriage. If they accept his proposal, he is invited to join them in a wedding feast. If they don't, he leaves."

The next method was Pinto's personal choice. "After first hiding himself in a tree or bush near his intended's tepee, the suitor sings to her in a loud voice, declaring his undying love and describing his great bravery and strength. Or, if he prefers, he plays a tune on a wooden flute. Following the serenade, the amorous brave brings gifts to his loved one's family, but as he does, he completely ignores his intended and directs all of his attention towards her parents. If they approve of him, his proposal and presents will be accepted. Personally, I think that this approach is by far the most romantic of the three choices," Pinto opined. "It's certainly better than having dirt thrown in your face or giving your loved one a dead animal." Juan agreed, whereupon Pinto graciously offered to give him flute lessons.

Courting Flute
(Courtesy of the Center of Southwest Studies Fort Lewis College, Durango, CO.)

"Actually, Juan, I'm a fine musician," he declared modestly. "I'm sure that you'll be playing the flute beautifully after I give you a few lessons." And so it was to this end that Juan and Pinto began to sneak into the woods to practice playing the flute. But after the third agonizing, ear-torturing session of screeches and squeals, Pinto clasped his hands over his ears and begged Juan to stop.

"It's hopeless," he said. "It's obvious that you'll never entice a mate by playing the flute." But then, after a moment's reflection, he solemnly declared. "But actually, now that I think about it, that might not be entirely true. For, even though it's spring and the wrong time of the year for such passion, I wouldn't be a bit surprised but what an amorous cow elk might suddenly appear in response to your seductive mating call. Or, what's probably even more likely, an enraged bull elk with fire in his eye will come charging out of the woods to challenge you for his mate's affections."

Following this unkind remark, the flute was replaced by vocal lessons. Unfortunately, Juan's singing ability was not much better than his flute playing. It just wasn't quite as shrill and ear splitting. Apparently music in any form was not one of Juan's strong points. Nevertheless, he opted to use the latter approach.

Pinto laughed, "You know, Juan, if Tsashin still agrees to marry you after hearing you sing, it'll be sure proof that she loves you."

And apparently she did, for the very next day, Juan serenaded his loved one with a number of discordant songs to the accompaniment of Pinto's flute, and after they had all stopped laughing, Tsashin and her parents joyfully accepted his proposal.

Immediately after their marriage, Chief Moara announced to Juan that he and the members of their tribe intended to escort the newly-weds on their way to Santa Fe to be sure they were not attacked by marauding Comanche bent on avenging the death of Cuerno Verde. Juan thanked him and told him that both he and Tsashin would be grateful for their protection.

And so it was that early in the morning on the first day of June 1780, Juan and Tsashin left the hot spring of Pagosah accompanied by over fifty Ute braves, women, children, their horses, and all of their belongings. It was much later in the year than Juan had originally planned on leaving, and he had hoped to travel fast and light in order to reach Santa Fe in about a week. But as it turned out, it took considerably longer than he expected, largely because of the lackadaisical manner in which the Utes traveled. But finally, after fifteen frustratingly slow days of travel, Juan, Tsashin, and their Ute escorts stood on the summit of a cedar-covered hill overlooking the sun-baked adobe Villa of Santa Fe. As it was already late afternoon, Chief Moara, Quana, Pinto, and the rest of their tribe hurried off in the direction of their intended campsite to settle in before dark. They promised to visit Juan and Tsashin in the Villa de Santa Fe on the following day.

Standing alone on their vantage point, Juan pointed out some of the familiar landmarks of the little town to Tsashin. The most imposing structure to catch the eye was the Church of Our Seraphic Father St. Francis, with its well-occupied cemetery bordering it on the east. A narrow dusty street began at the west gate of the cemetery and continued westward for about four hundred to five hundred varas, passing in front of the church and along the south side of a small, dusty plaza. Juan called Tsashin's attention to an adobe building near the church. It was a small inn that had been built many years ago by a Spaniard named Alarid La Fonda. He was a very gracious man, and through the years had offered his hospitality to many a passer-by. Even though he had long since died, his descendants still lived there and continued to carry on the tradition of opening their home to strangers in need.

Juan pointed out a much larger structure extending along the entire length of the plaza on the north. This, he explained, was the thick adobe-walled Presidio de Santa Fe, residence of Governor de Anza and his family as well as the military troops under his command. A few small shops and adobe homes belonging to the settlers bordered the remainder of the plaza. In its center was a forlorn water well surrounded by some equally forlorn looking trees. West of the plaza, several dusty alleyways led to a number of small adobe houses. One of these was the home of Juan's Uncle Bartolome and his Aunt Estrella.

Beyond the settlement, through the gathering dusk, they could see many small ranchos, each surrounded by greening fields of vegetables, melons, and corn. Juan pointed out to Tsashin the two ranchos at the western outskirts of the settlement where his sisters and their families lived. At last count, there were close to twelve hundred people living in the Villa de Santa Fe, including Governor Anza, the five members of his family, two hundred and twenty-nine Spanish families, and forty-two Indian families that lived like the Spaniards and were known as "Genizaros."

Standing alone in the gathering twilight and looking down upon the little village, Juan and Tsashin were filled with excitement and anticipation — mixed with apprehension — as each wondered what the future might have in store for them. It was not the first time that they had wondered these things — how Juan's family and the other people of Santa Fe would accept Tsashin as a person and as his wife, or if Father Zarte would agree to marry them. They had discussed it many times over, and Juan had always assured Tsashin that there would be no problem — that everyone would love her and welcome her with open arms. But now that the time had arrived when they would find out for sure, they were both filled with doubt and apprehension. So much depended on the next few minutes and hours. Would Tsashin really be accepted and welcomed as Juan's wife, or would she be rejected? If it went one way, all would be well, but should it go the other, their lives would be entirely different from what they had so confidently planned — but how different and in what way? They would soon know as they began the short ride down the dusty hillside to the Villa de Santa Fe.

❊ PART TWO ❊

SHADYCROFT FARM
LITTLETON, COLORADO
NOVEMBER 4TH 1932 TO EARLY MARCH 1933

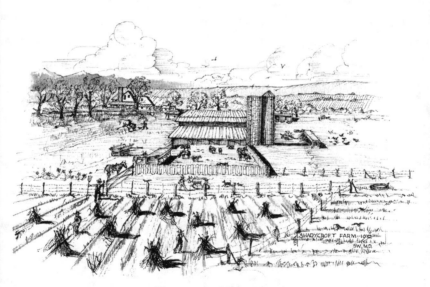

(A pen and ink drawing by Doctor Seymour Wheelock)

CHAPTER 8

Friday, November 4, 1932

The black shroud of night enveloped me so that I could scarcely see. Yet, if I looked closely, I could make out the ghostly outline of my home at Shadycroft Farm. It was there that I'd just seen something that frightened me.

My grandparents, Herbert and Mona Johnson, had purchased Shadycroft Farm from Henry Harper Curtis in 1902. The original owner, Charles R. Bell, homesteaded the 365 acres of farmland in June 1877. After acquiring the land, my grandparents immediately set about building a large barn and enlarging the original farmhouse to accommodate their family of five children, later to be eight, of whom my father, Julius, was the oldest. Julius, in turn, purchased Shadycroft from his father in 1917, and ever since that time had been busily, and for the

Shadycroft Farm, Pond, and Orchard on the left, house is hidden among the trees in the background. Chicken houses are on the right.

(Picture taken by Julius Johnson Sr. - circa 1929.)

Shadycroft Farm House, circa 1920.

(Photograph is from the Johnson family album.)

most part happily, engaged in farming. That is, he was, up until the time of my story.

There were four of us in our family — my dad, my mother (Grace), my brother (J. J.), and me. Actually, my brother's name was Julius, same as Dad's, and to begin with my folks called him Julius, or Julius Jr.. or, sometimes, just Junior — except Mother — she still called him Julius Jr.

Our farmhouse at Shadycroft was a large, comfortable home with a gabled roof and wide, shady porches. It was set in the midst of numerous large cottonwood and elm trees, and ordinarily I would have derived a good deal of comfort from its reassuring presence, but tonight was different. Accompanied by Rab, a big, black German shepherd, I was returning from an afternoon and evening of play with Charley Vogel, the boy who lived in the house at the head of the lane.

At that time of my life, next to Rab, Charley was my very best friend. There were several reasons for this. First of all, he'd just turned ten years old and I was a little over nine months older, making me, in my considered opinion, much his superior in most every respect. Second, he had an older sister, Abigail, and just recently I had begun to realize that there were some very interesting differences between boys

Grace Reed Johnson
Robby and J. J.'s mother, circa 1921.
(Photograph is from the Johnson
family album.)

Julius E. Johnson Sr.,
Robby and J. J.'s father, circa 1921.
(Photograph is from the Johnson
family album.)

and girls. Third, his mother, who was a widow lady, made really great
chocolate cookies; and fourth, and maybe most important, there was no
other playmate to be had for miles around.

I should have gone home long ago on strict orders from my parents. On this particular Friday night, they and J. J. were in town attending a meeting at the Grandview Grange. Ordinarily I would have gone
with them, but that afternoon they had agreed to let me stay and play
at the Vogel's, just as long as I promised to be home well before dark.

Perhaps I should point out that this concession on the part of my
parents had come only after an unusually eloquent appeal on my own
behalf in which I pointed out that, being as how I was almost eleven
years old, I was perfectly capable of taking care of myself — especially
without the help of my fifteen-year-old brother. To my considerable
surprise, they had agreed, but only after I had assured them that I would
be home well before dark and that I would comply with my mother's
long list of "do and don't do" instructions regarding my behavior.

Later that afternoon, just as the sun was disappearing behind
Mount Evans, Mrs. Vogel suggested that perhaps I should give serious

thought to leaving because it would soon be getting dark. But, inasmuch as I appeared to be well on my way to winning all the wooden kitchen matches in a spirited poker game with Charley and Abigail, I could see no compelling reason to hurry my departure. So I chose to ignore Mrs. Vogel's comment regarding the rapidly approaching night. I ignored, too, her gently added reminders that my mother's wrath, when aroused, was a significant force to be reckoned with, and, besides that, it was getting dark and she was sure that it was going to snow.

After another forty-five minutes of play and after losing most of my hard-won matches — to a girl, of all people — Mrs. Vogel's admonitions finally arrived at the reasoning part of my brain — particularly the part about my mother's wrath. Belatedly, I decided that it really was time to go home — well past it, as a matter of fact. So here I was, shrouded by the blackest of nights, wishing fervently that I had not been so successful in convincing my parents that I could take care of myself without their help — or maybe even my brother's.

I was standing at the end of Windermere, the narrow, rutted road leading to Shadycroft Farm from the small town of Littleton about

Julius E. Johnson Jr. and
Robert Reed Johnson.
J. J. and Robby, circa 1929.
(Photograph is from the Johnson family album.)

Rab
(Photograph taken by Julius E. Johnson Sr. circa 1931.)

three miles to the north. I was staring intently down the lane at the shadow of my home a quarter of a mile away. I thought I had seen a faint glimmer of light coming from the east end of the house, right where the kitchen window was situated. It was there for only an instant and then gone. Had I really seen anything? Surely it was my imagination. Halloween was just a few days past, and I succeeded in convincing myself that it was only my recent involvement with ghosts and witches and my rampant imagination that led to my disquietude. That my imagination was rampant had been pointed out to me on innumerable occasions by my parents as well as by my brother, all of whom were frequently not pleased, and often downright critical, of the end products of my active, and what I considered rather creative, mind.

Grateful for Rab's reassuring presence by my side, I resumed my walk down the lane but with noticeably less enthusiasm. The wind was cold and sharp and out of the north. It whispered ominously through the dried and shriveled leaves of the cottonwood trees that overhung the lane, composing a sinister symphony that contributed mightily to my increasing feeling of unease. I thought briefly of returning to the haven of the Vogel's warm and safe kitchen, but I immediately gave up the idea on the mistaken belief that whatever might await me down that dark and forbidding lane couldn't possibly be worse than the humiliation and teasing I would be forced to endure, should I timidly return to the shelter of my friend's home. How wrong I was!

Two thirds of the way down the lane, I stopped again — abruptly — and so did my heart. I felt certain that I had again seen a faint yellow glow flicker very briefly, this time from the small dormer window in the attic directly above the kitchen where earlier I had seen, or at least thought I had seen, the first glimmer of light. Except for storage, the attic was seldom used. It was accessed from below by a stairway from the laundry room that adjoined the kitchen, as well as by a door from the upstairs hall. Surely it was a gleam of reflected light, I told myself, although from what source I couldn't possibly imagine, black as the house and the world around it now were. My heart had commenced beating again, and for that I was most grateful. But where were my parents? They should have been home long before now — and besides that, how come they let a ten-year-old kid talk them into going to the Grange meeting, leaving him home alone to fend for himself against all manner of scary things? — I wished now that I hadn't been so persuasive.

The temperature was dropping rapidly, the ever-increasing wind driving sharp needles of snow, stinging my face and forcing the bitter cold through the layers of my clothing. It was not a time to dally. I had to decide, and decide very soon, whether I should go on to my home, which now was very near by, or seek some other shelter from the storm. My options were few. I had already dismissed going back to the Vogel's house for reasons that I foolishly still thought valid. I considered trying to get to the Williamson's house, perhaps a third of a mile farther west in the lee of the bank of the Highline Canal, where it wound its way through our property. Clyde Williamson worked for my dad and lived in the tenant house on our farm with his wife, Ada, and their two daughters, Blanche and Frances. I had seen them leaving in their old Star touring car during the late afternoon, and I was pretty sure that they hadn't come back yet. I could see no light in the direction of their house, but by now the blowing snow limited visibility to no more than a few feet.

I thought briefly of taking shelter in the barn on the other side of the canal or in one of the chicken houses. I had spent many hours working and playing in our barn. It could be scary enough in the day time, but at night, in a storm, with the wind howling through the rafters like a banshee, I was certain that it was no place for me.

The chicken houses were even less inviting. Somehow the thought of snuggling up to thirty or forty whiterock hens and roosters wasn't particularly appealing — due, in part, to the intimate knowledge of our chickens' unsanitary habits I had acquired through seemingly endless hours spent cleaning up their messes. Let me tell you — chickens are not neat. Even in the brief time spent considering these options, the temperature had dropped several degrees and the wind seemed to double in intensity. I had no other choice — I had to go into the house.

Actually, all seemed peaceful and serene in the big house now. Certainly there was no sign of a light anywhere that I could see, and I became more and more convinced that I had only imagined that I had seen anything worrisome. Retrieving the door key from where it was hidden on the ledge over a nearby window and keeping Rab close beside me, I stepped cautiously onto the porch and walked to the front door. After taking a deep breath, I reached out to insert the key into the lock, but at the slightest touch, the door slowly swung open to reveal the pitch-black interior of the entry hall. The door was already unlocked! It wasn't even closed tightly.

Anxiety flooded over me. I couldn't stop shaking, whether from fear or from the cold, I couldn't be sure. I forced myself to breathe. No sound was to be heard, other than the wailing of the wind through the cottonwoods. Nothing moved — including me. I stood riveted to the door threshold. After what seemed an eternity, I whispered softly to Rab and was relieved to feel the reassuring pressure of his big head nudging my leg. As far as I could tell, he wasn't a bit concerned. Taking a deep breath, I groped inside the doorjamb searching for the light switch. The click of the switch sounded like a rifle shot, but how I welcomed the flood of light that filled the entry hall, revealing nothing more sinister than our hall tree festooned with a variety of familiar hats and coats.

Turning on every available light as I went, I entered the living room and flopped down on the sofa — Rab flopped down beside me. I had to think — why didn't my parents lock the door when they left like they usually did? Probably, I thought guiltily, it was because they were counting on me to lock up when I came home before dark as I had promised.

Up until then, there never had been much crime in Littleton and the farms around it. Except for a robbery at the Littleton National Bank back in 1928, it had always been quiet and peaceful. According to the write-up in the *Littleton Independent*, George Malcolm was working in the bank that day and according to him, the bankrobber stole over eleven thousand dollars — neither the robber nor the money were ever seen again. But just in the last year or two lots of hobos had been coming to Colorado from Kansas and Oklahoma after they were forced to leave their farms and home by the drought and blowing dust. Most of them just wandered from house to house, asking for food and money and didn't cause any trouble. But every so often, I'm sorry to say, one of them would rob somebody or somebody's home. And according to my folks, there was another reason that so many homeless people were showing up around Littleton back then. It was on account of what they called the depression — and it wasn't just in Colorado. People all over the country were out of work and hungry — farmers and townspeople alike. Partly it was because of the drought and partly it was due what my folks called the failed economy.

But it was the bootleggers that worried me the most. According to my friend Joe Wilkinson, a gang of them was making moonshine whiskey in a house up on Windermere, less than two miles north of our farm. I don't know how he knew that, but he swore it was gospel truth. So I guess it wasn't too surprising that my folks had started locking the house whenever they were going to be away — except for today, of course, when they were counting on me to lock up when I got home.

But how come the door wasn't even shut completely? Could somebody have come in the house after we all left? But why didn't they close the door? Were they afraid it'd make some noise and someone inside the house would hear it? Could they still be in the house?

And where were mother and dad and J. J.? They should be home by now. At least they could have called me on the telephone to tell me they were going to be late. Of course, maybe they did and I wasn't here to answer. But I probably was worrying needlessly. Except for the storm outside, everything was quiet and peaceful in the house, and all I had to do was just sit tight and wait for my folks to get home.

Actually, there was something I could do. I could ask the telephone operator to call the Grange hall so I could talk to my folks if they were still there — just hearing their voices would make me feel better. It was Friday night and Myrtle should be the operator on call. I liked Myrtle. She was nice and right then the thought of hearing any familiar voice was mighty appealing. The telephone was on the desk in the entry hall. I quietly lifted the receiver from the hook in order not to avoid alerting anyone or anything that might be lurking on the other side of the door that opened into the east part of the house. I waited for the operator to answer and ask me what number I wanted. Nothing! Not a sound could be heard. Apprehensively, I jiggled the receiver hook up and down several times, but all I could hear was the sound of my heart beating faster and faster as I held the receiver tight to my ear. There was nothing, no sound at all — only silence. The line was dead.

I knew very well what had happened. A tree branch, burdened by the weight of the snow, must have broken and fallen across the telephone wire snapping it in two, leaving me cut off from the outside world and, except for Rab, completely alone — or so I sincerely hoped. It had happened many times before, and I knew the line wouldn't be repaired until tomorrow at the very earliest. Accompanied by Rab, I slowly returned to the sofa and sat down. He laid his big head in my lap and wagged his tail reassuringly, as though to tell me that he would keep me from harm. I hugged him around the neck, grateful for his presence.

Well over an hour crept by and still no sign of my parents — I was getting more and more anxious by the minute. I felt sure that they had tried to get home and had gotten stuck in a snowdrift somewhere between here and the Grange hall. Windermere was deeply rutted even in the best of weather, and now, with the ruts buried by a heavy blanket of snow, it would be difficult to keep the car from slipping off the road. But even if that had happened, I was sure they'd take shelter at one of the farmhouses along the way. So I really wasn't worried about my parents or J .J. — partly because I knew they were safe — but mainly because I had enough problems of my own to worry about.

CHAPTER 9

The storm was steadily increasing in fury. At times, when the wind subsided, I would hear the sound of breaking tree limbs and the harsh rasp of wind-driven snow against the windowpanes. At irregular intervals, a disturbing thumping noise came from the direction of the kitchen, creating mental images of something huge and fearful attempting to force its way into the house. "It's only the wind banging a branch of that old box elder tree against the side of the screened porch," I told myself unconvincingly.

Abruptly, my anxiety was increased a hundredfold by a momentary flicker of the overhead lights. I'd forgotten. If the telephone line could break, so could the power lines, and at any moment I might find myself in total darkness. It happened every time we had a bad snowstorm. As far as I knew, all our flashlights, kerosene lamps, and candles were in the kitchen and dining room. Both were places I definitely did not want to go. Hoping that there was one at this end of the house, I decided to make a search — maybe I'd get lucky and find one — although the thought of doing it while there might be an intruder skulking in the house was worrisome to say the least. (I had recently learned the word "skulking" while reading one of my favorite Zane Grey books.)

Mustering what little courage I had left and keeping Rab close by my side, I carefully explored the newer part of the house, both downstairs and up, through more rooms than I seemed to recall the old house having. Happily, my search was successful, for I found a flashlight in a bureau drawer in my parent's bedroom at the southwest corner of the upstairs hall. It was a welcome sight.

My most exciting discovery, however, was a .44 caliber Colt revolver, sheathed in a well-worn leather holster and cartridge belt hanging from a hook on the back of the closet door. I recognized it. It was the gun my Granddad Johnson had used back in the 1880s, when he carried the mail on horseback from a small town on the eastern plains of Colorado called Longmont to a little community in the mountains called Estes Park. I remember him telling me once how grateful he was that he'd never had to use it to shoot a bad man — I found that very disappointing.

I remember my dad calling it a "hogleg" because of the shape of the grip. He also mentioned that the one and only time he'd ever shot it, the recoil had taken most of the skin off the palm of his hand. I could just imagine what my mother's reaction would be should she realize that I had found this treasure and what I thought I might do with it — I'd be in big, big trouble. My dad would be in even bigger trouble, however, for having left it where I could find it. The rest of his guns, including my own .22 caliber Winchester and 410 shotgun, were securely locked in a cabinet in the entry hall closet. They'd all been put there on strict orders from my mother right after Dad shot a hole in the kitchen door while cleaning a twelve gauge shotgun he thought was unloaded. The fact that no one had been hit was a minor miracle: that Mother had agreed to his keeping his guns at all was a major one.

I was sure it was on account of the recent robberies in Littleton that Dad had hung the revolver in their bedroom, figuring it would be a handy and safe place to keep it in case he ever needed it. Obviously, he had forgotten my tendency to investigate — snoop was the word my brother would have used. Anyway, I was sure that Dad would hear from my mother in no uncertain terms when she discovered that I had found it, but right now it seemed like a gift from heaven.

Dragging it down from the hook, I strapped it about my waist. Fortunately, Dad was a small man, and the extra holes he had poked through the belt to make it fit his waist just barely sufficed to keep it hanging precariously from my own scrawny hips. I pulled the revolver from the holster with some difficulty. It was real heavy, and I doubted that I could actually shoot someone, even if the need arose. I'd be far more likely to shoot off my foot or some other valuable body part. At that moment, however, such a possibility didn't particularly concern me as I loaded the gun with bullets from the cartridge belt, put it back into the holster, and, cowboy fashion, swaggered back into the hall and down the stairs, certain that I was the spittin' image of Buck Duane.

Buck was my current cowboy hero, having recently seen Zane Grey's *The Last of the Duanes* at the Gothic Theater in Englewood, a small town several miles to the north of us between Littleton and

Denver. Actually, Buck and I might easily have been mistaken for brothers, except that Buck didn't seem to have the annoying problem of having his gun belt fall down around his ankles as he walked. Fortunately, I hadn't come across any unwanted visitor during my search, although the thought had been foremost in my mind. Unhappily, I had found only one flashlight. All of the others, along with the lamps and candles, were in the dining room or kitchen.

As I returned to the living room sofa, my stomach growled loudly, reminding me that I hadn't eaten since lunch and was hungry. On top of that, the temperature inside the house was dropping rapidly, making it obvious that the furnace in the cellar needed stoking. Well, I'll tell you right now, there was no way I was going down into that dark, dank dungeon and add coal to the furnace. Compared to that gloomy, black widow-infested region, a visit to the kitchen was like a pleasure trip. In the kitchen, a big wood-burning range would make short work of the cold, and in the dining room, the "Round Oak" stove with isinglass windows in the door would do likewise. And, best of all, there was plenty of wood in the wood box, coal in the coal bucket, and food in the pantry. It was becoming more and more apparent that, despite what I hoped were my silly imaginative fears, I had to venture into the kitchen to avoid starvation and to keep from freezing to death.

The storm was abating. I no longer could hear the tree branches banging on the side of the house. In fact, there was no noise at all — silence enveloped the entire house. I should have been grateful, but, while the racket from the storm had been frightening, the complete quiet seemed far more unnerving. I whispered to Rab. He responded by thumping his tail on the rug, grateful that I had acknowledged his presence but not nearly as grateful as I was for his company.

With resolve, I rose from the sofa. It was time to put an end to my foolish fears as well as to my hunger and cold and go to the kitchen. With Rab close by my side, I walked towards the entry hall, but the moment I entered, the light in the hall flickered once and then went out, leaving a terrifying darkness in its stead. I couldn't believe it. Now the power line was down — what else could go wrong? I wondered if perhaps this was an omen that the dining room and kitchen were not safe places to go. But what else I could do — other than sit in the living room in total darkness, shaking with cold, and fear, and hunger.

Taking the flashlight from my jacket pocket, I pressed the switch and watched in horror as a sickly, yellow shaft of light extended from it for no more than a foot or two before it vanished in the black interior of the entry hall. The battery was weak, almost gone! After turning off the flashlight in order to conserve what little power was left, I stood shaking with fright in the suffocating darkness.

Up to this point, I had succeeded fairly well in overcoming my earlier anxiety, but now the prospect of having to search for the lamp and matches in total darkness raised new and fearful specters in my mind. What if some fearsome creature should leap upon me in the dark! The thought terrified me. But I still had no other choice: I had to find the kerosene lamp and light it before the power in the flashlight died completely. To avoid using the flashlight until I really needed it, I groped in the dark — first for Rab's reassuring presence, and then for the door leading into the dining room. I was surprised when I took hold of the doorknob. For some reason it felt wet and sticky, almost slimy. But I thought little of it at the time as I peered into the black interior of the dining room. The lamp should be on the table in the center of the room, but I wasn't so sure about the matches. Stepping cautiously in the dark, I bumped into the edge of the table sooner than I had expected, creating an unnerving squeak as its wooden joints rubbed together.

Reaching out carefully in the dark, I moved my hand back and forth across the tabletop until I found the lamp, but, search as I might, I could find no matches. I had to use the flashlight. Praying fervently, I pressed the switch and sighed in relief as a weak ray of light dimly illuminated the surface of the table. My hand was still sticky from touching the doorknob, and, without thinking, I directed the weak beam from the flashlight towards it. I stared in horror — my hand was covered with blood!! Dropping the flashlight, I began to shake uncontrollably. My initial impulse was to escape — to get out of that room, out of the house — anywhere but here. And if it hadn't been for Rab, that's probably what I would have done, but somehow his comforting presence allowed me to think more clearly, and I decided to stay — at least until I could decide what to do next.

First off, I had to find the matches and light the lamp. Fortunately, when I dropped the flashlight, the light had gone out, so, with any luck, there would still be a little life left in the battery. Groping about in the dark, I found it and pressed the switch. With relief, I saw a dim beam of light shine forth. I quickly directed it at the big coal-burning stove and then to the small table beside it. My spirits soared. There was the box of matches.

Retrieving it, I returned to the table and inspected the lamp. Fortunately there was plenty of kerosene and a good wick, so the lamp lit readily, and, as the soft, warm glow spread throughout the dining room, my courage rose rapidly. Of course, I was still very much aware of the serious problems that confronted me, and that hunger and cold were the least of them. Now I knew for sure that I was not alone. Someone or something was in the house, and whoever — or whatever — it was had been injured. (Unlikely as it was, my rampant imagination kept insisting that it might possibly be some fearsome creature left over from Halloween.)

The smart thing for me to do was to put aside my pride and go back to the Vogel's, and I was strongly tempted. But something was stopping me. Could it possibly be someone I knew? What if the injured person was one of my parents — or maybe my brother — who had come home without my knowing it and was lying on the kitchen floor, injured, weak, bleeding, and in desperate need of help? Although it didn't seem very likely, it was a possibility that I couldn't ignore.

But if that were so, why didn't he — or she — turn on the lights? The flickers of light I'd seen from up on the lane lasted for only a brief moment and then were extinguished. Maybe whoever it was was too badly hurt to reach up to the light switch. But if that were so, why did I see a light in the attic window? Whoever it was must have had enough strength to climb the stairs — and why would anyone even want to go to the attic? I had many questions, but no answers. Courage had never been one of my greater attributes, and now was certainly no exception, but I really had no other choice. As frightening as it would be, I had to find out whose blood it was on the dining room doorknob.

This was the older part of the house. It was heated by the Round Oak stove in the dining room and the wood-burning kitchen range, and on a night such as this the bedrooms and sleeping porch would be bitter cold. But nevertheless, even though it was unlikely that I'd find anyone, I still had to be sure that no one was lurking in one of the bedrooms waiting to bushwhack me. ("Lurking" and "bushwhack" were some other swell words I'd learned when reading Zane Grey.)

My frosty breath floated about my head, as I cautiously opened the door of first one bedroom, then the other, and finally the sleeping porch, allowing the lamplight to shine into each in turn — nothing was amiss. I did find another flashlight, however, and this time I was careful to check it — the beam shone forth brightly. Shoving it into my rear pocket, and holding Dad's gun with one hand and the lamp with the other, I walked towards the swinging door into the kitchen and pressed on it with my shoulder. The door silently swung open into the black void beyond. Holding my breath, I listened intently for any sound. I heard nothing but the pounding of my own heart. Holding the lamp high up in front of me, I watched as the pale yellow lamplight spread throughout the room. As far as I could tell, the kitchen was empty. To be certain, I put the gun and the lamp on the table and, using the flashlight, checked around the stove and woodbox and under the zinc-topped table. Nothing was amiss. I did find another kerosene lamp, though, which I lit and set on top of the range. As the light in the room increased, so did my spirits. Feeling increasingly safe and at ease, I further explored in and under the washtubs in the laundry room and around the icebox and cabinets in the pantry. I found no one. All seemed secure. I did find two burned matches on the floor by the kitchen table that I thought must surely be the source of the flickering lights I had seen when coming down the lane. I was relieved to have that mystery explained. At least I could be sure that the blood on the doorknob was that of a human being. (Certainly no creature I'd ever heard of could strike a match. But then my imagination pointed out that perhaps there was one that I'd never heard of.) My courage grew rapidly as I realized that my earlier fears were groundless. I'd seen the lights in the window long before the worst of the storm, so whoever it was must have left and gone elsewhere after finding that there was no one here to help him. And now I knew for sure that it wasn't my brother or one of my parents.

What a relief. The crisis was over, and now I could get back to the important needs of my life. As usual, my stomach had first priority. I'll eat first and then get a fire going in the kitchen range, I told myself. After loading a tray with milk and cheese from the icebox and bread from the breadbox, I carried it to the kitchen table. Intent on ending my long fast, I failed to notice that Rab had disappeared. As a matter of fact, I was in the middle of my second sandwich when I heard him whining and growling and looked about to discover that he was no longer in the kitchen. The growling was coming from the laundry room, and upon directing the flashlight beam in that direction, I spotted him just inside the doorway on the left side of the laundry room. I almost choked on my sandwich. How could I have been so stupid? I'd totally forgotten that I'd seen a second flicker of light coming from the dormer window in the attic directly above my head. And now, to add to my escalating alarm, Rab was growling and dancing about excitedly directly in front of the door to the stairs that led to the attic.

My fear and anxiety skyrocketed. Obviously, the intruder was still in the house — and most probably in the attic, not thirty feet away. As my panic slowly subsided, questions came into my mind. Why in the world would anyone who was injured and in need of help go up to the attic when it would have made a lot more sense to remain in the kitchen where there was food, warmth, and help when it became available? I wondered if whoever it was might possibly be hiding, and if so, from whom or from what? In any event, I knew that if I were to stay in the house any longer, I had to find out just who it was and why he was hiding — and I had to do it soon before I lost what little nerve I had left.

CHAPTER 10

After tying a short rope to Rab's collar so he couldn't dash up the stairs when I opened the attic door, and after summoning what little courage I had left, I hitched my dad's revolver higher up on my hips, picked up the flashlight, and slowly and quietly opened the door and directed the rays of the flashlight up the stairwell leading to the attic. It was empty. Keeping a tight hold on Rab, I slowly crept up to the landing at the top the stairs and swept the beam of the flashlight across the black void of the attic, staring intently and apprehensively as its contents were revealed. A black, rectangular object caught my attention. It was the large steamer trunk that belonged to my mother, and it appeared to be undisturbed. Several other long forgotten items came into view as the light spread over the dusty, cobweb-shrouded room. My grandmother's old dressmaker's dummy gave me a start as the light revealed it leaning against the opposite wall but, other than that, nothing seemed threatening.

Rab, however, appeared to think otherwise. He was straining hard to get loose, dragging me irresistibly along the walkway while at the same time whining and growling in a very unnerving fashion. From the landing at the head of the stairs, a walkway doubled back for about ten feet before it turned to the right and headed across the attic to the door that opened into the upstairs hall. Except for the part covered by the walkway, the rest of the attic floor was not floored over, making it easy to step between the floor joists and plunge a foot through the plastered ceiling of the pantry. I swung the light back and forth across the attic floor to see if I might have overlooked something. But other than a burned-out match on the landing in front of the dormer window and several others scattered along the walkway, I found nothing alarming. The matches further convinced me that they were the source of the mysterious lights I had seen earlier. Other than that, nothing was unusual, and once again I decided that the intruder had left our house before the worst of the storm, hoping to find help elsewhere.

But Rab was not of the same opinion. He was tugging insistently on the line, seemingly interested in the folded remnant of an old rug lying just off the walkway a few feet ahead of us. As I was dragged closer and the light revealed it in greater detail, I could make out the worn, threadbare pattern quite clearly. Then to my horror, as the light shone over the far end of the rug, I became aware of an unblinking, bloodshot eye staring fixedly at me with a malevolent glare. My heart did its usual stopping and starting thing again, but I hardly noticed, absorbed as I was in trying to decide whether to die on the spot or to leave and die someplace else. So far, I had seen no sign of movement, and, as far as I could tell, the eye still hadn't blinked. It was set in a dirty, disheveled head belonging to what appeared to have been a sorry, disreputable looking man. As happens altogether too often, my curiosity overcame any good sense I might have had, so while keeping a close hold on Rab, I moved slowly and cautiously closer in order to get a better look. Could it really be a dead body? I'd never seen anybody that was dead before, but I bet if I had, he would have looked just like this. I decided that he must have bled to death, although, except for a little on the rug, there were no other signs of blood.

I took a step or two closer — at Rab's insistence. He was growling and lunging at the body in a very determined fashion, and I was having trouble restraining him. As I directed the light more closely, and the face was more fully revealed, it seemed strangely familiar. Had I seen this man before? His hair was mostly gray, streaked with black, although it was hard to tell, dirty and matted as it was. His face was even dirtier than his hair, and deep wrinkles showed beneath the scruffy stubble on his cheeks and chin. His mouth was an ugly slash below his bent nose. His thin lips were parted to reveal uneven, snaggly, tobacco-stained teeth, and he seemed to be leering up at me with a sinister sneer. Even in death it was an ugly and frightening countenance, and I'd seen all I wanted — much more than I wanted, as a matter of fact. As I was turning away to return to the sanctuary of the kitchen, I was both startled and terrified to hear a hoarse grating voice.

"Get that damned dog away from me, Boy, and help me get out of this here rug."

This seemed a surprising request to be coming from a dead man, and for a moment I stood frozen from shock and fear. After a long period of silence, I managed to stammer in a weak voice, "Yes sir, I'll try."

Actually, I was already attempting to drag Rab back towards the stairway landing, using every bit of strength I could muster, but I had no intention of helping him get out of the rug. I had succeeded in making no more than a foot or two of headway, when from out of the shadows again came the raspy whisper.

"What's yore name, Boy?"

I turned, shining the light back onto his face. He had turned his head more towards me, and was feebly trying to pull the rug away from his body — then came the whispered question once more.

"Damn it, Boy, cain't you talk? What's yore name?" Somewhat reassured by the knowledge that I was not having a conversation with a dead man, I answered in a tremulous voice, "I'm Robert Johnson." (Actually, I answered to a number of different names. My mother always called me "Robert," my dad either "Son" or "Robby," and my brother called me "Robby," along with a number of other names I'd rather not mention.)

"What's your name, Mister?"

Crazy Sam.
His horse, Maude, is pulling the buggy.
(A pen and ink drawing by Doctor Seymour Wheelock)

"I'm Sam," he whispered. "I knows your daddy, Boy. That's why I come here. He's always treated me good, and he don't think I'm crazy like a lot of them other folks in town do. How 'bout you, Boy? D'you think I'm crazy?"

Suddenly I remembered who this man was. It was Crazy Sam, and I really didn't know if he was crazy or not, but I sure wasn't going to let him think I had any doubt in the matter. I wasn't the crazy one around here. And so, with what I hoped sounded like great sincerity, I stammered, "No, sir, you're sure not crazy. I know that for a fact."

Crazy Sam had been a fixture around Littleton for as long as I could remember. He was hard to overlook as he drove about Littleton and its surrounds in his dilapidated buggy, drawn by an equally dilapidated horse. Sam apparently dressed with the hope of conveying the appearance of a gentleman, for his attire might have been one of sartorial splendor had it not been so worn and so dirt covered. His grimy trousers — once gray with a black pinstripe — were torn in several places and completely worn through over the knees, revealing the dirty long johns that he wore both winter and summer. Presumably, at one time his shirt had been white, but it had long ago lost any such claim and was now a basic gray, aggrandized by a limp, black string tie encircling his scrawny neck.

A filthy frock coat hung loosely from his small, gaunt frame, one pocket torn and hanging in a flap by his side, while the other was crudely pinned in place with a safety pin. It had originally been black, but now it, too, was a faded gray, except where it was brown from the accumulation of years of dirt and grime. Surmounting it all was his hat, and he had two of them. A tired and beaten up derby was his choice for ordinary days, and for what Sam apparently considered formal occasions, he would don a top hat that was surprisingly intact. It provided a startling contrast to the rest of his attire.

Sam's main pastime appeared to be driving about in his buggy for hours on end with no apparent destination. At times, he would seem to be having an animated and occasionally heated conversation with another individual. That would have been just fine, I suppose, except that there never seemed to be anyone else around to hold up the other end of the discussion.

The kids at school and, I'm sorry to say, even an occasional grownup, took delight in teasing Sam and calling him "crazy" over and over again with taunting voices. They did so at their own peril, however, for if any tormentor was close enough, Sam would inevitably retaliate by directing a copious quantity of spit, mixed with a generous portion of tobacco juice, at the target with surprising accuracy. And, if the victim wasn't familiar with Sam's mode of attack, he was almost certain to be hit squarely in the face. It was rare for anyone to tease Sam a second time, particularly if he was anywhere within range. I had never been one of those that taunted Sam, for which I was very thankful — especially so under the present circumstances. As we were growing up, Mother and Dad had taught J. J. and me to always respect our elders. Even those that seemed different — and Sam sure was different.

No one seemed to know him very well. Actually I doubted that anyone wanted to know him well — or at all for that matter — except maybe my dad. I think that he was acquainted with him better than most of the folks around Littleton. Dad had always said that Sam wasn't really crazy, but for some strange reason he wanted people to think he was.

Apparently no one knew where Sam had come from or just how he came by the money that he always seemed to be spending in the stores in Littleton. He had never been observed doing any sort of work — certainly not work that would have earned him money. He lived in a little ramshackle house about three-quarters of a mile north of Shadycroft Farm, just a little south and east of where Lee Gulch crosses Windermere.

Crazy Sam's House.

(A pen and ink drawing by Doctor Seymour Wheelock)

Sam's house fit him like a glove, at least that's the way it appeared to us as we drove past on Windermere. That it was small was an understatement. There appeared to be no more than one or two rooms, judging by the sparsity of windows. And just how Sam remained dry during a rainstorm was questionable, for the roof was missing a considerable number of shingles and even some boards. The southern wall of the house leaned outward at an alarming degree, and this created an unusual, even jaunty, angle to the decrepit roof. A screened porch graced the front of the Sam's abode and, as though to counterbalance the southern cant of the rest of the structure, it slanted north. The house truly did seem the perfect habitat for Sam.

There were times, however, when Sam would disappear for several days in a row and was nowhere to be found — assuming anyone was actually looking for him. Where he went and what he did there, no one seemed to know — or care, for that matter.

Sam had finally succeeded in extricating himself from the rug and was standing unsteadily on the walkway — a pathetic sight to behold. His frock coat was even dirtier and more wrinkled than usual, as were his pants and as was Sam. His right arm hung limp at his side. Dried, clotted blood caked the sleeve of his coat. He appeared to be anything but threatening as he stood there, weaving back and forth, and I felt a great sense of relief as my fear fell away to be replaced by pity for this unfortunate man. Even Rab seemed to share my feelings, wagging his tail in a tentative gesture of friendship.

"What are you doing here, Sam, and what in the world happened to you?" I asked as curiosity replaced my fear.

"I ain't gonna tell you that, Boy," he replied. "You don't need to know. It'd just get you in a heap of trouble. Where's yore daddy? It's him I needs to talk to."

"Mother and Dad and my brother went to the Grange meeting, and I guess they couldn't get home on account of the storm. But I'm sure they'll be here in the morning after Windermere is plowed out."

"Damn," Sam spluttered. "I need your daddy to help me get away from them."

"Who is it you're trying to get away from, Sam?" I asked, hoping he'd forgotten that he wasn't going to tell me. But no such luck.

"Quit askin' that, Boy. Like I told you before, I ain't gonna tell you and I still ain't. We're jest gonna hafta wait 'til your daddy gets home. So quit pesterin' me."

"Yes, sir," I replied, "but you can't just stay up here in the attic, Sam. It's so cold you can see your breath. Why don't we go down to the kitchen? I'll get a fire going in the stove so we can get warm."

This suggestion apparently appealed to Sam, for he started to shuffle towards me while holding his right arm close to his side. He was so weak he could barely walk, and he obviously was hurting a lot. But finally, with Rab leading the way and me propping him up, we made it safely down the stairs and into the kitchen.

CHAPTER 11

As the welcome warmth from the stove spread slowly throughout the room, the kitchen would have seemed almost cozy had it not been for the company of my peculiar companion, who was not only of questionable sanity but also appeared to be on the verge of dying. Sam seemed to be looking for something as he sprawled in a chair by the kitchen table and stared out the window — I wondered what or who it was.

Thinking Sam must be hungry, I fetched more bread, cheese, and milk from the pantry and set it on the table in front of him, but he wasn't interested in food. Instead he stared at my midriff.

"What in tarnation are you doin' with that there gun, Boy? I bet you cain't even haul the damned thing out of its holster, let alone shoot it. Yore mamma'd tan yore hide good if she knowed you was packin' it, and if she didn't, I reckon yore daddy would. Right now I ain't got the strength to shoot it neither, but I wouldn't even if I could. Guns generally jest cause folks a whole lot of grief, so go hide the damn thing before you get yoreself kilt and most likely me along with you."

It was a long speech, considering Sam's weakened condition, but it was good advice. I'd already decided I wasn't cut out for the life of a gunslinger — I'd leave that kind of stuff to Buck Duane. At least his gun belt and holster didn't have the annoying habit of falling down around his ankles. I hid the gun, with its belt and holster, in the back of a drawer in the pantry, figuring that when this ordeal was finally over I could sneak it back into the closet where I'd found it — that way Mother and Dad would never suspect that I'd borrowed it. I was a strong believer in the saying, "What my parents don't know won't hurt me."

Sam seemed agitated when I returned to the kitchen. "I hate gettin' you mixed up in this mess, Boy, but I reckon I's got no other choice, 'cause I's afeared yore daddy's not gonna get here in time. Yore gonna have to hide me someplace where they cain't find me, 'cause if they do, they'll kill me — that's for damn shore."

"What are you talking about, Sam? Who's gonna kill you?"

Sam really did seem terrified. "I's gonna tell you what all happened to me last night, jest like I was figurin' on tellin' your daddy if'n he'd of been here. But I ain't gonna tell you who they is, on account of knowin' that could get you in a whole peck of trouble." Sam was becoming increasingly upset as he continued.

"I seen them shoot my buddy, Cliff Alexander. They'd kilt him deader'n a damn doornail."

"Who's Cliff?" I interrupted. I didn't know that Sam had ever had a buddy — either dead or alive. Sam hesitated, then apparently decided to answer.

"Like I already said, Boy, Cliff was my friend. Me and him had jest pulled up in my buggy behind his house. It's the second house on Windermere t'other side of the ridge. He was jest gettin' out of my buggy and I was tellin' him how I'd be seein' him come mornin', when we seen these three guys standin' out back of the house jest north of Cliff's place. They was all wearing black hats and long black coats, and I could see where they'd been loadin' a whole bunch of whiskey bottles into the trunk of a big car. Two more guys was parked in a second car on the street out front.

"I was pretty damned sure I knowed who one of them guys was. Well anyways, when they seen me and Cliff watchin' them load up, I guess they figured we'd go tell Sheriff Haynes that they was bootleggin', so they shot Cliff and kilt him right off — then they shot me in the shoulder. I think the damned bone's busted, 'cause it hurts like hell."

After that Sam fell silent and went back to staring out the kitchen window into the black night. This was really scary stuff, and I wished more than ever that my dad and mother were here. But they weren't, and I was, so I asked him a question.

"Sam, how come you came way out here to Shadycroft to hide instead of going to tell the sheriff?"

"That's none of yore business, Boy."

"Well, then," and I blurted out two more questions in rapid succession, "where's your horse and buggy, and how did you get into our house? It was supposed to be locked."

These questions seemed to be acceptable. At least Sam answered them. "Like I said, I know'd who one of them guys was, but I sure as hell warn't never gonna tell nobody — 'specially not the sheriff. I jest wanted to get out of there as fast as I could. So I left old Maude and my buggy in back of the house and run like hell. If I hadn't, I'd of got kilt. Them three guys out back come a hotfootin' it after me along with the two other guys what was waiting in a car out front. But I fooled the whole damned pack of them. I run like a scared jackrabbit, pretendin' I was headin' back towards town, then when I was out of sight, I hid out in an empty rain barrel 'til they passed me by.

"After that I doubled back, like a smart old fox, and walked all the way out here to yore place, hopin' I could get yore daddy to help me. But there warn't nobody around when I got here, so I got the key from off'n the ledge over the window and let myself in." Then, obviously embarrassed, he added, "I knowed where the key was hid, Boy, 'cause a while back I seen where yore daddy hid it."

After a short pause he continued. "By now I's shore the colonel knows I never went into Littleton, and has figgered out which way I really did go. They's most likely checkin' all the houses on Windermere south of the ridge right now, hopin' they'll find me. And when they do, they's gonna shoot me dead — jest as sure as hell." Now I wish Sam had stuck to his original plan and hadn't told me about his problem — especially after it occurred to me that I'd get shot dead right along with him.

"Who's the colonel?" I asked. He hadn't mentioned him before.

"None of yore damn business, Boy," he snapped back, "jest forget I ever mentioned him."

Sam sure didn't look or sound crazy as he was telling me all this. Maybe my dad really was right about Sam being a lot smarter than he let on.

Sam wanted me to hide him where he couldn't be found, and from what he'd said, it sounded like a smart idea — but where? The coal bin down in the cellar wouldn't work. It'd be one of the first places they'd look. Hiding him in the barn or chicken house wouldn't work either, 'cause he'd freeze to death. So it had to be in the house somewhere — then Sam interrupted my thoughts.

"What's in that old trunk up there in the attic, Boy?"

"Why, I don't know, Sam. Probably just old clothes."

"Well, go check it out. It might be a mite snug, but I reckon I can squeeze into it if I have to."

"OK, I will. It sounds like a good idea."

Guided by the flashlight, I carefully tiptoed across the floor joists to the leather steamer trunk on the far side of the attic. It was over three-and-a-half feet long, two-and-a-half feet wide, and almost two feet tall. It appeared to be plenty big enough to hold Sam if he folded himself up. I'd never seen inside the old trunk and was curious as to what I'd find. I hoped it didn't have a lot of stuff in it that would take a long time to hide. As it turned out, it didn't. In the top was a removable storage tray partially filled with old clothing — more old clothes were in the compartment below. Fortunately, it took only a few minutes and two trips to carry everything from the trunk to a store room off the upstairs hall and put it where it wouldn't look out of place.

Then, after rolling up the rug Sam had wrapped himself in so that the blood didn't show and putting it where it was less noticeable, I examined the trunk. Its walls and floor were made of wood and covered with black leather, as was the rounded top — but there was a problem. If I didn't cut airholes in the bottom of the trunk, Sam would run out of air, and if I was going to do it, I had to be quick about it: Daylight was fast approaching, and I didn't have much time.

After a quick trip through the snow to our toolhouse, I selected a small saw and drill and quickly returned to the attic. Putting air holes in the trunk was easier than I had expected, and I was quite pleased with the end result. My mother, on the other hand, was going to be anything but pleased when she discovered what I'd done to her favorite steamer trunk. Returning to the warm, cozy kitchen, I found Rab sleeping peacefully by the range. Sam was still staring out the window and he sure looked bad. He was so pale and weak, I wondered if he could even make it back up the stairs to the attic. As a matter of fact, I'd been wondering why he'd gone there in the first place. So I asked him.

"Sam, how come you went up to the attic? It's the coldest place in the house."

"I wanted to be where I could keep a close watch on Windermere and still be able to hide quick if I seen somebody acomin'. I'd keep lookin' out that little window up there 'til I got so cold I couldn't stand it no more, then I'd wrapped myself up in the rug so's to get warm — but it didn't do a hell of a lot of good. I damn near froze to death."

Following that, Sam and I sat quietly, each immersed in his own thoughts, and as I recalled the events of the last twelve hours, I began to wonder about some of the things he'd told me. What if he hadn't been telling me the truth? What if it was Sam that shot Cliff Alexander and the police were looking for him — not the bootleggers? It was a worrisome thought and one I wished I hadn't had. But if Sam was really the murderer, why would he come here to ask for Dad's help? And there was something else that puzzled me. Sam usually talked with a drawl and used terrible grammar, but sometimes he'd talk a lot better. He never talked that way for long, though, and it only seemed to happen when he was excited about something, and I wondered why.

CHAPTER 12

It had been many hours since last I'd slept, and as I sat and watched alongside of Sam, I had to fight to stay awake. At long last, a faint glow in the eastern sky brought the promise of the approaching dawn. My drowsiness faded along with the night, and as the daylight slowly increased, so did my apprehension. I knew that Sam was worried, too, for he had become increasingly alert as the trees along Windermere gradually emerged from the darkness.

The sky was leaden. High clouds shrouded the sun, muting its warmth and radiance as it revealed the bleak and shadowless landscape outside the kitchen window. Broken, snow-laden branches dangled tenuously from the ragged stubs of limbs in the cottonwood trees, swaying and twisting in the breeze like so many grotesque Christmas ornaments. Occasionally one would break free and crash through the branches below in an explosion of snow, adding to the clutter at the base of the tree like discarded wrappings of the green gifts of summer. Beyond the trees stretched snow-covered fields, sculptured by the wind into a tapestry of brown and white.

Shadycroft Farm was at the south end of Windermere, so it would take a long time for the snowplow to reach the head of our lane. That was worrisome, but what worried me more, a car with extra-high clearance might get through ahead of the snowplow. Unfortunately, Dad and Mother's car didn't have it, so they'd have to wait until the road was plowed — but what about the colonel's? His cars might be able to make it through. That thought didn't add any to my peace of mind.

Sleep was about to overtake me when Sam suddenly exclaimed, "Wake up, Boy, somebody's comin'. Look down yonder just the other side of those trees. What do you see?"

Although it was at least a half-mile away, I could see what had aroused Sam's attention, but drifted snow made it impossible to tell just what it might be. It soon became clear, however, as a large, black sedan inched past a grove of cottonwoods. Two men were outside of the car, alternately shoveling the snow from in front of it and then struggling to the rear so they could push.

As we watched, Sam became more and more agitated. "That's them for shore, Boy. That's the car I seen up on Windermere, and they're moving fast, so it won't be long before they get here."

I agreed. At the rate they were coming, it was only a matter of minutes before they reached the head of our lane. Then a second car pulled up behind the first, and a third man got out to help the two that were already digging and pushing. Counting the drivers, that made five men, just like Sam had said, and I became more alarmed than ever.

"Gosh, Sam, they sure are comin' fast. You'd better get back up to the attic."

"Not jest yet, Boy." He seemed to have calmed himself somewhat. "I 'spect I can wait awhile longer. It's gonna be damned cold in that there trunk, and I shore ain't in no hurry to start freezin' to death."

We watched with increasing apprehension, as the two cars grew closer to the end of Windermere and pulled into the Vogel's driveway where they stopped, and all five men got out of the cars. After what appeared to be a brief discussion, two of them returned to the lead car and drove it into the Vogel's driveway and out of sight behind their barn — no doubt thinking correctly that the tracks would soon be drifted over by the wind. Then they returned and drove the other car in back of the Vogel's barn, while at the same time the other three started down our lane on foot. I had supposed that the other three men would wait to make sure that Sam wasn't hiding at the Vogel's house before attempting to drive their car down our lane. I think Sam thought so, too, for I heard him cursing under his breath.

The lane was bordered on the north by the bank of the canal, and whenever it snowed heavily and the wind was from out of the north, as it had been since the onset of the storm, our lane was always blocked by deep drifts, making it virtually impassable. It appeared to be that way now, leading us to assume that we were not especially pressed for time. But we were wrong, for although the colonel and his men were obviously having a difficult time of it as they pushed their way through the snow, they were nevertheless making alarming progress. Sam and I were galvanized into action. As he was struggling to his feet, I grabbed hold of his arm to help him, for he was wobbling back and forth and I was afraid he would collapse on the floor.

In a weak voice he mumbled, "Thank you, Boy. I shore do appreciate how yore helpin' me."

"You're welcome, Sam," I answered.

My heart ached for Sam right then, and I became even more determined to keep the colonel from finding him. As I urged him towards the attic stairway, Rab must have sensed our fear, for he awoke from a sound sleep and bounded over to accompany us. I doubt Rab's presence made Sam feel any safer, but it sure did me. Without Rab, I doubt I could have weathered what was yet to come.

With considerable effort on both of our parts, we made it to the top of the stairs and carefully worked our way across the floor joists to the trunk, where I watched as Sam painfully climbed inside.

"How are you doing, Sam?" I asked after he was settled.

"Wal, to tell you the truth, Boy, it's a mite snug, but I reckon I'll make it. Jest shut her up tight, and get back down to the kitchen real fast afore they gets here. And good luck, Boy — I's countin' on you."

He sounded so weak and pitiful I almost cried as I hastily shut and locked the trunk and pocketed the key, intending to hide it when I got back to the kitchen.

Rab and I returned to the kitchen, where I hurriedly glanced out the window to see what progress the colonel and his men were making. They were nowhere to be seen! Then, before I could even think, I heard the door to the screened porch squeak as it swung open and the sound of stomping feet on the porch floor outside the kitchen door. They were already here! It was the moment I had been dreading. Pushing Sam's chair back into the table, I looked quickly about the room for other telltale signs that he had been here. There were none that I could see.

A forceful knocking rattled the kitchen door to the accompaniment of Rab's agitated barking. Telling Rab to be quiet, I opened the door. Two men were on the porch. I had been expecting three and wondered what had become of the third until I saw him wading through the snow in the direction of our barn. Of course, I thought, he's making sure Sam isn't hiding in one of the outlying buildings.

Without introducing themselves, the larger of the two men demanded in a harsh, unpleasant voice, "Where's your dad and mother, Kid? We want to talk to them."

"They're not home, Mister. The storm came up while they were in town last night, and I guess they got stuck somewhere and couldn't get home. But I'm sure they'll be back soon," I added hopefully.

The big fellow seemed to be the one in charge. "Stand aside, Kid, we're comin' in. It's mighty damn cold out here," he announced gruffly as he and his companion pushed into the room.

My parents had given J. J. and me strict instructions to never to let strangers come into the house — especially when they weren't at home. But right now I had no choice — they came in without an invitation. Maybe, I thought, if I act real friendly and answer all their questions, they'll leave once they get warmed up. So, trying to smile convincingly, I said, "Come over by the stove and get warm, Mister," and I stepped back out of their way.

"Does your dog bite, Kid?" the big man asked in a snarly voice as they walked over to the stove and held their hands out to the warmth.

"Naw, not very often," I answered, hoping that this time would be the exception.

By now I'd taken a good look at the two men, and they were not a reassuring couple, especially the big man. He looked to me like an old guy — at least fifty — maybe more. He'd taken off his heavy black over-coat and tossed it on the table, revealing a powerful frame under his rumpled gray suit. He still had his hat on, but, judging from what I could see of it, his hair was a dirty gray color — and greasy. His mouth was small and his lips thin and turned down at the corners in a constant sneer. I don't think he'd shaved for a couple of days, 'cause his chin and jowls were covered with blue-black stubble. His squinty, yellowish eyes glared from beneath dark, bushy eyebrows, and it seemed to me that he was reading my innermost thoughts and fears. The other man was a welcome contrast. He was a good deal smaller and younger, probably in his twenties, I thought. He was nice looking and had blond hair and a friendly smile. The other guy was real scary.

As they stood soaking up the warmth of the stove, I decided that maybe I should be saying something.

"How come you're lookin' for my folks, Mister — 'specially in such bad weather? Wouldn't it have been a lot smarter to have waited and come on a nicer day?" Apparently my questions irritated the big man, for he answered in an angry tone of voice.

"It's not your folks we want, Kid. We're looking for a murderer that gunned down one of my deputies last night. He took some shots at us, too, but fortunately missed. Then he took off running down the road. We shot back, and I'm sure we wounded him, because we found blood on the ground close to where he'd been standing. Anyway, I know that he's hiding somewhere close around here, 'cause we found his tracks in the mud just this side of Ridge Road, and they were pointed in this direction. We've already searched all the other houses and barns south of the ridge without finding him, so your house is the only place left where he could hide."

"Well, he's not here, Mister. If he was hiding anywhere in this house, I'd sure know it."

But now I was really puzzled. In some ways his story was a lot like Sam's, except this fella claimed that Sam had murdered Cliff, and Sam had said it was one of this gang that did it. So how could I be sure which one was telling the truth — this fella or Sam? Maybe if I asked some more questions I could learn more about my unwanted visitors.

"Say, who are you fellas, anyway? I don't ever remember seeing either of you around Littleton before. And if you're looking for a murderer, how come Sheriff Haynes isn't with you? He's the sheriff here in Arapahoe County, you know."

The big man hesitated, obviously annoyed by my questions and trying to decide whether or not to answer them. But eventually he did. "I'm Colonel Pettigrew, head of the state constabulary, and this here is Jack Hall. He's one of my deputies. We're lawmen out of Denver. Not that it's any of your damn business. And just so you'll know it, we've got a legal right to investigate whoever and wherever we damn well please without havin' to ask permission from some local, two-bit sheriff and especially from a snot-nosed kid like you — you got that?"

I nodded that I got it, thinking, "Wow, if Sheriff Haynes had heard him say that, he'd sure be mad."

The colonel continued, "The only reason I'm talking to you at all is because I'm pretty damned sure you know where the man we're after is hiding, but for some reason you don't want to tell us. One thing's for sure, though, and you'd better get this straight, Kid, I'm not answering any more of your damn fool questions."

Well, that did it. My mind was made up. I was going to believe what Sam told me. There was no way I was gonna believe the colonel. I didn't trust this Colonel Pettigrew, and I didn't like him either. Unfortunately, I have never been good about knowing when to keep my mouth shut, and I decided to try one more time to convince the colonel that Sam wasn't hiding in our house.

"Well, whoever it is you're lookin' for, Colonel, he isn't anywhere around here, and I'm not lying. I've been the only one in the house since late yesterday afternoon, and I haven't seen anybody, and nobody could hide here without my knowing about it. I was awake all last night on account of the storm, so if somebody tried to break into the house I'd have heard it. You'll just be wasting your time if you look for the murderer around here."

The colonel's face was getting redder and redder. "Damn it, Kid, I'm sick and tired of listening to you. I don't know why I bothered trying to explain anything to a mouthy kid like you in the first place. I'm sorry I did now. And you damn well better get this straight — *I'll* be the one that decides whether or not we will search this house — not you."

"Yes sir," I answered meekly, "but I still think that Sheriff Haynes should be here with you. He's a good friend of my dad's, you know, and Doctor Harrod, the mayor of Littleton is too."

Well, for some reason that didn't go over too well with the colonel. "I don't give a tinker's damn who your dad knows, Kid. And I'll say this just one more time — we're Denver lawmen, and if you've got a brain in your stupid little head, you'd better damn well cooperate with us." With that he raised his hand as though he was going to strike me. Sensing the colonel's anger and the implied threat, Rab growled and stationed himself between us.

The colonel slowly lowered his hand. "I know you're lying to me, Kid. I think the guy we want is hiding here, and you know damned well where he is. As a matter of fact, I'll bet that he's some kin of yours, like maybe your dad, or brother, or somebody you know, and you're trying to protect him." If he'd said that to shake me up, it sure did work. I was afraid that he might do something bad to my family. But then, Jack unexpectedly came to my rescue.

"I think the kid's tellin' the truth, Boss. At least what he's saying makes sense to me."

"The hell he is, Jack," snarled the colonel. "I know damn well he's lyin', and he's good at it, too. I'll give him that much."

That seemed pretty high praise to be coming from the colonel, but I didn't really know whether or not to be flattered — probably not. I guess it's a questionable talent, but it sure comes in handy at times.

Then Jack spoke up again. "Well, if he really is here, Colonel, hadn't we best start lookin' for him? It won't be long before they get the road open, and we want to be long gone by then."

The colonel looked out the window. "We'll wait for the other men, to be sure he wasn't hiding in an outbuilding or their hired man's house. They'll be here most any minute now. Then we'll go through this house with a fine-toothed comb. He's hiding here somewhere all right — I can feel it in my bones."

Unfortunately, his bones were right about Sam, and they were also right about his men, for almost immediately the other three members of what I now had decided must be an outlaw gang stomped into the kitchen.

CHAPTER 13

The colonel didn't waste any time giving orders. "Jack, you stay here and keep an eye on the road, and give us a holler if you spot the snowplough or anybody else coming. The rest of you boys come with me, and Kid, just in case you're figuring on runnin' off, you're comin' with us."

"Can Rab come too?" I asked hopefully.

"Hell, no. Tie that damned dog to the leg of that table and be quick about it."

Over Rab's protests, I did as he said. Then I followed the colonel and his men as they entered the dining room and methodically searched the main floor of the house, the colonel assigning different rooms to each of the men as we went along. We were proceeding much more rapidly than I had expected, and I was praying hard that we'd hear Jack holler out that someone was coming.

After checking the first floor, they went down the narrow stairway into the cellar, dragging me along with them. With so many men looking, they made short work of the cellar, and ordinarily that would have pleased me for, as I have explained before, the less time I spent in the cellar the better. But this time was different, and I wished I could think of some way I could prolong it. But I couldn't, and in only a few minutes we were trudging back up the squeaky cellar steps and those leading to the second floor, where they rapidly searched the bathroom, sewing room, a bunch of closets, and six bedrooms, including the one that was used for storage.

A door at the east end of the upstairs hall opened into the attic space where Sam lay huddled in the dark confines of the trunk, awaiting his approaching doom. As it swung open, I watched the rays of the flashlights cast eerie shadows about the dark interior of the room as one object after another came into view. I was terrified, and I knew Sam must be far more so as he listened to the sounds of his pursuers growing louder and closer. I sure hoped he was good at praying. I was getting better at it with every step I took.

The moment the rays of the colonel's flashlight revealed the trunk and hovered there, it was obvious that the colonel knew that he'd finally found Sam's hiding place. Now Sam's and my final moments had come, and there was nothing more that I could do or say. I was too paralyzed by fear to even think, so certain was I that neither Sam nor I could expect the slightest shred of mercy from the colonel.

"What's in that trunk, Kid?" he asked, although I suspected that he already knew the answer from the anxious expression on my face.

"I don't know, sir. Probably just a bunch of old clothes and stuff like that."

"Well, we'll just damn well see," snapped the colonel as he escorted me to the trunk, stepping from floor joist to floor joist while holding me none too gently by the arm. The colonel lifted one end of the trunk by its handle.

"It's too damn heavy to be clothes," he said as he unbuckled the leather straps and attempted to lift the trunk lid while his men held the flashlights. He examined the lock carefully.

"Where's the key, Kid?"

A sudden panic erupted within me as I remembered that the trunk key was in my pocket. I had forgotten to hide it when I was in the kitchen. Praying that the colonel wouldn't search me, and hoping to delay the inevitable for a little while longer, I stammered, "I don't know for sure, but I think it's in a drawer of a dresser in one of the downstairs bedrooms."

"Okay, go get it, Kid, but be quick about it. George, you go with him, and be damned sure you don't let him con you into doin' something stupid."

George followed me down the stairs. He looked to be a little younger than Jack. Rab was delighted to see me when we came into the kitchen and began to jump about expectantly. Even Jack seemed happy to have his vigil interrupted.

"What the hell's goin' on up there?" he asked.

"The boss thinks Sam's hidin' in a big trunk up in the attic," George replied, "but it's locked up tighter'n a tick, so he sent me and the kid down here to find the key."

I was startled to find that they knew Sam's name. For some reason, I had thought they didn't know who it was that they were after.

"Well, I hope to hell he gets a move on," Jack said anxiously. "We've stayed here too damn long as it is. We're sure as hell gonna get caught if we don't leave soon."

All of a sudden I was becoming quite fond of Jack — especially so when he was saying things about leaving. I only wished that he were up in the attic where he could tell the colonel what he thought.

Thinking that I might help out in that regard, I suggested, "Jack, why don't you watch for the snowplow and cars from the window in the attic? You can see a lot farther down the road than you can from here."

"Thanks, Kid, that's a good idea. I'll see if the boss goes along with it." Then he got up from his chair and headed for the attic. I just hoped he'd tell the colonel what he'd said about leaving.

George and I went into one of the bedrooms off the dining room, where I pretended to look for the key. After searching for as long as I thought wise, I suggested to George that maybe we had better check the bedroom next door. He grunted his approval. I was beginning to think that George wasn't too bright, and that maybe I could stall for a few more minutes before the inevitable trip back to the attic. Accordingly, I carefully examined the icy cold sleeping porch, the entry hall, and even the living room before it occurred to George that perhaps it was taking too long, and we should return to the attic before the colonel came looking for us.

"What the hell took you so long, Kid?" was the colonel's warm greeting.

I was grateful when George answered. "There was a whole bunch of drawers to check out, Boss. We hurried as fast as we could."

"Well, give me the key, Kid." The colonel held out his hand. He seemed sort of uneasy, and I wondered if maybe Jack had worried him some by speaking his piece about leaving.

"I couldn't find it," I mumbled in a weak voice.

"Damn," the colonel spit back. "I bet you were just stalling for time down there. But it won't do you any good, Kid, 'cause now I'll just have to shoot the lock off."

I was in the first stages of panic when I heard Jack say, "Boss, I don't think that's a good idea. You know we don't have any legal right to be here, and if Sam really is in the trunk, you'll most likely shoot him right along with the lock. And if he's killed, how are we gonna get rid of his body and all the blood? And besides that, what are we gonna do about this kid here?"

Yeah, what about the kid? I'd been wondering the same thing myself and was most grateful to Jack for pointing out the problem to the colonel. Then Jack added convincingly, at least he sure convinced me, "Besides, Boss, we ain't got time to fool around. We've gotta get back to our cars before the sheriff gets here, and that's likely to happen most any second now. If they catch us here, we'll be in a heap of trouble, 'specially if Sam and the kid are dead."

"Hell, we've got plenty of time, Jack. Our cars are well hidden back of that barn up the road, and we can sneak back to them real easy by walking in the bed of the canal — that way they'll never see us." Having said that, the colonel drew a pistol from a holster inside his coat and was turning towards the trunk when Jack called out urgently.

"Don't do it, Boss! It's too late. We've gotta get out of here right now, and fast. The snowplow's comin' up Windermere, and there're a couple of cars right behind it, and one of them's the sheriff's."

After looking quickly out the window to confirm it, the colonel immediately started down the stairway, dragging me along with him. As he was throwing on his coat and heading for the door, he snapped a sharp warning.

"Kid, if you don't want your folks to get hurt real bad, all you'd better tell that damned sheriff is that we're lawmen from Denver and that we had a warrant from a judge giving us the right to search this house for the man that killed my deputy. You tell them anything other than that and you'll be damned sorry you did — your folks will be even sorrier. You got that straight?"

On that less that comforting note, they all set off in the direction of the canal with the colonel in the lead.

CHAPTER 14

Oblivious to the cold, I stood in the open doorway of the kitchen and watched as the five men struggled through the deep snowdrifts blanketing the driveway between our house and the Highline Canal. Upon reaching the canal road, three of them dropped down into the bottom of the ditch and disappeared from sight, but Jack and the colonel remained standing on the bank — they appeared to be having a heated argument. At one point in the discussion, the colonel stretched out his arm and pointed in my direction. A sudden chill came over me. I wondered if he'd changed his mind and was trying to persuade Jack to return and kill Sam and me after all. The longer they argued, the more anxious I became. I was scarcely able to breathe. At long last, the colonel whirled about and stomped angrily to the edge of the canal where he vanished from sight. Jack followed with obvious relief.

The moment they disappeared, I fell to my knees and hugged Rab tightly to me. At long last my ordeal was over and my fears could finally be put to rest. Getting back to my feet, I re-entered the kitchen and collapsed in a chair by the table. In a moment or two, I looked out the window and was delighted to see my parents standing beside their car at the end of Windermere as they watched the snowplow clear the snow from the Vogel's driveway.

Shortly, they were joined by the sheriff and two of his deputies and soon after by my brother and the Williamsons. Together, they all walked in the direction of the Vogel's house. I'm sure they assumed that, as usual, I had ignored their instructions to be home before dark and, with the onset of the storm, spent the night at the Vogels. I was sure, too, that the moment they discovered I hadn't, they'd make fast tracks down the lane — especially when they learned that the colonel and his men had gone there after leaving the Vogels. I wished I could have kept on watching, but I couldn't — not until I got Sam out of the trunk and down to the kitchen — if he was still alive. He'd looked half-dead when he got into the trunk, and that was a long time ago. Picking up the flashlight, I called to Rab and hurriedly returned to the attic. As I tightroped across the creaky floor joists, my apprehension grew. Taking the key from my pocket, I unlocked the trunk and slowly lifted the lid, directing the rays of the flashlight into the dark interior to reveal Sam's pale motionless body. My apprehension skyrocketed. Sam is dead, I thought, as the light reflected from his ashen face. I found myself holding my own breath as I tried to see if he was breathing. I tentatively reached down to poke him with a cautious forefinger.

"What the hell are you doin', Boy?" erupted from the depths of the trunk. Startled, I jumped back, almost putting a foot through the lath and plaster ceiling of the pantry.

"I'm sorry, Sam. I just wanted to see if you were dead."

I guess Sam thought that a somewhat insensitive remark, for he snapped back, "Wal, I thank you for askin', Boy, but I don't think so. I'm not too shore, though, 'cause I's feelin' mighty bad. Sometimes it seems like my head's afloatin' around somewheres out yonder, like I's gonna pass out."

As if to illustrate this point, Sam suddenly began to talk real weird, saying things that didn't make any sense. He acted like he could see somebody else in the attic besides Rab and me, and this time he wasn't pretending. He started sobbing as he was talking to whoever it was, mumbling something about how it was all his fault. Then he started moaning and over and over begged to be forgiven. After that, he seemed to be trying to say something else, but he couldn't get it out. He just kept sayin', "I - ah - ah - please no God - no - no - no - don't let him do it!" — then all of a sudden Sam collapsed, and I thought that maybe now he really was dead. It seemed unlikely, though, 'cause I could hear him breathing, sort of raspy-like. I wondered what it was he'd been trying to say. Whatever it was, it must be about something really awful. Maybe it had something to do with his friend, Cliff, getting killed. But for some reason I couldn't explain, I had a strong feeling it wasn't that, but that it was something even worse that had happened to Sam in the past.

I was abruptly aroused from my speculation by Sam's hoarse whisper. He seemed to be back in his right mind again. "What kept you so damn long, Boy? The colonel must of skedaddled hours ago."

"It hasn't been that long, Sam. After they saw the snowplow coming with my folks and the sheriff following right behind, they cleared out of here in a real big hurry. The last time I looked, the sheriff and my family were up at the Vogel's place at the head of the lane, but I'm sure they'll be down here real soon. But right now, Sam, I've got to get you out of this trunk and down to the kitchen where it's warm. You're awful pale and shaky, and I'm afraid you're getting sick. But you needn't worry, Sam; when my folks and the sheriff get here, they'll know what to do."

"Now jest wait a damn minute, Boy," Sam interrupted in a weak but agitated voice. "I reckon it'd be best if'n I stays put in this here trunk 'til after the sheriff heads back to town."

"But why, Sam? The sheriff is looking for the colonel, not you."

"Never you mind, Boy — I got my reasons. But jest as soon as he's gone, get me down from here real fast, that is if'n I ain't kicked the bucket by then. I shore will be happy to see your daddy, Boy. He'll be able to help me if anybody can."

Having said that, Sam curled up on the floor of the trunk, a sad, sick, caricature of a man with no apparent reason to live — and what was even sadder, with no one to even care if he lived or died. Then I suddenly realized — except for me, that is.

I really felt sorry for Sam, and I wanted to help him all I could, so I said, "Sam, I promise, I won't tell anybody you're here until after the sheriff's gone. And I'll keep my promise. You can count on it."

After closing the trunk lid, I descended to the kitchen, escorted by Rab, and looked out the window at a welcome sight. The snowplow was almost to the end of the lane, followed closely by the sheriff's car, then my parents' Studebaker and the Williamson's Star bringing up the rear. I briefly considered standing out in the driveway to meet them, but I quickly dismissed the idea for fear they would get the ridiculous idea that I'd been scared. I knew that's what my brother, J. J., would think. So, seein' as how I so closely resembled Buck Duane, I figured I'd best act like him and be calm and cool. But I was anything but calm, let alone cool, as I stood on the kitchen porch and awaited the arrival of my family.

A few minutes later, the plow pushed its way past the large drifts blocking the drive by the pump house and scraped the snow from the driveway in front of our house so that the cars could park. Then it turned around and headed back toward Windermere and Littleton. The second the snowplow left and the cars were parked, my parents' car doors flew open and my brother leapt out, followed closely by my mother, my dad, and, to my considerable surprise, by the Vogels and the Williamsons. The sheriff and his deputies brought up the rear.

My Buck Duane image was being severely tested as I struggled to hold back tears of joy. I sure didn't want them to see me crying — especially J. J., and double-especially Abby. But it wouldn't have mattered, even if I had, because the ladies got all teary-eyed and sniffly the minute they saw me, and right off started kissing and hugging me. Even Abby was crying and dabbing her eyes with a hanky.

Then, everybody started talking at once, asking a lot of questions without ever giving me a chance to answer. Nobody had ever made such a fuss over me before, and it was sort of nice. In fact, I was beginning to like it, but then Sheriff Haynes' loud voice drowned out everyone else's and quickly ended my moment of glory. He obviously didn't have time for such foolishness, 'cause he started right in asking me a bunch of questions.

"What became of those men that came down here this morning, Robert? We saw their tracks in the lane. Did they hurt you or give you a hard time in any way?"

"No, sir," I hurriedly replied, relieved that he hadn't started off by asking me anything about Sam. If he had, I wasn't sure which would be worse — to lie or to tell the truth and break my promise to Sam. It seemed to me that I'd be wrong either way. But right now, Sam really needed a friend, and I wasn't going to let him down. So I decided if the sheriff did ask me about Sam, I'd lie and tell him that I hadn't seen him and didn't know where he was, even though I knew I'd be in big trouble with my folks and the sheriff later on. Besides, I had a plan. If I hurried up and told the sheriff everything that had happened last night without ever mentioning Sam or giving him a chance to ask any questions, maybe he'd think I'd told him everything I knew and would leave without asking me any more questions. At least it was worth a try, so I hurriedly began to recount the events of the day with a few notable exclusions.

"There was this big guy that was the boss. He said his name was Colonel Pettigrew and that he was a Denver lawman. He sure wasn't very nice, though. I didn't like him and neither did Rab. He told me they were lawmen from Denver and that they were looking for a bootlegger who had shot and killed one of his deputies last night when they were raiding his still up on Windermere. I told him there sure wasn't any murderer around here, but he didn't believe me and made me go with them while they searched the whole house — even down in the cellar. And I don't know why, but for some reason the colonel was afraid that you might show up, Sheriff, 'cause he had one of his deputies stay in the kitchen and keep watch so he could give him a holler if he saw you comin'. But by the time he'd hollered, they'd finished searching. 'Course, they never did find any murderer."

I could tell that the sheriff was wishing I'd quit talking so he could ask me some questions, but I kept on jabbering away like my life depended on it — mine didn't, of course, but maybe Sam's did.

"The colonel never did apologize for busting in like that. He and his men just cleared out of here in a hurry when they saw you were coming. And boy, were Rab and I ever glad to see them go. They all headed off towards the barn and got down in the bottom of the ditch so you wouldn't see them as they were going back to where they'd hid their cars in back of the Vogel's barn. They sneaked right past you while you were coming down the lane." One time, when I quit talkin' for a second so I could take a breath, the sheriff tried to say something, but I hurriedly broke in…

"Oh, yeah, I almost forgot, Sheriff. Right before he left, the colonel said to tell you that he had a paper from a Denver judge giving him permission to search our house. But I knew he was lying, 'cause earlier on I'd heard one of his deputies tellin' him they should be leaving, 'cause they didn't have a legal right to be searching our house, and that they'd be in big trouble if they got caught doing it."

To my amazement, my plan worked. After I'd quit talkin', the sheriff didn't ask me many more questions, and none about Sam. Maybe he really was sick of hearing me talk. I know everyone else was — except Abby and Charley. They'd listened to every word like I was some kind of hero. It made me feel pretty proud until I saw my brother's skeptical look. He hadn't believed a thing I'd said.

My thoughts were interrupted when the sheriff said, "Julius, I'm sure the man Robert said was the boss was Colonel Pettigrew, and he's certainly no lawman. He couldn't get a search warrant from a judge in

Colorado or anywhere, else for that matter. A while back, though, he really was head of the state constabulary in Kansas and was in charge of enforcing the prohibition laws and tracking down bootleggers. But, as it turned out, he got caught making his own moonshine on the side and ended up spending a few years in jail. After he was released, he came here to Littleton where, believe it or not, he started a bootlegging operation out east of here on Dry Creek Road. We found their still and broke it up, but we never have been able to catch up with the colonel. They're rumors going around that he and his gang are back making moonshine liquor again, but so far we haven't figured out where. We'll get him eventually, though. By the way, Robby, just how many men did he have with him?"

"There were four of them, sir. Besides the colonel there was Jack, George, and two others."

"He's right, Sheriff," one of the deputies volunteered. "We found the tracks of five men going up towards the barn and down into the bottom of the ditch. They were headed back towards the Vogel's place, just like he said."

Then the sheriff rose from his chair and reached for his coat. "Well, boys, I guess we'd better be on our way. There's nothing more we can do here. We'll be getting out of your hair so you can all get settled, Julius. Your boy's been through a lot, and I'm sure he's tuckered out."

"Thanks a lot, John," my dad said. "We sure do appreciate your help in checking on Robby. I'll be coming into town a little later to get some tractor parts, and I"ll probably stop by your office to see if you've caught up with the colonel by then."

What a relief — they were actually leaving, and the sheriff hadn't once mentioned Sam. He must not have been looking for him after all, and there never was any reason for me to worry. But then — just as they were going out the door — I overheard the sheriff's instructions to his deputies.

"OK boys, after we get back to town, you two can pick up the other car and keep on looking for the colonel and his bunch, and I'll keep looking for Crazy Sam. He's bound to be around here somewhere." Shocked, mouth agape, and unable to speak, I stood and watched as they waded through the deep snow to their car.

CHAPTER 15

So the sheriff was looking for Sam after all — but why? What had he done to make the sheriff want to find him? Was he really the murderer after all? Now I began to have second thoughts about the promise I made to Sam. I probably should have stopped the sheriff from leaving and told him where Sam was hiding the moment he mentioned his name. But I didn't, and now it was too late, and I was stuck with it. Then, even though I knew it might make matters worse, I decided to wait to tell my parents about Sam until after the Vogels and Williamsons had left. I figured a few more minutes couldn't make that much difference, and that right at that moment the fewer people that knew about Sam, the better it would be for him — and for me.

Fortunately for Sam, but unfortunately for me, it didn't quite work out as I had planned. My mother had been unusually quiet all during the time I was talking to the sheriff. That in itself was quite remarkable, and if I'd had time to think about it, it would have set off the alarm system that I had developed from past encounters of a similar nature. But now that I did think about it, it occurred to me that she had been observing me with an unusual degree of interest, and I wondered what it was that had aroused her curiosity. I didn't have long to wonder, however, as she asked me in what I knew to be her inquisitional tone of voice, "Robert, just what is it that you're not telling us?"

I have never been able to figure out how she invariably knew when I was telling a lie, or, as in this case, when I wasn't quite telling all of the truth. Resigned to my fate, I was about to confess my knowledge of Sam's whereabouts when my dad came to my rescue.

"Now, Grace, don't be hard on the boy. You know he's had a bad time of it, and I imagine he's mighty tired and hungry. Don't you think we should at least wait until after he's eaten and rested up before we talk to him?"

I was most grateful to my dad right then and did my very best to look even tireder and hungrier than I really was.

Surprisingly, my mother agreed. "I guess you're right, Julius, but you know how that boy's mind works. He's really good about forgetting to tell us things he doesn't want us to know about. Have you forgotten how only last week he found that baby skunk in the woodpile and hid it in the tack room in the barn? He told us he was planning to make a pet out of it and was feeding it eggs and hamburger without even telling us it was there."

My dad looked thoughtful. I sure hoped he wasn't having any second thoughts, especially after she added, "We probably wouldn't even know about it now if Clyde here hadn't found it when he was getting the harness. I doubt that he'll ever forgive Robert, and I won't blame him a bit if he doesn't."

As one, the entire Williamson family glared at me in unison and in a most unfriendly way. It seemed to me that Mother was making entirely too much of the whole affair. Besides, Mr. Williamson didn't smell much at all anymore. I decided that I had better change the subject before the Williamsons became any more hostile.

"Dad, how come the sheriff is looking for Sam?"

The moment I spoke I realized that I had made a major strategic error. I should have said "Crazy Sam," instead of just "Sam," as I always had in the past when talking about him. Even the sheriff had called him "Crazy Sam," and everybody knew that Sam and I weren't on such familiar terms that I would be calling him by anything other than his full name.

My dad picked up on it right away. Glancing at my mother, who was looking at him with a "See, I told you so" look, he asked, "Son, do you know something about Crazy Sam that you should be telling us?" (Was it Robert Burns or John Steinbeck who said something about how "The best laid plans of mice and men often get messed up." Well, little kids' plans get messed up too.)

There was no other way out for me. Even though the Williamsons and Vogels were still with us, I had to confess that I knew where Sam was hidden. This was going to be a tougher confession than usual, with all those skeptical eyes glaring at me. Especially so when I could see how much pleasure my brother was getting out of seeing me squirm. After a few deep breaths, I commenced recounting the events of the past night and morning, except for the part about finding Dad's revolver. I could see no reason to get my dad in trouble, and I already had enough problems without adding more. After first telling them how Sam was shot in the shoulder by Colonel Pettigrew and his gang of bootleggers, I explained how he'd come to Shadycroft hoping that Dad would help him. But when nobody was here, he'd let himelf in and hid in the attic. Then I explained that the reason I didn't tell Sheriff Haynes about Sam was because I had promised him that I wouldn't reveal his hiding place, and I didn't want to go back on my word. I also explained that I didn't tell them about Sam right after the sheriff left because I wanted to wait until after the Vogels and Williamsons had left, 'cause I figured the fewer people that knew about Sam the better.

At that point in my discourse Dad interrupted. "Well, where in the world did you find a place in the attic to hide Sam, Robby? There's nothing up there but a lot of old clothes and such."

After swallowing hard a time or two, I confessed, "He's in Mother's old trunk."

"You hid him in my what?" interrupted my mother, her voice an octave higher than usual.

"In that old trunk. The one that's been up there forever." Then, before she could question me in greater detail about her prized trunk, I hastily added, "But I think Sam's real sick. At least the last time I saw him, he felt awful hot and was talking funny, like he was out of his head, or something." Fortunately for both Sam and me, my dad intervened before Mother could say anything more.

"Well, why didn't you say so sooner, Son? If Sam's that sick, you should have told us long before now. We'd better hurry and get him down to the kitchen and not waste any more time."

Without waiting for me to reply, he said, "Come on, Clyde, grab that flashlight and give me a hand." With that, both my dad and Mr. Williamson headed for the attic with J. J. and me close behind. Abby and Charley started to follow but were stopped by their mother, despite their vigorous protests.

Dad and Mr. Williamson hurried over to the trunk and, with obvious concern, opened the lid and peered inside. "He sure looks bad, Clyde," my dad said softly. "The sooner we get him out of here and downstairs the better. I think it would be best if we carry him down while he's still in the trunk. That way he won't get shaken up so much."

Dad closed the lid of the trunk and with seemingly little effort, he and Mr. Williamson lifted it by the leather handles on either end and carried it carefully down to the kitchen, placing it gently on the floor by the stove. As Dad lifted the lid, everyone stared into the trunk with various expressions of revulsion mixed with pity and concern.

"How terrible," my mother said in a barely audible whisper. "He looks so pale and blue, Julius. Do you think he's dead?"

"I don't know, Grace," my dad said as he gingerly reached inside of the trunk and gently shook Sam by his shoulder with no noticeable response. "He looks mighty bad. You can see where he was shot. His right arm and shoulder are caked with blood."

Mr. Williamson craned forward to get a better look and at the same time suggested, "Julius, don't you think we should get him out of the trunk so we can examine him?"

"You're right, Clyde," Dad replied. "We'll put him on the kitchen table where we can work on him better. J. J., you and Robby go and get some blankets we can use to pad the table."

It was obvious that neither my dad nor Mr. Williamson were at all enthusiastic about having to touch Sam in order to lift him from the trunk. Even seen at his best, Sam was pretty repulsive looking, and now he looked a hundred times worse. But they did it. After the blankets were covering the table, Dad took hold of Sam's left arm and leg while Mr. Williamson held onto the right leg. My mother and Mrs. Williamson, looking almost as pale and sick as Sam did, helped to steady his head and right arm. Then all four slowly lifted him from the trunk and gently laid him on the kitchen table. Dad felt carefully for Sam's pulse.

"By golly, his heart's still beating — in fact, his pulse seems fairly strong. He's breathing, too, but just barely, and in short, little breaths. Robby was right — he feels mighty hot. I'm sure he has a high fever." Mother was standing on the other side of the zinc-covered table, looking down with obvious distaste at Sam's unkempt form as she muttered under her breath, "I wonder if he's ever had a bath." Then, in a loud, clear, and determined voice, she added, "I'm sure that his bullet wound has gotten infected — that's why he's so feverish. I really hate having to do it, but we're going to have to clean up his shoulder and some of the rest of him as well. Otherwise, the infection will get worse, and Sam will surely die."

Everyone appeared to agree with her, but no one volunteered to do the job, and I could certainly understand why. After a prolonged period of silence, Mother reluctantly assumed command and galvanized everyone into action.

"Julius, you and Jerome take his shirt off and cover him with a blanket so he doesn't chill. J. J., you, Robert, Abigail, and Charles get busy and build up the fire in the kitchen stove and start one in the stove in the dining room, too. We're going to have to have it nice and warm in here. Ada (that was Mrs. Williamson's first name), why don't you and your girls put some water on the stove to boil, and Vera (that was Mrs. Vogel's), maybe you can help me find some washcloths and bandages."

I knew from ten years of personal experience that my mother was a great organizer, but I was nevertheless surprised to see everyone spring into action with what appeared to be enthusiasm.

It wasn't long before the dining room was toasty warm, water was boiling on the stove, and the kitchen was getting downright hot. Sam had yet to be relieved of his shirt, however. It was very obvious that neither Dad nor Mr. Williamson were looking forward to removing it, in as much as it obviously required touching both the shirt and its repulsive occupant. They did remove it, however, and to their surprise and grateful relief, they discovered that under his filthy shirt, Sam was relatively clean. As he covered Sam with a blanket, Dad announced that he thought all was in readiness.

My mother, however, was nowhere to be found. No one had seen her leave the kitchen, and we were about to start a search when she burst abruptly out of the pantry and my heart flip-flopped. She was carrying a box of bandages in one hand, but in the other was Dad's Colt .44, complete with holster and cartridge belt. "Oh no!" I thought, "not now." Just when I thought I was out of the woods, I was back in trouble again. Dad looked worried, too, as he looked first at the gun, then at me, and then at my mother. "Where'd you get that, Grace?" queried my dad.

"Why don't you ask your youngest son?" she responded sharply. "I imagine that he can tell you even better than I can. I thought that you had locked all of your guns in the gun closet, Julius." My dad looked at me — none to kindly, I thought.

"They were all locked up, the last I knew. Where did you find that revolver, Robby?"

"Hanging in your bedroom closet," I mumbled, feeling that I had betrayed my dad. "I saw it when I was looking for a flashlight, and I thought it might be a good thing to have to protect myself. I hid it in a drawer in the pantry so the colonel wouldn't see it."

"Ha!" exclaimed my mother. "You're lucky you didn't blow your foot off!"

I didn't tell her that the same thought had occurred to me. I just wanted to forget the entire affair. Fortunately she had other things on her mind right then, so she let the subject drop. I just hoped she'd forget it for good.

Apparently Dad was as eager to change the subject as I was, for he promptly brought our attention back to the sorry soul lying on our kitchen table.

"Come on, Grace. We'd better be getting on with attending to Sam." Then he turned to Mrs. Vogel. "You're a nurse aren't you, Vera?"

"Why, yes," she answered, obviously suspecting that this might be leading her into a trap. "I fill in now and then at the Swedish Hospital in Englewood when they're short a nurse or need extra help."

"I thought so." My dad looked pleased. "That's just great, Vera. I'll bet you know exactly how to fix Sam's shoulder, so why don't you go ahead and do whatever it is that needs to be done, and just let us know when there's something we can do to help."

I thought that this was a stroke of genius on my dad's part, and except for Mrs. Vogel, I'm sure everyone agreed. Of course Mrs. Vogel agreed to do it, but with obvious reluctance. She did a great job of fixing Sam up, though — at least he was a lot cleaner. When she was scrubbing off the layers of clotted blood from his shoulder, the flesh around the bullet hole looked sort of greenish black in color, and some yellow, goopy stuff was oozing out of the hole. It made my stomach queasy to look at it, and some of the others looked a little greenish, too. But after Mrs. Vogel finished slathering Sam's shoulder with tincture of Merthiolate and bandaging it, we all felt a lot better — except Sam.

When Mrs. Vogel had finished, everybody complimented her on doing such a good job. That obviously pleased her, 'cause she blushed and stammered some as she said, "Well, thank you. I did the best I could, but now I really think a doctor should look at Sam just as soon as possible. The bullet is still in his shoulder and, if it's not removed soon, I doubt the infection will get any better."

"You're right, Vera," my dad said as he started towards the entry hall. "I'll see if the phone is working now. If it is, I'll give Doctor Sims a call and ask him to come and take a look at Sam."

CHAPTER 16

As Dad hurried to the phone in the entry hall, I felt the sudden surge of panic that always came over me whenever I heard Dr. Sims' name mentioned. It's not that I didn't like him — I really did. It's just that hearing his name always triggered memories of an experience I would prefer to forget. Perhaps I should explain.

It was a cold day in November 1930 when I was awakened by my father early in the morning.

"Robby, wake up and get dressed. Your mother and I have an appointment with Doctor Sims in half an hour and we want you to come with us."

"You mean I can't even eat breakfast?" I asked in alarm. "I'll starve to death, Dad."

"We don't have time for that, Robby. Now hurry up and dress. We want to leave in ten minutes."

I pouted all the way to Littleton. After parking in front of the Coor's Building on the corner of Main Street and Nevada, my folks got out of the car.

Looking east up Littleton Main Street towards Courthouse Hill - Ca. 1930. The large building on the left is the Coors Building.
(Picture courtesy of the Littleton Historical Museum.)

"Come on, Robby. Let's hurry. We don't want to keep Doctor Sims waiting." Dad seemed very uneasy. I followed my parents up the steep, narrow stairway leading to the doctor's second-floor office above the Littleton Drug store and entered his small waiting room where Doctor Sims' nurse greeted me.

"Good morning, Robby, it's nice to see you again. Just have a seat. The doctor will be right with you." "Mornin'," I mumbled glumly as I started to sit down. Then it hit me. She'd said "you," meaning "me"— ME! How come she'd said that? Turning to my dad, I asked in a panicky voice, "How come *I've* gotta see the doctor? There's nothin' wrong with me. You said you and Mother had the appointment."

"Don't you remember all of those earaches and sore throats you've been having, Robert?" my mother answered. "And you know how you breathe through your mouth all the time. You may not realize it, but you snore a lot. Your brother has been complaining that you keep him awake every night, even though he sleeps in the room next door to yours."

"You mean I've gotta see the doctor just 'cause J. J. can't sleep?" This seemed mighty unfair, and I was about to protest further when Doctor Sims came in from the adjoining room and joined in the discussion.

"Robby, you remember all of the earaches you've had lately, don't you — especially the times when your eardrum ruptured?"

Come to think of it, I did have earaches sometimes. When I did, my folks would heat up some oily stuff in a little, dark blue bottle and pour it in my ear. It was supposed to help the pain, but it didn't always work, and sometimes my eardrum would bust and a bunch of green stuff would run out of my ear. I guess that's what Dr. Sims meant by a ruptured eardrum.

But then came the shocker. "If you keep on having all of those ear infections, Robby, you're sure to lose some of your hearing. So the last time it happened, I told your folks that you should have your tonsils and adenoids removed."

Immediately, alarm bells went off in my head. Removed meant "cut out!" I was well informed on the subject of cutting out tonsils. Ivy Hunt, a friend of mine at school, had his tonsils taken out recently, and he'd spared no detail in describing his terrifying experience. According to him, after they cut his tonsils out, he couldn't swallow anything for over a month — not even water — and it was a miracle he was even alive to tell of his agonizing ordeal. But Doctor Sims had said something about taking out my adenoids, too. I'd never even heard of adenoids, and I was pretty sure I didn't have any. But even if I did, I sure didn't want them cut out.

I turned toward my dad in dismay. "How come you didn't tell me why we were coming here, Dad?" "Well, Son, you know how your imagination always makes things a whole lot worse than they really are. So your mother and I decided it would be best if we waited to tell you until just before Doctor Sims operated. It was the only way we could think of to keep you from eating before surgery or making yourself sick with worry."

Then, even before I could ask Doctor Sims what adenoids were, his nurse led me (dragged me, would be a more accurate way of putting it) into the next room and stretched me out on a table. The next thing I knew, she was holding a mask over my nose while dripping some kind of liquid from a can on to it, saying, "Now take deep breaths, dear."

"I'm going to die," I thought, as I fought to get off the table. I couldn't move either my arms or legs, and I had decided that this must be the strongest lady I had ever encountered, but then I realized that I was strapped to the table both top and bottom. Even though I struggled, I had no choice but to breathe the fiery fumes that were pouring through the mask and into my lungs. Later, when I was back among the living, Dad told me it was called "ether."

Very shortly, a dark cloud came over me, and I remembered nothing more until I awoke on the black leather couch in the doctor's waiting room. "Are you all right, Robert?" I heard my mother's anxious voice somewhere off in the distance. I opened first one eye, then the other. The room was whirling about in an alarming fashion, with my mother's face centered above me.

"How are you feeling?" she asked again.

"Not too good," I whispered. It was a major understatemen, considering my present circumstances. I seemed to see two of my dad through the blur, and the one on the right said, "Just lie here until you feel better, Son. Your mother and I are right here if you need us." I immediately put him to the test as he held a shiny pan in front of my mouth as I repeatedly, but unsuccessfully, attempted to empty my already empty stomach.

My mother had often told me that all things, both good and bad, eventually come to an end. This was really bad, and it finally did end — but it sure took its time doing it. After an hour or so, I slowly came to the conclusion that I actually wanted to keep on living, and I struggled to my feet with my mother holding one arm and my dad the other. Then, as the world whirled about me, my parents guided me down the narrow stairway, into the car, and back to Shadycroft where, a month and a half later, I was able to take nourishment and drink fluids again.

Perhaps now you can understand my apprehension when my dad returned to report that the phone was back in service and that the doctor was on his way.

CHAPTER 20

Sam was no better, maybe even worse, and my parents were obviously worried about him —especially Mother. "I hope the doctor gets here soon, Julius. I'm sure the infection is getting worse. Did he say how long it would be?"

"Try to be patient, Grace. The doctor will get here as soon as he can. He was at Fort Logan on a house call, so it's likely to be quite awhile before he gets here. In the meantime, we'll take care of Sam as best we can."

I'm sure Dad's comments did little to lessen Mother's anxiety, but it did serve to spur her into action. "Julius, why don't you and Clyde move a bed into the kitchen so Sam will be more comfortable when he regains consciousness? And boys, first bring in some wood for the wood box and then go to the cellar and stoke the furnace so the rest of the house will be getting warm. Ada, why don't you and the girls get some sheets and make up the bed, and then get some water heating on the stove. And Vera, you can look after Sam and help me fix breakfast. I'm sure we're all hungry."

The trip to the cellar with Charley and J. J. would have been almost pleasant had it not been for my brother's nosy questions. He was amazed that I had survived not only my encounter with the colonel, but the ones with Mother as well. He just couldn't believe that she wasn't more upset by my putting Sam in her beloved trunk.

"How did Sam get any air to breathe in there?" he asked.

"I cut the holes in the bottom of it in a place where the colonel couldn't see it."

"Man - oh - man, are you ever gonna catch it when Mother finds them. That's her favorite trunk."

From the tone of J. J.'s voice, it seemed to me that he was looking forward to seeing me catch it with an unbrotherly degree of pleasure.

"Well, I couldn't let Sam run out of air, could I?" I said defensively.

"No, I suppose not, but I'd sure hate to be in your shoes when she finds out." Fortunately, by this time we were nearing the kitchen, thus putting an end to any further inquisition and dire predictions.

Moving a bed into the kitchen proved to be a good idea, for Sam was some quieter, and a lot easier to take care of. Breakfast was a great idea too, as we all voraciously attacked the fried potatoes, sausage, eggs and toast. Having eaten and done all they could to help, Mr. Williamson announced that he and his family were leaving — he had chores to do. No one seemed a bit upset by their departure. In fact, everyone in the room except Sam, and he was unconscious, was more than happy to see them go, for, as the warmth of the kitchen increased, so did Mr. Williamson's aroma. And I'm sure it wasn't just my imagination that I was getting some extremely dirty looks — especially from the Williamsons. You know, I'd never realized before just how long that skunk smell could last.

After eating, we waited for the doctor and worried about Sam. He seemed to be getting worse. He was sweating heavily, thrashing about on the bed and talking really crazy-like, even for Sam. It was hard to understand what he was saying. Sometimes it sounded like he said something about his daddy, but nobody could make any sense out of it. Once he even said something about gold.

Then, finally, after what seemed like forever, but was probably no more than an hour, we were relieved to hear the sound of Doctor Sims stomping the snow from his boots out on the screen-in porch.

"I got here just as soon as I could," Dr. Sims said as he set his black bag on the table and shook hands with all the grownups. Wasting no time, he removed Sam's bandages and carefully inspected his shoulder. He looked very worried.

"This really looks serious, Julius. The wound is badly infected, and I'm sure he has blood poisoning. That's why his fever's so high." Then he removed the thermometer he had placed under Sam's good arm and looked at it. "Good heavens! His temperature is over a hundred and six."

"Can you do anything for him, Harry?" my dad asked anxiously.

"Well, first, we've got to get him cooled down some before his fever goes any higher and injures his brain. He's already in a coma. Once he's cooler, we'll take the bullet out of his shoulder. Vera's right — it didn't go all the way through. In fact, I think I can feel it deep in the muscle here on the back of his shoulder. Let me show you, Julius — feel right here."

With that, he took Dad's hand in his and put it on Sam's shoulder, showing him where to feel. Initially Dad didn't seem to be particularly happy to find himself a consultant on this case, but after gingerly poking Sam's back with his forefinger, he nodded his head and looked quite pleased with himself.

"I can feel it, Harry. What are you going to do now?"

"Well, first, before we do anything else, we have to scrub this table-top real well and disinfect it with alcohol before we work on Sam." Dad had grown noticeably pale when Doctor Sims had used the pronoun "we" on several occasions, but he was obviously relieved when the doctor added, "Vera, would you mind helping me? It would be good to have a trained nurse as an assistant."

"Of course I'll help, Doctor, but wouldn't it be better if we do it at the hospital?"

"It would take too long to get him there, Vera, and it's too risky to move him. The sooner we get the bullet out and establish drainage, the better chance we have of saving him. For right now, at least, Sam will be a lot better off if he stays right here until he's strong enough to be moved."

Now it was my mother's turn to become pale. I'm sure a houseguest was the last thing she wanted — especially if it was Crazy Sam.

As instructed by Dr. Sims, Dad and J. J. wrapped Sam in cold, wet sheets in an attempt to lower his temperature while my mother sterilized the doctor's instruments by boiling them on the stove. At the same time, Mrs. Vogel scrubbed the tabletop with soap and water and then wiped it down with alcohol. When all was in readiness, the doctor, assisted by Dad and J.J., moved Sam from the bed to the tabletop where Mrs. Vogel scrubbed Sam's shoulder, both front and back, and slathered iodine over the entire area.

Boy, it's a good thing Sam's unconscious, I thought, 'cause that stuff hurts – A LOT! I knew that for a fact, 'cause iodine was my parent's favorite remedy for cuts and scrapes, and my brother's and my very least. After Mrs. Vogel was done killing germs, Dr. Sims asked Dad to help him turn Sam onto his stomach. That surprised me and, forgetting my fear of the doctor, I asked him how he could take the bullet out of Sam's shoulder with him lying on his stomach when the hole was in the front.

Mother was aghast, "Robert, you and the rest of you children stay back and don't interrupt the doctor again. In fact, I think you'd better all go into the dining room until this is all over."

Never had my popularity level with my brother, Abby, and Charley plummeted so low, and I was facing certain brotherly abuse. But happily, Dr. Sims came to my rescue.

"Now, Grace, it's fine with me if the children watch, just as long as they stay well back — and it's good that they ask questions." Then he explained how if he were to probe for the bullet through all of the pus and infection in the front of Sam's shoulder, it would spread the infection and make it worse. Instead, it would be much better and easier to remove the bullet by going through the back where there was no infection. Then the shoulder could drain from both sides and would heal more rapidly.

Mother, only slightly mollified by Doctor Sims' countermand of her order, instructed all of us to stay well back out of the way while Doctor Sims and Mrs. Vogel got ready to operate. After tying white masks over their noses and mouths and giving one each to Dad and Mother, the doctor and Mrs. Vogel scrubbed their hands with soap, rinsed them with hot water, and dried them with clean towels. After arranging the sterilized instruments on a clean white towel close by Sam's shoulder, Dr. Sims picked up a knife and quickly made a cut on Sam's shoulder over the place where he'd felt the bullet. With Vera busy moping up blood and handing the doctor the instruments, and Mother and Dad preoccupied by holding onto Sam, all us kids slowly crept closer and closer to the table, hoping no one would notice.

We'd failed to reckon with my mother's peripheral vision, however, for without appearing to even look in our direction, she said firmly, "You children stay back out of the way."

But, as luck would have it, my mother's warning came too late to prevent our witnessing the grand finale, for at that very moment the doctor pulled the bullet from Sam's shoulder. After showing it to us and stopping the bleeding, Doctor Sims put a big bandage on Sam's shoulder, and then he, along with everyone else in the kitchen — except Sam — heaved a big sigh of relief.

As I have already explained, my prior experience with Dr. Sims had not been particularly pleasant, but now that I had witnessed him in action on a body other than my own, it occurred to me that being a doctor might even be more exciting than being Buck Duane. There was a lot more fun and excitement in this doctor business than I had originally thought. I hoped it wouldn't hurt Buck's feelings too much, but I just might have to give careful thought to being a doctor instead of a cowboy. I imagine it would be a lot easier, too, 'cause you wouldn't have to learn how to roll cigarettes and chew and spit tobacco. That part of being a cowboy never had appealed to me much.

As Dr. Sims was packing his things back into his bag, he turned to Mother. "Grace, I'd surely be grateful if you and Julius would be willing to keep Sam here at Shadycroft for awhile — at least until he's strong enough to move to the hospital."

Mother and Dad looked at one another with obvious distress. Apparently neither one of them could think of a diplomatic way not to grant the doctor's request. After a long period of quiet, Mother responded, but with a notable lack of enthusiasm.

"Why, of course, Harry, we'll be happy to help out in any way we can. Neither Julius nor I have had much experience along those lines, however."

Dr. Sims smiled. "I realize that, Grace, and I have a solution to that. That is, I do if Vera is willing to help out, too. If you're not working at the hospital right now, Vera, would you be willing to help Grace and Julius by taking care of Sam for a while? I'm sure I can arrange it so you can be paid for doing private duty nursing by either the sheriff's department or the hospital."

Now it was Mrs. Vogel's turn to look distressed. Obviously she was no more enthusiastic than my parents over the prospect of spending any great amount of time in Sam's company. But on the spur of the moment, she was no better than Mother or Dad in coming up with a plausible excuse.

"Well, I suppose I could help out for a few days, Doctor, but heaven knows how long Sam will require constant care. I'm sure it will be for quite a while, and I just don't know how long I can do it. I have my children and my house to look after, you know."

My mother was obviously delighted with this new development. "It surely would be nice if you would agree to help us, Vera. You and the children are welcome to stay here with us. We have more than enough bedrooms upstairs, and I'll be glad to do the cooking and help you in any way I can. And I know Julius will be willing to give you a hand with Sam when you need it, as well as drive the children to school and help you keep track of your house. Besides that, Vera, I'm sure Abigail and the boys will be happy to help you take care of Sam when they're not in school or busy doing homework or chores."

That last part came as a shock. I didn't recall volunteering to be Sam's nurse, and from the expressions on Dad and J. J.'s faces I was sure that they didn't either. But before any of us could lodge a complaint, Abby gushed enthusiastically,

"Oh, I think it would be wonderful if we could help that poor, helpless old man."

And then, to make matters worse, Charley said, "Oh yeah, it'd really be swell if we could stay here and help take care of Sam. It'll be a lot of fun."

I just couldn't believe he'd said that. It was the stupidest thing I'd ever heard him say and he'd said lots of them. The only possible explanation I could think of was that Abby had somehow gotten control of his mind. And then Mrs. Vogel ended any hope I had of a reprieve when she said,

"Well, Grace, it looks like you're going to have a lot of house-guests."

After that my dad finally said something, and I was hoping he'd thought of a way out of this mess. But he hadn't. Instead he turned to Doctor Sims and said, "I'm sure it's a good idea for Sam to stay here, Harry — at least for the time being. But before we go making too many plans, shouldn't we first check with Sheriff Haynes to be sure he agrees?"

"Of course, you're right, Julius, but I'm almost positive that he will want Sam to stay here. It would be very risky to move him right now. I'll stop in to see John when I'm back in town. But before I do, I'll go by Jerome Burnett's place on the way to see how he's coming along with his pneumonia."

Dad chuckled. "I hope you're not to late, Harry. Grace, Julius, Jr., and I spent last night with the Burnetts while we were waiting out the storm, and it seems that Cleota didn't think your treatment was getting Jerome well fast enough. So despite his loud protests, she insisted on putting a mustard plaster on his chest, and now it's one gigantic blister."

Dr. Sims rolled his eyes. "I can believe it, Julius. Cleota is convinced that she knows more about medicine that any doctor — especially me. I'd better get over there before she tries some other old wives' remedy." Saying that, Dr. Sims hurried to his car, grumbling something about old wives as he went.

Sam appeared to be cooler after the doctor left, and we were all much relieved — that is I was until I heard Dad say, "Grace, now that the crisis is over, I'm going into Littleton so I can talk to the sheriff and see what he says about Sam staying here. Once we know that for sure, we can start making plans of our own." Then he looked at me. "Robby, I want you to go with me so you can explain to the sheriff why it was you didn't tell him that Sam was here at Shadycroft. Right now he's wasting his time looking for him somewhere else."

Lulled by the drone of conversation, I had been on the verge of dozing off. But when I heard my dad's request, I was instantly blasted into a full state of consciousness and extreme anxiety. Frantically, I tried to think of some reason I shouldn't talk to the sheriff, but for once my imagination failed me: I couldn't think of a single excuse. Actually, it would have made no difference if I had, for there was obviously no question of my compliance as Dad took my coat from a peg on the wall and gave it to me. "I'll be back in an hour or so, Grace," he said as he headed toward the car.

I reluctantly followed, and as I was wading through the knee-deep snow, it suddenly occurred to me that Dad had said "I'll be back" instead of "We'll be back." Did he use the singular pronoun on purpose? Then I had a terrible thought. Maybe I wasn't coming back.

As I climbed into the front seat alongside of Dad, I got to thinking: Do they ever put little kids in jail? How long will I be in for? Probably a year at least, I decided. Then I had a real frightening thought: What if the food in jail isn't good? What if they make me eat spinach and drink milk with gloppy cream in it? Dad broke into my thoughts.

"You're awfully quiet, Robby. What's bothering you?"

"Dad," I asked in a quavering voice, "will they put me in jail for not telling the sheriff about Sam?"

I was startled to see a broad smile spread over my dad's face. What's he smiling about, I wondered. Maybe he's happy I'm going to jail. He must be glad he's gettin' rid of me. My self-pity level had risen to an alarming degree by the time Dad answered.

"Oh, I don't think so, Robby. The sheriff will probably just give you a talking to about how you should have told him everything when he was there and not held anything back, like the fact that you knew where Sam was hiding."

"But Dad," I explained, "I'd promised Sam that I wouldn't tell, and I didn't want to break my promise. You always told J. J. and me that once you promise something, you should never go back on it."

"That's right, Son. You should always do your best to keep your word. But before you make a promise, you have to be very careful that you know what it is you're agreeing to keep secret. First, know all the facts — otherwise you could make a mistake and promise something you shouldn't. And if that happens, you might be forced to make a decision as to whether you should keep a bad promise or break it. Breaking it is certainly what you should have done in this case — mainly for Sam's sake. He might have died if he'd stayed in that trunk much longer. I don't know just why it is that Sam doesn't want the sheriff to find him, but it should have made you wonder if he had done something wrong, and that was the reason he didn't want the sheriff to know where he was." Then he smiled and added, "But I'm sure you did what you thought was right, Robby, and I don't think Sheriff Haynes will hold it against you."

That made me feel better, but only until my imagination had a chance to revive and point out that what Dad thought and what the sheriff thought might not be the same.

The day was bright and sunny as Dad and I climbed the steps of the Arapahoe County Courthouse, high up on the hill overlooking the railroad depot and downtown Littleton. It was a big, gray brick

Arapahoe County Courthouse circa 1920 — built in 1907.
(Picture courtesy of the Littleton Historical Museum.)

building several stories high, with a big cupola perched on top. Up 'til now, I'd always liked how it looked, but for some reason on this particular day it seemed dark and forbidding, even in the bright, noonday sun. As I walked down the long, dimly lit corridor my anxiety increased rapidly as I searched the gloomy shadows for signs of the jail. Around every corner I expected to see meanlooking men leering at me through the bars of their cell. Despite Dad's repeated assurances, I was certain that my fate was already decided — the jig was up. (Whatever that meant — I'd read it in a Sherlock Holmes story just a few days ago.)

A number of important looking people stood in the hall outside of the sheriff's office, and as we approached, every last one of them glared at me accusingly. Sheriff Haynes stood as we came in and shook Dad's hand — then he smiled at me.

"Well, Julius, I see that you brought your boy along. I didn't expect to see you again, Robby — at least not quite this soon. How are you doing?"

Not too good, I thought, but I lied. "Just fine, thank you, sir."

I think Dad chuckled a little, which was certainly uncalled for. Then he said, "John, Robby has something he wants to tell you."

Nothing like getting right to the point, I thought, as the sheriff invited us to take off our coats and sit down. I was speechless for a spell as I tried to make words come out of my mouth, but eventually I succeeded in stammering out a full confession, while hanging my head as though waiting for it to be chopped off by the executioner's ax.

Expecting the worst, I sat and waited for judgment. Surprisingly, no one said a word, and I looked up to see the sheriff smiling at me. Amazed, I wondered if he hadn't heard what I'd said, and I was about to restate my case when he broke the silence.

"You really did have a tough night, didn't you, Son? You should've told me about Sam when I was out at your house. It would have saved me a lot of running around. I've been looking for him, but not because he's broken the law or anything like that, and I really don't know why he didn't want me to know that he was out at your place. Sam's a little peculiar, you know. But I can certainly understand why you didn't want to tell me about him, so don't worry about it. I'm not going to press charges or anything like that."

I could hardly believe what I was hearing. My anxiety was instantly replaced by a joyful sense of relief. I wasn't going to jail after all.

After listening carefully as Dad was explained how Dr. Sims wanted Sam to stay with us at Shadycroft until he was well enough to be moved, Sheriff Haynes nodded his head and said, "I agree with Harry, Julius — not only for that reason, but for another one just as important — maybe even more so. If the colonel really did kill Cliff Alexander as Sam said, he will undoubtedly try to kill Sam, too, to make sure he can't testify against him. So, it's extremely important that no one knows that Sam is recuperating at your place — except for those who already do know, of course. Hopefully, Robby was successful in convincing the colonel that Sam isn't at Shadycroft, but if he ever finds out that he's really there, not only will Sam's life be in great danger, but your lives will be, too."

That was real scary to hear, and it didn't help any when I heard Dad say, "I'm sure you're right, John. I'll make certain that we warn everyone who was there this morning to keep absolutely quiet about this entire affair. Fortunately, I'm positive no one has left the farm except Harry Sims. He was going by the Burnetts on the way home from our place, and he's coming here after that. I only hope he didn't tell the Burnetts. Cleota has never been known to keep a secret in her whole life. If she found out about Sam, everybody on her party line will know about him by now."

"Well," interrupted the sheriff, "if Harry did tell them, which I doubt, I'll be sure to put the fear of the law into Cleota and anyone else she might have told. He'll be getting here soon and we can ask him."

"Sooner than you think, John," Dr. Sims commented as he walked into the room. "Julius, you should know that I would never tell Cleota anything about Sam — he's my patient."

"I'm sorry, Harry," my dad apologized. "I didn't think you would, but we had to be sure."

As Dad and I were about to leave, the sheriff warned us again how important it was that no one know of Sam's whereabouts. "Robby," he said, knowing full well that I was the weak link in the room, "be sure not to tell your friends at school about Sam, and be sure that your brother and the Vogel kids know how important it is for them to keep quiet, too. Sam's life, and maybe even your own, depends on it."

"Both Robby and I will make that very clear to them, Sheriff, and I'll be sure to tell the Williamsons, too," my dad assured him. "But I just remembered — I made a phone call to Harry about Sam. Clara is the operator I talked to. I hope she didn't overhear us talking and tell someone else."

"I'm glad you thought of it, Julius. I'll be sure to talk to her right away. Now you'd better be getting on back to the farm so you can warn the others to keep quiet." As we were leaving, Dr. Sims told us that he'd be out to check on Sam that evening, just as soon as he was through seeing patients at his office.

For some reason, the courthouse corridor didn't seem to be nearly as long or as gloomy as when Dad and I had come in. And when we I walked into the brilliant sunshine outside, the town and surrounding countryside were beautiful, peaceful, and quiet under a sparkling white mantle of snow. In exposed places, it was already beginning to melt under the warm autumn sun, and it was difficult to believe that any danger could mar such a lovely day. But dark, towering clouds were beginning to boil up from behind the high peaks in the west — a threatening reminder that peace, like the weather, could change rapidly and without warning.

Fortunately, no one at Shadycroft had told anyone about Sam, and upon hearing the dire consequences that might ensue if they did, I was sure no one would. Dad left to warn Mr. Williamson and his family to keep quiet. As for me, I went to bed and promptly fell into a long, deep sleep.

CHAPTER 18

And so it was that Sam and the Vogels became members of our Shadycroft Farm family, and it wasn't as bad as I had at first imagined — but it came close. Everyone had to shift for themselves a lot more than before. Mother was so busy cooking and cleaning that she had time for little else. But she didn't complain, having made up her mind — and ours — that this was the right thing to do.

By now, Sam had improved somewhat and was able to take sips of water and broth, and at times he'd even say something we could understand. He still had fever, however, and kept slipping in and out of his right mind, although at times it was difficult to tell which of his minds was the right one.

After the first week, we moved Sam to an upstairs bedroom where he'd be more comfortable and out of sight should anyone pay us an unexpected visit. There were six bedrooms on the second floor, and, after we'd transferred everything that was in the storeroom to the attic, all of the rooms were filled to capacity, as they were in the days of my grandparents and their eight children.

It didn't take long for us to settle into a daily routine. Of course, Dad and Mr. Williamson were kept busy running the farm. J. J. and I helped them with chores like milking, and feeding the horses, cattle, chickens, and such. Mother did most of the housework, but all of us kids were expected to keep our rooms picked up and the beds made, as well as to help out with the laundry and cleaning. Mrs. Vogel was busy nursing Sam and helping Mother whenever she could. As it turned out, Abby was a really good cook, especially pies, cookies, and all kinds of desserts. It was about that same time that my opinion of Abby improved considerably.

My brother's did, too, but for different reasons. Abby was just a year or so younger than my brother, and I was pretty sure she was sweet on J. J., 'cause she was always smiling and fluttering her eyelashes at him. I figured she'd probably seen some movie star batting her eyelashes like that and thought it would make her look prettier, so my brother would be more likely to notice her. I thought she looked really dumb and was amazed when J. J.'d get all red in the face and act like he really liked it. Charley agreed with me when I told him I thought my brother had most likely lost his mind.

In the beginning, we all helped take care of Sam with varying degrees of enthusiasm, but Abby did the most. But before long, the novelty began to wear off, and J. J., Charley, and even Abby got to where they just looked in on Sam now and then, and then mainly to say hello and goodbye. I was quite a bit more faithful than the others, however. Maybe it was because I had a special feeling for Sam, being as how I'd saved his life and all. I really didn't do anything for him other than sit by his bedside and talk to him most every day. But he seemed to enjoy it a lot and looked forward to it — and so did I.

Of course, my main job was going to school at the red brick schoolhouse on Rapp Street in Littleton — at least it was according to Mother. I was in grade 5-A back then, and reading and writing were my favorite subjects—they appealed to my imagination. But, according to my dad, using your imagination isn't much help when you're doin' your arithmetic. In fact, it could get you into a whole lot of trouble — especially if you're a businessman. At least I didn't have to worry about that, 'cause I sure wasn't good at arithmetic.

But the thing I liked best about school was recess, especially in the spring of the year. The school playground was divided almost in half by a six-foot high chain link fence. The girls played on one side and the boys on the other, which suited me just fine 'cause, except for Abby, I'm leery of girls — I didn't know there were so many of them 'til I started going to school. Every recess when the weather was nice, Charley Ammons, Al Thompson, Clark Skinner, and I headed out to the playground to shoot marbles, play tag, or have spittin' contests. I guess it wasn't anything to be proud of, but I was the spittin' champion of my class — at least I was until Mr. Bradley, our principal, made us quit.

Right after Cliff Alexander's murder, the kids at school were making all kind of wild guesses about who had done it and why, and it was hard for us to keep pretending that we didn't know anything about it. But eventually the excitement died down and everything returned to normal — as normal as it ever got with Sam and the Vogels living in our house.

The days stretched into weeks and the weeks into months as Sam struggled for his life. He ate less and less and, as his physical strength slowly waned, his already emaciated body wasted away to little more than skin, bones, and stringy hair. Everyone was real worried — especially Dr. Sims. He did everything he could to control the infection in Sam's shoulder, but despite his and Mrs. Vogel's very best efforts, the infection continued and Sam kept getting weaker and weaker. Dr. Sims thought that for some reason Sam didn't really want to get well, and, if something didn't happen soon to change that, he'd die — that made me feel awful. I didn't want Sam to die 'cause, even though I'd never admitted it to anyone, I was really fond of him. He was my friend.

But even as his body weakened, Sam's mind stayed surprisingly clear, and what he liked to do most was to talk to people, and for some reason nobody could understand, he especially enjoyed talking to me. I figured it was on account of I'd helped him and he was grateful, but more than that, I think he enjoyed talkin' to me 'cause he knew I really liked him. I don't think he had many friends now, and I wondered if he'd ever really had any. As a matter of fact, I got to wondering about Sam's life in general and how he got to be the way he was.

And so it was, that every day after school and on weekends, I began to spend time talking to Sam about his childhood and some of the things that had happened to him in the past. He didn't have the strength to talk very long each day, so when he'd tire and begin to drowse, I'd tiptoe out of the room. The next day I'd have to remind him where he'd left off the day before.

Mrs. Vogel thought I might be tiring him too much and that maybe it wasn't good for him, but Mother thought it was just about the only thing Sam had to look forward to and that it might even be perking him up a little. Dr. Sims agreed with Mother, so Sam and I continued our daily talks.

As a matter of fact, I started writing down a lot of what he told me. One day he asked what I was doing, and I explained how I was keeping a record of what he told me each day so I wouldn't forget it. Sam said he was glad I was doin' that, 'cause his very best friend in this whole world had kept a diary for most all of his life, and then, when he got older, he'd used it to help him write a story telling about all of the exciting things that had happened to him during his lifetime. Not long before his friend died, he'd given the journal to him. It was over at his house in an old metal box, and maybe someday I could go get it so I could read it to him. In addition to the journal, he wanted me to bring him his top hat, because he was afraid somebody might break into his house and steal it. I couldn't imagine why anyone would want to go anywhere near Sam's house, let alone break in and steal his hat — of course, I didn't say that to him. I just let the matter drop.

I thought he'd forgotten all about the journal and hat, but several days later he mentioned it again. He told me he'd decided for sure he wanted them and that he'd like for me to go his house and get them for him. I said, fine, I would — just as long as Dad could go with me. Sam agreed, so that night I told Dad what Sam wanted and, to my surprise, he agreed to go. He suggested that we go the very next morning, right around first light, so that no one, especially the colonel, would see us. Unfortunately, the sheriff still hadn't been able to catch the colonel, even though several people had reported seeing him recently in the vicinity of Littleton.

A little before sunup, Dad got me out of bed. It was a frigid Saturday morning in late January, and the mercury was hovering well below the zero mark. Warmly dressed, we stepped out into the crisp, cold air. Frozen clouds of breath floated in front of our faces, and our feet squeaked in the snow as we walked to the car. The car engine turned over stiffly a number of times before it reluctantly coughed and started. A cloud of frozen vapor belched from the tail pipe and hung suspended in the air as we drove up the lane and down Windermere towards Sam's house.

There was no sign of life anywhere, but, to be sure nobody saw us, we parked the car some distance from his house and walked to the back door, where Sam had told us the key was hidden. The door groaned as it slowly swung open. It seemed even colder inside the house than out, and we lost little time in searching for the journal and hat. Fortunately, they were right where Sam said they'd be. The black metal box that held the journal was on top of the icebox and the top hat was on top of a beaten-up chest of drawers. Taking them with us, we made a hasty retreat to the car.

It was only later, after we returned home and had warmed up a little, that Dad remarked, "You know, Robby, it seems peculiar, but now that I think about it, Sam's house looked surprisingly neat and clean. There was even a bathtub. Now that's really odd, considering how filthy Sam looks all the time. And not only that, I noticed several books on the table. One of them was Shakespeare and another was an old, well-read Bible. I was surprised to find books like that in Sam's house."

"I noticed that too, Dad, and there's another thing I don't understand about Sam. He doesn't seem to cuss and use bad words nearly as much now as he did before he got sick. Sometimes he even uses pretty good grammar. Why do you suppose that is?"

"I don't know, Son. I guess it's just one more thing about Sam that is puzzling."

Sam seemed delighted when we returned. "Thanks a lot, Boy. I shore do appreciate you and your daddy fetchin' these here things to me. I'm gonna feel a whole lot better, now that I have my friend's journal and my top hat where I can keep a close eye on them and be shore they're safe."

Actually, Sam did seem a lot brighter and happier, and he seemed to be talking more. I wondered if maybe the journal and hat really were helping him perk up some. I sure hoped so.

"How come you've got this top hat, Sam?" I asked as I picked it up from the bed and inspected it. I'd always wondered why he had it. I couldn't imagine anyone less likely to own a top hat than Sam. For some reason he seemed strangely upset that I was examining his hat, and, ignoring my question, he took it from my hand, set it on the far side of the bed well out of my reach, and changed the subject.

"Hand me that metal box, Boy." He seemed deeply moved as I handed it to him, and there were tears in his eyes as he opened it and withdrew a thick roll of yellowed papers. He obviously treasured them highly. "This here's my friend's journal I was tellin' you about." He clutched it to his chest as though it was something sacred. "My eyes ain't none too good no more, so maybe someday I can get you to read me what my friend wrote in it. I don't want nobody but you to read it, though, 'cause it's got a lot of secret stuff in it. But I trust you a heap, Boy, and I knows you won't tell nobody else."

Surprised, I asked, "You mean if I read it, I can't even tell my dad? I'm sure he wouldn't tell anybody. Not unless you wanted him to, Sam."

"I knows that, Boy, but for right now, I want this to be between jest me and you."

"Well OK, Sam, I promise not to tell anybody what it says unless you say I can." After that, I continued to visit Sam almost every day, but he didn't mention the journal again for over two weeks. I had about decided he didn't want me to read it after all, until one day when I walked into his room he greeted me, "Boy, I's glad to see you. Awhile back I reckon I come mighty close to meetin' my Maker, and I shore is glad I didn't, 'cause before I do that, there's some important things I's got to tell you about myself. But, before I do that, I want you to read my friend's journal out loud to me, so's you'll understand some of the things I'll be tellin' you about my own life. I haven't always been a dirty old bum, you know. But before you start readin' it, I's gotta explain how come my friend wrote it and how it all came about."

And that was the beginning of the most amazing part of my life — up 'til then, at least. Listening to Sam and reading his friend's journal was a lot like hearing and reading history, but not the dry kind of stuff my mother and teachers wanted me to read. It was a lot more exciting.

SAM EXPLAINS

"My friend's name was John Reynolds. He was born in late December 1843 and growed up on a Texas cattle ranch what his daddy owned in the hill country a little ways north of a town called San Antonio. He had an older brother named Jim. In the summer of 1859, right after he turned twenty-one, Jim told his daddy he was sick and tired of workin' on the ranch all the time and wanted to head up north to Colorado, so's to try his luck in the gold fields. A friend of his what had jest come back from there claimed a feller could get rich in no time at all and without doin' hardly any work. Jim's daddy told him his friend was tellin' him tall tales and that he'd best not go, but Jim didn't give a tinker's damn what his daddy thought or said. He was gonna go up to Colorado come hell or high water.

"Even though he warn't quite sixteen, John wanted to go along, too, and finally, after beggin' and pleadin' long and hard, he got his mamma and daddy to agree. But before they left, his mamma made him promise her that he'd keep a diary tellin' what they did and what all happened to them whilst they was gone. That way, when he'd got home, he could tell her all about it — and besides that, it'd make him keep practicing his writin'. John's mamma had done her level best to teach him, but he still warn't no great shakes at readin' and writin' — sort of like me, I reckon.

"Anyways, come mid-September, right after the fall roundup, Jim and my friend John headed north to a place in the Colorado mountains called Tarry All City where, according to Jim's friend, the miners what was workin' in the placer mines was gettin' rich overnight."

Interrupting, I asked Sam what placer mines were. I'd never heard about them before.

"Wal, Boy, that's what you calls it when you use water to wash the gold out of the sand and gravel of a river bank or to help get the gold out of ore what's been dug out of a vein or maybe a big mother lode." I interrupted again, even though I knew my questions were irritating Sam. "Well then, what's a mother lode, and what's a vein?" 'Course, I knew I had veins in my body, but they had blood in them — not gold.

"Damn it, Boy, don't you know nothin' about minin'? A vein is a crack in a rock what's filled full of gold, and a mother lode's what the vein is called where the gold is comin' from. Sometimes, it can be as much as twenty-five to sixty feet wide, like the one at the Phillip's mine up near Buckskin Joe — you calls that kind of lode a 'bonanza.' It's a strike like that what keeps men huntin' for gold. Now quit buttin' in all the time, and let me finish tellin' you about placer minin'.

"Them big operators, like the ones up at Buckskin and later on at Alma, pumped big, powerful streams of water through hoses so's to wash the sand and gravel of a river bank down into a long, wooden trough called a 'sluice.' Sluices is usually about a foot and a half wide and sometimes as much as a hundred feet long. Little boards what's called 'battens' lay crosswise in the bottom of the sluice, and the nuggets and gold ore, bein' heavy, hangs up topside of them battens where the miners can collect it. The lighter sand, gravel, and rocks flushes on down to the end of the sluice.

"And sometimes, if'n a miner's lucky, he'll find a place where heavy rains and snow melt has washed gold out of a mother lode and down into a crick bottom where the miner can collect it by pannin'. That's what it's called when the the miner uses a shallow pan to scoop up sand and gravel from the crick bottom, along with water from off'n the bottom of the crick, and swirls it 'round and 'round 'til it's all sloshed out, leavin' the heavy gold in the bottom of the pan. 'Course, it's usually nothin' but a few flakes or a little dust, but sometimes, if he's lucky, he'll find some nuggets. When that happens, the prospector most likely will head upstream, lookin' for the mother lode the gold is comin' from.

"That's what Jim and John Reynolds done. They spent most all their time prospectin' on a crick east of the Tarryall Mountains. An old Mexican feller named Ramon had told them about it and claimed his granddaddy and his granddaddy's brother had found a big bonanza in a crick they called Lost Crick — that was 'way back in 1779. John and Jim had helped the Mexican get back to his family in Texas, and he was so damned grateful, he gave them a faded out old map what was supposed to show the whereabouts of his granddaddy's bonanza. But I reckon I best let you read about that in my friend's journal, 'cause I's gettin' a mite weary now."

Sam had been talking for a long time, and I'm sure he was enjoying it, but now his voice was growing weaker and he was obviously very tired. About that same time, Mrs. Vogel came into his room to check on him, and when she saw how exhausted he looked, she became alarmed and shooed me out saying, "Robby, you must try to be more careful not to tire Sam so much. If we're not careful, he'll get sick again. Now you run along and wait a day or two before you visit him again." So I thanked Sam for all that he'd told me and promised him I'd come back just as soon as Mrs. Vogel said I could.

CHAPTER 19

The next morning I was up bright and early. It was the second Saturday in February and quite warm for that time of year. That wasn't too unusual, however, for every few years we'd have what my dad called "the February thaw." Sometimes he could even do some plowing before the spring rain and snows made the soil too wet to work. But since the big blizzard back in November, there had been almost no snow or rain, and now Dad was worried that his winter wheat, what little had sprouted, would be blown clear out of the ground by the strong winds that often came in March.

I always looked forward to the coming of spring and warm weather, for it was the time of the year that Buck Duane and I would hightail it out to the dryland so's to clean out all the rustlers and no-good varmits what had snuck in over the winter. And that's what I was figurin' on doing that morning. After gulping down breakfast as rapidly as my mother would permit, I hurried up to my room where I changed into my cowboy outfit, thereby revealing my true identity — the steely-eyed, formidable gunslinger, fearless guardian of the open range. Then, fully outfitted, I'd swagger up to the old corral where, with a running leap, I would vault onto the back of my spirited, fire-breathing steed and gallop fearlessly off into the great unknown — side by side with my intrepid companions, Buck and Rab. That is, I would if I could catch my mare, Molly.

Perhaps I should be more explicit. According to J. J., some aspects of my attire left a few things to the imagination, and he may be right. Of course, Buck Duane always dresses entirely in black, from his high-crowned Stetson right down to his high-heeled boots, except for the grips of his Colt .45s — they're pearly white. Regrettably, my overalls are not black — they don't even come close. Both my overalls and my shirt are a torn and faded blue. Nor is my cowboy hat black. Although properly high crowned, it's white. I have no cowboy boots, so my Red Goose shoes have to provide support for the one mail order spur I have left — the other one is somewhere up on the dryland. But the part of my outfit I like the best is the .32 caliber Smith and Wesson revolver that my Granddad Reed gave me after filing off the firing pin. It's remarkable, but despite all of the other shortcomings of my attire, the moment I strap it about my waist, I am miraculously transformed into the spitting image of Buck Duane. I'm real proud of my horse, Molly. She's a pretty little buckskin with a white blaze on her nose, and I'm sure she's the finest horse in Arapahoe County. At least she is now, after I straightened out a few basic misunderstandings that we had early on.

Robby on Molly
(Picture taken by Julius E. Johnson Sr.)

I was just a little kid when my folks bought her, and to begin with, Dad would have to saddle and bridle her and hoist me up into the saddle every time I wanted to go riding. But that got old in a hurry, so he dug a trench a horse and a half long and one horse wide at the west end of our vegetable garden. Then he showed me how to get Molly to unclench her teeth so I could put the bit of the bridle in her mouth by offering her a mouthful of Omalene, a mixture of oats and molasses that she loved dearly. Once the bridle was buckled in place, I'd lead her into the trench, get up on the bank, put the blanket and saddle on her back, cinch it up tight, and climb on — at least that's the way it was supposed to happen. But Molly didn't agree. She wasn't about to let a scrawny little kid tell her what to do. 'Course, the scrawny little kid thought the opposite, and that was the start of our problems.

Molly was an expert blanket snatcher. Blanket snatching is when your horse reaches around and snatches the blanket off with her teeth after you've put it on her back and are reachin' around to pick up the saddle — or sometimes she'd just shudder a little and shake it off. But the trick Molly liked the best and I hated the most was when I'd be standing on the edge of the trench with one foot up on her belly, pulling on the cinch stap with all my strength, and she'd take a real deep breath and puff up her belly like a toad. Then, thinkin' it was tight, I'd buckle it into place, stick my foot in the stirrup, and start climbing onto the saddle. But the instant I did, she'd let out her breath and deflate her belly, the saddle would turn, and I'd end up in the bottom of the trench. That was bad enough, but it was a whole lot worse when she waited to deflate until we were up on the dryland, galloping along at top speed. That was both disastrous and painful, as I had demonstrated on several occasions. Happily, Omalene was the solution to both of those problems as well.

After two days of chasin' rustlers off'n the *dryland* — that's what we call the unirrigated part of our land above the Highline Canal — I asked Mother if it was all right with Mrs. Vogel, could I please go up and talk to Sam. Mother seemed surprised.

"You seem to be spending a lot of time with Sam, Robert. What on earth do you two talk about?"

I guess I should have expected her question. It probably was a little difficult for her to understand why a supposedly normal eleven-year-old boy would want to spend time talking to an illiterate old man like Sam. At least my brother, J. J., had expressed considerable doubt about my intelligence in this regard. But then, he questioned my intelligence in most anything I did, so that didn't bother me much.

"Oh, Sam's just been telling me some things about when he was a boy down in Texas," I told her, hoping she would let it go at that.

Fortunately, she did. "Well, I guess it's all right. Just be sure you don't neglect your homework."

With Mrs. Vogel's permission I entered Sam's room, and it was obvious that he had been waiting impatiently for me to arrive. "Where the hell have you been, Boy? You ain't come to see me for two whole days, and now this morning's damn near shot, too."

"It's only nine o'clock, Sam, and I came as soon as I could. Mrs. Vogel wouldn't let me 'til now."

"Wal, OK, I guess. It's jest that I's been hankerin' to hear more of what my friend writ in his journal. I's sorry I fussed at you, Boy. But this time I ain't gonna spend so damn much time 'splainin' things. I plumb tuckered myself out last time we talked."

"I know, Sam. From here on, I'll just read your friend's journal to you so you won't have to talk. And I promise not to ask you any questions — unless it's about something I've really got to know."

So that's what I did, and well over two months passed before I finished reading the journal to Sam. Most every day, after I'd read only a few pages, Sam would grow weary and fall asleep in the middle of the most exciting part. I could have gone ahead and read more while he was sleeping, I guess, but I knew he'd feel better if I waited so we both could read it together and, for that matter, so would I. Readin' it in fits and starts like that sure took a long time, though, so now I'm going to tell it to you without any interruptions, starting with the time John and his older brother, Jim, headed north to make their fortunes in the gold fields of the Colorado mountains.

PART THREE

THE JOURNAL OF JOHN REYNOLDS
1859-1915

SOUTH PARK - FIVE MILES TO WATER

(A pen and ink drawing by Doctor Seymour Wheelock)

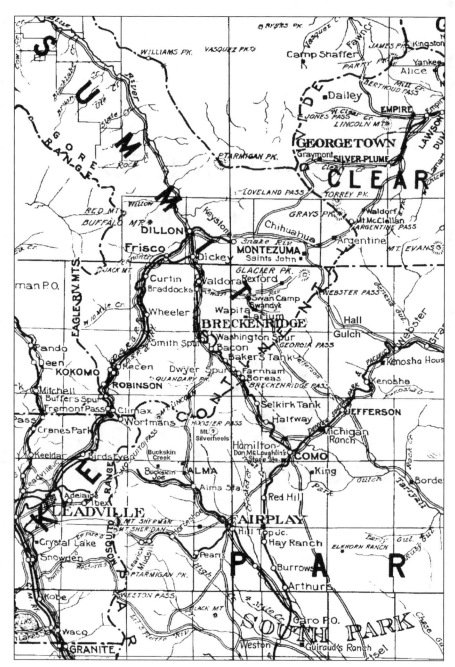

Map of Central Colorado
This is a portion of a map taken from The Denver Westerners Brand Book of 1956.
With their permission, the author has modified the map in places so that it better illus-
trates his story.

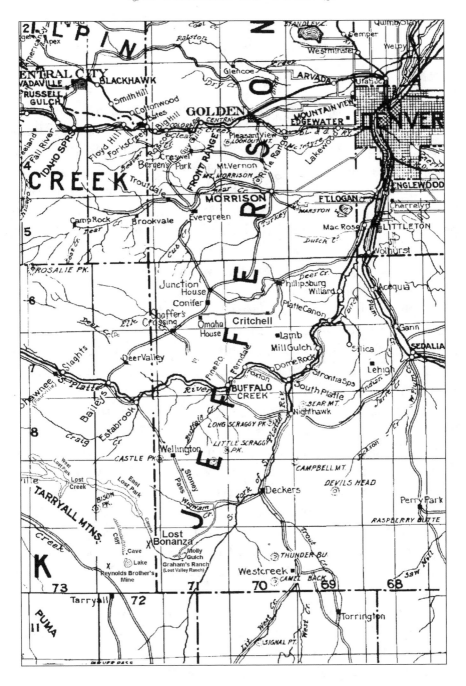

CHAPTER 20

It was the twenty-fifth of September 1859 when me and Jim left our folks' ranch in the hill country of Texas and lit out for Colorado. Before we left, our daddy gave us a couple of good ridin' mares and a burro, plus enough money and gear to get us to where we was goin'. From then on we was on our own. First off, we headed west to an army fort close to the town of El Paso, and from there headed up the Rio Grande Valley past Santa Fe and Taos to Fort Garland in the southern end of the San Luis Valley. We figured we'd hole up in one of them places if the weather turned bad. But we was lucky. The weather stayed good, and we rode the whole way up without a speck of trouble, 'cept'n that Jim's horse, Blaze, throwed a shoe a little ways outside of Fort Garland. But that evening, the blacksmith at the fort fixed her up good as new, and the next mornin' we took off bright and early, passin' by the west side of some big sand dunes what lay at the foot of the biggest mountains I'd ever seen. Their tops was all covered with fresh snow.

That night we camped 'long side a little lake at the north end of San Luis Valley and the next day headed over Poncha Pass and down into the Arkansas River Valley. When we come to the river, we rode downstream ten or twelve miles 'til we found a place we could cross. From there, we headed north to a pass over a low mountain range where we looked down on a monstrous mountain valley what stretched into the north for what looked like forever. Big mountains bordered it on both the east and west, and way off to the north we could see the tips of snowcovered peaks stickin' up over the horizon. We figured it was South Park for shore.

After settin' up camp on top of the pass, we was frying up some antelope steaks, when along comes an old Mexican hombre riding a scrawny little burro. His name was Ramon Sanchez. He claimed as how a couple of seedy lookin' miners had beat him up and stole his other burro what was loaded with most all of his gear, including his bedroll and all of his grub. And I reckon he was tellin' the truth, 'cause his clothes was all tore up and he was bruised bad around his face. But he still figured he was lucky, 'cause they hadn't kilt him or stole the burro he was ridin'. 'Course, it was easy to see why they didn't 'cause it was a mighty sorry lookin' critter. Jest a few days back, Ramon had been workin' at a saloon at the Tarryall Diggin's and doin' a little prospectin' on the side, and now he was headin' home to Santa Fe before heavy snows closed the passes out of the park.

Well, I tell you no lie, Ramon was a sad sight to see, and we both felt sorry for him. Jim told him he could eat supper and bed down with us for the night if he liked, and it was sort of pitiful to see how grateful the old man was, 'specially so after we'd fixed him up with some spare blankets and gave him some grub to help him get home. I hope he made it. I'm shore he never would have if'n we hadn't helped him. After supper Jim asked him a whole passel of questions, like which way we should go to get to Tarryall City and who we should see about gettin' a job when we got there.

I reckon Ramon must of had real good schoolin', 'cause he talked American even better'n me. He told us we was camped in a saddle jest a few miles west of Currant Creek Pass, and that it was South Park we was lookin' down on, jest like we'd figured, 'ceptin' he called it "Valle Salado." Seems the early Spanish explorers started callin' it that after they found a salt marsh on the west side of the park. Indians had been gettin' salt there for centuries, and jest lately ranchers and miners was usin' it too. When the fur trappers and mountain men started comin' here, they'd called it "Bayou Salado." Then the miners showed up and they called it "South Park" on account of there was two more big moun-tain parks farther on up north.

Accordin' to Ramon, it'd take us two days to get to Tarryall City, and that a good place to spend the next night would be at Adolph Guiraud's ranch. It was right on the road to the Tarryall district. But if he was us, he said, instead of goin' straight to the Tarryall Diggin's, we'd best check out a brand new minin' camp what was poppin' up close to where Beaver Crick runs into the South Platte River. It'd been named "Fair Play" by some tenderfoot miners what figured they'd got cheated up at the Tarryall Diggin's. Seems as how, even though all the good claims was already taken by the time they'd got there, the newcomers figured the claim own-ers ought to be nice and share their claims with them.

'Course the claim owners didn't see it that way — as far as they was concerned, them Johnny-come-latelys could complain all they wanted, but it warn't gonna do them a damned bit of good. They warn't about to share their claims with nobody. 'Course, that upset the newcomers considerable, and they was all for changin' the name Tarryall Diggin's to "Graball," 'cause them selfish claim owners had grabbed it all. After that the newcomers hustled on down to the new strike on the Platte and named it "Fair Play." They figured namin' it that would make them greedy miners at the Tarryall Diggin's feel real ashamed. 'Course it didn't do no such a thing.

Old Ramon really took a shine to us when we told him we was Texans, and even more so when he found out we was from down around San Antonio way. Seems he had kinfolks down in them parts. After we'd finished eatin' supper that evening and was settin' by the campfire, Ramon told us we'd been so nice to him, he was gonna tell us about a lost gold mine his granddaddy'd found when he was up in these parts nigh on to ninety years ago. 'Course that got me and Jim's attention in a hurry, and we told him we was all ears.

It seems as how Ramon's granddaddy, Juan, and his younger brother, Pedro, was in these parts back in 1779. They was scouts for a Spanish and Indian army what was out to put an end to the rampages of a renegade Comanche Indian chief named Querno Verde. Once they'd finished doin' that, the rest of the army headed for home, but Juan and Pedro stayed behind so's to look for a rich bonanza an old trapper had told them about. They found it all right, and it was even better than they'd been hopin', but not long after they'd found it, things went to hell in a hurry. Pedro was damn near kilt by a cougar and died whilst Juan was trying to get him out of South Park and back to Santa Fe. Ramon's granddaddy didn't make out too good, neither. He got busted up bad by an avalanche and would have died if it hadn't been for some kindly Ute Indians what found him and took care of him 'til he got well — 'ceptin' for bein' crippled. A beautiful Indian girl named Tsashin was the one that helped Juan the most. She was the granddaughter of a Spanish lady what was kidnapped by the Apache when she was a little girl and traded to a tribe of Ute Indians for two horses and a mule. The chief of the tribe and his wife adopted her and raised her like she was their own daughter. When she was growed up, she married and had a daughter named Quana, and Quana was the mother of Tsashin and Pinto. Their daddy was a Ute warchief named Moara. Whilst Tsashin was takin' care of Juan, they'd fallen in love with each other, so after he could get around purty good, they went down to Santa Fe so's to get married and so Juan could go into business with his uncle. They raised a big family, too — seven children — all girls, and thirty-five grandchildren — Ramon was their only grandson. When Juan got old and was about to die, he told Ramon about the bonanza. After that, he gave him an old map what was supposed to show him how to find it, but he made him promise not to go there to look for it 'til he was growed-up, on account of it was such rough and dangerous country.

But, bein' as how he was thirteen years old and gettin' interested in the señoritas, he warn't much interested in gold, so he'd put the map away and forgot all about it. Over the years he'd got married, raised a family — all girls, and jest like his granddaddy and daddy, he'd made a good livin' in the tradin' business. He'd plumb forgot about the map and the bonanza 'til the spring of 1857, when he was fifty-five years old.

He was rummagin' through a drawer of his dresser, tryin' to find a clean shirt, when he'd come across the old map and spread it out on the table so's he could study it. It was drawed on parchment made out of deer hide and was yellowed and faded so bad with age it was hard to make out what was writ on it. But still, along with the map and what he recollected his granddaddy tellin' him, Ramon figured he'd have a pretty good chance of finding the gold, and the idea of bein' rich began to get real appealin'. Not long after that, he'd outfitted hisself and spent the next three summers and falls lookin' for the bonanza on Lost Crick — but he never did find it. The map didn't help him one damned bit, 'cause he never could match up the markin's on the map with the lay of the land. He figured rains and floods must have changed things around a lot since his granddaddy was there. And another thing he never could figure was why his granddaddy had wrote "lechuzas doble" on his map. 'Course, it meant twin owls, but how could owls have anything to do with the gold?

But even if he didn't find the bonanza, at least he'd hadn't wasted his time, on account of he'd found enough gold to make it well worth his while in the meadow downstream from the place where Lost Crick comes out of an openin' in the rocks and flows down the valley. But now he was done lookin' — he was goin' back to Santa Fe and stick to the tradin' business. Then Ramon handed Jim a leather folder with his granddaddy's map inside it, sayin' he doubted it'd do us any good, but that we was welcome to it anyhow. At least it'd show us how to get out of South Park and into the watershed of Lost Crick on the far side of the Tarryalls. Then he pointed to the range of mountains on the east edge of South Park and said, "That's them over there."

CHAPTER 21

Next mornin', after a quick breakfast, Ramon thanked us for our help, picked up the lead rope of his pitiful little burro, told us good-bye, and headed south in the direction of Santa Fe. I shore hoped he made it, too, 'cause Ramon was a nice old man. After he'd left, me and Jim climbed on our horses and rode down the mountainside into South Park and from there, headed north in the direction of Fair Play. It shore was a pretty ride. Whole hillsides looked like they was painted bright yellow with splashes of red here and there. It made the day seem bright and sunny, even when the sky was gray.

That night we stayed at the Guiraud's, and they was mighty nice folks. After we'd stabled our animals in their barn, we ate supper with Adolph and his wife, and after that bedded down in their spare bedroom. At breakfast next mornin', Adolph gave us the name of a man we should see at the Fair Play Diggin's. His name was William Coleman, and he was plannin' on stakin' out a town site and sellin' off lots. Accordin' to Adolph, Fair Play was bound to grow fast, 'cause the gold ore there was so high grade it was bringin' seventeen dollars an ounce, 'stead of the twelve and fifteen dollars at most other places. When Jim asked Adolph what he knowed about the country around Lost Crick on the far side of the Tarryalls, he shook his head. All he knowed was hearsay, he said, 'cause he'd never been there, and he didn't know if there was any gold there or not. But if what he'd heard was true, we'd best stay clear of it, 'cause it was a mighty rough, dangerous country.

It was almost dark when we got to Fair Play, but it was easy to find Mr. Coleman, 'cause there was only ten or twelve shacks plus maybe two dozen tents scattered around an area the size of a big corral. Mr. Coleman let us bunk in with him for the night, for which we was grateful, 'cause it'd turned mighty cold in jest the last hour. Jim figured that me and him had best be findin' a place we could settle in for the winter, and we'd better be findin' it fast, if we didn't want to end up spendin' the winter sleepin' in a tent. I agreed. Somehow spendin' the whole winter shiverin' didn't sound too appealin'. Mr. Coleman said if he was us, he'd head up to the Tarryall

Diggin's. Just last July, a miner made a rich gold strike up near the forks of Deadwood Gulch and Tarryall Crick, and by the first of August there was miners all over the place. They was mainly from out of Denver and Gregory Gulch. A lot of buildin' was goin' on about two miles below the diggin's, so we'd most likely could find a place to hole up 'til spring. Not only that, he was shore we could get jobs, 'cause a bunch of the miners up there had left and come to Fair Play or gone down to Denver City.

Early next mornin', we left Fairplay and headed northeast to the Tarryall Diggin's. The air was crystal clear, and you could see for miles across the flat, grassy park. As we went, we passed big herds of antelope, deer, and elk grazing peacefully in the tall grass and watched the eagles as they floated in the blue, blue sky up above our heads. What a beautiful day! We figured it must be the beginnin' of somethin' good.

Tarryall Diggin's was close to fifteen miles from Fair Play, but it was easy goin', and 'long about mid-afternoon, we rode into a little settlement of log cabins, shacks, and tents what was built, or was bein' built, along Tarryall Crick. Right off, we met up with a Mr. Holman. He said he was stakin' out a new town and was gonna call it Tarryall City, and he wanted to sell us a site for a cabin. But Jim told him we jest was lookin for a place to hole up for the winter so's come spring we could do a little prospectin' of our own. Mr. Holman didn't have no rooms to let and, as far as he knowed, nobody else in the camp had any either, but he told us about another settlement about a half-mile upstream on the far side of the crick. He was shore we could find a place there. A Mr. Earl Hamilton could more'n likely help us.

Fordin' the crick was a mite tricky, but we made it in good shape, and a short ride later we rode into another little camp about twice the size of the first. A few miners was settin' around passin' the time of day, and we asked one of them where we might find Mr. Hamilton. Turns out we was already talkin' to him, and in no time at all we was stashin' our gear in a upstairs room of his cabin. Besides that, there was a place to stable our horses and burro a short piece down the trail.

Accordin' to Mr. Hamilton, there was fourteen claims, each a hundred feet wide, what miners had staked out about a mile and a half farther up Tarryall Crick, and he was shore we could find work there. So the next day me and Jim rode up the crick, and it warn't long before we come across a miner what was buildin' a sluice box. He was a medium tall, stocky fella, and I could scarce tell what he looked like on account of the dirty old hat he'd pulled down clear to his eyebrows — the rest of his face was hid by a long shaggy beard. He seemed like a mighty nice fella, though. He said his name was John D. Cranor, and that he was glad to see us, 'cause the two fellas what'd been helpin' him had left him high and dry a few days back. They'd taken off for Fair Play, hopin' they could stake out their own claim.

Mr. Cranor offered to pay us a fair day's wage for a good day's work, and Jim said fine, that we'd be glad to help him out, jest as long as he understood that come spring, we'd be quittin' to go prospectin' on our own. Mr. Cranor agreed. Come spring, a passel of greenhorns would be comin' up from Denver, and he was shore he could find somebody to give him a hand — most likely for less wages.

So now me and Jim had a job and lodgin's, and we was feelin' pretty good. We figured we was all set for the winter. And jest in time, too, 'cause the very next day it started to snow. The snow fell and the wind howled for the next two days, and when it stopped there was close to two feet of it on the level. But there warn't much level, on account of the wind had blowed the snow into big drifts what most buried our cabin. When the storm let up on the third day, we helped Mr. Hamilton dig a pathway out to the stable and to some of the other miner's cabins, includin' the store what was owned by Wing, Doyle and Company. The sun came back that same afternoon, and things began gettin' back to normal.

That was the start of a long, hard winter. Mr. Cranor, or J. D. like he'd asked us to call him, was a tough old buzzard, and he'd shore meant what he'd said about our doin' a good day's work. But he was a real hard worker hisself and mighty strong, and it was hard to keep up with him. At first me and Jim was afraid old J. D. was gonna have us clear the snow off his whole damned claim, but as it turned out, it was just the sluice and the gravel bank where he was workin'. Jest doin' that gave of us both permanent backaches, and they got a lot worse after we started diggin' and shovelin' gravel into the sluice so's J. D. could wash it down with the water he'd piped from upstream a piece. It warn't too bad a claim either, 'cause he was takin' out two, maybe three, ounces of gold a day — at times a good deal more. Jim figured at eighteen dollars an ounce, J. D. was doing pretty damned good for hisself, and he could hardly wait 'til spring so's we could go make a strike of our own.

I didn't think that winter was ever gonna end, but it finally did 'long about the end of April, so we started makin' plans to head out on our own. Jim asked Mr. Hamilton what he knowed about the country on the east-side of the Tarryalls and explained how Ramon had told us about it — 'course, he didn't say nothin' about the bonanza. Mr. Hamilton jest laughed and said he knew all about that crazy Mexican what claimed he was gonna find a rich lode in that godforsaken country along Lost Crick. Other prospectors had tried to explore that hellhole, and they'd never found a damned thing. They was lucky they'd even made it out of there alive — and so was Ramon. If he was us, he said, he'd stay right where we was, on account of he'd already laid out a townsite and named it Hamilton in honor of hisself. Now he was busy buildin' cabins to sell to the new miners what would be pourin' in come spring. He claimed he could use a couple of hard-workin' Texans like us, and that he'd make it well worth our while. We'd most likely make lots more money without havin' to do near as much work.

But what Mr. Hamilton said didn't make one bit of difference to Jim. We was goin' to Lost Crick come hell or high water, 'cause he was shore that Ramon warn't lyin' about the big mother lode his granddaddy found on Lost Crick. We had a map what showed us where to find it, and even though it was wrote in Spanish and faded some in spots, we could still make it out without much trouble.

It was toward the end of May, and Tarryall Crick was still runnin' high with the spring runoff. Most all the ice was gone from the banks of the crick and the south slopes of the mountains, but on the north slopes and on the shady sides of rocks and trees where the sun didn't hit, there was still a considerable snowpack. But that didn't make no difference to Jim. He was sick and tired of waitin' and figured it was time we was headin' up to Lost Crick, so we headed over to Wing, Doyle and Company to outfit ourselves and damned near went broke in the process. We already had our tent and bedrolls and some cookin' gear, but we still ended up havin' to buy a lot more equipment, as well as all our grub. Mr. George Wing helped us get outfitted. He sold us what he figured we'd need, 'long with a few things I reckon we didn't. We even had to buy a second burro, 'cause we couldn't pack it all on jest one.

CHAPTER 22

Come sunup, we said our good-byes to Mr. Hamilton and lit out for Lost Crick. Followin' the map and his directions, we rode 'long side Tarryall Crick 'til we come to another little stream Mr. Hamilton called "Michigan Crick." From there we headed southeast and climbed up the west slope of the Tarryalls to a pass overlookin' South Park. We camped there for the night and next mornin' headed south, followin' along the tops of the Tarryalls 'til we come to a pretty little lake. A little crick was runnin' out of it towards the southeast. Figurin' it most likely was Lost Crick, we followed it on down the mountain, and shore 'nuff, 'long about midafternoon we rode out into the upper end of the meadow Ramon and Mr. Hamilton had called "Lost Park." By this time Lost Crick was a fair sized stream, so after settin' up camp, we spent the rest of the day checkin' the crick in the meadow for gold, but there warn't any. The next mornin', we followed a game trail into the upper end of what the map called the "Cañon Diablo." It was a damn good name for it, too, but it didn't come nowheres close to tellin' how bad it really was. That damned trail never did stay on the level. It was always headed either straight up or straight down. The horses was havin' a terrible time tryin' to keep from slidin' down the hill on the loose gravel, so me and Jim got off and led them, but that warn't too good neither. All that horse flesh jest waitin' to slide down on top of us got to be downright unnerving, so we switched to leadin' the burros and trailin' the horses, 'cause the burros was a lot more surefooted. After that the goin' got a mite safer — but no easier.

Ramon had told us how that damned crick keeps goin' in and out from under the rocks, and he was right. At times it'd disappear for up to a quarter mile at a time before it popped out again. I reckon that was why Ramon's granddaddy named it Lost Crick. But luckily, the trail always took us back to open water, where me and Jim would check it for gold. But we never did find any.

Late in the afternoon on the fourth day out of Hamilton, we final-ly come to the end of that god-awful canyon and rode out on top of a hill overlookin' the upper end of a meadow. The sun had already set in back of the Tarryalls and the light was fadin' fast, but if we looked close, we could still see the silvery sliver of Lost Crick as it wound its way down the meadow 'til it disappeared behind a far-off hill. We both gave a big cheer. We figured it must be the place where Ramon found his gold. Hopefully our luck was gonna change.

That night we'd finished rollin' out our bed rolls 'long side of the crick and was fixin' to crawl in when we heard the most god-awful caterwaulin' comin' from way down the valley, and a few seconds later, an answering scream — a whole lot closer and louder. Twice again that night, them big cats let out with those damn heart-stoppin' screams, and each time it came it sent cold shivers runnin' down my spine — 'specially when I recollected what all had happened to Ramon's granddaddy's brother.

Next mornin', after a quick breakfast, me and Jim started pannin' the crick and right off collected a couple of nuggets and a good show of color. Now we was shore we'd found the place Ramon had told us about. We was even more shore when we seen the place where Lost Crick flows out of an openin' between the rocks and into the upper end of the meadow. We both gave a cheer! Jim said that now he was shore we was gonna find the mother lode — he could feel it in his bones.

Wal, his bones was dead wrong. We spent most a month lookin' for the bonanza up and down the west side of Lost Crick upstream from the meadow, 'cause accordin' to the map, that's where it was supposed to be, but nothin' on the ground matched what was on the map. For one thing, the map showed a stream comin' down the west slope of the Tarryalls and runnin' into Lost Crick, but we looked and we looked 'til we damn near dropped, and we never could find it. Most of the time we couldn't even find Lost Crick, 'cause it was flowin' under the monstrous rocks on the valley floor.

And another thing we couldn't figure out was why Ramon's granddaddy wrote "lechusas doble" on the map. What could owls have to do with a bonanza? It didn't make any sense. Jim said he was beginnin' to wonder if there really was a bonanza — maybe the old man had made the whole thing up. But I figured that warn't likely, 'cause why would Ramon's granddaddy lie to his own grandson and send him off on a wild goose chase? But if he warn't lyin', where the hell was it?

We rolled up in our blankets that night and the next morning, after a good night's sleep, things seemed a little brighter. Jim said as he recollected, Mr. Hamilton had told us how Lost Crick runs into the South Platte River downstream from the meadow, and that he'd got to thinkin' that it might be worth our while if we was to check for gold 'long that stretch of crick — maybe we'd have better luck down there. So that's what we did. We worked our way down the north bank of Lost Crick 'til we come to the Platte, then we went back up the south bank 'til we got back to the meadow. It took us three weeks, and all we found was three puny nuggets and a half-ounce of gold dust. We was wore out and discouraged and thinkin' about goin' back to Hamilton and workin' for wages. Jim claimed we'd make more money and it'd be a hell of a lot easier. But then — all of a sudden — things got better.

As we was comin' back into the lower end of the meadow, we'd come across a little stream what was emptyin' into Lost Crick from out of the west. It was in the bottom of a gully, and we'd missed seein' it when we was headed downstream. Wal, I tell you no lie, that perked us up considerable. But by then it was gettin' too dark to do any more pannin', so we set up camp, ate supper, and crawled into our bedrolls. Come mornin', we'd start checkin' the new little crick for gold.

Close to a quarter mile up the crick, we come to a place where the water was runnin' slow and clear. It seemed a likely place for gold — and, as it turned out, it was. In the very first pan I found a good show of color, and by the time we quit for lunch, we calculated that between us we had close to half an ounce of dust and three fair-sized nuggets. It warn't a lot, but it was a hell of a lot more than we'd been findin', and we was hopin' we'd find more the farther we went up stream. Maybe we'd even find the mother lode it was comin' from. I figured it might be comin' from Ramon's granddaddy's bonanza, but Jim said "no way"— this crick warn't nowheres close to the one marked on the map.

The lower end of the stream was anglin' across the east slope of the Tarryalls from out of the northeast and was easy to pan for gold, but the higher up we went, the tougher it got, 'cause up there the crick was comin' straight down the mountainside in the bottom of a deep ravine. The fast runnin' water made it a lot harder to check, but, as it turned out, it was worth it, on account of we kept findin' a fair amount of gold.

By the time we quit that evenin', we'd collected over four or five ounces of dust and a passel of nuggets. Things was finally lookin' up!

That night we camped on a grassy shelf south of the ravine. Jim called it a "bench." From there, we could look down and see last night's campsite and Lost Crick as it wound its way down the valley. Lookin' north and halfway up the mountainside, a rocky cliff stretched 'long the side of the valley for as far as we could see — it looked to be close to a 150 feet high in spots. Next mornin', jest as we was fixin' to head back into the ravine and start pannin' again, I spotted a waterfall spillin' over the edge of the cliff. It was sparklin' in the bright mornin' sunlight and easy to see. It was mighty pretty, but if it was the same crick what we'd been followin' up, checkin' it for gold was gonna be a mighty tough job.

We worked our way up the crick, pannin' the likely pools and riffles, and by the time we got to the upper end of the ravine, we'd collected four or five nuggets and close to an ounce of gold dust. We was feelin' good about the way things was shapin' up. We figured the mother lode the gold was comin' from was somewheres further on up the stream, and it was beginnin' to look like it was a big one. At the upper end of the ravine, the crick spilled off the bench and down into a crystal clear pool where three more nuggets was waitin' to be picked up. That lit a fire under us, and we hustled up the game trail to the top of the bench where we was in for a surprise — the bench was a lot bigger than we'd been expectin'. Not only did it stretch for over half a mile north across the face of the cliff, splittin' it into an upper and a lower part, it also went south along the side of the mountain for well over half a mile.

Jim said it looked to him like a part of the bench south of the cliff had been a lake at some time in the past, but that it must have been a long time back, judgin' from the size of the ponderosa pines growin' out in its middle. Back then, the lake most likely filled with water from the same little crick we'd been followin' up, 'ceptin' it was comin' down the mountainside south of the cliff and into the lake before goin' down into the ravine. But then somethin' happened higher up on the mountain to change the course of the stream and make it start spillin' over the edge of the cliff, across the bench, and into the ravine like it was doin' now. I reckon Jim most likely was right, 'cause if you looked close, you could see an old dried up crick bed comin' down the mountain south of the cliff and into the dried up lake.

Jim figured it'd be best if only one of us checked for gold in the stretch of water comin' down the cliff and across the bench. Then the other fella could take our critters to the top of the cliff and wait for the other to join him — that way our animals would be safe. I figured that made good sense — 'til I found out I was the one elected to check out the crick — and I never even got to vote.

Checkin' the part comin' down the cliff was hard — awful wet, too — but I got the job done, and I didn't find no gold. Checkin' for gold in the crick on the bench warn't too easy neither, 'cause it kept goin' in and out from under monstrous big rocks like Lost Crick was doin' down in the canyon. It took me over two hours to check it, and all I found was a few specks of gold, and a big scary cave.

I'd come to a place where the crick disappeared under the rocks, and, whilst I was scramblin' around tryin' to find where it came out again, I come across a little path. I followed it and it led me to a passageway beneath two big rocks what was leanin' up against each other. I kept on goin, hopin' it might take me to the crick, but the farther I went the darker it got, 'til finally it was gettin' hard to see. It was gettin' spooky, too. Then a little ways further on I come to a solid wall of rock, and I figured that was as far as I could go. But I was wrong. When I got to the wall, the path turned off to the left. I followed it and walked right into a big cave. The walls and ceilin' was solid rock and the floor was hard-packed dirt. What little light there was was comin' through a crack between the rocks at the far end of the cavern. It was real dark and scary and I could hardly wait to get out of there — 'specially so after I found big piles of bear scat in two or three places on the floor of the cavern, and some of it looked mighty damned fresh. That shore shook me up, and I got out of there in a hurry, prayin' as I went that I wouldn't run into the bear. But I didn't, and I finally found the crick again and finished checkin' it for gold. After that, I hightailed it to the top of the cliff where Jim was waitin' with our animals. I told him I didn't find no gold, but I shore did find a spooky lookin' cave chock full of bear scat.

CHAPTER 23

There was still plenty of daylight left, so we kept on workin' our way up stream. We kept on findin' good color and a nugget now and then, so we was still hopin' to find the mother lode, but it was gettin' less and less likely all the time. Late in the day, we camped in a grassy openin' in amongst a grove of big aspen. From there to the top of the Tarryalls looked to be no more than half a mile, and next mornin', Jim decided that instead of breakin' camp and movin' to a new spot, we might jest as well make this a permanent camp whilst we finished checkin' out the rest of the crick. That sounded good to me. Packin' and unpackin' burros and settin' up and breakin' camp every night warn't a whole lot of fun. Besides that, there was plenty of good grass, water, and shelter for our animals.

Come next mornin' we was back at work pannin' our way up the crick, still hopin' we'd find a promisin' outcroppin' of gold-bearin' ore. But, 'ceptin' for a little gold dust, we found nothin', and we was both mighty discouraged. But there was one thing to be happy about — at least accordin' to Jim there was. When it come time for us to leave these parts, all we had to do was to head over the divide to the west slope of the Tarryalls, drop down to Tarryall Crick, and head back to Hamilton from there. Goin' that way, we wouldn't have to go back to Lost Crick and up that god-awful canyon.

A little ways above our camp, the crick split into two branches. The north branch was carryin' most of the water and was headed straight up the mountain to the top of the Tarryalls. The other branch was jest a trickle of water comin' down a gulch from out of the southwest. We figured our best bet was to keep on pannin' the north branch. So that's what we did, and it was a mistake. After spendin' two more hours pannin' promisin' lookin' sands and not findin' so much as a speck of color, we decided we was pannin' up the wrong crick.

Jim was ready to quit. I hadn't been keepin' track, but accordin' to him, we'd been gone from Hamilton for close on to four months and had damned little to show for it. We'd collected some small nuggets and a few ounces of gold, but it didn't amount to a hill of beans, considerin' all the work and time it'd taken us. Besides that, we was low on grub, so Jim figured we'd best go back to Hamilton and work for wages instead of wastin' our time prospectin'. I had to admit that shore sounded good. I was tired of grubbin' around in water and dirt day after day, and I was 'specially tired of eatin' Jim's and my cookin'. But I warn't quite ready to quit yet — not 'til we'd checked the south branch of the crick. I wanted to be shore we didn't miss nothin'. Jim figured it'd be a waste of time, but he finally agreed to it, so come next morning that's what we did.

Like I said, there warn't but a speck of water in the south branch, so we was surprised when we started findin' good color again. The higher we went up the gulch, the more excited we got. But then, all of a sudden, the gulch up and petered out, and the little crick disappeared under a big bank of dirt. We figured our prospectin' days was over for this year, but I'm happy to say we was wrong. The water what was seepin' out from under the bank had made a little pool before tricklin' on down the gulch. The water was crystal clear, and we couldn't believe what we seen. The bottom of the pool was covered with gold nuggets. Both me and Jim gave a big whoop and scared our horses so bad they damn near bolted. Once they was quieted down, we checked the pool, and out of that one little pool alone we collected way, way over the amount of gold we'd found up to now. One nugget must of weighed over a quarter pound. After that, we checked the bank where the spring was comin' out and found lots more gold — some lyin' free, some bound up in a quartz outcrop. After that Jim started chippin' away at the outcrop with his pickaxe, whilst I shoveled the loose rocks and dirt over to one side of the pool. When we had a good-sized pile, we started takin' turns — one bustin' up the bigger rocks with the sledgehammer, and the other pannin' the crushed up rocks and gravel for gold. The more we worked, the more excited we got, 'cause we was findin' big nuggets and chunks of high-grade gold ore. It was late afternoon when Jim finally called a halt, and I shore was ready to quit. My back was hurtin' something awful, and my hands was blistered bad. That night we got in our bedrolls right after we'd ate, but I couldn't sleep. I was too damned excited.

The next few days we worked even harder, and by the end of each day we was so tired we could hardly move. But come mornin' we was up and at it again, 'cause we knowed snow and cold weather was comin'. We didn't have much time left to work, and we wanted to get as much gold as we could before we had to leave. By now we'd dug eight to ten feet back into the quartz outcroppin', and we was shore we'd found a mother lode. We was followin' up a vein of gold ore close to six inches wide — even more in some places — and it seemed to be gettin' wider the deeper we dug. 'Course, as mother lodes go, I guess it warn't a real big one, but it shore warn't nothin' to sneeze at neither. Jim figured we was gonna have to start shorin' up the tunnel soon, 'cause if we didn't, the walls and ceilin' was likely to cave in on us. It was gonna take a lot of time and be a lot of work, but we didn't have no other choice, 'cause I shore didn't cotton to the idea of bein' buried alive.

A thick stand of pines was growin' close-by, so for three days me and Jim cut off tree trunks and big branches and hauled them back to our mine on our burros. After trimmin' off all the branches, we set the sturdiest logs on either side of the mine shaft. Then we used the bigger branches for overhead cribbin', so's loose rocks wouldn't come fallin' down on our heads. Once we was finished with that, we went back to diggin', haulin', and pannin' ore. But the deeper we dug into the hill, the harder it got, on account of the face of the tunnel where we was workin' was nothin' but solid rock — so we was gonna have to blast.

We'd brung along some black powder and some fuses, but neither of us had ever used it. But Mr. Hamilton had explained how it was done, so Jim figured it was worth a try, 'cause if we didn't blast, we warn't goin' to get much more gold. We used a star drill and a sledgehammer to make holes in the rock wall at the end of the mineshaft. I held the drill whilst Jim hit it with the sledge. The idea was to cut a hole into the rock deep enough to hold a charge of black powder. After that, one end of a fuse was stuck in the powder and the other end was lit. The explosion was supposed to loosen the rock so's we could get to the ore. Well, I'd like to go on record as sayin' that warn't my favorite job — not by a damn site — I was lucky my hands and head didn't get busted up by the sledge. After drillin' several holes close together, we cleared out the rock in between them so's to make a little pocket where we could pack in the black powder.

At first Jim wanted to make more'n one hole and blast two at a time. He figured it'd get the job done quicker. But when he found out how much work it was makin' the first hole, he used jest one. And it was a damned good thing he did, on account of that one charge caved in the far end of our tunnel, and we spent the rest of the day cleanin' out the rubble and shorin' our mine shaft back up.

Lately things had been goin' along real good. The weather was stayin' good. We'd collected what we figured was a small fortune in gold, and we was only forty feet into the hill. In fact, we had a lot more gold than our animals could carry out in one load, and one load was all we could make, 'cause it was already early fall and could start snowin' most any time now. So we was gonna have to leave and leave soon. But first we had to find a place to hide the gold we couldn't take with us, so's it'd be safe 'til we come back in the spring. The mine tunnel wouldn't work, 'cause somebody might come by and find it. 'Course, that warn't likely to happen, but if it did, and they seen the tailin's pile, they might start snoopin' around and find our gold. Then I thought of the cave, and I figured it'd be the perfect hiding place. When I told Jim, he wanted to go see it. Findin' it again was a whole lot harder than I'd expected, but I finally did, and when Jim seen it, he agreed that it'd be a good place to hide our gold.

So's not to overload our burros, it took us seven trips and two full days. The passageway into the cave was too narrow for our critters to get through, so me and Jim hauled the gold the rest of the way ourselves. We piled it on top of deer and elk hides. The last time we left the cave, we used pine branches to wipe away our footprints, so's to make shore nobody'd see them if they happened to come by. It warn't too likely, I guess, but it don't hurt to be careful when you're hidin' a small fortune in gold. We was about to run out of supplies. All we had left was a little coffee, salt, dried fruit, and beans. Our salt pork, jerky, and bacon was long gone, same as our flour, and we was even gettin' low on fresh meat. But, even though it was early October, the weather was still holdin' good, so we decided to stay a few more days so's to mine a little more gold. As it turned out, we should have left. The next day we was back at the mine, blastin', haulin', and crushin' rock like usual, and it warn't long until we had another load of high-grade ore to take to the cave. So we spent the next day doin' that. For some reason, Jim never could find the cave without my help. He claimed he was gonna draw us a map so's to help him find it, but he never did, and neither did I — leastwise not 'til later on.

After we'd got back to camp that evenin', I headed over to a draw near our camp and shot a fat spike buck. After guttin' it, I brung it back to camp and hung it from a branch of a dead pine tree so's it'd cool 'til we had time to butcher it. Early next mornin', we was back at the mine and worked 'til late evening, so's to get enough gold for one last trip to the cave. It was jest about dark when we got back to camp and found everything in a terrible mess. Our gear was scattered all over the countryside, and our tent and bedrolls was ripped to shreds. What was left of our grub was either nowheres to be found or ground into the dirt, and our pots and pans was mostly smashed flat. The carcass of the buck had been torn out of the tree along with the branch it was tied to. Somethin' had eaten most half of it, and most of what was left warn't fittin' to eat.

To make matters worse, our saddlebags was tore up so bad they couldn't hold nothin'. But at least we still had all our animals — we was thankful for that. We always took them with us whenever we left camp, jest to be shore they didn't get kilt or run off by a bear or cougar, but we'd leave our saddle bags, figurin' they'd be safe and sound. But now they was anything but sound, and neither was anything else.

It was too dark to do anythin' more, so we staked out our animals close by the campfire and took turns sleepin', jest in case the critter decided to come back. The next day, we spent the whole mornin' cleanin' up the mess and tryin' to save what was left of our gear. We didn't have no trouble figurin' out what had done it, 'cause monstrous bear tracks was scattered all around our camp. There was other sign, too, like a big pile of scat and some claw marks high up on the trunk of the pine tree where we'd hung the buck. They was over ten feet above the ground. Jim said that black bear never got anywheres near that big, so he was shore it was a grizzly, and a big one, too. Neither of us had ever seen a grizzly, but we'd shore heard a lot about them from the miners around Hamilton last winter. They was sayin' as how a grizzly could kill a horse with jest one swipe of his paw and knock in a cabin door with no trouble at all, if'n he was of a mind to. Me and Jim always kept our rifles loaded and close by after hearin' that. Jim figured this old bear was probably tryin' to fatten herself up for the winter, bein' as how they spent most of it sleepin' in a cave.

I'm shore that old grizzly figured it was nice of us to furnish her with a free meal, but what puzzled me was why she'd tore up our camp so bad. That was a damned ungrateful thing to do. I hoped she'd had a bellyache from eatin' too fast. Jim said as how we'd best pack up what was left of our gear and get the hell out of camp before the bear decided to come back for the rest of the buck — or for one of our animals, or for us. I couldn't have agreed more. We managed to scrape up a few handfuls of beans, dried fruit, coffee, and a little salt from off'n the ground. 'Ceptin' for that, we was plumb out of grub. We'd managed to patch up one set of saddlebags to where we could put a few things in it, but the other bags was too tore up to even try fixin'. After tyin' what was left of our tent, bed rolls, and clothes behind our saddles, we rode out of camp jest as quick as we could. All the way up to our diggin's we kept lookin' around for any signs of the grizzly. Accordin' to Jim, they could outrun a horse jest as easy as pie. I shore wished he hadn't told me that.

Now, not only was our camp and equipment all busted up, but a pile of our richest gold ore was settin' outside of the mine, and all we had to carry it in was two beat-up saddle bags. We'd been figurin' on takin' the richest gold with us when we went back to Hamilton and leavin' the rest of it hid in the cave 'til we come back next spring. 'Course, now we had to change our plans, but I warn't expectin' what Jim had in mind, and I warn't quite shore I agreed with him. He claimed as how the old grizzly had actually done us a favor, 'cause now we was gonna have to leave most all our gold in the cave instead of takin' it with us. And that was good, 'cause that way the miners in Hamilton wouldn't find out about our strike. Then, if we didn't file on our claim or tell anybody about it, we could come back in the spring with a string of pack animals and haul it all out in jest one trip.

But for now, Jim added, we'd only take with us what gold we could carry in our pokes and in the bottoms of our sorry saddlebags. We'd hang our pokes around our necks and tuck them inside our shirts so's nobody'd know they was there. Then, when we got back to Hamilton, we'd get jobs and go back to workin' for wages like we was broke. 'Course, we could live high off the hog if'n we wanted to, but Jim figured we'd best play it safe. If they knowed we'd found gold, they'd be likely to jump our mine and steal it from us. I agreed. We'd best not take any chances with claim-jumpers.

After takin' the rest of the gold ore we'd dug to the cave, we put most all our tools inside the mine shaft and caved it in with a charge of blasting powder a little ways back from the entrance. Then we scattered the tailin's pile out a mite and put weeds and a few little bushes on top, so's to make it look like an old, abandoned tailin's dump. Lastly, I took the pickaxe, prybar, and shovel we'd been usin' a couple of hundred feet down the hill and pitched them behind a thicket of wild currant, where they'd be out of sight. It was dark by the time we finished, so we ended up havin' to spend the night takin' turns sleepin' and stayin' awake, so's to stoke up the fire and keep a sharp look-out for the bear.

Breakfast was a mite sparse come mornin' — just a few boiled beans and coffee. We'd bent our coffeepot and a pitiful, beatup pan back into good enough shape so's we could at least make that. After first checkin' to be shore we didn't see any sign of the bear anywheres, we took off a little after sunup, ridin' our horses and leadin' our pack animals. We headed up to the ridge of the Tarryalls and dropped down the west slope into South Park. After crossin' over what we figured must be Tarryall Crick, we followed it north 'til it got too dark to ride.

CHAPTER 24

We broke camp at first light next mornin'. By our reckonin', it was the sixteenth day of October 1860. The sun was low in the southern sky, and even though the days was gettin' short, we was hopin' to make it into Hamilton before sundown. And we most likely would have, if we hadn't stopped 'long about midmornin' to eat and jaw a mite with a couple of hombres what was workin' their claim at a placer works they called "Nelson's Bar." They said their names was Bill and Tom. They never did say their last names. It shore was good to talk to somebody other than our critters and ourselfs for a change, even though they was both real scruffy lookin' — 'course, come to think of it, so was we. They told us how they'd jest got back from pickin' up their mail and supplies in Hamilton, and they filled us in a little on what all had been happenin' since we'd left.

Mr. Hamilton had left last week on the Denver and South Park Stage. He was plannin' on spendin' the winter in Denver. And J. D. Cranor was gone too. About a month ago, he'd sold his claim and went back home to Shreveport, Louisiana. There was a lot of talk goin' around right now about a possible war between the southern and northern states over people's rights to own slaves. So he'd figured he'd best get back to his kinfolk in Louisiana whilst he still could. Well, this was news to us. 'Course, we'd knowed there'd been a lot of talk about whether or not folks should own slaves. But there warn't many slaves in the part of Texas where we'd growed up, so we'd never had to give any thought about it bein' right or wrong. But no matter which way it was, if a war started between the North and the South, we'd fight for the South whatever the reason, 'cause it was our home. But the fellas we was talkin' to seemed to feel jest the opposite, so me and Jim figured we'd best keep quiet and not say too much. They had plenty to say though — mostly bad about us southern boys.

They claimed there was a lot of Johnny Rebs in South Park right now, 'specially up around Buckskin Joe. We asked them where that was. We'd never heard of Buckskin Joe. Bill explained how it was a new little minin' town about nine or ten miles north of Fair Play, and that it'd been named after Joseph Higganbottom, an old miner who always wore buckskins. Back in September of 1859, he'd been the guide for five prospectors what found a lode up along Buckskin Crick. A month or so after that, a fella named Phillips made a rich gold strike in the same gulch, but then he'd took off for parts unknown and nobody'd seen him since or knowed why he left.

Then, jest last spring, Higganbottom had laid claim to the water rights at the Phillips Lode and started workin' it. But it seems that he warn't too fond of hard work and a little too fond of hard likker, and I reckon he warn't too good at dickerin' neither, 'cause he sold the lode to four other fellas — Miles Dodge, Jacob Stansell, J. W. Hibbard, and Griff Harris — for a horse and a gun. Then he gave them all the water rights for payin' off his whiskey bill and took off for the San Juans. The Phillips Lode turned out to be a rich bonanza with a vein of gold runnin' through it from twenty-five to sixty feet wide. Jacob Stansell, the man in charge of the operations there, was a doorman at the theater in Oro City before he got into the minin' business. Now he was the richest man in town and, accordin' to Bill, one of them damned rebels.

It was the middle of the afternoon when we got on our way again. Now that Mr. Hamilton and J. D. Cranor had left Hamilton, Jim figured we'd be smart to winter over in Buckskin Joe. It sounded like a mighty up and comin' town, and besides that, a bunch of southern boys was livin' there. That night we camped 'long side of Tarryall Crick and the next day rode up to Hamilton so's to stock up on supplies before headin' over to Buckskin. As it turned out it was a good thing we did, 'cause when we was buyin' supplies at the Wing, Doyle and Company store, one of the miners we'd met last winter come up to us and told us he'd been holdin' some letters for us since August. His name was Daniel Witter, and he was the postmaster of a new post office what had opened in Hamilton not long after we'd left last spring. He was glad to see us, 'cause nobody seemed to know where we was.

The letters was from our folks. Me and Jim had both wrote them letters before we headed out prospectin' last spring and put them on the Denver and South Park Stage, hopin' they'd make it to San Antonio and then on to our folks. They'd got them all right, and Mamma had wrote back to let us know how things was with them. They'd been missin' us a heap, she said, and she'd been prayin' every day that we'd come home real soon. Our daddy had busted his leg when a horse fell on him last winter, and he'd been laid up for a spell. His leg was jest fine now and he was gettin' around pretty good, but accordin' to Mamma, he'd shore be happy if we'd come back and help him out with the chores. She was hopin' we'd come home, too, on account of it was awful lonely there without us.

Readin' them letters shore made me homesick — guilty, too, for not goin' home when we said we would. Jim claimed he missed them, too, but that we couldn't change our plans now — not and leave all that gold we had hid out in the Tarryalls. So we both wrote letters, sayin' how we was doin' jest fine and that we missed them a lot, too, but that we warn't gonna be home 'til sometime next year — probably midsummer. 'Til then we'd be here in South Park, most likely at Buckskin Joe. We didn't tell them about our findin' gold — we figured we tell them about all that when we got home. 'Course, we was figurin' on comin' back in '62 so's to work our claim, but we didn't tell them that either.

Buckskin Joe (Laurette), circa 1860.

(Courtesy of the Colorado Historical Society.)

We spent that night at a boardin' house in Hamilton and the next night at a hotel in Fair Play, 'ceptin' the folk livin' there now was callin' it the Fairplay Diggin's. Come morning, we headed north up the Platte River Valley for six or seven miles, then a few more miles up Buckskin Crick 'til we come to Buckskin Joe. After stablin' our animals, we took a look around town. Let me tell you, as minin' camps go it was a real humdinger. Close to two thousand miners was strung out along Buckskin Crick that summer, and a lot of them was still there. We talked to some what was workin' at the Phillips Lode. They said as how the vein there was so damned wide and rich that, instead of a tunnel, they was diggin' the ore out of a big pit eighty, maybe a hundred feet wide. To start out with, they'd crushed the ore up in arrastras, but that was too damned slow, so they'd brought in a steam-driven stamp mill.

We asked one of the miner's there where we could find Mr. Stansell, and he pointed towards a shack settin' 'long side of the pit. When we went in, he was behind a desk at the far end of the room. He was a big man, most likely in his mid-thirties, and right off he treated us like we was good friends — and when he found out we was from Texas, he jumped up and damn near shook our hands off. After that, we talked for over an hour. He asked us if we had a place to stay and did we have a job, and we told him no, we didn't have neither. He said the boardin' house where he was stayin' was passable and the food was jest fair, but it was the best Buckskin had to offer. He knew they had some rooms open right now, so why didn't we go down and see Mrs. Perry about stayin' there. We couldn't miss it. It was called the O.K. House and was right across the street from Billy Buck's Saloon. And as far as a job was concerned, that warn't no problem either, 'cause he had plenty of jobs at the Phillips Lode.

Everything was workin' out great. Me and Jim could hole up in Buckskin 'til maybe mid-April, or at least until most of the snow was out of the high country. Then we'd buy our pack animals and fetch out our gold. With any luck, we should be back in Texas by early next summer. Was we ever wrong!

The boardin' house warn't too grand, jest like Mr. Stansell said, but it shore beat sleepin' on the ground. The livery stable was next door, so's our animals was taken good care of, too. After that, we both got jobs

Dance Hall and saloon in Buckskin Joe in the 1860s.
(Courtesy of the Denver Public Library Western History Collection.)

workin' the sluices at six dollars a day. It was hard work, and it didn't make it no easier knowin' that we didn't really have to do it, 'cause come spring we'd be richer than most anybody in Buckskin — 'ceptin' maybe for the fellas what owned the Phillips Lode.

Actually, there warn't much to do in Buckskin 'ceptin' work. 'Course, for some of the miners that warn't entirely true. Once they got off work, they'd head straight to one of the saloons or dance halls in town and have a high old time gamblin', drinkin', and whoopin' it up. There was always a bunch of ladies in them places, and I never could figure why the miners fancied them so much. They shore didn't look too pretty to me. In fact, most of them was downright ugly. They was so painted up, a fella couldn't even tell what they really did look like. I couldn't see what all the attraction was, so I asked Jim to explain, but his explainin' warn't too clear. Mainly he said I was too damn young to understand and that he'd promised our mamma he'd keep me from get-tin' into trouble with women like that. I told him I warn't figurin' on gettin' into no trouble. I was jest tryin to find out what it was about them painted-up ladies that made the miners think they was so great.

But one of the ladies was different. She'd come to Buckskin in the spring of '61, not long after me and Jim started workin' at the Phillip's

Lode. The miners called her "Silver Heels." When she got off the stage, her face was covered with a veil, and she was wearin' slippers with high silver heels. And when she took off her veil, I thought she was the prettiest lady I'd ever seen. So did most everybody else. She got a job right off and was dancin' at Billy Buck's saloon when me and Jim left Buckskin later that year.

Years later, when I was back in South Park again, I asked an old miner whatever had become of Silver Heels, 'cause she warn't around Buckskin no more. He told me that the same year we'd left Buckskin, she'd been takin' care of some miners what had caught the smallpox from a couple of Mexican sheepherders what'd come through town. It turned into a real epidemic, but Silver Heels jest kept on nursin' them poor sick miners 'til she finally caught it herself. She didn't die, but after she got well, I guess she warn't too pretty to look at no more, 'cause whenever she left her cabin, she'd always wear a heavy veil. Father Dyer and all of the miners had taken up a collection to show how grateful they was for all she'd done for them, but when they took the purse full of money up to her cabin so's to give it to her, she was gone.

Silver Heels warn't never seen again. She'd jest up and left Buckskin without tellin' anybody goodbye. Some folks claimed her pretty face was scarred up so bad from the pox that she didn't want nobody to see it. Even though they couldn't give her the money, the miners was so grateful to her that they'd named a big mountain up northeast of Buckskin "Mount Silver Heels" so people would always remember her kindness. It was strange, though, 'cause for several years after that, some of the folks in Buckskin swore that they'd seen a veiled lady visitin' a miner's grave in the cemetery. They was shore it was Silver Heels.

The winter of '60-'61 started out mild. Up until early January, there was only three or four light snows. But then things changed in a hurry, and it seemed like it was going to snow and be cold forever. It stayed below freezin' most all the time. Some days the thermometer was way below zero. The snow never melted, just kept stackin' up until by the end of March, there was five or six feet on the level and drifts up to twenty feet deep in some places. Nobody could work the mines. It was hard enough jest gettin' out of the houses. Tunnels and deep trenches was dug from house to house and to the stores and saloons so's people could move around some. A lot of the miners had left before the snow got too deep, but them of us what stayed was stuck there from the first of February to the middle of March. Nobody was gettin in or out of Buckskin — not even Father Dyer.

Father Dyer had first come to Buckskin in July of '60, not long before me and Jim got there. His given name was John, same as mine. He was a Methodist circuit minister with a flock what was scattered all over South Park and the camps the other side of Mosquito Pass. But preachin' didn't pay too good, so's to keep from starvin' to death, Father Dyer got a second job carryin' the U. S. mail.

Goin' from camp to camp deliverin' mail warn't too bad in the summertime, but durin' the winter it was somethin' else again — 'specially climbin' over Mosquito Pass. It was over thirteen thousand feet high and hard to get over even in the summer, let alone in a winter like we'd been havin'. But Father Dyer warn't one to let a little snow stop him. He took to makin' his rounds on long skis, eight or nine feet long. On the level it was easy goin', but goin' uphill it got a lot tougher. Sometimes, in places where there warn't much snow, he could put his skis over his shoulder and climb up the hills. In places where there was a lot of snow, he'd strap them on and side step up the mountain. That was hard. 'Course goin' downhill was easy if he didn't try to turn, and if he didn't get goin' too fast and fall. To keep that from happenin', he'd drag a long pole in the snow along side his skis, so's it'd act like a brake.

But this winter Father Dyer warn't workin', and neither was any of us miners. Instead, we was spendin' our time settin' around talkin' to each other and waitin' for the snows to melt. We talked to a lot of miners around town, but mostly to Jacob Stansell. I think he took a shine to us on account of we was fellow Texans, and he knowed we'd be rootin' for the southern states to win if it ever came to war between the North and the South. Jacob was born in Charleston, South Carolina, like his daddy before him. But, back in the '30s when he was eleven years old, him and his family moved out to west Texas where his daddy was hopin' to make his fortune in the cattle business. Jest like me and Jim, Jacob had growed up on a ranch, and when he'd heard about the gold strikes up in Colorado, he'd decided to try his luck in the gold fields. That was a little over a year ago.

Jacob had two aunts, an uncle, and a passel of cousins still living in Charleston, and his cousin, Hattie, wrote to him now and again so's to keep him posted on what was goin' on back home. Accordin' to Hattie, the Yankees had a garrison of soldiers stationed at Fort Sumter, which was settin' smack dab in the middle of Charleston harbor, and judging from what Hattie had wrote, there warn't a lot of love lost between the folks in town and the Yankee soldiers. In fact, Hattie'd wrote how most of the folks livin' in Charleston would sooner spit on a Yankee than talk to him. The last letter he'd got was way back in January, on account of the snow was keepin' Father Dyer from fetchin' the mail from Fairplay. But, from what she'd wrote then, it sounded like things was likely to explode most any time now. Jacob told us he wouldn't be a bit surprised but what the war had already started.

Quite a few of the folks livin' in Colorado was from the South and had kinfolk there what owned slaves, and that's was what was causin' all the ruckus. Seems as how a lot of folks up north figured it warn't right for one person to own another human bein' no matter what color their skin was. 'Course, most of the folks down south — 'specially ones what owned slaves — didn't see nothin' wrong with it. They claimed they'd paid good money for their slaves and they was their property — like their land and houses, and they'd be damned if they'd let the Yankees take away from them what was rightfully theirs. And if they tried to they was gonna have a fight on their hands. Accordin' to Jacob, close to a third of the folks in Buckskin sided with the South. The rest either favored the North or jest plain didn't give a damn.

One of the southern fellas Jacob introduced us to was a friend of his from Shreveport, Louisiana, named Cy Killgore. Cy was different from a lot of the rough-cut miners in camp, and me and Jim liked him a lot. He warn't like most miners, 'cause he always shaved regular and looked neat and clean, even whilst he was workin'. Not only that, he talked good too — a lot better'n me and Jim. Cy was a crackerjack hard-rock minin' engineer, and not long after Jacob and his partners bought the Phillips Lode, Jacob had wrote to him, askin' him to come to Buckskin so's to help them figure out how to mine it. Cy had brought his pretty wife, Mary, along with him, and they was livin' in a little cabin 'long side of Buckskin Crick. A time or two, they'd asked me and Jim to come eat supper with them. It was the first home cookin' we'd tasted in a long, long time, and it was mighty fine eatin'.

Cy had talked most of the southern boys around camp into formin' a company of volunteers he called "The Buckskin Joes," and he wanted me and Jim to join up. He claimed it'd give us southerners a lot more say about how things was bein' run in Buckskin. We'd tell the rest of the folks in Buckskin that we'd formed it so's to defend ourselfs against Indian and outlaw attacks. 'Course, the real reason was to make shore the Yankees didn't get too rambunctious and try to stir up trouble. Cy even had the uniforms figured out — the officers was to wear gray shirts and trousers, and the enlisted men would wear gray shirts with overalls. After hearin' him out, Jim thanked him kindly and told him we'd like to, but we couldn't, 'cause we had some urgent business to tend to come spring and would be leavin' Buckskin right after the snow melted.

And finally it did. 'Long about the first week in April, the sun come out warm and strong, the snow began to melt, and it was a good thing, 'cause us folks in Buckskin was about out of food. A bunch of the miners, includin' me and Jim, started clearin' snow from the road to Fairplay, hopin' that the road between it and Denver would open and that the supplies we was needin' would be waitin' for us when we got there. As it turned out, they was along with a letter from our folks.

Mamma wrote how they'd had a cold winter down in Texas but, other than that, everything was goin' good. Our daddy's leg was doin' OK, and his brother was givin' him a hand on the ranch. The big news was that Texas had left the Union and was part of the Confederate States of America. 'Course, that meant that war was likely to start most any day now, and that we should be headin' back to Texas. And that's what we was figurin' on doin', right after we'd finished bringin' our gold down out of the Tarryalls. Leastwise, that's the way we had it figured.

But we had a problem. Even though the snow was meltin' good in South Park, it was still deep in the high country. 'Ceptin' where the wind had blowed the ground bare, there was still several feet left in a lot of places, and some drifts was a lot deeper — 'specially on the north slopes. With all that snow, we'd never be able to get a string of pack animals up to the cave, and the way the weather was actin' lately, we was likely to get more heavy snows clear up to the end of May. So we ended up goin' back to Buckskin and workin' at the Phillips Lode again. But at least this time we was runnin' a stamp mill. It was still hard work, but not near as bad as workin' the sluices.

The news come to Buckskin on April twenty-sixth, 1861: Southern artillery had fired on Fort Sumter jest two weeks before. After that, the North didn't waste no time in declarin' war on the Confederate States, and the fat was in the fire. By now all the southern states had pulled out of the Union, and the Yankee folks up north was callin' us southern boys "Rebels." Well, if that's what we was, we was proud of it. Cy figured that me and Jim could help the southern cause a lot more if we was to stay in Colorado instead of goin' to Texas and joinin' up with the Confederate army. He claimed a lot of southern boys was already bein' trained to fight right here in Colorado at a place called Mace's Hole in the foothills of the Wet Mountains, about twenty miles south-west of Pueblo and a little over a hundred miles southeast of Buckskin. A colonel by the name of John Heffiner was the officer in command there, and when they was a big enough outfit and was trained good enough, they was plannin' to take over all the gold mines in Colorado, New Mexico, and Utah. That way, the Confederacy would have the gold to buy guns and ammunition and all the other things they'd be needin' to whup the Yankees.

Cy had first heard about the plan from a Mr. A. B. Miller when he was down in Denver last December. For the past six months, Mr. Miller had been gettin' southern sympathizers in and around Denver to enlist in the Confederate army, and sendin' them down to Colonel Heffiner in Mace's Hole. Mr. Miller talked Cy into doin' the same thing in the mining camps around South Park and California Gulch.

And now, seein' as how me and Jim was stuck in Buckskin waitin' for the snows to melt, Cy was hopin' we'd do him and the Confederate cause a favor by goin' down to Denver and askin' Mr. Miller if he was still needin' recruits, and if so, how many, and whether Cy should send them to Denver or direct to Mace's Hole. He'd go hisself, he said, but he couldn't right now, on account of the Phillips Lode was jest gettin' fired up, and he had to stick around to help supervise. Right off, Jim told him that we'd be glad to do it. At the time, it upset me some that he hadn't asked me for my opinion, but later on, after Cy had left, Jim explained that the reason he agreed so quick was on account of it gave us a good excuse for goin' to Denver. 'Course, we'd talk to Mr. Miller like Cy wanted, but the main reason we'd go was so's we could buy a string of ten or twelve burros to pack out our gold. He figured if we was to buy that many pack animals in South Park, folks might start suspectin' that we'd made a big gold strike.

We stayed in Buckskin and worked at that damned stamp mill for two more weeks to be shore we had enough money to buy the pack animals and all the supplies we'd be needin'. But, finally, on the thirty-first of May, we climbed onto the Denver and South Park Stage and headed for Denver.

McClellan's Spotswood Stage en route to Denver.
(Courtesy of the Colorado Historical Society.)

CHAPTER 25

It was late Sunday afternoon when we crossed over the Platte River and pulled into Denver — tired and sore after a long, rough ride. The meltin' snows had made the stage road muddy and even more rutted and bumpy than usual, but that didn't slow the driver down none. Half the time I warn't shore he was on the road. Jim figured the driver must have a pretty girl waitin' for him in Denver. I figured he was drunk.

Denver was considerably bigger than Buckskin, and there shore was a bunch of groggeries — or "deadfalls." That's what the proper folks of Denver was callin' saloons. Most of them was also gamblin' houses. One that was 'specially popular with the southern boys was the Criterion House down on Larimer Street, which was owned by a southerner named Charley Harrison. Charley was a mighty fancy dresser and had a real soft voice. When we met him, he seemed like a real pleasant gentleman, but later on we found out he really was a hard case and could be tougher'n nails when he had to be — sometimes even when he didn't. We'd heard tell he'd boasted that he'd kilt seven men. He'd claimed they was all in self-defense, but accordin' to some folks that warn't necessarily so. And they most likely was right, 'cause once when he was a mite liquored up, we heard him braggin' how he was gonna kill hisself an even dozen men before he died, jest so's he'd have a jury of his peers in hell.

We got settled into a boarding house right off. Mrs. Meridith ran it, and she seemed like a right nice lady. She said she wouldn't put up with no drinkin' or foolin' around by her boarders whilst they was stayin' in her house. The food there was a big step up from what it'd been at the O.K. House in Buckskin — which suited us jest fine. After we'd got settled in, we looked around town and it shore was a big step up from Buckskin, too. In a few places, they even had board sidewalks so folks wouldn't have to walk in the mud. There was a lot more exciting things to do in Denver than there was in Buckskin, and I figured I was really gonna like it, 'specially so when I seen some pretty girls talkin' and laughin' with each other on their way to church. I suddenly had a hankerin' to hear some good preachin', but Jim said no, we had to find Mr. Miller instead.

And he warn't hard to find, 'cause he'd been makin' a reputation for hisself in Denver, and to some folk's thinkin', it warn't a good one. He'd been goin' around Denver and the nearby minin' camps gettin' volunteers to join up and fight for the Confederates. That didn't make him particularly popular with the two thirds of folks in Denver what favored the Union. We found him at his boardin' house on the street jest north of Cherry Creek. He was middlin' tall and on the heavy-set side, with a black beard what covered most of his face. He was a real friendly feller and seemed happy to meet us, 'specially so after we'd told him how Cy and Jacob was recruitin' Confederate volunteers from up in Buckskin and the other minin' camps around South Park.

It was a good thing we'd showed up right when we did, he said, 'cause if we'd come any later, we'd of missed him. He was fixin' to leave on the mornin' stage to Central City so's to raise recruits for the South, and he asked us to go with him if we didn't have no other plans. Mr. Miller figured the miners at the Gregory Diggin's would be more likely to listen to us than they would to him, on account of we was miners, like them. We told him we'd go. We'd heard a lot about Gregory Gulch and was glad to get a chance to see it. It was almost the end of June before we got back to Denver. We'd talked to a passel of miners and close to forty agreed to sign up. They was to meet at Mr. Miller's boarding house no later than the fifteenth of July so's they could all ride down to Mace's Hole together.

When I asked Mr. Miller how come it was called Mace's Hole, he explained how it was a hidden valley southwest of Pueblo. It was surrounded on all sides by high hills, and accordin' to Alexander Hicklin, an old-time rancher in southern Colorado, it was named after a fella named Jose Mace. It seems that Mace had a habit of helpin' hisself to all the stray cattle he could find on the open range, then he'd hide them in Mace's Hole. I reckon he couldn't see too good, 'cause he never seemed to see their brands. But he'd finally got caught by a posse and strung up to the branch of a cottonwood tree, and now, instead of rustled cattle, Mace's Hole was full of southern boys bein' trained to fight Yankees.

Mr. Miller asked if we'd do him a favor. He'd be real appreciative, he said, if me and Jim would ride herd on the new recruits to be shore they made it to the Hole in one piece. He couldn't do it hisself, 'cause he had business to take care of in Denver. But if we did agree to go, we'd best not go direct to Mace's Hole. There was two good reasons. First, we most likely couldn't find it, and second, we'd get shot if we did. Instead, we should go first to Hicklin's ranch on Green Horn Crick. It was close to twenty miles southwest of Mace's Hole, so it'd take us a little longer. But once we got there, Hicklin could take us to the Hole without our gettin' shot by the sentries. When we got there, we was to tell Colonel Heffiner what all Mr. Miller was doin' up in Denver, and ask if he should keep sendin' recruits to Mace's Hole. Then he wanted us to go up to Buckskin and tell Cy Killgore to do the same. After that we should come back to Denver and report to him, and from then on we could get on with whatever it was we'd come to Denver to do in the first place.

Then Jim surprised me. He asked Mr. Miller if me and him could talk it over in private — he warn't shore we could spare the time right now. That was the first time Jim had ever asked me for my opinion or wanted to talk over something important with me before and it surprised me. Mr. Miller agreed and after he'd left the room, Jim asked me what I thought we should do. I told him how I figured we should do what Mr. Miller asked. If we left with the recruits on July 15 or 16 like he'd said, we should be able to get to Mace's Hole, go up to Buckskin, and be back in Denver in about three weeks. That'd put it around the first week of August, which would give us plenty of time to buy our pack animals, get our gold, sell it for cash, and get down to Texas by the end of October. 'Course, I mainly wanted to go so I could see what Mace's Hole looked like, but I didn't tell that to Jim. He told me that I'd figured good and that he agreed.

As it turned out, it was the end of July before the thirty-two volunteers finally showed up — most all from the Gregory Diggin's. A few of them come by the middle of July like they was supposed to do, but mostly they jest straggled in. But it turned out that was a good thing, 'cause Mr. Miller was havin' trouble findin' enough equipment to outfit them. Guns and ammunition was hard to come by in Denver right then, and horses was even scarcer. But finally all the recruits showed up, and on the twenty-ninth of July we rode out of Denver. Five days later, we rode up in front of Hicklin's ranch house. It was settin' on a little knoll up above Green Horn Crick. Mr. Hicklin's first name was Zan, short for Alexander, but most folks called him "Old Secesh" on account of he was a southern sympathizer from Missouri. That's how come he was helpin' the South by takin' volunteers to Mace's Hole by way of his ranch. Hicklin's wife was a pretty, young Spanish girl named Estafana Bent. She was the daughter of Charles Bent, the first civilian governor of the Territory of New Mexico, and her mother was the sister of Kit Carson's wife.

Hicklin was a mite past middle age, and he was a tall, nice-lookin' fella. His face was brown like an Indian's, and his skin was leathery like wrinkled-up cowhide. His hair was white, and gettin' sparse on top. At first he acted sort of suspicious of us, but when he found out that Mr. Miller had sent us, he got real friendly and said he'd be happy to take us to Mace's Hole.

It was close to a three-hour ride to Mace's Hole. We headed northeast from the Green Horn Valley 'til we come to a narrow cut in the hogbacks where we seen a sentry stationed high up on top of the ridge. He was checkin' us out with a telescope, and I guess he must have recognized Mr. Hicklin, 'cause he hollered to somebody down below and behind him, then he waved for us to ride on in. After passin' through the cut, we come to a big grassy meadow what was bordered on all sides by high hills. It was easy to see why they called it a "hole." There was two big tents at the upper end of the meadow and close to a couple of hundred pup tents strung out in front. Mr. Hicklin told the recruits to stay put whilst he took me and Jim to the command tent.

A Confederate captain named Alvin Miller rode out to meet us. He was a mighty friendly fella, — 'specially so after he'd seen the new recruits — and by the time we got to the command tent, he'd damn near talked our ears off. Colonel Heffiner looked to be in his late thirties, maybe a mite older. He was thin and stood real tall and straight, dressed in his gray uniform with gold stripes runnin' down the sides of the pant legs. His hat was wide brimmed and also gray. He told us the new recruits was a welcome sight, 'cause he was fixin' to send a message to

General Sibley in Texas tellin' him how things was goin', and this would be more good news to give him.

After supper that evening, Jim asked the colonel if he'd mind explainin' what he was plannin' to do with all the troops he was trainin'. He was curious on account of both Cy Killgore and Mr. Miller had said somethin' about a plan to take over the gold mines up around South Park so's to send gold down to the Confederacy. And he hoped the colonel wouldn't be too upset by his askin', but jest how in the hell did they think they could do it? 'Course he knowed there was southern sympathizers in the minin' camps, but they was outnumbered two to one by the Yankees and them odds didn't seem too good to him. The colonel chuckled and told Jim he could see why he wondered, but there was a lot more to the plan than jest gettin' the gold, and that he figured it had a good chance of succeedin'. Then he told us the whole plan, and it was a real humdinger.

Back in 1857, four years before the war started, a southerner named John B. Floyd was secretary of war under President Buchanan. In 1860 he was forced to resign because of a money scandal, but in the years before that, he must have knowed that a war between the North and the South was likely to happen, 'cause he'd arranged for surplus supplies to be sent to some of the storage depots in New Mexico, figurin' that the Confederate army could use them during an invasion. And on top of that, he'd also arranged for a lot of the Union forts in the New Mexico Territory to be commanded by officers what was sympathetic to the South. He figured that when the war started, most of them would resign their commissions in the Union army and join up with the Confederate army, taking the men in their commands with them.

Colonel Heffiner told us that he didn't know this for a fact, but he suspected that Jefferson Davis, the future president of the Confederate States of America, had most likely helped Floyd with some of the plannin'. He'd been a senator from Mississippi when Floyd was secretary of war, and in 1853 he was Buchanan's secretary of war, so Floyd and Davis was bound to have knowed each other real well.

Colonel Heffiner had come to Colorado on the orders of a Confederate brigadier-general named Henry Sibley. He was the officer in command of Fort Union in northern New Mexico when the war started, and, after resignin' his commission in the Union army, he joined up with the Confederate Army and was commissioned a brigadier-general.

Not long after that, Sibley received orders from Jefferson Davis and members of his cabinet to raise an army of Texas volunteers and to invade the Territory of New Mexico and claim it for the Confederacy. After that, he was to take most of his army out to the west coast and capture California and Oregon and claim them for the Confederacy as well, while at the same time, Colonel Heffiner and the rest of the army would head north into Colorado, Utah,

General Henry H. Sibley, Commanding General of the Southern forces during their invasion of the Territory of New Mexico. Taken from Battles and Leaders of the Civil War. *Century Press, 1887.*
(Courtesy of the Colorado Historical Society.)

and Nevada and take over the gold mines. General Sibley was expectin' a lot of the gold miners to join up with Heffiner's forces and when they was strong enough, they could capture the three territorial governments and make them part of the Confederacy.

In that way, the Confederacy would control the western part of the country as well as all of the Pacific ports up and down the California and Oregon coasts. And then, using the gold from the Colorado, Utah, and Nevada gold mines, they'd be able to purchase the arms and supplies they so desperately needed from England and the European countries — arms and supplies they couldn't buy now, because the Union navy was blockading all of the Pacific Ocean and gulf ports.

Accordin' to Colonel Heffiner, the campaign to take New Mexico from the Yankees had already begun before General Sibley ever got to Texas. When the war started, the Union officer in charge of the military forces in Texas transfered control of all of the Union forts, armaments, and supplies under his command to a group of Texans called

"The Commissioners on Behalf of the Committee for Public Safety." When General Sibley got there, they turned it all over to him. Then, jest last July, a Confederate lieutenant colonel named John Baylor had taken a brigade of Texas Rangers down to El Paso, where they captured Fort Bliss from the Yankees. From there they marched up the Rio Grande River and took Fort Fillmore. After that, he declared all of New Mexico south of the thirty-fourth parallel to be a part of the Confederate States of America and named it the Territory of Arizona. After sayin' that, Colonel Heffiner stood up and said as far as he knowed, that was the whole plan, and in his opinion it was likely to succeed. Jim said that now that he had heard the entire plan, he agreed — it jest might work.

Come mornin', right before we took off for Buckskin, the colonel stopped by and asked if we'd do him a favor. When we got to Buckskin, he wanted us to tell Cy Killgore that he had close to three hundred trained troopers, but that he could still use more — jest as long as they made it to Mace's Hole by the first of October. That way, he'd have time to train them and get them in shape to fight in the campaign, which should be startin' early next year if all went as planned — when we got back to Denver, we was to tell Mr. Miller the same thing. We told him we'd be happy to — then we said our good-byes and left.

We was already over two weeks behind in our plans to get to Texas and we figured that, goin' by way of Buckskin, it'd take us close to a week more to get back to Denver. After that, we'd have to buy our pack animals, bring our gold down out of the Tarryalls, have it refined at the smelter, and sell it. To do all that, we was gonna have to make fast tracks so's to get home by early October. But when we got to Buckskin, Cy and Jacob warn't nowhere around. Jest that mornin', they'd left on the stage headin' for California Gulch and Oro City and warn't expected back for at least a week. Well, that was a big disappointment, 'cause there warn't nobody else in Buckskin we could give the message to, so we was gonna have to wait and cool our heels 'til they got back.

The mines around Buckskin was really hummin' that summer of '61. The O.K. House and all the other hotels and boardin' houses in Buckskin was chock full of miners, so it looked for a time like we was

Augusta Pierce Tabor
(Courtesy of the Colorado Historical
Society.)

Horace Austin Warner Tabor (H.A.W.)
(Courtesy of the Colorado Historical
Society.)

gonna have to sleep on the ground in our bedrolls, and that warn't too appealin'. But then we had a turn of good luck – we met up with the Tabors. A brand new store had opened up in Buckskin not long after we'd left last spring, what was owned by a nice lady named Augusta Tabor and her husband, Horace — "H.A.W." was what most folks in Buckskin called him. When they heard how me and Jim was friends of Cy and Jacob, the Tabors let us sleep in a room in the back of their store and eat most all our meals with them, too. And they wouldn't let us pay them, either. So we helped them as much as they'd let us by cleanin' up around the store and puttin' their sales stuff on the shelves.

'Ceptin' for bein' quite a bit younger, the Tabors reminded me a lot of our folks, and it made me sorta homesick. I 'specially liked talkin' to Horace, and he did a lot of it. By the time we left Buckskin, I reckon we heard his whole life story. Then he tried to talk us into doin' some prospectin' with him as a partner. He claimed he'd be happy to grub-stake us for a fourth of whatever gold or silver we'd find. But Jim thanked him for his offer and told him we couldn't, 'cause we had business to attend to in Denver jest as soon as Jacob and Cy showed up.

The remains of the Tabors' store in 1930, as verified by N. Maxey Tabor. (Courtesy of the Colorado Historical Society.)

Twelve days later they finally did. After apologizin' for keepin' us waitin', Cy explained that they'd been out recruitin' for the Confederacy, and it'd taken them longer than they'd figured. After we'd delivered Mr. Miller's and the colonel's messages to Cy, we said our good-byes to Jacob, Cy, and the Tabors, and told them that we'd most likely be seein' them later on that summer. As it turned out, we never saw any of them again.

CHAPTER 26

We hightailed it to Denver jest as fast as we could go. Even though we was runnin' way later than we'd planned, we figured that once we got to Denver, we'd still have time to buy the pack animals and supplies we needed, fetch our gold down from the Tarryalls, process it, and get home to Texas by late October. We spent the night at the Kenosha House on the east side of the pass, and the next day headed down the north branch of the South Platte, crossed over to Apex, and took the Gregory Toll Road down to Denver. It was gettin' dark and startin' to rain as we was fordin' the Platte a little ways downstream from Cherry Crick. As we was ridin' up Larimer Street, we seen a ruction goin' on in front of the Criterion House. Mr. Miller was standin' in the middle of the street arguin' with a man 'most twice his size. By then it was rainin' hard and they was both soakin' wet, along with all the rest of the folks what was standin' around watchin' the fuss — even the rain warn't coolin' the argument down none. When we got closer we seen that the man Miller was arguin' with was a fella named John Chivington.

We'd never met him, but we'd heard him preach at the Methodist Church, and his sermons was mighty convincing. If you warn't already a Christian when he started in to preach, you'd shore better be one by the time he got through — not so much out of fear of the Lord, as out of fear of John Chivington. He was six feet, four-and-a-half inches tall, a big bear of a man with a voice to match, and it was easy to see that him and God was on a first-name basis. If I was Mr. Miller, I'd of picked somebody smaller to argue with. We couldn't tell what the argument was about, and they broke it off not long after we'd rode up. Most likely they'd finally figured out it was jest too damned wet for argufyin'.

We was about to head to the livery stable, when Mr. Miller spotted us and hollered for us to wait up so's he could talk to us. The mucky street didn't bother him none. He jest waded through the deep mud over to where we was settin' on our horses. We asked him what the argument was about. He told us he'd tell us about it later, but that first we should stable our critters. After we'd done that, he wanted us to come over to his boardin' house so's we could talk.

After stablin' our animals at Sumner's Livery Stable on Cherry Creek, we sloshed the six blocks to Mr. Miller's boardin' house. Mrs. Meridith's boardin' house was right on the way, so we stopped in hopin' we could get a room, but she was all full up, so we jest kept on walkin' and sloshin' 'til we come to Mr. Miller's. Besides bein' wet, the rain was cold, and it shore was good to get into a warm, dry house. Even though it was only the twenty-sixth of August, there was a bite to the wind, and it felt like fall warn't far off. We was in a hurry to report to Mr. Miller, buy the pack animals, and get on with bringin' our gold out of the Tarryalls.

First off, we told Mr. Miller what all Colonel Heffiner, Cy Killgore, and Jacob Stansell was up to, and he was mighty pleased to hear how good the recruitin' and trainin' was goin'. He was glad to get some good news for a change, he said, 'cause ever since the first of the year, the situation in Denver had been goin' to hell in a hurry — at least that's the way he seen it. On January twenty-ninth, President Lincoln had made the new state of Kansas out of the eastern part of the Kansas Territory. To do that, he'd taken the west end of the Kansas Territory below the fortieth parallel and joined it to the west end of the Nebraska Territory above the fortieth parallel. Then he added to it the part of the Utah Territory west of the continental divide, along with the northern part of the Territory of New Mexico, including the San Luis Valley. After all them pieces was put together, the president named it "The Colorado Territory."

Not long after that, President Lincoln had appointed a fella named William Gilpin to be governor of the territory, and it was him what was upsettin' Mr. Miller. To hear him tell it, Governor Gilpin figured he could do most anything he damn well pleased jest on his own authority. One of the things he'd done was to organize the First Regiment of Colorado Volunteers. He was recruiting Yankees from all over the Colorado Territory and payin' them with worthless scrip what he printed hisself, on account of the Union government wouldn't give him any money. To make matters even worse, he was figurin' on askin' the first general assembly to make him commander of all the volunteer troops in Colorado when they met in September, jest two weeks away.

Gilpin had already appointed his own military staff and was buildin' a trainin' camp he called "Fort Weld" on the banks of the Platte River about two miles south of Denver. On top of that, he'd bought up all of the shotguns, rifles, and ammunition he could lay his hands on. Mr. Miller was more'n a little upset about that, 'cause now he was havin' a hard time findin' any equipment and supplies for his own recruits. In fact, he was havin' a hard time findin' recruits. Apparently Governor Gilpin was havin' a lot better luck with his recruitin', 'cause he'd already raised ten companies of Colorado Volunteers.

Gilpin had appointed John P. Slough, a Denver lawyer, to be the colonel in command of his ragtag militia and Samuel Tappen to be the lieutenant colonel and second in command. All ten companies of volunteers was bein' billeted at Fort Weld. Two or three other companies was down at Fort Lyons in the Arkansas River Valley east of Pueblo. And, to make matters even worse, Mr. Miller had jest learned that there was two more independent companies of volunteers at Cañon City. James Ford was the captain of one and Theodore Dodd the other. It was them companies what worried Mr. Miller the most. They was too damned close to Mace's Hole.

Jim asked Mr. Miller how come Governor Gilpin was recruitin' his own army. From what he'd heard, there was already enough federal troopers down at Fort Lyons on the Arkansas and at Fort Garland in the San Luis Valley to handle most any problems that might come up, such as Indian attacks and the like. Mr. Miller told Jim he was right. Gilpin was claimin' his militia was needed to guard against Indians, but the real reason he was doin' it was so's to keep us southerners in line.

But what really got Mr. Miller upset was when the governor ordered his militia to arrest any southern sympathizers they suspected of speakin' out against the North. That was what him and Chivington had been arguin' about. Mr. Miller didn't like John Chivington, mainly on account of — besides bein' a Yankee and a rabid Republican — he was a major in Gilpin's militia and was trainin' new recruits how to fight. Now that, in Mr. Miller's opinion, was a downright unchristian thing for the presiding elder of the Methodist Episcopal Church in Colorado to be doin'.

Accordin' to Mr. Miller, the First Regiment of Colorado Volunteers was a big joke to the folks in Denver. They was callin' them "Gilpin's Pet Lambs" and sayin' they was nothin' but a bunch of no-good loafers what couldn't make a go of it in the minin' camps and figured soldierin' was a lot easier than workin' for a livin'. They was a real rowdy bunch, and any time they warn't playin' soldier out at Fort Weld, they was whoopin' it up here in Denver. Some of them figured if confiscatin' was OK for the governor, it was OK for them, too. Most every night they'd be out scourin' the streets of Denver and Auraria, helpin' theirselfs to chickens, pigs, eggs, hams, and whatever else they could lay their hands on. A writer for the *Rocky Mountain News* called them "no good chicken thieves." And to make matters even worse, when they got finished raiding the town, the troopers would party and carouse and make so much racket the good folks of Denver couldn't sleep.

After Mr. Miller finished tellin' us about all his problems, Jim finally got a chance to ask him where we could get a string of about ten good pack animals. They could be horses, mules, or burros, we didn't care which, jest as long as we got them quick. Mr. Miller looked unhappy and shook his head. There warn't no way in hell we was gonna find even one animal for sale in or around Denver, let alone ten. The governor had already confiscated all of the critters to outfit his damned militia. He'd been tryin' to find some horses hisself but so far hadn't had no luck.

The Rocky Mountain News *building on the west bank of Cherry Creek. It was destroyed by flood waters on May 19, 1864. The* News *was founded by William Byers in 1859.*
(Courtesy of the Denver Public Library Western History Collection.)

That was a terrible shock. 'Course, me and Jim already had four animals, but we'd be ridin' our two horses, so our two burros would have to carry all our gear plus some of our gold. That'd be better than nothin', but what we wanted was enough pack animals so's we could bring all of the gold out at one time. In three days it'd be the first of September, so we only had time for one trip. But then Mr. Miller told us about a wagon train what was comin' from Kansas what was supposed to be gettin' to Denver in about ten days. He'd heard they was bringin' a small remuda with them, so maybe if we was to ride out to meet them before they got into town, they might sell us whatever horses we was needin'. He was figurin' on doin' that hisself, but bein' as how we'd been so much help to him, he'd give us first crack at it. That was good news to me and Jim, and we decided to wait for the wagon train, even though it was gonna put off our leavin' 'til even later in the year.

In the meantime, we needed a place to stay. Jim figured we'd best find a good hotel instead of lookin' for a boardin' house, on account of we was gonna be in Denver such a short time. Mr. Miller said there was eight hotels to choose from, but the one he'd recommend was the Broadwell House, 'cause it was the nicest one in town. Then — once we was settled in and had time to kill — maybe we could give him a hand with his recruitin' down at the Criterion saloon. 'Course, we'd have to be damned careful who it was we was talkin' to, so's to keep from bein' put in jail or kicked out of town. Mr. Miller claimed he was a good friend of Charley Harrison, and he was shore that he'd let us sound out the men what come into the Criterion to drink and gamble. Besides that, he could tell us which of them was southern sympathizers and which ones was Yankees. Jim promised Mr. Miller that we'd check with Charley Harrison first thing in the mornin'.

The Broadwell House was the plushiest place I'd ever been in, and I was all for stayin' there. But Jim said no — it was too damned expensive. We didn't know how much money we'd need to buy our horses and supplies, so we'd best not spend any more than we could help. We still had most all the money we'd got from workin' in Buckskin, and when we sold the gold in our pokes, we'd have a whole lot more. So I figured we could afford it easy. As usual, we ended up doin' what Jim wanted and checked into the Vasquez House on the west side of Cherry Creek in Auraria.

The Broadwell House, built at 16th and Larimer Streets by James Broadwell in 1859 - 1860.
(Courtesy of the Colorado Historical Society.)

I was real disappointed. Here we was, richer than most folks in Denver, but we had to pretend like we was poor. I'd wanted people to know how rich we was, 'specially the pretty ladies me and Jim had met at the Criterion and Progressive saloons. The ones at the Criterion was the nicest. Sunny Sadie was jest a few months younger than me and I liked her best, but Redstockin' and the Colonel's Daughter was nice, too. I'm happy to say we didn't stay but one night at the Vasquez House. Not after fightin' bed bugs and cockroaches all night. So we ended up stayin' at the Broadwell House like I'd was wantin' to do in the first place, and it was a real nice place — no bugs and a lot closer to the Criterion.

Me and Jim spent a lot of time recruitin' at the Criterion after that, and we got to know Charley Harrison pretty well. He seemed real nice, but he shore did have a hot temper, and it warn't too good an idea to do or say anythin' what made him mad. Like I said before, we'd already heard how he'd shot and kilt seven men, and we shore warn't hankerin' to be numbers eight and nine. But he always was real nice to us and helped us out a lot by pointin' out the fellas what was partial to the South. Quite a few of the ones we talked to ended up talkin' to Mr. Miller.

The bar girls was mighty friendly, and we got to know them pretty good. Redstockin' told me how she was from Texas and that she really liked Texas boys. They was her favorites, she said. That seemed nice, I thought, but it did seem a mite peculiar when a little later on I heard her tellin' another fella that she was from Georgia and really liked Georgia boys — they was her favorites. I reckoned maybe she was jest a mite mixed up. But then Jim told me that they really warn't nice ladies like I'd been thinkin', and that we shouldn't even be talkin' to them, 'cause if Mamma ever found out she'd most likely skin us both. It sort of shook me up some when Jim told me how they made their livin', but I noticed he still kept on talkin' to them same as me.

A week went by real quick, and we was gettin' more and more worried. Nobody seemed to know when, or even if, the wagon train was gonna show up. Jim said that if we didn't hear somethin' in the next few days, we'd best quit waitin' around and take what animals we had and head for the Tarryalls. Maybe we could buy some pack animals in the minin' camps along the way. As it turned out, we should've left right then.

It was Saturday night, the eleventh of September, and as usual Gilpin's Pet Lambs was whoopin' it up in town. Only this time, they was even rowdier than usual. A bunch of them showed up outside the Criterion, and they was lookin' for a fight. 'Course, the southern boys at the Criterion was happy to oblige them. 'Specially so after some of the militia fellas tried to push their way into the Criterion. Charley and his boys wouldn't let them come in, and that started the fight for shore. At first it was mainly fist-fightin' up and down Larimer Street, but it warn't long before some of the Yankee soldiers pushed their way into the Criterion and started bustin' up chairs and tables.

Charley pulled a shotgun from in back of the bar and shot up towards the ceilin', hopin' it would get their attention so's he could ask them politely to quit fightin'. All it did, though, was to blow a hole in the ceilin' and scare the folks in one of the upstairs bedrooms damned near to death. Things started goin' downhill from there, and it turned into a free-for-all fight between the First Regiment and the boys what was rootin' for the South, along with a few other fellas what was jest fightin' for the hell of it. Mostly it was still fist-fightin', but 'long towards the end of the fracas, Charley and a few others started shootin' off their handguns. That ended the battle mighty quick. There was three militia and two southern boys what got hurt, but luckily none was busted up too bad. In fact, after it was all over, Charley was offerin' free drinks to everybody — southerners and Yankees alike.

Me, Jim, and Mr. Miller, 'long with a few others includin' the bar girls, had stayed at the back of the room pretty much out of of the fight. Now and again, though, I seen Jim take a swipe at a Yankee soldier what come within range. One time I even saw Sunny Sadie stick her foot out, trip a fella, and then bop him over the head with a whiskey bottle. I had a feelin' that maybe she had a personal score to settle with that soldier, and that it didn't have much to do with the North and the South.

It was a great fight, but it didn't end up too good. I reckon it warn't no coincidence that the sheriff and his deputies didn't show up 'til the fight was over, and when they did get there, they arrested all of the wrong people — me and Jim, to mention two. I think Governor Gilpin and the sheriff had been waitin' for somethin' like this to happen, so's they could get rid of what they was callin' the "undesirable element" in Denver. Anyways, besides me and Jim, they arrested Charley Harrison, Mr. Miller, and a few other fellas what was openly for the South. For some reason, they'd even arrested Sunny Sadie.

It didn't take a whole lot of figurin' to see how this was gonna put a big crimp in our plans. We'd be lucky jest to get out of jail, let alone get out in time to fetch our gold from out of the Tarryalls before the snows fell. Now, even if the wagon train did show up, we couldn't buy any pack animals whilst we was in jail. Mr. Miller would have done it for us, I'm shore, but he'd been arrested same time as us.

About a week after our arrest, we heard that Charley Harrison had been fined five thousand dollars and released from jail on strict orders to get out of Denver and never come back, unless he wanted to be locked up for good. Not long after that, Mr. Miller and some of his southern cronies was also let out of jail and told to leave town after bein' given the same warning. I couldn't understand why they didn't let us go too, but Jim figured the sheriff was holdin' onto the two of us so's to make an example of what happened to southern sympathizers in Denver. Mr. Miller and Charley Harrison was probably let go on account of they was a lot better known in Denver than we was. Governor Gilpin most likely was afraid it'd make martyrs out of them if they was kept in jail, and that would make southern supporters in Denver hoppin' mad.

On the first day of October it snowed 'most a foot, puttin' an end to any hopes we had of bringin' out our gold this year. We was still in jail, and as far as we knowed, nobody even gave a damn. We'd asked to see a lawyer, and a Mr. William Zeigler showed up. He was a real nice fella, but he warn't in no hurry to take our case to court. Jim was shore he was a Yankee, and that he was waitin' 'til a lot of the southern sympathizers left Denver and went back home before goin' to court. That way, there wouldn't be a lot of fuss when we was tried and convicted for supportin' the enemy.

It warn't all bad, though. The jailer was a Texas boy named Billy Joe Barlow. He told us that he didn't like the way we was bein' treated, and he for shore couldn't figure out why they'd locked up Sunny Sadie. It jest warn't right to treat a nice little lady like that — she hadn't done nothin' wrong. Jim choked a little when he said that, and I was afraid he was gonna say somethin' bad about Sadie, but he didn't, he jest asked Billy Joe if they let her loose or if she was locked up like us. Billy Joe said she was still locked up, and that he didn't know why. It seemed to bother him a lot.

Billy Joe was 'specially nice to us after he found out our daddy's ranch was in the Blue Mountains less than a hundred miles north of his home in San Antonio. After that, he brought us extra food and checked on our animals for us. Accordin' to Billy Joe, he was fed up with the goin's on in Denver and was givin' serious thought to goin' back to Texas before it got any worse. 'Course, it didn't take but a second for me and Jim to figure how it'd be nice if we was to go along with him, and before long we had Billy Joe thinkin' the same thing. After that, Billy Joe come up with a plan as to how we could leave without getting caught.

Sunday night would be the best time to leave, 'cause he'd be on guard duty from nine at night until seven the next mornin'. On Fridays and Saturdays, the jail was likely to be overflowin' with boys from the First Colorado Regiment what had got a little too liquored up and rowdy. But by Sunday night they most always was all back at Camp Weld, and the jail would be empty — 'ceptin' for us. Then, 'long about ten o'clock, when most folks in Denver was off the streets, Billy Joe would give us back our money and belongin's and unlock our cell door. He was to pick up our animals from Sumner's Livery Stable, then meet us in a vacant lot over on Cherry Creek about three blocks south of the stable. We'd already gave him a bill of sale for our two horses and the two burros, along with our saddles, saddlebags, and such. Most folks already knowed he was thinkin' about goin' back to Texas, so when Mr. Sumners seen the bill of sale, he'd jest figure we'd sold Billy Joe our horses and gear to use on his way back home.

CHAPTER 27

Everything went jest like we planned, 'ceptin' for one thing. When Billy Joe showed up with our horses, Sunny Sadie was with him. That shook me and Jim up considerable. We hadn't figured on havin' to nursemaid no female on our way back to Texas, 'specially not a softlookin' girl like Sadie — and a bar girl at that. Jim asked Billy Joe why in tarnation he'd brung her along. She'd slow us down so much we'd end up gettin' caught, jest as shore as hell. We argued with him for ten minutes or more, but he didn't budge. It was either we take Sadie with us, or he was gonna go straight to the sheriff and tell him he'd caught us escapin'.

Besides, he added, she warn't like them shady-ladies what was always hangin' around the Criterion and the other saloons. She was a really nice girl. Well, me and Jim didn't believe that for a minute. We jest figured Billy Joe and Sadie was sweet on each other and he didn't want to leave her behind. It was easy to see why he'd taken such a fancy to her, but I shore couldn't see what Sunny Sadie could see in him. Why, Billy Joe was even older than Jim and sort of fat to boot. Anyways, me and Jim finally figured that we might as well make the best of it and take her along, even though she was gonna slow us down somethin' awful. Billy Joe was stuck on her, and we was stuck with her, and that's jest the way it was.

Was we ever wrong. Sadie kept up with us every step of the way all the way back to Texas. In fact, lots of days she wanted to keep goin', even after the rest of us was plumb wore out and ready to quit. Not only that, she was a great help with the cookin' and packin' and never complained — not even once. It warn't long before I was beginnin' to envy Billy Joe. It was hard not to. I done my level best not to pay any attention to her, but sometimes when she warn't lookin', I couldn't keep from watchin' her, 'cause she was jest downright pretty.

She warn't very big, the top of her head comin' jest up to my shoulder, but what there was of her shore was arranged good. I figured I could reach clear around her waist with both of my hands, but it bothered me considerable to think about doin' it, so I tried not to. She was curved in and out in all the right places, and her arms and legs was mighty shapely, too. Her hair fell in gentle waves to jest above her shoulders and was almost the color of the gold what me and Jim had been diggin' out of the ground — but a whole lot prettier. It looked real soft, and I figured it'd shore be nice to touch. But what I liked best was her face. It was jest the prettiest thing I'd ever seen, with a cute rounded chin, a perky little nose, and real pretty lips and mouth. Her eyes was a color I'd never seen before — sort of like the color of the violets my mamma liked to grow. And when she smiled, it was like her whole face lit up. It was easy to see why she was called Sunny Sadie.

Billy Joe and Sadie never did seem too lovey-dovey when me and Jim was around, but I never knowed what was goin' on when we warn't, and I gotta admit it bothered me. Jim could tell it was eatin' at me and told me I'd best let it go, 'cause she was Billy Joe's girl, not mine. And besides, our mamma would drop dead in her tracks if'n I ever brought a whore into her home, 'specially if she knowed I was sweet on her. I knowed Jim was right, so I started keepin' as far away from Sadie as I could, which was hard to do, on account of all the time we was ridin', she'd keep steerin' her horse up close 'long side mine. And a lot of times when we was restin', she'd set close to me, too. All I could figure was that she liked talkin' to me, on account of we was close to the same age.

After leavin' Denver, we rode jest as hard and fast as we could all the rest of that night, stoppin' only a few times to rest. It was moonlight, and that helped considerable, but it was still slow goin' and by sunup we'd only rode about twenty-five miles. That day we holed up in the shade of some cottonwoods growin' 'long side a little crick what was tricklin' down the bottom of a gully. We knowed that by now a posse was shore to be out lookin' for us, so that whole day we took turns keepin' watch from the top of the bank so's to be shore nobody could sneak up on us. The rest of us what warn't on watch tried to rest and sleep a little in the bottom of the gully. But an icy wind was blowin' from out of the north, so we had to keep movin' around some, so's to keep from freezin'. Billy Joe wanted to make a fire, but we couldn't for fear somebody'd see the smoke. And it was a good thing we didn't, too, 'cause 'long about midafternoon, when Sadie was standin' watch, she hollered down to us that a bunch of riders was comin' our way from up north.

We all clambered up to the top of the bank, and jest like she'd said, there was eight riders travelin' fast and comin' our way. It was a posse, and they was lookin' for us. Well, I tell you no lie, the next few minutes was tense. We was all hunkerin' down jest below the rim of the gully, keepin' watch and prayin' they wouldn't come close enough to see us. For a while there, it looked like they was gonna ride right over us, but at the very last minute our prayers was answered. They changed direction jest enough to take them a little to the east of us and passed us by ridin' hell bent for leather towards the south.

Four days later we was all settin' around a table palaverin' with Zan and Estafana Hicklin 'long with two Confederate officers by the names of Daniel Ellis Conner and John Buckmaster. They was both on their way back to Texas, same as us. They seemed real happy to see us — 'specially Sadie. I reckon there warn't many pretty women livin' in the Greenhorn Valley right then. Sadie warn't but a few years younger than Estafana, and they got to be good friends right off. It was nice to see Sadie talkin' to a nice lady for a change — I was hopin' some of the nice would rub off on her.

As it turned out, it was a good thing that we'd come by the Hicklin's instead of goin' to Mace's Hole, 'cause if we had, we'd have ended up in a peck of trouble. Jest last week, the Hole had been attacked by a passel of Yankee troopers from out of Fort Garland in the San Luis Valley, and some of the colonel's recruits and a few of his officers got caught. That was the bad news. The good news was that the colonel and most of his regiment had escaped and was already safe and sound back at Fort Bliss.

Then Mr. Hicklin laughed. The Yankees had even arrested him and accused him of operatin' a rebel outpost at his ranch on the Greenhorn. They'd took him to Fort Garland and was gonna put him in the stockade, but after he'd started talkin' and actin' like he warn't quite right in the head, the Yankee colonel decided to release him instead. He said he was shore Hicklin was harmless and warn't no threat to the Union, bein' as how he was half-witted. But before the colonel let him go, he'd asked him to take an oath of allegiance to the United States and promise to be a good citizen. Accordin' to Mr. Hicklin, the conversation went somethin' like this.

"Take what, Kurnel?"

"Why, take an oath of allegiance."

"Wal now, Kurnel, what kind of a thang is that?"

"Why, it's to solemnly swear to support the constitution of the United States and not to aid or encourage its enemies."

Then Mr. Hicklin tried to look real serious and foolish at the same time and stuck up his left hand and said, "Swar me."

After that the colonel ordered a lieutenant to give him the oath and told Hicklin to raise his right hand. Mr. Hicklin stuck up his left hand again, and when they told him it was the wrong hand, he raised both hands and solemnly repeated the oath while holding them high over his head.

After he'd finished swearin', Mr. Hicklin asked, "Does that get me in, Kurnel?"

"Into what?"

"Why, into the United States."

"Yes," the colonel answered, "that lets you in."

"Clear in?"

"Yes, and see that you live up to it."

Mr. Hicklin said his partin' remark was, "My God, Kurnel, I feel like I jest got religion."

Both Conner and Buckmaster were on the run from the Yankees. When the Yankees raided Mace's Hole, Conner was hidin' out at a spread in the Green Horn Valley what was owned by a rancher friend of his named Bo Boyce. Buckmaster had escaped from the Federal military prison in Santa Fe jest the week before. He'd been accused of stealin' the U. S. mail up on Raton Pass a few months back. He didn't do it, and the Yankees couldn't prove that he did, but they went ahead and sentenced him to be shot by a firing squad anyways. But, luckily, he'd managed to bribe a Yankee guard into lettin' him escape, and he lit out for Mace's Hole so's to report to Colonel Heffiner.

But luck was with him again, 'cause on his way there, he'd run into sixteen confederate recruits hidin' out in Apishapa Canyon west of the Green Horn Valley, and they'd filled him in on what had happened at Mace's Hole. Now they was tryin' to figure out a way to get to Fort Bliss without gettin' caught by the Federals. Major Buckmaster told them he'd go with them, but first he had to buy a new mount from the Hicklins, 'cause his horse had gone lame. They was figurin' on leavin' Apishapa Canyon three days from now and we was all welcome to ride along with them if we liked, 'cause the more southern boys in the party, the better. Then he looked at Sadie and added, "and southern ladies, too, ma'am."

Jim told the major we'd be happy to go with them — it seemed like a gift from heaven. Then he told how we'd been put in jail up in Denver for bein' southern sympathizers, and how we'd escaped. But now we had a posse hot on our tail, so the sooner we got out of Colorado and back to Texas the better. A little later on, when me and Jim was alone, I asked him if he figured it'd be safe for Sadie to be ridin' with all them men, bein' as how she'd be the only lady. Jim laughed and said she'd be jest fine. He was shore she could look out for herself, and besides that, she warn't no lady. It didn't seem to worry Billy Joe none either, which seemed real peculiar to me, 'cause I didn't like her sleepin' with all them men, and she warn't even my girl.

Accordin' to Mr. Hicklin, it was close to fifty miles from his ranch to Apishapa Canyon, and the goin' would be a mite rough in spots, so we was gonna have to push hard to get there in three days. But, as it turned out, we made it in good time, and before long we was on our way to Texas.

We got to Fort Bliss on the fourth of November and right off we run into Colonel Heffiner. He filled us in on what all had been happenin' since we last seen him. It seems that a Yankee colonel by the name of Edward R. S. Canby had been put in charge of all the federal troops in New Mexico Territory. When Canby learned that the

Colonel Edward S. Canby, Commander of the Union Forces in the Colorado and New Mexico Territories – circa 1850s and '60s.
(From *Battle Leaders of the Civil War*, Century Press, 1887. Courtesy of the Colorado Historical Society.)

Confederates was figurin' on invadin' the New Mexico Territory, he'd upped the number of men under his command to close to eight thousand troopers. Half of them was up at Fort Craig and the rest was in Albuquerque, Santa Fe, Fort Union, and the other Union forts in northern New Mexico.

General Sibley only had half that many in his army, but accordin' to Colonel Heffiner, that didn't worry the general none, on account of all his men was Texans, and one Texan could whup three or four Yankees — even on a bad day. The colonel figured the general might be right, 'cause a lot of the Yankee soldiers was new recruits what come from little towns and farms around New Mexico, and they'd most likely scamper off like a bunch of scared jackrabbits the minute the fightin' started. And besides that, the general was shore that a lot of Yankee soldiers was gonna switch sides and join up with the Confederates once the invasion had started — 'specially when their commandin' officers switched first. Colonel Heffiner was hopin' that me and Jim would enlist, 'cause he figured that, bein' as how we was miners ourselves, we'd be a big help in gettin' the Colorado miners to join up and fight the Yankees.

"Where do I sign up?" I asked. I was enlistin' — there warn't no doubt in my mind.

Jim told the colonel he'd enlist, too, but first we had to visit our folks. Then, without so much as a by yore leave, he told the colonel not to count on my enlistin', on account of my mamma would say I was too young. Now that was downright humiliatin'. Sayin' it to the colonel and Billy Joe was bad enough, but Sadie had heard it, and that was a whole lot worse. I knew she was Billy Joe's girl, but I still didn't want her thinkin' I needed my mamma's permission every time I wanted to do somethin'.

Then Billy Joe told the colonel that he was gonna enlist, too, right after he'd visited his folks in San Antonio. Now that really surprised me, and early next mornin', jest as we was fixin' to leave, Billy Joe surprised me again. He asked if it'd be all right with me and Jim if him and Sadie went with us up to our folks' ranch and then go down to San Antonio from there. He didn't say why, and we didn't ask, we jest told him it'd be fine with us. But I shore couldn't figure why they'd want to go so far out of their way. If'n it was me, I'd have married Sadie as quick as I could and I shore as hell wouldn't go off and fight in a war right after I done it.

The trip back to our ranch was hot, dry, and tiring, but we made it in good shape, and, twenty days out of Fort Bliss, we rode into the shade of the oak trees in front of our adobe home.

CHAPTER 28

Mamma come runnin' out of the house when she seen us ridin' in, and the second we was off our horses she threwed her arms around us and hugged everybody — includin' Billy Joe and Sadie. I'd never seen her so happy. She said our daddy and a couple of his cowhands was up north in the Blue Mountains roundin' up stray cattle, but that they should be gettin' home most any day now.

Accordin' to Mamma, the cattle business in Texas had been boomin' ever since the start of the war — mainly on account of the Confederate army was needin' lots of beef these days. The last two winters was real mild, and the calf crop better'n usual, so Daddy'd hired two Mexican vaqueros and a black man to help with the roundup and brandin'. But our daddy was thinkin' of keepin' them on permanent, 'cause they was such good workers — 'specially the black man. His name was Jake Jefferson, and he'd been a slave on a cotton plantation in Louisiana before he'd come to Texas. Accordin' to Jake, his master had always treated him good. He'd even gave him his freedom so he could go live up north if he wanted, but Jake told him he'd druther stay down south with his kind of people. He didn't want to have no truck with them Yankees.

Mamma and Sadie hit it off great the minute they met — it was like they'd been friends for years. Mamma claimed she didn't have a chance to talk to a lady very often, 'specially one as nice and sweet as Sadie. That worried me a lot, and later that night, I asked Jim what he figured was gonna happen when Mamma found out that Sadie warn't really a nice lady. He told me not to worry. She warn't gonna find out, 'cause come mornin', Sadie'd be leavin' with Billy Joe, and Mamma would never see her again. He doubted that Mamma would visit the parts of San Antonio where she'd be likely to run into Sadie. I told him I figured marryin' Billy Joe would make Sadie into a nice lady, but Jim jest grinned and said, "In a pig's eye it will."

But come mornin', me and Jim was in for a shock. Mamma had invited Billy Joe and Sadie to stay on for a day or two more so's they could rest up some before goin' down to San Antonio, and they'd both told her they'd be happy to. So for the next two days me and Jim was settin' on pins and needles, prayin' that Mamma wouldn't find out that Sadie was a whore. But she didn't, and finally, after two days of worryin', Billy Joe told us him and Sadie was leavin' first thing in the mornin'. You could of heard me and Jim's sighs of relief two miles away. Even though I knowed it'd make me feel awful, I got up next mornin' so's I could tell them both good-bye. When I went out the door, I seen Mamma givin' Billy Joe some food to take along, but I didn't see hide nor hair of Sadie — her horse warn't nowheres around, neither. When I asked Billy Joe where Sadie was, he told me how my mamma had invited her to stay on awhile longer, and Sadie had said she'd be happy to. Well, that really shook me up — I warn't shore if I should be glad or sad. When I told Billy Joe how I'd been thinkin' all along that him and Sadie was goin' to San Antonio so's to get married, he jest laughed and asked me where I'd got that crazy idea — Sadie was jest a good friend, and he'd helped her out same as he'd helped out me and Jim. Then he rode off whilst I stood there with my mouth hangin' open, collectin' flies.

'Course, I've gotta admit, I was happy that Billy Joe and Sadie warn't gettin' hitched, but I knowed that Jim was gonna be awful upset 'cause she warn't leavin'. I was afeared of what he might say or do. And I was right — he warn't a bit happy and he had a lot to say, none of it good. He didn't like havin' Sadie pretendin' she was a nice lady when she really warn't. He was afeared that Mamma would get real fond of her and then be hurt bad when she found out the truth. Jim figured that I should be the one to tell Mamma that Sadie was a shady lady, bein' as how I was the one what was sweet on her. But I told him he was crazy. I warn't sweet on her, and even if I was, I warn't gonna tell our mamma that Sadie was a whore. If he didn't do it, nobody would. After we'd argued back and forth for a time, we finally decided we'd wait and tell our daddy about Sadie when he got home and let him be the one to tell Mamma. In the meantime, Mamma kept gettin' fonder and fonder of Sadie.

Two days later, Daddy finally came ridin' down out of the hills with a herd of cattle strung out in front of him. Me and Jim rode out to meet him. We told him we was real happy to see him. Daddy said he was happy to see us, too, 'cause come mornin', he was fixin' to drive a big part of his herd down to the stockyards in San Antonio where he had a buyer from the Confederate army lined up. The herd was likely to number close to a thousand head, and he was gonna need our help, 'cause up to now he'd only had four drovers, countin' him, Jake, and the two vaqueros — but now he had six. Then he gave us a big toothy smile — our daddy never was one for sentiment.

First chance he got, Jim hauled me off to one side and told me how this was the answer to our problem. We'd take Sadie along with us on the cattle drive and give her back to Billy Joe in San Antonio — that way our folks would never know the truth about her. But we had to work fast before Sadie could twist Daddy around her little finger, like she'd done with me and Mamma. I told him he was wrong. I didn't care a whit about Sadie. 'Course, I did — I jest didn't want to admit it.

That night after supper, whilst we was settin' in front of the fire-place havin' a nice chat, I guess Jim must have figured it was a good time to tell our folks how we was gonna take Sadie along with us on the cat-tle drive and give her back to Billy Joe in San Antonio. That way she wouldn't have to ride down all by herself later on — and besides, she'd be a big help on the cattle drive. Well, for some reason, that didn't go over too good. Mamma was upset, and that's puttin' it mildly. She jest couldn't believe that her sons would let a sweet girl like Sadie go ridin' off in the dust behind a herd of smelly cows. She'd never heard of such a stupid idea, and that we should both be real ashamed of ourselfs. The very least we could do was to apologize to her. Then Mamma gave Sadie a little hug and told her she was welcome to stay for as long as she wanted. And if she ever did decide to go to San Antonio, it'd be when she chose to go, not when some dumb, ungentlemanly, ill-bred cowboys said she should. Not only that, the two of us would escort her.

Then my daddy chimed in: Didn't we have no manners at all, and didn't we know how to treat a nice lady? 'Specially one who's mamma and daddy was both dead? Well, that was news to me, and I guess to Jim, too. Sadie must have been tellin' our mamma and daddy things about her past life, and I wondered how much she'd told them about how she'd been makin' her livin' up in Denver. Sadie never had told me nothin' about her folks bein' dead. 'Course, come to think of it, I'd never asked. After that, to make matters worse — if'n that was possible —

Sadie spoke up, sayin' as how she shore didn't want to stay where she warn't welcome, and that she figured it really would be best if she rode to San Antonio behind the herd, like we was wantin' her to do. Then she started cryin', and that got our folks even more upset. This whole thing jest warn't workin' out like we'd planned it.

After what seemed like hours, they all quit talkin' and fussin' and jest sat there glarin' at us. Jim started stammerin' and finally managed to choke out somethin' about how we shore hadn't meant to hurt Sadie's feelin's, and that we'd be happy to wait and take her down to San Antonio after the cattle drive. Well, that jest made Sadie cry a whole lot harder and louder and Mamma get even madder. She told Jim she'd heard enough of this nonsense. He obviously hadn't heard a thing she'd said, and that we was both to excuse ourselves from the table and leave the room before she really lost her temper. For some reason, she was jest as mad at me as she was at Jim, and I hadn't said a word.

I followed Jim out to the front of the house where we sat down on a bench under one of the big oak trees. Jim was feelin' sorry for his-self and mad at everybody — 'specially me. He claimed it warn't fair what our folks had said, 'cause he was jest tryin' to keep Mamma from bein' hurt. He even blamed me for all what'd happened. He claimed if I hadn't been so damned nice to Sadie on our way down from Colorado, she never would have got sweet on me. I asked him where in tarnation did he get that fool idea — she warn't sweet on me. I'd figured all along that she was Billy Joe's girl. Jim said he jest couldn't believe I was so damned dumb. If'n she was sweet on Billy, then how come she kept stickin' so close to me all the way down from Denver? She'd even slept close to me at night. If'n it was Billy Joe she liked, why didn't she stay close to him instead? Well, that really shook me up. What if Sadie really did like me? What was I gonna do? 'Course, I liked her a lot, but I shore couldn't be in love with a whore — but then again, neither could I stop likin' her.

The cattle drive went off without a hitch. We left at sunup and four days later turned the herd over to the buyer for the Confederate army in San Antonio. Daddy hadn't spoke much on the drive goin' down. As a matter of fact, he'd seemed downright unfriendly. But once the herd was sold and he had the money in his pocket, he was back to his old self again and went off to visit some friends in San Antonio whilst me and Jim headed out to see Billy Joe Barlow.

He was real glad to see us. He'd been enjoyin' his visit with his folks, but now he was ready to go back to Fort Bliss and enlist. Jim told him to be back at our ranch no later than the thirteenth of December, so's we'd get to Fort Bliss in plenty of time to enlist and leave with the brigade. When Billy Joe asked me what all my folks had said about my enlistin', I told him I hadn't asked yet. I'd been afeared of what they'd say, but that I was plannin' on askin' my daddy on the way back to the ranch, 'cause if he agreed to it, I was pretty shore Mamma would, too. I already knowed what she'd say if I asked her first. 'Course, now that she was so mad at me, she might be happy if I did enlist.

Billy Joe asked how come our Mamma was upset with me on account of Sadie — what'd I do to make her mad? Nothin', I told him, it's jest that me and Jim figured that Mamma and Sadie was gettin' too fond of each other, and we wanted to take her with us on the cattle drive so's that wouldn't happen. Billy Joe shook his head like he couldn't believe what he'd heard and asked why in the hell shouldn't our mamma be friendly with Sadie. Then Jim explained how me and him didn't want Mamma to get real attached to her and then feel bad when she found out she was a whore. Billy Joe looked at Jim like he was crazy. Where in God's green earth did you ever get that stupid idea? he asked. Sadie was the farthest from bein' a whore than any lady we could ever hope to meet.

Then he explained how Sadie was the daughter of Sam Hardin, a professional gambler friend of Charley Harrison. Not long after Sam and Sadie had come to Denver, Sam was shot and kilt after he'd caught another gambler dealin' from the bottom of the deck — I reckon maybe Sam was a better gambler than he was a gunfighter. Jest the year before her daddy got kilt, Sadie's mother had died of smallpox back in Kansas, so now, with her daddy and mother both gone, she was left all alone with nobody to look after her — 'ceptin' for Charley Harrison. Before Sam Hardin died, Charley promised him that he'd take care of Sadie 'til she was growed up and to see to it that she didn't get into no trouble. Billy Joe thought Charley had done a good job, too, 'cause even though she danced with some of the men what come into the Criterion and served them drinks now and then, she for shore warn't no prostitute like them other ladies. I asked Billy Joe if'n that was true, why didn't the sheriff in Denver let Sadie out of jail 'long with Charley? Billy Joe said he warn't real shore, but most likely the sheriff figured that as long as Sadie was in jail, Charley wouldn't cause no trouble for fear of what might happen to her. If they'd let her loose, he might have stayed around Denver and talked the southern sympathizers into riotin'. I reckon that made sense.

Early next mornin' we lit out for the ranch. Daddy wanted to get back to his chores, and I wanted to apologize to Sadie. On the way home, me and Jim explained to Daddy how the reason we'd wanted Sadie to come on the cattle drive was to keep our mamma from bein' hurt. After we'd told him why we'd figured she was a whore, Daddy said he could see why we jumped to that conclusion, and that he hoped it would teach us not to judge a person without first knowin' all the facts about him or, in this case, her. If we'd jest taken the time to find out more about Sadie, we'd of knowed she warn't no whore. Daddy couldn't believe that we'd never once asked her anything about her family or how come she was livin' in Denver — why, we didn't even know she was an orphan. We'd jest figured right off that she was a whore on account of she worked in a saloon. But at least he was glad we'd tried to keep our mamma from gettin' hurt, and he promised to explain it all to her once we got back to the ranch — but that it was up to us to explain it to Sadie, 'cause he shore as hell warn't gonna do it.

Daddy got real quiet when I told him I wanted to enlist in the Confederate army and fight Yankees. He jest sat on his horse lookin' sad — not sayin' a word. Finally, after what seemed like forever, he told me if that's what I really wanted, it was all right with him, even though he knowed it would make my mamma mighty unhappy. He told me how he agreed with the folks what thought slavery was wrong, 'cause he figured it jest warn't right for one person to own another, and that everybody should be free to go his or her own way no matter what color their skin was. But there jest had to be a better way to solve the problem than by fightin' a war. 'Course, now that the Union armies was attackin' the Confederacy, it really didn't matter no more what had caused it, and he was gonna do everything he could to help whup them Yankees. After that, Daddy told us how proud he was of both of us for wantin' to defend our home, and that he'd be countin' on us to take care of each other and to come back home safe and sound. Then, without sayin' another word, he spurred his horse and rode on up the trail.

As it turned out, it was Sadie what was the most upset about our goin'. Mamma didn't like it, but she said it didn't surprise her none. It made her proud to know that both of her sons wanted to fight for the South, 'cause it was important for a person to fight for the things they believed in. 'Course, she'd worry about us a lot whilst we was gone, and she'd be prayin' every day for us to stay safe and sound and to come home soon.

Then she told us about our Aunt Sarah's son, Mosely. He'd joined the Confederate army jest last July, right after the South won a big battle at Manassas in Virginia. In early August, the South won another battle what was fought on Wilson's Creek up in the state of Missouri. The southern troops had been fightin' under the command of General Ben McCulloch, who'd been a Texas Ranger in his younger days. Accordin' to Mamma, a red-haired Yankee general named Nathaniel Lyons was kilt in the battle at Wilson's Creek on the tenth of August, and on that very same day Mosely was kilt — jest two weeks after he'd enlisted. I remembered playin' with Mosely at my aunt's home in Austin when I was a youngster. He was a year older than me and I liked him a lot. Mamma told us that, even though his folks was sad, it made them feel better to know that he'd died for a good cause.

I don't know as how hearin' about Mosely made me and Jim feel a whole lot better, though. 'Specially not after Sadie busted out cryin', blowin' her nose, sobbin', and sayin' how she didn't want me and Jim to get kilt. I felt bad seein' her carryin' on so, and I put my arm around her shoulder hopin' it would help — but it jest made her cry harder. I didn't know what to do when she throwed her arms around my neck and said she warn't never gonna let me go.

After Mamma had peeled Sadie off'n me and got her to calm down some, she told her she was shore the Good Lord would be lookin' out for both of us, and that we'd be back home in no time at all. In the meantime, Sadie'd be welcome to stay at the ranch with her and my daddy for as long as she liked, if she didn't have some other place to go.

She'd always wanted to have a daughter, and now she had Sadie. After that, Sadie busted out cryin' again, sayin' how sweet we all was, and how happy it made her feel to know that they wanted her to stay with them. First she was cryin' 'cause she was so sad, and now she was cryin' 'cause she was so glad. I decided that girls certainly was peculiar.

Jim was amazed that Mamma hadn't fussed at me about wantin' to join the army. But he claimed he was glad I was goin', 'cause if everythin' worked out like Colonel Heffiner figured it would and his outfit captured the gold mines up in Colorado, maybe we could bring our gold down out of the Tarryalls at that same time. I told him maybe we could look some more for Ramon's lost bonanza at the same time, but Jim said to forget it — that damned bonanza warn't nothin' but an old man's pipe dream.

It seemed like me and Jim was jest gettin' settled in when it came time for us to leave. We'd been helpin' our daddy out around the ranch a lot, gettin' things set for winter, fixin' barns, mendin' fences and the like. I'd forgot what hard work it was, and I warn't too sorry to be leavin' it behind — but I shore did hate leavin' Sadie. It'd been embarrassin', but right after we'd got back from San Antonio, I'd explained to her how come me and Jim had wanted her to go with us on the cattle drive. I apologized and asked her to forgive us both. I told her I couldn't believe I'd been so stupid as to think she was a shady lady. She hugged me and kissed me on the cheek. She said she could see why me and Jim had figured the way we did and that I should forget about it — she already had. All Mamma ever said about that sorry affair was that I should make shore I knowed all the facts about a person before I judged them. And then — even if they'd done wrong — we should forgive them if they was sincerely tryin' to change their lives and do the right thing, 'cause that's what Jesus wants us to do.

It was the day before we was to leave, and Billy Joe hadn't showed up yet. We was afeared we was gonna have to leave without him, but 'long about dark he come ridin' up on the sorryest lookin' horse I'd ever seen. His mare, Betsy, the one he'd rode comin' down from Colorado, had stepped in a prairie dog hole and busted her leg. He'd shore hated doin' it, he said, but he had to shoot her to keep her from sufferin'. He'd bought the old nag he was ridin' at a ranch about thirty miles away, and it was a wonder she'd ever made it this far. My daddy fixed him up with a new horse.

That night, Sadie and I had a long talk. I told her not to worry about me. I was shore I'd be comin' home real soon, and I was gonna miss her somethin' awful 'til I did. She promised to wait, no matter how long it took for me to get back. Then she kissed me right smack on the lips, and my heart damn near jumped out of my chest. By now I was head over heels in love with Sadie, but I jest couldn't get up the nerve to tell her. I'm shore she knowed it, though.

Me and Jim both felt bad about leavin' our folks again so soon after we'd come home, but at least Sadie would be stayin' there with them, and we was glad of that. They warn't near as young and spry as they used to be, and we figured that Sadie would be a big help to them — 'specially to Mamma. But most of all, I was glad she'd be there so she could help mend the empty places in their hearts.

Next mornin' a little afore sunup, we said our good-byes and start-ed back to Fort Bliss. It was the twenty-second day of December. Before we left, Mamma asked us all to bow our heads whilst she prayed to the Lord, askin' Him to keep a close eye on us whilst we was gone and to bring us home again, safe and sound. As we was ridin' off, I thought I heard somebody cryin' softly, but I couldn't tell whether it was Sadie or Mamma. I was pretty shore it warn't Daddy.

CHAPTER 29

We rode into the parade ground at Fort Bliss on the fourteenth of January, and it was damn near deserted. When we checked in at the headquarters buildin', the officer of the day gave us a message from Colonel Heffiner sayin' that him and General Sibley was up at Fort Thorn and that me, Jim, and Billy Joe was to join him there. Seems that General Sibley had got to Fort Bliss towards the end of December, and not long after, he'd ordered Colonel Baylor to take his brigade up the Rio Grande to Mesilla Valley and set up camp near Fort Fillmore. But there was an outbreak of smallpox at Fort Fillmore, so the brigade headed forty miles farther north and set up camp on the east bank of the Rio Grande River jest opposite Fort Thorn. Then, three days ago, Colonel Heffiner, the general, and the rest of his army had joined them. The general was figurin' on stayin' there for the rest of January and the first part of February so's to train his troopers before headin' farther upriver to fight Yankees.

The next day, we was ridin' out the front gate of the fort when a Confederate major named Trevanion T. Teel caught up with us. He was the gunnery officer in charge of General Sibley's artillery batteries and was headin' to Fort Thorn, too. Bein' as how it was gonna take us close to three days to get there, the major wanted to ride along with us. Me and Jim told him we'd be happy to have his company and, as it turned out, we was, 'cause what he told us was mighty interestin'.

It seems the major was comin' back from a special assignment in

Major Travanion T. Teel, Artillery officer in General Sibley's New Mexico forces in 1862.
(Courtesy of the Colorado Historical Society.)

Austin so's to report to General Sibley on the outcome of a meetin' between representatives of the Confederate States of America and those of the Republic of Mexico. The southern representatives was hopin' to

Map of the Rio Grande Valley from El Paso to Santa Fe. From a War Department Military Map issued in 1857.

(Courtesy of the Colorado Historical Society.)

make the northern Mexican states of Chihuahua, Sonora, and Baja California a part of the Confederate States of America, either by buyin' them from Mexico or, if necessary, takin' them by force. The southern leaders figured that Benito Juarez, the president of Mexico, would most likely be happy to sell them, on account of he was havin' big problems of his own lately. Seems that some of the folks in Mexico warn't 'specially fond of their president and was tryin' to overthrow his government. 'Course, President Juarez didn't want that to happen, but his army warn't very big and his troops was porely equipped, so jest lately he'd been givin' serious thought to cedin' the three Mexican states to the Confederacy in exchange for money and supplies.

The southern leaders had ordered the major to instruct General Sibley to proceed at once with the conquest of New Mexico, California, and Colorado. And after he'd done that, he was to begin serious negotiations with Benito Juarez for the purchase of Chihuahua and the other two states. Then — once that'd happened — hopefully the rest of Mexico, along with Cuba and Central America, could be persuaded to join the Confederacy, too. And if they wouldn't, force might be the answer there, too.

Lt. Commander William R. Scurry.
An officer in General Sibley's forces in New Mexico in 1862.
(Courtesy of the Colorado Historical Society.)

It was late afternoon when we joined the brigade. After Colonel Heffiner finished swearin' me, Jim, and Billy Joe into the army, we was outfitted with double-barreled shotguns, ammunition, backpacks, and other gear. We already had our own horses, revolvers, rifles, and bedrolls. All three of us was assigned to a company of the Second Texas Mounted Rifles, commanded by Major Charles Pyron. It was part of Company C of the Fourth Texas Mounted Volunteers, under the temporary command of Lieutenant Colonel William Read — "Dirty Shirt"

— Scurry. I never did know why they called the colonel Dirty Shirt. His shirt warn't no dirtier than mine or any of the other troopers.

Me and Jim had been hopin' to serve under Colonel Heffiner, but, as it turned out, we couldn't, on account of he was an aide to the general and would be helpin' direct troop maneuvers. But he promised us

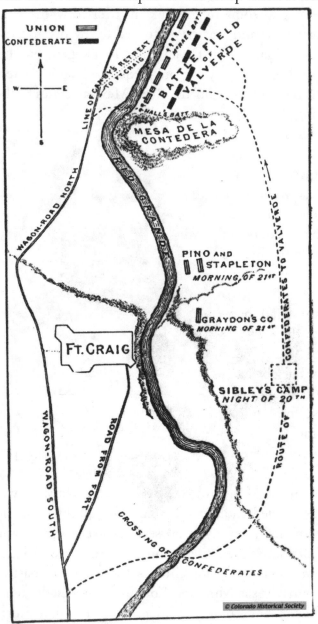

Map of the Fort Craig locality, showing the location of the fort as it relates to the Battle of Valverde. Taken from Battle Leaders of the Civil War. *Century Press, 1887.*

(Courtesy of the Colorado Historical Society.)

that we'd be in his command for shore when he went up to the Colorado gold fields. Accordin' to the colonel, we should be proud to a part of the Second Texas Mounted Rifles, on account of it was a great outfit. And we'd be likely to see a lot of action, 'cause Company C of the Fourth Texas Mounted was to be the vanguard throughout the campaign, and the Second Texas Mounted Rifles was gonna be the spearhead in all of the battles. That was a real honor.

Colonel Heffiner shore was right about that first part — the Second Texas Mounted Rifles seen a lot of action. We spearheaded most all of the attacks and had more casualties than any other outfit. Now that I look back on it, it was an honor I could have done without. In fact, I'd jest as soon forget about that whole damned campaign, but I reckon I'd best tell you about some of it, 'cause it'll help explain what happened to Billy Joe, and why Jim got to actin' the way he did later on.

On the mornin' of February seventh, the Fourth Texas Volunteers headed north up the old wagon road to a few miles south of Fort Craig, where we bivouacked and waited for the rest of our brigade to catch up. The fort was out in the middle of a cactus-and-sage brush-covered desert about three-quarters of a mile west of the Rio Grande. The wind was blowin' somethin' fierce, and it was hard to see with all the dust and tumbleweeds whizzin' by, but we could see good enough to know that there warn't no way to sneak up close to the fort without gettin' shot to pieces by rifle fire and by all them cannon what was mounted on the bastions. We found out later that most of them was "Quaker Guns" what was made from the trunks of trees.

We sat around twiddlin' our thumbs for two whole days waitin' for General Sibley and the rest of our troopers to show up, and so far we hadn't seen hide nor hair of the Yankees. We was all bored and itchin' for action — 'specially Jim. He wanted to kill Yankees. Five days later Jim got what he wanted —in spades. On the twenty-first of February, we rounded the east end of the Mesa de la Contedera and headed west along its north slope towards the river. Our outfit was in the lead. A little ways before we got there, our thirsty horses smelt the water and took off like they was shot out of a cannon. Whilst we was all hangin' onto our saddle horns, prayin' we wouldn't fall off, we routed a company of Yankee militia. They skedaddled without even firin' a shot. Jim figured they most likely was raw recruits and that we'd been lucky, 'cause if they was regulars, we most likely would have all got kilt.

After that, we took cover in a grove of cottonwoods below the west end of the Mesa de la Contedera, right above a river crossin' called the lower ford of Valverde. As the rest of our troopers showed up, we kept movin' our company's position further to the north, takin' cover in amongst the cottonwoods that lay between the river and another smaller mesa to the northeast. Our new position overlooked the upper ford of Valverde. Not long after that, the Yankee artillery started cannonadin' the clumps of cottonwoods where we was hidin'. Then their sharpshooters joined in the fun, and the bullets started buzzin' through the trees like swarms of mad bees. We didn't waste no time in fallin' back to where we could hunker behind a low ridge of sand at the edge of a dried-up river channel.

That was the beginnin' of what folks now are callin' "The Battle of Valverde." All the rest of that mornin' was spent in a heavy artillery duel. Our Texas gunners gave more than they got and made it hot for the Yankees — 'specially the batteries of Major Travanion T. Teel and his junior officer, Lieutenant John Riley. Late in the mornin', our sharpshooters forced one Union battery to abandon its position and move to the north end of the battlefield, where they mounted their six artillery pieces on the east side of the river about seven hundred yards downhill from our positions. We found out later that the battery was under the command of Captain Alexander McRae. Even though he was a southerner, he'd stuck with the Union army and refused to join the Confederacy, and I shore wish he'd switched, 'cause he was one hell of a gunnery officer. I'd of much rather had him on our side.

They'd lined up their artillery pieces a little ways back from the river's edge right behind some big piles of sand. Then they started shellin' our positions with a vengeance. Our own artillery was firin' back, and I was damn near scared to death by all the noise and the smoke and soldiers on both sides of the river screamin' in pain when the shells hit in amongst them. This kind of fightin' warn't quite what I'd been figurin' on. I jest sat there hunkered down behind a little pile of dirt, shakin' with fear and prayin' that I warn't gonna get blown to smithereens. I figured it must be a lot like the hell Mamma now and then told me and Jim we was goin' to if we didn't shape up.

Then all of a sudden their cannonadin' stopped, and a minute or two later, a whole passel of Yankees come chargin' across the river and up the slope towards our positions — but we was ready and waitin'. We'd double-shotted our guns so's they'd be twice as deadly, and our rifle and cannon fire soon stopped their charge as the Yankees scattered, searchin' for whatever cover they could find. After that, there was a lull in the fightin' and, 'ceptin' for the cries of the wounded, it got quiet. When I looked down at the river, I could see a dozen or more dead bodies floatin' downstream.

Durin' the fightin', a company of Yankee soldiers wearin' gray blouses with red stripes across the chests had crossed over the river not far below our position, and they shore made it hot for us. We dasn't stick our heads up above the bank for more'n a second for fear of havin' them blowed off. We found out later that they was from Company K of the Colorado Volunteers and was led by Captain Theodore H. Dodd. Last time we'd heard, they was up in Cañon City, and I shore wished they'd stayed there.

After that, it was quiet for a time. Even the cannon was silent and, 'ceptin' for a few rifle shots, it was almost peaceful. It was hard to believe that jest a minute ago I'd been tryin' to kill other men. I warn't shore whether I'd really kilt anybody or not. One or two of the fellas I'd been shootin' at had fell, but maybe they was jest duckin' to take cover and warn't hit at all. I hoped so. That was the first time I'd ever really got to thinkin' about what it'd feel like to kill another man, 'specially one what had never done me no harm. Somehow it didn't seem right, and it bothered me considerable.

I asked Jim how he felt about it, and he said it didn't bother him one damned bit. There warn't no such thing as a good Yankee — they all needed killin', and how I was gonna get myself kilt if I kept on feelin' sorry for Yankees, 'cause they shore as hell didn't feel sorry for me. I know Jim was worried about me, 'cause I heard him tell Billy Joe how they'd best keep a close eye on me to be shore I didn't do somethin' stupid the next time we was in a skirmish. After that, I jest sat there thinkin' to myself — thinkin' how goin' to war didn't seem near as great as I'd thought it was gonna be. I thought about Sadie, too, and how much I missed her

It was midafternoon when the Yankee artillery started shellin' us again, and the six-gun battery below us was givin' us fits. Colonel Scurry ordered the Texas Mounted Volunteers to charge the Union lines in an all-out attack. Our end of the line was to attack the crack six-gun battery what had been givin' us so much grief, and it ended up in a terrific fight — almost too terrible to talk about. We started out shootin' at the Yankees with rifles, but when both sides got close up and all mixed together, there warn't no time to reload, so we ended up fightin' hand to hand with bayonets and Bowie knives.

That part of the fight only lasted a few minutes, but it seemed like forever. I was right in the thickest part of it, with Jim on one side of me and Billy Joe on the other. We was gradually pushin' the Yankees back towards the gun emplacement, when we was attacked by four Yankees comin' at us with fixed bayonets. Jim kilt one right off and was fightin' another whilst Billy Joe was busy with a third. The fourth Yankee was headed in my direction. He looked to be twice my size, and I could tell he was figurin' on makin' short work of me. And there warn't no doubt in my mind but what he could do it, as I braced myself for his attack — but it never came. Billy Joe'd knocked the man he was fightin' from off'n his feet and was jest about to finish him off, when he'd seen I was in danger and rushed over to give me a hand. Before the big Yankee even knowed what was happenin', Billy Joe drove his bayonet deep into his chest and clean though his heart, killin' him deader'n a doornail.

I'd jest started to thank Billy Joe for savin' my life, when a shot rang out and he dropped to the ground with blood oozin' from a gapin' hole in his head. I looked around to see where the shot had come from, and I seen the Yankee Billy Joe had been fightin' strugglin' to get up from the ground. Smoke was still curlin' up from the muzzle of his rifle barrel, and I knowed it was him what had shot my friend. After he'd made it back on his feet, he come runnin' at me with his bayonet held out in front, but I knocked it to one side with my rifle and thrust with my Bowie knife and felt the big blade sink deep into his chest. He screamed and fell back to the ground. Whether I kilt him or jest wounded him I'll never know, 'cause right then Colonel Scurry ordered our company to secure the gun emplacement and turn all the cannon around and point them in the opposite direction so we could use them to kill Yankees.

Not long after that the battle ended. The Union troops broke and ran like a passel of frightened rabbits tryin' to get to the west side of the Rio Grande. Their officers was tryin' to form a new line of defense on the opposite bank. At the same time, Colonel Scurry was ordered to get his troops ready to make a frontal attack across the river. I gotta admit, the idea of crossin' the river whilst them Yankees was firin' point blank into our ranks didn't appeal to me one little bit. It was bound to be risky and bloody, and a lot of us was gonna get kilt or wounded. So I was mighty relieved when a Yankee soldier rode forward carryin' a white flag. Colonel Canby was requestin' a truce so both sides could take care of their wounded and bury their dead. General Sibley, bein' a real southern gentleman, granted their request, and we watched as the Federal troopers carried their dead and wounded inside the walls of Fort Craig. But, as it turned out, all the rest of the Yankee soldiers went with them, takin' with them all of their equipment and some of ours what they'd captured. But they'd left behind a lot more than they took, and we spent that evenin' and the next mornin' collectin' the guns and other equipment what they'd discarded. The biggest prize was the six cannon from Captain McCrae's battery. They was brass twelve-pounders and Captain McRae and his troopers must have figured they was pretty special, 'cause they gave their lives tryin' to defend them. They was all mighty brave men — even if they was Yankees.

That evenin' we collected our dead and laid them all in a row — and it was a long one. We'd had 197 casualties in all — 150 wounded and 47 kilt. We figured the Yankees had lost a lot more. Me and Jim was put on burial detail 'long with several other troopers from our company. The first one we buried in the dry, rocky ground at the foot of the mesa was Billy Joe. He'd been a good friend to both of us, and he'd gave his life to save mine. And now there was nothin' I could do to repay him, 'ceptin' to tell his mamma and daddy what a fine friend and brave man he was. Jim told me to quit grievin' so much, that I should forget about Billy Joe. In a war, people got kilt, and I'd damn well better get used to it. But I told him he was askin' me to do the impossible. I could never forget Billy Joe — not even if I tried.

Burials over, we stopped to eat and rest. Some of the other troopers looted the knapsacks of the dead Yankees and was eatin' light-bread and washin' it down with whiskey what they'd found in some of the Union canteens. I jest couldn't bring myself to eat dead men's food or drink their whisky. Jim said I'd come to it soon enough, but somehow I doubted it.

That night everythin' was quiet. You couldn't hear a thing, 'ceptin' a couple of coyotes serenadin' each other way off in the distance. Nobody felt like talkin'. We all jest lay on our backs, lookin' at the stars overhead and thinkin' about the battle what was comin' in the mornin'. I'd already seen enough killin' to last me for the rest of my life, and I knowed that tomorrow would most likely be even worse than today. I don't know about all the others, but I was scared — scared I was gonna get kilt like Billy Joe, scared I'd never see Sadie again. I don't think I slept at all that night. I jest lay there lookin' up at the stars in the heavens and wonderin' if maybe Sadie was lookin' at them, too, and thinkin' of me. And I prayed a lot. I asked Jesus to keep a close eye on Sadie and keep her safe whilst I was gone. I prayed for me, too, that I wouldn't get kilt or wounded, and that I could go home to her real soon.

We was up well before the sun next mornin' so's to get ready for what we figured was gonna be a long, bloody day. But that's not the way it turned out. General Canby and his whole army stayed inside the walls of Fort Craig. When it got to be late mornin' and the Yankees still hadn't come out, General Sibley sent some officers with a white flag up to Fort Craig. They was to tell General Canby to either surrender unconditionally or come out and fight — but General Canby didn't do neither one. I figured he'd lost his nerve, but Jim said no, Canby knowed our army was short on food and was hopin' we'd all either leave or starve to death. Either way he'd win.

And Jim was right: We was short of food and if we didn't find more and find it quick, we was gonna have to call off the campaign and head back to Texas. So, instead of fightin' like we'd been expectin', we spent the rest of that day restin' and early next mornin' lit out for Socorro, where we spent a day settin' up a hospital for our wounded. After that, we headed a hundred miles north to Albuquerque, where there was plenty of food waitin' for us, courtesy of Secretary of War John Floyd.

But when we got there, all the food and supplies we was countin' on was gone — and so was the Yankees. Accordin' to the natives in town, they'd all moved over to Santa Fe, takin' all the food and supplies they could carry with them. What they couldn't carry, they burned. So we headed double time over to Santa Fe and the same thing had happened there. The supplies was burnt up and the federal troopers had moved — lock, stock, and barrel to Fort Union on the far side of Glorieta Pass. The territorial government had moved to Las Vegas.

On the twenty-second of March, Lieutenant Colonel Scurry and the Fourth Texas Mounted Volunteers headed down to the little settlement of Galisteo close to twenty miles southeast of Santa Fe, where they was to prepare for the attack on Fort Union. The six hundred troopers in the Second Texas Mounted Rifles was to encamp at Johnson's Ranch at the mouth of Apache Canyon. Our orders was to picket the stretch of the Santa Fe Trail between there and the top of Glorieta Pass and to alert Colonel Scurry if we seen any Yankees comin' our way. General Sibley and his staff had stayed back in Albuquerque.

CHAPTER 30

Fort Union was built on the high desert of northeastern New Mexico, so's to protect folks travelin' the Santa Fe Trail from Indian attacks. It was the biggest and strongest fort in New Mexico. And now we was supposed to capture it, and I doubted it was gonna be near as easy as General Sibley said it'd be. I told Jim I was tired of spearheadin' all the attacks — I figured we was doin' more than our fair share of the fightin'. But Jim didn't agree. He said he liked bein' spearhead, 'cause he liked killin' Yankees, and that way he could kill more of them — the more the better. That shore didn't sound like the Jim I'd knowed talkin', and it shook me up some. Killin' other men made me sick, even though I knowed we had to do it if the South was ever gonna win this damned war.

Four days later, Jim got the killin' he'd been hopin' for, and for the next eight hours, it got downright lively. 'Long about midday, two of our scouts came ridin' into camp, their horses puffin' and all lathered up. They'd been talkin' to a Mr. Alexander Valle', the owner of the Pigeon's

Pigeon's Ranch in the 1880's. Photograph taken from Colorado Volunteers in the Civil War, by William P. Whiteford D. D.

(Courtesy of the Colorado Historical Society.)

Ranch hostelry up on Glorieta Pass. Folks in these parts named it that on account of the way Mr. Valle' strutted like a pigeon whenever he danced. Accordin' to Mr. Valle', four hundred Yankee troopers was comin' our way over Glorieta Pass from Kozlowski's ranch. They was headin' for Santa Fe so's to take it back from the Confederates.

In less time than it takes to tell, we was headed up Apache Canyon, haulin' our field artillery pieces with us. Major Pyron was figurin' on interceptin' the Yankees near the top of the pass. He claimed it'd be easy pickin's. And he was right, the pickin's was easy all right, but for the Yankees — not for us — and late that afternoon we was back at Johnson's Ranch, lickin' our wounds. A hundred and fifty of our troopers was missin'. But how many was dead and how many wounded or captured, we couldn't tell — we'd had to leave them all behind. The Yankee officer in command of their outfit was ridin' a big black horse, and I'd swear he had a charmed life, 'cause a bunch of us was shootin' at him, but he never once got hit. He looked sort of familiar, too, but right then I didn't have any time to think on it.

Major John M. Chivington, Colonel Slough's successor as commander of the First Regiment of Colorado Volunteers. Picture was taken from Colorado Volunteers in the Civil War.
(Courtesy of the Colorado Historical Society.)

Colonel John P. Slough, Commander of the First regiment of Colorado Volunteers. Picture taken from Colorado Volunteers in the Civil War.
(Courtesy of the Colorado Historical Society. Colonel Slough's photograph loaned to them by Mr. Samuel C. Dorsey of Denver.)

Back at camp that night, I remembered who the Yankee officer was. It was John Chivington, the Methodist-Episcopal minister, the man Mr. Miller was argufyin' with up in Denver out in front of the Criterion saloon, 'ceptin' now he was a major in the First Regiment of Colorado Volunteers. No wonder we'd had such a tough time: We'd been tanglin' with "The Pike's Peakers" — the tough miners from the Colorado gold fields. When we told Major Pyron who it was we'd been up against, he told us not to worry, 'cause Colonel Scurry was already on his way with reinforcements and once they got here we'd whup them Yankees for shore. That was what he'd said last time — I hoped this time it'd be true.

Shore enough, right at daybreak, Colonel Scurry, two battalions of troopers, and a wagon train loaded with supplies and ammunition joined us at Johnson's Ranch, and we spent the rest of that day gettin' ready to lick the Yankees up on Glorieta Pass. We had close to 1400 men along with our artillery batteries to back us up, so we figured we was unstoppable.

Come sunup on the mornin' of the twenty-eighth, we started up Apache Canyon towards Glorieta Pass. Three hundred troopers and one artillery piece stayed behind so's to guard our animals and supplies in the rock corral at Johnson's Ranch. A little before we got to the pass, one of our scouts told Colonel Scurry that close to 700 Yankees was waterin' their horses about a mile down the road — and so far, they hadn't spotted us. We found out later that their commander was Colonel John Slough. Last time we'd heard about him, he'd been a lawyer up in Denver.

The colonel ordered us to advance up the wagon road to a grove of trees about 800 yards west of the ranch. Once we got there, we split into three columns. Major Pyron took the companies in his command — includin' ours — over to a ridge south of an arroyo. Once we was in position, the artillery battery under the command of Major Raguet opened fire. A few seconds later, we heard bugles soundin' and saw the Yankee troopers formin' battle lines in amongst a thick stand of cedar and pinyon pines near Pigeon's Ranch. Then the bugles sounded a second time, and the Federals started comin' towards us. We was hunkered down behind rocks and trees waitin' for them and, when they got close enough, both side started shootin' at each other with pistols and rifles, and the artillery batteries on both sides kept firing their cannon. The noise was terrible — it felt like my head was gonna split open.

It seemed like hours, but I'm shore it was only minutes until the cannonadin' stopped and the Federal lines split into two separate columns. One come chargin' at our position, and for a while it looked like they'd run right over us, but then our artillery drove them back. The other column of Yankees tried to outflank Colonel Scurry's troopers on the north side of the arroyo. But it didn't work and they fell back to a new position west of Pigeon's Ranch, where there was a lot of rocks and trees they could hide behind. We was in for one hell of a fight. On Colonel Scurry's orders, Major Pyron led our outfit to a position across the arroyo and onto the side of the canyon north of the battlefield where we could overlook the Yankees' position. But the Yankees, seein' what was happening, repositioned themselves so's to counter our move and started shootin' at us with their artillery and rifle fire. As best we could, we kept dodgin' from tree to tree and from rock to rock, until we was finally right in amongst the Yankees. It took a lot of bloody, hand-to-hand fightin', but we finally pushed them back onto a rocky ridge above Pigeon's Ranch.

Right after that, we was ordered to make an all-out attack on the Yankee positions — so that's jest what we did. We went screamin' and yellin' down the hill, hoppin' from rock to rock right in the face of cannon and rifle fire. A few of the Yankees panicked and started runnin' back down the hill, and I reckon I might have got a mite carried away, 'cause I jumped up and started chasin' down the hill after them. But then I heard Jim hollerin' at me, and I looked back and seen him wavin' at me to get down and take cover. Then, all of a sudden, he gave out a loud yell and fell back on the ground. That shook me up somethin' awful. I could tell he'd been hit hard, and I scrambled over to where he was lyin' jest as fast as I could go. When I got to him he was holdin' onto his right shoulder, tryin' to stop the bleedin' and at the same time cussin' up a storm.

As best I could, I kept pressure on Jim's shoulder whilst me and another trooper dragged him to the rear of our lines, but he still lost an awful lot of blood. After givin' him a big dose of laudanum, a medic cut the bloody shirt from off'n his shoulder and got the bleedin' stopped by holdin' thick gauze pads over the bullet holes, front and back. The bullet had went clear through and, accordin' to the medic, that was good. But it'd busted up the bone real bad jest below the shoulder and that warn't good — in fact, it was terrible, 'cause Jim most likely was gonna have to have his arm cut off at the shoulder. When Jim'd heard the medic say that, he damn near exploded.

"The hell you will!" he shouted. "Nobody's gonna cut my arm off. I'd druther be dead than have that happen."

"I'll have Doctor Akers, our surgeon, look at you," the medic said, tryin' to calm him down. "He's a mighty good doctor. Maybe he can do something to save your arm." Then he disappeared and came back a few minutes later, followed by the doctor.

"Hi. I'm Dave Akers," the doctor said. "Let's take a look at your shoulder, soldier." Then he took off the dressing and inspected the wound carefully. "The medic's right, Son," he said looking at Jim kindly. "It's a mighty bad wound, and by rights I should take yore arm off. It'd save you a lot of misery, but if you're willin' to put up with a long, hard recovery and a crooked, stiff arm that won't work too great, I think I can probably save it. So it's up to you. What do you want me to do?"

"Don't cut it off, Doc." We could scarcely hear Jim's whisper. "I'd sooner be dead than lose my arm. I'll do anything to keep it. I'm gonna need it so's I can get even with them what done this to me." Then, while the medic held guaze over Jim's nose and dripped ether on it, Doctor Akers went to work on him. After he'd finished, he put a splint on his shoulder and arm so's to hold the bones in place.

Then he put his hand on my shoulder saying, "Well, Son, I did the best I could to fix your brother's shoulder, and I think it will most likely heal up all right — as long as it doesn't get infected. But it's going to be a long time in healing, and I'm afraid it's never gonna look too good, or work too well."

After thanking the doctor for all he'd done, I headed back to where the fightin' was goin' on — prayin' that I wouldn't be the next to get shot. The battle went on without let up for over seven hours. Then, late in the afternoon a quiet fell over the valley what was almost scary. It seems that Colonel Scurry had asked for a temporary cease-fire so's both sides could take care of their wounded and bury their dead.

Colonel Slough, the Yankee commander, agreed to it and extended it to the mornin' of the second day. And then, for some reason we couldn't understand at the time, him and his troopers went back to their encampment at Kozlowski's Ranch and on to Fort Union from there. The next day we found out why. That night we bivouacked at Pigeon's Ranch. We'd had 123 casualties — thirty dead and the rest wounded. The next mornin' we started buryin' our dead, but before we'd even finished diggin' the graves, one of the troopers what had been guardin' our supplies at Johnson's Ranch come ridin' into our camp hellbent for election with a message for Colonel Scurry. As soon as the colonel heard it, he ordered us to finish buryin' the dead and then head double time back to our encampment at Johnson's Ranch. We was to take all our wounded with us. We couldn't believe it. Here we'd been beatin' the britches off'n the Yankees and now we was ordered to retreat. It didn't make no sense. 'Course, they warn't whupped yet, but we never doubted that we could do it. Not a one of us troopers wanted to quit, but orders was orders, so we obeyed.

That evening, we found out the reason for the order. That mornin', whilst we was fightin' at Glorieta Pass, over 400 Yankee troopers had worked their way across the rugged cedar-covered hills south of Glorieta Pass for over ten miles. From there, they headed north to a hill overlookin' our supply base in Apache Canyon and skidded down the steep slope to the bottom, where they'd spiked our cannon and kilt or captured most all our guards. After that, they burned or blowed up all eighty-five wagons what was loaded with all our food, ammunition, and other supplies. Then they kilt all six hundred of our horses and mules with their bayonets and went back to Kozlowski's Ranch the same way they'd come.

One of our guards what had managed to escape, told us that the Yankee major in command of the attack was the same one what was leadin' the fight in Apache Canyon three days ago. When we told them his name was Chivington and that he was a preacher from out of Denver City, they jest wouldn't believe us. They'd figured it was the devil come up from hell.

CHAPTER 31

Most all us troopers in Colonel Scurry's command was in real sorry shape. We was hungry, discouraged, tired, and now, on top of that, we had to hustle back to Santa Fe jest to keep from starvin' to death. It was 'specially hard for the sick and wounded. Jim was way too weak to walk and he couldn't ride, so me and some other troopers took turns carryin' him on a stretcher. Several times, when we was carryin' it over rough ground and the stretcher tipped back and forth, Jim would go clear out of his head with pain. It got a whole lot worse when we run out of laudanum.

When General Sibley heard what all had happened at Johnson's Ranch, he'd hightailed it over to Santa Fe so's to take stock of what supplies and equipment he had left. And there warn't much — 'cause, accordin' to Colonel Heffiner, the general had sent most all of the army's food, guns, ammunition, and horses down to Colonel Scurry and his outfit at Galisteo. Now that they was gone, he was gonna have to call off the campaign and head doubletime back to Texas. There warn't no other choice.

Jim had been worryin' me a lot lately. There was times when it seemed like he was gettin' better, but then, all of a sudden, his shoulder and arm would start hurtin' him again and he'd take a turn for the worse. He was takin' laudanum pretty regular, and lots of times he acted real strange and had terrible nightmares about battles and people gettin' shot. Then he'd holler and thrash around somethin' awful. After we got back to Santa Fe, he got even weirder, and it warn't jest from his wound. 'Course, he was shot up pretty bad but, accordin' to the medics, the wound warn't infected and most likely would heal up all right. But that's not what was worryin' me. It was the way Jim was actin' and talkin', like he hated the whole world — and 'specially the Yankees. He swore he was gonna find a way to pay them back for what they'd done to him, even if it took him the rest of his life. Lots of times he claimed he didn't like me — his own brother! We'd always been best friends before he got shot, but now when I'd come to see him, he'd tell me he hated me and to get the hell away from him and leave him alone.

He even blamed me for his gettin' shot up on Glorieta Pass. He claimed it never would have happened if I hadn't been so damned stupid as to stand out in the open so them Yankees could shoot at me. If he hadn't stood up and hollered at me to get down, he never would have got shot, and he was sorry now that he'd done it — he should have let me get kilt. Hearin' him say that tore me up somethin' awful, 'cause even though I knowed it warn't really my fault that he'd got shot, I still felt guilty. With all them bullets flying around, either one of us could have got shot most any time. I finally decided it was the laudanum what was makin' him act that way, but I still couldn't stop feelin' guilty.

Even though it'd be a hard thing to do, we was gonna have to leave some of our sick and wounded troopers in Santa Fe, 'cause they never would have made it if they'd went with us. The wives and daughters of the good folks that lived there already had been treatin' our boys real nice, and I'm shore they'd keep on doin' it after we left — even though we was their enemy. Mrs. Canby, the wife of General Canby, was one of the ladies what was takin' care of Jim, but he claimed he hated her more than any of the others.

I told Jim he'd be a lot better off if he stayed in Santa Fe 'til his shoulder was healed, or at least 'til it quit hurtin' him so bad. I explained how he was too weak to walk and that we didn't have no horse he could ride. I even offered to stay with him so's we could both go home together after he got better. But I reckon that was the wrong thing to say, 'cause he got so damned mad he wouldn't listen to another word I said. He claimed I was jest tryin' to get rid of him like I done up at Glorieta Pass, and how I wanted to steal his share of the Tarryall gold — but that it warn't gonna work. If he couldn't ride, he'd walk, and if he couldn't walk, he'd crawl. He'd rather rot in hell than be left behind with all them Yankee witches — they was gonna torture and kill all the sick and wounded Texans the minute the rest of us left.

On the fifth of April, we started our long retreat back to Texas, and Jim went right 'long with us. I'd figured we was finished with the fightin', — but I was wrong. The Fourth Texas Mounted Volunteers was in two more skirmishes. The first was at Armijo's Mill on the east end of Albuquerque, and the second was at a ranch near Peralta what was owned by Mr. Henry Connelly, the territorial governor of New Mexico. Neither one amounted to a hill of beans.

On the twelfth of April, General Sibley and most all of his army crossed over to the west side of the Rio Grande and headed downriver from Albuquerque to the little town of Los Lunas. Jim and a few other troopers what was sick or injured went with them. What was left of the Second Texas Mounted Rifles joined them there a few days later, after buryin' some of our cannon in Albuquerque so's the Yankees couldn't find them and after the skirmish at Mr. Connelly's ranch. For two long days after that, our troops marched down the west bank of the river, whilst at the same time the Union troops, led by General Canby, went down the east. All that time both armies was in easy rifle range of each other, but neither one ever fired a shot.

Right about then, Jim was doin' a little better health-wise, but mind-wise he warn't doin' worth a damn. He could walk pretty good on his own, and even though he warn't hurtin' near as much as before, he was still takin' a lot of laudanum. I figured he was takin' way too much and told him he should quit it, but that jest made him mad. As a matter of fact, he was mad at the whole world and snapped at most everybody around him — 'specially me — and usually for no reason.

The evenin' of April seventeenth, we encamped on a bench a little ways back from the Rio Grande, about a day's march upriver from Socorro. After settin' up camp as usual, we built up our campfires, ate our slim rations, and rolled up in our blankets. A little past midnight we was rousted out and ordered to break camp quietly and move off to the west. Several troopers stayed behind to keep the campfires burnin' so's the Yankees would think we was still there, then a little before dawn they hightailed it to catch up with our army. We left most all our sick and wounded behind without nobody to take care of them and without medicines and hardly any food. It seemed like a terrible thing to do, but I'm shore General Sibley figured the Yankees could take a lot better care of them than we could, and he was right — but I still didn't like it, and neither did Jim. He swore as how they'd have had to shoot him before he'd stay behind and let them Yankee devils capture and torture him. I told him they wouldn't do that, but he jest told me to shut up and that I was a Yankee lover.

Next mornin' come reveille, the Yankees was in for a big surprise. We was gone, and as far as I knowed they never did follow us — leastwise, if they did, they never caught up. Most likely General Canby was countin' on the desert to do the killin' for him and, as it turned out, it did. We first swung close to twenty miles west from the river, then back to it about seventy miles above Mesilla, close to thirty miles south of Fort Craig. In all we struggled for well over a hundred miles, makin' a big detour through the most god-awful desert it'd ever been my misfortune to see, and I hope and pray I'll never see again. That was as close to hell as I ever want to come. We started out with only enough food and water for five or six days, and it was ten whole days before we got back to the river. We straggled along under a hot sun over benches and across miles and miles of scorchin' hot sand. There warn't no water, nothin' to eat — just miles and miles of sand, sagebrush, chaparral, and rattlesnakes.

It was terrible for Jim. The second day out, his shoulder started to get red and swollen, and it hurt him somethin' fierce — I'm shore he had fever, too, even though I'd been givin' him most all of my water ration. Jim's nightmares had come back, too, only a lot worse. There was times when he went plumb out of his head, and me and a couple of other troopers would have to take turns carryin' him. Sometimes he'd get to jerkin' around so much we couldn't even hold him, and we'd have to set in whatever shade we could find 'til he calmed down some. Whilst he was like that, he'd talk real crazy and cuss out the Yankees, sayin' how he was gonna kill every damn one of them. A time or two he even cussed me out and said it was my fault he'd got shot and that he was gonna get even with me for doin' it. 'Course, that shook me up, but when he started cussin' out God and blamin' Him for all his troubles, it shook me up a whole lot more. I figured the laudanum was makin' him talk that way.

After stragglin' up and down hills for what seemed like forever, we finally crossed over to the west side of the Sierra Magdalena and worked our way through the Sierra de San Mateo 'til we come to the dry bed of the Rio Palomas. From there the goin' got easier, and a day later we stumbled down a long slope to the banks of the Rio Grande where there was plenty of food waiting for us, courtesy of the troopers from Fort Thorn and the nice folks from Mesilla. That night we held a prayer meetin' so's to thank God for our deliverance. I was right there in the front row, but Jim didn't go. He said he warn't gonna to pray to a god that didn't give a damn about him.

Me and Jim got to Fort Bliss on the fourth of May. For at least a week after that, more troopers kept stragglin' in, and when it come time to take count, out of the 3,700 Texans what'd left Fort Thorn on February seventh lookin' for fame and glory, there was only 2,000 sorry survivors left. Figurin' the wounded what we'd left behind in the Yankee hospitals, the captured, and them what was kilt, we'd lost close to 1700 men — damn near half of our outfit. Many of our troopers was still lyin' out on that godforsaken desert, their bodies food for the coyotes and vultures.

I don't know how he done it, but Jim somehow managed to stay alive across that hellish desert where so many other troopers had died. I reckon it most likely was his hate for the Yankees what was keepin' him goin'. He still was blamin' them for his gettin' shot and swore that he'd live to even the score. I'd never seen anybody what hated Yankees as much as Jim did. It jest warn't natural. He hadn't said anything lately about my bein' to blame for his gettin' shot or that he wanted to kill me — I shore hoped he'd got over that crazy notion. When we got to Fort Bliss, I took Jim straight to the hospital. He was as hot as a two-dollar pistol, and his shoulder was red and swollen. The doctor said it was a miracle he was still alive. When I told him how Jim was sick in the head, too, and explained how he'd been actin', he told me not to worry. Now that he was back in Texas, he'd most likely get over it real quick.

A few days later, I run into Colonel Heffiner when he was comin' out of regimental headquarters. He'd been helpin' General Sibley draft a report to President Davis and the southern leaders in Richmond, explainin' why the campaign had failed. The general claimed it was partly due to the lack of support from the folks what lived in New Mexico and to the terrible, rough country and lack of food. But mainly he blamed the Pike's Peakers for destroyin' his supplies up at Johnson's Ranch. He claimed if it warn't for them, he wouldn't have had a bit of trouble in completing the rest of his mission.

When the colonel heard Jim was in the hospital, he asked if he could go see him. I told him yes, but he might be pretty grumpy. When we got to Jim's room, he was lyin' on his bed scowlin' up at the ceilin'.

But when he seen Colonel Heffiner, he brightened up and, right off, asked the colonel when he was figurin' on makin' a raid up in Colorado. The colonel smiled and told him he had no plans at the moment, but if he ever did go, we'd be the first to know about it. But for right now, he was goin' to San Antonio with General Sibley so's to help him muster his men out of the army. After that, he warn't quite shore what he'd do. More'n likely he'd go with the general when he got a new command.

Well, that warn't what Jim wanted to hear, and he got real upset. In a raspy whisper I could scarcely hear, he told the colonel he didn't give a tinker's damn what he did — he could rot in hell as far as he was concerned. When he got strong enough, he was gonna do it with or without the colonel's help, 'cause he had a score to settle with them rotten Yankees for all the grief and misery they'd caused him, and he had another score to settle, too — then he looked straight at me. 'Course, that shook me up considerable, and I'm shore it did the colonel, too, 'cause he didn't say another word to Jim, 'ceptin' that he hoped he'd get well quick. Then he said good-bye and left. It was a mighty short visit.

After we was outside Jim's room, I apologized to the colonel for what Jim had said. I explained how he'd been actin' strange ever since he'd got shot, and how sometimes he seemed mad at the whole world — even mad at me. But what I couldn't figure out was why Jim hated the Yankees so much for shootin' him. 'Course they'd shot him — jest like he'd been tryin' to shoot them, but that's what soldiers is supposed to do. The colonel shook his head and said it was strange how the war affected some people more than others, but that he was shore Jim would get over it once he got home. That was the same thing the doctor had told me, and it warn't a bit of help. Before we parted company, I told the colonel how he could get in touch with us in case he ever did make a raid up to Colorado. Then we said good-bye and that was the last I ever seen or heard of Colonel Heffiner.

On the fourteenth of May, jest four months after they'd marched up the Rio Grande with their minds filled with dreams of glory, General Sibley and what was left of his little army began the long march back to San Antonio. 'Course, me and Jim didn't go with them. Colonel Heffiner had fixed it so we'd be mustered out of the army at Fort Bliss after Jim got strong enough to head for home. A little over a month later, he was, and we did. Horses was in real short supply, but I finally managed to scrape up a couple of sorry lookin' nags. They was both considerably older than me, but I figured they'd most likely get us home all right, and they did — but just barely. Jim warn't in no better shape than the horses — maybe not even as good — but I figured them old horses should work out jest fine, seein' as how we was gonna have to take it slow and easy.

As it turned out, it was mainly slow but not too easy. The fourth day out of Fort Bliss the wind come up, and it started to rain hard and steady. For the next five days and nights it never let up, and I was beginnin' to think Mamma was wrong when she told us how God had promised never to send another great flood. But finally the rain did stop and the sun come out — then it got hot and muggy — and there shore warn't no rainbow like there was in the Bible story. Another reason it was slow goin' was on account of we had to stop a lot so's Jim and the horses could rest. Every day, Jim kept gettin' weaker and his pain kept gettin' worse. The doctor had gave me a big supply of laudanum before we left Fort Bliss, but by the second week I was havin' to give it more'n more often, and I was afeard it was gonna run out.

Then Jim's fever come back, and sometimes he'd rant and rave like he was plumb out of his mind — cussin' out me and God and anythin' else he could think of. I tried spongin' him off so's to cool him down, but then I got to worryin' we'd run out of water and he'd die of thirst before we got home. But we didn't, and he didn't, and finally, late one afternoon, after a little over a month in the saddle, we was home.

CHAPTER 32

Jim and our horses looked like they was damn near dead, and I reckon I didn't look a whole lot better. Whilst I was strugglin' to get Jim down off'n his horse, everythin' was quiet 'til Sadie came around the corner of the house carryin' a bucketful of water. When she seen us, she gave out a loud whoop and come runnin' over to us whilst sloshin' most of the water out onto the ground. First off, she threw her arms around me and gave me a big kiss on the mouth — then she started to go over to Jim so's to give him a hug, but she stopped short when she saw how sickly he looked. He'd got so skinny his bones was stickin' out like a skeleton, and his skin was pale and ghostly lookin', even though he'd been ridin' for weeks out in the sun and wind. Before he'd got shot, he was a good bit heavier than me — I was a mite taller, but he had a lot more muscle. But now he was leanin' on his pore old horse, tryin' to keep from fallin' down, and it was hard to tell which one of the two looked the sorrier. As a matter of fact, I think they was both proppin' theirselfs up on each other, hopin' the other one wouldn't fall over. Once Sadie got over the shock of seein' Jim, she hustled over to him and gave him a gentle hug and a peck on the cheek. You could tell she was real worried, but she didn't ask no questions, jest put her arm around him to keep him from fallin' as he tried to walk towards the house. I got on his other side, and between us we got him into the kitchen and seated in a chair by the table. I asked Sadie where our folks was, and she told me our mamma was out back of the house, feedin' the chickens, and daddy was down by the barn doin' chores. When Mamma seen me comin', she was so happy I hated to have to spoil it for her by tellin' her about Jim — but I did and she took it pretty well. I think she'd been expectin' even worse — at least he warn't kilt, she said. After that, Mamma headed for the house to see about Jim, whilst I went to find Daddy. Like always, he didn't seem 'specially upset when I told him about Jim.

When we got back to the house, Mamma was tryin' to get Jim's shirt off so's to see how bad he was hurt. Sadie was helpin' her, and it warn't long before they had him cleaned up and stretched out on his bed in our old room. Jim looked better already, and I could tell he was mighty glad to be home. In fact, it seemed to me that he was likin' Sadie's attention a lot more than I figured he should, and I've gotta say it didn't please me none.

After Jim was asleep, I told our folks and Sadie what all had happened to us since we'd left. 'Course, they was all sad to hear about Billy Joe gettin' kilt, but Sadie was the most upset. She said she hoped he'd knowed how grateful she was to him for helpin' her out up in Denver, 'cause if it hadn't been for Billy Joe, she'd most likely still be in jail. When I finished tellin' them how Jim had got shot and about that terrible march across the desert, Mamma shook her head and said what a terrible thing war was, and how foolish. She was shore that most all the differences amongst men could be settled peaceably if only they'd jest take the time to talk to each other. If they was to do that, and both sides was willin' to settle for a little less than what they wanted, more'n likely they could come to some kind of understandin' without all of the needless bloodshed and killin'.

After we'd been home a few days, things pretty much settled into a routine. I spent most of my time helpin' out with the chores, and it warn't long before I was gettin' mighty damned tired of mendin' corral fences, herdin' cattle, and brandin' calves. But it was work what had to get done — leastwise that's what my daddy kept sayin'. All the time I was workin, Jim was slowly gettin' better, and even though his body was mendin', he still had a terrible anger inside him. But at least he'd quit blamin' me for his gettin' shot, and I was glad of that. But I shore didn't like the way things was goin' between him and Sadie. I figured that Jim was enjoyin' Sadie's attention way too much, and that he warn't tryin' very hard to get well. In fact, I was pretty shore Jim was sweet on Sadie. 'Course, that bothered me some, but what bothered me the most was that Sadie seemed to be enjoyin' takin' care of Jim a lot more that I figured she should. I fretted about it so much I could hardly think of anything else, 'til finally I couldn't stand it no more, and I told her flat out how I felt. She jest laughed and said I was bein' silly, but I still warn't convinced.

Not long after that, Jim started gettin' worse, and I felt guilty for havin' such thoughts. He'd stopped eatin', his fever come back, and his shoulder and arm was hurtin' him real bad again. He talked crazy, too — like he was fightin' the Yankees back at Valverde or Glorieta Pass. Sometimes he'd holler out and talk like he was shootin' at somebody — cussin' and sayin' things what was awful to hear — like he was havin' a nightmare. But most of the time his eyes was wide open, and he kept lookin' around the room like he was scared of somethin' or someone. Then all of a sudden that would stop, and he'd jest lie there starin' up at the ceilin' with his eyes wide open — not even blinkin'. Sometimes it was hard to tell if he was alive or dead.

It was real scary to see him like that and nobody knowed what to do. Mamma and Sadie was about wore out, and me and Daddy was havin' to spell them more'n more often so's they could get some rest and keep from goin' crazy theirselves. We'd been givin' Jim laudanum what my folks kept on hand at the ranch in case of an accident, and we was about out, so Daddy asked me to hightail it down to San Antonio so's to get some more and to ask Doctor Wheelock if he would come up and take a look at Jim.

I rode jest as fast as I could go, stoppin' only a few times to rest my horse. Doctor Wheelock agreed to go back to the ranch with me, and whilst he was gettin' ready to go, his wife, Janet, fed me a real good meal. After that we took off for the ranch. When we got there, the doctor took one look at Jim's arm and said it was a wonder he was still alive. The bone in his upper arm what was busted by the bullet was infected so bad that it rightfully should be taken off — but if he did, he was shore Jim would die. He told us that Jim's chances for livin' was mighty slim, no matter what he did, but there was a few things we could try that might help. If Jim was real tough, he might jest make it.

After a big dose of laudanum for the pain, the doctor cut away the part of Jim's shoulder muscle what was gangrenous. When he'd finished with that, he gave my mother a red liquid and told her to flush out the wound with it three or four times a day. Then he took a little jar filled with maggots out of his bag. After Mamma finished flushin' out Jim's shoulder, the doctor put three or four of them ugly things in the wound and told her to leave them there for three or four days, so's they could eat up the rotted flesh. Then she should put on some new ones. Them maggots looked jest like the little white worms I'd seen crawlin' on dead critters at the ranch, only they was bigger. If Jim had knowed what the doctor was doin' he'd have died right off. But as it turned out, by the time he knowed what was goin' on, the maggots had done their job — and believe it or not, it worked.

A month later, Jim's fever was gone and he was slowly gettin' better. Even though his right arm was real crooked and stiff, it was finally healin'. But Jim never got anywheres close to normal after that — leastwise, not in his head. We'd got home from Fort Bliss about the middle of July 1862, and Jim didn't get out of bed until January '63. And even then, all he could do was to set around and mope. By the middle of August, he was finally able to help out around the ranch some — or would have been, if he was of a mind to. Now'n then he'd do a little chore, but mostly he jest sat around complainin' and feelin' sorry for hisself.

After Jim had got most of his strength back, Mamma and Sadie quit doin' things for him and started treatin' him same as they treated the rest of us. From then on Jim got restless and even more irritable and would get mad and argue over little no-account things — not jest with me, but with Mamma and Daddy, too. I knowed they was worried about the way he was actin', but they never let on that they was. 'Ceptin' for one time, when Mamma'd told me how she figured the war had changed the way Jim felt about life somehow and that she felt real sorry for him. Sadie was the only one he was always nice to, and if we was close by when she was there, he was always nice to us, too.

One day in early October of '63, Jim told me he was gonna go crazy if he stuck around the ranch any longer doin' piddlin' little chores for Daddy. He was sick of it and needed some real action. He was fig- urin' on ridin' down to San Antonio and wanted me to go along so's I could help him learn the whereabouts of Colonel Heffiner and see if he still figured on raidin' the gold fields up in Colorado. He claimed we'd be gone for two weeks. It sounded great to me — I was tired of doin' chores, too, and besides that, maybe if he was to get away for a spell, it'd help him get back to his old self again. I figured our folks was gonna be upset when they heard me and Jim was goin' to San Antonio — Daddy 'specially, on account of he'd be losin' two of his work crew. But I was wrong — they was happy we was goin' — most likely on account of they figured it'd be a big relief to have Jim gone for a spell. Sadie shore didn't like it, though, but I couldn't tell which one of us she was gonna miss the most, and it bothered me. 'Specially so when, jest as we was leavin', I gave Sadie a hug and a kiss, and then Jim up and kissed her and hugged her, too. That upset me. But she seemed to like it. Now that made me mad. It was the middle of October when we got to San Antonio, and the first thing I wanted to do was to go say hello to Billy Joe's folks. For a long time now, I'd wanted to tell them how Billy Joe had lost his life whilst savin' mine, and how he was a real hero. I asked Jim to go 'long with me, but he said I could do what I damn well pleased. He was gonna spend his time doing what he wanted to do, not visitin' some old folks he hardly knowed. He was headin' for the nearest saloon to see if he could find some of his old army buddies. Before we split up, we agreed to meet later in the day in the lobby of the San Antonio Hotel — that's where we figured we'd be stayin' whilst we was in town.

The Barlows was mighty happy to see me — 'specially so after I'd explained to them what a hero Billy Joe was and how he'd saved my life. Nobody had ever told them that before, and they was mighty proud to hear it. Billy Joe was their only child, so now they was all alone, and I'm shore they was real lonely. They wanted me and Jim to stay with them whilst we was in San Antonio. They seemed so excited by the idea, I jest couldn't say no, but I told them I doubted Jim would take them up on their offer, 'cause I was pretty shore he had other plans.

After supper, I went to the hotel to see Jim, but he warn't anywheres around, so I asked the desk clerk if he'd checked in yet. He hadn't, so I waited in the lobby. But when he hadn't showed up by nine o'clock, I left a message with the night clerk sayin' I was spendin' the night at the Barlows and that I'd see him at the hotel come mornin'. Come mornin', Jim still hadn't registered, and as far as the night clerk knowed, nobody'd even seen him. Well, that got me to worryin' — maybe somethin' bad had happened to him.

San Antonio warn't too big a town, so I figured it shouldn't be too hard to find him. First off, I went over to the jail and talked to the sheriff, but he didn't know nothin' about him and suggested I check the other hotels and boardin' houses in town. I doubted Jim would have gone to any hotel other than the one we'd talked about, so I decided I'd first check out all of the saloons in town. That's where Jim said he was headin', so maybe he was still holed up in one of them. It warn't somethin' he'd ordinarily do, but then he'd changed considerable.

There shore was a lot of saloons in San Antonio, but I finally found him settin' at a table with four other fellas in the back of the Red Rooster Saloon. He looked terrible, like he hadn't slept all night, and I guess he hadn't. He hadn't shaved since leavin' the ranch, and his lower face was covered with the straggliest set of whiskers I'd ever seen. His clothes was stained with spilled food and whiskey, and his eyes was bloodshot and bleary. I couldn't tell whether they was that way from lack of sleep or from the booze. When he seen me, he raised his hand, waved me over to the table, and told me to join them. That didn't appeal to me a whole lot, but I sat down anyway — and I want to tell you, that was as tough a lookin' bunch of hombres as yore ever likely to see, Jim included. Each of them was holdin' a handful of greasy cards. A loose pile of poker chips was out in the middle of the table, and each player had a stack in front of him, 'long with a dirty whiskey glass. An overly plump bar girl kept fillin' them back up jest as quick as they was drained.

I'd never seen anythin' quite like her before, and I won't mind a bit if I never do again. She had more rouge and paint on her face than I'd ever seen on any of the girls at the Criterion in Denver, or anywhere else for that matter. Her dress was so skimpy and fit so tight it looked like parts of her was gonna pop out of it 'most any time. I ain't gonna say which parts.

I really didn't care to make their acquaintance, but Jim introduced me to his four buddies anyhow. They was a mighty sleazy bunch, and I hate sayin' it, but Jim was the sleaziest of the lot. One of them was a long, lanky cowboy named Owen Singleterry and another's name was Tom Holliman — both of them was pretty forgettable characters. The third fella's name I've plumb forgot, but I shore do remember the fourth one. His name was Rafer Rathbone, and even though he warn't a fella I 'specially wanted to remember, I had no choice, 'cause — 'long with Singleterry and Holliman — I was to meet him again at a later time and another place, and much to my regret.

Rathbone was tall and skinny. His shoulders was hunched forward and his chest sort of caved in, makin' him look like he was walkin' into the wind even when he was standin' still. His face was thin, his cheeks sunken, and his dark, muddy lookin' eyes glared out of deep, cadaverous eye sockets overhung by shaggy, black eyebrows. His hair was black, too, and slicked down with some kind of grease. His clothes hung loose on his scrawny frame, and his ugly appearance was equaled only by his surly attitude and lack of good manners. He had all the charm and personality of a rattlesnake. All things considered, he shore warn't a fella you'd want to take home to meet yore family, and I couldn't understand why in tarnation Jim seemed so attracted to him.

I hung around the Red Rooster Saloon 'til Jim's poker game finally broke up. He was pretty pleased with hisself, 'cause he'd come out a winner by close to fifty dollars. I told him about the Barlows' hospitable offer, but Jim said to forget it — he'd rather hang around with his new-found buddies. He hadn't been able to locate Colonel Heffiner, but somebody'd told him that he'd left San Antonio for good and gone back East somewheres. So if we was gonna go up to Colorado so's to liberate gold for the southern cause and bring our own gold down from the Tarryalls, we was gonna have to get together a bunch of men and supplies and make the raid ourselves. I told Jim we'd best think it over for a while. I didn't ask him, but I had a feelin' what Jim had in mind was to recruit his poker playin' buddies as part of the raidin' party and that didn't appeal to me one damned bit.

I told Jim that I'd be in San Antonio for two or three more days and then head back to the ranch. I'd already seen all I wanted of city life. He told me if I went, I'd be goin' by myself then, on account of he was stayin' close to the Red Rooster Saloon so's he could keep gamblin'. He said I should check back with him in a couple of days, jest in case he'd changed his mind. When I checked two days later, he was still winnin' and was gonna stay put for awhile longer, and if I still wanted to leave, I could go without him — so that's what I did. The next day I got my horse from the livery stable, told the Barlows good-bye, and headed back to the ranch.

CHAPTER 33

Sadie had seen me comin' and was waitin' for me when I rode up, and the second I was out of the saddle she started huggin' and kissin' me and tellin' me how happy she was I'd come home. Well, I gotta tell you, that made me feel like I was ten feet tall — at least it did 'til she quit huggin' and kissin' me and started lookin' around for Jim. When she didn't see him, she looked real worried, like she was afeared somethin' bad had happened to him and I got to wonderin' if she'd been missin' him more than me. That bothered me a lot, and lookin' back at it now, I reckon it was pretty stupid — but it didn't seem so right then. But I didn't say nothin', I jest told her Jim had stayed in San Antonio so's to visit some friends and that he'd be gettin' home later.

For the next couple of days, I tried not to think about Sadie and Jim, but I might as well have tried to forget about breathin'. I jest couldn't put it out of my mind, and it kept eatin' at me 'til I finally couldn't stand it no more, and I asked Sadie flat out how she felt about Jim. Was she in love with him? After I'd finished sayin' my piece, Sadie jest stood there shakin' her head.

"What in the world ever gave you that silly idea, John? I thought you knew by now that it's you I love. I fell in love with you the first time I saw you at the Criterion up in Denver. You were always so nice to me and treated me like a lady — some of the others didn't. And I'm even more in love with you now since I've gotten to know you better. Of course, I like Jim, too, but more like a brother."

From that time on, if I'd had my druthers, I'd have spent all my time with Sadie. 'Course, I couldn't, 'cause I was so busy doin' chores. Right after me and Jim had left for San Antonio, some spooky horses had knocked down a corral fence and Daddy wanted me and Jake to mend it. Jake was the freed slave I talked about earlier, and we got to be real good friends. He was the blackest fella I'd ever seen, and when he smiled — which was a lot — his teeth was the whitest I'd ever seen, too. He had black, smiley eyes and even blacker curly hair, which was cropped real close to his scalp. Jake was most a head taller than me, and that's sayin' a lot, 'cause I'm a little over six foot myself. And was he ever strong. He could lift me easy — like I was a feather — and back then I weighed close to 180 pounds.

When Jim finally showed up, it was close to Christmas, and the first thing he did was to give Sadie a real tight hug and a kiss on the cheek. That got me all upset again. Mamma got all excited thinkin' he'd come home to help us celebrate Jesus' birthday. But then he told us he'd jest come by to tell us hello and good-bye, on account of he had somethin' important to do somewheres else — he didn't say what or where. Jim was dressed fit to kill in brand new store-bought clothes, shiny new boots with silver spurs, and a fine lookin' ten-gallon hat. Not only that, he was packin' a pair of pearl-handled Colts that turned me pea-green with envy. Mamma asked him how he'd come by the money to buy all them fancy duds and guns, but Jim wouldn't say. Later, after he was gone, I told Mamma I figured he'd most likely won the money gamblin', but I warn't entirely shore that was true. I had a bad feelin' that Jim and his mangy friends had been helpin' theirselfs to other people's money.

The next time Jim come to the ranch was over three months later, in early March of '64. To tell you the truth, I hadn't missed him much — mainly on account of I was busy most all the time. Between sparkin' Sadie and keepin' Daddy happy, I didn't have time to worry about what my brother was up to. When Jim did show up, he didn't come alone. There was eight other men with him, and they shore was a rough lookin' lot, and I'm sorry to say I recognized four of them. They was the same hombres I'd met at the Red Rooster Saloon in San Antonio, and I warn't at all happy to be meetin' up with them again. I could tell that Mamma and Daddy warn't happy to be meetin' up with them for the first time. I told Sadie to keep out of sight as much as she could, 'cause I didn't want any of Jim's bunch gettin' crazy ideas. She said not to worry, she could take care of herself — but I noticed she took my advice anyway, and stayed close to me or my folks whenever they was around.

Jim and his bunch was headin' for a place over near Austin, but he didn't say what for. He claimed he'd come by to see how we was doin' and to tell me that he hadn't forgotten about goin' to Colorado. He was still plannin' on leadin' a raid up South Park, so's to get gold for the Confederacy and to bring our own gold down out of the

Tarryalls — but that it was gonna have to wait 'til late summer, 'cause he needed time to recruit more men. So far he had ten signed up, not includin' me and him, and he was hopin' to find at least ten or twelve more, but that it was gonna take time to find men he could trust. I wondered what made him think he could trust the ones he already had — 'specially that Rathbone fella. And I shore didn't want any of this bunch of toughs knowin' where our gold was hid. When I pointed that out to Jim, he said for me not to worry — they was jest comin' 'long with us so's to help out on the raid, and that we'd figure out how to bring our gold out later.

Jim and his bunch stayed at the ranch for two nights and a day, and we was all mighty happy when they left — 'specially me, 'cause Jim kept shinin' up to Sadie. After they was gone, Jake asked me who them fellas was, that they shore was a mean lookin' bunch, 'specially that skinny Rathbone fella. He was the spittin' image of what he figured the devil would look like if he ever had the misfortune of meetin' up with him face to face.

By now Jake was my very best friend. I trusted him like he was my own brother — a lot more, as a matter of fact. I told Jake how me and Jim had been hopin' to collect our gold in the Tarryalls when we was up in South Park with Colonel Heffiner's outfit. But when that fell through, I was figurin' that we'd wait and do it after the war was over. But now I had serious doubts that would happen, 'cause I was pretty shore Jim and his buddies was figurin' on stealin' my share of the gold so's they could divvy it up amongst theirselfs, and there was no way in God's green earth I'd let that happen.

Jake asked me why Jim would want to share our gold with all them fellas when he could jest spilt it half and half with me. I told him I didn't know for shore, but I figured he owed a lot of gamblin' debts to some of the fellas in his gang and was plannin' to use my share to pay it back. Jake was still puzzled. If that was true, why would Jim want me to go 'long with them? He'd know I'd make a big ruckus if he tried to give them my half of the gold. Jim and his gang could jest as easy go up to Colorado, get my gold and go back to Texas without my ever knowin' about it — and when I found out it was gone, I'd never be able to prove it was them what took it.

I told Jake he was right, but I figured Jim needed my help in findin' the cave where the gold was hid. Back in '60, when we was workin' our mine, Jim never could find it without me showin' him how, so he probably figured he'd still need my help. Jake said he reckoned that made sense, but he still couldn't believe Jim would do such a rotten thing to his brother jest to get more gold. I told him I shore hoped he was right, but that there was somethin' else what worried me even more. Then I explained how Jim had blamed me for his gettin' shot up on Glorieta Pass, and how he'd threatened to kill me so's to even up the score. 'Course, he hadn't said nothin' about it lately, and I was hopin' it was the laudanum what made him talk that way. But I had a strong feelin' he'd really meant it and was figurin' on killin' me so's to get even and steal my share of the gold at the same time.

Well, that really shook Jake up. He couldn't believe that Jim would kill his own brother — no matter what the reason. But after I reminded him of the Bible story about Cain and Abel, he scratched his head and said well, maybe to be on the safe side, I'd best not go, but he still didn't think Jim would do that. I told Jake I shore hoped he was right, but whichever way it was, I was goin'. I'd worked too damned hard for that gold to lose it now, not if I could help it. Jake shook his head. He still didn't think I should, he said, but if I was set on goin', he was gonna ask my daddy if'n he could go 'long with me so's to keep me out of trouble. I told Jake I'd be mighty grateful if he did, but that I doubted my daddy would be willin' to let his best hand go. As it turned out, I was wrong. I reckon Daddy didn't trust Jim's gang any more than I did, 'cause he agreed to Jake's goin' right off — jest as long as we made it back in time for the fall roundup.

The rest of the spring of '64 went by real quick, and in no time at all it was June. We hadn't seen hide nor hair of Jim and his gang since they'd left the ranch, but when I heard about a big bank robbery over in Austin where a couple of bank guards got kilt, I wondered if by any chance Jim and his gang had somethin' to do with it. I wondered even more after readin' a two-month-old article in a San Antonio newspaper what said there was nine men in the gang. As far as I knowed, my folks and Sadie never saw the article, and I burned it to make shore they wouldn't. I did tell Jake what I suspected, though. It was mighty good to have a friend to share my worries with. 'Course, I spent 'most all my spare time with Sadie talkin' a lot about our future. I told her what I wanted most in this world was for me and her to get married, live in a home of our own, and fill with it love and children — but it was gonna have to wait 'til after I got back from Colorado. Then I explained to her how me and Jim would be makin' a raid up in South Park so's to help the Confederacy right after him and his men got back to the ranch — and that we'd be bringin' our gold down out of the Tarryalls at the same time. A little later that day, I told Mamma the same things I told Sadie. 'Course I never told either of them what all I'd told Jake — I didn't want them worryin' none. But they worried anyway — 'specially Mamma. 'Course she'd seen the bunch of hard cases Jim was ridin' with, and she warn't stupid — far from it. I'm shore that she, like me, had been won-derin' what kind of mischief Jim was up to. She told me I shouldn't go, and that I should forget about the gold, marry Sadie, and settle down here on the ranch. There was a lot of things in this world more impor-tant than wealth. Then she told me I should talk it over with my daddy, and I told her I already had, and how he'd said he didn't think I should go either, but that he wouldn't try to stop me, on account of I was growed-up now and should make my own decisions. Mamma didn't say nothin' after that, 'ceptin' to tell me how she'd be prayin' for us to come home safe and sound.

We didn't have much longer to wait. Two days later, jest as we was settin' down to supper, we heard the drummin' of horse's hooves and looked out to see close to twenty riders reinin' their horses to a stop in front of the house. After the cloud of dust settled, Jim got off of his horse and come swaggerin' towards us. He was wearin' the same fancy clothes as before, 'ceptin' they looked a mite ragged and covered with dust. And he was still packin' his pearl-handled revolvers, but now he was wearin' them slung low and tied to his leg — gunfighter style.

Jim stomped onto the front porch, dustin' off his clothes with his hat as he come. He didn't waste no time sayin' hello or anythin' friend-ly like that. He jest told us they'd be leavin' early next mornin' and for Mamma to fix him and his men supper. It sounded like he was givin' her an order, and I could tell it upset her — but she didn't say nothin'. After that, Jim told me him and his outfit would be leavin' at sunup and for me to be on time, 'cause they shore as hell warn't gonna wait for me. When I told him that I'd be there and so would Jake, Jim didn't seem too pleased. I was pretty shore Jim didn't want Jake goin' with us, and I knowed why.

All the time he was there, Jim didn't say a word to our folks — 'ceptin' to give them orders — that made me mad. Instead, he spent most of his time sweet-talkin' Sadie — that made me a whole lot madder. He told her how she was gettin' prettier every time he'd seen her and some other real flatterin' things, and I was about to tell him to cut it out when one of his men called to him from outside and he left. I could tell my folks was upset by the way Jim was actin', but they didn't say nothin'. They jest set back down at the table and started pickin' at their cold supper.

After Mamma and Sadie had fixed food for Jim and his men, they took it out to them. I went along so's to lend them a hand. Jim didn't even say thanks — he jest told Mamma to have breakfast ready real early next mornin', 'cause they'd be leavin' right at sunup. The rest of that evenin' we didn't see much of Jim, and whenever he did show up, it was to give us orders and flirt with Sadie. I could tell my folks was sick at heart over the way he was actin', 'cause they headed off to bed a lot earlier than usual. They claimed they both was feelin' poorly. Mamma had tears in her eyes.

Later that evenin' Jim stopped me when I was goin' out to Jake's cabin. He told me that if me and Jake was goin' on the raid, we'd have to sign a pledge of loyalty and swear an oath of allegiance to the Confederate States of America. His men had already signed it. That was so we could prove we was makin' the raid on behalf of the Confederacy if we got caught by the Yankees up in Colorado. At the time, I didn't say nothin' to Jim, but I figured it'd take a mighty dumb Yankee to believe that. After that, Jim reached into his pocket, pulled out a little logbook, and handed me a piece of paper. He told me to sign it. I told him maybe I would, but I'd best read it first. This is what it said: "I swear Allegiance to the Confederate States of America and to its President and all its officers appointed over me. I swear to aid or assist all true Southern men and their families, wherever they may be, at a reasonable risk to my own life whether in the army or out of it. So help me God." I couldn't see any good reason not to sign it, but I doubted the oath meant the same to some of the hard cases in Jim's outfit as it did to me.

After I'd signed it, I asked Jim what made him think any of his gang was gonna honor that oath. From what I could see, they warn't nothin' but a bunch of no-good scoundrels he'd dredged up from the San Antonio saloons and whorehouses, and I was shore that not one of them low-lifes gave a tinker's damn about the Confederate cause. They'd end up keepin' all the gold and loot for theirselves. And I shore as hell didn't want them knowin' where our gold was hid — 'specially that scruffy Rathbone fella. They'd no doubt steal it and kill us, too. Jim damn near bit my head off. He said it didn't make a damned bit of difference to him what I thought of his men, and that I had them figured all wrong. They really was fine fellas — jest a little rough around the edges — and Rafer was the smartest one of the bunch. At least Jim was right about that last part. Rafer was smart, all right — a lot smarter than Jim.

After I signed the pledge, I took it over to Jake's cabin so's he could sign it, too. I figured I'd have to read it to him and show him where to make his mark, but as it turned out, he could read as good as me — maybe better. Now I'd come to think about it, he talked a lot better than me, too. After Jake finished signin', I asked him where he'd learned to read so good. He told me how the folks what had owned him back in Louisiana had taught all of their slaves how to read and write, even though it was against the law. They really didn't like ownin' slaves, but they had no other choice, 'cause without them, they couldn't raise cotton. His owner's name was Jefferson, and his parents used it for their name, too — that's how come Jake's last name was Jefferson. A lot of other slave families had done the same.

After that, I went back to the house so's to talk with Sadie. Even though I knowed she'd do it anyway, I asked her to keep a close eye on my folks whilst we was gone. They warn't gettin' any younger, and I knowed they was worried about Jim and his gang — 'specially now that I was ridin' off with them. I told Sadie she needn't worry about me and that I'd be back in no time — and after that, we'd all be rich. She gave me a hug and told me she didn't care one whit about bein' rich, all she wanted was for me to come back safe and sound. Then she helped me get my outfit together and after that we talked — neither one wanted to tell the other good-bye. We jest sat there holdin' each other tight. It was real late when we finally said good night.

The next mornin' I was up well before rooster crow, but Sadie was already out in the kitchen fixin' breakfast for the whole bunch of us, and it warn't long before Mamma, Daddy, and Jake joined us. Jim never did come in to eat with us. He never even said good-bye to our folks, and I could tell it made them feel real bad. After we'd finished eatin', Mamma asked us all to get down on our knees and bow our heads whilst she prayed for our safe return. I could tell she was real worried 'bout us, 'cause her voice broke a time or two whilst she was askin' the Lord to bring us safely home. After she finished and said amen, we all said our amens, too. After that nobody said much. Actually there warn't nothin' left to say — 'ceptin' good-bye.

CHAPTER 34

Come dawn, me and Jake mounted up and rode over to where Jim and the rest of the men was waitin'. Our folks and Sadie followed us out. At a signal from Jim, they all mounted up and rode off, headin' north in the direction of Colorado. Jim waved to Sadie and blew her a kiss, but he left without so much as a thank-you or good-bye to our folks. He didn't even look at them. Then me and Jake said our final good-byes and rode off after them. It was the twenty-third day of June 1864. All told, there was twenty-two of us in the raiding party.

For the next few days, we rode hellbent for leather from long before sunup 'til way after dark. We hardly even stopped to rest. I asked Jim how come we was in such a hurry, and he explained that we was tryin' to get to Raton Pass on the border between Colorado and New Mexico by the sixteenth of July so's to intercept a Yankee wagon train. It was comin' out of Fort Lyons up in Colorado, carryin' supplies to Fort Union, Santa Fe, and the Union forts along the Rio Grande. But, accordin' to Rafer's cousin in the disbursing department at Fort Lyons, it also was carryin' a forty thousand dollar payroll down to the troopers in New Mexico. Seems that, even though Rafer's cousin was a corporal in the Yankee army and supposedly loyal to the Union, he was even more loyal to Rafer.

Now this was more what I'd been hopin' for — maybe this raid would be for the good, after all. This way, we could take the payroll from the Yankees, head to the Tarryalls, collect our gold, and be back in Texas before the Yankees ever figured out what was goin' on. But I'm sorry to say that warn't how it happened. We got to Raton Pass by the sixteenth all right, but I'm not gonna tell you much of what happened there, 'cause it's somethin' I'd like to forget. When it was over, I counted twelve dead bodies — none of them ours. Our bunch kept on killin' Yankees, even after they was wavin' a white flag. The whole affair made me sick. I'd already seen too much killin' at Valverde and Glorieta Pass.

After bustin' up their guns and pitchin' them into a ravine, we took their horses a far piece off and scattered them where the Yankees

couldn't find them. Then we loaded all the loot on our mules and headed north into Colorado. Two days later, we rode past the Hicklin's ranch
house in the Greenhorn Valley, but the Hicklins warn't there. I was
glad, 'cause I didn't want them seein' the sorry lookin' bunch of no-
goods I was ridin' with. We camped there for the night and next
mornin' rode up to Mace's Hole and hid most all our loot where it'd be
easy to pick up on our way back to Texas. After that, Jim and Rafer
counted the money in the strongbox, and it came to a little over 35,000
dollars — some in currency, but most of it was in gold eagles. We took
the money and the strongbox with us, figurin' we'd hide it up in South
Park so's it'd be close by if we had to head back to Texas in a hurry. The
next night we camped on top of Currant Crick, and the night after that
we was the uninvited guests of Adolph Guiraud and his wife. First off,
they seemed happy to see us again, but then they seen the roughlookin'
bunch we was with, and they warn't near as friendly after that. 'Specially
after Rafer Rathbone and a couple of his cronies started talkin' nasty to
Mrs. Guiraud and treatin' her like she was a shady lady. I told them to
quit it and that she was a really nice lady, but Rafer jest laughed and told
me to simmer down — they was jest funnin' around. I was about to say
more, but I didn't have to, 'cause right about then Mr. Guiraud started
loadin' his shotgun with buckshot. Rafer and his cronies quit foolin'
around with her real quick after that.

By now I was sorry I'd ever come on this damned raid — I was
ready to quit and go home. I told Jim how I felt and how I figured we'd
best go back to Texas before we got caught and strung up by the
Yankees. We already had thirty-five thousand dollars and all the loot
we'd stashed at Mace's Hole, and I figured that was plenty. Jim told me
to forget it. He was the leader of this outfit, and we'd quit and go home
when he said and not before. Besides, Mr. Guiraud had told him about
a big gold strike at the New Orphan Boy Mine up near Buckskin, and,
if what Adolph told him was true, Billy McClelland's Denver and
South Park stage would be leavin' Buckskin early next mornin', carryin'
bars of gold bullion and currency to be deposited in the Denver banks.
If'n it was on time, it should be pullin' into the stage stop at
McLaughlin's Ranch 'long about noon, and Jim figured we'd meet it
and save them the trouble of havin' to take it all the way to Denver.

'Course, we'd both knowed Billy back in '60 and '61 and knowed where the stage stop was up near Hamilton — leastwise, where it was back then. It'd been owned by a fella named Stubbs. I wondered how Jim got Mr. Guiraud to tell him all that, but I didn't ask. I doubted I'd like hearin' the answer. After Mrs. Guiraud fed us supper that night, we all bedded down in their barn, and come mornin', she fed us breakfast and we left — but, I'm sorry to say, not before two of the no-goods in our outfit stole the Guiraud's money and one of their horses. One of them — I 'spect you know who — even promised Mrs. Guiraud that he'd be stoppin' by on his way back to Texas so's they could have some more fun and good times together.

After leavin' the Guirauds, we hightailed it to the north end of the Park so's to get to the stage stop before the stage. When we got there, we tied up Dan McLaughlin, the stage stop owner, and Major H. H. DeMary, a fella what was waitin' for the stage. He claimed he was the owner of a rich gold mine over in California Gulch on the west side of Mosquito Pass. But Rafer and his buddies figured he was lyin', 'cause he only had a measly hundred dollars in his wallet. Then they stole it, his hat, and his wallet and started pushin' him back and forth between them. But, luckily for the major, the stagecoach showed up right then, so they quit messin' around with him and trussed him up along side Dan.

Even before the dust had settled, we all rushed out and surrounded the stagecoach — some of us pointed our rifles at the doors and others at Abe Williamson, the driver. Billy McClelland, one of the owners of the stage line, was the only passenger. We made both of them get down off'n the stage and come inside the station, where we tied them up. Whilst we was doin' it, Billy looked first at me, then at Jim. Then he hollered over to Dan.

"Say, Dan, don't these two fellers look kinda familiar?"

"They shore as hell do, Billy," McLaughlin hollered back. "Them's the Reynolds brothers what was in these parts a few years back. That there older one is Jim. I don't recollect the young one's name."

Bein' recognized didn't make me feel too good, but it didn't seem to bother Jim a bit — leastwise, it didn't stop him from stealin' 400 dollars, a revolver, and a fancy gold watch from off'n Billy. Then we dragged the strongbox out from under the driver's seat and lifted it down to the ground. It was real heavy, so we figured there must be a lot of gold in it — and we was right. There was close to thirty gold ingots in the bottom of the box, and on top of that was stacks of paper currency — mostly in hundred dollar bills. All together, it came to a little over thirty thousand dollars.

After loadin' the gold and money on our mules, our gang mounted up and rode off towards the northeast end of the Park. Me and Jake was bringin' up the rear and ridin' slower than the rest, so's to let them get ahead of us. When they was clear out of sight, we headed back to the stage stop. I was afeared that Rafer had tied the major's arms and legs up so tight that the ropes was keepin' the blood from gettin' into his hands and feet. As it turned out, I was right — he was bad off. His hands and feet was all swole up and blue, so I loosened the ropes a little. I figured in time he could work hisself loose — then he could free the others.

Before we left, I apologized for the way we'd treated them, and explained how me and Jake had come on the raid thinkin' we was gonna steal gold to help the Confederacy win the war. But, as it'd turned out, some fellas in our outfit was stealin' the gold for theirselves. And, besides that, they was treatin' people bad — somethin' a real southerner would never do. Me and Jake wished now that we could quit and go back to Texas — but we dasn't, 'cause if we did, some the leaders of our gang would kill us.

As we was leavin', they all thanked us for our help and promised that they'd put a good word in for us when we was caught so we wouldn't get hung. Well, that got me to thinkin': Up to then, I'd never thought about what would happen to me if'n I was to get caught. I'd jest figured it'd never happen, but now I warn't so shore. Before long, everybody in South Park was gonna hear about our gang, and we'd have a posse of mad Yankees hot on our trail. We'd be lucky to get back to Texas without gettin' our necks stretched. They'd no doubt hang us right off, and Major DeMary's kind words about us would come way too late to do us any good. I told Jake what I was thinkin' about and he agreed.

We was ridin' fast, so's to catch up with our raidin' party, when we seen Jim and Rafer hightailin' it back in our direction. They asked us what the hell we'd been doin'. I asked Jim what his problem was, we'd jest had to stop a little ways back so's to relieve ourselfs, and now we was hustlin' to catch up — but neither of them believed me. Jim knowed I didn't like the way things was goin' on this raid, and he'd probably figured that me and Jake was on our way back to Texas, and if we was, I couldn't show him where the cave was hid. 'Course, I still warn't entirely shore that's what Jim had in mind, but somethin' was shore makin' him antsy. That night, we set up camp at the northeast end of the Park near the bottom of Georgia Pass. That was to be our base of operations for the next couple of days.

After supper that evenin', Jim told me that come mornin', him and Rafer was gonna take the gold and currency we'd collected and hide it in a safe place where it'd be easy to pick up on our way back to Texas. He figured the cave was a good place to do it, and he wanted me and Jake to go 'long with them so's I could show him how to find it. 'Course, that's exactly what I figured was gonna happen, but his sayin' it still made me mad. I told Jim that there was nothin' this side of hell that'd make me help him find the cave – 'specially not if Rafer was goin' with us. Well, Jim got so mad I thought he was gonna explode. He was cussin' and yellin' at me somethin' awful, sayin' as how Rafer was goin' with us whether I liked it or not — that is, he was if I didn't want somethin' bad happenin' to Jake.

Even though I'd been expectin' it to happen, it was still hard to believe that Jim would do anything that terrible. All of the years we was growin' up together, he'd been my very best friend. Back then he never would of threatened to hurt nobody — 'specially me. He didn't like killin' things any more than I did. But then the war had come along and Jim'd changed into somebody else — somebody entirely different, somebody I'd never knowed and didn't want to know now.

But I didn't doubt for a minute that Jim and Rafer would kill Jake if I didn't do what they asked. 'Course, once they got their greedy hands on the gold, they'd no doubt kill us anyway. Then they'd fix it so nobody'd ever know what they'd done — 'specially not our folks and Sadie. So I really didn't have no choice. Come mornin' I was gonna have to go with them, and all I could do was hope and pray that somethin' would happen between now and when we got to the cave so's me and Jake could get away from them. But that warn't likely, 'cause that night

Jim and Rafer took turns stayin' awake so's to make shore me and Jake couldn't talk to each other or try to slip away. I didn't sleep a bit — I jest lay there prayin' and thinkin' and prayin' some more. Mainly I asked God to show me some way out of the terrible fix we was in.

Early next mornin', Jim explained to the others in our outfit how the four of us was gonna go and find a place to hide our loot where it'd be safe 'til we was ready to go back to Texas. Owen Singleterry was to be in charge of the rest of our gang 'til we come back, and whilst we was gone, they was to raid the Michigan House stage station over near Hamilton, 'long with some of the nearby ranches.

A little ways out from camp, where the rest of the men couldn't see what was happenin', Rafer made me and Jake give him all of our ammunition for our pistols and rifles. He claimed he'd give it back to us later if we didn't make no trouble. After that, the four of us took off headin' south with Jim in the lead, me and Jake in the middle, and Rafer bringin' up the rear. Both Jim and Rafer was leadin' a mule loaded with loot and kept their rifles across the front of their saddles, jest in case we made a break for it. We followed the same route what me and Jim took back in 1860 when we left our mine and went back to Hamilton, 'ceptin' this time in the reverse direction. By now, me and Jim's old mine really did look like an abandoned tailin's dump. The little crick was flowin' out from under it and down into the gully, jest like before. I told Jim how I figured our old mine shaft would be a lot better place to hide the loot than the cave, 'cause it'd be quicker and easier to get to if we ever had to leave these parts in a hurry. But Jim said I warn't foolin' him none: I jest didn't want Rafer findin' out where our gold was hid. He was right.

It was beginnin' to get dark when we'd got to the mine, so we camped there for the night and next mornin' come sunup, we headed down the mountainside to the dry lakebed. Jim told Rafer and Jake to wait there with the horses and pack mules whilst me and Jim looked for the cave. Back in '60, a narrow path leadin' to the cave had wandered in and out amongst the monstrous rocks on the bench below the cliff, but there shore warn't no sign of it now.

We spent over three hours lookin' for it, but we never found anythin' that even came even close to lookin' like a path. I told Jim that without the path, there warn't no way I could find the cave, so we'd better hide the loot in our old mine shaft after all. But he said like hell we would, and that I'd damn well better find the cave — with or without the path — and find it quick if I didn't want somethin' bad happenin' to Jake. 'Course, somethin' bad was gonna happen to both of us, even if I did find the cave, but stayin' alive, even if it was only for a few more hours, or even minutes, seemed mighty appealin' right then. So I kept on lookin' 'til my eyes was about to drop out of my head. And after close to two more hours of lookin', I finally did find it, and I figured that now me and Jake was goner's for shore, 'cause now Jim and Rafer didn't need us no more. But as it turned out they did — they needed us to lug the loot from the dry lakebed over to the cave, which was hard on account of all the rocks and rubble what'd fallen from off'n the cliff. One big rock was perched on a ledge right above the path, and it looked to me like a little nudge would make it fall, and if it did, it'd make it well nigh impossible to get into the cave — or even find it. I wished I could have toppled it right then. 'Course, I couldn't — not with Jim and Rafer keepin' such close watch over us.

Once we got inside the cave and Rafer seen all that gold, his greedy face lit up, his shifty eyes bugged out, and you could jest see his evil mind thinkin' of all the ways he could spend my gold. It was a mighty ugly sight to see. It made me feel like cryin'. All my dreams of riches and a wonderful life with Sadie was about to come to a sudden and terrible end, and I got to wonderin' how Jim was gonna explain to Sadie and our folks why me and Jake didn't come home with them. I was shore he'd make up somethin' real believable — most likely makin' hisself out to look like a hero. Then my imagination really got goin', and I got to thinkin' how, after Sadie quit mournin' over me, she'd fall in love with Jim, get married, and the two of them would have a wonderful time together whilst they was spendin' all my money. That really upset me.

One time whilst I was carryin' loot into the cave, I'd noticed the wooden box where me and Jim kept the black powder we'd used for blastin'. It was settin' up on top of a pile of gold ore right where we'd left it back in '60. I wished there was some way I could get Rafer to set down on it so's I could blow him to kingdom come. 'Course, there warn't no way I could make it happen.

After we was finished stashin' the loot in the cave, I figured my life and Jake's was over for shore. I reckon Rafer did, too, 'cause he pulled his six-gun out of its holster and ordered us to get over by the side of the cave. But before he could shoot us, Jim told him to stop, there was somethin' they had to talk over first. Then, after orderin' me and Jake to stay in the cave, Jim and Rafer went outside. They picked a place to talk where they figured we couldn't hear what they was sayin' — but they was wrong. We could hear everythin' they said loud and clear through a little openin' in the rocks.

Rafer sounded mad. He asked Jim why in hell did he stop him from killin' us. Jim told him to jest calm down, he'd still get to do it, but it'd be later on, not right now. Then he explained how if they was to go back to camp without me and Jake, the rest of their gang would wonder what'd happened to us and get suspicious. They might even suspect the truth — that they'd kilt us so's they wouldn't have to give us our share of the loot, and that the same thing was gonna happen to them once the raid was over.

Jim said he figured the smart thing for them to do was to take us back to camp and keep close watch over us so's we couldn't escape or warn any of the others about what was goin' on. That way, him and Rafer would have time to figure out how to kill us and make it look like an accident so's the others wouldn't suspect anythin'. Rafer argued a lot, and he finally agreed to go along with Jim's plan, but he still didn't like it. He wanted to kill us right off and be done with it, but if he couldn't do that, he was gonna keep such a close watch on us we couldn't even bat an eye or take a deep breath without his knowin' it. That didn't sound too appealin', but at least me and Jake would be amongst the livin' for a little longer. I thanked God for that and asked Him to keep it that way, if'n it warn't too much trouble.

CHAPTER 35

Whilst we was gone, the rest of the gang had raided the Michigan House stage station and close-by ranches, like Jim had ordered them to do, but all they'd got for their troubles was a few ounces of gold dust and a little Yankee currency. That didn't improve Jim's disposition none — and it warn't too good to begin with. I don't think he'd liked havin' Rafer argufyin' with him. The next few days went by in a blur, mainly on account of Rafer was watchin' me and Jake so close nobody could tell us what was goin' on.

On the twenty-ninth of July, the whole gang rode over to the east side of Kenosha Pass to a stage stop called the "Kenosha House." It was close to the junction of the main road and the one up Hall Valley, and Jim and Rafer was figurin' on holdin' up the west-bound stage out of Denver. Whilst we was waitin' for it to get there, a real nice lady from Texas named Mrs. Harrington fed us a good, home-cooked dinner. After we'd finished, most of the fellas in our outfit, includin' me and Jim, paid her for our meals. Then Rafer and a couple of other no-goods stole it all back from her — along with all the money she had stashed in her safe. But a fella from Oklahoma named Dick Hawes took up a collection from some of the others in our outfit and raised enough money so's he could give her back most all of what Rafer and his cronies had stole. I don't rightly know why Hawes done that, but I was glad he did. Most likely he didn't like for anybody to steal money from a nice lady — 'specially one from from the South.

I've never mentioned it before, but for some time now, I'd been wonderin' if Dick Hawes and some of the other fellas in our outfit figured that we really was makin' this raid to help the South win the war. Maybe they didn't know how Rafer and some of his cronies was outlaws and that they was figurin' on keepin' all the loot for theirselfs. I wished I could ask Hawes about it, but I dasn't — not with Rafer watchin' me so close.

When the Denver and South Park stage finally pulled up outside the Kenosha House, Jim and Rafer, along with some of the others in the gang, went out and relieved the passengers and driver of their valuables. Then they busted open the strongbox and helped theirselfs to its contents. I never knowed how much they stole, 'cause right after that we took off down the road headin' east, and for a time there I was afeared that Jim was figurin' on raidin' Denver. But as it turned out, I needn't have worried, 'cause we only went as far as the Junction House, then turned around and went back to the Omaha House close to Conifer, where we spent the nights of the twenty-ninth and thirtieth.

Whilst we was there, Jake somehow managed to swipe some food and hide it in our saddlebags, figurin' it'd come in handy if we ever got away from Jim and Rafer. He even liberated some ammunition for our Colt revolvers and our rifles. How he did it and who he took it from he never said and I never asked, but I shore was happy he'd done it.

On the last day of July, we headed back towards Kenosha Pass. After passin' by Shaffer's Crossin' and a little town called Bailey, we'd stopped at Slaght's freight station and was eatin' breakfast when a fella come bustin' in and told us there was two posses comin' at us from opposite directions. I never knowed why he warned us — might be he was a southern sympathizer. Anyways, he told us how Major DeMary was comin' from the west over Kenosha Pass with over thirty mad miners in his posse, and a company of cavalry led by a Captain Maynard was coming at us out of Denver from the east. It didn't take us long to figure out that we was right in the middle.

Well, that shore lit a fire under us. We headed lickety-split up the road toward Kenosha Pass, goin' jest as fast as our horses could take us. But after we'd gone less than a mile, we spotted DeMary's posse coming down the road towards us, so we swung our horses around and rode in the opposite direction to where the upper Deer Crick road takes off. We followed it north for a few miles past the end of the road, where we hid out in the woods 'til early afternoon.

As soon as our scouts told us the posses was gone, we hightailed it back to the main road and headed back toward Kenosha Pass to where the Hall Valley road turns off and heads north past Handcart Gulch to Webster Pass. Jim figured Handcart Gulch would be a safe place for us to hole up 'til things quieted down. But we found out later it warn't, on account of a third posse of about twelve men led by a fella named Jack

Sparks was comin' hellbent for leather over Webster Pass, headin' south. The posse was from out of the Swan and Snake River country over near Breckenridge. We hadn't done nothin' to bother folks in those parts, so I figured there warn't no reason for them to be mad at us, but I reckon they must not have seen it that way.

Late in the day, we was settin' around three campfires we'd built out of dry pitch pine so's they wouldn't smoke much and give away our hidin' place. But as it turned out, it didn't help none, 'cause once it got dark, Sparks and his bunch seen the light from our fires, snuck up real close, and started shootin' at us. All them bullets whizzin' by scared us damn near to death, and we scattered — every man for hisself — and ran for our horses jest as fast as we could go. Jest as me and Jake was takin' off, I seen one of our bunch go down like he'd been hit. I found out later, it was Owen Singleterry and that he was kilt. Then, jest as we was hightailin' it out of there, I seen Rafer raise his rifle and take a quick shot at me. It missed, but not by much, and I didn't wait around to see if he tried it again. I took off.

This was me and Jake's big chance to escape, and we took off and rode jest as fast as we could go back to the main road and up to the top of Kenosha Pass. From there, we left the road and headed across a big meadow jest south of the pass. After ridin' in the dark for close to three more miles, we finally called a halt — mainly so's our horses could rest, but also so's to figure out what to do next. It looked like we'd gave the posse the slip, at least for the time bein', but I knowed that sooner or later they'd figure out which way we'd went and be back hot on our trail. I jest hoped it was later. I told Jake how we'd best clear out of these parts jest as fast as we could, but that before we did, there was something I had to do. Even though it was risky, I wanted to fix it so Jim and Rafer couldn't find the cave and get their greedy hands on the loot — 'specially on my half of the gold. Jake warn't shore it was a good idea. He figured we'd be a lot smarter if we was to get back to Texas jest as fast as we could, before everybody in the territory knowed we was on the run. More'n likely, Jim and Rafer had already been caught by a posse, but even if they hadn't and they found the cave on their own, they still couldn't take much gold with them, 'cause they only had two horses.

Jake might have been right about Jim and Rafer gettin' caught, but we couldn't count on it. If we'd could get away from the posse, so could Jim and Rafer, and if they had, I wanted to fix it so's they couldn't get their greedy hands on the gold — not one solitary ounce. They had no right to it. 'Course Rafer never did, and now neither did Jim — not after what he was figurin' on doin' to us. I knowed we'd be takin' a chance. We might run into them or the posse and have a fight on our hands, but I still wanted to fix it so they couldn't find the cave. Once we'd done that, we'd head back to Texas.

Jake still didn't think we should do it, but if we did, at least now we had ammunition for our guns and could put up a good fight if we had to. I told Jake I was mighty grateful to him for providin' the bullets, but I hoped and prayed we'd never have to use them, 'cause there warn't no way I'd ever shoot my own brother — no matter what he might have tried to do to me.

"In that case," Jake said, "if'n it ever does come to a gunfight, I reckon you'd best aim at Rafer and leave Jim to me."

That night we holed up by the pond at the headwaters of Lost Crick and, at the first whisper of dawn, headed out again, stayin' high up in the Tarryalls 'til we come to me and Jim's old mine. We went there first instead of goin' straight to the cave, so's to get the shovel, pickaxe, and prybar I'd hid in the bushes downhill from our mine's old tailin's pile. I figured they'd be a help to us when we was hidin' the cave.

It was late afternoon when we got to the cave, but I figured — if we worked fast — we could still load the gold into our saddlebags, block up the path leadin' into the cave, and be out of there before it was too dark to ride. Jake agreed, so like we'd already planned, he picked up his rifle and clambered up on a big rock so's to keep watch for unwanted visitors. Then I went inside the cave and loaded our saddlebags with as much gold as I figured our horses could carry and still carry us. I only took our own high-grade nuggets — I wanted no part of the loot our gang had stole. Besides the gold, I helped myself to some packets of blastin' powder and fuses from the box I'd seen when we was here with Jim and Rafer. I figured it'd come in handy when we was blockin' up the entrance to the cave. I only hoped it was still good after bein' in the cave for the last four years. It looked good and seemed dry, but the proof would be if, and when, it exploded.

After I'd loaded the saddlebags, it took me and Jake two trips to lug them out to where our horses was tethered in the dry lake bottom. The bags was heavy, but we finally got them loaded onto the horses and still had plenty of daylight left to see how to go about blockin' up the entrance to the cave. Jake claimed it'd be easy — all we had to do was use the prybar to topple the big rock on the ledge down into the pathway. He figured it'd block up the entrance to the cave completely. That way, we wouldn't have to use blastin' powder, and nobody would ever know we was there. That sounded good to me, so we both leaned on the prybar with all our weight, tryin' to tumble that damned rock — we tried, and we tried, and we tried again, and I finally told Jake that it jest warn't no use. We was gonna have to use blastin' powder.

Well, I'm here to say that black powder worked great. We took our horses back a piece and tied them to some trees, so's they couldn't bolt and run off at the sound of the blast. Then we stuffed a couple of packets of the powder in the crack under the bottom of the rock on the side facin' the path. After lightin' the fuse, we scrambled behind a big rock, thinkin' we'd be plenty safe — but as it turned out, the blast was a mite more powerful than we'd been expectin'. After the powder went off, it seemed like the whole damn mountain was comin' down around our heads. Pieces of rock and dirt showered down on us like we was in a hailstorm, and both me and Jake got bruised up some. Other than that, it worked jest fine. The pathway was blocked up so solid you couldn't tell it was ever there, and there warn't no sign of the cave. As a matter of fact, it was blocked up a little too good. It was gonna be a mighty big job to clear all that rubble from the entrance to the cave when we come back — assumin' we ever did come back, that is. And assumin' we could find the cave if we did.

Before goin' back to our horses, we hid the bent prybar and other tools a far piece off from the cave to make shore Jim and Rafer couldn't find them. They'd be a dead giveaway as to the whereabouts of the cave if they did. Jake figured if we was to hide them a certain distance and direction from the cave, they might help us to find it again, if we was to come back. So that's what we did. We stashed them about 200 feet due west of the cave, right close to the base of the cliff and in front of a monstrous big rock what had a little pine tree growin' from a crack on its front side. I felt better. Now, even if Jim and Rafer did figure out where the cave was hid, they still couldn't get to the gold without a lot of work, and that would take time, and right now that was somethin' they didn't have any more of than we did.

It was twilight as we hurried back to our horses, and we had to get movin'. But before we did, I wanted to make a map showin' the location of the cave and some landmarks to help us find it again. I didn't have no paper or anythin' to write with, so I used my skinnin' knife to make some deep scratches on one of the leather flaps of my saddle bag to mark the whereabouts of some trees and rocks what was close to the cave. My map warn't too good, but I figured I could copy it on some paper later on.

Whilst I was doin' it, I'd been leanin' on a big rock out in the middle of the dry lake bottom. It was close to seventy yards due south of where the opening to the cave had been, and it gave me another idea: If I was to chisel a deep mark onto the rock, it'd make a good landmark. So Jake hustled back to where we'd hid the tools and fetched the pickaxe, and it worked jest fine. We chipped a big X on the rock about waist high off'n the ground. It was about a foot high, and we put it where it warn't too easy to see less'n you knowed where to look. After makin' another X on a rock about fifty feet north of the first, I marked them both on my map so's to show where the two rocks was settin'. Now, if a person was to sight 'long a line runnin' from one X to the other X, and then on to the north about two hundred feet, give or take a little, it would mark the exact spot where the gold was hid.

Jest as I finished, Jake gave me a nudge on my arm and pointed up the hill to the west where I could jest barely make out two black specks movin' fast down the mountainside in the gatherin' dusk. Even in the fadin' light, we could tell it was Jim and Rafer, so we quick mounted up and headed off, goin' south jest as fast as we could go. As we rode out of the lakebed, I tossed the pickaxe behind some big rocks where nobody'd be likely to find it. We was pretty shore that Jim and Rafer hadn't seen us, but they couldn't have helped hearin' the blast and figurin' out what it was, who'd done it, and why. If they ever caught up with us now, it'd be the end of me and Jake for shore.

It'd clouded over durin' the day, so there warn't no moonlight, makin' it hard to see where we was goin'. I was hopin' our horses could see better than us, but after they stumbled a few times, we dismounted and began leadin' them single file across the side of the mountain with Jake in the lead. I swear he had eyes like a cat. He'd lead us around rocks and up and down gullies that I couldn't even tell was there, so I jest kept hold of the tail of his horse and followed along in the dark, hopin' and prayin' that we wouldn't walk off a cliff.

But we never did, and, after several hours of gropin' our way in the dark, we decided we'd best stop and rest 'til sunup. We didn't make a fire that night, jest in case either Jim or Rafer could see in the dark as good as Jake did and was followin' us. Besides that, we took turns standin' watch, jest to be shore nobody could slip up on us in the dark. It didn't seem likely, but we couldn't take no chances. But even when it come my turn to sleep, I couldn't. I jest sat there thinkin' about what all had happened and how great it'd be when I was back home with Sadie.

Our trip back to Texas was long and slow, 'cause we tried to stay off the main roads and away from people as much as we could. When we finally got down to El Paso, me and Jake felt like we was already home, even though we still had a lot of long, hot miles ahead of us before we got back to my daddy's ranch. We got there on the third day of September 1864.

CHAPTER 36

I was jest gettin' off'n the saddle when Sadie come sailin' out the door with Mamma followin' right behind. She hugged me and kissed me and held on tight to me like she warn't never gonna let me go and — I didn't want her to, neither. After that, Mamma hugged both me and Jake — then she asked me where Jim was. I told her he'd most likely be gettin' back a little later. I wanted to talk to my daddy before tellin' her what all had happened up in Colorado. I was hopin' he'd help me explain it all to her. Accordin' to Mamma, my daddy was down by the barn and he was gonna be mighty happy to see us. I figured she was right, but mainly on account of me and Jake got back in time for the fall roundup.

Sadie went down to the barn with me and Jake, and whilst we was walkin', I told her about Jim and what all had happened on the raid. How he'd turned outlaw and how, if they'd hadn't got caught by a posse, him and Rafer would be showin' up at the ranch most any day now, and when they did, they'd kill both me and Jake on sight. I didn't doubt that for a minute. I explained to her how I was dreadin' havin' to tell my folks what all had happened, 'cause I knowed it'd make them feel terrible — 'specially when I told them how Jim was figurin' on killin' his own brother. But, even though I hated tellin' them, I figured it was somethin' I had to do.

Then Sadie put her arm around my waist, gave me a little hug, and told me that maybe I'd best not tell them about it — leastwise, not jest now, and maybe never. Hopefully, Jim and Rafer would never show up. Then she explained how right after me and Jim left, my folks had tried to figure out why Jim had acted so mean and nasty. They'd talked it over with her and between theirselfs for a time, and finally decided that it warn't really Jim's fault. It was the war and his gettin' shot at the battle of Glorieta Pass what'd changed him so much and how, in time, Jim would get over it and be back to his old happy self again. Only yesterday, whilst they was eatin' supper, they both was sayin' how happy and proud it made them feel to know that both me and Jim was helpin' the South win the war.

We found Daddy in back of the barn shoein' his favorite mare, and when he seen us comin' he dropped his tools and started walkin' towards us, smilin' from ear to ear. He seemed so happy, I figured maybe he really had missed us and was glad to see us, and not jest on account of our helpin' him with the roundup. As a matter of fact, I think he really had been worried about us — he even gave me a hug — first time he'd ever done that. Then he hugged Jake, and he didn't say one thing about our havin' to do any work. It was hard to believe, but it seemed like Daddy was lettin' his feelin's show a mite. That was a big change, and I wondered if maybe it had somethin' to do with Sadie's stayin' with him and Mamma. It'd be mighty hard for anybody to stay grumpy with her around.

After what Sadie'd said, I jest couldn't bring myself to tell Daddy about Jim, and I shore warn't gonna tell Mamma. Maybe we'd be lucky like she'd said and they'd never show up. Anyways, rightly or wrongly, I jest couldn't make my folks unhappy. Most likely, if I waited a while longer, Jim would do that for hisself. Daddy and Jake walked back to the house with us, and a little before we got there, I took Jake aside and explained how I'd decided not to tell my folks the truth about Jim. Jake said he was glad, 'cause he knowed it'd be real hard on them if I did.

Back in the house, me and Jake spent the next couple of hours tellin' Mamma, Daddy, and Sadie what all had happened since we'd left. 'Course, we left out some things and changed a few others so's my folks wouldn't know the truth about Jim. When we'd finished talkin', Mamma hugged both me and Jake. Then she thanked God for bringin' us home safe and sound and prayed that He'd do the same for Jim. I hoped I warn't bein' too disrespectful, but I was prayin' for jest the opposite.

There's jest no words I can use to tell you how good it was to be back. I told Sadie, if'n I had my druthers, I'd never leave these parts again. I'd been thinkin' a lot about my life lately, and I'd decided that I already had somethin' a lot more more valuable than gold. What could be better than livin' on this beautiful ranch with the people I love more'n anythin' else in the world and bein' able to make a honest livin' from the land I loved so much? That was all I could ever ask for, and bein' rich would most likely spoil it. I told Sadie I'd decided I didn't want no part of the gold anymore — Jim and Rafer could have it all. After that Sadie kissed me and told me she couldn't agree more.

But I gotta admit, not long after that I come across Ramon's granddaddy's old map showin' where the bonanza was supposed to be hid, and I started havin' second thoughts. It was in the bottom drawer of a dresser in me and Jim's old room. Jim must have put it there back in '61, the first time we'd come back from Colorado. After that, I made a copy of the map what I'd scratched on the flap of my saddlebag showin' where the cave was hid and put it in the drawer 'long side of Ramon's. You jest never know, someday I might change my mind about not goin' back for the gold.

Sadie and me set the date for our wedding in early June at the Baptist church in San Antonio, jest like my mamma wanted. My folks was tickled pink when we told them we was gonna get married. I'm shore they could hardly wait for us to start havin' their grandkids. Mamma was probably thinkin' how much fun she'd have fussin' over them and playin' with them. Daddy, on the other hand, was most likely figurin' how they could help out with the chores once they got old enough. But then, might be I was misjudgin' him, 'cause — like I said — he'd changed a lot lately.

The fall and winter of '64 went by fast. Me and Jake was kept busy helpin' my daddy and the vaqueros with all the ranch chores. Sadie helped my mamma a lot, and as I look back, I think that was most likely the happiest time of my whole life. We never heard a word from Jim, which didn't upset me none. I'm shore none of us had forgot him, though, 'specially my folks.

Almost before we knowed it, winter was gone and spring flowers was beginnin' to pop up through the greening grass that covered the hills and valleys of the Blue Mountains. Big V-shaped flights of geese honked overhead — all of them headed due north. Us men folks was kept busy checkin' the arroyos and mesquite brakes for newborn calves and their mammas, so's we could bring them down to where they'd be safe from coyotes and wild cats. Them longhorn mammas was mighty tough and most times could take care of their younguns jest fine, but when a pack of coyotes took out after them, the coyotes 'most always won.

This was usually the happiest time of the year on the ranch, what with the cold winter days givin' way to bright, sunny warm ones. But this year it was different, and we all felt sad, 'cause a rider had come by the ranch about the middle of April and told us some real bad news. The South had lost the war. On the ninth of April, General Robert E. Lee had surrendered to the Yankee general, Ulysses S. Grant, at a place in Virginia called the Appomattox Court House. 'Course, for some time now, we'd knowed it was gonna happen, but still it was hard news to hear.

But we didn't stay sad for long, 'cause me and Sadie's big day was comin' up fast, and it warn't gonna be long before we'd be headin' down to San Antonio so's to get hitched. By now, Sadie was not only the prettiest and most wonderful person I'd ever met and the love of my life, she was my very best friend, and every day I thanked God that it was me she loved and that she was gonna be my wife.

Besides keepin' busy with all the ranch work, my daddy, Jake, and the vaqueros helped me build a nice adobe house where me and Sadie figured on livin' after we was married. We built it on Sadie's favorite spot on the top of a little hill about a quarter mile east of my folk's place. There was plenty of water from a nearby spring, so we'd have enough for the house as well as a vegetable garden. It shore was a pretty spot, too, settin' up on the hill like it was. From the front porch, you could see for miles across rollin' hills covered with grass and mesquite, and every spring it seemed like the whole world turned a beautiful shade of blue. All the earth in every direction, stretchin' as far as you could see, was carpeted with bluebonnets and pink and red paintbrush. In some places, it was even hard to tell where the bluebonnets ended and the sky began.

It seemed like it was a long time comin', but the day finally come for us to head down to San Antonio so's me and Sadie could get married. 'Course, Jake was comin' to the weddin', too, along with Pedro Sanchez and his family. Pedro had been livin' on the ranch with his family and workin' for my daddy for several years now, and they was jest like our own kinfolks. Jose Fernandez, Daddy's other vaquero, hadn't been workin' for us near as long, so he stayed behind to mind the ranch whilst we was gone.

My folks, Jake, and the Sanchez family was figurin' on bein' gone about a week, but me and Sadie would be stayin' an extra week for our honeymoon. After gettin' to San Antonio, we all checked into the San Antonio Hotel. Once we'd finished doin' that, we all headed over to the

Baptist church so's to talk with Pastor Childers. He was a young fella, not much older than me. His first name was Howard, and we already knowed him, on account of up to a little over a year ago, he'd been a circuit-ridin' preacher and would come by our ranch at times. He still dropped in now and then, jest to be shore we warn't gettin' into no trouble. He was a big friendly fella — always smilin' a lot. He told us he'd be happy to marry me and Sadie, so we set up a time two days from then on a Friday night, June the sixth, 1865.

After that my mamma and daddy took off to look up some their town friends so's they could invite them to the weddin'. Whilst they was doin' that, me and Sadie went out to see the Barlows, Billy Joe's folks. Jake 'long with Pedro and his family, took off to do their own thing — whatever that was. The Barlows was mighty happy to see us, 'specially so after we invited them to come to our weddin'. This was the first time they'd met up with Sadie, and right off they fell in love with her. They treated us jest like we was family. Mrs. Barlow even offered to fix a weddin' supper for us. After visitin' with them for awhile longer, me and Sadie took off to see the sights of San Antonio. They might not have seemed like much to city folks, but they shore looked great to us.

The wedding went off without a hitch and supper at the Barlows was real nice, too. Two days later my folks, Jake, and the Sanchezes headed back to the ranch, whilst me and Sadie spent another wonderful week honeymoonin' in San Antonio. One day, whilst we was eatin' lunch in a little downtown cafe, I was surprised to see Dick Hawes settin' at the table next to ours. He was the fella from Oklahoma, the one what gave back the money some in our gang stole from that nice lady at the Kenosha House up in Colorado. When Dick seen me, he got up and come over to our table. He seemed happy to see me again and acted real friendly, 'specially so when he found out that me and Sadie was married. Dick and his buddy, Howie Kelsall, had escaped from the posse and got back to Texas by way of Huerfano Butte on the east side of the front range. They'd went there so's to stock up on supplies before they they hightailed it back to Texas. I told him me and Jake had done the same, 'ceptin' by a different route. Dick seemed surprised when I asked him if he knowed what'd happened to Jim and the other fellas in our outfit. Then he looked sad and told us that Jim was dead. He'd been kilt up in Colorado, along with four others of our gang. I guess I should have been expectin' it, but hearin' it still shook me up somethin' awful — Sadie, too. When I asked him if he knowed how Jim had died, he looked even sadder. Then he explained to us what all had happened after we was jumped by the posse up in Hall Valley. Most of what Dick knowed, he'd read in an article in an Austin newspaper a few months back, tellin' 'bout a bunch of Confederate raiders what had stole over sixty-five thousand dollars up in Colorado. And there warn't no doubt but what it was our bunch it was talkin' about, on account of it told what all we'd done and it even gave the names of some of our men — includin' me and Jim's.

After the posse attacked us up in Hall Valley, Dick and Howie took off on their own instead of meetin' up with the rest of the gang in Mace's Hole, like they was supposed to do if for some reason they got separated from the others. And it was a damned good thing they didn't go there, 'cause that's where Jim and the others got caught. That surprised me. Jim and Rafer had never told me and Jake about a rendezvous — most likely on purpose, hopin' we'd get caught by a posse if we got away from them. Accordin' to the article, Jim and the four other men was taken to Denver, but it warn't too clear what happened after that. Supposedly they was taken secretly to Fort Lyon, where they was to be tried as Confederate spies by a military court. But they never made it that far, and nobody seemed to know for shore what really did happen to them.

The officers and men in the army escort claimed that all five of them was shot whilst tryin' to escape. But accordin' to a write-up in the Denver *Rocky Mountain News*, the folks in Denver seriously doubted that story. They figured there'd been some kind of foul play. Uncle Billy Wooten, the owner of the toll road over Raton Pass, claimed that on his way up to Denver, he'd seen the bodies of five men at the California Ranch on Cherry Crick, not far from the site of Russelville. All five of the pore souls was trussed up to trees and had bullet holes in their heads. That was the exact same place the guards claimed the prisoners had tried to escape, but if what they'd said was true, then how come their bodies was all tied to trees? The *Rocky Mountain News* claimed the whole story sounded mighty fishy, and Dick agreed. It sounded to him like it was out and out murder.

Me and Sadie visited with Dick for a little while longer. Then, jest as we was gettin' up to go back to the hotel, he remembered somethin' he'd forgot to tell us. He'd seen Rafer Rathbone in a saloon in Austin not long after he read the article. He was drunker'n a skunk and was talkin' crazy, sayin' how he was figurin' on goin' back to Colorado to look for a cave full of gold. Well, that shook me and Sadie up considerable. It was goin' on eleven months since I last seen Rafer and I'd pretty much forgot 'bout him — I'd figured he most likely was dead. But even if he warn't, it hadn't seemed likely he'd show up after all that time. But I reckon I was wrong. Rafer was still amongst the livin' and talkin' about tryin' to find the cave where my gold was hid. I shore wished he didn't know where we lived, but he did, so he knowed right where to find me and try to make me show him where the gold was hid. Me and Sadie talked it over after we got back to the hotel and decided that there warn't no use in our worryin' 'bout it. More'n likely Rafer never would show up, but if he did, we'd jest have to figure out what to do when it happened.

A few days later, me and Sadie was back at the ranch and beginnin' our lives together in our new little home on the hill. I really hated havin' to tell Daddy and Mamma what'd happened to Jim, but I did, and they both took it a lot better than I'd expected. My daddy said it didn't surprise him none, but at least he'd died whilst he was helpin' the Confederacy, and that made him feel a whole lot better and proud, to boot. Right then, I was mighty glad I'd never told my folks the truth about Jim, 'cause now they'd never need to know how he was jest lookin' out for his own self and never gave a damn about the Confederacy.

CHAPTER 37

The years went by fast after that. Some was good, some not so good, and some jest downright bad. One way or the other, though, our lives went on pretty much like before — at least they did in the beginnin'. The price of beef had dropped considerable after there warn't no Confederate army to sell it to. That made money harder to come by, but when a lot of new folks started movin' to Texas after the war, and they all liked eatin' beef, we still made enough money to live on, and we was happy. Now and again, when things got tight, we'd have to use some of the gold what me and Jake'd brought back from Colorado, but it couldn't last forever, and later, after it was all used up, things got considerably tighter — mainly on account of the drought what hit our part of the country 'long about the end of '65, and all through '66. The grass dried up 'long with most all the water holes, and we lost 'most half our herd, and the half what was left was so scrawny, they was damn near worthless.

In March of '67, Daddy had to let Jose Fernandez go — we just couldn't afford him no more. But at least Jake and Pedro Sanchez was stayin' on, even though we couldn't pay them as much as before. Bless their hearts, they both told us how this was their home, too, and that they'd rather be here than any other place they could think of — and besides, the hard times warn't gonna last forever. I shore hoped they was right.

Now and again, and 'specially now with the hard times comin' on us, I'd get to thinkin' about all that gold what was hid up in the Tarryalls and how nice it'd be if me and Jake could jest hop up there and bring back some of it. But then I'd talk it over with Sadie, and she'd remind me of why I couldn't do it — and she was right. My folks needed me and Jake to help out around the ranch, and she needed me even more. Besides that, if me and Jake went to South Park we'd be likely to run into somebody what'd recognize us and string us up to the nearest cottonwood tree.

I didn't argue none with Sadie. By now I'd learned to always take her advice — well, 'most always that is. I don't know what I'd of done durin' all those hard times if I hadn't had Sadie. She was the light of my life, always cheerful and happy. As a matter of fact, she seemed to light up the life of everybody what was livin' at the ranch in those days.

Then, in the spring of '66, Sadie's light got to shinin' a lot brighter when she told me I was gonna be a daddy. That was one of them happy times I talked about. Actually, it was about the happiest we'd been for a long time. We broke the news to my daddy and mamma, and I don't recollect ever seein' them so happy — either before or after. It made us forget all the other troubles we was havin', and we could hardly wait 'til it come time for the baby to arrive. Finally, on the fifth of January 1867, John Reynolds Jr. was born, and he was the finest little boy baby I'd ever had seen. 'Course, I'd never seen one before, either boy or girl — leastwise not up close. But if'n I had, I'm shore he'd of been the best of the bunch. What's more, to prove it, Sadie and both of my folks agreed with me.

Before little Johnny was born, me and Sadie talked a lot about what to name the baby. We'd agreed right off on "Hannah" if'n it was a girl, 'cause that was my mamma's name. If'n it was a boy, I wanted to name him James after Daddy and my brother, 'cause I had a lot of good memories of Jim, even though he went bad at the end. But Sadie was set on namin' him after me. Well, I reckon you know who won out. I'm shore my mamma and daddy would have been happy even if'n we'd named him Rover, jest as long as they had a little grandson to play with and spoil.

The next two years was some better or maybe they jest seemed that way on account of we had little Johnny to take our minds off'n our troubles. He was doin' jest fine, too, and was growin' into a fat-cheeked, strong and sturdy toddler. Before Johnny'd come along, Sadie warn't quite as sunny and cheerful as she was in the early days. But now that we had little Johnny, our sweet, happy, Sunny Sadie was back with us again. Then in the early summer of '67 Sadie got pregnant again. Everybody on the ranch was tickled pink with the news, and all went well 'til about three months later, when she lost the baby. That was a big disappointment to all of us, but especially to Sadie, and I think it was right about then that some of her sparkle started to fade out a mite.

By now the drought had ended, and you'd of thought things around the ranch would be gettin' better. But you'd have thought wrong. For one thing, some big cattle outfits had started grazin' their cattle on the same range our cattle had been usin' for all these years, and whilst the grass was growin' good again, there still warn't enough to go around. We figured we had claim to the grasslands on account of we was there first, but the other ranchers didn't see it that way, and we warn't a big enough outfit to argue. On top of that, cattle rustlers had begun showin' up, and it warn't long before our herd was cut in half again — first by drought, and now by them low-down cattle thieves.

After the fall roundup of '67, we'd drove a part of our herd down to San Antonio to be sold in the local markets. The drive went without a hitch, and we got a fair price for our herd. That was good, but then my daddy had to let Pedro go 'cause we couldn't afford even the little bit we'd been payin' him. We all hated to see him and his family leave — it was like we was losin' part of our own family.

By now, the bigger ranchers was takin' their herds up north and sellin' them in the cattle market in Abilene, Kansas. From there, the critters was loaded into boxcars and shipped by train to cities back East, where Texas beef was bringin' higher prices than what they was gettin' in San Antonio. They followed the Chisholm Trail. It was named that back in 1866 after a cattleman named Jessie Chisholm, who was the first rancher to take a herd along that route. It would have been easy for us to use it, too, on account of it passed by a little east of our ranch. But we couldn't, on account of me and Jake would have had to go 'long to help out on the drive, leavin' my daddy to take care of the ranch all by hisself. 'Course, there warn't no way he could have done that.

We was all real worried about Daddy. Even though he'd never been a big man, he was always real wiry and strong, but back in '66 he'd come down with some sort of sickness, and now he was nothin' but skin and bones. So that fall, when we drove the herd down to sell in San Antonio, Mamma, my daddy, Sadie, and little Johnny went with us. Jake stayed behind so's to mind the ranch. Mamma had been wantin' my daddy to see Doctor Wheelock for some time now, and he'd finally agreed — but not without a heap of arguin'. Sadie went along, too, on account of I was wantin' her to see the doctor. She'd lost still another baby, and I was real worried about her. I figured somethin' must be wrong with her, and maybe the doctor could tell us what it was and how to fix it.

But Doctor Wheelock warn't much help. First off, he told us that my daddy had consumption, and there warn't a lot we could do to help him, 'ceptin' to keep him quiet and restin' all of the time and to be shore he got lots of good food and fresh air. He gave him some sort of tonic to take three times a day. Daddy got so he really liked takin' it, and after I tasted it I found out why. It was mainly drinkin' alcohol. I didn't tell Mamma, on account of she was strictly against whiskey, no matter what it was used for, but I 'spect she knowed what it was anyways. The doctor warn't of much help to Sadie either. He jest said flat out that he didn't know why she was losin' all her babies. But he told her that for one thing, she shouldn't work as hard as she'd been doin', and for another, if she got pregnant again, she should stay in bed 'til the baby'd come.

Well, you most likely can imagine what happened after that. My daddy said there warn't no way in hell he was gonna stay in bed — there was too much work to be done. My mamma said, "Oh, no, there isn't," and, "Oh, yes, you are gonna stay in bed, jest like you was told." A considerable amount more was said, but it was pretty clear from the beginnin' that my daddy was gonna lose the argument. I didn't make out that good with Sadie. She was jest as stubborn as Daddy — even more so. If she got pregnant again, there warn't no way she was gonna stay in bed. I knowed there warn't no use arguin' with her, 'cause it wouldn't have done a damned bit of good.

After sellin' the cattle and seein' the doctor, we stayed three more days in San Antonio before headin' back to the ranch. The second day there we went to see the Barlows, and they was real happy to see us — 'specially little Johnny. Mrs. Barlow told us what a fine lookin' boy he was, the best lookin' child she'd ever seen. We all agreed that she was a mighty fine judge of children.

Whilst our folks went to the hotel so's to rest up, me and Sadie wandered around town. We was surprised when we come to a lumberyard what was owned by Dick Hawes. We was even more surprised when we found out Pedro Sanchez was workin' for him. That evenin', me and Sadie ate supper with Dick and his brand-new wife, Elsie. Dick told us the lumber business had been goin' great lately, on account of all the people what was movin' here from back East and buildin' new homes and businesses. In fact, it was goin' so great Dick was lookin' for a partner and wanted me to come in with him. I told him I'd like to, but there warn't no way I could. With my daddy bein' so sick, I had to stay around and take care of the ranch. It shore was a temptin' offer, though, 'cause we shore could have used the money. But deep down I knowed that I never could work in town — even if my daddy warn't sick — 'cause ranchin' and love of the land was too much in my blood.

Dick had heard some recent news about Rafer Rathbone, and this time it was good news. Seems that Rafer and some other fellas had kilt a guard whilst they was robbin' a bank out in Arizona. But this time they'd got caught, and Rafer was locked up tight inside the Arizona Territorial Prison and was gonna be there for a long, long time. Nothin' me and Sadie could have heard would have pleasured us more — 'ceptin' maybe that they'd hung him. The next day we all headed back to the ranch, but when we got there, we got some bad news. Accordin' to Jake, the rustlers had hit us again, and this time they'd stole most all our best breedin' stock what we'd been countin' on to help us build our herd back up. It was a terrible shock to us all.

From then on, things didn't get no better. Sadie got pregnant again in the early part of '68, and, jest like she'd said, she didn't stay in bed or quit workin' like the doctor had told her to do. I fussed at her, tryin' to get her to take it easy, but she told me she couldn't — there was too much work to do. I couldn't argue, 'cause she was right — there was a lot to do. My mamma was wearin' herself to a nub frettin' over Daddy, and she warn't lookin' none too good herself. Me and Jake was kept busy ridin' herd and doin' all the ranch work. So, besides takin' care of little Johnny, Sadie had to do all the cookin' and housework. I 'spect you guessed it: She lost our baby, jest like Doctor Wheelock said she would. Not only that time, but twice more in the next two years. Sadie told me how she thanked God every day that we had little Johnny, 'cause she was pretty shore we warn't never gonna have no more babies.

Before we knowed it, another year had passed on by, and it was comin' up on 1870. We was jest barely scrapin' by, but so far, at least, we hadn't had to sell the ranch to one of the bigger outfits like some of the other smaller ranchers in these parts had done. We'd had some pretty fair offers, but my daddy'd swore that hell would have to freeze over before he'd ever sell his ranch.

Then, after all these years, Jake left us — but not because he wanted to. In fact, we almost had to force him to leave. He claimed he'd been a part of our family for so long, he'd feel like he was desertin' his own kinfolks. But we knowed he'd been offered a good job at Dick's lumberyard, and on top of that, he had a lady friend in San Antonio that he was figurin' on marryin'. So he finally agreed to go, but he told us if we ever needed his help in any way, all we had to do was to let him know, and he'd be there.

My daddy never did get back to where he could work around the ranch again like he was always wantin' to do. It seemed like every day, he was lookin' a little more puny and a little bit older. My daddy and mamma was both in their mid-sixties by now, but they looked a lot older — all them hard years on the ranch had taken its toll on both of them. During them days, Mamma spent a lot of time readin' her Bible and prayin'. Most every night, after all our work was done, we'd sit 'long side my daddy's bed whilst she read us a chapter or two from the Scriptures. Then we'd all join hands and ask for the Lord's blessin' on us all, but 'specially on my daddy.

The main joy in our lives was watchin' Johnny growin' up, which he was doin' mighty fast. He was always a real happy little fella — well, 'most always. Now and then he'd get hisself into a little mischief and end up gettin' a spankin' from his mamma. Most of the time, though, he'd play with our old hound dog out in the shade of the oak trees or tag along after me whilst I was workin' around the place. He was learnin' to talk, too. In fact, it got so he'd never shut up. Half the time I couldn't figure out what he was sayin', but that didn't bother him or me none. We understood each other real well. Then one day he went away — and he warn't never comin' back.

It was a Monday afternoon in early December when a peddler pulled his wagon up in front of our ranch house. He'd brought his wife and two little boys along with him whilst he made his rounds sellin' pots and pans and what not. Sadie asked them to join us at supper. Then they bedded down for the night in our front room, 'cause it was cold and rainy outside. The next mornin', jest as they was fixin' to go back to San Antonio, the peddler told us they was gonna have to see the doctor when they got back to town, on account of their youngest son's throat was hurtin', and he was feelin' a mite hot. I didn't give it a second thought 'til three or four days later, when Johnny started actin' droopy. Sadie thought he felt hot — like he had fever. I felt his forehead, and she was right. His cheeks was a fiery red, and he felt like he was burnin' up. Later that day, he started havin' trouble breathin' and couldn't swallow or talk too good. I didn't wait a minute longer. I hitched our horses to the buckboard, and with Sadie holdin' Johnny in her lap, we lit out for San Antonio jest as fast as we could go.

I knowed it was a long chance, and that he might not be alive when we got there, but what else could I do? I figured Johnny most likely had quinsy and that he might choke to death most any minute. A circuit-ridin' preacher had come by a few days back. He'd told us how there was a lot of it makin' the rounds, 'specially down around San Antonio, 'ceptin' down there they was callin' it "diphtheria."

We drove night and day — as fast as we could without killin' the horses. Johnny was still alive when we pulled up in from of the doctor's office, but not by much. We'd been tryin to get him to drink all the water we could, but he'd got so's he couldn't even swallow. He was strainin' to breathe, and his breath was comin' in short little gasps. We kept spongin' him off with cool water, tryin' to drop his fever, but it didn't do much good. When we carried him into Doctor Wheelock's office, he took one look at him and rushed him into another room. He told us later how he'd made an openin' into his windpipe low down in his neck so's he could breathe. But it was too late. Our little Johnny was gone, and our lives warn't never gonna be the same.

When we'd got back to the ranch, Mamma come out to meet us, and I'd never before seen her look so tired and wore out. I knowed that her and my daddy had been prayin' most night and day ever since we'd left. The minute she seen the little pine box in the back of the wagon and realized that Johnny was dead, she dropped down on her knees and started sobbin' and callin' out his name over and over again. By that time me and Sadie was about cried out, but we knowed jest how she was feelin'. We picked her up and carried her back into the house, and then I had to go in and tell Daddy the terrible news. He didn't say nothin', jest lay on the bed starin' up at the ceilin'. I'm shore he'd been expectin' to hear the worst but was still hopin' for a miracle.

Well, a few months after that a miracle really did happen — at least it seemed like one to us. Sadie got pregnant again, and this time she didn't lose the baby. She claimed that now she knowed how Abraham and his wife, Sarah, must have felt when God gave them baby Isaac after they was both real old. I told her she warn't near as old as Sarah, and I shore as hell warn't as old as Abraham.

I reckon God must have heard all our prayers, 'cause on the fifth of May 1874, He gave us little Jimmy so's we'd stop grievin' so much over losin' Johnny. That's right, we named him James Reynolds, after my daddy and my brother. Daddy was mighty proud and happy. He said it was good to know that there'd be a little youngster named Jimmy runnin' around the ranch again. Right then I was 'specially glad that me and Sadie had never told my folks the truth about Jim.

After Johnny died, my folks had taken it real hard, and me and Sadie was awful worried about them. But now — now that we had little Jimmy — they was back to their old selfs again — leastwise, Mamma was. My daddy, even though he seemed a lot happier and more content, jest gradually kept gettin' weaker and sicklier lookin' as he slowly faded away. Doctor Wheelock had told us to make shore little Jimmy never went in my daddy's bedroom, or got anywheres close to him so's he wouldn't catch his consumption. 'Course, that made my daddy real sad.

Whenever it was sunny and warm, Daddy liked to have us carry him outside in front of the house where he could set in the sun or, if it was too hot for that, set in the shade of one of the big spreadin' oaks. As Jimmy got older, we'd let him play in the dirt where his granddaddy could keep an eye on him. He loved to watch him as he crawled about and later toddled around whilst explorin' all the things in the outside world what was new to him. My daddy died on June 22, 1876, and we buried him 'long side little Johnny on the top of a shady knoll not far from our house. It was a real peaceful spot, where you could look for miles across the rollin' hills and see the wind as it blew in waves across the prairie grasses. There was a patch of bluebonnets right next to their graves, which was nice, 'cause Daddy always loved them so much. I had a feelin' he still did.

Mamma didn't do too well after that. She tried her best to be helpful and act happy, but many was the time we'd see her jest settin' and starin' off across the prairie — like she was expectin' to see Daddy come ridin' up on his old sorrel mare jest like he used to do. Maybe she really did see him — I shore hoped so. It didn't seem too likely, but there was times when I got to thinkin' I could almost see him myself.

Lots of times in the evenings after the day's work was done, we'd all go up to the top of the hill where my daddy and Johnny was buried, and Mamma would read to us out of her old, worn Bible. I think her most favorite verses was the ones what Matthew, Jesus' apostle, had wrote down. She knowed them by heart, 'long with a lot of other parts of the Bible, and I learned them, too. Like the part where Jesus was sayin', "Come to me all ye that labour and are heavy laden, and I will give you rest. Take my yoke upon you and learn of me, for I am meek and lowly in heart, and you will find rest unto your souls. For my yoke is easy and my burden is light."

Then, on October 25, 1880, not very many years later, a time came when I figured my mamma was most likely seein' Daddy jest fine. That was the night she gave up her burdens and drifted off to sleep, never to wake again. We laid her to rest 'long side of Daddy and little Johnny on the crest of the hill overlookin' their beloved ranch.

Now that my mamma and daddy was both gone, me and Sadie didn't seem to get near as much pleasure out of workin' around the ranch, and I got to wonderin' if there warn't some better way to make a livin'. I even started thinkin' about the gold up in the Tarryalls, and how if I could jest find the cave and figure out some way to get into it, all our problems would be over. But if I went up to Colorado, I'd have to leave Sadie and Jimmy on the ranch all by theirselfs, and there warn't no way I would do that. I felt guilty jest thinkin' about it.

Every so often, all three of us would ride down to San Antonio so's to get supplies and visit our friends. We 'specially enjoyed seein' the Barlows. They liked seein' us, too, and we usually ended up stayin' with them. They treated us like we was family. I'm shore it was Jimmy they liked seein' the most, and they always fussed over him, like he was their own grandson. 'Course, it was good to see Dick, Jake, Pedro, and Jose, too, but I gotta admit, it bothered me some, 'cause they was so much better off than me and didn't have to work near as hard. I wished now that I'd taken Dick up on his partnership offer, but back then I couldn't and now it was too late, 'cause Dick already had a partner.

One of the times we was down in San Antonio, I think it was in the spring of '83, I got to tellin' Jake about all the troubles we was havin' on the ranch — how I still loved the old place, but that things was a lot different now than they was in the old days, and ranchin' warn't near as much fun. After listenin' to all my complainin', Jake asked me if I'd ever gave any thought to goin' back to Colorado so's to look for the gold. After this long a time, he doubted that anybody in South Park would be likely to recognize me, so it should be pretty safe for me to go there.

I told Jake how he must have read my mind, 'cause I'd been thinkin' a lot about the gold lately. But there warn't no way I could go and leave Sadie and Jimmy alone at the ranch, and I couldn't take them with me, either — the Tarryalls was too rough a country. Jake scratched his head a mite like he always did whilst he was thinkin'. Then he told me that maybe, if'n I could find somebody to take care of the ranch, Sadie and Jimmy could stay at the Barlows whilst I was gone.

Well, I figured that was a great idea, and, after thankin' Jake for the suggestion, I hustled back to the Barlows so's to tell Sadie what I was plannin' to do. They was jest settin' down at the supper table when I got there, and when I told them my plan, the Barlows got real excited. They said they'd be tickled pink to have Sadie and Jimmy stay with them 'til I got back. But then Sadie spoke up, and what she said really surprised me. There warn't no way I was gonna go off by myself and leave her and Jimmy here to wonder and worry if'n I was alive or dead — she'd been through that too many times already. But, if I really was set on goin', why didn't her and Jimmy jest pack up and go with me? We could sell the ranch and move to some little town up in South Park where I could get a job and look for the cave in my spare time. The more Sadie talked about it, the more excited she got. She claimed it'd be like we was startin' our lives all over again. My wife shore was full of surprises.

Jimmy figured it was a great idea, too. He was nine years old, goin' on twenty-one, and he figured he could ride and drive a wagon even better than me. His mamma had taught him how to read, write, and cipher pretty good, and jest lately he'd been readin' books about trappers and miners, so he figured he knowed most all about everythin' —

'specially how to find lost caves full of gold. After talkin' it over for a spell, me and Sadie decided it'd be best if we waited 'til spring before leavin'. That way, we wouldn't have to risk travelin' through the Colorado mountains so late in the year, and it most likely would be easier for me to find a job then. Besides that, there was a lot things we had to do before we left, and it'd give me time to grow a beard and let my hair grow long so's the folks up in South Park wouldn't be as likely to recognize me.

Sellin' my folk's old ranch and all the memories that went with it was somethin' I hated to do it, but the owner of the spread jest east of ours paid us a real good price for it, and that made it a lot easier. The hardest part was figurin' out what things we should take with us and what we'd should leave behind, but Sadie did most of the decidin'. The main things I made shore we took with us was our tools and the two maps what showed where the gold cave and the bonanza was hid. I made copies of both maps and hid them in my bedroll, then I locked the originals in our strongbox and shoved it under the front seat of the wagon. The stuff we couldn't take with us we gave to our friends in San Antonio or auctioned off — all the rest we packed in our wagon. Jake and one of the fellas from Dick's lumberyard made the wagon's sides higher and fixed some wood struts to go over the top. After that, they stretched a tight canvas cover over the struts, makin' it look like a Conestoga wagon, 'ceptin' that it warn't near as big. What we couldn't get into the wagon, we loaded on our three new bought mules. I figured they'd come in handy later for haulin' our gold from out of the cave in the Tarryalls, if we ever found it.

When we was finally finished packin', it gave me a peculiar feelin' to know that everythin' we owned in this whole world was stashed into one wagon and on top of three lop-eared mules. Everythin' else we'd had — our friends included — we was leavin' behind us in Texas — forever, as far as we knowed. The hardest part was sayin' good-bye to our friends in San Antonio — 'specially Jake, Dick Hawes, and the Barlows. Sadie told them she'd write to them often, and that any letters they wrote to us should be addressed to John and Sadie Hardin and sent to the post office in Fairplay, 'til we was settled down permanent. She explained how "Hardin" had been her last name before we got married, and that we warn't usin' our real last name on account of me and my brother havin' been arrested in Denver back in '41 for bein' Southern sympathizers. 'Course that was a long time ago, but we figured it'd still be best if folks in South Park didn't know my real name. I didn't tell them about the raid in '64, 'cause it'd be a lot harder to explain. 'Course, Jake and Dick Hawes already knowed about it.

On the tenth of May 1884, jest five days after Jimmy's tenth birthday, we left the ranch. I had a lump in my throat bigger than the mare I was ridin', and I couldn't keep from cryin' a little whilst I was standin' on the top of the hill, tellin' my mamma and daddy and little Johnny good-bye for what I figured was the very last time. I hope Jimmy didn't see me cryin', 'cause he figured growed-up men never cried — but this one shore did. Sadie gave me a little squeeze and a kiss on the cheek. Then I climbed on the seat of the wagon, picked up the reins, and we was on our way to Colorado.

CHAPTER 38

The trip up was a long one, but it went without a hitch. It shore brought back memories as we was goin' over Raton Pass past the Greenhorn Valley and Mace's Hole and into South Park. Some was good memories, and I shared them with my family — but others was bad ones, like what happened at Raton Pass and Adolph Guiraud's ranch in South Park. I'd never told Sadie what'd happened at those places, and I figured it'd be best to keep it that way. Some things are best kept to yoreself.

Not long after we got to South Park, we was ridin' past a new little town called "Garo." I wondered if maybe it'd been named after the Guirauds, 'cause it warn't very far from there to their ranch house and their names was pronounced the same way. After passin' by Garo, we headed north to Fairplay, crossin' over the South Platte River a little ways south of town. Back in '61, the water in the river was crystal clear and sparkled bright in the midday sun as it flowed past Fairplay and wound its way across the grassy meadows of South Park. But now it was

Gold dredge working near Fairplay in the 1800s.
(Courtesy of the Denver Public Library Western History Collection.)

an ugly yellow color, and as far as I could see, there was big piles of rock and gravel on either side of the stream what'd been dumped there by gold dredges. It made me feel sick when I seen it. 'Course, might be there was another way of lookin' at it, 'cause if it warn't for them ugly dredges and all the money and jobs they'd brung to Fairplay, the town would most likely have shriveled up and died off a long time ago, like so many other little minin' towns had done.

We was checkin' into the McLean House on Main Street at the north end of town, when me and Sadie'd got to chattin' with the manager of the hotel. He was a young fella named Frank Hamilton, and he shore did enjoy hearin' hisself talk. All we'd asked him was if he figured Fairplay was a good place for us to settle. We told him we'd come up from Texas, and how I was hopin' to find work in the placer mines so's to make a livin' for me and my family. I figured that Frank would most likely say Fairplay would be a fine place for us to settle, bein' as how he lived there hisself — but he didn't. Instead, he told us about a whole passel of little towns what had sprung up along the Denver, South Park and Pacific Railroad lines after it'd had come into South Park back in 1879. One was named Alma, and he figured it'd be the perfect place for us to put down roots, 'cause if he had his druthers, that's exactly what he'd do hisself. Fairplay was too damned crowded.

After that, Frank told us all about the railroad — how it was a narrow gauge, and how after leavin' Denver, it went south past a little farm town called Littleton, then up the South Platte Canyon, over Kenosha Pass, and down into South Park. Jefferson and Como was the first new towns to spring up — they was northeast of Fairplay on the way to Kenosha Pass. From Como, they'd run the tracks southwest to the station at Red Hill and then on south to Garo. Accordin' to Frank, that upset the good folks of Fairplay considerable, 'cause they figured it should have come through their town instead, bein' as how it was the seat of Summit County.

You'd have thought Frank would have got tired of talkin', but he never did. He jest kept on chatterin' away, tellin' us how when Alma was founded back in '73, the town fathers had named it after Alma Janes, the daughter of a local storekeeper. It was located seven miles north of Fairplay, right where Buckskin Crick flows into the South Platte River.

I didn't let on to Frank, but I knowed the exact spot he was talkin' about, 'ceptin' there shore warn't no town there when me and Jim was in Buckskin in '60 and '61. I asked him if he'd ever heard of Buckskin Joe — that I'd been wonderin' where it was, on account of I knowed a fella down in Texas what claimed to have lived there in '61. Frank said there was a town called that back then. It was jest a few miles up Buckskin Crick from where Alma was now, but that it'd gone bust back in the late '60s. Now all that was left of it was a few old ramshackle houses and the cemetery.

Accordin' to Frank, there was close to nine hundred people livin' in Alma now. There'd been 'most that many there back in 1878, but a little later that same year, nearly threefourths of them took off over Mosquito Pass so's to work in the silver mines in California Gulch up above Leadville. They was hopin' to strike it rich like a fella named H. A. W. Tabor had done there. 'Course, I'd knowed H. A. W., so I asked Frank how he'd got rich. Frank explained how, when H. A. W. was a storekeeper in Leadville, he'd grubstaked some miners and they'd ended up findin' the Little Pittsburg Mine. It'd produced close to 3.8 million dollars in 1878 alone. I was happy to hear that, 'cause the Tabors deserved it — they was mighty fine folks. At least they'd shore been nice to me and Jim.

From what our talkative hotel man told us, there was still a lot of minin' activity goin' on up around Alma — mostly gold, but also silver and lead, so the town was really boomin'. The Alma Placer Company had a big operation jest south of town on the Platte River, and back in 1881, a railroad line had been built from Garo north to London Junction, about two-and-a-half miles south of Alma. That really started business boomin', and over twenty new business places had opened up in jest the last two years, includin' a bank, four hotels, five saloons, and a photography shop. And not only that, there was a fine school in Alma and a pretty, young schoolteacher named Miss Lydia Smith. Jimmy didn't seem 'specially happy about that, but me and Sadie shore was.

I told Frank my friend down in Texas had asked me to check and see if Jacob Stansell and Cy Killgore was still livin' in these parts. 'Course, they'd been friends of me and Jim back in '60 and '61, but that was before the raid, so I didn't know how they'd feel about me now and

I didn't 'specially want to find out. In fact, I was hopin' they'd left these parts, and accordin' to Frank, they had. He'd never even heard of Cy, but he had heard of Jacob Stansell. He'd been one of the foundin' fathers of Alma, but he'd left a few years back and was livin' in Denver now. That was good news, 'cause with both of them gone, Alma should be a pretty safe place for us to live.

One time when Frank quit talkin' so's to catch his breath, Sadie spoke up and said it

Placer mining using a sluice to separate gold from a gravel bank.
(Courtesy of the Colorado Historical Society.)

sounded to her like Alma would be a good place for us to go visit, so why didn't we go up to our room and get some rest so we could leave early in the mornin'? I'd figured it was jest an excuse to leave so we wouldn't have to listen to Frank talk any more — but I was wrong, she really did want to take a look at Alma. She said it sounded to her like it'd be a good place for us to live. And I agreed, 'cause it'd most likely be easy for me to find work there. Besides that, it warn't too far to the cave where our gold was hid, so we could go look for it whenever I had a few free days off in a row. 'Course, it'd be a long day goin' and another comin' back, so it'd take some plannin', but I was shore we could manage it.

So come mornin' that's jest what we did — we went up to Alma and signed in as Mr. and Mrs. John Hardin and son Jimmy at the St. Nicholas Hotel. Frank had told us that they had the best food in town

— and he was right, the food was good, but the mattresses was too damned lumpy, and we could hardly wait to get our own home. That's where the money we'd got from sellin' the ranch come in handy. We bought a little house at the south edge of town and was able to move right in, on account of the owners had taken off in such a hurry they'd left most all their furniture behind.

Once we was settled in, me and Sadie took off in different directions so's to find work we could do, and it warn't long before we both had a job. Sadie'd got a job helpin' out a lady named Sarah Watson what owned one of the boardin' houses in Alma. I ended up doin' pretty much what I'd done when I was in these parts before. I got a job workin' at the Alma Placer Company's hydraulic operations on the Platte River below town.

Even Jimmy got a job stockin' shelves, sweepin' floors, and doin' other odd jobs at Harry Singleton's Mercantile Store. He took to it like a duck to water, and before long, to hear him talk, he was runnin' the whole shebang. His mamma told him he could do his job before and after school 'cause, even though he was a successful businessman, that didn't mean he warn't gonna get an education. That didn't please Jimmy none — not 'til he seen his teacher, Miss Lydia Smith. She was a

Main Street in Alma in 1885, Mount Bross above clouds in the distance.
(Courtesy of the Denver Public Library Western History Collection.)

mighty good lookin' young lady and not a whole lot older than Jimmy. I noticed he quit complain' about goin' to school after that.

All of us liked livin' in Alma, even in the winters, which was long and cold. And we liked what we was doin', too. We made a lot of friends in town, but lots of times, no sooner than we got to know them, they'd hear of a new strike somewheres else and take off for what they figured was greener pastures, thinkin' they was gonna strike it rich. Most of them never did. But we never had the itch to move, 'cause we knowed we was gonna get rich by stayin' put — that is, we was if we could find the cave where our gold was hid.

Whenever I could get away for at least three or four days, me, Jimmy, and usually Sadie would light out for the Tarryalls so's to look for the cave. But the first time we went there I was in for a shock, on account of the two big rocks I'd marked with Xs was out in the middle of a lake under who knows how many feet of ice cold water. Back in '60 and again in '64, when me and Jim was there, the little crick was spillin' over the edge of the cliff and down to the bench where the cave was hid. But it'd changed course, and now it was comin' down the mountain and goin' into the lake south of the cliff, like it most likely was doin' when the lake was first formed. And it was easy to see what had changed it, 'cause a little ways above the cliff, a big pine tree had fallen across the channel of the crick, blockin' it up. Then rocks and gravel had washed down from the mountainside above, dammin' it up even more and changin' the direction of flow. Now the crick was goin' south of the cliff and into the lake, like it was in the beginning. That was gonna make findin' the cave a whole lot harder.

After that, we looked for the cave every chance we got — I 'spect we must have spent at least five or six days climbin' around in amongst all them big rocks tryin' to find it. 'Course, we had my map, but it warn't worth a damn without knowin' where the rocks with the Xs on them was at. But they was too far out in the lake to spot from shore, and none of us knowed how to swim — even if we had, we'd have froze to death in that icy water. Jimmy figured it'd be easy to find them. All we had to do was to dig the outlet of the lake deeper, so's the water could drain out. But I told him that wouldn't work, 'cause the outlet warn't nothin' but solid granite. Then he figured we could do it with dynamite. Awhile back Miss Smith had told his class how a Swedish fella named Albert Nobel had jest recently invented it, and how the miners had been usin' it to do heavy blastin' on account of it was a lot more powerful than black powder. But I knowed all about dynamite, and there warn't no way this side of hell that I'd use it — I was too fond of livin'. It was real touchy stuff — sometimes it'd explode when you'd least expected it, and blow you and everything around you to kingdom come.

By that time Jimmy'd run out of advice, so we went back to pokin' around in amongst the rocks, hopin' we'd get lucky and stumble onto the cave — but we never did, and we finally quit lookin'. Now we go to Lost Crick jest to have a good time. Me and Sadie always enjoy gettin' away from people, cookin' over a campfire, and sleepin' under the stars, and Jimmy loves it too.

One time, when we was ridin' by the old mine me and Jim found back in 1860, Jimmy started askin' me questions about it — things like how long was the mineshaft and how come we'd caved it in. Whilst I was answerin' his questions, I got to thinkin' how it most likely wouldn't be too hard to open the mine up again. There still was a good showin' of gold when we'd closed it up, so maybe it'd be worth workin' it in our spare time. I wondered why I hadn't thought of it before. When I told Sadie and Jimmy what I was thinkin', they both got excited. They figured it was a great idea and that it'd be a lot of fun. I told them that muckin' around in a cold, wet mine warn't quite my idea of fun, but if they didn't mind workin' hard, it jest might pay off.

Money-wise we was gettin' 'long pretty well, what with all of our jobs and the money what was left from the sale of the ranch. But still, fattenin' up our account at the Bank of Alma seemed like a good idea. When we'd first come to Alma, I'd opened an account for me and Sadie and another one for Jimmy in his own name, bein' as how he was earnin' his own money. Two Englishmen, E. P. Arthur and C. G. Hathaway, was the founders and owners of the bank, and it seemed to be doin' jest fine. They was handlin' large amounts of currency, plus silver and gold bullion from all the mines thereabouts.

After outfittin' ourselfs with the tools and equipment we needed, we headed on up to the mine. It was late spring of 1889. By now I'd staked a claim and filed on it, so if somebody found out what we was doin', they couldn't jump our claim — leastwise, not legally. It took us a fair length of time to clear out the entrance to the tunnel and to shore it up with new timbers clear on back to where the vein was located. Even though workin' in that wet, cold mine tunnel warn't a whole lot of fun, Jimmy never complained and neither did Sadie, the times she'd helped. They was both hard workers. The lode was holdin' out real good and even seemed to be gettin' a little wider the deeper we got into the mountain. The ore was pretty high grade, too.

So's not to stir up a lot of talk, each time we'd come back to town, we brung only as much ore as we could pack in the saddle bags on one burro, and I'd take it straight away to the Alma Placer Company where I was workin'. I had an arrangement with the manager there to let me throw what little ore we had in with what they was sendin' to the smelter in Alma, what was owned by the Boston and Colorado Company of Blackhawk. Then, after the placer company was paid the money what was due them, he'd give me my fair share — less a little for their trouble. It was all fair and square and worked out real good. After bein' paid, I'd hustle over to the bank and deposit the money, and as far as I knowed, nobody in town ever knowed about our mine.

After the panic of '93, Alma's population dropped down to around 300 people, and all the smelters in town closed, includin' the big one what was owned by the Boston and Colorado Company. Along about then, a lot of our friends left Alma and went lookin' for work in other places. The problem was that the price of silver had dropped way down when the country went off the silver standard, and it really knocked the props from under the economy around these parts. In 1894, Davis Waite held a big rally in Alma — he was governor of Colorado at that time and was runnin' for re-election on the Populist ticket. The Populist Party's candidate for president of the United States was William Jennings Bryan, and all the miners was rallyin' to his side on account of he supported the free purchase of silver. Fortunately, the metal what kept Alma goin' through them hard times was gold, not silver, so we didn't have it near as bad as folks in some of them other places was havin'.

When the smelter in Alma closed, the Alma Placer Company started shippin' their gold, 'long with ours, down to the Boston and Colorado Company's new Argo Smelter in Denver. So, despite the panic, life for me, Sadie, and Jimmy went along pretty much like before. In 1902, the Snowstorm Hydraulic Company bought the old Alma Placer 'long with a lot of the other placer claims along the Platte, both above and below Alma. That didn't affect us much either, 'cause I jest started workin' for the Snowstorm outfit, doin' the same kind of work as before, 'ceptin' now I was one of their foremen. I even had the same manager, so we could still send our ore to the smelter, jest like we'd been doin'.

Things had changed for Jimmy, though. He warn't livin' with me and Sadie no more — hadn't since back in '97, as a matter of fact. He was workin' as a cashier at the bank now and was sleepin' nights in a little back room so's to keep an eye on the place. That same year, the bank had been bought by Harry Singleton. Harry'd come to Alma in '80 and was in charge of a freightin' business for a time, but two years later he opened a mercantile business, Jimmy'd been one of his clerks. In '88, Harry'd sold his business to James Moynahan and went to bein' head cashier at the bank. Then he'd bought the bank from Arthur and Hathaway in '97 and asked Jimmy to come work for him. Jimmy'd jumped at the chance.

Me and Sadie was real proud of our son. He'd done real good in school and could read, write, and cipher most as good as Miss Smith. He was a good worker, too, and everybody seemed to like him. One little gal named Lilly Larkin liked him better'n most, and Jimmy seemed to feel the same way about her. That didn't make me and Sadie too happy, 'cause Lilly had the reputation around town of bein' somethin' of a floozy. She was different from the other girls in Alma — that's for damned shore. Before Lilly showed up, Jimmy'd never seemed to like one girl any more than the next — but, like I said, Lilly was different, and it warn't long before she had Jimmy all tangled up like a fly in a spider's web.

They was married in May of 1905. Jimmy was thirty-one years old, and Lilly claimed to be twenty-four. Sadie figured that she was really a lot older. I've gotta admit she shore did look it, but I jest figured she'd had a real hard life. After they got married, they lived in a house not far from where me and Sadie was livin'. We never got to know Lilly very well, which most likely was a good thing, 'cause she never seemed to like us much — mainly Sadie. But she shore did like the other fellas around town — 'specially a sheriff's deputy in Alma named Ben Bellew, and gettin' married didn't change that at all. I don't know why, but Jimmy never seemed to figure out what all was goin' on, until finally, two years later, Lilly run off with a patent medicine salesman from out of Denver. It bothered both Ben and Jimmy a whole lot, and it took Jimmy over a year to get over it. I don't know how long it took Ben. But it shore didn't bother me and Sadie none. We never did like Lilly, and I shore didn't like that travelin' salesman. The stuff he was sellin' warn't nothin' but alcohol with a fancy label on the bottle — and it didn't do my rheumatiz one damn bit of good.

CHAPTER 39

After Jimmy's marriage broke up, he'd started spendin' more time with me and Sadie again. We hadn't gone much to the mine since Lilly'd showed up, but now we made up for lost time. We didn't work near as hard at it, though — my stiff back and knees seen to that. Mainly we went so's to enjoy the peace and quiet of the Tarryalls. Sometimes Miss Lydia would go 'long with us, and she shore was a pleasure to have around. Even though she was five or six years older than him, Miss Lydia and Jimmy got along real good together. Whenever Jimmy'd go fishin', more often than not she'd go with him. As for me and Sadie, we just liked bein' alone with each other, surrounded by all the beauty of those rugged and awesome mountains. Those was the happiest times we'd had in a long, long time.

One day, whilst I was goin' through my things, I'd come across the old map what Ramon had gave me and Jim so many years ago. I'd never showed it to Jimmy, and when I did he got real excited — 'specially so after I told him how it was supposed to show the whereabouts of the lost bonanza Ramon's granddaddy and uncle claimed to have found. Jimmy asked what the words wrote on the map meant. I explained about the ones I knowed and told him how "lechuzas doble" meant twin owls in American, but that I didn't know why it was writ on the map and I shore as hell wished I did.

Jimmy said it couldn't mean real owls, 'cause they wouldn't stay put. So it must mean somethin' else, and the next time he went fishin', he was gonna keep his eyes peeled — maybe he could figure out what it really did mean. Then he made a copy of the map to take with him. But Jimmy never did find no owls, 'cause he was too busy helpin' Sadie take care of me.

Each year I'd been gettin' more and more stove up with rheumatiz, and by the time 1908 rolled around, I knowed it warn't gonna be too much longer before I'd have to quit workin' at the placer mine. By then I was sixty-four years old, and in the mornin', when I was gettin' out of bed, I felt every last one of them. But even though I warn't near as spry as I used to be, I kept on workin', 'cause now I was a foreman and didn't have to do some of the tougher jobs at the placer works. So all things considered, I was gettin' 'long pretty damn well — for an old coot, that is. Sadie kept tellin' me I should quit workin' and start takin' things easy. We had all the money we'd ever need to live out the rest of our lives, so she figured it'd be nice if I quit so's we could spend time together. But I reckon I was jest too damned stubborn to admit I was too old to work. As usual, I should have listened to Sadie.

After the Snowstorm Hydraulic Company bought out Alma Placer, they'd started usin' two big hoses with seven-inch nozzles 'long with one six-incher. The force of the water comin' out of them hoses was somethin' you'd have to see to believe. It was a lot more powerful than what we'd been usin', and it took some gettin' used to. The stream of water tore up the banks of the Platte somethin' awful and left deep pits where the gravel and sand had been washed into a sluice over three feet wide. When you was

workin' around them big hoses, you had to be mighty damned careful not to get hit by the full force of the water. I learned that the hard way on the second of July 1908, and it shore did ruin my Fourth of July celebration.

That day, like usual, I'd got to the placer works a little earlier than the rest of the men, so's I could figure out where our hose was to be located. I'd climbed down onto the bank and was standin' in front of one of them seven-inch nozzles when some damned fool fired up the pump. Before I

Hydrological placer mining, Alma, circa 1880s. From stereoptican slide by R. C. Miller.
(Courtesy of the Colorado Historical Society)

knowed what was happenin', a stream of water came shootin' out of the nozzle and blowed me twenty feet 'long the bank and into a big boulder. I hit so hard it busted both of my legs, not to mention the scrapes and bruises on the rest of my body. Not only that, I damn near drowned to death before somebody seen what'd happened and shut down the pump. I never did find out who'd turned it on, and nobody ever told me. It wouldn't have made no difference anyways, so I reckon it was best for me not to know.

There warn't no doctor in Alma right then, so they hauled me down to Fairplay in the back end of a wagon. Sadie and Jim sat in the back with me, whilst one of the placer workers drove. I'd never noticed before how rutted and bumpy that damn road to Fairplay was. It was seven miles of pure hell, and I was wishin' I was dead long before we got there. I wished it even more after the doctor went to fixin' my legs.

The doctor was a nice young fella named H. C. Cowen, and he seemed downright happy to see me — mainly, I think, on account of his gettin' what he'd called a new Roentgen machine jest the day before. It'd been brought up from Denver on the train, and he could hardly wait to use it. He claimed it'd let him see through the skin and muscle to the bones in my legs and show him right where they was busted. It was hard to believe, but later on he showed me the pictures, and damned if he warn't right.

Doctor Cowen told me that both of my legs was broke, and the left one was busted up real bad. He showed me on the X-ray where it was busted clear through up near the hip joint, and the two parts was lined up crooked and overlappin' instead of end to end like they was supposed to be. The right leg was busted in the same place, but not near as bad. The doctor explained how he was gonna try to get the two parts of my left leg lined up as good as he could, and after he'd done that, he'd put a plaster cast all around my body from my belly button down to my toes on the left leg and a mite below my knee on the right. That way I couldn't move my legs none whilst the bones was healin'.

Well, that didn't sound like it was gonna be a whole lot of fun — and it warn't. The doctor's wife, her name was Mary, held a bunch of gauze over my nose and started drippin' ether onto it from a can. Whilst she was doin' that, Jimmy and Sadie was holdin' tight to my shoulders whilst the doctor was pullin' on my leg, tryin' to get the bones lined up straight. Then he took another X-ray to see how he'd done. After one more round of pullin' and X-rayin', he told Jimmy to keep a tight hold on my leg whilst he slathered close to a ton of plaster-soaked rolls of gauze on the lower half of my body. After he'd got done doin' all that, and the plaster was beginnin' to dry, everybody in the room heaved a big sigh of relief and relaxed — everybody but me, that is. I was jest heavin'.

Once I was able to think good again, Doctor Cowen told me he'd done the best he could, but that he warn't too pleased with the end results. My leg bone was lined up better than before, but he couldn't get it near as straight as he'd wanted. He was pretty shore it would eventually heal up all right, but it was gonna take a long time doin' it and most likely was gonna end up crooked. Then he looked real unhappy and put his hand on my shoulder as he told me how he was afeard I might never be able to walk on it again — leastwise, not without crutches.

That was terrible news. I figured I'd be better off dead than to be a cripple for the rest of my life. But Sadie, bless her heart, told me she was shore that everything would work out all right if I jest had the patience to stay quiet in bed 'til the broken bones healed. With God's help, she was shore I'd eventually be able to walk on my own. In the meantime she'd do my walkin' for me. Jimmy told us he was gonna move back in and help us out 'til I got so's I could help myself. They done everything they could to cheer me up, but right then nothin' anybody could have said would have made me feel a bit better. I figured there warn't no sense in livin' if I never could walk again.

After the doctor finished patchin' me up, he gave me some laudanum to take if the pain got too bad. He said he'd be up my way in a couple of days, and that he'd stop in to see how I was doin'. And it was a damned good thing he did, 'cause by the time he got there I was about to run out of laudanum. I'd used over half what he'd gave me goin' back to Alma over that damn bumpy road.

I thanked God every day — several times most days — for Sadie and Jimmy. I'd of never made it without their love and help. It was way over a year before my busted up body was healed. Sadie was right, though, I can walk some, but not without usin' a crutch. Sometimes whilst I was healin', I'd get to feelin' like I was gonna go crazy if I didn't find somethin' to do to fill up my time. We had a few good books what I read over and over, and Miss Lydia loaned us some of hers, so I did a lot of readin'. I read the Bible through at least twice. One of the parts I liked most was the part about Job — I figured me and him had a lot in common. But I couldn't read all the time, and at times I'd get bored and start fussin' at Sadie for no good reason. One time, when I was complainin' to her and sayin' how this was a hell of a way to live, Sadie'd come up with a bright idea that made the time pass a whole lot better.

All the years since 1859, after me and Jim left our folks' ranch to come to Colorado, 'most every night, jest before I'd go to sleep, I'd jot down in the little diary my mamma had gave me what all had happened that day. 'Course, I'd missed some days and had to catch up later, but I'd pretty much made a record of my life for the past forty-nine years. I'd filled up several diaries and a good many loose sheets of paper with scribblin' that nobody but me could figure out what it said — leastwise, that's what Sadie claimed. Her idea was for me to write down in a journal what all had happened to me over all them years. And I should try to write as good as I could so's other people could read it, 'cause I'd had some interestin' experiences that would make real good readin'. Besides that, I'd be so busy writin', I wouldn't have time to fuss at her.

Well, at first it sounded like a good idea, but then I got to thinkin'. Some of the folks in Alma now was livin' in these parts back at the time of the raid, and I doubted they'd be too happy when they heard how they'd been livin' 'long side a member of the Reynolds gang for the past twenty-four years. Sadie told me not to worry, her and Jimmy would be the only ones to read the journal for now. Then later on — after I was dead and gone — other folks could read it, too. I don't know as how I liked hearin' the part about me bein' dead, but I reckon she was right — by then it wouldn't make a damned bit of difference who read my story.

It's taken me several years, 'cause I's done it in fits and starts, but today is the twenty-fourth day of September 1914, and I've finally finished writin' down most everythin' what's happened to me and to Sadie — up to now, at least. I reckon from here on, it's not likely that anythin' will happen worth writin' about. But if anythin' excitin' does come along, I'll be shore to write it down, jest like I've been doin' for all these years.

CHAPTER 40

Early Afternoon
September 20, 1915

Almost a year's gone by since I last wrote in this journal, mainly on account of nothin' has happened worth writin' about since then. Besides that, by the time I'd finished writin', I was sick and tired of doin' it. I'm able to get around pretty good now, 'ceptin' I can't walk worth a damn without usin' my crutches. Now I come to think on it, I can't walk worth a damn with them. My left leg's two or three inches shorter than the other, and it's more a bother than a help. But I can ride my horse pretty good, and I still have Sadie and Jimmy, so I'm shore not complainin' none. The Lord has been mighty good to me. I'm seventy-one years old, and I'm grateful for every new day He lets me keep on livin'.

My friend Harry Singleton died not long ago, and his son, Fred, is runnin' the bank in Alma now, whilst his brother Jack runs the one down in Fairplay. A month ago, Fred hired a second cashier named Tobe Taylor and made Jimmy his chief cashier. So now that Jimmy can be away from the bank for a few days, we're all goin' campin' at our favorite spot in the Tarryalls. We're figurin' on leavin' early in the mornin'. The aspen trees should be a mighty pretty sight 'long about now. We've only been there twice this summer, and now that September's 'most half gone, we want to make one more campin' trip before winter sets in. We asked Miss Lydia to go 'long with us, but she can't, on account of later on today, she's leavin' to go to Denver so's to visit relatives.

Speakin' of Miss Lydia, she shore has been a good friend and a big help all the time I was laid up — before and after, too. It's almost like she's me and Sadie's daughter. I don't know why such a sweet, pretty little lady ain't never got married, but she hasn't, and I think maybe Jimmy's glad of it. In fact, I'm pretty shore he's sweet on her, even though she's a few years older than him. He won't admit it, though, and I don't rightly know how Miss Lydia feels about him, but I do know that me and Sadie wouldn't mind it a bit if someday they'd decide to hitch up with each other.

Anyways, like I was sayin', come tomorrow mornin' we're goin' campin' up by our old mine in the Tarryalls. Nowadays we don't work it no more, 'cause the vein of gold we was followin' has mostly petered out — it don't produce enough good ore anymore to make it worth our while. Besides that, I'm too stove up to work it, and Jimmy'd rather fish. But we like to go there anyway, so's we can get away by ourselves for a spell and enjoy God's great creation.

For that, there's no better spot I know of than right up there in the Tarryalls. At night, when I'm lyin' 'long side of Sadie in my sleepin' bag, smellin' the sweet vanilla scent of the ponderosas, I look up at the stars over our heads, and, if I didn't know better, I'd swear they was tangled up in the top branches of the trees. Then you hear an owl hootin' away off in the distance, or maybe a coyote howlin' at the moon, and you feel so peaceful and content — you jest know that everythin's fine with the world and that your Maker is right there with you, standin' by yore side.

Same Day — Eight O'clock in the Evening

Dear God, how can this be happenin' to us? I can't believe it! Jest a few hours ago, I was writin' how my Maker was standin' beside me, and now it's not the Lord standin' there — it's the Devil. At least he was 'til he went out to the kitchen to get hisself something to eat, leavin' me locked up in the bedroom 'long side of Sadie and Jimmy. More'n likely you've already guessed who it is — and if you guessed Rafer Rathbone, yore right. Right now he's out in the kitchen, 'long with two other mean lookin' men. Here one minute I'm writin' about God's peace and contentment, and the next thing I know I'm in hell.

Earlier this evenin', we'd finished packin' our campin' gear and was fixin' to go to bed when there comes this heavy poundin' on the door. When I opened it, there stood Rafer Rathbone lookin' jest as mean as ever and twice as ugly. 'Course, he's a lot older now, but he shore ain't no prettier, and he don't have no better manners either. He's shrunk up considerable over the years. His face is real wrinkled, his hands is all knobby, and he walks sort of bent over, but other than that,

I'm sorry to say, it's the same old Rafer. I wondered how and when he got out of prison. I'd been hopin' he'd stay there 'til he'd rotted, but I reckon that was too much to hope for. The two men with him are big and mean lookin'. One of the big men with him has greasy black hair, bushy eyebrows, and black glowerin', bloodshot eyes. He looks real evil and nasty, and when I first seen him I figured that, 'ceptin' for bein' heavier-set, he looked a lot like Rafer did when I first knowed him. And I was right — he is Rafer's son and his name is Jud. The other fella's name is Rube Blackburn.

When I opened the door, I tried to keep them from comin' into the house, but they pushed right past me like I warn't even there. When I asked Rafer what he was doin' here and what he wanted, he looked at me like he figured I was crazy and said I shore shouldn't have no trouble figurin' that out without his havin' to tell me. 'Course, he was right — I knowed right off he'd come to get the gold and loot in the cave. He figures I've already found it, and now he wants me to give it to him, and if I've already cashed it in, he wants all the money I got for it. If I don't do what he wants, he'll tell the local sheriff about my part in the raid. I tried my best to explain to Rafer how we couldn't find the cave, on account of the lake and all the changes in the Tarryalls since the time of the raid, but he wouldn't believe me. Somehow he knows that me and Sadie have a big savin's account at the Alma bank, and he says I shore as hell didn't get all that money by workin' in the placer mines, so it's bound to be from the cave. When I told him the money in the bank was from the gold mine me and Jim had found back in '60, he wouldn't believe that either.

When I asked Rafer how he'd found us after all these years, he jest laughed and said it was easy. When he was down in San Antonio a little while back, he'd dropped in on the Barlows and asked them real polite like where it was we'd moved to — and they'd been real obligin'. After a little gentle persuasion, they was downright happy to tell him where we was livin' and what name we was goin' by. That made me sick. I shore hope Rafer didn't do anythin' to hurt the Barlows. Then I asked him how come he knowed about the money we had in the bank, and he claimed that was easy, too — you jest had to ask the right person. He never told me who that person might be.

Come mornin', Rafer is gonna have Rube tie Sadie to a chair so she can't escape, and put a gag in her mouth so she can't holler out if somebody comes to our door. That makes me so damn mad I'd kill him if I could — 'course, there's no way I can do that. But even if I could, it wouldn't do any good, 'cause then Jud would be in charge, and it'd most likely make our problems a whole lot worse. So I really don't have no other choice and neither does Jimmy. Come mornin', we've got to go with Rafer and Jud, 'cause if we don't, something bad will happen to Sadie — and to me and Jimmy, too.

So it's gonna be a long, long night for all of us, and I doubt that any of us can sleep. Leastwise I know I can't. Right now I'm settin' here in my rockin' chair writin' all this down in my journal, 'cause I don't know when I'll get a chance to write in it again. Jest as soon as I've finished, we're all gonna get down on our knees and pray — pray that the Good Lord has mercy on us all. After that, we'll wait 'til sunup.

 # PART FOUR

SHADYCROFT FARM
LITTLETON, COLORADO
MARCH TO AUGUST, 1933

(A pen and ink drawing by Doctor Seymour Wheelock)

CHAPTER 41

March 1933

I couldn't believe it. John Reynolds' journal up and ended right when it was beginning to get exciting again, and here I was sittin' alongside of Sam, wondering if John and Jimmy had gone up to the Tarryalls the next day with Rafer and Jud Rathbone, and if they did go, what'd happened. As usual, Sam had gone to sleep right after I stopped reading to him, so I was gonna have to wait 'til the next day to see if Sam knew what had happened. I sure hoped he did — it'd be awful if he didn't.

But as it turned out, it was over two weeks before I could talk to Sam again, 'cause a little later on that day, he came down with the flu and then double pneumonia. I had plenty to do in the meantime, though — my mother and dad saw to that. Except for when we were going to school and doing homework, we were kept busy doing chores, and that didn't leave much time for the fun stuff. So one day, when we were pulling weeds in Mother's vegetable garden, I started complaining to J. J. about how much work we were havin' to do. But J. J. told me to quit gripin' and that I should do all I could to help our folks, 'cause they were going through some real hard times right now. Dad wasn't making enough money to pay all the expenses of running the farm and feeding his family — 'specially when the prices for feed and food were so high.

Well I knew that to be a fact, at least the part about food, 'cause a few days back I'd gone grocery shopping with Mother at the Piggly Wiggly store in Littleton. As usual, she made me practice my arithmetic by listing the prices of her purchases and then adding them up to get the total cost. Mother was always figuring out sneaky ways to make me do math. Anyway, as it turned out, a ten-pound sack of flour cost twenty-one cents; ten pounds of sugar, forty-six cents; a large can of peaches, fifteen cents; tomatoes, ten cents; and a two pound can of Hills Brother's coffee (the kind Dad likes best) was thirty-five cents. I tried to talk her into buying a quart of chocolate ice cream — it was only fifty cents — but we couldn't on account of she'd run out of money.

Michie, J. J., Rab, and Robby in the front yard at Shadycroft — circa 1932.
(Photograph was taken by Julius E. Johnson Sr..)

'Course, living on a farm, we could grow a lot of our own food, and that helped a lot. Besides eating our own vegetables and fruit during the summer and fall months, Mother would preserve them in Mason jars and store them in the cellar for us to eat during the winter — we stored carrots, potatoes, and other root crops in the root cellar — but that was in the good years. What with the drought and all the last two years all of our crops — including vegetables and fruits — had been pretty sparce and we'd been havin' to buy a lot of our food at the store — including meat. Most years, Dad and Mr. Williamson would butcher a hog or steer so we could make our own sausage, hamburger, steaks, and chops, but lately we'd were buying most of our meat at Lemke's meat market in Littleton. That's on account of it cost more to buy hay and grain for our feeder stock than it did to buy meat at the market. One good thing, though, we had plenty of chickens and eggs — and now and then we could add to our meat supply by goin' jackrabbit hunting on the prairie east of a big cattle ranch called "The Diamond K Ranch." It's called that because its brand is a diamond with a big K inside it.

I knew that our folks had been through droughts and hard times before, but I'd never seen them this worried. Lots of nights I'd see them sitting at the kitchen table talking quietly. I never could hear what they were saying, but it looked like they were going over a whole bunch of important lookin' papers with lots of numbers written on them. I'd wondered what was bothering them, so I asked J. J. what was going on. He said that he didn't know much, 'cause our folks didn't like to talk about it, but that he was pretty sure it was about not having enough money.

He explained to me how farm prices, especially that of wheat, had been great during all the years America was at war with Germany, but that they went to pot after the war ended in 1918. All during the twenties our folks had struggled to make ends meet, and they'd gone into debt in the process. Then in 1930, not long after the start of the big economic crash in 1929, Dad borrowed ten thousand dollars from the Federal Land Bank of Wichita, Kansas, so he could pay off all his other smaller debts and put them into one big loan at a lower rate of interest. That most likely would have worked out fine if it hadn't been for the depression and the drought. When the stock market crashed in 1929, the value of the dollar dropped to next to nothing, and all over the country businesses went broke and folks lost their jobs.

On top of that, the terrible drought and winds we'd been havin' for the past few years had dried up and blown Dad's wheat and dryland crops right out of the ground. The same thing happened to his corn, alfalfa, and other irrigated crops. They'd dried up, too, on account of the irrigation water in the Highline Canal had been next to nothing. For the last few winters, there'd been so little snow in the mountains there wasn't any snowpack to melt and run off come spring. There was no rain, either. The mountains were bone dry, and the water in the South Platte River was down to a trickle.

So, according to J. J., it wasn't surprising that our folks didn't have any money. For the past two years, Dad hadn't been able to grow enough forage crops to feed his feeder cattle — let alone enough to sell any — so he'd had to sell all of his feeder cattle. And, besides that, he'd been havin' to buy feed for his milk cows and horses. With all of these extra expenses, and no income, it was easy to see why our folks were so worried. Just last night J. J.'d overheard Dad telling Mother that the next payment on the bank loan would be coming due in late April, and if they couldn't find a way to raise the money soon, we were gonna lose Shadycroft Farm. Well, that shook me up something awful.

'Course, we weren't the only ones having trouble. According to an article by Mr. Houston Waring, the editor of the *Littleton Independent*, it was a lot worse for the farmers in eastern Colorado, Kansas, and Oklahoma. Back there, not only was it hot and dry, but the wind was blowing all of their topsoil away. I knew that was true, 'cause most of it was coming our way. Some mornings when we'd get up, it'd be bright and sunny. Then all of a sudden the sky would get dark, almost like night, and when we looked to the east, we could see a towering cloud of dark, yellowish-colored dust blocking out the sun.

Then, a little while later, the wind would hit us, and some of our own topsoil would be added to the dirt that already filled the air. Sometimes it was so bad you couldn't go out of the house without a bandanna tied around your nose and mouth to keep you from choking on the dust. But that didn't do a whole lot of good, and once you got back inside the house you'd have to cough and spit a lot to get all of the dust out of your lungs. But dirt came into the house, too — under the doors, around the windows and through every crack and crevice until it sometimes seemed like there was more dirt inside the house than out. And up on the dryland it was a whole lot worse. There, the relentless wind scoured the dust and tumbleweeds from the fields and piled it in deep drifts along the east side of our fences, until only a few tips of posts were left exposed.

And another problem we'd been havin' for the past few summers was grasshoppers. In some places they'd cover the ground, making it seem like the earth beneath your feet was moving. Wherever you'd step, they'd squish under your shoes, and wherever they went, they'd eat everything in sight. They even chewed bark off the wood fence posts! Dad put out poison bait with arsenate of lead in it, but it didn't do any good. It killed some, of course, but there were always plenty more to replace them. At least the birds were well fed — even the magpies seemed satisfied.

Now that I knew why our folks were worried, I was real worried, too, and big tears started rolling down my cheeks. As I was trying to wipe them away with the back of my hand, J. J. put his arm around me and said, "Don't worry so much, Robby. We haven't lost Shadycroft yet, and I'm betting that our folks will find a way to keep it from happening. In the meantime, we should do everything we can to help them."

'Course bein' as how I was only eleven years old and sort of scrawny, there weren't many farm chores I could do other than feeding chickens, picking apples, mowing grass, and the like But there were a few, and the one I liked the best was to get up on top of a haystack and spread out the dry, sweet smelling hay after the stacker dumped it. Putting up ensilage wasn't near as much fun. That's what you call ground-up corn or other forage crops. After attaching a heavy leather belt to the flywheels on my dad's Twin City tractor and the grinder, the tractor is fired up, the grinder chops up the corn — stalks, leaves, cobs, and all — and blows it up a pipe into the silo. Our two brick silos, both close to forty feet tall, have slot-like openings up and down their west sides with metal rods set in them like the rungs on a ladder. My job is to climb up the slot to the top of the ensilage, get into the silo, and put boards over the opening in the slot so the ensilage won't spill out as the level increases. Besides that, I spread out the ensilage to keep it from piling up in one spot, and at the same time do a little dance to keep from gettin' hit by the chunks of corncobs that are rainin' down from above like bullets shot out of a gun.

Milking cows is another thing I like to do — if I don't have to do it too often. Milking time comes twice a day at five in the morning and five in the evening — day in and day out — year in and year out. The doors from the corral into the milking parlor are opened, and the cows file in one by one. Each cow knows to go to its own station, where a metal stanchion is snapped shut around her neck to keep her from backing out when she finds out what's going on at her other end. Then, after all the cows are contentedly munching silage from the trough in front of the stanchions, Dad and Mr. Williamson sit on three-legged stools and do the milking — and so do I, now that I've figured out how to get the milk out of the cow and into the bucket.

My very favorite job is driving our herd of feeder cattle from one pasture to another. Molly likes it, too, 'cause she's a trained cutting horse and loves to cut a steer out of the herd or to chase it back in — whichever needs doin'. It's a fun job, and I like doin' it, except for the times she unexpectedly turns and goes off to the right, or left, while at the same time I keep goin' straight.

It's not a job, but another thing I like to do is to cloud watch from on top of Indian Lookout. That's the name my Grandmother Johnson gave to the little knoll on top of a hill just west of our farm back in 1902, after she found arrowheads and flint chips on it. But back in the mid-1910s, folks in Littleton started calling it "Jackass Hill," on account of a fella started raising jackasses on the slopes of the hill and sellin' them to the U. S. army to use in the war against Germany. But I think the name Indian Lookout fits it a whole lot better 'cause the Indians were using it as a lookout and making arrowheads there long before the first white man showed up. And it's easy to see why they chose that place to do it, 'cause from the top of the knoll they could see all up and down the Platte River Valley, from Pike's Peak in the south to the Wyoming border in the north, and keep watch for signs of game or enemy Indians. 'Course, the real Indians are long gone now, but if you have the time for it and a good imagination, on warm summer days you can still sit with your back leaning against the trunk of a cottonwood tree and look up into the vast blue sky to watch the cloud Indians drifting by on their gossamer horses in slow pursuit of puffy, white buffalo — or perhaps other Indians.

CHAPTER 42

It was the morning of March twenty-ninth. Over two weeks had passed since I'd last seen Sam, and as I walked into his room, he greeted me.

"Where the hell have you been keepin' yourself, Boy? I's missed seein' you."

"I wanted to come see you, Sam, 'cause I've really been missin' you, too, but Mother and Mrs. Vogel wouldn't let me 'til now. How are you feeling?"

"Pretty good, Boy. In fact, I feels damn near as good as I did afore I got shot."

"Gosh, that's great Sam. It's the best news I've heard all winter."

Then I took a deep breath and asked the question that had been worrying me. "Sam, ever since we finished reading John Reynolds' journal, I've been wondering what happened when John and Jimmy went with Rafer and Jud to look for the cave. I've been worrying about Sadie, too, 'cause she was bein' held hostage. Do you know what happened after that? I sure hope nothin' bad happened to any of the Reynolds."

When I had finished, he lay quietly for a while like he was thinking. I could tell that he didn't want to talk about it — but finally he did.

"Wal, I wish I didn't have to tell you this, Boy, 'cause it hurts me every time I think about it. But I 'spect I owes it to you to finish the story and not leave you hangin' in midair. But you ain't gonna like hearin' about it any more'n I like tellin' it, 'cause it don't have a happy endin'."

"You mean something really bad happened, Sam?" I was beginning to wish I hadn't asked.

"Jest quit interruptin', and let me get on with what I'm gonna tell you. I want to get it over with," he said in a choked voice.

SAM'S STORY

"I'm shore you recollect, Boy, how John's diary jest up and ended with Sadie, Jimmy, and him all settin' there in the bedroom, waitin' 'til sunup.

Wal, come next mornin', way before sunup, after Sadie'd fixed breakfast, Rafer told Rube to tie her to a chair in the front room and keep her there all the time they was gone. That way she couldn't run off and tell the sheriff what was goin' on. 'Course, if she'd did, then he'd tell the sheriff in Alma how John Hardin was really John Reynolds, and how he'd been one of the Reynolds gang back in 1864. Then John would end up either gettin' hung or spendin' the rest of his life in jail.

"After eatin' breakfast, Rafer, Jud, John, and Jimmy went out to the barn in back of the Reynolds' house, saddled up their horses, mounted up, and rode off in the direction of the Tarryalls. It was mid-afternoon when they got to where the cave was hid, and after he'd seen all the water in the lake and spent four hours lookin' for the cave, Rafer finally had to admit that John had been tellin' him the truth when he told him why he couldn't find it. By then, it was gettin' dark, so they all climbed on their horses and headed back to Alma.

"It was midafternoon when they finally got there and untied Sadie from the chair. John and Jimmy was happy that Rube hadn't hurt her none, but Sadie was madder'n hell. Right after they'd got there, Rafer and his two cronies took off for parts unknown, and the Reynolds all heaved a big sigh of relief. They figured they was gone for good and that it was damned good riddance.

"But they was wrong. Four days later, all three of them was back. That devil, Rafer, had come up with a brand-new scheme. I reckon you recollect how John wrote how Jimmy was head cashier at the Alma bank now. Well, a few months before Rafer showed up, Fred hired another cashier named Tobe Taylor. He was supposed to be Jimmy's assistant, but he was really in cahoots with Rafer and had told him how, come the end of the month, the bank vault would be full of currency what the mine and placer owners around Alma used to pay their workers' wages. On top of that, there'd be a lot of gold and silver bullion in the vault waitin' to be shipped to the Denver mint. All told, it'd come to over a hundred thousand dollars. When Rafer heard that, his greedy mind started figurin' a way to force Jimmy and John into helpin' him rob the bank.

"Seein' as how Jimmy and Fred Singleton was the only ones what knowed the combination to the vault, Rafer needed Jimmy go to the bank with him and Jud, so's to unlock it for them. John was to go 'long, too, and if Jimmy didn't do like he was told, somethin' real bad was gonna happen to John. To make it even more certain that Jimmy and John would cooperate, Rube was gonna tie Sadie up like he'd done before and stand guard over her. And if they didn't do what Rafer told them to do, he was gonna kill Sadie real slow and painful like and enjoy hisself whilst he was doin' it. Then Rafer took John and Jimmy's guns from them, so's to be shore they didn't try to do somethin' stupid." Right then I forgot I was not supposed to interrupt.

"Sam, how come you know all this stuff, and how come you have John Reynolds' journal? John never mentioned you in his journal, but somehow you seem to know everything that happened to him and his family." Before I'd even finished talkin', I was sorry I'd asked it. Sam was really upset.

"Damn it, Boy, I asked you not to interrupt! I already told you how John was my very best friend. And not only that, Sadie and Jimmy was my good friends, too — I spent lots of time talkin' to all three of them, so you've no call to be so damned nosy. I really don't know why John never mentioned me in his journal, and it was Sadie what gave it to me, but it's none of your damned business why she did. Now jest set there like a good boy and keep your damn mouth shut so's I can finish tellin' you my story."

"I'm sorry, Sam. I promise I won't interrupt any more," I mumbled.

Seemingly appeased, Sam began again. "John and Sadie's cabin was at the south edge of town, a far piece from any of the other hous-es, so's it warn't likely anybody'd notice their unwanted guests. But, jest to be on the safe side, Rafer told Rube to take all three of their horses to the livery stable in Alma and spend the night in town, so's folks wouldn't start wonderin' what all them horses was doin' in the Reynolds' corral. Then Rube was to bring the horses back the next day 'long about midafternoon, that'd be the thirtieth of September — the day they was figurin' on robbin' the bank.

"Rafer and Jud stayed at the Reynolds' house that night and all the next day 'til Rube come back with their horses. All that time, the Reynolds was kept locked up in the back bedroom to be shore nobody'd take off and warn the sheriff that the bank was about to get robbed. Jimmy told Rafer his scheme warn't gonna work, on account of Fred would come lookin' for him if he didn't show up. But Rafer jest laughed and told him not to get his hopes up, 'cause Taylor had already told Singleton that he warn't comin' to work that day on account of he was sick.

"That night of the twenty-ninth and all the next day 'til it come time for the robbery, the Reynolds had to stay in the back bedroom waitin' and worryin' about what was gonna happen, 'ceptin' for the times one of them had to answer a call of nature. And even then, Jud would go 'long with them so's to stand guard by the outhouse to be shore nobody would try to sneak away and go for the sheriff."

It seemed to me that Sam was getting more and more nervous as he began to tell me what'd happened next. He'd wring his hands together like maybe they were hurtin', then he'd rub them on the bedcovers. I could tell that he really hated having to tell me whatever it was, and I figured it must be the part Sam had said I wasn't gonna like to hear. He was right — there were some things I wished I'd never been told.

"That afternoon, Rube and the horses showed up jest a few minutes before the bank closed. After tyin' Sadie up and orderin' Rube to keep close watch over her, Rafer gave John and Jimmy their guns back — minus bullets — and told them to strap on their gun belts and holster their guns. Then all four of them mounted up and rode over to the bank. Jimmy and John was in the lead and Rafer and Jud was bringin' up the rear. After tyin' their horses to the hitchin' rail in front of the bank, Rafer stayed settin' on his horse whilst Jimmy and John went inside. Jud was followin' close behind, holdin' a six-gun in each hand. Fred Singleton was in a little room over to the right, settin' behind his desk, tallyin' up the day's deposits and withdrawals. Taylor was in the cashier's cage tryin' to look busy. Fred looked up from his work, and when he seen it was Jimmy and John walkin' towards him, he smiled and was fixin' to stand up and say somethin'. And then, before Fred knowed what was happenin', Jud come up behind him and hit him a hard rap on the head with the butt of his gun. Fred dropped like a flour sack and lay on the floor lookin' like he was dead, but, as I found out later, he was jest knocked out cold.

"Then Jud made Jimmy open up the vault. Right after that, Taylor come out from where he'd been cowerin' in his cashier's cage and started carryin' the currency and bullion outside to where him and Rafer could put it into the saddlebags. Jud made John and Jimmy help, too, and it warn't long before they had the vault emptied out of everything what was worth takin'…

"I don't know if'n I can stand tellin' you what happened next, Boy," Sam said in a low, trembly voice. It looked to me like he had tears in his eyes, but I was probably just imagining it, 'cause I figured a grown man like Sam wouldn't cry. Then he started talkin' again, and his voice got sort of husky, and he had to clear his throat now and then.

"After all the bullion and currency was loaded into the saddlebags, Jud told John and Taylor to stay inside the bank, whilst him and Jimmy went outside to where Rafer was waitin' with the horses. Then Jud took Jimmy's empty gun from its holster and ordered him to mount up and wait 'long side Rafer. After reloadin' Jimmy's gun, Jud handed it up to Rafer, then he mounted up hisself. After that, all three of them jest kept settin' on their horses outside the bank, waitin' for what was gonna happen next.

"From where Jimmy was settin', he could look through the bank's window and see what was goin' on, and he couldn't believe what was happening." Now Sam's voice got all choked up, and I was sure I could see tears in his eyes as he struggled to go on. Finally he blew his nose hard, cleared his throat, and began to tell his story again. "Taylor was standin' over near the open door of the vault, and John was jest a few feet in front of him. Then Jimmy seen Taylor pull his revolver out of his holster and shoot my daddy dead, straight through his heart."

Sam lay quietly for a few seconds after that, then continued in a tear-choked voice. "After Jimmy'd seen his daddy drop dead on the floor, he jest set there on his horse like he was in a daze. He couldn't move. All he could do was to keep on watchin' whilst Taylor took John's gun out of the holster, loaded it, shot it once up into the ceiling of the bank, and put it into John's dead hand. After that, Taylor come runnin' out of the bank, figurin' he'd get on John's horse and escape, but the very second he come out of the door, Rafer shot him right through his head, usin' Jimmy's gun to do it. Taylor dropped like a rock on the ground in front of the bank — deader'n a doornail.

"Next, Jud got down from off'n his horse, took Taylor's gun from its holster, and put it in his hand, to make it look like Taylor had been tryin' to keep the robbers from gettin' away. Then Jud took Jimmy's gun from Rafer and dropped it in the dirt by the hitchin' rail, so's to make it look like Jimmy was the one what shot Taylor. After that, he climbed back on his horse. Everythin' happened so quick, it was over before Jimmy could figure out what was goin' on. And before he knowed what was happenin', Rafer'd grabbed his reins and started leadin' him at a fast gallop back to the Reynolds' house, so's to get there before the town folks had time to figure out what was goin' on."

By now Sam wasn't crying any more, and his voice sounded harsh and angry as he told me what happened next. "Rafer had it all figured out. He knowed it warn't gonna be long before the sheriff would be comin' to the Reynolds' home lookin' for Jimmy. 'Long with most everybody else in Alma, the sheriff would know it was Jimmy's gun what was lyin' there in the dust, 'long side Taylor's body, makin' it look like Jimmy was the one what had robbed the bank and kilt Taylor. And not only that, the way Rafer had fixed it, everybody'd think that John was one of the bandits and that Taylor had kilt him before he'd got kilt hisself. It was a real slick scheme to make the sheriff and everybody else think that Jimmy was the one they was after.

"The second they got to the Reynolds' house, Rafer climbed down off'n his horse and rushed into the house, draggin' Jimmy with him. Whilst Rube was untyin' Sadie, Rafer warned her not to tell the sheriff or anybody else how he'd forced John and Jimmy to rob the bank, 'cause if she did, when he heard about it, he'd kill Jimmy — then he'd come back and kill her — real slow and painful like. Then, before Sadie or Jimmy had a chance to say a word to each other, Rafer and Rube pushed Jimmy out of the house and made him get on his horse. Then they all headed south towards Fairplay, ridin' as fast as their horses could go."

Sam was quiet for a long time after that. He jest lay there not sayin' a word and looking like his thoughts were a zillion miles away. He'd forgotten I was even there. I figured that this must be the end of the Reynolds' story, and I wondered if Sam knew what had happened to Jimmy after he rode off with Rafer and Jud. I wondered, too, if he knew what had become of Sadie. But I decided I'd best not ask. I'd already made him mad once today, and I shore didn't want to risk doin' it again. So I got up and tiptoed out of the room. I don't think he even knew when I left.

CHAPTER 43

I had a lot to think about. Sam's story was like something out of a book by Zane Grey, except that all the good guys kept gettin' shot dead and nothin' bad ever seemed to happen to the bad guys. One thing that Sam had said, however, struck me as being sort of peculiar. Not far from the end of his story, jest after his friend John Reynolds got shot by that rat, Taylor, Sam had said, "He'd shot my daddy," and it seemed to me he should have said "*his* daddy," meanin' Jimmy's daddy. Right when he'd said it, I didn't give it much thought. I figured it probably was jest a mistake, or maybe on account of John seemed like a daddy to him. But now that I had more time to think about it, I'd begun to wonder if it'd been a slip of the tongue, and that maybe it really was true — John Reynolds actually was Sam's daddy. But if that was so, why wouldn't he want me to know about it? 'Ceptin' for Jimmy, I was pretty shore that John and Sadie didn't have any living children — at least Sam had never mentioned anything about Jimmy havin' a brother, 'ceptin' for little Johnny, and he'd died long before Jimmy was born.

Then all of a sudden I figured it out. I'd bet anything that John Reynolds really was Sam's daddy, and that Sam was really Jimmy. That way it would explain how come Sam knew so many little details about what all had happened to John and Sadie Reynolds, and to Jimmy, too. Not only that, it would also explain why Sadie gave John's journal to Sam. I was shore I was right. Now the only problem was did I dare ask Sam if what I was thinkin' was true? I knew that sooner or later, I'd have to ask, and I decided that sooner was better. But, as it turned out, it was later — a week later, as a matter of fact.

Unfortunately, unbeknownst to me, my mother and my teacher'd had a discussion, and the subject of the talk was me. My teacher seemed to have the mistaken notion that I hadn't been payin' attention in class and had fallen behind in my schoolwork. She also said that when I was speakin' in front of the class, my language would at times include some unusual words such as "warn't," "whilst," and "ain't," and that I'd totally given up puttin' the "g" on the end of words endin' in "ing." She even claimed that another student in my class had overheard me usin' the word "damn." I'd shore like to know who it was that tattled on me. I bet it was Grace Simon, 'cause she's mad at me, even though it wasn't my fault.

Grace sits at the desk right in front of me at school and has real long, blonde hair sort of like a horse's tail, only it's fluffier and floats around a lot. On this disastrous occasion, that hair was my downfall. Our whole class was lined up and moving towards the front of the room where Miss Hamilton was handing out report cards to take home to our parents. I was doing my very best to stay back and not get close to Grace, 'cause it's common knowledge that all girls have cooties. I know that for a fact, 'cause Joe Wilkinson told me so, and he should know, 'cause he has sisters. 'Course, I'm not real sure what a cootie is, but I'm sure it's something bad. Anyway, like I said, I was stayin' as far back from Grace as I could, but Al Thompson was right behind me in line, and he kept shoving me up close to her and snickering, like he thought it was funny. Finally, after what seemed like forever, we got to the teacher's desk, where Grace received her report card and started to walk off, and then — to my horror and embarrassment — I discovered that some strands of her hair had become entangled around the middle button of my shirt, and I was firmly attached to Grace — cooties and all.

I considered dying on the spot, but before going to that extreme, I tried to free myself by jerking at the hair that bound us together. Grace did not appreciate this. In fact, she became downright hostile. So I tried a more humane approach and attempted to unwind her hair from my button. By now, the rest of the class had gathered about and were enjoying themselves immensely, laughing and saying very unkind things at Grace's and my expense. Finally, Miss Hamilton came to our rescue and managed to untangle our golden tether. I appreciated that greatly, but I sure didn't appreciate her poorly suppressed giggles.

But, other than that short swear word spoken at a moment of extreme emotional stress, I didn't think my talkin' had changed none at all. However, what I thought didn't really matter, and what my mother thought did. And what she thought I'd rather not say, except that she had the ridiculous idea that the alleged flaws in my speech had somethin' to do with my seein' so much of Sam. Ignorin' all my protests and denials, she said that from now on I warn't — wasn't — to see Sam any more, or to ride my horse, and that all of my free time was to be spent in readin' and practicin' how to write good, uh, well. After a full week of such unreasonable treatment, I appealed to a higher authority and spoke to my dad. He said that while he seriously doubted that his authority was higher than my mother's, he'd at least listen to what I had to say. Then I told him how all I wanted to do was to explain to Sam why I hadn't been comin' — coming — to see him. 'Course, it was mainly because I wanted to ask Sam if he really was Jimmy Reynolds, but I didn't say that to Dad. I just told him how Sam seemed to look forward to my visits, and how Mrs. Vogel was pretty sure my visits were helpin' Sam get better faster.

Dad smiled a little and told me that he would talk with Mother and see if she'd agree to let me visit Sam again, as long as I was careful to watch my grammar from now on. Then he explained how the reason he and my mother wanted J. J. and me to work hard in school and get a good education was so we could find good jobs when we got older. He said that both of them, and especially my mother, didn't want either of their boys to be farmers, 'cause it was such a hard, uncertain way to make a living. I don't know what Dad said, but whatever it was worked, for on the morning of April fifth, Mother told me I could start seeing Sam again whenever I wanted as long as I did my homework assignments and chores first. I was surprised when she agreed so readily. Maybe she figured that Sam's and my talks really were helping to shorten the stay of her star boarder. Actually, in another way, things were already improving for Mother. After Sam had recovered from the flu and pneumonia, the Vogels had started spending most evenings and nights at their own home, and, believe it or not, I missed them. By now the Vogels seemed like part of our family, and I think J. J. thought so, too — 'specially Abby.

"Where the hell have you been the past week, Boy?" Sam greeted me as I entered the room. "I's been missin' you." After I explained why my mother hadn't let me visit him because of the way I was talking, Sam looked real guilty.

"Yore mamma's right, Boy, and first chance I get I's gonna 'pologize to her for gettin' her upset. I reckon I do mangle the English language a mite, but from now on I's gonna try to talk better."

Sam asked what all I'd been up to since the last time he'd seen me, and first off I said, "Not much." But then I decided to tell him about all the troubles my folks had been having — like the drought and depression. I even told him what J. J. had said about my folks owing the bank a lot of money, and how if they couldn't pay the upcoming interest payment, we most likely were gonna lose our farm. By the time I'd finished telling Sam about our troubles, I was close to cryin'. And I'm sure he could tell how unhappy I was 'cause he put his arm around my shoulder, gave me a little hug, and told me how he shore wished he could help us. Of course, there was no way he could, but it was a real nice thought anyway, and I thanked him for saying it.

I asked Sam how he was feeling, now that he'd gotten over the pneumonia. "Jest fine, Boy. Really fine — I's damn near back to my old self again." I didn't figure that getting back to his old self was anything to brag about — of course, I didn't tell him that.

"That's great, Sam. I bet it won't be long before you can start coming downstairs."

"I shore hope so, Boy, 'cause to tell you the truth, I's gettin' mighty tired of lookin' at these four walls."

Now was the time — if I was ever gonna ask Sam if he was really Jimmy Reynolds, I had to do it now while I still had the nerve. I was afraid he'd get mad at me and think I was accusing him of lying about who he really was, but I still had to ask. So, after taking a deep breath and crossing my fingers, I did. "Sam, do you remember telling me how John Reynolds was shot to death by Tobe Taylor?"

"'Course I do, Boy. You think I was makin' all that up?"

"Oh, no, Sam. No, 'course not. But when you were telling me about that, you said how Taylor had shot *my* daddy. When you said it, I just figured you'd made a mistake, and meant to say his daddy, meaning Jimmy's daddy, not yours." And then, taking another deep breath, I continued. "But then, when I got to thinking about it later, I started wondering if maybe it really wasn't a mistake after all, but a slip of the tongue. Now please don't get mad at me for saying this, Sam, but ever since then I've been wondering if maybe all the time you were talking about Jimmy you were really talking about yourself, and that you're really John and Sadie's son, Jimmy Reynolds — not Sam. If that's true, it would explain how you know every little thing that ever happened to them, and how come you ended up with John Reynolds' journal." After I'd finished talking, Sam sat there propped up in bed, not saying a word for the longest time. Then he finally broke the silence.

"I was wonderin' when you'd figure it out, Boy. I had an idea you'd been thinkin' along them lines. Wal, yore right, 'cept my name is really Jimmy Reynolds. I reckon I should've told you a long time back, but I've been playin' the part of Crazy Sam for so long, that now it's hard for me to admit to anybody who I really am. I was named James after my granddaddy and Uncle Jim. It's my middle name what's Samuel, after my mamma's daddy, Samuel Hardin. After my daddy was kilt in the bank robbery and I was on the run, I started usin' Sam for my first name and Baker for the last. But hardly anybody's ever asked me my name — nobody cared a tinker's damn who I was."

"Well, I'm sure glad to know that you really are Jimmy, Sam. I'll really be glad when you let me tell my dad about your daddy's journal and all the other things you've told me about. He'll be amazed, even though he's always said you were a lot smarter than everybody thought."

"Wal, now, I's mighty pleased to hear yore daddy said that, Boy. I's always knowed he was a real smart man — and yore mamma's real smart, too, you know. But I doubt either of them is gonna like it when they find out the man they's been hidin' is wanted for murder up in Alma."

"But you didn't do nothin' wrong, Sam," I protested. "You didn't rob a bank, and you sure didn't kill anybody — Rafer just made it look like you did."

"True enough, Boy, and, as a matter of fact, most of the folks livin' up in Alma don't think I did, either — even Fred Singleton, the owner of the bank, don't think I did it. But the sheriff still thinks I done it, and I's sorry to say, it's what he thinks what counts."

"By the way, Sam, there's another thing I've been wondering about. When's the last time you saw or heard from your mother? She must be real worried about you."

There was a catch in his voice when he answered, "Last time I heard, Boy, Mamma was doin' jest fine, but that was more'n a month afore I got shot. 'Course, since I's been here at Shadycroft, there's no way I can know how she's doin', and it worries me somethin' awful. She'd be eighty-eight years old now. 'Course, she ain't near as spry as she used to be, but her mind's jest as sharp as it ever was — leastwise, it was last time I was in Alma.

"You remember my tellin' you how my teacher, Miss Lydia Smith, was my mamma's best friend?" I nodded. "Wal, since comin' to Littleton, I's kept in touch with Mamma by writin' letters to Miss Lydia — then Miss Lydia writes back, tellin' me how Mamma is doin'. She sends the letters to my post office box in Englewood. She's been livin' with Mamma, ever since my daddy got kilt, and that gives me a lot of comfort. She's shore been a good friend to me and my momma."

"Sam, a little while back you said something about the last time you'd seen your mother up in Alma. How could you do that without getting caught by the sheriff?"

Sam chuckled. "Wal, Boy, maybe I'd best go ahead and tell you the rest of my story. I'll start where I left off — right after all of them terrible happenin's at the Alma bank the day my daddy got kilt."

CHAPTER 44

SAM'S STORY CONTINUES:

"I reckon you remember me tellin' you, Boy, how all four of us — me, Rafer, Jud, and Rube — was ridin' hellbent for election towards Fairplay jest as fast as we could go. I was ridin' jest as fast as the others 'cause I figured that no self-respectin' posse was gonna stop and ask me polite-like how come it was my gun what was lyin' in the dust outside the Alma bank 'long side Taylor's corpse. They'd either shoot me or hang me right off, without askin' me any questions, and, if they didn't, I was shore that either Rafer or Jud would do it for them to make sure I did-n't escape.

"A few miles before we got to Fairplay, we turned off the road on to a rock outcrop where our tracks wouldn't show and rode cross coun-try over the hills, headin' a little north of due east in the general direc-tion of Kenosha Pass. I'm shore Rafer was figurin' on gettin' to Denver jest as fast as he could so's he could hole up 'til things quieted down some. 'Ceptin' for the times we swung wide around the little railroad towns of Como and Jefferson, we followed 'long side the tracks of the Denver, South Park and Pacific. Rafer made me stay in the lead — I reckon he was afeared I'd take off in a direction of my own choosin' if I'd been bringin' up the rear. One time, when we stopped to give our horses a breather, I heard Jud talkin' to Rafer, and I got a sudden sinkin' feelin' in the pit of my stomach.

"Pa, he said, "why don't me and Rube jest shoot Jimmy right here and now? We can dump his body in that dry wash over there? This is as good a place to do it as any."

"I said a prayer, braced myself, and sat there in the saddle waitin' for the bullet to hit. But it never come. That was the first and only time I ever felt grateful to Rafer, when I heard him say, 'Naw, not now, Jud — we're gonna be needin' Jimmy's help when we go lookin' for that cave in the Tarryalls where the loot and gold is hid. The money we got from the bank is jest chicken feed compared to what's stashed in the cave.'

"That didn't make Jud a bit happy. I could tell he was itchin' to shoot me, and I reckon I should have thanked Rafer for keepin' him from doin' it — but I didn't. I thanked God instead. I was shore it was Him what put them words in Rafer's mouth, unlikely as it seems.

"But Jud warn't gonna give up. 'What makes you think Jimmy'll help us find the cave, Pa? He'll jest stall us along pretendin' to look for it, hopin' that somethin' will happen so's he can sneak off. Then he'll come back later and find the gold for hisself.'

'Damn it, Jud! Jimmy's not stupid. He knows damn well if he don't do jest what we tell him, we'll pay a little visit to his mamma — one that she won't like and neither will he. That'll keep him from runnin' off. Ain't that right, Jimmy?' I nodded my head.

"That's right, Rafer, I'll do jest what you say.

"By the time we'd got to the top of Kenosha Pass, the sun had long since set, but there was a full moon that night, so there was plenty of light for us to see where we was goin'. At the top of the pass, we left the railroad line and started ridin' down the road on the east side of the pass towards Grant and Bailey. But after goin' about a quartermile, we seen by the light of the moon close to ten or fifteen riders comin' fast in our direction. But there must have been some other riders even closer that we couldn't see for the shadows, 'cause all of a sudden I heard gun shots, and then the zing of bullets whizzin' past my ears.

"Let me tell you, Boy, that got my attention in a hurry, and I didn't waste a second in wheelin' my horse around and headin' back towards the top of the pass jest as fast as I could get my horse to go. Rafer's horse was faster than mine, and he was passin' me by when all of a sudden I seen him throw up his arms, pitch forward out of the saddle, and hit the ground in a heap. I figured he was dead for shore, and I found out later I was right. I would have gave a cheer for the fella what shot him, but right then I was too busy tryin' to keep from gettin' shot myself. Jud was ridin' right behind me, and I kept thinkin' he'd take a shot at me now that his daddy couldn't stop him. But right then I reckon he had other things on his mind. When we got to the top of the pass, Jud and Rube went west down the road to South Park, whilst I headed south, ridin' through the rocks and trees in the moonlight jest as fast as I dared. There warn't nobody followin' me, so I figured the posse most likely hadn't seen me turn off and had took off after Jud and Rube. I shore hoped they'd catch them. But they didn't, as I found out a long time later.

"I rode hard 'til I figured I was in the clear, then I slowed down a mite and kept on goin' 'til a little before noon on the following day, when I come to the old mine my daddy and Uncle Jim had dug back in 1860. I spent the rest of that day restin'. That night, after it got dark, I lit out again and headed back to Texas. It was a long hard trip, and I doubt I'd have made it if Rafer hadn't stuffed some of the money from the bank robbery into one of my saddle bags 'cause he couldn't get it all in his. I hated to do it, Boy, but I had to 'cause I needed it to buy supplies and food along the way. I didn't use much, though, and the rest of it is hid under the floorboards of my old shack on Lee Gulch — 'ceptin' for what I used when I couldn't get my money the usual way."

When I asked Sam how it was that he usually got his money, he looked surprised and said, "Why, from my mamma, of course." Then he told me to hold up with the questions 'til he'd finished tellin' me what all happened in Texas.

"The first thing I done when I got to San Antonio was to go see the Barlows. I was afeared that Rafer and Jud had kilt them or hurt them real bad whilst they was tryin' to make them tell where me and my folks was livin'. But, I's happy to say, they was alive and kickin' — 'course, they was both gettin' on in years. In answer to my questions, Mrs. Barlow told me how they'd beat up Mr. Barlow so bad she couldn't stand it no more. She told them where we was livin' and whatever else they wanted to know, but now she felt terrible, 'cause my daddy'd got kilt on account of what she'd done — then she started cryin'. I told her not to feel bad 'cause there warn't nothin' else she could have done. If she hadn't told them, somebody else in San Antonio would have, and my daddy would have still got kilt.

"When I asked Mrs. Barlow how come she knowed my daddy was dead, she told me my mamma had wrote to her, tellin' her about it and askin' her to be on the lookout for me. After Mamma heard how I'd escaped from the posse up on Kenosha, she figured I'd most likely head for San Antonio, and if I did, she was shore I'd come by their place to check up on them. Mamma wanted me to write her and address the letter to Miss Lydia Smith so's the sheriff in Alma wouldn't know I was sendin' it.

"The sheriff's name is Ben Bellew, and he's dead set on catchin' me — dead or alive. Preferably dead. I reckon I'd best explain why. Mainly, it's on account of he claims I stole his girl. Most likely you recollect how my daddy's journal told about my marryin' Lilly Larkin up in Alma and how she left me for a travelin' salesman. Well, Ben was in love with her, too, and it'd upset him somethin' awful when she married me instead of him. 'Course, unbeknownst to me, our gettin' hitched didn't make a bit of difference to either Ben or Lilly — they kept on seein' each other and doin' whatever it was they'd been doin' before we was married. But for some reason I can't figure out, Bellew blames me for her runnin' away, and he's hated me ever since. Back then, he was deputy sheriff and what he thought didn't matter much, but now that he's the sheriff in Alma, it matters a lot. And ever since the bank robbery and murder of Tobe Taylor, Ben's been doin' his damnedest to catch me. He claims he's positive I did it, and that he's gonna keep on bein' sheriff 'til I's caught and hung. I'll tell you more about him later, Boy, but first I'll finish tellin' you what all happened to me down in San Antonio.

"I lived in San Antonio from the fall of 1915 'til the spring of '23. I stayed with Jake and his wife, Rose, 'til I found a place of my own and got a job as a salesman at Dick Hawes's lumber company what was bein' run by his son, Bruce. Dick and Elsie and Jake and Rose was all retired now and livin' quiet lives. Jake was close on to seventy-four — same age as my mamma — and it shook him up somethin' awful when I told him how my daddy was kilt. He said John Reynolds was the finest man he'd ever knowed and that he'd been a real good friend. When I told him what'd happened to Rafer, it perked him up some — he said as how the world was a lot better place without him in it. Then he asked what had happened to Jud and I told him I didn't know — but I shore as hell wished I did.

"Three or four times whilst I was in Texas — usually it was in the spring — me and Jake would ride up to our old ranch so's to pay our respects to my granddaddy, grandmamma, and little Johnny. Whenever I went, it always left me feelin' sad. As I stood on top of the hill where little Johnny was buried 'long side my grandfolks, and looked out over the rolling green hills of the ranch they loved so much, I'd get to wonderin' what it would have been like to have had an older brother — pretty nice, I 'spect.

"All things considered, the years I spent in San Antonio was good ones. The people was real nice, I liked my job, and I'd joined a real fine Baptist church. Howard Childers was the pastor, and I got to know him and his wife, Sondra, real well. They was mighty fine folks and it gave me a lot of comfort jest to talk to them. When I told them what all had happened to me and my folks up in Colorado, and how my mamma was livin' in Alma and that Miss Lydia was livin' with her, Sondra asked me how I kept in touch with Momma.

"When I told her how I wrote her letters and addressed to Miss Lydia, she shook her head. 'That's really sad,' she said. 'Your momma must be very lonely. I'm sure she's worried sick about you. Maybe you could find a way to be closer to her and still not get caught by the sheriff. What do you think, Howard?'

'Sondra's right, Jimmy.' Howard agreed. 'Your Mamma most likely isn't going to live for very much longer, and that way you'll be close by her if she started havin' trouble. If you don't go, and she dies, I suspect you'll regret it for the rest of your life.'

"Wal, that got me to thinkin'. Like Howard said, Mamma was nigh on to seventy-five years old now, and if I didn't see her soon, I might never see her again — not in this life, anyhow. So I started to figure how I could work it so's I could be somewheres close to her and still keep from gettin' caught by that damned Sheriff Bellew. Then one day a letter come from Miss Lydia, sayin' that my mamma warn't feelin' good, and how she'd taken her to see Doctor Cowen down in Fairplay. He couldn't find nothin' serious wrong with her — jest old age. But Miss Lydia was pretty shore that my mamma's problem was mainly on account of she was pinin' for me and was afeared she might die without ever seein' me again. Now I knowed for shore it was time for me to head back to Colorado and find a place to live where I'd be close to Mamma. 'Course, I shore couldn't go back to Alma — not while Ben Bellew was still around — and none of the other little towns in South Park would be good, either, 'cause a stranger would stick out like a sore thumb. What I needed to do was to find a small town close enough to Alma so's it'd be easy to go see Mamma without bein' recognized. And that's when I remembered Littleton.

"Two or three times whilst I was livin' in Alma, I rode to Denver on the Denver, South Park and Pacific Railroad, and I recollected how, not too long after the train comes out of the mountains, it'd stopped at Littleton before goin' on into Denver. I remembered one of the conductors tellin' me how Littleton was jest a mile or so south of the place on Little Dry Crick where a fella named William Green Russell discovered gold back in 1858. Accordin' to him, that gold strike was one of the reasons the "Pikes Peak or Bust" Colorado gold rush started the following year. But mainly I remembered how Littleton was a pretty little farmin' town with a courthouse settin' high up on the hill, and I figured it would be the perfect place for me to settle down. It was the right size, easy to get to, and not too far from Alma. Now all I had to do was figure out a way I could do it without bein' recognized.

"It was the twenty-fifth of December 1922, and I was celebratin' Christmas with Jake and his family when I told him how I was figurin' on movin' back to Colorado so's to be closer to my mamma. He warn't surprised, he said, and that it was long overdue, but that I was gonna have to figure out a way to stay clear of the law and of folks what had knowed me when I was last there. I told him I was plannin' on doin' jest that. 'Course, I'd changed considerable, but not near enough to keep me from bein' recognized by somebody I knowed. I told Jake how I was figurin' on growin' whiskers like my daddy had done back in '84 when our family moved up to Alma. Jake scratched his head a mite and said, yeah, it'd help some, but for me not to count on it, 'cause the minute I opened my mouth to say somethin', anybody what had knowed me back then would recognize it and know it was me, 'cause my voice sounded different from other folks'.

"I'd always noticed how my friends always knowed it was me jest by hearin' me talk, but I'd never gave it much thought. But I reckon my voice does sound different from most other folks' voices — sort of low and gravelly like. But what could I do to fix that? There warn't no way I could change the way my voice sounded — leastwise, not all the time. Finally I come up with an idea. Maybe if I was to grow a real bushy beard, wear dirty clothes, and warn't too clean lookin', folks would figure I was jest a scruffy old bum and wouldn't be likely to talk to me, and I wouldn't be havin' to talk to them.

"Jake said he liked the idea, but that I'd have to be awful damn disgustin' 'cause some folks warn't too particular who they talked to. Then he come up with the idea of my chewin' tobacco and spittin' it at people — that'd keep people away if anythin' would. So that's what I did, and it took me two weeks to get over gettin' sick every time I took a chaw, and even longer before my aim was any good. But I finally got the hang of it and now I's pretty good at it — even if'n I do say so myself.

"Not long before I left San Antonio, I got togged out in some old, wore-out clothes, smeared some dirt on my face and hands, took a big chaw of tobacco, and went over to see what Jake thought of my disguise. He approved — I even disgusted him. I took that as a compliment. My friends in San Antonio gave me all of their old, cast-off clothes to use for disguises. My favorite outfit was the old wore-out suit of formal clothes and beat up top hat what Dick Hawes gave me. I figured it made me look real elegant in a pitiful sort of way. 'Specially, after I'd improved it by rippin' it up some and rubbin' some dirt on it. It's the outfit I liked most whilst I was ridin' around Littleton in my buggy.

"By that time my whiskers had growed out so much I doubted even mamma would be able to tell it was me. Jake agreed. He was shore that all them nice, respectable folks in Littleton wouldn't want to come anywhere close to a dirty old bum like me, and, as it turned out, he was right. It worked pretty damn good, 'specially after I added a few extra touches. My favorite was when I'd talk crazy and pretend I was havin' an argument with somebody in my buggy when there warn't nobody there.

"A few days before I left, Jake'd come up with another bright idea. Maybe I couldn't change the way my voice sounded, but I could at least change the way I talked. Up 'til then, I talked pretty good. I'd had a pretty good schoolin' — my mamma and Miss Lydia had seen to that. Not near as good as you and yore folks do, Boy, but closer. So I decided to take Jake's advice, and I started talkin' like I do now. Learnin' how warn't too hard, 'cause it's the way my daddy used to talk. Trouble is, I's been talkin' that way for so long now, it's hard to go back to talkin' good again.

"On the twenty-third of May, 1923, I packed all my stuff in a beat-up trunk the Barlows had gave me, said good-bye to my friends in San Antonio, and boarded the train to Pueblo, Colorado, where I got off, bought my horse and buggy, and drove north a hundred miles to Littleton. I got here on the twenty-eighth of May and I've been here ever since — 'ceptin' for the times I'd go to Alma to visit my mamma. My disguise worked great. Nobody on the train would even come close to me, and folks in Littleton didn't want anything to do with me, either. And I reckon I was lucky, 'cause right after I got here, I seen an ad in the *Littleton Independent* sayin' that the little shack on Lee Gulch was for sale. I rode out there as quick as I could, and the minute I seen it I knowed that me and it was meant for each other."

I was curious about something Sam had said, so I asked, "Sam, you said something about visiting your mother. How did you do that without getting caught by the sheriff?"

"I was jest comin' to that, Boy. Times I'd go to see Mamma, I'd first write to Miss Lydia, tellin' her when and how I'd be comin' and where she should pick me up. We had a code worked out, givin' the times and places I'd get there. That way, even if that damned sheriff got nosy and read the letter, he'd figure it was jest a newsy little note from a friend of Miss Lydia's. I always mailed it at a post office in Denver, so's Bellew couldn't trace it, even if he did get suspicious.

"Not long after I'd come to Littleton, I went into Denver and bought myself a '22 Chevy truck. I parked it in back of a farmer's barn on the outskirts of Englewood. On the night I'd be leavin', I'd wash up good, comb my hair and whiskers, and put on clean clothes. Then I'd hitch my old horse, Maude, up to my buggy and drive over to the farm, where I'd pick up my truck and head up over Kenosha Pass to Fairplay. The farmer looked after Maude whilst I was gone. I'd generally get to Fairplay early the next mornin' and leave my Chevy parked behind a gas station on the outskirts of town. I figured it'd attract too much attention if I drove it into Alma. A few times I drove a rented rig up to Alma and hid it in Mamma's barn, but most times Miss Lydia would come down to Fairplay and pick me up.

"I never could figure out why, but for some reason back in 1917 Mamma bought herself a big four door Premier tourin' car. She shore never needed a car that big, but I gotta admit, it was a joy to ride in it. It had jump seats, a fold down top, and isinglass windows you could snap in place for the winter. It even had a magnetic gear shift, so's you could change gears jest by pushin' little buttons on a box what was mounted 'long side the steerin' wheel column. Whenever I'd come to visit, Miss Lydia would snap on the windows so's folks couldn't tell who it was in the car with her. All the time I was visitin' Mamma, I'd stay inside the house — 'ceptin' for visitin' the outhouse.

"I'd generally stay for two or three days. I figured if I stayed longer, somebody might get suspicious. Then, the day before I left, Mamma would go to the bank and draw out some money from her savings account so's I'd have enough cash to keep me goin' 'til I could come back. Then, after it got real dark, Miss Lydia would take me down to Fairplay where I'd pick up my Chevy truck and drive to the farm south of Englewood. And then, after puttin' the truck in the barn, I'd hitch old Maude up to the buggy, and head back to my shack on Lee Gulch. I'd generally get there well before sunup.

"After awhile, I got tired of sneakin' in and out of Alma like I'd been doin' and told Mamma how I was thinkin' of comin' in the broad daylight, but Mamma put the kibosh on that. She said I dasn't — not while that crazy Sheriff Bellew was still lookin' for me. Jest a few days back, he'd told Fred Singleton how he warn't gonna quit lookin' for me 'til he'd caught me and put me behind bars — or better yet, hung me.

"Right after the robbery, Mamma had explained to the sheriff and Fred Singleton how Rafer and Jud had forced me and my daddy to go to the bank with them, 'cause if we didn't, somethin' real terrible was gonna happen to her. Well, Fred believed her, but the sheriff shore didn't — he was dead certain that me and my daddy was in on it from the start. Fred and Mamma did their best to change the sheriff's mind, but he wouldn't budge. He was positive that poor Taylor was forced to shoot my daddy to keep daddy from killin' him, and that I'd kilt Taylor so's to get even. Then I'd had to leave in such a hurry I'd accidentally dropped my gun in the dust and didn't have time to pick it up. He claimed it was as plain as the nose on his face. Well, I've gotta admit Ben's nose is big and easy to see, but the rest of what he was sayin' shore warn't. That damned sheriff's mind is shut up tighter than a bank vault, and there's no way anybody's gonna change it.

"And then for some reason, Mamma told Bellew that my daddy's name was really John Reynolds, not John Hardin, and how him and his brother, Jim, 'long with Rafer, was members of the gang what raided South Park back in 1864. Mamma admits it was a stupid thing to say, but right at the time, she was tryin' to get the sheriff to understand what a terrible man Rafer was. And now that my daddy was dead, she didn't think there'd be any harm in tellin' him about it. But that was before she knew what an idiot Bellew was gonna turn out to be.

"Anyways, as far as Bellew was concerned, that proved beyond any doubt that my daddy was an outlaw and that we was both in on the bank robbery — 'like father, like son,' he'd said. So maybe now, Boy, you can see why I's had to go to so much trouble makin' shore that nobody knows I's back in these parts — 'ceptin' for Mamma, Miss Lydia, and you."

"I sure am glad you trust me, Sam, but I sure wish you'd let me tell my dad about all this. I'm positive you can trust him to keep your secret."

"I knows that, Boy, and one of these days I'll most likely tell him, but for right now, let's jest keep it a secret between me and you." Then, with a big sigh, Sam lay back on his pillows and put his hands behind his head. "Well, that's about it, Boy. By now you know my whole life's story. I jest wish I knowed what is gonna happen to me next. But I reckon I'll know soon enough — I's jest gotta be patient. Now you'd best go do yore chores, Boy, 'cause I's a mite tuckered out and needs to take a little rest."

CHAPTER 45

It was three days before I could talk to Sam again. School, chores, and my mother kept getting in the way. When I finally was released from bondage, I hurried up to his room. I had another question.

"Sam, have you ever tried to find the cave where your daddy and Uncle Jim hid their gold? You've never said anything about it."

Sam thought for a minute. Then he answered, "As a matter of fact, I did, Boy. I've went there quite a few times, but I never could find it, 'cause them rocks with the Xs carved on them was still out in the middle of that damned lake, under who knows how many feet of icy cold water, and without them, there's no way to find the cave. Besides the map for the cave, I'd always take along the old map showin' where the bonanza Ramon's granddaddy'd found back in 1779 is supposed to be hid. But I never could find it, neither. But I'd always take along my fishin' pole and go fishin', so I had a good time anyways — 'ceptin' for the last time I went when, I seen a couple of things what really shook me up. That was six years ago, and I ain't been back since."

"What are you talking about, Sam? What shook you up?" At first he seemed reluctant to answer, but he eventually did. "Wal, the first time it was when I come across a little road a couple of hundred feet up the hill above Lost Crick. I'd never seen it before and, when I followed it up, I found two beat-up cabins right at the end of the road. A bunch of scruffy lookin' fellas was livin' in them. I never knowed who they was or what they was doin' there, but they shore was a rough lookin' lot. They claimed they was huntin', and might be they was, 'cause they had some haunches of venison hung up in the cave where Lost Crick comes out from under the rocks and into the meadow. It's a piece down the hill from them cabins, and it's colder'n hell inside — jest like an ice box."

"Sam," I broke in, "I know right where you're talking about. For years my family has been going there to camp and fish but we call it "Goose Creek" — not Lost Creek."

"Why hell, Boy, they's both the same crick! The upper end is called Lost Crick on account of the way it keeps poppin' in and out from under the rocks, and the lower end is called Goose Crick, but damned if I know why. As far as I know, there ain't no goose within fifty miles of the place."

"I can't believe it, Sam. All the times you and your daddy's journal talked about Lost Creek, it was Goose Creek you were talking about. I even know the place where the creek comes out of the cave in the rocks — J. J. and I call it 'the ice cave.' But the road and the cabins have been there since way before I was born. You must have missed seein' them when you were fishing along Lost Creek — I like that name better than Goose Creek. According to Dad, the road and cabins were built by The Lost Park, Antero Reservoir Company sometime around the turn of the century. They were tryin' to dam up Lost Creek where it flows underground so they could store the water in a reservoir and sell it to farmers along the Highline Canal for irrigation during the summer months. They tried damming it in several different places, but the water always leaked out, so they finally gave up and built the Antero Reservoir up in South Park instead."

Sam scratched his head. "I jest cain't see how I missed seein' the road or them cabins when I was fishin' down 'long Lost Crick."

"Probably it's because they're so high up on the hill, Sam. They built them that way so they wouldn't get washed away by floods."

"Well maybe yore right, Boy, but I shore wish they hadn't done it. There's too damn many people clutterin' up the mountains as it is and now that there's a road in there, they'll be goin' to Lost Crick in droves. It'll ruin it — 'specially the fishin'." I guess Sam was right, but I was still glad they'd built it, 'cause if they hadn't, I most likely would never have gone there.

"Sam, you said that there were two things that shook you up the last time you were at Lost Creek. What was the other one?"

"It's the main reason I's been afeard to go back, Boy. Last time I was there, it looked to me like somebody had been diggin' around in amongst them big rocks close to where the cave is hid. There was places where the smaller rocks was moved around some, and there was piles of dirt what warn't there last time I come. It looked to me like whoever done it was lookin' for somethin' — most likely the cave. 'Course, might be it was the fellas what was livin' in them cabins, but I doubted it. I figured it was Jud come back to look for the gold."

"What do you mean, Sam?" I asked in alarm. "Is Jud around here somewhere?"

"I reckon he is, Boy. I hadn't seen hide nor hair of him since me and him parted company so quick up on top of Kenosha Pass — and that was fine with me. To tell you the truth, I'd been hopin' he'd died and gone to hell. But I reckon he's so damn mean, even the Devil don't want to fool with him. In fact, I's pretty damn shore that Jud is hidin' out someplace close to Littleton, hopin' he can find me and make me show him where the gold is hid."

"You mean you have three people looking for you, Sam?" I interrupted with dismay. "I thought there were only two. You told me about Colonel Pettigrew and the sheriff in Alma, but you've never told me anything about Jud. That's awful!"

Sam hesitated for a moment, then he answered, "I reckon it is, Boy. I warn't figurin' on tellin' you this, but maybe it's best if I explain some things to you." What Sam told me next really shook me up. "It's really jest one fella what's lookin' for me in Littleton, but God knows he's mean enough for two. What would you say if I told you that Colonel Pettigrew really ain't a colonel, that his name really ain't Pettigrew,and that his first name is really Judson? I 'spect you can guess what his real last name is."

"It's Rathbone!" I almost shouted. "You mean the colonel is really Jud?"

"That's right, Boy. I'd been wonderin' some if he warn't hangin' around these parts somewhere, but I never really knowed it for shore 'til that night my friend Cliff was kilt and I got shot." Then he went on to explain. "After Jud escaped from the posse in South Park, he made it down to Denver and from there went back to Kansas, where he lived for four or five years. Whilst he was there, he changed his name from Rathbone to Pettigrew, so's nobody — 'specially the law — would know who he really was. At least he was smart enough to do that. I done the same thing myself. But then he started makin' bootleg whiskey and that was downright stupid. It was a shorefire way to get the attention of a Kansas sheriff and end up in prison, and that's jest what happened.

"And then, after four years in prison, Jud got out and come to Littleton so's he'd be close to the gold, and I's pretty damn shore that he's holed up somewheres close around, hopin' he can find me and make me show him where the gold is hid. For some fool reason, Jud figures I knows where to find it. You'd think he'd be smart enough to know that if I did know where it was, I'd have already got it and that I wouldn't be hangin' around Littleton lookin' like a bum. I tell you, Boy, that Jud is nowheres close to bein' as smart as his daddy, Rafer, was."

Some of what Sam had said puzzled me. "Sam, how come you didn't know that Jud was in Littleton until the night you were shot? I would have thought you would have seen him sometime when you were driving around town in your buggy."

"Wal, Boy, I's wondered that myself. And I reckon yore right. I must have seen the colonel from a far piece off a dozen or more times, but up 'til the night I got shot, I'd never seen him up close and personal. Besides, he's changed a lot since I last seen him, makin' him hard to recognize from a distance. He's heavier now and a hell of a lot uglier — if you can believe that."

"Sam, there's one other thing I've been wondering about. How come you know so much about the time Jud was in Kansas? It seems to me that you know everything that went on back there."

"Wal, that part was easy, Boy — I knows it 'cause Cliff Alexander told me. Cliff was a member of Jud's gang back then, but I doubt he knowed his real name was Judson Rathbone — he'd knowed him as Colonel Pettigrew. Anyways, when Cliff got to Littleton, he quit bootleggin' and went to workin' for Rudy Lemke at his meat market on Main Street in downtown Littleton. Jud didn't like that, most likely 'cause he was afeared Cliff might tell Sheriff Haynes how he was makin' moonshine out on Dry Crick. I 'spect that's why he shot him."

After that, Sam grew quiet and sat staring out the window like he was thinking, and I thought his eyes looked a little misty as he said, "You know, Boy, I never did tell you everythin' what happened that night I got shot. It's a mite different from what I told you and Sheriff Haynes before — not much, but a little. Anyways, this is the way it really happened. I'd got to know Cliff Alexander not long after I come to Littleton. First time I met up with him, I was buyin' some meat at Lemke's Market, and I got to know him pretty well after that. I reckon he was the only fella in Littleton what knowed I warn't really crazy —

'ceptin' maybe for your daddy, and I 'spect he never really knowed for shore. Cliff never did try to pry into my affairs. I guess he figured that, whatever the reason I was actin' peculiar, it warn't none of his business.

"Anyway, that night we'd jest got back from seein' a movie at the Gothic Theater in Englewood. I was drivin' my buggy around in back of Cliff's house so's to let him out, when these three fellas come out the back door of the place jest north of Cliff's. He was jest about to get out of my buggy, and I was tellin' him good night, when I heard this loud voice sayin', 'Well, I'll be damned. If it ain't Jimmy Reynolds. I'd know that voice anywhere. And lookit who's with him, boys — it's Cliff Alexander. Now ain't that nice and convenient?' I 'spect I don't have to tell you, that got my attention real quick. I was pretty damned shore I knowed who it was talkin', but I had to be certain, so I leaned forward in the seat a mite so's to get a better look. The light in back of that old house was comin' from a little yellow light bulb danglin' down inside the screened-in back porch. It warn't worth a damn, but there still was enough light so's I could tell it really was Jud what was standin' there with an evil lookin' grin on his ugly face.

"Then I seen him put his right hand inside his coat, and I knowed right off he was reachin' for his gun. Cliff had already got out of the buggy and was standin' on the side closest to Jud. I started scramblin' out the other side, and at the same time hollerin' at Cliff to get the hell out of there. But jest as I was turnin' to run, I seen Jud point his gun straight at Cliff and pull the trigger. Cliff fell backwards towards the buggy like he'd been hit with a club, and I could see where he'd been shot right through the head. At the same time, I heard one of the other men with Jud cry out, 'My God, Colonel, you kilt Cliff. Why'd you do that?' Right after that, Jud started shootin' at me, and I reckon the only reason I's here to tell the tale is that the few seconds it took Jud to shoot Cliff gave me the time I needed to clear out of there before Jud could aim good at me. If it hadn't been for Cliff, I wouldn't be here talkin' to you now.

"Back then, I figured that Jud had shot Cliff on account of he'd quit his gang, and that Jud was tryin' to kill me, too, now that Rafer warn't here to stop him. But now that I've had time to think on it, I doubt that Jud really wanted to kill me. As a matter of fact, I doubt he wanted to kill me when I was in your mamma's trunk. I gotta admit, though, it shore seemed so at the time. I figure if he really did want to kill me, he wouldn't have wasted time havin' you look for the trunk key when all he had to do was to shoot the lock off'n the trunk and kill me at the same time. But he didn't, and I doubt he was even figurin' on doin' it. 'Course, if he had kilt me, he would have had to kill you, too, Boy."

Well, "Boy" had already thought of that, but I still didn't understand why Sam didn't think Jud wanted to kill him. From where I'd been standing, it sure sounded like that's what he had in mind.

I asked Sam, and he smiled. "Oh, I reckon he wants to kill me all right, but not 'til I shows him where the gold is hid. As I figure it, Jud was so shook up that night by seein' me and Cliff together that he jest blasted away at me without givin' it no thought. But then later, once he'd calmed down a mite, I reckon he recollected how he needed my help in findin' the gold. 'Course, might be I'm wrong — maybe he'll kill me first chance he gets. I 'spect I'll find out for shore when Doc Sims tells me it's time for me to leave Shadycroft."

After that, Sam grew quiet again and stared unseeingly out the window. I asked him what it was he was thinking about, and he jumped a little as though I'd startled him. Then he took out his handkerchief, wiped his eyes, blew his nose, and said in a husky voice, "Aw, I was jest thinkin' about my mamma, Boy. I's been worryin' a lot about her lately. Last time I seen her was way back in September, and I shore wish I knowed how she's doin'. She'll be eighty-nine years old come this fall — leastwise, she will be, if'n she's still amongst the livin'. I 'spect she is, though, 'cause she's a real tough lady, and besides that, I's been countin' on the Good Lord to look out for her. I's been prayin' for Miss Lydia, too. It comforts me, knowin' that she's helpin' Him keep take care of Mamma."

I felt really sorry for Sam right then. It must feel awful to be cut off from everybody you love or who loves you. But I figured that it probably wouldn't be very much longer before Sam could leave Shadycroft, so I asked him what he was planning to do when he left our farm.

After a few seconds of hesitation, he answered, "Wal, Boy, what I'd like to do most is to go see my mamma and Miss Lydia, but I can't risk it, not while Ben Bellew is still lookin' for me. Besides, I's been too damned easy to recognize ever since Mrs. Vogel shaved off my beard and cut my hair back when I was too sick to stop her. 'Course, I reckon one thing I could do is to go live with my friends down in San Antonio, but that way I'd be too far away from Mamma. So to answer your question, Boy, I don't know what I's gonna do. More'n likely I'll jest go back to my shack on Lee Gulch and wait to see what happens.

"I 'spect you'd best leave now, Boy — I's feelin' a mite wore out and need to get some rest. Besides, by now you know most everythin' what's ever happened to me and my folks, and I reckon yore ears are about wore off. But I shore hope you'll still come to see me now and again, 'cause I gets mighty lonely cooped up in this here room all by myself."

"Don't worry, Sam. I'll come see you every day, if my mother and Mrs. Vogel will let me. I promise. But I still wish you'd let me tell my dad all that you've told me — about Jud, your mamma, and all the rest. I'll bet he'd know what you should do. Besides that, I'll bet my folks would know a way to check on your mamma for you — maybe Mother could write to her and tell her what all's happened to you. Anyway, Sam, whatever you do, please don't worry. I'm sure it's all gonna turn out all right."

Sam just sat there in his chair, staring out the window. Big tears were running down his cheeks.

CHAPTER 46

Mother was putting dinner on the table when I came into the kitchen, but I didn't feel much like eating. Besides being worried about Sam, I was even more worried about what was going to happen to us if we lost Shadycroft. But I ate as much as I could, hoping to avoid my mother's inevitable lecture. Unfortunately, I didn't quite make it.

"Robert, be sure to eat everything on your plate. We mustn't forget all those poor, unfortunate folks who are starving in Oklahoma and Kansas."

I never could figure out how my eating everything would fix it so those folks back there would get more to eat, and my mother never did get around to explaining how it worked. But I did the best I could for them — with Rab's help — and after I'd finished eating, I excused myself from the table and went outside into the warm spring sunshine.

It was a beautiful day — very warm for April. I was anxious to catch up with my dad so I could ask him if he knew what was gonna happen to Shadycroft. Rab ran back and forth excitedly as I hurried up to the horse corral where Molly was munching contentedly on some hay that I'd thrown out for her earlier that morning. When she saw me comin', she quit munching and started looking around for some way to escape. But after a few minutes spent chasin' her around the corral, I finally got her cornered and managed to get a rope around her neck.

Once I'd done that, she pretended like she'd given up and just stood there quietly, actin' like she was tickled pink we were gonna go for a nice ride. But all the time I was saddlin' her, I could tell she was watchin' me out of the corner of her eye, just waitin' for me to relax my guard so's she could make her move. But by now I'd figured out all of her sneaky little tricks. After I finished bridling her, I vaulted (translation: struggled) into the saddle and, with Rab happily leadin' the way, rode off to the dryland in the direction I'd seen my dad take in his truck.

When I found Dad, he was sitting on the running board of his truck, reachin' down with his hand to pick up some of the dust near his feet and then lettin' it trickle through his fingers and back onto the ground. He waved when I rode up and signaled for me to join him. After tying Molly to the back bumper, I sat down alongside him.

"Whatcha doin', Dad." I asked, thinkin' that he looked awful sad.

"Not a whole lot, Son," he answered. "I'm just seeing how my spring wheat's doing."

Even I could tell it wasn't doing well. Because of the drought and winds, the fields were a terrible sight to see. But it wasn't always like this. I remembered many times in years past when Dad and I would drive out to the dryland to check on his crops and we'd sit alongside of each other in his truck looking out across the fields — then he'd start talkin' to me.

Dad was usually a quiet man and kept his thoughts to himself, but I guess sometimes he just needed somebody to talk to about how he felt about this land that he loved so much and how wonderful it was to plant a crop, to see it grow to maturity, and finally come to harvest. He'd said that, to his way of thinking, there weren't many things in this world more beautiful than a field of wheat — no matter what the season of the year. He'd told me how much he loved the way the fields changed in appearance from that time in the fall when the fields of last summer's stubble were plowed, disked, harrowed, and planted, right up to the time the ripe grain was harvested the following summer and the fields once again turned to stubble.

At first, you'd have to look real close to see the tender green rows of newly sprouted grain pushing through the brown earth, all in parallel lines like a huge army of soldiers marching across the fields. Then — as the spring passed and the warm rays of a summer's sun shone down — a miracle would happen, and a lush carpet of wheat would spread over the rolling countryside, billowing in the breeze like green waves on a restless sea. But the best was yet to come, Dad said, when the green waves turned to a shimmering gold as the wheat ripened in the hot August sun. And then — after the combines had come and gone, like a final encore — the rows of stubble would be left standing at stiff attention, a golden reminder of the fruits of the summer's labors.

I think that, maybe, I loved this land almost as much as my dad did. At least I knew just how he was feeling as he looked across his parched and withering fields. He'd planted his winter wheat last fall, and for a time it had seemed to thrive. The heavy snow in November had soaked deep into the ground, and the seeds, warmed by the late fall and early winter sun, had sprouted and grown until the brown earth was covered with a rich, fresh mantle of green. But then the snows stopped, the wind blew, and the ground dried and cracked, leaving the fragile roots of the seedling wheat exposed and dying under the hot sun. By the end of January, the sprouts were wind dried, brown, and dead. The past winter had been so warm and dry that the ground had never really frozen. What little frost there was had completely thawed, so that by the first week of February, Dad had been able to plow again and replant with spring wheat — all the while hoping and praying that the snows and rains would return and bring life back to the land.

But the snow and rain never came — only more winds and drought and heat. So now Dad sat on the running board of his truck, grimly looking at the few stubborn sprigs of wheat clinging to little mounds of cracked and windblown earth. Oh, how I wished there was something I could do to help. I knew his heart must be aching as he saw his hopes and dreams of a bumper crop shriveling before his very eyes. I felt like crying myself, and I wished I could say something that would make him feel better — but I couldn't think of a thing. We sat there a little while longer. Then Dad stood up, brushed the dust from his hands and trousers, and opened the door to the truck, saying, "Well, Robby, I guess I'd better be getting back to the barn so I can help Clyde with the chores."

I untied Molly and led her alongside the truck to the cab where Dad was sitting. I wanted to ask him if he'd be able to make the bank payment when it came due at the end of the month. It'd been worrying me a lot. When I asked, Dad smiled a little, but I could tell he was forcing it as he told me not to worry — he was certain we'd be able to meet this next payment all right, and hopefully the one that was due in October, too. He explained that he was planning to hold an auction later this month and sell off some of the equipment we didn't need, along with most of his milk herd.

With his crops failing, he was having to buy feed for his herd of milk cows, and he wasn't even making enough money from selling the milk to pay for their feed. I told Dad selling the milk cows would solve one of my problems, 'cause milk wasn't high up on my list of favorite foods. Dad smiled again, but this time it was more for real.

"I know that, Robby, but I'm afraid you'll still have to keep gagging it down, because we're keeping two or three cows so we'll have enough milk for the Williamson family and us. Clyde and I will spell each other with the milking and feeding, so maybe we can go camping and fishing now and then." I was about to climb back into the saddle when I had another thought. "Dad, what about the land below the ditch where you always plant corn or alfalfa? Couldn't you use the money you get from sellin' those crops to make the October payment?"

"I wish that was true, son, but barring a miracle, we won't be able to grow much of anything on the irrigated land, either. You see, Robby, there's so little snowpack in the mountains this spring, there won't even be enough runoff water in the Platte River to wet the bottom of the Highline, let alone irrigate crops. And whatever runoff there might be will have to be used to satisfy the priorities of the older ditches further down the Platte — so I'm sure we won't get a drop."

I'd about run out of things to hope for, and I'm sure Dad could tell how worried I was, 'cause he put his arm around my shoulders and gave me a little hug. "I know how much you love Shadycroft, Robby, and that you can't stand the thought of losing it. I feel the same way. But I wonder sometimes if maybe God is just trying to teach us that it's not good to get too attached to material things. Of course, if we do lose Shadycroft, it will be an awful way to learn that lesson. But if it does happen, maybe it's just God's way of pointing out to us that the way we live is a lot more important to Him than where we live or the things we own."

"Well, maybe a miracle will happen, Dad. Maybe if we pray a lot, God will make it rain."

"That'd be nice, Robby, but don't count on it. The last few years I've pretty much given up hoping for miracles. Your mother and I have done more than our share of praying, but it seems like God just isn't listening these days." He sounded a little bitter, like maybe he was mad at God, and that frightened me. "Please don't give up on God, Dad. I'm sure He hasn't given up on us. I'll bet things are gonna turn out fine, just you wait and see."

"I hope you're right, Robby," my dad muttered, "I sure do hope you're right." With that, he started the truck and drove off in the direction of the barn.

After Dad left, I climbed onto the saddle and rode off, intending to patrol the range for rustlers and outlaws, but my heart wasn't in it, so I headed back to the barn. Molly approved. For some strange reason, she's always a lot more spirited and wants to run more when she's headed toward the barn than when she's goin' in the opposite direction.

The next couple of weeks went by fast. I saw Sam every day, like I'd promised. I told him how my dad was plannin' on holding an auction, and he was hopin' he'd make enough money to pay the interest on the loan in April and again in October. But that he seemed real discouraged, like he didn't really believe it would happen, and I was afraid he'd even given up on God.

"I knows jest how your daddy's feelin', Boy. A little ways back I was feeling that way myself. As a matter of fact, I still have a hard time bein' patient and waitin' for God to fix my problems. But whenever I start feelin' that way, I recollect how my mamma told me that God is always in charge, no matter what happens, and He always answers the prayers of folks what love Him and put their faith in Him. 'Course He don't always do it the way we might want, but it always seems to work out for the best in the long run. Rememberin' that always makes me feel better."

"Gosh, that's great, Sam. I'll tell my dad what you said. But have you thought any about asking my folks to read your daddy's journal and telling them everything that's happened to you? I sure wish you would."

Sam smiled, "I's been thinkin' on it, Boy. I'll let you know when I decide."

Somewhere around the middle of April, Doctor Sims told Sam that he could start coming downstairs, and maybe, in another few weeks, he'd be able to leave Shadycroft if Sheriff Haynes agreed. Sam didn't seem a bit happy to hear the doctor say that and neither was I, but my mother sure was. "Finally," she said, "I can start getting my life back to some semblance of normal." Course, she didn't say that in front of Sam.

It was the twentieth of April — the long awaited day of the auction. There was no wind or dust for a change, and the morning sky was a deep, deep blue with flocks of white clouds hovering overhead — we all hoped the beautiful day was a sign of great success. People came out to the farm in droves. Most were farmers and ranchers, but there were some that looked like town folk. I suspected that they had come mainly out of curiosity and wouldn't buy anything. I'd never been to an auction before, and I was amazed at how fast that auctioneer could talk. Mother told me it was called a chant, and that it was a special way auctioneers had of talking in order to get folks to bid on whatever it was they were selling. It was midafternoon before everything was auctioned off and all the people had left. Our folks were settling up with the auctioneer, and they didn't look happy. I wondered if maybe the auction hadn't raised as much money as they'd hoped, so I asked J. J. if he knew. He said they'd made enough money for the bank payment at the end of April, but that it was way short of what they needed for the one coming

Our barn and milk house where the auction was held.
(Photograph taken from the Johnson family album.)

up in October. I asked J. J. what was gonna happen if we couldn't pay it, and he said he didn't know for sure, but he thought that our folks would probably have to sell Shadycroft so they could get enough money to pay off the bank loan and their other debts. If they didn't, the bank would foreclose on the loan and we'd lose the farm anyhow. When J. J. said that I started cryin', and he put his arm around my shoulder and gave me a hug.

"I wouldn't worry too much yet, Robby. A lot can happen between now and the end of October. I'll bet our folks will find some way to keep from losing our home. But even if they can't and we lose Shadycroft, we'll still have each other, and no matter what happens, we'll weather it together. In the meantime, we can keep on doing our very best in school and help our folks out more around the farm."

CHAPTER 47

Abby and Charley Vogel had been listening to everything J. J. had said, and they were almost as upset as I was. Abby burst into tears. She didn't want us to move away from Shadycroft, she said, 'cause we were like part of her own family. I was pretty sure it was mainly J. J. she didn't want to move away, but it still was nice to hear her say it. At least there was one thing I'd learned from all this: It's really great to have a family and good friends to help you through the bad times in your life. It'd be awful if you had to go it alone. Then I thought of Sam and all of the trouble he was having, and — believe it or not — I felt even sorrier for him than I did for myself.

Sam had stayed out of sight inside the house all during the auction, and I knew he must be wondering how it had turned out, so I went up to his room to report. When I entered, he was sitting by the window, reading his daddy's journal for what must have been the zillionth time. Other than his memories, that wrinkled-up packet of papers was all Sam had left to remind him of his family, and it made me sad.

"How'd the auction go, Boy? Did yore folks get enough money to pay on their loan?"

"Enough for the payment in April, Sam, but not near enough for the one in October. So, unless a miracle happens, we're gonna lose Shadycroft, and we'll have to move."

With that, I burst into tears and began to sob uncontrollably. Sam stood up quickly and came over to me. Putting his arm about me, he held me quietly until I finally grew quiet. Then he pulled a handkerchief from his pocket — a clean one, fortunately — and handed it to me so I could blow my nose and dry my tears.

I guess he could tell I was embarrassed for crying, 'cause he smiled and said gently, "It's OK to cry, Boy. I's cried lots of times myself — 'specially after my daddy got kilt. In fact, I feels like cryin' right now, and I would if I could, but I reckon by the time you gets to my age, it's a lot harder to do, 'cause yore tears are most all used up." Then he surprised me. "At least what you said helps me make up my mind about one thing. I's decided to ask yore folks to read my daddy's journal. Then, once they's done that, I'll explain to them how Jimmy was really me and what all has happened since the bank robbery — jest like I done with you. I's hopin' that once they know all about me and the trouble I's in, they'll help me check up on my mamma — I'd be mighty beholdin' to them if they did."

"Hey, that's great, Sam. I'm sure my folks will be happy to help you. 'Specially once they know the whole … "

"And another thing, Boy," Sam interrupted, "I'd shore be grateful to yore folks if'n they'd let me stay on here at Shadycroft for awhile longer. That way, I'll feel a lot safer. Then, maybe come summer, if they's of a mind to, me and yore folks can head up to the Tarryalls so's to look for my daddy's and Uncle Jim's gold. If we can jest find that damned cave and figure out how to get into it, I reckon your folk's money problems will be over for good."

"You mean you'd share your gold with my folks, Sam? Gosh, that's really swell of you! And J. J. and I can help you look for it — man-oh-man, I can hardly wait. We're all gonna be rich!" My imagination was already busily engaged in listing all of the absolute necessities that poverty had been forcing me to do without, such things as cowboy boots, a new saddle, and a black cowboy hat. But before I could finish compiling my list, Sam started laughing and raised his hand.

"Whoa there, Boy. Jest you hold yore horses. Don't forget, yore folks don't know nothin' about any of this yet, and when they do, they's likely gonna figure it's jest some wild story cooked up by Crazy Sam. And even if they do believe me and want to go to look for the cave, we still cain't go 'til I gets stronger — and besides that, yore daddy's got a lot of work what needs doin' right here on the farm. As a matter of fact, I reckon it'd be best if we waited 'til June to go anyways. The weather in the Tarryalls is likely to be better by then, and it'll give me and yore daddy time to figure out how to go about lookin' for the cave. Besides that, by that time you boys will be out of school. 'Course, even then, yore mamma's not likely to want her boys grubbin' around in the dirt and rocks, lookin' for a crazy old man's gold."

Well, that last really shook me up. Not once had it ever occurred to me that my folks might not let J. J. and me help them look for the gold. But I made a quick recovery. "Oh, no, Sam, I'm positive our folks will let us go. I'll die if they don't. And besides, I can be a big help to you, 'cause I'm so skinny I can squeeze through narrow places between the rocks where the rest of you can't go. Man-o-man, won't it be great? After we find the gold all our problems will be solved, and everything will be perfect." Sam smiled and shook his head. "Wal, maybe not all yore problems, and I'm shore things won't ever be perfect. Lots of time, gold and the things it can buy can cause a whole lot of grief, and it shore as hell don't always bring happiness — that's for damn shore. That's one of the reasons I took so long in decidin' whether or not to tell yore folks about it. Look at all the troubles it's caused already. First with Ramon's granddaddy and his brother, second with my daddy and Uncle Jim, and now me. As I figure it, that Tarryall gold has already kilt three men and crippled another. Sometimes I wonder if there ain't some kind of curse on it. Maybe it'd be best if we jest let it be."

As Sam was speaking, I was edging slowly towards the door of his bedroom. "See you later, Sam. I've gotta find my folks and tell them about the gold and everything. Boy, are they ever gonna be happy?"

"Now jest hold up a minute, Boy. You'd best not go runnin' off half-cocked and tellin' them how Crazy Sam is gonna fix it so's they'll be rich. They won't believe a word you say. They'll jest figure we's both crazy as loons. You'd best let me be the one what tells it to them. But first, I's gonna ask them to read my daddy's journal, and once they've done that, I'll explain it all to them, jest like I done to you. Maybe after they know all that, they'll believe me and help me look for it." Of course, I knew that Sam was right. Coming from me, my folks would-n't believe a word I told them, seein' as how my reputation for telling the truth was a trifle tarnished.

"I guess you're right, Sam, but could I at least tell J. J., and maybe Charley and Abby? I'm just bustin' to tell somebody, and they're bound to hear about it sooner or later."

Sam thought it over for a moment. "Wal, Boy, I reckon you can tell J. J., jest as long as he promises to keep it to hisself, but you'd best wait to tell Charley and Abby. They'd be likely to tell it to their friends, and it might get back to Jud somehow. Then he'd know for shore that I's hidin' out at yore folks' place."

The Littleton Café on Main Street — circa late 1920s.
(Picture courtesy of the Littleton Historical Museum.)

I rushed back to the barn, hoping to tell my folks that Sam wanted to talk to them about somethin' real important, but they were nowhere to be seen. I asked J. J. where they were.

"You just missed them, Robby. They went to the Littleton Café to have supper with the Burnetts and won't be home 'til late tonight. I sure hope it perks them up some, 'cause they're really down in the dumps."

I was disappointed, but at least I could tell J. J.. Except that I doubted he'd believe what I told him, based on his frequent past encounters with my imagination. I was right. As soon as I started talking, J. J. got that look on his face like he always gets when I'm tellin' him one of my true stories about how Buck Duane and I captured a bunch of cattle thieves up on the dryland. But the more I talked, the more he quit smirkin' and began to listen to me like he'd never done before.

It was almost dark by the time I finished telling the whole story as best I remembered it, and never once did he accuse me of makin' it up. It was a new experience for me, and it felt sort of good to have J. J. believe me for a change. After I'd finished, he told me it was the most amazing story he'd ever heard, and that he figured it most likely was true, 'cause nobody could ever make up a story that fantastic. Then he looked at me and thought a bit and shook his head. "Naw, not even you,

Robby." Then he asked if I thought Sam would mind if he looked at his daddy's journal and maybe the maps. I told him I wasn't sure. Why didn't we go ask him?

When we got to the house, Sam was in the kitchen, heating up leftovers for our supper. After Doctor Sims told him he could be up and around, Sam had been helpin' Mother some with the cooking and even the cleaning now and then. He was pretty good at both — 'specially the cooking. I guess he'd had a lot of practice when he was livin' by himself. Mother was pretty startled when Crazy Sam asked if he could help her, but once she found out how good a cook he was, she was real pleased. Of course, any time visitors pulled into the yard, Sam would head up to his room so nobody would know he was there.

Sam told J. J. he'd be happy to let him read his daddy's journal, but that he wasn't gonna show us the maps 'til after he'd talked to our mamma and daddy. I told J. J. not to feel bad, 'cause he'd never let me see the maps either. After we'd finished eating, J. J. went with Sam so's he could give him the journal, and I went to my room. I started doin' some homework, but I couldn't keep my mind on it. All I could think about was how great it was gonna be when we found all that gold, and my folks wouldn't have to worry any more. Finally, I put on my pajamas, climbed into bed, and read *Riders of the Purple Sage* by Zane Grey until I couldn't stay awake any longer.

When I awoke it was just getting light. Dressing quickly, I rushed down to the kitchen to tell my folks the good news. Mother and Dad were just sitting down to breakfast when I walked in, and I lost no time in telling them that Sam wanted to talk to them about something real important. I told them I knew what it was, and that they were really gonna like hearin' it, 'cause it might even keep us from losing Shadycroft. After I finished saying that, nothin' happened. I'd figured they would be real happy and excited, but they weren't — not even a little bit. Mother just smiled and said, "That's nice, Robert. Now sit down and eat your breakfast." Dad didn't say a word. They obviously didn't think anything Sam could tell them would be important, 'specially if I said it was.

Right after that J. J. came into the kitchen. When I told him how Mother and Dad didn't believe me about what Sam was gonna tell them, he said, "Well, I'm not surprised. I was pretty sure they wouldn't." Then he went on to tell them that he thought it really was important for them to listen to what Sam had to say, on account of he was sure he was telling the truth. And you know what? They believed him.

Dad said, "Well, I guess Sam really must have something important to tell us after all." Well, that's the same thing I'd just told them, so how come they believed J. J. and not me?

I was just about to complain about brotherly discrimination, when Sam came into the kitchen and Dad said, "Sam, according to the boys, you have something important to tell us, but neither of them will tell us what it is."

"That's right, Julius, and I reckon it jest might be a way out of all the troubles you folks are havin' — you'll have to be the judge of that. Yore boys have told me how you and Grace have a bank payment comin' up in October, and that right now it don't look like you're gonna be able to pay it, and if'n you don't, you'll most likely lose the farm. Is that right?"

Dad looked first at J. J. and then at me, like we'd been talking out of turn. Then he answered, "I'm sorry to say it is, Sam. Right now, I can't think of any way I can come up with the money for the loan payment short of robbing a bank. And even if by some miracle we're able to make the one in October, we'll still be short of cash when the next payment comes due at the end of April next year. We won't have any crops to sell until later on that summer, and we might not have any then if this drought keeps up." Sam had looked a little startled when Dad mentioned robbing a bank, and he'd looked at J. J. and me like maybe we'd told our folks about the Alma bank robbery — but then he nodded his head.

"Wal, that's a shame, Julius, but it jest might be I have a way to fix yore problems. I 'spect both you and Grace will have a hard time believin' what I want to tell you, and I hope you'll hear me out. But it's a long story, and it'll take a considerable time to tell it. So, bein' as how you've got chores to do, why don't we jest eat breakfast, and maybe I can talk to you later on today when you've got more time."

So later that day that's what he did, and it was two long days before they said a word about gold or about what Sam had told them. In the meantime, J. J. and I could think of little else. But finally, one evening after supper, Dad relieved our suspense.

"I suspect you boys are wondering what your mother and I thought of Sam's story." We both nodded our heads in unison. "Well, it's a fascinating story, and it certainly explains a lot of the things about Sam that we've been wondering about. Of course, we may not be able to find the cave where the gold is stored, but your mother and I agree that it's certainly worth the time and effort to try. In fact, Sam has offered to share his gold equally with us. But Sam, Grace and I have talked it over, and while we appreciate your offer more than we can possibly say, we feel that you're being far too generous. It would be a godsend just to be able to pay all of our debts. We'd be more than happy with that — the rest of the gold should belong to you."

Sam shook his head vigorously. "No, Julius — my mind's made up. You jest don't know how much I appreciate what all you and Grace and the boys have done for me. So it'll make me feel a whole lot better if'n we jest split it half and half right down the middle. It's the only fair thing to do. 'Course, first we's got to find it, and that ain't gonna be easy."

"Well, all right Sam, if your sure that's what you want to do, we'll accept your offer. Grace and I certainly do appreaciate it."

"We surely do, Sam, " my mother added, "and we'll still appreciate it even if we don't find it."

As yet, no one had said a word about J. J. and me helping them to look for the cave, and J. J. couldn't stand the suspense any longer.

"Can Robby and I help you look for the gold, Dad?"

"Yeah," I chimed in, "please let us. I'll bet J. J. and I can be a big help."

Dad smiled, "Why sure, boys. Who do you think is going to do all the digging and hard work while Sam and I are fishing down on Lost Creek? But don't get too excited. There's a lot of work to do around Shadycroft, so it's likely to be a month or two before we can go. And besides that, Sam hasn't recovered fully yet."

Then mother chimed in. "Now you two boys calm down. Don't forget — your schoolwork comes first. If we do go to look for the gold before school lets out for the summer, whether or not you boys go with us will depend on how much homework you have." At times I wished my mother had never taught school — it'd messed her thinkin' up something awful. "And Julius, you haven't said a thing about Sam's mother. You know how we decided last night to check on her before we did anything else. That poor woman must be worried sick. She probably thinks that her son is dead. I declare, all you and Sam seem to think about is gold and fishing. You're even worse than the boys."

"Now, Grace, don't get so upset. Sam and I have already talked that over and — if it's all right with you — you and I will go to Alma and bring her back to Shadycroft for a visit this coming weekend."

"Well, I'm sorry — perhaps I spoke too hastily," my mother said. "This weekend should be just fine."

"Can we go, too?" J. J. and I spoke in unison.

"It will depend on how much homework you have, Robby, and I'm sure you can't go, Junior. You have that long history report to write."

J. J. looked unhappy, and I didn't feel so great either, 'cause Miss Olds usually loaded us down with homework for the weekends. But as it turned out, she was kinder than usual, so early the next Saturday morning, my folks and I headed up Deer Creek to Turkey Creek and drove over Kenosha Pass to Fairplay — then north to Alma. Following Sam's directions, we pulled up in front of his mamma's house about ten o'clock that morning, and Dad got out and went to the door. A moment

Robby, Mother, J. J., and Michie standing by our 1929 Studebaker – circa 1930.
(Photograph was taken by Julius E. Johnson Sr.)

after his knock, a tiny little lady with snow-white hair opened the door, and the minute I saw her, I knew we'd come to the right place.

I'd always pictured Sam's mother as a small lady with blond hair and blue eyes, but of course she was eighty-eight years old now, so I guess it wasn't surprising that she'd changed some. But the name "Sunny Sadie" still fit her like a glove. Once she realized who we were and why we'd come, a bright smile lit up her face, and she asked us to come into the house. She sure was spry for such an old lady, too — she walked across the room like she was no more that half her age. Of course, her face was wrinkled up some, but you forgot that right off when she smiled. Her bright blue eyes shone with a kind of inner light that made you feel good just to be near her.

Miss Lydia was there, too, and once we were all inside the house, Sam's mamma introduced us to her. She was white-haired like Sam's mamma and just as slender, but a little bit taller. She had a nice smile, dark brown eyes, and a real soft voice. Her face was beautiful, and she looked a lot younger than I thought she would. In fact, she looked younger than Sam, even though she'd been his teacher. They both were mighty relieved and happy when they heard that Sam was alive and well and staying with us at Shadycroft. They'd been sure that something bad had happened to him, 'cause it wasn't like him not to keep in touch with them. Then Dad explained to them that Sam didn't come with us on account of he'd been sick, but he didn't say anything about his getting shot and what all had happened to him. He figured Sam could do that for himself. My folks had invited the two of them to go back with us and visit him at Shadycroft, and they both accepted with pleasure.

It was sundown when we pulled into the gravel drive in front of our house. Sam, J. J., and Rab were all waiting for us on the screened porch when we arrived, and the minute they got out of the car, Sam and his mamma started huggin' and kissin' each other on their cheeks. Then Sam let loose of his mamma and started huggin' and kissin' Miss Lydia, only the kisses were on her lips. You could tell she liked it a lot, too, and I got to thinkin' that Sam seemed almost happier to see Miss Lydia than he was to see his mamma — and I could see why. Miss Lydia was mighty pretty and not much older than Sam, and it looked to me like they were sweet on each other. It was hard to imagine how any lady could be sweet on Crazy Sam, but maybe I just hadn't seen him at his best.

Sadie and Miss Lydia stayed with us the whole week, and it was swell having them there. Every evening, after the chores were done and after we'd had supper, we'd all sit in the living room and they'd tell us about their lives. I especially liked the stories Sadie told us about the old days — it was like John Reynolds' journal had come alive.

CHAPTER 48

The week Sadie and Miss Lydia spent with us went by fast, and before we realized it, Friday evening came and their visit was over. Sam, J. J., Rab, and I were to leave in the truck next morning well before sunup — our destination, Lost Creek. Dad and Mother would meet us there later after they'd taken Sam's mamma and Miss Lydia back to Alma. We planned to spend the rest of Saturday and most of Sunday getting the lay of the land around the cave before returning to Shadycroft.

That night, after waiting 'til well after dark to be sure that Jud or any of his men couldn't see us, Sam, Dad, J. J., and I loaded all of our camping equipment and the tools we'd be needing into the back of Dad's Ford truck. The first thing Dad put in was his fishing equipment, and that seemed odd to me, 'cause I thought we were going to Lost Creek to look for the gold. When I mentioned it to Sam, he grinned.

"Wal, Boy, I reckon yore daddy's takin' his fishin' equipment 'long with us to be shore we don't run out of grub. It never hurts none to be careful, you know."

Even though it was pitch dark when we left in the mornin', to be doubly sure that one of Jud's gang wouldn't see Sam leaving, J. J. did the drivin' while Sam hid under a tarp in the back end of the truck. Only a few days ago, Mother claimed that she'd seen a suspicious lookin' fella standin' behind a willow tree up on the ditch bank, and that it looked like he was keeping watch on our home while at the same time trying to stay out of sight. Of course, Mother's imagination is almost as good as mine when it comes to matters like that.

After we'd driven a few miles outside of Littleton, Sam knocked on the rear window and hollered that he wanted to ride inside the cab with the rest of us. When he got in he took over the driving, but after we'd gone another mile or two, he stopped the truck and said he couldn't take it no more — not with all three of us, plus Rab, packed into the cab. It was just too damned crowded and, besides that, Rab smelled real "doggy." I wondered what he expected him to smell like. He smelled all right to me. I could tell Rab was pretty offended when he'd heard Sam say that. He was even more put out when he found out he was gonna have to ride in the back of the truck along with all of our gear.

It was close to fifty miles from Littleton to Lost Creek, and Sam drove most of the way, except for the times J. J. managed to talk him into letting him drive. He'd gotten his driver's license just a few days before and claimed he needed the practice. I wasn't too sure if J. J. knew what he was doin', but it was obvious that he needed practice. And before long I got to wishin' he'd do his practicing some other place and some other time and without me in the car — 'specially on the Critchell Cutoff. It was a real narrow shelf road with a hundred foot drop-off on one side of it. It's mighty scary, 'specially if J. J. is driving.

The fifty or so miles from Shadycroft to Lost Creek — or Goose Creek — whichever it was called — was slow goin'. A lot of the way was steep and rocky — 'specially the part goin' over "Stoney Pass," down to Wigwam Creek, and along the east slope of the Kenosha Mountain range to a saddle between two mountains. From there, the road dropped down a steep, gravel covered hill and leveled off beside the sparkling, clear water of Lost Creek.

As we slowly worked our way up the valley, we had to stop a number of times to repair places in the road that had been washed out by heavy rains. But two hours later — after what seemed like four hours of work — we parked the truck at the end of the road in front of the two dilapidated cabins that were abandoned by the workmen of the failed Lost Park Antero Reservoir project.

Sam picked a spot for our campsite on a grassy flat close to the cabins. It was two or three hundred feet up the hill from Lost Creek and was sheltered by tall ponderosa pines. It was a nice spot to camp, but I asked Sam why he hadn't picked a place down by the creek. There were some real pretty campsites down there, too, and we wouldn't have to go near as far to haul water — and besides, he'd be closer to the fishin'. Sam smiled and said, "I reckon yore right, Robby. It'd be easier, but its safer to stay up here. If it rains hard upstream from us and we was camped down by the crick, we might be caught in a flash flood and get drownded." That seemed like the very last thing we'd have to worry about, considering how dry it'd been lately, but Sam claimed that you never could tell what was gonna happen weatherwise, and how it never hurts to be careful. He sounded a lot like my mother.

After setting up the tents, one for my mother and dad and the other for Sam, J. J. and me, I told Sam I was gonna sleep out in the open under the stars. But Sam didn't agree.

"We'd best not to take any chances, Boy. You never can tell in these mountains. A storm can come up out of nowhere when you least expect it." Then, just to make his point, he made J. J., and me dig a trench all around the tents to keep the rainwater from getting inside them.

After we'd finished, I announced to Sam, "Well, I'm still gonna sleep outside. I don't want to sleep in a stuffy old tent."

"Suit yoreself, Boy. I jest hope you don't get et by b'ars or cougars. Oh, and be shore you takes along that manila rope what's in the truck, so's you can lay it on the ground around your bedroll. It'll keep the rattlers from bitin' you." That's really dumb, I thought to myself — there aren't any rattlesnakes this high up in the mountains.

After setting up camp and eating lunch, J. J. and I were all set to go and look for the cave, but Sam said, "No, it's best if we wait 'til yore mamma and daddy gets here. They's bound to be worried if we ain't close by when they shows up. 'Til they do, though, I reckon I'll jest string up one of yore daddy's fishin' poles and mosey on down to the crick, so's I can catch us a nice mess of trout for supper."

J. J. and I moseyed on down to the creek, too, but for another reason. If we couldn't hunt for the gold cave, we could at least explore the ice cave. It's called the "ice cave" for reasons I'll explain a little later. Rab ran ahead of us as we headed down the hill towards a spot not far below our camp. In the distant past, huge granite boulders had fallen from a cliff over halfway up the mountainside on the west side of the creek and lodged together in such a way that they created a cavern. Its entrance was large enough to let a full-grown man walk into it without stooping over, and it was even wider than it was high. It's from out of this cavern that Lost Creek flows into the upper end of the meadow, before continuing its meandering way down the valley.

The level of water in the creek was low, leaving a wide, sandy bank along both sides, making it easy to walk back into the cavern. J. J. led the way, and Rab and I followed close behind him. About twenty feet in from the opening, the passageway narrowed, the overhead rocks lowered, and the footing became much more difficult. We were forced to climb over and under broken tree branches and other debris that had been washed from further upstream and lodged in amongst the rubble that lay on the floor of the cavern. At this point, Rab decided that he was tired of explorin' caves and went off to do his own thing — most likely porcupine hunting.

The farther J. J. and I went into the cavern, the darker and gloomier it became — colder, too. Thirty or forty feet from the entrance to the cave, the creek turned abruptly to the right and flowed through a narrow corridor between two massive boulders. There the water deepened, the current became swifter, and there was no longer a bank we could walk on. After checking the depth and temperature of the frigid water, I was all for turning back — 'specially when I started thinking about what Sam had said about flash floods. But J. J. didn't want to quit yet, and I wasn't ready to admit I was scared, so we hung our shoes around our necks by their laces, rolled up our pant legs and waded on up the stream. The water was a little over knee deep and icy cold. Besides that, there was water drippin' on us from the rocks above our heads, and it wasn't long before I was soaked to the skin and about to die of the cold.

Besides that, we couldn't see — it was totally dark. J. J. lit a match and held it out in front of him, hoping to see what was further on up the creek. But all we could see was cold, black water, rugged rock walls — then complete darkness. J. J. showed me where the light from the match was reflecting off a thick layer of ice that coated the rocks on either side of the pool. It sure was spooky and cold. No wonder the men working for the reservoir company had used this cave for an icebox — I was becoming a piece of frozen meat myself. In fact, I'd had it — to heck with my pride. I was ready to get out of there, and I'm pretty sure that J. J. was relieved when I suggested it. At least he didn't argue any, and before long we were standing in the bright sunshine outside the cave, and did it ever feel good. I figured I'd had enough cave exploring to last me for the rest of my life but, as it turned out later, I was wrong. I whistled for Rab, and he joined us halfway up the hill, panting and puffing with his tongue lolling out of his mouth. And — to our considerable relief — quill free.

Our folks hadn't arrived yet, and there was no sign of Sam, so we decided to explore upstream from our camp to see if we could find where Lost Creek went underground before coming out again from the entrance to the ice cave. Accordingly, we climbed the small hill in back of the cabins and looked down from its summit on an amazing sight. The entire floor of the canyon was covered with massive boulders of every shape, size, and form. It was as though some giant hand had tossed them helter-skelter in a huge game of chance. Some were stacked one on top of another like fat, rocky pancakes, while others leaned at odd angles against neighboring rocks to create arches and passages that would take a lifetime to explore — what a place for a kid with a rampant imagination!

A game trail led down the hill where we were standing and into the middle of that great maze of rocks. We followed it, and after weaving our way through the boulders for perhaps a quarter of a mile, we came to a grassy plot about the size of our front yard at Shadycroft. It was nestled amongst huge rocks that bordered it on all sides. As we quietly entered the tiny glen, we startled five mule deer — a fat buck and his harem of four does. The buck snorted, then they all bounded down the game trail, tails flagging alarm, and vanished. Rab bounded down the trail after them, but he came back panting a few minutes later in response to our calls and whistles.

At the upper end of the glen, the crystal clear waters of Lost Creek emerged as though by magic from an opening under the boulders and flowed quietly between its banks until it disappeared beneath the rocks at the lower end of the grassy hollow. Fat cutthroat trout floated lazily in the quiet pools, their heads all pointed upstream in the hungry hope that a fat and reckless mayfly would come fluttering by. Boy, I thought, would Sam ever like to be here. It made me wish that I'd brought my own fishing pole.

A few years back, Dad apparently decided that I was old enough to learn how to fly fish. He'd tried earlier to get J. J. interested, but without much success. At first, I think Dad thought I was hopeless. He'd given me one of his old Granger bamboo rods. It was long and heavy, and it took quite a while before I could cast it without snapping the fly off the line or getting it tangled. Every time we'd go fishin', Dad would spend half of his time unhooking my line from tree branches and straightening out my snarls. It's a wonder he didn't give up on me, but I guess I was his last hope, at least I was his last son. So he stuck with it 'til I finally got the hang of it, even though he about went broke buying new leaders and flies and repairing broken rods.

By now the sun was low in the west and about to slip behind the Tarryalls, and J. J. decided that we'd best get back to camp in case our folks had arrived and were looking for us. Sure enough, they had, and Mother was already worrying about where her boys were. Dad was fishing down on Lost Creek.

It was almost dark when he and Sam came up from the stream with a creel half full of natives, rainbows and brookies. And, after a meal of trout rolled in cracker crumbs and fried crisp in bacon grease, we all sat around the campfire listening to Dad and Sam swap stories and lies about all the big fish they'd caught. After that, they argued about which was the best fly to use if you wanted to catch big fish. For a time, it was a standoff between Dad's Rio Grande King and Sam's Yellow-bodied Greyhackle, but finally they agreed on the Adams fly as a compromise. It was pretty boring, and the rest of us were relieved when they finally got around to talking about our plans for the following day.

"I reckon we'd best get a real early start come mornin'," Sam allowed. "That'll give us 'most a full day to look for the cave before we head back to Shadycroft. Julius, I reckon 'bout all we'll have time to do this time is to get the lay of the land and figure out how best to go about findin' the cave when we come back, so all we'll be needin' to take with us is a couple of shovels and a pickaxe." Having said that, Sam stood up, stretched, told us good night, and headed off in the direction of our tent.

J. J. and I were about to follow, when Dad stopped us. "Wait a minute, boys. Your mother and I want to remind you of a couple of things to be careful of whenever you're out camping like this." Oh boy, I thought, here it comes again, lecture 101. J. J. rolled his eyes, and I knew he was thinkin' the same thing. Every time we go camping, 'specially when Mother is along, we can count on at least a ten-minute talk about how to stay out of trouble in the mountains. Dad didn't waste any time getting started, with Mother keepin' track to be sure that Dad didn't skip anything.

"You know, boys, the water flow in Lost Creek is unusually low right now because of the lack of winter snow and the long-lasting drouth, but even now a cloudburst followed by a flash flood could come along at any time. So remember, it's always a good idea to keep a sharp eye out for any signs of a heavy thunderstorm upstream — it might save your life. And another thing, be very careful not to get lost. It's easy to lose your bearings in these mountains, so pay attention to where you are and which way you're going, and be sure not to stray too far from the rest of us."

Then he finished up with the old familiar "and don't ever forget, boys, whenever you leave a campfire, always be sure to douse it with water to be sure it's completely out. We sure don't want to start a forest fire. Dry as it is right now, it'd burn forever." So that's what we did. J. J. and I soaked the campfire with so much water next morning Dad had to build the fire in another place.

That night I found a good place to sleep on a grassy flat not far from the tents. After clearing away a few small rocks and sticks and digging a shallow hip hole for my bottom to fit in, I unrolled my sleeping bag. Then I put all the stuff from my pockets into one of my shoes that I'd taken off and put close by. It was early May, and the nights up here were still cold, so I decided to sleep with all my clothes on. That way I wouldn't freeze when I got up in the morning. Not long after I'd crawled in, I heard footsteps comin' up behind me, and I saw J. J. walking towards me, carrying his sleeping bag.

"I thought you were gonna sleep in the tent," I said as he drew near.

"I was, but Sam's sound asleep and snorin' so loud the whole tent's shakin'." I'd forgotten how loud Sam could snore. Sometimes at Shadycroft I could hear him from clear down the hall. I figured he must have tonsil problems.

"Well, there's a good flat spot right over there," I said, and I pointed to a place ten or fifteen feet away. Fortunately, there was a three-quarter moon that night, so it was easy for J. J. to see what he was doing. It wasn't long before he was snuggled down in his sleeping bag, and we were both fast asleep.

I don't know what time it was, but the moon was about to set behind the Tarryalls when I was suddenly awakened. I was sure that I'd heard a sound. But it seemed quiet now, so I decided I must have dreamt it. Then it came again. First a little rustling sound, then louder noises, like something heavy was walking not very far away. I immediately thought of what Sam had said about hoping I wouldn't get et by a bear or cougar, and my imagination went wild. As I stared into the fading moonlight, I was certain I saw something move. I was too scared to get out of my sleeping bag and head for the tent, so I did the next best thing and whispered, "J. J., wake up, there's somethin' movin' around out there." It took me three more whispers, each one doubling in intensity, before J. J. roused enough to sleepily say, "Whatcha want, Robby? How come you woke me up?"

"There's something out there," I whispered in a shaky voice.

J. J. was quiet for a little bit. "I sure don't hear nothin'. It's just your stupid imagination. Go back to sleep." That seemed to me to be a very unsatisfactory response, but I had little choice but to accept it. So I lay there breathing shallowly so I wouldn't make too much noise and waited for the cougar to attack.

I hadn't long to wait. After a minute or so of silence, a loud cracking noise came from the same direction as the last time. It sounded as though something, or someone, had stepped on a stick and broken it.

"Did you hear that?" I whispered hoarsely. To my relief, this time he had, and now he sounded real scared, too.

"Yeah, I guess you weren't imagining it after all, Rob. Wait a minute — I brought a flashlight. Now, when I tell you I'm gonna turn it on, be ready to get out of your sleeping bag. And if it turns out to be a bear or lion or something like that, run as fast as you can to the tent."

I figured to heck with that, I was gonna head for the tent right now, but before I could get started, J. J. said, "Now!" and turned on the flashlight. The beam searched rapidly in the direction from which the sound had come and almost immediately illuminated a massive animal standing at the edge of the clearing, its eyes glowing red in the reflected light of the flashlight. I was about to set a new speed record on my way to the tent, when the beam of light shifted and revealed a big, red Hereford, placidly chewing her cud while squinting into the light to see what in the world all the commotion was about.

"Jeez," J. J. exclaimed irreverently. "All this fuss over a stupid old cow. Now will you get back into your sleeping bag and go to sleep? It'll be morning before we know it."

Get back into the sleeping bag I did — sleep I did not. Rab, incidentally, had slept soundly thoughout the whole dumb affair.

Right at daybreak the next morning, my dad came out of their tent humming a tune under his frosty breath. He came over to stand beside us and chuckled a little as he said, "Morning, boys. I see the lions and tigers didn't eat you." I didn't think that was particularly funny. I just hoped J. J. was gonna keep his mouth shut about that stupid cow. 'Course, it wasn't just me that was scared. He was, too — but I knew he'd never admit it.

"It's time to get up. It looks like it's going to be a beautiful day," Dad continued in a cheery voice. "We want to get an early start so we'll have more time to look for the gold."

An hour later, after eating and attending to a few other necessaries, I felt much better. J. J. hadn't said a word about the cow episode, for which I was extremely grateful. I figured he was most likely just as embarrassed as I was. Along about seven o'clock, we headed down to Lost Creek, crossed it, and started climbing up the east slope of the Tarryalls. Sam was leading the way with the rest of us strung out behind. Even Mother had decided to go along. She hadn't said as much, but I think she was just as excited as the rest of us about looking for hidden gold. A few hundred feet up the mountain, we came to a wide gully with a little trickle of water flowing through it. Sam pointed to it.

"This here's the crick my daddy and Uncle Jim was followin' up when they was lookin' for Ramon's granddaddy's bonanza back in 1860. Last time I was here, there was a lot more water in it than there is now. Now it's damned near dry on account of the drought. It starts out close to the top of the Tarryalls and runs down the mountain and into that lake where my daddy's landmarks is hid. From there it comes out of the lake and down into that deep ravine." Sam pointed to a deep cut on the mountainside northwest of where we were standing. "That there ravine is a damn sight deeper than it looks to be from here, and the water in it runs fast and straight down the mountain 'til it gets closer to the valley floor, then it slows down and angles off to the south into the gully we's standin' in now. From here, it goes southeast 'til it runs into Lost Crick, close to a half a mile south of here. The cave where my daddy's and Uncle Jim's gold is hid is on a bench right below that rocky cliff up there." Sam pointed to a high, rocky wall halfway up the mountainside and northwest of where we were standing. "I reckon everything's pretty much like it was when me and my daddy was lookin' for the cave back in the late '80s and '90s."

The further we climbed up the mountain, the steeper and tougher it got. Part of the problem was the thick layer of loose gravel that covered the slopes — my dad said it was decomposed granite. Whenever we'd take a step up, it seemed like we'd slip back two, so it was slow goin', and it wasn't long before we were all puffing and having to stop and rest and catch our breath. All but Rab, that is. He was having a wonderful time, bouncing up and down the mountain like he thought he was a jackrabbit. Every now and then, he'd come sliding down the hill in a big wave of gravel. He was obviously enjoying himself a lot. The rest of us weren't — 'specially me after I tripped over a rock and skidded down the mountainside on my stomach, while at the same time painfully plowing gravel with my nose. Happily, other than my pride, nothing was damaged, except for a few parts of my body that no longer had skin. Mother patched up my scrapes as best she could and delivered her standard "be more careful speech" at the same time. Then we kept on climbing.

It was midmorning when we came to a grassy tree-covered bench, where the slope leveled off and we could stop and rest. Sam pointed down into the valley.

"I reckon this here's the place my daddy was standin' when he wrote in his journal how he could look down and see the place in the valley where they was campin' the night before."

Sam was right. From where we were standing, you could look around you and see Lost Creek where it was coming out of the ice cave and our campsite on the hillside above it. Up the hill from us a rugged-looking cliff stretched northward along the east slopes of the Tarryalls. Below the cliff, we could see the outer edges of the benches where the lake stood and the place where the cave with the gold was hidden. And beyond that, we could see a tree-covered slope rising to the tops of the Tarryalls. It was like John Reynold's journal had come alive.

Our excitement grew as we kept going up the mountain. Eventually, we climbed out onto another bench. This one was considerably larger than the one we were on earlier and was partly covered by a pretty little lake. To the north, the bench continued, much like a shelf dividing the cliff into an upper and lower part. There, the bench was covered with huge granite boulders of all sizes and shapes — according to Sam, it covered an area of at least twenty acres. Some of the boulders closest to the cliff were partly buried by dirt and gravel that had washed down from above.

"Maybe now you all can see how come me and my daddy never could find that damned cave," Sam said as he waved his arm in the direction of the rock-strewn bench. "It's out in the middle of all them rocks out there, and there's no way on God's green earth we's ever gonna find it, 'lessen we first find them rocks with the Xs scratched on them."

After resting for a bit, we all walked around the lake, hoping to be able to see the landmark rocks, but it was hopeless. The icy water was way too cold to swim in and too deep to wade, and the only rocks we could see were close in to the shore. Sam shook his head and pointed to the lake.

"This here's what I've been tellin' you folks about. Them rocks with the Xs is way out in the middle of this lake under God knows how many feet of water, and if we don't find them, we's got a better chance of findin' a snowflake in the Texas panhandle in the middle of July than we do of findin' the cave. But I's been givin' it considerable thought, and it appears to me that the only way we's gonna find them rocks is to lower the water level of the the lake. 'Course, it'll be a lot of work and take us a long time to do it, but if'n we don't, we might jest as well give up and head on back to Shadycroft." So that's what we did — or at least tried to do. To begin with, we all dug with considerable enthusiasm, but when we discovered that the whole outlet was nothing but solid granite with a foot or so of dirt on top of it, the excitement of this gold hunt wore off real quick — at least it did for me. But Sam still wanted to dig it as deep as we could for now, so at least some of the water could drain out. Then the next time we came back, we could use dynamite to make it deeper. So like it or not, we went back to pecking away at the outlet, and by three o'clock in the afternoon, we'd managed to chip out a trench about three feet wide, a foot and a half deep, and close to twenty feet long, and the water was flowing through it real well — at least for now.

The rest of us were ready to quit for the day, but not Sam. He wanted to hide the ditch before we left, so if somebody was to come snoopin' around, they couldn't figure out what we'd been doin' and why. Both Mother and Dad agreed that it made good sense, and so did I, after I remembered how Sam had suspected that Jud had been up here looking for the cave. So, following Sam's instructions, we spent the next two hours collecting debris and breaking and cutting branches off trees and shrubs and using them to hide the outlet. Sam said he wanted it to look real natural, and it finally did — it looked about like it had before we'd deepened it, except that it had more water runnin' through it. We all heaved a big sigh of relief and wearily skidded back down the mountain, where we still had to break camp, load the truck, and drive home to Shadycroft. It had been a long two days and a lot of hard work, but at least we'd made a start in lookin' for the gold and were planing to go back the next weekend. But — I'm sorry to say — that's not what happened.

CHAPTER 49

It was over a month before we went back to Lost Creek, and then it was without Mother and Dad. On Wednesday afternoon, three days after our return from Lost Creek, Mrs. Vogel came to pick me up from school. Then, after picking up J. J., she took us both to Porter's Hospital and Sanatorium in Englewood where our mother was waiting for us. Dad was in surgery and it was doubtful that he was gonna live.

He'd been kicked in the head while helping Clyde Williamson shoe a horse, and Mother and Clyde had rushed him to the hospital, where he was now in the operating room. Doctor Sims and another surgeon, Doctor Robert Weaver, were trying to save his life. According to Mrs. Vogel, Doctor Weaver was a brain surgeon and a real good one, and if anyone could help him, he could. I told her I sure hoped she was right, but I was still gonna to do a whole lot of praying, 'cause I figured that God could help him even more than the doctors. Mrs. Vogel smiled, gave me a little hug, and said, "Of course you're right, Robby. I'm sure that God is in the operating room right now, helping the doctors take care of your daddy."

We joined Mother in the waiting room. She'd been crying and her eyes were all puffy, but she managed a weak smile and hugged and kissed us both. Then began the very worst time of my whole life, and I know it was just as bad for Mother and J. J.. Mrs. Vogel stayed with us the whole time, and after awhile the Williamsons and Burnetts joined us. After four hours of waiting, worrying, and praying, both Doctor Sims and Doctor Weaver came into the waiting room — they both looked exhausted and grim. Doctor Weaver did most of the talking. He said that Dad was still alive, but just barely. He was unconscious and there was nothing more we could do now but to wait and pray that he would regain consciousness and that his brain wouldn't be permanently damaged. He couldn't say just how long it might be before we'd know anything for sure. It might be a few hours, or it might be days — even weeks.

It was hard to hear him say all that, but at least Dad was still alive. I prayed like I'd never done before and hope I never have to do again.

My mother, J. J., and everyone else in the room were praying just as hard as I was. Doctor Sims was gonna spend the night at the hospital — unless he had to leave for an emergency. Doctor Weaver would be back in the morning — sooner if he was needed.

Three days later, our prayers were answered. Dad had regained consciousness! Not only was he alive and awake, he even could talk and move all the parts of his body. The doctors were both delighted and amazed, and they told us that, unless something unforeseen came up, they thought that Dad was going to be all right. I can tell you, there were a lot of thanksgiving prayers said that day and every day since then for that matter. Somehow, gold isn't very important when something like that happens to someone you love.

All the time Dad was so sick and we were afraid he might die, it was 'specially hard on Sam, because he was alone at Shadycroft with nothing to do but sit and wonder and worry how Dad was doing. I think that by now, Sam considered himself a part of our family. I'm not sure how my mother would feel about that, but I'm sure my dad would be very pleased. Anyway, Sam sure was relieved and happy when we told him that Dad was going to live.

We didn't forget about the gold entirely, though, and as Dad slowly began to recover, we started making plans to go back to Lost Creek. Now we needed the gold even more than ever. Besides the loan payment coming up in October, there were all the hospital and doctor bills to pay. Both Doctor Sims and Doctor Weaver told Mother not to worry — we wouldn't have to pay them anything until after Dad was back on his feet and able to work again. I think Doctor Sims must of known that we were about to lose Shadycroft, 'cause he told Mother we didn't have to pay him one solitary cent until all our other debts were paid — no matter how long it took.

Mother said it surely was nice of the doctors to offer to do that, and that it would help a great deal, but that, despite the doctors' generosity, things still didn't look good. Then she hugged J. J. and me and told us not to worry, 'cause what really mattered was that our dad was alive and getting better and that we were still all together. She felt certain that everything would eventually work out for the best. After that, she smiled and told us it was a miracle that our dad hadn't died, and perhaps we should all hope and pray for another one that would keep us from losing Shadycroft. I'm sure she was thinking how great it'd be if we could only find the gold.

According to the doctors, Dad wouldn't be strong enough to do any work for several more months, so that just left Sam, J. J., and me to look for the gold. With only a weak old man and two kids to do the work, it seemed pretty unlikely that we would find it in time to make the payment on the first of October. It was already the end of June, so only three months were left in which to find the cave.

Mrs. Vogel had been a huge help to us all the time Mother was stayin' with Dad in the hospital. She, along with Abby and Charley, had moved back to Shadycroft so she could fix our meals, clean house, wash our clothes, take us to school, and do all sorts of things like that. Sam helped out a lot, too. Like I'd said before, he was pretty good at cookin' — 'specially if it was meat and potatoes. But he sure wasn't any great shakes at cleaning house and washing clothes. Of course, he couldn't take us to school, for fear Jud would see him and figure out that he was stayin' with us.

Before Dad got hurt, I'd never realized how many of the Littleton folks were friends of my mother and dad, or how nice people could be when times got tough and you needed help, especially all the folks in Dad's Masonic Lodge and Mother's P.E.O. chapter. They brought us more food than we could ever eat. But Mrs. Vogel, Abby, and Charley were the ones that helped us the most. Until they moved back in with us, I didn't know how much I'd missed them. Believe it or not, I'd especially missed Abby, and I got to thinkin' that something was seriously wrong with me. I guess maybe J. J. must have missed her, too, 'cause ever since she'd moved back in, he'd been actin' goofy again, like he was doin' when she was livin' with us before.

Dad came home on the twenty-fourth of June after being in the hospital for over a month and a half. He was still mighty wobbly and couldn't walk much on his own, but at least he was back at Shadycroft again, and that was great. The doctors said that he'd done a lot better than either of them had expected, and in another four or five months, he should be pretty much back to normal. For awhile, they'd both been worried that he wouldn't be able to talk or think like he could before the accident, but now they said it looked like there wasn't going to be a problem after all.

After Dad came home, Mother still needed a lot of help, so the Vogels stayed on with us, which was good for them, too, 'cause their well had gone dry. For the past several months, they'd had to haul water from our well to use for drinking, cooking, washing, and such. According to Dad, quite a few of the shallower wells around these parts were dryin' up because of the drought. But he said that we were lucky, 'cause our well was over three hundred feet deep and wasn't very likely to go dry any time soon.

The well problem wasn't the only one that the Vogels were having. According to Charley, his mother hadn't been able to find near as many nursing jobs as she had before the depression. People were still gettin' sick, of course, but they didn't have enough money to pay her for taking care of them. It was so bad, she was even havin' a hard time making enough money for them to live on, and she was thinkin' they might have to move up north to Longmont, so they could live with his grandmother. When I told J. J. what Charley had said, he said we'd best ask Abby about it to be sure it was true, 'cause Charley had a way of stretchin' the truth like another kid he knew. Then he snickered a little, like he thought he'd said somethin' funny and hoped it'd make me mad. But I just ignored him and said how I thought talkin' to Abby was a good idea.

As it turned out, everything Charley'd told us was true. They really were havin' a hard time makin' a go of it and were moving to Longmont for sure, just as soon as our folks didn't need their mother's help any longer. Abby'd cried a little when she was telling us about all the troubles they'd been havin', and I knew just how she felt — I felt the same way whenever I thought about losing Shadycroft. That night, after the Vogels had gone up to bed, J. J. told Sam and our folks about the troubles the Vogels were having. They were all startled to hear it — especially Mother.

"Well, I declare. Vera never said one word to me about their having any troubles, other than the dry well. Of course, knowing Vera, I'm sure she thought we have enough troubles of our own and didn't want to burden us with hers."

My dad looked concerned. "Well, isn't there something we can do to help her, Grace? She'd be welcome to keep on living here until the depression lets up and they can get back on their feet again."

Mother smiled. "That surely is a nice thought, Julius, but have you forgotten? It won't be long before we'll be having to move, too." Dad looked startled and then real crestfallen. For just a few seconds, he'd completely forgotten that we were about to lose Shadycroft. For a while after that, everybody was quiet and thoughtful — then Sam broke the silence with what everybody thought was a swell idea.

"I reckon I knows what we can do — I'll jest split my share of the gold half and half with the Vogels. It'd make me mighty happy if I can repay Vera for all the help she gave me whilst I was so sick. I'm shore I'd never of made it without all her help — yores, too, of course."

Dad brightened up like a light had been switched on. "Why, that's a great idea, Sam, except that it wouldn't be right for you to share your half of the gold with the Vogels while we keep all the rest. Grace and I are just as indebted to Vera as you are — maybe more so. She not only helped us out when you were sick, but when I was laid up, too. So we should be the ones to divide our share of the gold with her and her family, and you keep a full half. After all, by rights, it should all be yours. Don't you agree, Grace?" Mother agreed wholeheartedly but before she could say anything more, Sam held up his hand and smiled.

"I'll tell you what we'll do, Julius. We'll jest split the gold into three parts. That way, we can all share equally — if'n we can find it, that is."

I asked if I could be the one to tell the Vogels the good news, and after a brief consultation with Dad, Mother told me I could. She said it would be interesting to see if they believed me, inasmuch as they all were well acquainted with my rampant imagination. (More of her warped humor.) So next morning at breakfast, that's what I did, but — just like she'd suspected — the minute I started telling them the good news about the cave with the gold in it, they started rollin' their eyes at each other and smiling like they figured how this time I'd really gone off the deep end. Sam finally took pity on me and convinced them that I was actually telling them the truth. Then he told them about the cave with the gold and how we were hoping to find it. After that, Abby and Charley got so excited that Mrs. Vogel had trouble calming them down

— especially after he told him how we wanted to share it with them. But she was just as excited as they were. "I just can't believe this is happening. I've been so certain that we would lose our home, and now ..."

But then, Mother — the perennial wet blanket — proceeded to dampen the Vogels' enthusiasm. "Vera, I hate to tell you this, but it's going to take a miracle for us to find the gold in time to save our homes."

After that gloomy prediction, Dad explained to them how Colonel Pettigrew was really an old enemy of Sam's named Jud Rathbone, and that there were actually two reasons he wanted to find Sam. The first they already knew — that Sam had been a witness to Cliff Alexander's murder — but the second and main reason he wanted to find Sam was so he could force him to show him where the gold was hidden. So it was doubly important they keep quiet and not tell anyone about it. He warned Abby and Charley to be especially careful not to say anything to their friends, for their lives might be in danger if they did.

"Wal, that settles it, then," Sam announced. "I'll be headin' up to Lost Creek to look for the gold jest as soon as I can. There ain't much time left between now and when the next bank payment comes due. With you out of commission, Julius, and with Grace and Vera havin' to stay here at Shadycroft so's to look out for you, it's gonna take me a lot longer to find the gold than I'd first figured."

At this point my dad interrupted. "Sam, I'm going with you. I'm feeling much stronger now, and I'm sure I can help you with the easy things."

"Oh, no you're not, Julius. You're going to stay right here where you can rest and get well — doctors orders." As usual, my mother's decree left no room for appeal.

"It'd shore be nice if you could come with me, Julius, but Grace is right. You'd best not take any chances. But I hope you'll let J. J. and Robby go with me. And Vera, if it's all right with you, I'd like to have Abby and Charley come, too — they'd be a big help to me, and I's gonna need all the help I can get. I'll keep a close eye on them so's to be shore they don't get into no trouble — you can be shore of that." To our great surprise and relief, our parents all agreed to our going — but only after we'd listened to Mother's standard "be careful" lecture about not gettin' hurt, stayin' out of trouble, and doing what Sam said.

CHAPTER 50

Three days later, after a big breakfast, lots of hugs, good lucks, good-byes, and good advice from Mother, Dad, and Mrs. Vogel, we drove up the lane just as the first glimmer of dawn edged the eastern horizon. Sam, J. J., and Abby were all ridin' in the cab, and Rab, Charley, and I were stuffed in the back, along with all our supplies and equipment, and there was a lot of it. Not long before Dad got hurt, he'd gone to the war surplus store in Englewood and bought a dozen army knapsacks that were left over from the world war back in 1915 to 1918. They were made of heavy canvas, and Dad figured they'd come in handy for packin' out the gold if we ever found it. Besides that, he gave us several of his irrigation canvases that he used to dam up the water in the ditches so it'd flow out over the field. It's tough stuff — I know, 'cause I've helped him irrigate with it.

To start with, J. J. drove the truck like when we went last time, while Sam squinched down in the middle of the seat trying to stay out of sight. Even though it wasn't likely Jud's men would be watching this early in the day, Sam still wanted to be careful. But once we got to the road up Deer Creek, Sam took over the drivin', and I felt a lot better.

It was midday when we got to the abandoned cabins on Lost Creek, and this time, instead of camping by the cabins like we did last time we were there, Sam wanted to camp closer to where we'd be working — he figured it'd save us a lot of time. So, right after lunch, escorted by Rab, we started hauling our equipment and supplies up the mountain and setting up camp by the north edge of the lake. Along about midafternoon, Sam told us that he was all tuckered out so he was gonna stay by the lake and rest. Whilst he figured out what we should do next, us kids could fetch the rest of our stuff up the hill by ourselves. So that's what we did, and it was evening by the time we'd finally finished haulin' the last load up the mountain, and for some reason, that hill got steeper with each trip. I figured we must be havin' one of those upheavals my dad had told me about.

I slept like a rock that night, and other than bein' a little stiff and sore the next morning, I felt great and was rarin' to start lookin' for the gold — and so was Sam. He was up at the crack of dawn, and by the time he rousted us out of our sleeping bags, he had breakfast all cooked and ready to eat.

"Come and get it, or I'll throw it out," he called as he went around kickin' our sleeping bags so's we'd wake up. "Come on, time's awastin'. We's got work to do." We all dragged out of our bags and, one by one, headed off into the trees to make ourselves more comfortable.

Rab and I walked alongside the lake on our way back to camp. I was still half asleep, but I woke up fast when I heard what sounded like a rifle shot echoing across the water. Rab jumped a little and started barking; I jumped a little and ducked behind a tree. "Jud's shootin' at us," was the first thought I had, but as I peeked cautiously from in back of the tree, I noticed a ring of waves spreading out over the water near the middle of the lake. Then I saw a beaver stick his head up out of the water and swim towards a big mound of sticks and branches that was sticking up out of the water, and I felt much better. I guess Rab and I must have startled him, and he'd slapped his tail on the water. According to my dad, that's the way a beaver warns other beavers that danger is nearby. The mound of sticks and branches was the lodge where the beaver lived.

As I was watching the beaver, I noticed something peculiar. The water level in the lake was about the same as it was a month ago before we'd deepened the outlet. When I got back to camp, the others were all wondering what had made that loud noise. After explaining how it was only an old beaver slappin' his tail on account of bein' upset with Rab and me, I asked Sam how come the water level wasn't lower. Sam looked startled and looked over at the lake.

"Wal, I'll be damned. How come I never seen that? I'll bet it's that damn beaver. He must of done it last night, 'cause yesterday, whilst you kids was fetchin' our stuff up the hill, I cleaned out a whole mess of sticks and mud what'd he used to block up the outlet. Now we has to do it all over again. Damn that stubborn critter — he must have worked all night blockin' it up again."

Following Sam's directions, Charley and I accompanied him to the outlet of the lake, taking with us two shovels, a pickaxe, and a prybar. He told J. J. and Abby to stay in camp and clean up from breakfast before joining the rest of us. That arrangement seemed to please them. Most likely they were happy to have some time together without two nosy brothers spyin' on them.

Sure enough, just like Sam had said, that old bucktoothed beaver had blocked up the outlet again, and he'd done an amazing job. I figured he must have had a whole army of beavers helpin' him, but according to Sam, it was only one — two at the most. The beaver'd cut down several good-sized aspen from higher up on the hill and hauled them down to the outlet. After choppin' off the branches, he'd stacked them across the outlet, then piled mud and sticks on top of that, blockin' it up so that only a little trickle of water was running out of the lake. That beaver was a real hard worker; I'm sure he figured that he'd do whatever it took to save his home. Then I thought about Shadycroft and how we were about to lose our home, and I sympathized with him. But Sam sure didn't — he was really ticked off. "That damned beaver," he muttered under his breath. "I'm gonna fix him."

I was afraid Sam was gonna shoot him. Unbeknownst to Mother, and I'm sure at Dad's suggestion, he'd brought along Dad's .38 special Colt revolver and his 1894 .25/.35 Winchester rifle. Sam claimed he'd brought the guns along just in case we were attacked by a bear or cougar, but I'm pretty sure what he really was worried about was a two-legged varmint named Jud. Sam assured me that he wasn't gonna shoot the beaver. He was gonna use dynamite to open up the lake's outlet so's that "damned paddletail" couldn't stop it up so quick.

"You mean you're gonna drain the lake, Sam? What'll happen to the beaver if you do that? You'll be ruinin' his home."

"Hell, Boy," was his unsympathetic reply, "that miserable critter will have the lake dammed up again in no time flat. Besides, we's not gonna drain all the water out, jest enough to fix it so's we can find them landmarks. Don't you worry none about that damned beaver. He'll make out jest fine."

After saying that, Sam left to get the dynamite, and Charley and I started tearing down the beaver's dam. Not long after he'd left, J. J. and

Abby showed up, shovels in hand and, with all of us workin', it wasn't long before we had the outlet pretty well opened up. And all the time we were doin' it, I could feel that old beaver's eyes glaring at us accusingly from the other side of the lake. When Sam showed up with the dynamite, he was still muttering about "that damned beaver."

"I ain't gonna mess around peckin' at this outlet little bits at a time. If I do, that stubborn critter will have it plugged up tighter'n a tick again by mornin'. No siree, I's gonna do it right the first time and put charges on both sides of the outlet and 'long either side of the crick down below it. That way, we can set them all off at the same time. I reckon that'll open up the outlet so's the water drains out in a hurry. That way, we can find them landmark rocks a lot sooner and it'll save us a lot of time— and that's important, 'cause we ain't got much of it left. Drainin' the lake's gonna be the easy part — findin' the cave and the gold is likely to take a lot longer."

Sam handed J. J. an eight-pound sledge and a metal rod he called a "star drill." It had a sharp, star-shaped end on it. He claimed as how him and his daddy had used one like it when they'd been workin' their claim, not far up the mountain from where we were now. It took the rest of the morning and part of the afternoon to get the dynamite charges set. Sam and J. J. did all the drilling. While Sam swung the sledgehammer, J. J. held the star drill, turning it a little after each blow. Once the holes were drilled, the rest of us put sticks of dynamite in them.

Boy, I thought, if Mother could see what Sam is lettin' us do, he'd really catch it — in spades — and so would we. That went without saying. We were real careful, though. In fact, I wouldn't be a bit surprised but what we set a new record for careful. By about three o'clock in the afternoon, all the holes were drilled, the charges were set, and Sam had attached the fuses. All we had to do now was light them. But before we did that, Sam showed us a place behind a big rock where we could all take cover. He told me to tie Rab up there, too, so he wouldn't get blown to pieces or run away. When I did, Rab acted real put out. I tried to explain to him why I was doin' it, but I don't think he believed me. He did a little later, though. There were eight charges in all, one on each side of the outlet, and three more goin' down each side of the creek. Sam, J. J., and Abby would each light two, and Charley and I were to light one apiece. Sam's final instructions were to light the matches on the count of one, light the fuses on the count of two, and then run like hell for cover.

That's exactly what we did, and it worked great. As a matter of fact, once the pieces of rock and tree limbs stopped raining down and the dust had settled, it seemed to me it might have worked a little too great — at least, from the beaver's point of view. The blast had opened up the channel at the east end of the lake into a big ditch, and a flood of water was pouring through it and down into the ravine. It looked to me like the beaver's house, and maybe even the beaver, was gonna get washed down the mountain. But Sam just laughed and told me I needn't worry about the beaver. He'd be just fine. More'n likely he was already busy figurin' out how to block up the outlet again.

It was gonna be quite awhile before the lake drained down to where we could start lookin' for the landmarks. 'Til then, we were going to have to wait. But that didn't seem to bother Sam a bit, and we soon found out why.

"Wal now, seein' as how there's nuthin' more what needs doin' right now, I reckon I'll jest have to try my luck fishin'. How about you kids? Any of you want to come along?"

"Sure, Sam, I do," I replied. "Charley, do you want to come along, too? We can take turns usin' my fishing pole." Charley agreed to go, but J. J. and Abby decided to stay in camp, and that didn't surprise me a bit, 'cause for some dumb reason I never could understand, J. J. liked bein' with Abby and talkin' to her more than he liked bein' with me.

Sam told us we should go down the north side of the ravine instead of the south. That way, we could get down to Lost Creek without having to ford the creek in the ravine while all the rampaging water from the lake was rushing down it on its way to join Lost Creek. As we drew closer to the floor of the valley, we came to a spot where the creek had split into two channels. Most of the floodwater was flowin' southeast down its regular channel like it did before, but a trickle was goin' down another little gully towards the northeast. Sam figured all that water rushin' down the ravine had opened up an old streambed.

After jumpin' over the new little stream, we headed down to Lost Creek, and it wasn't long before Sam was happily fishing further down the valley and I was busy trying to teach Charley how to fly fish. Fishin' was kind of slow that day, but we had a good time anyhow, and Sam was happy, 'cause he'd managed to catch enough trout for supper. It was late afternoon when we started back to camp. By then, the amount of water in the creek was getting back to normal, so it was easy to cross it and return to camp by our usual route. The water level in the lake had dropped considerably, and Sam figured that, come morning, we most likely could start lookin' for the landmark rocks.

As Sam had predicted, that stubborn old beaver had spent the entire night plugging up the outlet of the lake again, and the next morning the water level was no lower than it was the night before. But Sam still wanted to look for the landmark rocks — so that's what we did — and it wasn't any fun. Over the years, a thick layer of sediment had washed down from the mountainside above the cliff, covering the bottom of the lake with a foot or two of fine gravel and muck. Every step we took was like tryin' to walk in glue. On top of that, the water was still three or four feet deep in place, and that made it harder — cold and wet, too. To make matters even worse, there were hundreds of big boulders scattered about on the bottom of the lake and any one of them could have an X on it.

It was late in the afternoon when J. J. finally located the first one, and not long after that I found the second. By then, the sun had set behind the Tarryalls and it was twilight, but fortunately there was still enough light for Sam to take a sighting from the mark furthest south, to the mark on the second rock, and then across the boulder field to the place where the cave was hidden. I got the job of standing by the rock closest to the boulder field, holding my hand up over the X, so Sam and J. J. could line up the two marks. The water was icy cold and came to a little above my belly button, and I was frozen stiff by the time they finished. Accordin' to Sam, it'd worked out great. He was tickled pink — but I was cold and blue and could hardly wait to go back to camp and thaw out.

Once I'd quit shiverin' and shakin', J. J. showed me how if you were to draw a line through the two landmark rocks, it would line up with a huge rock on the north edge of the boulder field. Now all we had to do was to check along that line 'til we found the cave. But it wasn't gonna be easy, 'cause it was at least a quarter of a mile from the near edge of the boulder field to the big rock on the far side, and there were hundreds of places all along that line where the cave could be hidden.

I'd always heard that lookin' for a needle in a haystack was hard, but I'll bet it's nothin' compared to lookin' for a cave in amongst a bunch of rocks. By noon the next day, we were only a third of the way across the boulder field, and we were already tuckered out — hot, thirsty, and sweaty, too. I almost wished I was back standin' in the lake. It took us the rest of that day and all of the next to reach the big boulder at the north edge of the boulder field, and we never saw hide nor hair of a cave or an old path, or anything else that would be a clue as to the whereabouts of the cave. We were all tired and discouraged — especially Sam. He looked real pale, and the rest of us were worried that he was gettin' sick again and that we'd have to quit looking for the cave and take him back to Shadycroft.

But happily, come morning, Sam was back to his old self, and after eating breakfast he announced, "You know, kids, I woke up last night and got to thinkin'. J. J. and Robby, do you all recollect that part in my daddy's journal where it tells how him and Jake used some tools from their old mine to hide the entrance to the cave after they'd finished blowin' it up, and how they hid them close to the cave, thinkin' they'd make a good landmark?" We nodded our heads that we did. "Wal, if'n that's really so, I reckon they'd most likely still be here — 'ceptin' for the pickaxe they used to chip the Xs on the rocks — they'd pitched it down the hill — but the shovel and prybar should still be hid by the rock. They's most likely rusted up considerable, but if we can find what's left of them, it might help us find the cave. If I recollect rightly, my daddy wrote as how they was close to two hundred feet due west of the cave, 'long side of a monstrous rock what was right close to the base of the cliff. So maybe, if we can find them tools and step off two hundred feet due east from there, it'll put us right on line with the landmarks and real close to the cave. I reckon it's at least worth tryin'."

It sounded easy when Sam was tellin' about it, but it sure didn't turn out that way. First off, it was hard to pick out which one of the rocks at the base of the cliff was the one Sam's daddy had been talkin' about. They were all monstrous. But Sam pointed out four huge rocks he thought looked bigger than the rest, and we spent the rest of the morning pokin' and diggin' around them. Towards noon, Abby, J. J., and I were gettin' discouraged again, and it was obvious that Sam was, too. We were all tired and hungry and about to give up when Charley hollered out — "I found them!" We all gave a cheer and scrambled over the rocks headin' in his direction, and sure enough, he'd found the prybar at the base of a rock the rest of us had figured was too small to be the right one. But as it turned out, it was bigger than it looked, 'cause the lower third of it was buried in dirt and gravel, and when Charley started pokin' around in it, he'd uncovered one end of the prybar. Then we all pitched in and, after a fair amount of diggin', we found what was left of the shovel.

After that, we headed back to camp, had lunch, and, after resting up a little, went back to lookin' for the cave — all but Sam, that is. He was feelin' puny again and figured he'd better rest up some so he wouldn't wear himself out. We all thought it'd be a cinch to find the cave now that we'd found the tools, but were we ever wrong. We spent all the rest of that day tryin' to figure out how far a hundred yards was and which way was due east. Besides that, it's really hard to pace off a distance of a hundred yards at the same time that you're climbin' up and over and down and around rocks. By the time you get through pacing, you can't tell which way you've been goin', let alone how far.

The only exciting thing that happened that day, other than finding the tools, was when Abby's imagination got to runnin' wild. She thought she'd seen something move up on the edge of the cliff. The rest of us never could see anything, though, and after starin' 'til we were all buggy-eyed, we decided it was either a deer or elk or, what was more likely, she was just imagining it. Abby swore she hadn't been, that something really had moved, and she was sure it wasn't an animal. It looked more like a man. We all laughed and told her that now we knew she was imaginin' things and, can you believe it, she got mad. I don't know why. Why, for years people have been tellin' me that I imagine things, and I never get mad — well, hardly ever.

Sam seemed rested when we got back to camp — he'd already built a fire and was busy fixin' supper. J. J. explained to him how we'd looked and looked, but we never could find the cave, and that finding the tools wasn't gonna help after all. But Sam told him not to be discouraged, and that come morning, he'd go look for it himself. That evening, after a supper of trout, bacon, and fried potatoes, we all crawled into our sleeping bags and slept like hibernating bears.

Back at the boulder field next morning, we showed Sam where and how we'd looked for the cave. After doing some checking of his own, he told us that maybe his daddy was a mite mixed up on which way was due east, 'cause as far as he could tell, we'd figured things out pretty well. He'd remeasured it, and we'd figured the hundred yards right on the button. And we were right on line with the landmarks, too, so were was bound to be somewhere close to the cave. What we should do now was spread out and start lookin' along that line, goin' in both directions.

So that's what we did. Charley and I went back towards camp, while the others went in the opposite direction. We spent the rest of that morning climbing, crawling, and poking around amongst rocks of every possible size and shape, hoping to find some sign of the cave. It was noon and we were about to head back to camp for lunch when Charley and I came across a place where two big boulders had tipped together, makin' it look like they were leaning on each other. By the edge of the boulder nearest our camp, we found a chimney-like opening, and when we looked down it to the ground at its base, we saw what appeared to be the opening of a small passageway.

The chimney was narrow, 'specially near the top. I was pretty sure Charley could never squeeze through it, but it was easy for me on account of my bein' so skinny. By squeezin' a little, I managed to work my way to the bottom of the chimney. When I got there, I was surprised to find that the passageway was quite a bit bigger than it looked from above. In fact, it was big enough for me to stand up straight in, but as I began workin' my way along it, the rocky sides and ceiling kept closing in, and the passageway kept gettin' smaller and smaller. Finally, I was crawling, first on my knees, and then on my stomach — squirming along like a snake.

It was mighty scary. 'Specially after I got to thinkin' about snakes, but I kept on goin' anyway. Actually, I had to — partly on account of the little tunnel kept on goin', but mainly because I couldn't turn around. Then I started thinkin' about gettin' stuck and began to get panicky. I was just about to try squirmin' backwards, when I saw that it was getting bigger a little down the passageway, so I decided to risk it and keep on goin'. And I was sure glad I did, 'cause after goin' another ten or twelve feet, it opened up into a much bigger passage where I could easily stand up straight. A little bit of light filtered through small cracks in the rocks overhead, and I could see a path that followed along a rock-walled corridor for at least another thirty feet until it ended at a solid granite wall. Holding my breath in anticipation, I followed it.

At first I was real disappointed. I felt sure it was a blind alley, but when I got to the place where I thought the passageway ended, I discovered that it took a sudden turn to the left and opened into a large cavern. It was lit by a soft diffused light, that shone though a crack in the rocky ceiling filling the caven with a soft, diffused light. Along either wall of the cave, I could see piles of what I supposed was gold ore and several old saddlebags, also filled with gold. But what excited me the most was a large box at the far end of the cavern. It was marked "Property of the Army of the United States of America" on top. "YAHOO!" I shouted at the top of my voice. I just couldn't believe my eyes. But it was really true — I'd found John and Jim Reynolds' cache of gold, and we were all rich! Rich! RICH!

Charley and the others could hear me hollerin', but they couldn't figure out where it was comin' from. When I heard them shouting my name I shouted back, tellin' them that I'd found the cave. They still didn't know where I was, but they sure heard what I'd said, 'cause I could hear them whoopin' and hollerin' like a bunch of crazy folks. Fifteen minutes later, I'd managed to squirm back through the tunnel and climb up to where they were impatiently waiting for me to emerge. They wanted to go look at the cave right away, but I explained that none of them could make it through the passageway, 'cause they were all too big. That's the only time I can remember bein' happy because I was so skinny. After the excitement died down some, we marked the spot so we could find it again, then headed back to camp. We were too excited to eat much, and in less than an hour we were back by the cave, tryin' to figure out how we could get to the gold. There was no way I could drag it out through that little tunnel piece by piece. I'd be a hundred years old by the time I was finished. Sam didn't say much at first. He just kept climbin' back and forth over the rocks, goin' from the spot where I'd climbed down the chimney to another spot he figured was right above the cave. Pretty soon he sat down on a rock and scratched his head.

"You know, I reckon we's gonna have to use dynamite to blast open the passageway. I brung some of it with me when we left camp, but we's gonna have to be mighty damned careful how we use it so's not to blow the cave and the gold to smithereens." Or us, I thought apprehensively.

"How can we do that, Sam?" J. J. asked. "It sounds awful risky."

"Wal, J. J., for one thing, we'll use small charges, and for another, we'll start blastin' quite a ways back from the cave and work our way towards it a little at a time. First off, we'll set half a stick of dynamite in the passageway under them two leaning rocks."

Unfortunately, I was the only one skinny enough to get down the chimney, so I got the job of placing the dynamite charge, attaching the fuse, and lighting it. It was a long fuse, and after it was lit, I still had plenty of time to get back up the chimney and take cover, but right at the time it sure didn't seem that way. The explosion blew the rocks apart, just like Sam had hoped, and it was easy to climb down to the passageway, but when we got there and looked in, it was filled with rocky debris. We spent the next three hours clearing it out, and when we'd finished, the opening was still too small for anybody but me to get through. Sam figured we'd have to use the dynamite at least one more time, and that I was gonna have to make another trip down the tunnel to place the charge and light the fuse. This was gettin' old real fast, and I kept wishing I was a lot fatter.

As I was squirmin' down the passageway, I got to wonderin' what my mother would say if she could see what I was doin'. I figured it'd be best if she never found out — for Sam's sake as much as my own. After I lit the fuse, Charley and J. J. had to pull me out by my feet — then we all headed for cover in a hurry. The dynamite exploded only a second or two after we got to where Sam and Abby were hunkered down behind a big rock while keeping a tight hold on Rab. That was callin' it a little too close, I decided. Next time, somebody else was gonna get to light the fuse. But there wasn't a next time. There didn't have to be: That last shot opened up the passageway even better than Sam had expected, and once the rubble was cleared away, we'd have a clear path into the cave.

By that time it was late afternoon, and Sam decided that we'd best call it quits for the day. Tomorrow we'd clean the rubble out of the pathway so we could get into the cave and start haulin' the gold down to the truck. That night, even though we were all real tired, nobody wanted to go to bed. We were too excited. Instead, we sat around the campfire telling what all we were gonna do, now that we'd found the gold. 'Course, we all agreed that the first thing to do was to pay off the loan on Shadycroft and our folks' and Mrs. Vogels' debts. Then the Vogels could drill a new well, and after that the sky was the limit. My list was the longest, but the other's came close — 'specially Charley's. The only thing Sam wanted was to be able to go back to Alma and be with his mamma and Miss Lydia. 'Course he couldn't, 'cause he still had the sheriff in Alma and Jud to worry about, and the money wasn't gonna help him solve that problem. That put a damper on our celebration, and it wasn't long before we crawled into our sleeping bags. The moon was just disappearing in back of the Tarryalls, and as the world around us turned black, the sky above our heads gradually filled with zillions of stars. Some of them seemed so close you could almost reach up and touch them. We all slept well that night, and I'll bet every last one of us dreamed about gold.

CHAPTER 51

Early the next morning, we started clearing rubble out of the caved in part of the passageway. First, Sam and J. J. took turns bustin' the larger rocks into smaller pieces with a sledgehammer, then the rest of us hauled it away. By midmorning, we could crawl through it into the pathway beyond. Holding our breath in suspense, we worked our way along the corridor into the cavern and watched as the light from our flashlight spread throughout the rocky interior. It was as though we had stepped back in time to 1864 and right into John Reynolds' journal. The beaten up saddlebags filled with high-grade ore were right where Sam's daddy and Uncle Jim had left them, as were the ten piles of gold ore, each over three feet high and six feet wide. And way in the back of the cave, we found the U. S. Army box, and right next to it a smaller box marked "Property of the Denver and South Park Stage Line." It was the one the Reynolds gang stole from Billy McClelland's stagecoach back in 1864. When we opened it and saw that it contained over thirty gold ingots and packets of ten and hundred dollar bank notes, our spirits soared. They soared even higher when Sam and J. J. lifted up the lid of the US. Army box and found stack after stack of hundred dollar bank notes and boxes filled with gold coins.

"Them there coins is gold eagles," Sam told us. "Back then, each one was worth ten dollars — most likely they still is. But don't start celebratin', 'cause we shore as hell cain't keep it. We's got to give it all back to the U. S. government, 'cause if we don't, we's gonna end up in a peck of trouble. Them generals back in Washington don't look kindly on folks what steals army payrolls — even though it's been over seventy years since it happened. But maybe we'll at least get a nice reward." Then he thought for a minute and added, "You know, now I come to think on it, I reckon we'd best not tell the army how my daddy was one of the raiders what stole it — they's not near as likely to be grateful if'n they was to know that. But I reckon we can keep what all's in the stagecoach box, though, as long as we don't let anybody know we found it." Then Sam closed the lid on the strongbox, sat down on top of it, and stared at the contents of the cave for a few moments.

"The next thing we's got to do is to figure a way to get all this gold down the mountain and back to Shadycroft, and it's gonna be one hell of a job. There's a lot more gold ore here than I figured there'd be, and most of it's real high grade, so it's gonna be mighty damn heavy.

"First off, I reckon, we'll sort the ore into two piles, puttin' nuggets and highest grade into one pile and all the rest in the other. Then we'll take the highest-grade ore and what's in them strongboxes down the mountain and load as much of it as we can on the truck. We'll stash what's left in a safe hidin' place I found when I was fishin' down on Lost Crick. After that, we'll haul all the rest of the ore down the hill and hide it 'long side the other ore. That way, we can come back later and take it all back to Shadycroft a truckload at a time, so's yore daddy can take it to a smelter."

"Sam," I asked, "why can't we leave it in the cave 'til we come back and get it? It'll be a lot more work that other way."

"I wish we could, Boy, but we cain't risk it. Now that we's found the cave and opened it up, other folks is likely to find it." I was sure that by "other folks" he meant Jud. So we did what Sam said and spent the rest of that day sorting gold, and by late afternoon we were more than ready to quit.

We spent the next two days hauling the gold down the hill, and it was just as hard as Sam said it would be. Rab was the only one that had any fun and he didn't have to do any of the work. Except for short breaks to eat and rest, we all worked steadily from dawn to dark. J. J. and I hauled the gold in knapsacks from the cave to a flat place on the hillside just below the lake, where we dumped it on a canvas. After that, Abby and Charley skidded the canvas and gold down the mountain and dumped it alongside Lost Creek so Sam could load it into his knapsack, pack it across the creek, up the hill and stash it in the back end of the truck.

Sam wanted to do all the loadin', 'cause he was afraid if one of us did it, we'd overload the truck and break a spring or — even worse — an axle. He showed us how to check to be sure the springs weren't gettin' too flattened out, but he still didn't want us doin' it, for fear we'd make a mistake. After a couple of trips haulin' ore up the hill to the truck, Sam drove it down closer to the creek so it'd be easier to load. But he didn't bring it down all the way, and I asked him why, 'cause it'd be even easier if he had.

"I dasn't do that, Boy. The slope from the truck down to the crick is so damned steep, we'd never make it back up the hill with a heavy load of ore. I 'spect we's gonna have to do some chockin' as it is."

Chocking is what it's called when you put rocks in back of the rear wheels to keep the car, or truck, from slidin' back down the hill. The hills around Lost Creek are covered with a thick layer of loose gravel, and it can be a problem — especially when you're drivin' your car up a steep hill and both rear wheels start spinnin', like you were on ice. When that happens, the car grinds to a stop, and somebody — usually it's one or both of us kids — has to get behind the car and push it to get it movin' up the hill again. And if it spins out and stalls again, whoever's pushin' has to "chock" the two rear wheels to keep the car from slidin' back down the hill.

It was late afternoon when Sam told us we could stop. "Wal, kids, I reckon that's it for today. I's loaded as much ore on the truck as I can without bustin' an axle, and I stashed all the rest in a safe hidin' place downstream from here. So now, I reckon once we's finished hidin' the pile you kids jest brought down, we can head back to camp. Come mornin', we'll start bringin' down the strongboxes and the rest of the ore what's left in the cave and hide it 'long with the rest. With any luck, we'll be done by day after tomorrow at the latest. After that, we'll collect all our campin' gear and tools, put them on top of the ore in the back of the truck, and head back to Shadycroft." Boy, did that ever sound great! But unfortunately, that's not how it happened.

After that, we started hauling the gold to the hiding place, but not long after we started, Sam quit working and sat down on a rock. "I reckon I's not feelin' too good, kids. My back is hurtin' somethin' awful and I's real tuckered, so I 'spect it'd be best if we calls it quits for the day and head up the hill to camp. I'm shore I'll feel better after a good night's sleep, but right now I feels terrible."

He looked terrible, too, and he could hardly walk, so J. J. found him a sturdy stick he could use as a crutch. After that, we all took turns helpin' him up the hill — one of us on each side of him. But he kept havin' to stop and rest, and it took a long time, so it was almost dark by the time we made it back to camp. By the time we'd finished fixin' supper, Sam was sound asleep by the fire.

Up 'til now, the weather had been perfect — sunny and warm in the daytime, cool and crisp at night. But that evening it looked like a change was on the way, as somber gray clouds began to spill over the summits of the Tarryalls in the west. The sun had already dropped behind the rim of the mountains and, as the sky darkened, the forested slopes turned a deep indigo blue, as the last rays of the sun lit the canopy of clouds with a glorious explosion of brilliant reds and gold. As the afterglow faded, the clouds grew dark, and we watched in wonder as the wind cleft an opening in the lowering curtain to reveal an endless blue heaven beyond. It seemed to me that, could I but see just a little bit further into that limitless sky, I might see God smiling down at us. I didn't tell that to the others — they'd think I was crazy.

Sam wasn't the only one that was tuckered out that night. We all were, and we crawled into our sleeping bags right after supper and went right to sleep. But a little before dawn, Rab's barking woke us up. He was protesting loudly, and, at first, we couldn't figure out why he was so upset. But then, in the murky morning light, we saw a big black bear waddling along near the edge of our camp. She wasn't the least bit bothered by all the racket Rab was makin' – or by all the cussin' Sam was doin' as he struggled to pull his trousers on over his long johns. At least she wasn't bothered until Rab's leash broke. Then she was bothered a lot as he started circling about her, snarling and growling with the hair standin' straight up on the back of his neck. Rearing up on her hind legs, she kept turning as Rab circled around her, swiping at him with her front paws every time he came too close — but he always managed to jump back in time.

All of us kids were shouting at the tops of our lungs, tellin' Rab to come back and let the bear alone. Sam was still cussin', but now he was tryin' to load my dad's .25/.35 — but he kept droppin' the cartridges in the dirt. He wasn't havin' any better luck gettin' them into the magazine either, let alone into the chamber. But at least now he had his pants on, so he was makin' headway — or maybe bottomway, considerin' where he'd put his pants.

It all ended as fast as it began. The bear dropped back down on all fours, took a couple of more little swipes at Rab, then swung around and, without even a backward look, waddled off into the morning mist. I imagine she figured she'd had enough fun foolin' with that noisy critter. By that time Sam finally had the rifle loaded, but it was too late to shoot — the bear was gone and I was glad. I'm sure Rab was, too. I think he was beginnin' to suspect that he'd bitten off more than he should have.

Thanks to Rab and the bear, we were all wide awake and raring to go that morning — all but Sam that is. His back was still so stiff and sore it was a wonder he'd even been able to get out of his bedroll when the bear showed up. He looked awful, and I'm sure he felt terrible, but he wouldn't admit it. After we'd finished eating, J. J. told Sam that he thought he should stay in camp that morning and rest 'til we got back. We would keep on bringing ore down the mountain and hiding it with the rest, and we sure didn't need him for that. Then we'd come back to camp at noon to eat and check on him, and — if he felt better — he could help us after that. Sam argued a little, saying as how his back was already beginnin' to limber up some, and how we'd be able to head back to Shadycroft a lot sooner if he helped. But J. J. told him that if he did, it might make his back hurt so bad that he couldn't even ride in the truck. If that happened, we couldn't go back to Shadycroft 'til he got better, and that might take a long time. Sam didn't argue any more after that. I'm sure he knew J. J. was right. When we left, he was sittin' with his back to the campfire, keeping it warm while he sorted the flies in Dad's old tackle box.

We worked steadily 'til a little after noon. It was cloudy that day and not near as hot as the last few days had been, and for that we were mighty grateful. We worked hard all morning, and it was almost fun. We all felt wonderful, 'cause our trip had been successful. We'd found the cave a lot sooner than any of us expected, the first load of gold was in the truck, and by tomorrow night, we'd be back at Shadycroft, telling our folks the good news. We all felt like celebrating and were laughing and singing on our way back to camp, but when we got there a little after noon, Sam was nowhere to be seen.

CHAPTER 52

We checked all around our camping place, looking for anything that seemed out of place or different. But, as far as we could tell, everything was just as we'd left it. Sam's bedroll still lay by the burned out fire. Dad's tackle box was on a nearby rock, and his rod was leanin' up against a tree. Everything seemed in order. The .25/.35 was right where it had been, wrapped up in a blanket to keep dirt out of the barrel. Sam's knapsack was where we remembered it, too, with Dad's Colt .38 special still inside.

At first we were afraid that maybe the bear had come back, killed Sam, and dragged him off somewhere. But that seemed unlikely, 'cause there was no sign of a struggle, or blood, or anything else you might expect to find if that had happened. Not only that, nothing seemed to be bothering Rab. If there'd been a bear around recently, we figured he'd be real excited, and be sniffin' the ground like he always did when a skunk or porcupine had wandered by. But he didn't seem to be the least bit concerned. He was flopped down in the shade of a tree, takin' a snooze. Most likely he was pooped out from all the work we'd done that morning.

We looked everywhere for Sam, shouting his name at the top of our voices. We searched all around the lake, and J. J. and I even went all the way back to the truck, thinkin' that he might have decided to join us there, but that somehow we'd missed seein' him when we were comin' back to camp. But he wasn't there — he didn't seem to be anywhere. He'd just disappeared into thin air.

We didn't know what to do. We all talked it over, and I sure was glad J. J. and Abby were with us, 'cause Charley and I were both gettin' scared. Charley was even cryin' a little, and I was afraid I would, too. But J. J. told us to quit worryin'. Sam had to be around here somewhere, and most likely he'd be back most any time now and tell us where he'd been. Then J. J. snapped his fingers together like he'd just thought of something.

"Robby, I bet I know where Sam is. Do you remember that part in his dad's journal where it tells about the mine he and his uncle found here in the Tarryalls?" I nodded that I did. "Well, maybe Sam's back got better, and he decided to go visit their old mine. He told us that it was one of his favorite places to go. You know, if I'm right, I bet it won't be long before he'll be back, so why don't we all quit worrying and settle down and wait for him." That sounded like it made good sense, so we all relaxed and spent the rest of the afternoon playin' poker.

But when Sam didn't show up by dark, and he still hadn't come back by mornin', it was beginning to look like J. J.'s idea wasn't right after all. But he still figured it might be 'cause Sam just had to be around here somewhere, and where else could he have gone? Then he started guessin' again. Maybe Sam had gone up to the mine and his back had started botherin' him so much he couldn't even walk — maybe he'd even hurt himself. The more he talked, the more convinced he was that the two of us should take Rab and head up the mountain to see if we could find him. He told Abby and Charley to stay in camp just in case Sam came back while we were gone.

Well, we found the mine all right, but there was no sign of Sam. We hollered and shouted, both on our way up and comin' back down, but he never did answer. Hungry and tired, we got back to camp a little after noon. We were hopin' and prayin' that Sam would be there waiting for us. But he wasn't, and neither were Abby and Charley. Now they had disappeared, too. This was really gettin' weird and scary, with emphasis on the scary. We looked all around again and checked down by the truck just like we did before, but no matter where we looked or how much we shouted, we couldn't find hide nor hair of them. It was like the earth had opened up and swallowed them and then closed back up again. We discovered one strange thing, though. For some peculiar reason — even though it was broad daylight when Abby and Charley left — they'd taken the lantern and flashlights with them. At least, they weren't where we'd left them the night before.

"What are we gonna do now, J. J.?" I asked. "I sure wish our folks were here, 'cause they'd know what to do. Maybe we could go home and tell them what's happened. What do you think?"

But J. J. was clear out of ideas, except for sayin', "Naw, I don't want to do that Robby, not without knowin' what happened to Sam and Abby and Charley. So why don't we stay here one more night and if they're not back by noon tomorrow, we'll — well, we'll wait 'til then to decide what to do next."

That night, while we were eating, J. J. pointed out that we were about out of food — we were even out of trout — and he figured I should go fishin' so we'd have something to eat. I told him fine, I'd be happy to, as long as he went with me, but he claimed that he had to stay in camp in case Abby, Charley, or Sam showed up. I told him he had another think comin' if he figured I was dumb enough to let him get out of my sight and have him up and disappear like all the others. Either he was goin' with me, or I wasn't goin' at all. J. J.'s final words in the matter were, "OK, then — we'll just go hungry."

The past two days had been real cloudy, but so far it hadn't rained a drop. But late that evening, as we sat in the flickering firelight, we heard the rumble of distant thunder echoing back and forth between the rocky walls of canyons far to the north of our camp, and we could see the ghostly outlines of mountain ridges rimmed by the glow of sheet lightning. J. J. said it sounded to him like a big storm was brewing up near Kenosha Pass.

There was no comforting canopy of stars above us that night, only a suffocating darkness that seemed to smother the warmth of our campfire as well as to heighten our level of anxiety. As J. J. and I bedded down on opposite sides of the campfire, I saw him put Dad's .25/.35, still wrapped in the blanket, close by his sleeping bag where it would be handy should he need it during the night. Needless to say, that didn't add any to my peace of mind, and I made Rab lie down close beside me. I always felt safer when he was close by.

As I lay in my sleeping bag, watching the red tongues of our campfire licking at the night, I gradually grew sleepy and was about to drop off when I roused with a start. It seemed to me that I'd heard a faint, unfamiliar sound coming from the grove of aspen trees just outside our camp. It had sounded like the muffled snap of a brittle tree branch, followed by a furtive rustling, and then complete silence. Rab heard it, too, and by the glow of the fire, I could see the hair on the back of his neck standing erect, and I heard a low growl rumbling deep down in his throat. He was behaving exactly as he had when the bear paid us that visit. I grabbed him by his collar and held him tight, thinking, oh no, not the bear again. I whispered softly to J J. in a quavering voice. He roused, pushed himself up on one elbow, and asked me sleepily what was wrong.

"I think the bear's back, J. J., and so does Rab. At least he's sure actin' just like he was doin' then."

We both held our breath and listened intently to the forest sounds, muffled by a light rain that had begun to fall. Except for the forlorn, far-off hoot of a lonely owl, nothing could be heard. No matter how hard we both strained to see beyond the faint circle of firelight, neither of us could make out a thing. The forest beyond was dark and silent. The campfire was little more than embers now, glowing like tiger eyes in the night, and I could barely see J. J. as he quietly struggled to get up, while at the same time reaching for the .25/.35. But suddenly, before he could even unwrap the gun from the blanket, we were blinded by the brilliant rays of a flashlight, and we heard a raspy voice saying, "Well, looky here, Jack, if it ain't that mouthy Johnson kid. You might of guessed we'd find him here, considerin' how friendly he is with Jimmy, or Sam, or whatever the hell he calls himself."

I'd always read in books about how people's hearts would sink whenever something bad happened. Now I knew what they'd been talking about. My heart felt like it was somewhere in the vicinity of my belly button and was poundin' about a thousand thuds a second. I didn't even have to see his face to know that it was Jud Rathbone standing there in the dark. In a whisper, I told J. J. who it was, and we both lay paralyzed with fear, unable to move, and wondering what was gonna happen next. Both of us figured that this was most likely our very last moment on earth. Then, just to make that seem a lot more likely, a flash of distant lightning lit the forest around us with an eerie red glow, and we could see Jud standing there lookin' like the Devil himself, except you couldn't see his horns on account of he was wearing a hat.

"Both of you get your butts out of your bedrolls and keep a tight hold of that damned dog," Jud snarled. "If he makes one move in my direction, I'll have Jack here blow his damn head off, and while I'm at it, I might have him blow your heads off, too. You both got that straight?"

Unable to speak, J. J. and I both nodded. Then J. J. slowly got up and came over to snap the leash onto Rab's collar, so he could hang onto him while I was gettin' up. Rab was growling a lot and actin' real upset, but after we'd both told him to shut up and keep quiet, he stopped growling and sat down between us. He acted like he was waitin' to see what would happen next. We stood there with him, shaking with fright and wondering exactly the same thing. We didn't have long to wait, as Jud directed the beam of his flashlight full into J. J.'s face and asked in a menacing voice, "What the hell is your name, Kid?"

But, before J. J. could choke out an answer, Jack interrupted, "That's the older Johnson kid, Jud. His name's J. J. — he's one of the kids what helped Sam find the cave and haul the gold down the hill."

"Well, that was damn nice of him," Jud replied. "Nice for us, that is, 'cause come tomorrow, these snot-nosed kids are gonna come in real handy. Since they've already had all that practice, I reckon we'll just let them pack the rest of the ore down the hill and help us load it into the trucks. Now, both of you hurry up and put your shoes and pants on — you're comin' with us."

As he was speaking, Jud stepped in closer and gave me a sharp shove. Rab went instantly berserk. With a vicious snarl and bared fangs, he hurled himself towards Jud, fully intending to rip him apart. I don't know what would have happened next if J. J. hadn't jerked back on Rab's leash and held him close by his side, but whatever it was, it couldn't have been near as bad as what actually did happen.

Jud gave forth with a steady stream of cussing — words I'd never heard before and hope I never hear again. Then he aimed his revolver at Rab, and I'm sure he'd of shot him right on the spot if J. J. hadn't been right behind him, hanging onto the leash for all he was worth. After Jud calmed down some, and Rab was quiet again, Jud's voice got low and menacing.

"Jack, here's my pistol. Take that damned dog into that grove of trees over there and kill him. That's the last time he's ever gonna threaten me."

J. J. and I began to protest vehemently. I burst into tears, pleading with Jud in a choking voice not to kill Rab. "Please don't kill him, Colonel Pettigrew — he'll never do it again. He's my best friend, and I love him. He was just trying to protect me. He won't attack you again — I promise."

"You're damn right he won't, Kid, 'cause he won't be around to do it." Then he reached out, slapped me across the mouth, and commanded me to shut up.

Rab snarled and lunged at Jud again, and he repeated his order. "Damn it, Jack. Take this damned dog and get it over with. I don't want to stand out here in the rain any longer than I have to."

"You sure it's a good idea, Boss?" Jack asked. "It'll just upset these kids so much they won't do anything we ask."

"The hell they won't, Jack. They'll either do what we say or we'll do to one of them what you're gonna do to that damned dog. Now quit stallin'. Take this gun and get on with it."

With obvious reluctance, Jack took the revolver from Jud and, taking Rab's leash in his free hand, led him protesting into the dark night. As J. J. and I waited in shocked silence, Jud held me by the shoulder in a grip of iron and muttered ominously to J. J.

"Don't get any idea about runnin' off, Kid, 'cause if you do, I'll break your little brother's scrawny neck." As he spoke he put his other hand around my neck and squeezed briefly, but painfully.

Moments later we heard the sharp report of the gun, and after that, absolute silence, broken only by J. J.'s quiet weeping and my uncontrollable sobs. After several long minutes Jack reappeared. He looked grim and wouldn't look directly at either J. J. or me. He just handed the gun to Jud without saying a word and immediately left camp heading in the direction of the boulder field.

We all followed him, first J. J., then me in the middle — still sobbing — with Jud close behind. The flashlights helped some, but it was still hard to see where we were goin'. The light rain had turned to a cold, steady drizzle, and the rocks were wet and slick. We stumbled some as we tried to keep up, and now and then it seemed like Jack slowed down a little so we could keep up better. But every time he did, Jud hollered at him to get a move on, that he didn't want to spend the whole damn night gettin' there — wherever "there" was.

The further we went, the more obvious it became that "there" was the cave. As we approached the entrance of the tunnel and started walking down the pathway, we could see the flickering glow of a kerosene lantern. I stopped as we entered and tried to look about the gloomy cavern, but Jud gave me a sharp shove that sent me stumbling out into the center of the cave. After righting myself, I followed J. J. to the far end, just as far away from Jud as I could possibly get. What a relief it was when we saw Sam, Abby, and Charley in the back of the cave. They looked like they were all scared to death. Except for Sam — he was too far gone to be scared. His face was all bruised and his clothes were torn. I wasn't even sure that he was alive, on account of he was lyin' there starin' straight ahead, like he didn't even know we were there. Abby and Charley were happy to see us, though, but I sure couldn't see why, 'cause now J. J. and I were in the same sorry fix they were in. We couldn't help them none — that was for sure.

They were all tied up, both hands and feet, and it wasn't long before J. J. and I were, too. They tied our arms behind our backs so we either had to sit propped up against the side of the cave or lie on our sides on the rocky floor. Either way it was real clammy and cold — 'specially cold. I felt sick and miserable, but mainly on account of I missed Rab. I still couldn't believe he was dead. I knew that I'd never have another friend like him — ever.

That was the most miserable night I ever spent in my life, and I pray to God that I never spend another one like it. By the time morning finally came, I was almost wishin' I could die and be with Rab. I was cold, hungry, and thirsty, and I had to go real bad. I'm sure all the others were just as bad off as I was, but none of us dared say anything, for fear of what Jud might do. Twice during the night, Jack asked him if he could give us some water and feed us a little, or at least let us go outside the cave so we could relieve ourselves. But both times Jud just laughed and said, hell no, he liked seein' us suffer.

Besides Jud and Jack, there were three other men in the cave, and I recognized all of them. They were the same ones that had been with Jud at Shadycroft on that scary night last November. One of them was named George, I remembered, and I found out later that the other two were Chuck Collins and Gus Tobin. They were all a tough lookin' lot. Except maybe for Jack. Another time and another place, I might even have liked him — at least, I might have if he hadn't killed Rab. George didn't seem too bad, either — he just didn't seem too bright. The only good thing I could think of to say about any of them was that so far, at least, none of them had bothered Abby. Jud and his men all had lots to eat and drink and two blankets each to keep them warm — none of which made me feel any kindlier towards them. I know how the Bible says you should love and forgive your enemies — I think Jesus was the one that said it. But I got to wondering if He still would have said it if Jud and his gang had been hangin' around the holy land back in those days, sellin' bootleg whiskey to the Pharisees.

To my considerable surprise, come next morning we were all still alive. Sam sure didn't look like it, though. Off and on that night we'd heard the muffled rumble of thunder comin' from outside the cave, and I guess it was still raining, 'cause every now and then a drop of water would drip from the ceiling and splash on the rocks near where Sam was tied up. He was shivering and shaking from the wet and cold and was as pale as a ghost. I wished there was some way I could help him. Once, I even asked Jud if he would at least loosen Sam's ropes so he could move his arms and legs around some and try to get warm. He was way too weak to cause any trouble.

But Jud just laughed a mean little laugh and said, "Hell no, Kid. I'm not gonna untie him. He's just lucky he's still alive." Then, as the rest of us watched hungrily, Jud and his men bolted down a cold breakfast, washed down with bootleg whiskey. Finished with that, Jud stood up, stretched, and said, "Jack, Chuck and Gus and I are gonna head down the mountain to our trucks so we can drive them over to where they stashed the gold ore. Their truck's right up the hill from there, but we'll drive ours down closer to the creek, where they'll be easier to load. After the boys and I leave, you and George untie these kids and get them started packing the rest of this gold ore and the strongboxes down the mountain to where the boys and I can load it. And George, you stay here and keep a close watch on Sam, and be damned sure he stays tied up tight — I know from experience what a slick operator he is. He may look weak, but he's most likely just fakin' it. You can't trust him for a second." Then Jud unbuckled his gun belt from around his waist and handed it to Jack. "Here, Jack, take my revolver with you, and if any of these damn kids give's you any trouble, or are stupid enough to try to escape, just shoot 'em, and if you miss the runaway, shoot little missy here instead. I reckon that'll keep them in line."

Then, just as he was leaving the cave, Jud turned and pointed a dirty forefinger at me. "Jack, be damned sure you keep a close eye on that kid there, and don't believe a thing he tells you — he's the best damn liar I've ever seen. I'll bet you anything that this snot-nosed kid knew Sam was hiding in that trunk at his folk's place, and he just kept lyin' and stallin' around, hopin' and prayin' the sheriff would show up and we'd leave. Well, there's no sheriff to help him this time, and hopin' and prayin' ain't gonna do him a bit of good, 'cause later on today, once he's done haulin' gold, that kid's gonna get just what he deserves." If Jud said that to frighten me, he sure succeeded — in spades.

After Jud left, Jack did exactly what Jud had ordered him not to do. He untied us — but with a few welcome additions. Although I couldn't be real sure, I was almost positive that when it came my turn to be untied, Jack winked at me a little. Then he untied Sam — even though Jud had told him not to. That really surprised us. He told George that, even though Sam wasn't in any shape to give him any trouble, he still should keep a close eye on him to be sure he didn't try something stupid while we were gone.

Then Jack surprised us once again. He gave each of us a blanket to put around our shoulders and let us go outside the cave one at a time so we could relieve ourselves. Ever since then, I've understood why it's called that, 'cause it sure was a relief. After that, Jack gave us something to eat and drink, claiming it would give us the strength to haul gold. And finally, just as we were leaving with the first load of gold, he gave Sam a big cupful of bootleg whiskey: It was amazing to see how Sam perked up after that. Before we left, we all thanked Jack and George for their unexpected help.

Jack grinned and said, "Hell, I can't see no reason for you folks to have to suffer, so, seein' as how Jud won't be comin' back to the cave again, I figured it'd be safe to help you out a little. But don't go gettin' your hopes up any. George and I have to follow Jud's orders from here on out. If we don't, we won't be amongst the livin' much longer, 'cause Jud ain't a particularly understandin' or forgivin' man. Boy, was that ever a big understatement.

Something had been puzzling me. "Jack, how come Jud and the rest of you showed up right after we found the gold? How'd you know we were here? We did our best not to let anybody see us leavin'."

"Jud was sure that Sam was hidin' out at your folks' place, Robby, so he had one of his gang keepin' watch, and when he'd seen Doc Sims and the sheriff visiting your house, he was even more shore. Then, the times the lookout seen you folks sneakin' out early in the mornin', he reported it to Jud, and George and me would follow you up here. After we seen where you'd found the cave and was haulin' ore down the mountain, George stayed here to keep an eye on you while I lit out for Littleton so's to tell Jud the news. After that, I hightailed it back to Lost Creek, along with Jud and the rest of the gang."

So Mother was right after all. They really were spying on us at Shadycroft and had followed us up to Lost Creek when we'd come to look for the cave. And Abby was right, too, 'cause Jack and George really had been spyin' on us from the top of the cliff, just like she'd suspected.

One time when George wasn't listening, I asked Jack how come George did what he told him to do instead of followin' Jud's orders. He smiled and said, "I reckon George is a mite slow when it comes to thinkin' good, but other than that, he's a damned good man. Neither of us like Jud or the things he does — 'specially since he killed our friend Cliff Alexander. But we're in this with him too deep to quit now. If we did, he'd kill us both — that's for damned sure. So I figure me and George will stick with him 'til we get our share of the gold, and after that we'll clear out and go someplace where he can't find us. Oh yeah, I forgot to tell you. Besides that, George is my younger brother, and I promised my mamma that I'd always look out for him and keep him out of trouble."

It seemed to me that hookin' up with Jud was a peculiar way to keep his brother out of trouble. 'Course, I didn't say that to Jack.

That morning, we emerged from the gloom of the cavern into brilliant sunshine. Gone was the cloud cover of the prior day, replaced by fleecy wisps of white clouds floating in a deep blue sky. It was the kind of day that was meant to be enjoyed, and ordinarily I would have greeted it with enthusiasm, but this was no ordinary day. It was my last day on this earth, and not only mine, but J. J.'s, Abby's, Charley's, and Sam's last day, too, and I was scared spitless. When I stepped out into the bright morning sunshine, I almost whistled for Rab, like I thought I could call him back from the realm of the dead. I couldn't help cryin', 'cause I missed him so much. But at least there was one good thing — Rab would be waiting for me when I got up to heaven, and he'd probably be wanting me to go porcupine and skunk hunting with him. Of course, up in heaven, porcupines most likely don't have quills and skunks don't smell — Mr. Williamson would be happy to know that last.

The rest of that morning we hauled gold ore down the mountain just like before, but this time we hated it, 'cause we were doin' it for Jud. He made us haul it across the creek and dump it right next to the trucks, so it'd be easier for his men to load. It looked to me like they were figurin' on takin' all the gold out in just one trip, and I wondered if they knew what they were doin'. Even I could tell that they were way overloadin' their own trucks, and they'd moved Dad's truck down closer to the creek and were loading more gold ore onto it. From what Sam had said, they'd never be able to get my dad's truck back up the hill with all that extra weight on it, and I doubted they could their own — even though their trucks had more power than Dad's. Their springs were already flattened out straight, and they were still piling on more ore. And, even if they did manage somehow to get the trucks back up to the road, they'd most likely bust an axle the first time they hit a bump.

After a long morning hauling gold ore, Jack told us we could stop and rest in the cavern for awhile. But it would have to be short, so Jud wouldn't start wonderin' where we were and come lookin' for us. He even gave us some food to eat. That surprised us considerably, 'cause Jud had ordered him to take all the food that was left down to him and his men. But Jack, bless his heart, had held some back for us. I was actually beginnin' to like him, 'til I remembered that he was the one that killed Rab. The food perked up both our energy and our spirits, but I think what helped us the most was to see Sam's remarkable recovery — due in large measure, no doubt, to the occasional jolt of bootleg whiskey graciously provided him by George. And it was very obvious that George had shared in the libations as well; by now he and Sam had become the best of friends and were laughing and slapping each other on the back and swapping lies just like they'd known each other for years.

After we finished eating, Jack told George to come with him, and they both left the cave for a few minutes. It was the first time they'd ever left us by ourselves. We could hear them talking in the passageway outside the cave, and it sounded like George was protesting something that Jack had told him. I wondered if it had anything to do with the argument that Jack and Jud were having the last time we were down by the trucks. I'm pretty sure that Jud had been giving Jack instructions on how to go about getting rid of us once we'd finished hauling gold, and that whatever it was Jud had in mind, Jack didn't want to do it. Unfortunately, by the time the argument was over, it was obvious that Jack had lost, and now he was out in the passageway explaining to George what it was they had to do to us once Jud didn't need us any longer.

While I was sittin' there worrying, J. J. leaned over and whispered, "Hey, Robby, let's hide some of the gold ingots from the stage strongbox under those rocks over there," and he pointed to some nearby rubble.

So that's what we did. While Abby stood near the cave entrance so she could warn us when Jack and George were comin' back, Charley and I took turns tossing the ingots to J. J. where he was standing near the back of the cavern. After catching one, he'd hide it under a big, close-by rock, then replace its weight with another rock, so nobody would suspect what we'd done. After that, whoever's turn it was would toss him another ingot. By the time Abby announced that Jack and George were comin' back, we'd managed to hide at least ten or twelve ingots. After they came back into the cave, Jack told us that we'd best get a move on. If we didn't, Jud would come up to see what was holdin' us up, and he sure didn't want that to happen — and neither would we.

That afternoon, the weather couldn't seem to make up its mind whether to be sunshiny or cloudy. Gray, wind-driven clouds floated silently high above our heads, occasionally concealing the sun and sending a few drops of cold rain splashing down on our heads. It was midafternoon and our next to the last trip when we heard the rumble of distant thunder from out the north. As we watched, billows of black clouds boiled from behind the crest of the Tarryall range and scudded across the darkening sky like clumps of foam on a storm-tossed sea. To add still more to the eerie scene, the clouds were intermittently lit from within by fiery flashes of lightning, while at the same time the mountain quiet was rent by the echoes of clashing thunder. I sure hoped that the storm wasn't comin' our way — things were already bad enough down here.

It was the very last load of ore, and we were all dreading what was going to happen to us after we'd taken it down to the trucks. From then on,

Jud would no longer need our help, and he'd made it very clear that he had some very unpleasant plan in mind for us. As we reached the base of the mountain and started to cross over Lost Creek, Jud hollered, "Where the hell have you been, Jack? I was about to come lookin' for you."

As we drew near to the trucks and were dumping the ore, Jack answered. "Jud, these kids have been workin' their tails off all day, and they're plumb wore out, and…"

Before Jack could say anything more, Jud broke in, shouting, "Damn it, Jack, I'm sick of your bellyachin' and backtalk, and I don't want to hear any more of it. Here, take these sticks of dynamite and get these kids back up the mountain and put them in the cave with Sam. Then blow it up like I told you to do. And make damned sure that nobody can ever find it again — or them, either."

Jack kept tryin' to say something, but Jud wouldn't let him. "Shut up, Jack. Don't talk, damn it — just listen. Once you're positive they're all dead, get your butts off the mountain and back to your car. Then get the hell out of here. You and George go back to our hideout and wait for us there, and as soon as we get the ore processed, we'll join you with the gold. After that, we'll all light out for our old hideout in Kansas, where we'll be safe and can divvy it up."

We were all standin' there listenin' to Jud, and the more he said, the more frightened we became. We could scarcely breathe, let alone talk. We just stood there shaking, with fear. But God bless Jack. He was still gonna talk even though Jud told him not to, and the second Jud quit talkin', he started. "Jud, there's no way in hell I'm gonna kill these kids, and I ain't gonna kill Sam, either, and neither's George. I've figured out a lot better way to handle it." Jud's face got redder and redder. He looked so mad, I thought he was gonna explode, but Jack wouldn't stop talkin' 'til he'd had his say.

"Jud, if we blow that cave up with them in it, their folks are bound to know right where to look for them. They've been up here, too, you know, and they know about where the cave is hidden, so that'll be the first place they'll look for their kids. Most likely Sheriff Haynes and the Summit County sheriff will come with them, too, and with all their people lookin' for the cave, they'll find it in no time — no matter how much dynamite we use. Then they'll find their bodies, and when that happens, we'll have every damned lawman in the whole country hot on our tails, and they won't quit 'til we're all either swingin' from a rope or fryin' in the electric chair." Jud kept tryin' to break in, but Jack just kept raisin' his voice louder and louder until he was close to shoutin'.

"Me and George have a better plan worked out, Jud — now just listen to me, damn it. Our idea is to take them to our car, tie them up and haul them back to the hideout. We'll keep them there, while you and the rest of the boys take the ore to the smelter. Then — after you get back to the hideout with the money — we can all head for our old stompin' grounds in Kansas, just like you said. We'll dump the kids and Sam in some godforsaken place way out in eastern Colorado, where they won't be able to report to the law for hours. By that time we'll be in Kansas, divvyin' up the gold, and after that we'll split up and head for parts unknown. With all that money, we can go anywhere we want, and nobody'll ever find us. But I promise you this, Jud, if we do it your way, it's a surefire bet that we'll all be dead by the end of the year. The law will never quit lookin' for us."

Jack managed to finish sayin' his piece all right, but Jud had the final word. He was still so red in the face, I was hopin' he'd have a stroke or heart attack, but he didn't. Instead he shouted, "Gus, keep your rifle leveled at this —." I can't repeat what he said, 'cause if I do my mother will kill me. "If he makes one false move, shoot him. Jack, give me back that damned revolver, and get over there by the kids. You're goin' back to the cave with them, all right, but now you and George are gonna be inside it with them when we blow the damn thing up. I'm gonna light the fuses myself, and I'll damn well enjoy doin' it. I do thank you, though, for reminding me how their parents might look for their bodies in the cave. But that's real easy to remedy. Before we leave Littleton, we'll go by their places and get rid of all three of them, too."

When he said that, I felt like I was gonna throw up. The others looked like they might, too — and Charley did. I was trying to think of something we could say or do, but I knew that Jud wouldn't listen to me. It'd just make him madder. I wanted to run away, but that would've been stupid, 'cause they'd of shot me the second I tried. There was only one thing left to do. Pray, and boy did I ever do a lot of that. I could tell that the others were all prayin', too — even Jack.

Jud ordered Jack and the rest of us to cross over to the west bank of the creek and stay close to the water's edge 'til they finished loading the ore — that way, we couldn't jump them while they were workin'. Gus and Chuck were to take turns holding their guns on us to be sure we couldn't run away. They were to shoot us if it looked like any of us were even thinking about doin' it.

Following Jud's orders, we crossed over the creek and huddled together on the far bank. We all thanked Jack for sticking up for us the way he did, even though he must have known he'd pay for it with his life. He didn't say much, though — only that he figured we all had to die sometime, and he didn't want to go to his Maker with our deaths on his conscience. Then he apologized for getting our folks into trouble — he sure hadn't meant for that to happen. After that, nobody said another word. We just stood there, afraid to even move for fear that one of Jud's men would shoot us.

Then it started to rain. At first it was just a light sprinkle, but soon it began to rain harder, then harder, until finally it was a steady downpour. Although it was difficult to see clearly through the veil of rain, I could still make out Gus's rain-soaked figure standing in the lee of one of the trucks with his rifle pointed in our direction. I couldn't be sure which one of us he was aimin' at, and I wasn't anxious to find out — none of the others were either, I guess, 'cause we all stood perfectly still, afraid to move, lest he'd think we were trying to escape.

As the rain continued to increase, Jud and Chuck finished loading the ore. Then Jud joined Gus, and together they started working their way across the deepening waters of the creek, heading in our direction. At the same time, Chuck climbed into the cab of a truck, and I watched as it began to creep slowly up the hill toward the road. But, after going only a few feet, the rear wheels began to spin in the loose gravel and dig themselves in down to the hubs. Jud and Gus were already halfway across the stream, but when Jud realized what was happening, he paused and stood watching the truck, as though he was trying to decide whether to stay with Gus or go back to help Chuck.

By now, the storm was a full-fledged cloudburst. It fell in sheets, and there were times when I could see no more than a foot or two in front of me. The sound of the downpour was deafening as it pounded the ground and the surface of the swollen creek. Then we became aware of another sound mixed in with that of the falling rain. It was a low-pitched, ominous rumble that seemed to be gradually growing louder. J. J. was the first to react. "Flash flood!!!" he shouted. "Quick, get to high ground!"

Terrified, we all turned and scrambled up the mountainside just as fast as we could go. J. J. grabbed hold of Abby's hand and Jack grabbed me and Charley, as we all struggled up the hill together — each one helpin' the others. Just as we started to climb, I heard the sound of a rifle shot and heard the thud of a bullet striking the earth near my feet. That gave me wings, as I flew up the slope with the others, hoping to find shelter in the gully that came down from the lake. But when we got there, what had been a little trickle the last time we'd crossed it was now a turgid torrent fully ten feet across and at least three deep — and it was rapidly growing both wider and deeper. It was obvious that, if we didn't cross over it quickly, we never would. With Jack in the lead, we all joined hands to form a human chain and, with prayers on our lips, we struggled across the turbulent flow until we all were safely across. Then, though we were completely exhausted, we resumed our climb up the mountain.

CHAPTER 53

Although it seemed an eternity, I'm sure it was no more than a few minutes since the beginning of our flight until we were standing on a bench a hundred feet above the valley floor. Breathless, we turned and looked down the hill, where we could see Jud and Gus struggling to free themselves from the rising waters of Lost Creek. Jud was holding his rifle high above his head — obviously still bent on pursuing us. And though we could scarcely see him through the curtain of rain, Chuck was still in the cab of the truck, gunning the motor, and spinning the wheels as he tried to get up the hill.

Then, suddenly, the roaring sound doubled in intensity and the ground seemed to shake beneath our feet. We watched in horror as a deluge of water burst from the opening of the ice cave and shot forth into the valley with an unimaginable and indescribable force. Everything in its path was swept before it — men, trucks, gold ore, all gone in the blink of an eye. And then, as the torrent continued to spew forth from the mouth of the ice cave, it was increased threefold as even more water raged through, around, and over the boulders. Huge trees, rocks, gravel, and debris — anything that was not securely anchored — was torn up and carried away by the floodwaters.

As we stood watching those great forces of nature at work, the rain began to dwindle. Shortly it stopped completely, and as the black clouds in the west lifted to reveal an azure sky and the welcome orb of the golden sun hovering above the crest of the Tarryalls, we all said a prayer thanking God for sparing our lives.

As the cloudburst ceased and the torrent of floodwater subsided, Lost Creek slowly returned to some semblance of normal, becoming a rain-glutted stream instead of a raging torrent. Piles of sandy debris, gravel, and uprooted trees littered its banks as far down the valley as our eyes could see. In the distance, hundreds of feet downstream, we could see the remnants of the trucks lying upside down and sideways, like crumpled tin cans. Hoping that we might be able to salvage some of our lost gold ore, we slipped and slid back down to Lost Creek and walked along its water-soaked bank. But from what we could tell, recovery of the gold would be a hopeless task. The place where we had stored it was scoured clean, right down to the granite floor. All of the gold ore was gone — returned to the earth from whence it had come. Of course, many places were still underwater or buried by debris, so it was still possible that some of the gold was retrievable. But, according to J. J., even if it was, it probably wouldn't be worth the effort to even try.

We found no sign of Jud or his men, although I'll have to admit we didn't look very hard for them. We all figured they'd gotten exactly what they deserved, even though it was still a terrible way for them to die. But for the difference of a few seconds, the same thing would have happened to us.

After looking for the gold, we all headed up the mountain to see how Sam and George were doin'. I was sure they'd been worried sick, thinkin' about all that might have happened to us and how it most likely would happen to them, too — but as it turned out, they couldn't have cared less. As we approached the cave, they were laughing, singing, whooping, and having a high old time, and when we walked in the cave, they greeted us like they didn't have a care in the world. If either of them was worried about us, you sure couldn't tell it, and as soon as I saw them I knew why. Both Sam and George were sittin' side by side on a pile of our old irrigation canvases with a half-empty jug of moonshine beside them and cups full of whiskey in their hands.

When we told them about the flood, and how Jud and the others were killed, they just laughed and laughed like they thought it was the funniest thing they'd ever heard. I'm not sure they even knew it'd been pourin' rain that day, even though water was still drippin' from the ceiling of the cave. I tried to tell Sam how all the gold had been washed away by the flood, and he just giggled and said, "Now ain't that a shame."

All us kids thought they were funny, but it made Jack mad. He said they were pitiful, and that it was disgusting to see two grown men actin' like that. Then, despite their pathetic protests, he took the whiskey bottle outside the cave and smashed it on the rocks. Then he came back in and told us that he had to be gone for awhile, on account of there was something he had to do. He asked us to keep close watch over Sam and

George. They were both hung over and not feelin' too good, and he was afraid they might do something stupid.

At first we all thought Jack had left for the usual reason, but after he'd been gone for almost an hour and it was gettin' dark, we started worryin' about him and wonderin' where he could have gone and why. J. J. and I were afraid something bad might have happened to him, and we were gettin' ready to go look for him when we heard his footsteps outside the entrance to the cave. It sounded like he was talking to somebody. We couldn't tell what he was saying, and whoever it was he was talking to didn't answer back.

The first thing I thought and told the others was, "Oh no! It's Jud. He didn't drown after all." After that, nobody said a word — we just stood there, shaking, praying, and listening to the sound of the approaching footsteps.

Not wanting to see Jud's ugly face again, I squinched my eyes up tight and was bracing myself, praying that my end would be both painless and quick, when I suddenly found myself knocked down and pinned flat on the hard cavern floor. Then I felt a warm, wet tongue licking my face. I figured that was somethin' Jud would be unlikely to do, so I opened my eyes and there, to my joyful surprise, was my very best friend! Rab was standing over me, his tail wagging joyfully — very much alive and well. For a long moment I was unable to speak. I just lay on my back, wondering if maybe I could be dreaming. But Rab was no dream. He was really there, and I burst into tears of joy as I threw my arms around his neck and hugged him up close to me. J. J. was just as happy to see Rab as I was. He just didn't show it as much, and he sure didn't cry. Instead, he asked Jack how come Rab was alive, 'cause we thought he'd shot him right after Jud ordered him to.

Jack just grinned and said, "Hell, I like dogs too much to shoot one — 'specially a great dog like Rab. I just took him over to the other side of the lake and tied him up to a tree with his leash. Then I fired a shot into the air to make Jud think I'd kilt him. 'Course, back then I was hopin' I could talk Jud into lettin' me and George take you kids and Sam with us when we left, and let you loose later on our way to Kansas. I had it all figured out. After Jud and the others left with their trucks, I was gonna come back and untie Rab so we could take him with us. Then we'd drop him off somewhere close to your folks' farm when we got to Littleton. That way Jud never would know I didn't kill him."

After that, Jack told us we'd best eat a little of the food that was left and get some sleep, 'cause tomorrow was likely to be a long day, and he wanted to get an early start. Sam and George were already sound asleep and snoring, but that wasn't too surprising, considering all the moonshine they'd drunk. The rest of us weren't long in following their example. Sleepin' that is — I hope not snorin'.

It was still dark when Jack rousted us from our rocky beds next morning, and the flickering, yellow light of the kerosene lantern didn't do much to brighten the dismal interior. But nothing could have dampened our spirits that morning. Even a breakfast of rock-hard biscuits washed down with water seemed like a wonderful meal. I could scarcely believe it. Only yesterday I was certain that I'd never see my folks or Shadycroft again, and now we were headed for home. What a difference a day can make.

After eating, we packed what few belongings we had left into two ragged knapsacks. Jack carried one and J.J. the other. Then we all followed Jack and George down the dark passageway into the bright morning light of the newly risen sun and worked our way across the boulder field to our campground by the lake. We wanted to take Dad's .25/.35 and his fishing gear home with us. After hanging our bedrolls up where they would dry in the sun, we headed down the mountain with Rab bounding happily along beside us. When we came to the place where we'd crossed over the gully during the cloudburst, it was completely dry — not a drop of the water comin' out of the lake was runnin' through it. Sam said he figured that the floodwater must have opened up a new channel and that now all of the water was goin' down it instead of the old one. Most likely it was emptyin' into Lost Creek somewhere upstream from the ice cave.

When we got to Jack's car, all six of us plus Rab piled into it. It started right up, but we didn't go far, 'cause about a mile down the road we came to a washed out place, and, to quote Sam, it was a real "humdinger." Twenty feet of the road wasn't there any more — it was washed away by floodwater coming down the mountainside from above the road.

"Wal, we's shore as hell stuck now," Sam announced. "There's no way we's gonna get the car past this washout, so I reckon we's gonna have to walk out, and the closest place I know is Deckers. I reckon it's at least fifteen miles from here as the crow flies and more like twenty goin' by the road."

"We don't have to go near that far, Sam," J. J. pointed out. "Jim and Rhoda Graham's cattle ranch is no more than three miles downstream from here, and Lost Creek runs right past the ranch house. The Grahams are friends of our folks. They'll know Robby and me, too, and I'm sure we can call home from there. I'll bet Mrs. Graham will feed…"

"Uh – J. J.," Jack interrupted, "I reckon it's best if me and George stay clear of that ranch and head over to Deckers instead. When your folks find out how Jud and his gang was up here and what all happened, they'll tell it to the sheriff, and then him and his deputies will come up here with them — and when they do, they'll arrest me and George on account of they know we're part of Jud's gang."

We all agreed that going to Deckers would be the smart thing for them to do, so we started walkin' down the road, figurin' we'd split up when we got to the bottom of the steep hill where the road leaves Lost Creek. But we didn't get that far, 'cause after goin' about a mile, we saw five horses and their riders coming up the road in our direction. As they came closer and I could see who they were, I gave a big whoop and shouted — "Hey, Dad, Mother — it's us!" Then all of us kids and Rab started running towards them. Jack and George followed slowly and reluctantly, with Sam.

Besides Mother and Dad, the three other people were Mrs. Vogel, Mr. Graham, and one of his cowboys. They were just as happy to see us as we were to see them, and once they were down off their horses, everybody hugged and kissed everybody else — except for Mr. Graham and the cowboy of course, although judgin' from the way the cowboy was lookin' at Abby, I was sure he would like to have kissed her. I figured that was really disgusting — there's no way he could have been a real cowboy, 'cause they don't kiss ladies. They just kiss their horses.

After J. J. finished introducing Jack and George to our folks, Mrs. Vogel, and Mr. Graham, he told them that Jack and George were fishermen that'd been trapped by the flood on upper Lost Creek like we were, and that they'd offered to give us a ride out in Jack's car. But that we'd ended up havin' to walk instead, on account of the road was washed out. That surprised me 'cause I'd never heard J. J. tell a lie before. Maybe he wasn't so perfect after all.

After the introductions and huggin' and kissin' were over, all of us kids started talkin' at the same time, sayin' how happy we were to see them, but Mother interrupted. "I'm so sorry we didn't come sooner. We were all worried about you when you didn't come home as expected, and we wanted to go up to Lost Creek and check on you, but Doctor Sims was still afraid that your father might slip and fall and start bleeding inside his head again. Of course, that worried me, too, so we waited. But finally your father put his foot down and insisted that we come, and I'm awfully glad that he did. I never would have forgiven myself if something bad had happened to any of you, especially if it was something we could have prevented." She'd been snifflin' some all the time she was talkin', but now she burst into tears. I'd never seen Mother cry before, and it really shook me up — it shook Dad, J. J., and the others up, too, and we all did our best to comfort her.

By the time we arrived at the Graham's ranch house, Mother was back in firm control of her emotions —and of her family — again, and her first edict was for us to wash up. Not that we didn't need it: Except for an occasional handwash, none of us had felt compelled to disturb the ten-day accumulation of dirt and grime that covered us from head to toe. Of course, the cloudburst had removed a goodly amount of it, but not near enough to satisfy Mother. So we washed up as best we could, then we ate – and ate – and ate. That was a lot more to my liking, 'cause Mrs. Graham was a mighty good cook.

After we'd finished eating, we all thanked the Grahams for their help and headed for Shadycroft — all but Jack and George, that is. Mr. Graham had invited them to spend the night at the ranch so that, come morning, he could help them get Jack's car past the washout in the road. After that, they could go back to Littleton on their own.

I'd thought it was bad before, with seven people and a dog in Jack's car, but four adults and four kids crammed into Dad's Studebaker was a whole lot worse. Canned sardines have more room than we did. I was squeezed in next to Sam, and it wasn't long before I began to understand why Mother had wanted us to wash up. I guess it might have helped a little, but it was still pretty rank inside the car, even with the windows wide open. If I could have, I'd have ridden with Rab out on the running board in the fresh air, but that was Rab's spot. Dad had fixed an enclosure on the running board to keep him from fallin' off, and Rab really liked riding there — 'specially after Dad outfitted him with goggles so he wouldn't get dust in his eyes.

With everybody squinched up tight in the car, nobody did much talking on the way home, but that evening, we made up for lost time. Sam did most of the talking, with us kids chimin' in now and then. He told them the worst part first — about how we'd found the gold, and how Jud and his gang had stolen it from us and made us haul it down the mountain so they could put it on their trucks. Then he explained how Jud was planning to kill all of us, and would have if it hadn't been for the flood comin' along and washing him, along with two of his men and the trucks, down Lost Creek. So now, Jud was finally gone for good and, to quote Sam, it was damned good riddance. But unfortunately, all the gold had washed down Lost Creek too and most likely it was gone for good. The part about Jud getting killed didn't upset our folks and Mrs. Vogel a bit, but the loss of the gold sure did — and they were even more upset when Sam told them how he doubted we could recover enough of it to make it worth our while tryin'.

Then J. J. told our folks that Jack and George weren't fishermen, and that they actually were bootleggers and members of Jud's gang, but that he'd promised them that we wouldn't tell anybody, for fear Sheriff Haynes might hear about it and arrest them. Then he explained how Jack and George had saved all our lives — includin' Rab's — and how they weren't really the bad guys. Jud was the bad apple of the bunch, and he was dead. J. J was about to say somethin' more when Sam interrupted.

"Julius, accordin' to the boys, they snuck close to twelve gold ingots from out of the stage strongbox and hid them under some rocks in the cave, hopin' that Jud wouldn't notice. Each one weighs close to ten pounds, and the last time I checked, gold was bringing a little over twenty dollars an ounce after it was refined into coin quality. 'Course, that was last fall, and I don't rightly know what it's worth now. But fig-urin' it's the same, I calculate that each of them twelve ingots is worth close to 12,000 dollars, maybe more. I reckon that should solve some of yore and Grace's money problems for quite a spell — yore's too, Vera." For a moment Dad looked at Sam in amazement — then he started grinnin' from ear to ear and was starting to say something, when the perennial wet blanket spoke up.

"Now just hold on, Julius. Remember, that gold was stolen, so no matter how much it's worth or how much it might help us, we'll still have to turn it over to Sheriff Haynes so he can try to find the original owners. Perhaps we'll be able to claim it if no one else does but, unfortunately, by that time it will be too late to save Shadycroft or help the Vogels."

With that dose of cold water, everybody's spirits sunk to rock bottom — especially Dad's. He looked like he'd been kicked in the head by a horse again. After swallowin' hard a time or two like he had a big lump in his throat, he murmured in a barely audible voice, "I'm sure you're right, Grace, but maybe something might be worked out so we can still use it." But I could tell he didn't really believe it.

Our spirits rose briefly again when Sam said, "You know, Grace, I 'spect yore most likely right, but what if we was to sell it a little at a time so's nobody would suspect where it'd come from? That way, we could cash it in after all." It seemed to me like a great idea, and I suspect all the others thought so too, judging by the smiles on their faces. But Mother squelched that idea, too.

"Oh no, Sam, we will still all know that it was stolen, and our consciences wouldn't let us do a thing like that." The rest of us looked at one another and rolled our eyes. Obviously, our consciences weren't on near as high a plane as my mother's.

We'd returned to Shadycroft on the ninth day of July and, except for a few worthless sprinkles, it hadn't rained a drop since way last April — and, boy, was it ever hot. It was so hot, even the birds had quit singing, and the only sound you heard was the irritating drone of a bluebottle fly as it buzzed in circles around your head. According to Dad, the outside temperature had registered over ninety degrees in the shade every day for the past two weeks — a couple of days it even hit a hundred. On the dryland, you could see waves of hot air rising above the sun-baked fields, and it wasn't much better on our irrigated land. 'Course, we hadn't irrigated, 'cause there'd been no water in the

Highline since way last year. But at least the wind had died down so there wasn't so much dust in the air, and it always got a little cooler at night so most nights we could sleep — we were grateful for that.

All of us, but especially us kids, were chomping at the bit to get back to Lost Creek and check for the gold — and to get out of the heat. But Doctor Sims still didn't want Dad to do any work for fear he'd start bleeding inside his head again, and if that didn't scare my dad, it sure scared Mother. So ever since the doctor said that she'd been ridin' close herd on Dad to be sure he didn't do something he shouldn't, leavin' Mr. Williamson to do all the work around Shadycroft. 'Course, J. J. and I helped him as much as we could — or as much as Mother would allow. Abby and Charley helped some, too, but Mr. Williamson still did most of it.

It was two weeks since we'd come back from Lost Creek, and all us kids were sick of the heat, sick of the drouth, and sick of lookin' at each other. And we weren't the only ones that were grouchy — our folks were, too. 'Course, I'm sure they were sick of havin' us kids underfoot all the time, but I suspected what bothered them the most was money — or to be more accurate, the lack of it. Even though the October payment was still two-and-a-half months away, our folks were already making plans to move. They'd been trying to find a small house in Littleton where we could live — one they could afford. The Vogels were planning to move up to Longmont the following month.

I felt the sorriest for Dad, 'cause I'm sure he felt like it was his fault we were gonna lose Shadycroft. Of course, it wasn't. When he'd borrowed the money, he'd figured he could pay it back with the money he'd get by selling milk and wheat. Back then he had no way of knowin' how bad the drouth and depression were gonna be. But we weren't the only ones having trouble — other farmers were losing their homes and farms, too, and some of the folks in town were having as hard a time payin' their bills as we were. Almost nobody was making enough money.

The day after we got back from Lost Creek, Dad, Sam, J. J., and I went into Littleton to talk to Sheriff Haynes. Dad wanted us to tell him what all had happened, so he'd quit wasting time lookin' for Jud and his gang around Littleton and look for their bodies up at Lost Creek instead. But as it turned out, he wasn't there, and according to the deputy, he wouldn't be back 'til the end of the week. That was five days away. So we left a message for the sheriff with the deputy and went back to Shadycroft.

Later that same day, Sam got a letter from his mamma with some great news. Sheriff Ben Bellew had left Alma for good. It seems his term of office had expired, and the town council of Alma had decided they didn't need a sheriff anymore, bein' as how the population was down to less than two hundred.

Accordin' to the local gossips, the old buzzard had moved west to California. That suited her just fine, Sam's mamma said, but she'd have liked it a lot better if he'd gone a little farther west and drowned in the Pacific Ocean. After he'd left, the Park County sheriff reviewed the evidence in the bank robbery records and decided that Sam was innocent. He'd cancelled the warrant for Sam's arrest and told Sadie that the old sheriff was completely out of his mind to think that Sam was guilty. Sadie said she told him, "Well, praise the Lord. Finally, I can talk to a lawman who isn't crazy."

After what seemed like forever, the day finally came when Doctor Sims told Dad he could go up to Lost Creek, just as long as he was careful not to do any heavy lifting. The doctor needn't have worried – not with my mother watching him like a hawk. The following morning we started making preparations to leave, and this time we did it in broad daylight.

CHAPTER 54

A day or two before we went back to Lost Creek, I asked Sam if I could take along a copy of the old map showing the location of the lost bonanza — maybe I could find it and it would solve all our problems. Sam chuckled a little.

"Why shore, Boy, yore welcome to it, but don't go gettin' yore hopes up. First off it was Ramon, then my daddy and Uncle Jim, and then me – we all looked long and hard, and we never found nothin' that came close to matchin' up with some of them markin's on that map. In fact, I doubt there really is a bonanza. I don't rightly know why he'd have done it, but I figure Ramon's granddaddy made the whole thing up." Despite these discouraging remarks, I still wanted to take along the map, so I accompanied Sam to his room. He took his old top hat down from on top of the dresser and removed a piece of material that was hidden in back of the lining. Then he handed it to me.

"Here, Boy, yore welcome to it. I hope you have better luck findin' the bonanza than me and my daddy did." It was a thin piece of deer-skin, all stiff and yellow and cracked with age. It was about the size of a small dinner plate when it was unfolded. When I held it close to the light, I could barely make out some faded markings and a few words scribbled in what I supposed was Spanish.

I asked Sam what the words meant, and he pointed to one saying, "Wal, that there one means 'crick,' and this here one is 'twin owls' — but I'm damned if I know what them other marks is," and he pointed with his gnarled forefinger at some faint scribbles a little below the marks sayin' twin owls. "See what I mean, Boy? When you was up in them parts, did you ever once see anything what come anywheres close to matchin' up with these damned hen scratches?"

I told him I hadn't. I hated to admit it, but Sam was right, but I still wanted to take the map with me — it sure couldn't hurt any. After thankin' him, I left and hunted up J. J. so I could show it to him. But I didn't show it to Abby and Charley — it might get their hopes up, and most likely for no good reason.

Early the next morning we left for Lost Creek — the Vogels in their car, and our family and Sam in the Studebaker with Rab on the running board. With so many people goin', we were taking along a lot of food and camping gear. It was packed inside and on top of the cars, on the running boards and in the "Karry-Keen." That's a contraption you attach to the back end of the car sort of like a trunk, except it's hinged on the bottom so you can open it up like a clamshell, that way it can hold a lot more stuff.

Dad had made arrangements with Mr. Graham for the use of three of his packhorses to help us get all of our gear up to our camp. While we were busy loading, Mr. Graham told us some grisly news. Three of his men had been huntin' stray cattle on Lost Creek about two or three miles above his ranch house, and they'd found the bodies of two men. They were almost completely buried in the silt at the edge of the creek, close to half a mile below the wreckage of one of their trucks. Mr. Graham figured they were the bodies of two of the three fishermen we'd told him about the last time we were at his ranch. He'd reported their findin' them to the Park County sheriff, and a few days later he and two of his deputies came by to retrieve the bodies so they could take them to the morgue in Fairplay, where they could be identified. Mr. Graham had ridden up the valley with them, thinkin' he could be of some help, but he said he was sorry he did, 'cause both bodies were beat up so bad they were really hard to look at. Once the horses were fully loaded, we set off on foot, heading for our usual campin' spot up the hill from the ice cave, 'course we all carried our own backpacks. It was almost dark when we finished settin' up camp, and after a quick supper, Dad told us to crawl into our sleeping bags 'cause we'd be gettin' up early the next morning. I'm happy to say that we weren't attacked by any man-eating Herefords that night, so I slept soundly the whole night through.

It was still dark when Dad rousted us out of our bedrolls. I'm sure he was anxious to know if we'd be able to find at least enough gold to pay off our debts, as well as those of the Vogels'. He wasn't the only one — the rest of us were were hoping for exactly the same thing.

The first thing Dad wanted to do was to retrieve the gold ingots from the cave. Then we'd pick up our gear from our campsite by the lake, and after that we'd check along the creek for gold. Upon entering the cave, J. J. and I hurried over to where we'd hidden the gold, but to our great surprise and shock, the ingots weren't there. We couldn't believe it! We searched the entire cave, thinking that maybe we were mistaken about the location of the hiding place, but we still found nothing. The ingots were gone, and the only likely explanation we could think of was that Jack and George had seen us hiding them and had come back later and swiped them when the rest of us were back at Shadycroft. And here we'd been tellin' everybody what a couple of swell guys they were.

For some reason, Dad didn't seem a bit upset by the disappearance of the ingots. That surprised me. And he surprised me again when he told us he was glad that Jack and George had taken them, 'cause if they hadn't, he'd have been sorely tempted to use them to pay off his debts — even though he knew it was stolen and didn't belong to us. And he knew if he'd actually done that, he would have felt guilty for the rest of his life. But now that temptation was gone for good, and he was glad. Mother agreed with him wholeheartedly and so did Mrs. Vogel. The rest of us, includin' Sam, didn't.

Our campin' gear was pretty much like we'd left it, except that a pack rat had chewed a hole in one end of my bedroll and the kapok stuffing was leakin' out of it. After we'd collected our stuff, we were walking past the lake on our way back to Lost Creek when I saw the old beaver watchin' us from out in the middle of the lake. Now, I doubt you're gonna believe this next part — but it's true. When that critter saw that we were leaving without us messin' up his dam again, he heaved a great big sigh of relief. Then he waved good-bye to us with his tail.

We spent the rest of that day and all of the next looking for gold along Lost Creek — panning, hoping, and praying that we'd find enough to pay off our folks' debts. First, we went down the right side of the creek for well over two miles, then back up the left side to the ice cave, carefully panning the sand and debris as we went. But despite all our effort, other than a few traces of gold dust and one gold eagle, we found nothing of value. It was as though the gold had never existed. All along Lost Creek, for several miles downstream, broken branches and uprooted trees — some of them huge — littered the banks. The crumpled remnants of all three trucks lay half buried in the rocky debris, hundreds of feet from their original locations, mute testimony to the mighty power of the flood. It was late afternoon when we wearily dragged ourselves back into camp, exhausted, discouraged, and very, very unhappy — especially Dad. Now his last hope for saving Shadycroft was gone, and there was nothing more that he — or we — or anyone else could do.

But surprisingly, by that evening, Dad had made a remarkable recovery. He and Sam had gone fishin', and between them they'd caught enough fish for supper that night and breakfast the next morning. It was amazing to see how much Dad had perked up — he was actually happy. So, even though there was no reason for us to to stay any longer, we all agreed that we should stay for one more day so that Dad and Sam could fish. It'd been a long time since I'd seen my dad happy and havin' such a good time, and I wished it would last forever.

The next day, while Dad and Sam were fishing, us kids and Rab went exploring. J. J. and I wanted to follow up the west side of Lost Creek, starting where it comes out of the ice cave up to the place it

Dad fishing on Goose Creek — circa 1929.

(A picture from the Johnson family album.)

disappears under the rocks. We'd never done that before, and we were hoping we might get lucky and find the bonanza. So far we hadn't told Abby and Charley about it, and we decided to keep it that way. When we told Mother and Mrs. Vogel what we were plannin' to do, they agreed to it right off — in fact, they seemed downright happy to have us get out of their hair for awhile. After fixing us some sandwiches, Mother told us to go off and have fun, and she didn't even give us her usual cautionary lecture.

There was no game trail to follow on the west side of the creek, so we had to pick and choose our route up and around and over boulders, some of them as big as a house — and it was tough goin'. About four or five hundred feet upstream from the ice cave, we came to a pool at the base of some whoppin' big boulders. It was just west of where Lost Creek was flowing under the rocks. J. J. figured that this probably was the place where the water from the lake had been emptying into Lost Creek ever since the cloudburst changed its direction of flow.

After jumping over the creek, we worked our way a quarter of a mile or so upstream 'til we found the place where Lost Creek goes under the rocks before coming out of the ice cave. From there we kept goin' upstream, climbin' over rocks and up and down steep embankments for at least another mile. It took us most of the morning, and we didn't find anything that even came close to resembling a bonanza — 'course, neither J. J. or I had the foggiest idea of what a bonanza might look like, which probably made our findin' it even more unlikely.

But, even though we didn't find anything of interest, Rab did — of course, he's not too picky about his interests. Despite my strict instructions to stay right with us, he kept takin' off on little side excursions, and on one of these he hit pay dirt — at least to his way of thinking. He'd discovered a big fat porcupine ambling along in search of beetles, and immediately the peace and quiet of the forest was shattered by his happy, excited barks and growls. By the time we got to the site of the commotion, we found him dancing excitedly about the poor, befuddled creature. At the risk of collecting some painful quills of our own, and despite Rab's indignant protestations, J. J. and I managed to grab onto his collar and haul him away from the porcupine. Whereupon, no longer threatened by a noisy assailant, the prickly critter slowly waddled over to the closest pine tree and climbed unhurriedly to safety. Rab was outraged at what he considered our unsolicited intervention, and he refused to have anything more to do with us — until it came time for us to eat our sandwiches.

It was late morning when Abby announced that she was tired of exploring, and why didn't we go back to camp and play poker. I'll have to admit, right about then that sounded appealing — even though I always ended up losin' to Abby. J. J. and Charley agreed, so we all headed back to camp. On the way back, we stopped to eat and rest in the shade of a pine tree on top of a gravel covered knoll about sixty feet above the little pool I mentioned earlier. After we'd finished eatin', we sat with our backs against a large boulder and took turns chucking rocks down the hill and into the pool. It was fun watchin' the splashes, followed by the concentric circles of ripples that spread across the pool 'til they lapped the edges of the bank. For a time we vied with each other, trying to see who could come the closest to the center of the last ring of waves, but we soon tired of that and stood up, intending to head back to camp and the poker game. But then, just as we were turning to leave, Charley pointed down the hill and said, "Hey, lookit down there, you guys. Don't those two rocks look just like a couple of hoot owls?"

As you have no doubt guessed, that got J. J.'s and my attention in a hurry. We looked and, sure enough, there, poised on top of one of the huge boulders immediately in back of the pool, were two smaller boulders. And from where we stood they did, indeed, strongly resemble owls — twin owls, as a matter of fact! J. J. and I promptly did a happy celebration dance, hopping about on top of the knoll, laughing and hugging each another like we'd gone crazy. Abby and Charley obviously thought we had, and it took quite awhile to convince them otherwise. After I'd calmed down a little, I pulled Ramon's map from my pocket and showed them where the words "twin owls" were written on it in Spanish. Of course, they had no idea what they meant, but once we'd explained what a bonanza was and how the words "twin owls," combined with other marks on the map, were supposed to mark the location of a rich bonanza, they were just as excited as we were.

Seconds later, we were down by the pool, looking across at the two huge boulders that bordered it on the east. After studying it for a while,

J. J. told us there was something peculiar about the pool — it didn't have an outlet — at least none that he could see. And yet, even though the creek was runnin' into it, the pool wasn't gettin' any bigger. But the water had to be goin' somewhere, and the only thing he could figure was that it was seeping out underneath those big boulders. Then he tossed some pine needles into the middle of the pool, and sure enough, they floated straight over to its far side and clumped up at a spot right between the two big rocks. J. J. said he'd bet anything the outlet was right there. Then, like always, Abby agreed with him. She was obviously real impressed. I didn't say anything, but so was I. Maybe my brother was smarter than I'd thought.

Led by J. J., we all waded out into the water and started feeling under the edge of the rocks, hopin' we could feel some kind of opening, but we never could. J. J. said it must be there, though, 'cause he could feel a current in the water, and that meant that somewhere under the rocks, there was bound to be an outlet. After that we climbed on top of one of the boulders, hoping we could tell more from up there — but it was a waste of time. The boulder we were standing on was leaned up against the one next to it, so we lay on our stomachs and looked between them, hoping we could see what was down below — but all we saw was more rock. Abby called our attention to a soft noise that seemed to be coming from somewhere under the rocks, but whatever the noise was, it was so faint we couldn't be sure what was causing it. Abby thought it sounded like a big crowd of people talking, but somehow that didn't seem too likely. J. J. thought it sounded like a waterfall. Following that, we explored both upstream and downstream from the boulders, hoping to discover where the water went after it left the pool, but we never found a thing. So we went back to camp.

It was early afternoon when we arrived, and Mrs. Vogel was sitting on a campstool reading a book, but Mother was nowhere to be seen. According to Mrs. Vogel, she was off lookin' for wildflowers, and Dad and Sam were still fishing down along Lost Creek.

Upon hearing that, J. J. hurriedly said, "Well, in that case, why don't we go down by the creek and try our luck pannin' for gold — maybe we can find a nugget or two." After saying that, he grabbed four gold pans and hustled us out of camp. The rest went with him, but we couldn't figure out why he'd changed his mind — we'd thought we were gonna play poker. But then J. J. explained that he was afraid that one of us would say something to Mrs. Vogel about our finding the twin owls, and that he thought it would be better to wait and tell everybody about it at the same time. We all agreed and went down to Lost Creek, but instead of panning for gold, we sat by the creek and talked.

Now that we'd discovered that the twin owls actually existed and weren't just something Ramon's granddaddy had made up, J. J. and I were convinced that the map was genuine after all. And if it was, then the bonanza must be hidden somewhere under or behind the two huge boulders in back of the pool. Now the map really did make sense. In fact, when I looked at it closely, I could see that one of the little hen scratches actually marked the entrance to the ice cave. I showed it to J. J., and he agreed. He said that Ramon's granddaddy probably didn't want to put the Spanish word for "cave" on the map for fear it would make the bonanza too easy to find, so he made a scratch mark instead — one that only he and his brother would know what it meant.

Then J. J. came up with a really good idea. "Robby, how about if you and I go into the ice cave and see how far we can get up the underground channel? Maybe we can make it clear up to where we think the bonanza might be. We went pretty far up it the last time we tried it, and the water in the creek is a lot lower than it was then, so maybe we can…"

"Hey, that's a great idea, J. J.! When do we start?" I interrupted enthusiastically, while at the same time Abby and Charley were clamoring to go, too.

J. J. held up his hand. "Whoa, you guys. Let's not rush into this. Abby, we can't all go in the cave. We'll need you and Charley to stay on the outside so we can shout now and then, and then you can shout back and tell us where we are. And when we're getting close to the big boulder where we're hoping the bonanza might be, you can get up on top of it and holler at us to let us know we're there — and if the bonanza isn't, we'll know that we were wrong and that the map is a hoax after all. That way we won't tell Sam and our folks about it and get their hopes up only to have them disappointed again." Both Abby and Charley agreed to follow J. J.'s instructions, but they weren't happy about it: They didn't realize how lucky they were.

J. J. went on givin' us directions — he was beginnin' to sound a lot like Mother. "Robby, why don't you go back to camp and get our flashlight? We're gonna need it when we're inside the ice cave, 'cause it'll be real dark when we get way up in the channel."

I practically flew up and back down the hill. 'Course, all the time I was in camp I tried to act real nonchalant so Mrs. Vogel wouldn't get suspicious and ask me what I was up to. You know — I don't know why it is, but I always seem to have bad luck with flashlights, 'cause this one turned out to have a low battery just like the one on that scary night last November when I found Sam hidin' in the attic. I wanted to use it anyway, hopin' it'd last — but J. J. said "no," we shouldn't, 'cause if the flashlight fizzled out when we were deep inside the channel, we'd be stuck there in the dark, and that didn't sound like a whole lot of fun. Abby agreed — she told J. J. he shouldn't try it, and that we'd better wait and tell our folks what we'd found when they were all back in camp. I don't know why, but Abby always agreed with J. J., no matter what he said.

But then I came up with what, in my opinion, was a great idea. I remembered reading how one of my cowboy heroes had used pine branches for torches — it might even have been Buck Duane, but whoever it was, it worked real well and saved his and his pretty lady friend's lives.

I told the others about it, and at first J. J. was pretty skeptical, but after we'd argued back and forth for a while, he said, "Well, it just might work — at least I guess it won't hurt none to give it a try. We can use pine branches with lots of pitch in them and light them if the flashlight really does give out." But then he changed his mind again and said, "No, on second thought, we'd best not, 'cause we might not be able to light the torches when we're way back in the channel, 'cause it'd be too wet." As usual, Abby agreed.

But I wasn't about to give up that easily. I told J. J. that all we had to do was light a torch before we went into the ice cave. Then we could use it to light the others whenever we needed them. Then I had another brilliant idea. If we soaked some rags in the kerosene from one of our lamps back at camp, we could wrap them around the end of the branches and that would make them real easy to light. I guess J. J. thought it was a good idea, too, 'cause he agreed to give it a try, and it worked pretty darn well, even if I do say so myself. While I was getting the rags and kerosene, J. J. and the others gathered ponderosa pine branches from the piles of driftwood cast up on the banks of Lost Creek by the floodwaters. When I returned, we tied the rags around the ends of seven of the branches, soaked them in kerosene, and, except for one, tied them securely — three apiece — on top of our backpacks. When everything was ready, we lit the remaining branch and headed upstream in the direction of the ice cave.

Rab was still sulking over the porcupine episode, which was just as well, 'cause he couldn't come with us even if he wanted to. I made him promise to stay close to Abby and Charley. He promised, but I could tell he didn't mean it 'cause, all the time I was giving him his instructions, he was lookin' sort of shifty eyed. I'm sure he was thinkin' how, the minute we were inside the cave and couldn't see him any longer, he was gonna go hunt porcupines. Rab never has been good about keepin' his promises.

Just before we entered the cave, both J. J. and I carefully studied the sky —'specially up near the headwaters of Lost Creek. We were lookin' for clouds or anything else that might signal an approaching storm, but as far as we could tell, the weather was perfect. Reassured that there was no danger from another flood, we entered the ice cave. J. J. led the way with the flashlight, and I followed close behind, holding the burning torch high above my head.

I guess it was a little late for havin' second thoughts, but I had them anyway. I started wonderin' why in the world I'd ever figured that this was such a great idea. It'd sounded like a good idea when J. J. first talked about it, but now it was beginning to seem pretty dumb. But it was too late to back out now ,'cause if I did, it'd make it look like I was scared — which I was of course, but I couldn't let J. J. or the others know it — 'specially Abby. I did a considerable amount of praying, though, and I'm pretty sure J. J. did, too. Prayer had worked great the last time we were in trouble, and I was hopin' it would again. I was also praying that God would be patient with me, 'cause by now He must be real sick and tired of gettin' me out of all the scrapes I got myself in.

At first it was easy goin' as we walked along the bank of the creek. But the farther we went back into the cave, the narrower the banks became, until we eventually were forced to walk in the water where the footing was far more treacherous. Slippery moss covered the rocks under our feet and the water was really, really cold. As the passageway grew narrower, the rocky ceiling of the cavern grew lower, forcing us to walk stooped over in order to continue. Approximately thirty feet from the entryway, both the passageway and stream turned abruptly to the right and flowed between a solid rock wall on our left and an equally massive boulder on the right. The sunlight that had been gradually fading as we went deeper into the cave now vanished completely, forcing J. J. to turn on his flashlight.

As we followed the stream around the bend and through a narrow corridor between the two huge rocks, the frigid water deepened and the current grew much stronger, making the going far more difficult. Fortunately, the real narrow part of the passage was short, and we soon came to a noisy little waterfall that was splashing and tumbling over a jam of wet, ice-coated logs and debris that obstructed the flow of water. Beyond the jam lay a large, inky black pool of water.

Here, the passageway widened and the ceiling heightened while, at the same time, the channel turned back to a northerly direction. As J. J. directed the beam of his flashlight over the dark and forbidding pool, I half expected to see a horrible sea serpent rearing up from the inky depths. But if it did, I never knew it, for at that very same moment the light from the flashlight faded out completely and, but for the light of my torch, we would have been left in total darkness. J. J. quickly ignited another torch by touching it to mine, and together we raised them above our heads as we attempted to see what lay ahead. The black surface of the pool was smooth and tranquil and reflected the flickering gleam of our torches in such an unnerving fashion that my active imagination kept insisting that a monster was lurking just under it's surface — and that he loved to eat little boys. From what we could tell by torchlight, there were no banks bordering the pool that we could walk on — only perpendicular rock walls. If we went any farther, we'd have to wade up the channel. Although it was difficult to make out the far end of the pool, from what little we could see, the ceiling appeared to gradually lower until, at the far end, it was no more than a foot or two above the surface of the water.

"How deep do you think this pool is, J. J.?" I asked.

"I don't know, Robby. It sure looks deep to me. But we have to try getting to the upper end of it — it's either that or we'll have to turn around and go back, and we sure don't want to do that — not unless we have to. But we'd better do it soon, or we'll run out of torches and be stuck here in the dark."

After saying that, J. J. eased himself down into the icy water. It came to a little above his waist. After telling me to stay put 'til he told me it was all right to come on, he began to wade up the pool, carefully testing each step as he went while holding his torch as high above his head as the rocky ceiling would permit. I held my breath as I watched him, half expecting the monster to drag him under. I hadn't said anything about the monster to J. J.. I figured if he made it safely without gettin' gobbled up, it should be safe for me. Happily he did and, after reaching the upper end of the pool, he attempted to peer into the dark passageway beyond. Then, being careful not to extinguish his torch, he ducked under the low ceiling and disappeared — leaving me alone in the cavern with the monster. My panic level grew to new heights as I watched the weird patterns made by the flickering light of the torch reflecting from the surface of the pool and off the ice covered granite walls and ceiling. But then I saw the glow of J. J.'s torch, and he stuck his head back into the cavern.

"Hey, Robby, come on. You can make it OK — it's not even up to your shoulders! But hurry it up, 'cause if we don't get out of this water soon, we'll both freeze to death." After that less than reassuring remark, J. J. ducked back under the low ceiling and once more disappeared from view.

I carefully climbed down the logjam and slipped into the icy water, praying that I wouldn't step into a hole as I cautiously waded towards the upper end of the pool. J. J. was right, the water came only part way up my chest but, boy, was it ever cold. Carefully keeping my torch above water, I ducked under the low ceiling at the upper end of the pool and into the channel beyond, where I continued to follow J. J. up the underground creek. The water in this part of the channel wasn't nearly as deep. Further up the stream, the light from J. J.'s torch flickered from the icy walls of our subterranean crypt, creating ominous shadows that danced on the surface of the water. To my cold-benumbed mind, it

seemed like a scene from the halls of hell, except that it was much colder. I could even hear the sound of demon voices roaring at us from farther on up the channel. This was definitely not a good place for a kid
with an overactive imagination.

Moments later, the light from J. J.'s torch was suddenly extinguished, and I was afraid that he'd either fallen in a hole or been eaten
by monsters. I was on the verge of panic again when I heard him hol-
lering for me to hurry up — he'd found a place where we could get out
of the water. That was welcome news, and a few minutes later I sloshed
out of the stream into a large underground chamber enclosed by massive rocks. A ray of sunlight shone though an overhead opening
between the rocks, and I could see J. J. gathering a pile of driftwood left
by the flood on the sandy floor of the chamber. Before long, we were
gratefully warming ourselves beside a crackling fire. For a few minutes
J. J. and I just sat by the fire, waiting for our teeth to stop chattering.
When they finally quit and we were beginning to get dry and feel warm
again, J. J. asked, "Robby, when you were coming up the creek, did you
hear the noise that's comin' from somewhere upstream? It sounds sort
of like water splashin' over rocks." At first I told him I hadn't, but then
I remembered the noise the demons were making.

"Yeah, I guess I heard it after all. It's sort of spooky soundin'.
What's makin' it?"

"At first I was scared that it might be another flash flood," J. J.
answered, "but now, I'll bet you anything it's the noise made by a waterfall. And if that's what it is, it might keep us from goin' much farther
up the creek. Let's yell and see if Abby and Charley can hear us and tell
us where we are and how much farther we have to go 'til we get to the
twin owls."

So that's just what we did. We both shouted just as loud as we
could, and in a minute or two we heard them shouting back — they'd
seen the smoke from our fire pouring out through an opening between
the rocks. Abby told us that they sure were glad to know where we were
and that we were all right, 'cause they'd been real worried about us. We'd
been takin' so long, they were afraid we'd both drowned or that something else bad had happened to us. J. J. explained to them that it'd been
a lot slower goin' than we'd expected and that we both were OK, but

that we were afraid we might not be able to go much farther up the creek. Abby said she sure hoped we could go a little ways further, at least, 'cause from where we were now, it was less than thirty feet to the twin owls. That was great news. I don't know about J. J., but I was more than ready to quit this exploring stuff and get out of this gloomy dungeon and back into the sunlight again.

Then, after tellin' Abby, Charley, and Rab that we were starting to head upstream again, we lit two new torches and waded back into the cold waters of Lost Creek. A few moments later, we rounded the corner of yet another huge rock and were excited to see a bright glow reflecting from the surface of the water about twenty feet ahead of us. At the same time, the sound of the waterfall had increased considerably. We hurriedly waded towards the light, hoping that we could find where it was coming from, and when we did, we also found the answer to our prayers. We could scarcely believe our eyes!

We were standing at the entrance of another large chamber, much like the one we'd just left, but with several notable differences. This one was fully five times the size of the other one and was divided into both a lower and upper chamber by a rocky cliff close to thirty feet back from where we were standing at the edge of Lost Creek. The cliff itself was at least ten feet high. The upper chamber resembled a loft, and from where we stood, we could only guess at how far back it extended from the edge of the cliff or judge how large it might be.

The chambers were covered by a high, vaulted ceiling formed by several massive boulders that had wedged together in such a way as to block out the entrance of light, except for one brilliant shaft of sunlight that entered through an unseen opening high above our heads. It illuminated both chambers with a soft, diffused light. A noisy waterfall plunged over the edge of the cliff and splashed into a pool on the sandy floor below, creating a fine spray that floated upwards across the face of the cliff. Much of the cliff and walls of the cavern were covered by a coat of soft, green moss, creating a misty scene much like the one described in an Irish fairy tale I once read — a mystical grotto peopled by elves and fairies.

A placid stream of water flowed from out of the pool and meandered across the floor of the chamber until it emptied into Lost Creek, not far from where we were standing. Holding our breath in hopeful anticipation, J. J. and I hurried over and knelt by the edge of the pool and carefully examined its depths. We could scarcely believe what we were seeing. The bottom of the pool was literally covered with gold nuggets of every size and shape — some so large they boggled our minds. We were even more astonished when we looked about us and saw that there were hundreds of nuggets scattered over the sandy floor of the grotto, many of them even larger than the ones in the pool.

As we stood and stared in amazement, our gaze was drawn to the wall behind the waterfall where brightly lighted windows appeared to be gleaming through the velvety mantle of moss covering the surface of the cliff. Breathlessly, we began peeling the green covering from the face of the cliff and the more we removed, the more excited we became. It was truly astonishing: The entire back wall of the cavern was a quartz outcrop, and scattered throughout it were numerous veins of gold — one was well over seven feet wide. Except for a few grunts of wonder, J. J. and I didn't say a word to each other as we continued with our inspection. We were speechless at the sight of all that gold. At least we were until the initial shock wore off. Then we began to whoop and holler and dance about the floor of the cavern like a couple of wild Indians. We'd found it!!! We'd actually found it! We'd found the lost bonanza! After regaining our senses and quieting down some, we heard Rab's loud barking and Abby's and Charley's anxious shouts filtering down to us through the rocky ceiling of the cavern.

"What's wrong? Are you both OK? What are you shouting about?"

We both shouted back simultaneously, "Nothin's wrong! Everything's wonderful! We've found the bonanza, and it's a whole lot richer than we ever imagined it would be!" Upon hearing that, they had a celebration of their own, and while that was goin' on, J. J. and I filled our backpacks with nuggets.

Now that I'd calmed down some, I got to thinkin' that maybe it was too early for us to be celebrating. We were still entombed in Lost Creek's underground channel, and it was a long way back to where we'd be safe. Then I remembered how Sam had said this bonanza had already claimed four lives, and I got to worrying that J. J. and I might be numbers five and six.

All J. J. said when I told him what I was worried about was, "I wish you hadn't said that, Robby. This isn't a very good time to be bringing it up. But I doubt that anything bad will happen to us. Not if we're careful." I would have liked it a whole lot better if he'd used some other word than "doubt."

Before leaving, J. J. and I carefully examined all the cavern walls and the ceiling, hopin' we could find an easier way to get out so we wouldn't have to go back the way we'd come. But there wasn't any — we had to retrace our steps. After that I started worrying that I might fall in the creek and drown because I couldn't get up, weighted down by all the gold nuggets I'd stuffed in my pockets and backpack. When I told J. J. what I was worryin' about, he just told me to just be extra careful and that he wished I'd quit worrying so much — that wasn't a whole lot of help.

Just before we left, J. J. hollered up to Abby and Charley, tellin' them to go back to the entrance of the ice cave and wait for us there, 'cause we were heading back downstream. They both hollered back, tellin' us to be real careful. Rab didn't say a word — he didn't even bark. I guess he was poutin' again. For some reason, goin' back downstream wasn't near as bad as when we were headed the other way, even with all the extra weight we were carryin'. J. J. figured it was on account of we were goin' downstream and knew what was comin' up next. Abby and Charley were real happy to see us, and it was mutual. I'll bet Abby would have hugged J. J. if Charley, Rab, and I hadn't been standin' there watchin'. She might even have kissed him. What a yucky thought that was.

Abby and Charley could hardly believe it when they saw all of our nuggets. Rab wasn't a bit impressed by them, but at least he seemed happy to see us again. And at first, I figured that he'd finally forgiven us for spoiling his porcupine fun — but then I remembered it was gettin' close to his suppertime. Rab could be real sneaky at times.

J. J. and I wanted to find Dad and Sam so we could tell them the good news, but Abby thought it'd be a lot more fun if we waited 'til everybody was back at camp — that way they'd all be surprised at the same time. So that's what we did. When we got back to camp, Dad and Sam were still fishing, but Mother was there and waiting for us, and it wasn't long before she suspected that we were trying to keep something from her.

"What's gotten into you children? Why are you acting so fidgety and whispering to each other like that? Have you been up to something that you shouldn't have?"

Mother always was a hard lady to fool. She could always tell when J. J. or I were trying to keep something from her, and she generally assumed (usually correctly) that whatever it was we were hiding, it was bound to be something bad. Usually we'd break under pressure and end up confessing our sin, but this time was different. We all held our ground and answered, "Nothin' — No reason — and No" to her questions. After that initial setback, she enlisted Mrs. Vogel's help, and the two of them were busily engaged in devising a second inquisition when Dad and Sam returned to camp, happy and loaded down with fish. They'd had a good day, and now we were gonna make it a whole lot better.

CHAPTER 55

Now that we were all assembled, J. J. asked Sam and our folks to sit down, 'cause we had something important to tell them. Mother rolled her eyes a little, and I knew what she was thinkin', "Oh, Oh, here it comes. I knew they'd been up to some kind of mischief."

Then we all took turns telling them how we'd gone exploring that day, and how we'd found the twin owls that Ramon's granddaddy had marked on the map. After that, they started payin' closer attention to what we were sayin', and when J. J. started tellin' them about how the two of us had gone up Lost Creek's underground channel, Mother jumped up from the log she was sittin' on.

"You did what? You went where?" Fortunately, she must have been in some kind of shock, 'cause, before she could think of anything else to say, Dad interrupted.

"Now, Grace, the boys obviously made it back in one piece, so why don't we let them finish telling us about it before you get upset."

Before she had time to respond, J. J. hurriedly told them how we'd found the lost bonanza. Then, while the rest of us were showing them all the nuggets we'd brought back, he explained how the twin owls were directly above the bonanza, and that the map made sense after all. After that, Mother didn't say another word of complaint — at least not for a day or two. For a long moment, the sight of all that gold made them speechless. Then Sam jumped to his feet.

"Wal, I'll be damn — ah — jiggered," he added, looking at Mother. "If that don't beat all? I's been along this stretch of the crick dozens of times, and how I missed seein' them twin owls, I'll never know. And what's even more amazin', my daddy, Uncle Jim, and Ramon missed seein' them, too."

Our folks and Mrs. Vogel were just as excited as Sam was — just not as vocal about it. After everybody quieted down, Dad and Sam asked us to show them where we'd found the twin owls, so they could get the lay of the land before returning to Shadycroft. That way, they'd know what tools and equipment we'd be needing to get into the bonanza.

When we went back to the pool, Mother, Mrs. Vogel, and Rab went with us. They didn't want to miss any of the excitement. After J. J. once again demonstrated how the water in the pool was flowing underneath the two large boulders behind it, Dad studied the situation for a few moments then said, "You know, Sam, if we can get that big rock out from in front of these two boulders and clear the rubble out from between them, we might be able to get into that upper chamber J. J. and Robby were tellin' us about. In fact, I'll bet that's the way Juan and Pedro found the bonanza in the first place."

"I 'spect yore right, Julius. And I reckon I knows how we…"

"Julius," Mother interrupted, "don't forget what Doctor Sims told you. You're not supposed to be doing any heavy work." She was about to say more, but then Sam took his turn at interrupting.

"Now don't you go to worryin' none, Ma'am. Me and the kids'll do all the heavy work. In fact, like I was about to say, I figure if'n we was to set a stick of dynamite in jest the right place between them big rocks, it's likely to do a lot of the work for us. Leastwise, it's worth a try."

"Well, all right then, Sam, but if you do use dynamite, just be sure that Julius and the children are all safely out of the way." Compared to her usual admonition, this one was remarkably mild.

Before returning to camp, Dad took a topographic map from his pocket and spread it out on the ground where he and Sam could study it. He explained how they wanted to determine the exact location of the bonanza so they could mark it as accurately as possible, both on the map with ink and on the ground with stakes. That way, when he got back to the valley, he could go to the land office and register our claim. I asked Dad what would happen if somebody were to see the stakes after we'd left and pull them all out so they could jump our claim. I remembered how Jim and John Reynolds had been worried about that. Dad chuckled.

"You're letting your imagination take over again, Robby. Something like that isn't likely to happen nowadays. The main reason we need to register the claim is so we'll have the legal right to mine the gold. This is Pike National Forest and it's federally owned land, so we have to have the government's permission to mine on it."

After studying the map for a short time, Sam took some wooden stakes and a small sledgehammer from his pack. Then he and Dad set about measuring the boundaries of our claim and driving stakes into the ground to mark them. I asked Sam how come he'd brought the stakes and sledge along with us after he'd said that there wasn't any such thing as the bonanza.

Sam chuckled a little and said, "Wal, Boy, I reckon I was hopin' you'd prove me wrong."

Early the following morning, we broke camp, loaded our packhorses, and headed back to Graham's Ranch and then to Shadycroft. It was midafternoon when we got back, and after unloading our Studebaker, Dad and Mother left immediately in order to register our claim at the land office before it closed for the day. It was evening when they returned, and they were both smiling broadly as they told us that all had gone well — our claim was registered and we could legally mine the gold. They'd listed the owners as James Samuel Reynolds, Vera Vogel, and Grace and Julius Johnson, and named it "The Lost Creek Bonanza."

"How does that strike all of you?" Dad asked.

"Sounds great to me," Sam said, and the rest of us all agreed.

It sure was swell to sleep in a real bed again and to eat regular food. Camping and sleeping on hard ground gets old in a hurry — 'specially when all you ever eat is trout.

Next morning, after excusing myself from the breakfast table, I jumped up and headed in the direction of my room, intending to get my gun, cowboy hat, and spur so Molly, Rab, Buck, and I could go up to the dryland and chase outlaws. But Mother cut me off at the pass.

"Now, just hold on a minute, young man. Where do you think your going in such a hurry?"

"Why," I said apprehensively as I edged towards the door, "I'm just going to get my cowboy stuff so Buck and I can start cleanin' the rustlers from…"

"Well, I hate to disillusion you, young man, but the only things you're going to clean out today are the chicken houses." This came as a shock, and I frantically searched for something to say that might give me a reprieve, but I knew from prior experiences that anything I could say would be in vain.

I've already told you how my least favorite job is cleaning out our chicken coops, but I've never told you about the old banty rooster I call

"Lucifer." He's black as coal, has red eyes, and his disposition is a lot like Rafer Rathbone's — he hates me, and the feeling is mutual. His favorite trick is to wait 'til I'm concentrating on gettin' the eggs out from under a hen without havin' holes pecked in the back of my hands, then he sneaks up behind me, jumps high up in the air, and hits me on the backs of my legs with his claws and spurs. Sometimes, if I see him comin', I kick at him just as he launches his attack and loft him clean across the chicken house. After that, he stays clear of me for a few days, hoping I'll forget about him — but I never do. I told my mother how I figured he'd make good stew meat, but she said he was too tough even for that.

That same morning, Dad and Sam drove into Littleton and talked to Sheriff Haynes. That evening after supper, Dad told us what all had happened. First off, he'd explained to Sheriff Haynes how we'd come by to report Colonel Pettigrew's death to him ten days ago, but that he was out of town, and how ever since then we'd been up at Lost Creek and hadn't gotten back 'til late yesterday. As it turned out, the sheriff knew a lot more about Jud than we did. When he'd come back from Kansas, a message was waiting for him from the Park County sheriff, tellin' him how he and his deputies had found Colonel Pettigrew's body up on Lost Creek. Actually, they'd found two bodies. They were almost completely buried in the sand, and, when they dug them out, one of the bodies turned out to be Colonel Pettigrew's. 'Course, both bodies were beat up and decomposed so bad, nobody could tell who either of them was by lookin' at them. But the colonel's billfold was in the pants pocket of one of the corpses. His driver's license and some other personal papers were in it, so the sheriff was sure it was the colonel and that there certainly was no doubt that he was dead.

After that, Sam explained to the sheriff how he was really Jimmy Reynolds, not Crazy Sam, and how he started goin' by the name of Jimmy Hardin when his daddy and mother and him moved up to Alma from Texas back in 1884. He said the main reason they'd gone there was so they could look for a cave in the Tarryalls where his daddy and his brother, Jim, had stored a lot of gold from a mine what they'd found back in 1860. Then he told the sheriff about the Confederate raid into South Park in 1864 and the Alma bank robbery in 1915 when his daddy was killed and how that all came about. And finally, he told him how

Colonel Pettigrew was really Jud Rathbone, the son of Rafer, one of the leaders of the raid, and how Jud wanted to make Sam show him where the cave was hidden, so he could steal all the gold.

As it turned out, the sheriff already knew all about the Reynolds gang and their raid on South Park, including Jim Reynolds' death while being transported to Fort Lyons. He also knew about the Alma bank robbery and the warrant for the arrest of Jimmy Hardin for the crimes of murder and bank robbery. But he was real surprised to find out that Colonel Pettigrew was really Jud Rathbone, and that Crazy Sam Baker was really Jimmy Hardin and that Jimmy Hardin was really James Samuel Reynolds. The sheriff said he found all that a mite confusing, but that it didn't matter anymore what Sam's real name was, 'cause a few weeks back the Park County sheriff had dropped all the charges against him. Sam told the sheriff he already knew that.

After that, Dad told the sheriff everything that had happened to us up at Lost Creek, including how Jack and George had tried to protect us from Jud, and how they'd stolen the gold ingots. He even told the sheriff about our finding the bonanza and how we'd be heading up to Lost Creek in a day or two so we could figure out how to mine it. That really surprised me. I figured he should have kept that a secret.

CHAPTER 56

Three days later we headed back to Lost Creek. Dad, Sam, and J. J. drove up in Jerome Burnett's truck, while Mother, Mrs. Vogel, and the rest of us kids and Rab followed in the Studebaker. Both vehicles were packed with camping equipment, food, shovels, prybars, pickaxes, a wheelbarrow, and bunch of other stuff — including dynamite. Except for stopping a few times to repair the road, we got there in good shape and set up camp in our usual spot up the hill from the ice cave. After a quick meal, we spent the rest of that day haulin' our tools and equipment to a spot closer to the bonanza.

Both Dad and Sam wanted to get an early start come morning, so we all crawled into our bedrolls right after supper. But I was too excited to sleep, so I lay awake, listening to the mysterious sounds of the forest at night and breathing deeply the faint, vanilla-like scent of the ponderosa pines. I watched the endless procession of stars drifting through the tangled branches of the tree above my head. And far off in the distance, I heard the mournful call of an owl drifting up the valley like the wail of a lost and lonely spirit. It sent cold shivers up and down my spine, and I pulled my sleeping bag up over my head, fearful that it was Jud's hellbent soul wandering forlornly through the canyons of Lost Creek. Fortunately, my eyelids soon grew heavy and I was fast asleep.

The following morning, Dad had no difficulty in rousing us. We were all rarin' to get started, including Rab. He was jumping around, running back and forth, and acting like he was just tickled pink to be included in our group. I should have suspected that it was all an act, but I didn't, and that was a big mistake — for both Rab and for me.

Accordin' to Sam, the first thing we needed to do was to drill holes in the rocks on the front sides of the two huge boulders so he could put sticks of dynamite in them. As it turned out, the "we" Sam was talkin' about meant J. J. and me, and for the next hour and a half, "we" stood up to our hips in ice-cold water while "we" drilled a hole in the rock with a star drill. I got the job of holdin' the drill while J. J. hit it with a sledgehammer, and I gotta tell you, it wasn't a whole lot of fun, and "we" didn't enjoy it a bit. "We" got the job done, though, and ended up with holes in the rocks over a foot deep. After that, J. J. and I thawed out while Sam and the dynamite did the rest. It worked great, and nobody was killed or injured. After the explosion, the water level in the pool began to drop rapidly as it poured into the passageway between the two big boulders — just like Dad and Sam were hopin' it would. But there was still a lot of loose rock and debris that needed to be cleared away, and that's what we did for the rest of that afternoon. By the time evening came, we'd cleared eight to ten feet back into the passageway, and we were all tuckered out and looking forward to going back to camp and resting. So go back to camp I did — rest I did not.

As we were leaving, I whistled for Rab. When he didn't show up right away, I started hollerin' at the top of my voice. When he still didn't come, I was about to panic, thinkin' that maybe he'd been killed by a cougar or bear. But then I saw him comin' down the hill in our direction, and he was, without a doubt, the sorriest looking dog I'd ever seen. His muzzle and face had porcupine quills stickin' out in all directions: He looked like a big, hairy pincushion. There were quills in his front paws as well, so he walked with a limp, whining pitifully with every step. Every now and then, he'd stop and try to bite the quills out of his paws with his teeth, but he wasn't having much luck. He was eighty-five pounds of canine misery, and I felt real sorry for him — but Dad sure didn't. He was mad at Rab, and he was mad at me for not keeping an eye on my dog. It's a good thing Mother and Mrs. Vogel were standing there listening, 'cause if they hadn't been, I'm sure Dad would have used some rather creative language to describe his feelings. As it was, he did a good job of it without using words that would upset Mother.

"You dumb dog," he muttered. "Here I spend the whole day working, and now I have to spend half the night pulling quills out of a stupid animal that doesn't have enough sense to keep away from porcupines. Robby, take your dog back to camp and get my pliers out of the tool kit in the truck. Then find the alcohol and wait until J. J. and I get there. And for heavens sake, Son, from now on, keep your dog tied up whenever we're working so he can't get into any more trouble." I don't know why it is, but whenever Rab gets into trouble he's always "my" dog. All the rest of the time he's "our" dog.

So that's what I did. I took Rab back to camp, and after the others showed up, J. J. and I spent the next hour holding on to Rab for dear life while Dad pushed porcupine quills through the flesh of Rab's lips and then yanked them out with his pliers — sort of like a dentist pullin' teeth — all to the accompaniment of the most piteous whimpers and yelps you're ever likely to hear, not to mention a number of under-the-breath swear words — from Dad, not Rab.

After supper that night, I couldn't wait to get into my sleepin' bag, and if Jud's spirit was wailin' around in the valley, I sure didn't hear it. I was dead to the world, worn out by hauling rocks and wrestlin' with an upset German shepherd. Come morning, after a quick breakfast, we all hurried back to our claim so we could resume work on clearing out the passageway. All except Mother and Mrs. Vogel, that is; they came a little later.

Rab had made an amazing overnight recovery. He'd gone from a pitiful, whimpering mass of dog flesh to a happy, exuberant bundle of energy. He obviously assumed that he was gonna get to spend another wonderful day huntin' porcupines. I guess, maybe, he wasn't listening when Dad was tellin' me to keep him tied up — either that, or he didn't believe I'd do it. But whatever the reason, it came as a real shock to him when I tied a rope to his collar, and an even greater one when I tethered him to an aspen tree a little way up the hill from where we were working. He was outraged. He couldn't believe that his very best friend would treat him like that. I tried to explain that it was Dad's idea to tie him up, not mine, but he still wouldn't even look at me when I went down the hill to join the others.

After a couple of hours spent hauling rocks and debris from the passageway, Abby claimed that she saw a faint glimmer of light in the corridor directly ahead — and sure enough, she was right. But what was even more exciting, we could hear a muffled roar coming from the same direction. It was the unmistakable sound of a waterfall. That really fired up our enthusiasm, and after two more hours of labor, we stepped from the passageway into a large, rock-enclosed chamber. Warm rays of sunlight shone through narrow openings between the rocks in the ceiling, illuminating the interior with a soft yellow light and nourishing the lush green growth of grass on the floor of the chamber. The enclosed area was roughly fifty feet in length, thirty feet wide, and twelve feet from floor to ceiling. A few small boulders lay scattered about the chamber floor. After leaving the passageway, the little creek wound its way along one side of the chamber, paused briefly in a now roily pool, and then continued its flow until it disappeared from sight as it plunged over the edge of a cliff. For a moment we all stood transfixed, taking it all in — but not for long, as J. J. led the way over to the edge of the cliff, exclaiming at the same time. "Come on you guys. Down there at the bottom of this cliff is where Robby and I found all the gold." No one needed further urging, and a moment later we were all standing at the edge of the cliff, peering down into the chamber below. It was all exactly as J. J. and I had described it — the waterfall, the pool, and Lost Creek flowing quietly across the far side of the cavern. All Sam could manage to say was, "Wal I'll be jiggered. I must have walked past this place more times than you can count whilst I was up here fishin', and all them times this here gold was jest a stone's throw away."

After a few more minutes of excited conversation, Dad mobilized us into action. "Grace, why don't you and Vera stay here while the rest of us go back to camp and get some more equipment. It's a good thing that the boys told us that we'd need a ladder, so we'd know to bring along the materials to build one. Sam, I think we should build it inside the cavern. If we make it outside, I doubt we'll be able to bring it through that narrow passageway, and while we're at it, we'll bring along the rope and whatever else we think we might need. Oh, and Grace, while we're gone, why don't you and Vera fix us some sandwiches? I'm sure we'll all be hungry when we get back."

The second we emerged from the passageway, Rab spotted us and immediately started havin' a conniption fit. I felt sorry for him and asked Dad if I could take him with us, but he said no — I should take him inside the cavern and tie him to the big rock by the entrance instead. That way, Mother and Mrs. Vogel could keep an eye on him and make sure he didn't try to pull loose and follow us. So that's what I did, but not without another remarkably dramatic performance on Rab's part.

An hour later, when we returned, Mother and Mrs. Vogel had a surprise waiting for us. As they were fixing our food, Mrs. Vogel had noticed what looked like a piece of rusted metal sticking out from under a rock near the side of the cavern. She'd called Mother's attention to it, and between them they'd pulled away some of the other rocks until they found what was left of an old shovel. As they dug away more of the rubble, they discovered other pieces of rusted equipment but, except for the remnant of a pickaxe, most of it was too far gone to recognize. Digging further, they'd found a large pile of gold on top of the tattered remains of a deer skin, and as they cleared away more of the rock and debris, they realized that the tools and gold ore were hidden in a large crevice between two of the huge granite boulders that formed the wall of the cavern.

Excitedly, they checked the other crevices on the walls of the cavern and found a lot more ore — some of it appeared to be pure gold. Buried beneath that was a dried, badly cracked leather container. When they attempted to see what was in it, pieces broke off and crumbled to powder in their hands, revealing the contents to be gold — even purer than what they'd already found. They were tempted to continue exploring the other crevices, but decided to wait until the rest of us had joined them so we could all share in the discovery together — and in the work, too, I suspect.

We were hungry and looking forward to eating when we returned, but when we saw what Mother and Mrs. Vogel had found, all thoughts of food vanished, and we enthusiastically began to clear the rubble from all the likely looking spots on either side of the cavern. Before long, we had uncovered three more large leather containers. Sam told us they were called "panniers" and that they were used to carry stuff by slinging one on either side of a pack animal and filling them with what, in this case, was pure gold nuggets. A lot more high-grade ore was piled all around and on top of the panniers, and Sam said he couldn't even begin to guess what it was all was worth, but it was an awful lot.

As far as I was concerned, the two most exciting things we found were the rusted remnants of an old Spanish helmet and a flintlock musket. Lying alongside them was a piece of black leather that was studded with pieces of rusted metal. Dad was pretty sure it was a piece of leather armor that was used to protect the wearer's chest and back from Indian arrows and spears. Unfortunately, the moment we tried to pick it up, it crumbled into pieces. The helmet was rusted through in places, and all that was left of the musket were the rusted metal parts, and there weren't many of them. Sam said they probably had belonged to Pedro 'cause Juan would have taken his with them.

After all that excitement, we were too wound up to eat much — but Rab made out just fine, 'cause he got to eat all the leftovers. After that Dad and Sam made the ladder, and we all climbed down it to the floor of the lower chamber. For a long time our folks and Sam didn't say a word — they were overwhelmed by the sight of so much gold. GOLD!!! It was everywhere — in the sand on the cavern floor and in the pool below the waterfall. When Dad and Sam examined the quartz outcropping on the face of the cliff, they were amazed when they saw the width of the veins of gold that covered it.

"I jest can't believe my eyes, Julius. I ain't seen nothin' like this in all my borned days. This here bonanza's gotta be worth millions. Hell, I'll bet that old Phillips Lode up on Buckskin Crick back in my Daddy's time warn't as rich as this. Julius, I reckon yore and Grace's money troubles are over for good — yores too, Vera." While we were waiting for Mother and Mrs. Vogel to climb back up the ladder, I noticed a rounded rock partly imbedded in the sand of the chamber floor. Curious, I asked Charley to help me dig it out. After it was uncovered, it looked sort of like a bowling ball, except that it was quite a bit bigger — it even had a round hole on one side.

"What kind of rock is this, Dad, and how come it's got a hole in it?" I asked.

"I don't know, Robby. It's not quartz, and I don't think it's granite. At least it sure doesn't look like it, and I can't imagine what might have made that hole. It almost looks like there are rust stains around it. What do you think it is Sam?"

"I don't know what kind of rock it is, Julius, but I'll bet you anythin' it's a 'muller.' I 'spect if we look around some, we's apt to find another one jest like it. Do you all recollect seein' that big flat rock in the upper chamber what has what looks like the hub of a wheel with a scooped out trough runnin' all around it?" We nodded that we did. "Wal, I reckon that's what's left of an "arrastra" Ramon's granddaddy and his granddaddy's brother made to grind up the ore. Why don't we climb back up the ladder so's we can dry out and I'll tell you how it worked. This cold spray is makin' my rheumatiz hurt somethin' awful."

After we were all back in the upper chamber and warm and dry, Sam continued. "First off, they'd have chipped that there trough around the edge of the flat rock so's to leave the middle part of it stickin' up like a hub. Then they'd of drilled a hole in the center of the hub and pinned the trunk of a tall pine to it, so's the same length was stickin' out on both sides. Next, they'd of found two "mullers" like the one in the lower cavern, drilled a hole in both of them, and attached one to each end of the tree trunk with a chain — most likely one from a trap. After that, they'd of set the mullers in the trough 'long with some ore, harnessed one of their horses to one end of the pole and led it 'round and 'round the arrastra, so's the mullers could crush up the ore. All the arrastras I's ever seen had a stream of water piped into the trough so's to flush away the crushed up rock, leavin' the heavier gold behind — but there's no way Juan and Pedro could have rigged that. So I reckon what they did instead, was to scoop the crushed-up ore out of the trough with a gold

An arrastra on display at the South Park City Museum in Fairplay.
(Photograph courtesy of Doctor Howard Kelsall — taken in 2004)

pan, and wash away the dirt and crushed rock, usin' water from the crick — leavin' the gold in the bottom of the pan."

It was only midafternoon when Sam finished tellin' us about arrastras, but for some reason, Dad said we should quit work for the day and go back to camp. He claimed it was so we could all get some rest, but then — like it was somethin' he'd just thought of — he added, "And I'm sure we'll be needing more fish for supper, so I guess, instead of resting, Sam and I will have to go fishin'."

Sam tried to look surprised. "Why, I reckon yore right, Julius. As a matter of fact, we'll need some for breakfast, too." I couldn't believe it. They actually would rather go fishing than get rich collecting gold. Obviously, I'd forgotten the peculiar priorities of fanatic fishermen.

That evening, after eating and warming up by the campfire, I crawled into my sleeping bag and slept like the rocks around me. At least, I did until Rab woke everybody up, barkin'. It must have been way after midnight, and Dad and Sam rushed out of their tents, both were holding a gun and flashlight — figurin', I suppose, that it might be a bear or cougar. But after looking all around camp and finding nothing alarming, they went back into their tents. As they went, I heard Sam grumbling something about that stupid dog and his damned porcupines — 'course, by that time, Rab was sound asleep.

The next morning, everything in camp appeared to be in good order except for one thing. Before goin' to bed that night, Dad had hung a side of bacon from the dead branch of a ponderosa pine, and the next morning it was gone. So it wasn't a porcupine after all — unless they eat bacon, which I doubt. Dad figured it was a bear and Rab agreed with him, 'cause that morning after we untied him, he ran all around camp, sniffin' the ground and actin' real excited. The hair on the back of his neck was standin' up straight, and he was growling, just like he did that other time a bear visited our camp.

After a quick breakfast, we all hurried back to the bonanza so we could start bringin' gold out of the cavern and loadin' it onto the truck. Dad and Sam had been talking it over, and they'd decided that, before doing anything in the lower chamber, we'd take all of the nuggets and gold ore that Juan and Pedro hid in the cave down to the Denver smelter. Dad figured it'd take at least four or five trips just to get it all hauled, 'cause if we overloaded Jerome Burnett's truck, he'd be real upset, and Dad didn't want to lose a good friend. Dad must not have cared if I lost my best friend, 'cause he told me to tie Rab to the rock in the cavern again. So I did, and once again he gave a dramatic, award-winning performance, starting the minute I tied the rope to his collar and ending the second that he saw it wasn't gonna work. Mother and Mrs. Vogel stayed in the cavern and helped us load our knapsacks. Then we hauled the gold over to the truck where Dad and Sam could load it. At least that's the way Dad had it figured, until my mother intervened and, over Dad's strenuous protests, made Sam promise to keep a close eye on him to be sure he didn't lift anything heavy. With all of us working, it went a lot faster than I had imagined it would. At least, it was faster than when we were haulin' gold for Jud — or maybe it just seemed faster, 'cause this time we were doin' it for ourselves and not for that mangy Rathbone. It was close to noon when we finished the loading, and Dad told us that we could go back to the cavern and eat the sandwiches Mother and Mrs. Vogel had fixed for us. After that, we'd all go back to the truck, pack up our campin' gear, break camp, and head home to Shadycroft. Boy, did that ever sound great.

After we'd finished eatin', Mother suggested that we all take a short rest before leaving the cavern and — inasmuch as what Mother suggests we usually do — we did. All except Abby, that is. She had to step outside of the cavern for a couple of minutes, most likely to answer a call of nature. While the grownups were resting quietly and chatting with one another, the rest of us kids sat with our legs dangling over the edge of the cliff. We were chucking rocks and chunks of gold ore down into the lower chamber, tryin' to see who could come closest to a little rock at the edge of the creek. Rab was snoozing peacefully in the corner of the upper chamber just to the left of the entrance to the cavern, having finally resigned himself to being tied to the rock. Everything was quiet and peaceful. But then suddenly, without any warning, an ominous, raspy voice shattered the tranquil peace of the chamber.

"Well, now, ain't this nice. All my favorite people right here in the same place at the same time."

Startled, we jumped to our feet and stared in the direction of the familiarly evil voice. There, standing in the shadows of the cavern entrance, we saw an indistinct form. It approached us slowly until, in the dim light of the chamber, we were stunned when we beheld a ghostly apparition. But this was no ghost or apparition — it was a demon come up from hell. A demon that was very much alive and holding a shotgun leveled directly at us with its right hand, while grasping Abby firmly around her neck with its left. It was Jud Rathbone come back from the dead!!! God help us all.

Sam started to move in his direction, but Jud stopped him in his tracks. "Damn you Reynolds. Stay right where you are. Don't none of you move so much as a finger. You do, and I'll break little missy here's neck." Then, with a sneer in his voice, he added, "I reckon you're surprised to see me alive and well, and I know you're all real disappointed that I didn't drown in the flood like my two men did. But, I didn't — no thanks to you. I was lucky. That damned flood threw me up on top of a rock a little ways downstream, and I managed to pull myself out of the water. Otherwise I'd be just as dead as you're all gonna be, just as soon as I get finished talkin'.

"You didn't think that I knew what you kids were up to, did you? All that stallin' around you and that damned traitor, Jack, were doin' when you were bringing my gold down from the cave." And with that, he gave Abby a sharp shake. "You thought you were pretty damned clever, didn't you? Hidin' all them ingots like you did. But that didn't fool me none. The minute I started loadin' them I could tell from the weight that a bunch of them was missing, so I figured you'd hid them in the cave — and I was right. After the flood, I went back to the cave, and you know what? Damned if I didn't find twelve ingots hid under the rocks. You figured you were smart, but I'm here to tell you that I'm a hell of a lot smarter. And I'm rich now, too, and, if it hadn't been for that damned flood, I'd be a whole lot richer.

"After I found Gus's dead body, I switched my wallet with his, so now everybody thinks I'm Gus Tobin, and that it's Judson Rathbone that's dead and gone to hell. So now, once I've had the pleasure of disposing of all of you, I'll be home free — free and rich. Damn, how I wish my daddy could see me now. He'd be mighty happy to know his son is finally gonna be rich — even richer than he'd have been if he'd gotten his fair share of the loot and gold in the cave. 'Course, my daddy was figurin' on taking Jim and John Reynolds' share, too — that's what he had in mind doin' all along. Oh, and by the way, I almost forgot to say thanks for the bacon. You know, I could have killed all of you last night whilst you were sleepin', but I didn't. I figured I'd wait and let you load the truck for me first."

"Now hold on a minute, Jud, you…" Sam started to say.

But Jud cut him off short and, waving his shotgun in his direction, shouted, "Damn you, Reynolds, shut up. Don't you say another word — I'm doing all the talkin'. Now all of you get over to the edge of that cliff behind you — and don't forget, I can get three or four shots off with this scatter gun before you can get anywhere close to me, so don't try anything funny." Then he shook his gun at us in a threatening way, and immediately, Rab — who had up to now been quiet — began to snarl and lunge viciously at Jud. With each forward charge, he gradually jerked and dragged the rock in Jud's direction.

Jud turned and exploded. "Damn, that's the same dog as before! I thought he was dead. Damn that Jack. When I find where him and his stupid brother are hiding, it'll be the end of both of them. They'll be mighty damn sorry they ever crossed Jud Rathbone." Then Rab lunged again in his direction, and Jud snarled, "Well, at least you're gonna be dead now, damn your mangy hide," and with that he raised the shotgun and aimed it at Rab.

"NO!" I screamed at the top of my voice. "Don't shoot him!" And I hurled the chunk of gold ore I'd been clutching in my hand in his direction. I threw it just as hard as I possibly could, and no one was more surprised than I was when it struck Jud full in the center of his forehead, and he dropped the gun and staggered backwards towards the entrance to the cavern. J. J. reacted instantly — he raced across the cavern and tackled Jud, knocking him to the ground. Dad, Sam, and Charley immediately joined in the attack, and Abby already had.

Jud didn't have a chance, especially after Mother picked up the shotgun and handed it to Dad. In a loud voice, Dad told all of us to back away from Jud, and for a minute there, I thought he was gonna shoot him right on the spot. He sure was angry enough to do it, but Mother put a restraining hand on his shoulder.

"Now, Julius, calm down. Sheriff Haynes can handle it from here on out. Let's just tie him up securely and take him back to Littleton in the back of the truck, so we can turn him over to the sheriff."

Tying him securely would be putting it mildly compared to the way Jud was trussed up by the time we got through. We used all fifty feet of the rope we'd brought with us. We left his legs free so he could walk back to the truck, but from the waist up, he couldn't move a thing. He could still blink, but that was about all. Sam said it was a waste of good rope — we should of hung him with it instead. But Mother told him not to worry. She was sure the law would do that for him.

Before we could haul Jud back to Littleton, we had to first take enough gold ore out of the bed of the truck so it wouldn't be overloaded. Dad figured that Jud weighed close to two hundred pounds, so that's how much gold we unloaded. Then Dad and Sam tied Jud's legs together so he couldn't stand up. Then they heaved him up on top of the gold and packed our camping equipment and tools all around him. After that, everybody breathed a big sigh of relief.

But we weren't in the clear yet. Just as we were about to get into the car and truck so we could leave, we saw a long, black car coming down the road towards our camp. We all watched apprehensively as the car stopped a little way down the road and four big men climbed out of it. They were all carrying rifles and had handguns strapped to their waists. They started to walk in our direction, and my heart suddenly stopped in mid-beat. I'm sure everybody else's was doin' the same thing.

"Damn, it's some of Jud's gang, come to help him out," Sam whispered. "Quick, Julius, get your gun." Dad hastily handed the .38 special revolver to Mother, and both he and Sam grabbed for their rifles. He gave Jud's shotgun to J. J.. After taking cover behind our cars, we were bracing for the fight we were sure was coming, when Dad suddenly exclaimed, "Wait a minute! That's Sheriff Haynes and three of his deputies. Man, what a relief that is!"

To be real honest, I was gettin' tired of bein' scared all the time. I don't know how Buck Duane manages to stay so cool and collected, 'cause scary stuff keeps happenin' to him all the time. As the sheriff and his deputies drew near and Dad started to greet them, the sheriff interrupted.

"Thank God you folks are all right, Julius. I was afraid you'd be in a whole lot of trouble. Right after you and Sam told me how Jack had stolen the gold ingots, I started callin' the refineries and dealers that buy and sell gold. I asked them to notify me immediately if anybody tried to sell it. Then, just this morning, I called a dealer that I missed talkin' to before, and he told me that a little over a week ago, some fella had sold him twelve gold ingots, just like the ones you described. But, according to the dealer, the identification he showed him wasn't Jack's or his brother's, it was Gus Tobin's. Then he described the man to me, and — as it turned out — he was a big, heavy-set, rough lookin' man, about sixty years old, with blackish-gray hair. Well, of course that didn't fit Gus' description at all, 'cause he was in his thirties and wasn't especially heavy-set — but it fit Jud's description to a T. So my deputies and I rushed up here as soon as we could, so we could warn you folks that Jud is still alive and no doubt is gunning for all of you — especially you, Sam. But the rest of you better keep your eyes peeled too."

Dad smiled and thanked Sheriff Haynes for the warning. Then told him to take a look in the back of our truck, and when the sheriff saw Jud, he broke out laughing.

"Well, I'll be damned. Here I went and told all that to you and all the time you had Jud trussed up like a pig goin' to the slaughterhouse. Why didn't you say something sooner, Julius?"

"Well, I don't rightly know, John," Dad confessed. "I guess maybe I was just so glad to see you fellas I forgot all about Jud. And besides, you didn't give me a chance to get a word in edgewise."

After Jud was loaded in the back seat of the sheriff's car with a burly deputy sitting on either side of him, they all waved good-bye (all but Jud, of course) and drove off on their way back to Littleton, so they could lock Jud up tight in the Arapahoe County jail. As soon as they were out of sight, we reloaded the ore we'd taken out to make room for Jud and, while the others were doing that, I put Rab's goggles on him and fastened him securely in his perch on the running board. Then I told him we were goin' back to Shadycroft, and I can't ever remember a time when he looked so happy. In fact, I was pretty sure I was back to bein' his best friend again.

It's hard to describe the wonderful feeling of relief we all felt as we drove down the lane to Shadycroft — so I won't even try. Mother started crying, and I asked her what was wrong. I figured she should be happy. But she smiled through her tears and said, "Nothing, Robert, not one thing. I'm just so grateful to God for answering our prayers and for bringing our family home safe and sound. And that from now on — The Good Lord willing — Shadycroft will always be our home." We all said "Amen" to that.

❧ PART FIVE ❧

EPILOGUE
SHADYCROFT FARM
NOVEMBER 2ND, 1934

(A pen and ink drawing by Doctor Seymour Wheelock)

CHAPTER 57

It's Friday afternoon. In two days, it'll be exactly two years to the day since that scary night I found Sam hiding in the attic. A lot has happened since then, but you already know about that. One thing's for sure, though, I learned a good lesson — nowadays I come home well before dark. As usual, Mother and Dad are at the Grange meeting in Littleton this evening, and this time J. J. didn't go with them like he did two years ago. He and Abby went to a movie at the Gothic Theater in Englewood instead. Accordin' to Al Thompson, it's a yucky love story with lots of kissin' and huggin' and lovey-dovey stuff in it. I just can't believe my brother would ever take a girl to a dumb movie like that.

Of course, the first thing Dad did when we got back to Shadycroft was to pay all our debts — the second was to buy a new truck. First off, he checked out the Chevys at Emmett Stephenson's agency on Main Street in Littleton, but he ended up buying a Ford truck from my friend Ivy Hunt's dad, 'cause it could hold more ore than the Chevy. And we've been minin' the bonanza a little at a time, and doin' it real carefully so we don't mess up the mountainside like a of lot mine operators do.

The drouth is still going on, and in some places it's even worse than it was back in 1932. But, at least this spring, there was enough snowpack on the South Platte watershed so, between the runoff from that and a few showers last spring and summer, Dad was able to raise a few crops — at least enough to keep Mr. Williamson busy. We had a good apple crop this year, too, and Mother put up a lot of them in mason jars, while Dad made cider out of the rest. He'd put some bottles in the cellar, hopin' they'd turn into applejack. But he put them too close to the furnace, so they got too hot and fermented too fast, and a bunch of them blew up. We've been drinkin' a lot of sweet cider ever since.

Mother keeps on taking good care of her family and going to ladies meetings like the P.E.O. and Eastern Star. 'Course she still rides close herd on her boys — but mainly me, 'cause now that J. J.'s gettin' older, she doesn't fuss at him near as much as she does me.

I'm happy to say that the Vogels are still living in their home at the head of the lane, and they have a brand-new well with water to spare. Not only that, Mrs. Vogel bought a new Ford touring car. Abby and Charley haven't changed much, except that Abby seems to be getting prettier every time I see her, and Charley keeps getting bigger and harder to boss around.

Sam stayed at Shadycroft until after Jud's trial last December. Then he went back to Alma to live with his mother and Miss Lydia. He's putting an addition on his mamma's house, and installing central heating and indoor plumbing, so he has plenty to keep him busy.

Jud, I'm relieved to say, is in the Colorado State Penitentiary down in Cañon City, awaiting execution for the murder of Cliff Alexander — and why they haven't done it yet is a mystery to all of us. Dad says Jud most likely has a real smart lawyer who keeps appealing his case all the time, but that he's sure Jud will eventually get what's coming to him. I sure hope so, 'cause — even though I know he's locked up tight behind steel bars — it worries me that he's still among the living. But mostly I'll still worry even after he's dead, 'cause twice before everybody's figured that Jud was dead and gone for good, and both times he turned up alive and even meaner than before. I sure wish I didn't have such a good imagination.

Rab and I are still best friends — at least I know he's mine. The times when he isn't taggin' along with me, he's usually off hunting — preferably skunks — although for the life of me, I don't know why. You'd think the smell would bother him, but it doesn't seem to. It sure bothers the rest of us, though — especially my mother.

My life hasn't changed that much. I still do chores and go to school, and I actually enjoy it, 'cause Miss Ford is my teacher, and she's real pretty. But my main job still is clearin' the rustlers and outlaws off of our dryland — with Rab's and Buck's help, and Molly's, too, of course, when she's of a mind to. When we first came back to Shadycroft after findin' the gold, Molly was actually glad to see me — or she was 'til she found out I wanted to ride her. But at least she pays me a little more attention now, 'cause I've got two brand-new mail-order spurs. And besides that, I have a black hat and black cowboy boots, and Mother even made me some pants and a shirt out of black cloth. So now, when I get all togged out in my cowboy outfit, you can hardly tell which one of us is Buck Duane and which one is me. There's one thing that still bothers me, though. Buck's horse, Wrangle, is pure black, and Molly's a buckskin. Just lately, though, I've been givin' serious consideration to painting her black.

The Sheldon Jackson Memorial Chapel at Fairplay. Dedicated by Jackson in 1894.
(Courtesy of the Denver Public Library Western History Collection.)

Well, I guess that about does it. That's about all that's been happening since we found the bonanza — except for one other thing. Just yesterday we received a letter from Sadie, and enclosed with it was an invitation to attend the wedding of Miss Lydia Louise Smith and James Samuel Reynolds, to be held at the Sheldon Jackson Memorial Church in Fairplay on the second day of February 1935. Our family and the Vogels are invited to attend. Sam asked Dad to be his best man, and he accepted with pleasure, saying how he'd known all along that Sam wasn't crazy, and now his marrying Miss Lydia proved it. But now he wasn't so sure about Miss Lydia.

❧ PART SIX ❧

FACT OR FICTION?

(A pen and ink drawing by Doctor Seymour Wheelock)

As you may recall, I mentioned in the preface that this story is a compilation of both fact and fiction, stitched together by a thread of gold. I believe that the reference to the bonanza as the golden thread is obvious, but perhaps in other parts of the story it may not be quite so easy to distinguish the facts from fiction. So the following comments are included to help you in this regard.

The events described in Littleton and at Shadycroft Farm during the 1920s and early 1930s are, for the most part, true. Certainly the drouth, the depression, Dad's indebtedness, and the difficult times on the farm are factual, as is the presence of bootleggers in and around Littleton. Colonel Judson Pettigrew actually had a counterpart who operated a still on Dry Creek and was arrested and sent to prison. I have no knowledge of what became of him after he finished serving his jail term.

Unfortunately, my parent's indebtedness was not resolved in quite such a satisfactory manner as the one described in my story. We didn't lose the farm because of the debt, I'm happy to say, but how that came about is yet another story, and one not nearly as interesting and gratifying as my fictional account. It was an unhappy day for my whole family in 1948 when Shadycroft Farm was sold to Mr. Hugh Graham, the owner of Graham's Ranch. Another unhappy day came in the 1960s when our old farmhouse was torn down to make room for a modern, more elegant home. In 1998, the final vestige of our farm buildings disappeared when the old red barn was demolished.

All of the fertile, irrigated fields and dryland where I loved to roam as a boy while riding Molly in the company of Rab and Buck are now entirely covered by residential developments, as is much of the Diamond K Ranch, now known as the Highlands Ranch development. While the homes are very attractive, to my way of thinking there are none as beautiful as the home of my childhood. Sometimes I get to wondering if perhaps on drowsy summer afternoons, the current owners of homes on our old dryland ever wonder at the sound of galloping hoofbeats drumming across the sun-baked earth as Robby and Buck ride in pursuit of long-vanished cattle rustlers and desperados. It wouldn't surprise me a bit if they did.

Fortunately, when the farm was sold, my dad and mother kept fifteen acres along its north margin, where they built a small house and spent the remaining years of their lives. At the time of this writing, Tee and I, our oldest son Randy, his wife Carol, and their son Reed, as well as our daughter Pam, her husband Lester (Trey) Hay, and their children Elisabeth, Justin, and Andrew all have homes on the seven remaining acres of the original Shadycroft Farm. My youngest son Brad, his wife Patti, and their son, Peter, live in nearby Broomfield. As you may suspect, although it is considerably diminished in size, I still call our seven acres "Shadycroft Farm."

I stretched the truth somewhat in describing my mother, for she was a much more loving and warm person than I have portrayed her in my story. Dad, however, was much as I described him, as were my two faithful companions, Rab and Molly — although the term "faithful" is not entirely accurate when applied to Molly. Although he disagrees, I believe my brother, J. J., was much as I describe him in my story. As he recalls it, he wasn't nearly that nice to me as we were growing up. But as I pointed out to him, while I may have exaggerated somewhat when I suggested that he was sweet on Abby, I feel that the rest of my remembrances are fairly accurate, although somewhat enhanced by a rampant imagination. Of course, I may have erased some unsavory events from my memory.

My parents, of course, as well as my beloved friends Rab and Molly, have long since departed to a far better place, where the crops are always abundant, the flowers more profuse, the grass grows tall and sweet, the skunks don't smell, and the jackrabbits are easy to catch. Oh, yes — and the fishing is always good. I'm sure that my memories of all those dear people and creatures of the past will never fade — nor will J. J.'s, I suspect. I'm happy to say that Julius and his lovely wife, Sally, have moved back to Colorado from Midland, Michigan, and now have a beautiful home in nearby Roxborough Park.

❀

Most of the geographic references in my story are fairly accurate — at least they are to the extent of my knowledge and descriptive writing ability. However, while the terrain around Lost Park and Lost Creek is very wild and rugged as I described it, I did take the liberty of exaggerating it somewhat to better fit my story. In the 1970s, the federal government designated much of the Lost Park and Lost Creek (alias Goose Creek) region as the Lost Park Wilderness Area. However, all the references to a gold mine in the Tarryalls are entirely the product of my rampant imagination. As far as I know, no significant gold strike has ever been made on or near Lost Creek — not in 1779, 1859, in the 1930s, or at any other time.

❀

Graham's Ranch, now a popular guest ranch owned and operated by Bob Foster and his family, is known as "Lost Valley Ranch." In June of 2002, the Lost Creek Wilderness Area and the forests surrounding the ranch were ravaged by fire. But fortunately, except for the loss of a large herd of cattle and portions of the forests around them, Lost Valley Ranch survived with surprisingly little damage.

❀

Much of the account of Governor Juan Bautista de Anza's campaign against the Comanche war chief, Querno Verde, that is described in the prologue is taken from Colonel de Anza's diary. The references to the scouts, Juan and Pedro Vasquez, and the old trapper, Silas Smith, are, however, fictional. The part of the prologue describing the beliefs and customs of the early Ute Indians is as accurate as I could make it from my research, but the people and events are all fictional. Although a Ute war chief actually did accompany Governor de Anza on the campaign, I was unable to discover his true name, so I arbitrarily named him Moara — the name of one of the Ute chieftains that negotiated a treaty with Anza several years after the campaign. Another chief involved in the treaty signing was Pinto, and I bestowed his name on Chief Moara's son. I doubt that they really were related, however. The "Tsashin" in my story is named after the sister of Chief Ouray, the great chief of the Southern Utes who lived about a hundred years later. She was also called "Susan" and was the first wife of Chief Medicine Johnson (no relation to Robby or J. J. as far as I know).

Incidentally, many of the things that I describe in the parts of my story that pertain to South Park, Alma, Fairplay, placer mining, prospecting for gold, the Ute Indians, and the Denver, South Park and Pacific narrow-gauge railroad are nicely displayed at a historical museum called "South Park City" in Fairplay. It is the re-created main street of a mining town of the mid-to-late-1800s, and in my opinion it is remarkably authentic and well done. It enables the visitor to step back almost a century and a half into the lives of the miners, storekeepers, doctors, dentists, bankers, gamblers, and ordinary people that were living there at that historic time. The exhibits are realistically displayed in vintage buildings that have been moved to Fairplay from some of the other old towns around South Park. Among the many displays are a dentist's office, a doctor's office, a general store, a gambling hall, an assayer's office, a school, a newspaper office, a bank, and a narrow-gauge railroad station. The bank building is the same one that is depicted in my story as the site of the fictional bank robbery in Alma, in which John Reynolds was killed. Appropriately placed in the above buildings are collections of mining equipment, clothing, food, and medicines, along with many other household and office items that illustrate the way people lived in South Park during the mid-to-late-1800s.

Some of the main characters in my story are factual, but what they said and did may not be. A few of these are Doctor Harry Sims, Sheriff John Haynes, Jerome and Cleota Burnett, and the Williamson family. The Vogel family lived at the head of the lane at that time and were all much as I described them, but, for personal reasons, I gave them different first names. And, believe it or not, Crazy Sam really did have a counterpart in and around Littleton in the 1930s and 1940s. He drove a buggy, dressed as I described, and spit tobacco with amazing accuracy — but, unfortunately, the resemblance ends there. At least to my knowledge, the real Crazy Sam did not have such an interesting life as did the Sam in my story.

James Samuel Reynolds (Jimmy), alias Samuel Hardin, alias Crazy Sam Baker, and all of the events in which he was purported to be involved are entirely products of my imagination. However, the parts of the story concerning Jim and John Reynolds, their presence in South Park in 1859, and their arrests in Denver as southern sympathizers in 1861 are based on factual accounts, as is the description of their raid into South Park that culminated in the death of Jim Reynolds. There are various versions of that raid, and it is somewhat difficult to know which one is correct. For instance, the value of the money and gold stolen in the stagecoach holdup varies greatly from one account to another — from $3,000 to $30,000. The number of the raiders varies as well, from eight to twenty-two. In both instances, I chose the greater of the two numbers to enhance the significance of the raid in my story, although I suspect the lesser figures are likely to be more accurate.

Mr. A. B. Miller actually was a resident of Denver in 1861 and was arrested along with Charley Harrison at the same time that the Reynolds brothers were put in jail and for the same reason — all that is factual. But whether or not the Reynolds brothers assisted him in recruiting volunteers for the Southern forces is entirely conjecture on my part, as were their trips to Mace's Hole, their lives in Texas, and their later involvement in the battles of Valverde and Glorieta Pass in New Mexico. Although there is no documented proof that Colonel Heffiner was a bona-fide officer in the Confederate army, his efforts to recruit a Southern force in Mace's Hole in southern Colorado are factual. Incidentally, Mace's Hole is now called "Beulah," a pleasant residential community nestled behind the hogbacks about twenty miles southwest of Pueblo.

The description of Denver in 1861 is, for the most part, accurate. Certainly the Criterion saloon existed, as well as its notorious owner, Charley Harrison. Sunny Sadie, Red Stocking, and the Colonel's Daughter were all ladies' of pleasure in Denver at that time, but whether or not they worked at the Criterion is open to debate.

Major John Chivington, Governor Gilpin in Denver, and Zan and Estafana Hicklin, along with Colonel Heffiner in Mace's Hole, Captain Ellis Conner and Major John Buckmaster in the Greenhorn Valley, and Jacob Stansell and Horace and Augusta Tabor in Buckskin Joe in 1864, were all real people, but most of the conversations and comments attributed to them are solely the product of my imagination. All of the names and events mentioned in regard to the battles of Valverde and Glorieta Pass and the Confederate invasion of New Mexico are factual, however, some of my descriptions of the military maneuvers during the battles are also products of my imagination as are the parts played by the Reynolds brothers and Billy Joe Barlow.

With their consent, I have used the names of some of my friends for many of the fictional characters in my story. These include the late Doctor Dick Hawes and his wife Elsie; Reverend Howard and Sondra Childers; Doctor Seymour and Janet Wheelock; Doctor Homer and Mary Cowen; Doctor Al Miller; and Doctor Bill Ziegler. Other good friends whose names I used are the late Cy Killgore and his wife, Mary; the late John D. Cranor; and my Littleton cronies Ivy Hunt, Joe Wilkinson, Al Thompson, and Charley Ammons.

The two bad guys in my story — Rafer Rathbone and his son, Jud — are, I'm happy to say, fictional. I derived the name Rathbone from the movie actor Basil Rathbone, and Rafer is a name from my imagination. The name Jud, however, comes from two sources — the bad guy in the musical, *Oklahoma,* and from Jud Coon, a good friend and classmate of mine at Denver's South High School in the 1930s. At that time he was known as "Minor," but later, after becoming a renowned biochemist and head of the chemistry department at the University of Michigan in Ann Arbor, he changed his name to Jud.

※

And finally, the remarkable reasons behind the Confederate campaign up the Rio Grande River are purported to be true, and I can see no reason to doubt that the leaders of the Confederacy aspired to them and, but for the lack of adequate resources, might actually have achieved them. Had General Sibley accomplished what he set out to do, it almost certainly would have effected a remarkable change in the course of the

Civil War in America. Consider what might have happened if the South had succeeded in acquiring the gold fields of Colorado, Utah, and Nevada and had subsequently captured California and Oregon, thereby placing all of the western United States and the Pacific ports under their control. Then the struggling Confederacy would have had the means to buy the vital military supplies that they so desperately needed from Britain and other European nations — thereby bypassing the Yankee blockade of the Atlantic and Gulf seaports.

This in itself would have increased the size and strength of the Confederacy enormously, and especially so if the grandiose plans of acquiring the upper two provinces of Mexico had actually come about. If the latter had been achieved, the whole of Mexico, Central America, and even Cuba might have eventually been acquired as well. So, perhaps one can understand why the plan seemed so appealing to the Confederate president, Jefferson Davis, and to General Sibley. Had it not been for the lack of resources, the unforgiving New Mexican desert, and the devilish Pikes Peakers, America might now be two countries — the Confederate States of America, and its northern neighbor, the United States of America. Indeed, at the end of Margaret Mitchell's great novel, *Gone With the Wind*, the wind might have been blowing from the opposite direction.

R. Reed Johnson
July 2, 2005

GLOSSARY
(for Map on page 5)

Sierra — Jagged Mountain
Valle Paraiso — Paradise Valley
Querno Verde — Green Horn
El Aguage de los Utas — water of the Utes
Rio de Nepestle — Arkansas River
Rio del Norte — Rio Grande River
Sierra de Almagre — The Tarryall Mountains (mountains the color of red ocher.)
Rio del Sacramento — Fountain Creek
Las Lomas Perdidas — The Mountains of the Damned
Huajatolla — The Breasts of the World (The Spanish Peaks)
The Shining Mountains — The Rocky Mountains
League — approximately 3 statute miles
Genizaros — Indian-Spanish families living in Santa Fe in 1779. ("Half Breeds")
Gracias — thank you
Buenos Dias — good day
Vara — about thirty inches
Rio de los Conejos — River of the Rabbits
Orleans Nouvelle — New Orleans
Los Ojos Ciegos — the blind eyes
Lechusa Doble — twin owls
Valle Salado — Bayou Salado — South Park
Salado — salt

A Comanche Warrior
(A pen and ink drawing by
Doctor Seymour Wheelock)

SUGGESTED READING ABOUT THE PEOPLE AND EVENTS IN *A THREAD OF GOLD*

Part 1: Chapters 1-7, describe Governor Juan Bautista de Anza's campaign against the Comanche War Chief, Querno Verde. Also described are the customs and beliefs of members of the Ute Nation in 1779.

Dominguez, Fray Francisco Atanasio. *The Missions of New Mexico.* Translated and annotated by Eleanor B. Adams and Fray Angelico Chavez. Albuquerque: University of New Mexico Press, 1776.

Harrington, H.D. *Edible Native Plants of the Rocky Mountains.* Albuquerque: University of New Mexico Press, 1967.

Marsh, Charles S. *People of the Shining Mountains.* Boulder, CO: Pruett Publishing Co., 1982.

Moore, Michael. *Medicinal Plants of the Mountain West.* Santa Fe: Museum of New Mexico Press, 1979 edition.

Pettit, Jan. *Utes: The Mountain People.* Boulder, CO: Johnson Books, 1990.

Shikes, Robert H., M.D. *Rocky Mountain Medicine.* Boulder, CO: Johnson Books, 1986. Source of the legend of Pagosa Springs. Other sources include J. Lynch, "Pagosa Pagosa, Healing Water: A Legend from Grateful Utes." *Pioneers of the San Juans* 4 (1961): 452; Gavin, Ora, "Legend of Pagosa Springs." *Pioneers of the San Juans* 4(1961): White, L. C., "Pagosa Springs Co." Colorado Magazine 9 (1932): 88.

Smith, P. David. *Ouray: Chief of the Utes.* Ridgway, CO: Wayfinder Press, 1986.

Sully, Virginia. *A Treasury of American Indian Herbs.* New York: Crown Publisher, 1970.

Thomas, Alfred Barnaby. *Forgotten Frontiers: A Study of the Spanish Indian Policy of Don Juan Bautista de Anza, Governor, New Mexico Province: 1777 – 1779.* Norman: University of Oklahoma Press, 1932. Includes Don Juan Bautista de Anza's diary of the expedition against the Comanche nation.

Vogel, Virgil J. *American Indian Medicine.* Norman: University of Oklahoma Press, 1970.

Wood, Nancy. *When Buffalo Free the Mountains: A Ute Indian Journey.* Garden City, NY: Doubleday, 1980. Source of Ute creation story as related to Jean Allard Jeanion Ignacio in 1904 by Chief Buckskin Charley and Chief Nanice.

Part Three: Chapters 20-40, describe South Park and Denver in the 1860s, as well as the Reynolds brothers' raid, gold mining activity in South Park, early day Denver, and the Civil War activity in Colorado at that time. South Park in the 1880s is also described, particularly the parts around Alma and Fairplay.

Athearn, Robert. *The Coloradans.* Albuquerque: University of New Mexico Press, 1976.

Chamblin, Thomas S., ed. *Historical Encyclopedia of Colorado.* Vol. 1. [Denver]: Colorado Historical Association, 1960.

Conner, Daniel Ellis. *A Confederate in the Colorado Gold Fields.* Edited by Donald Barthrong and Odessa Davenport. Norman: University of Oklahoma Press, 1956.

Englert, Kenneth. *The Reynolds Brothers' Raid,* Denver Westerners Brand Book of 1956. Published by Johnson Books, Boulder, CO. The article entitled *Colorado Gold and the Confederacy,* pages 151-173, describes the Confederate raid into South Park that was led by Jim Reynolds in 1864. The Colorado map at the beginning of Part Three of John Reynolds' Journal is a modified version of a 1910 map that was prepared especially for the Denver Westerners Brand Book of 1956 by E. J. Haley. With the Denver Westerners permission, I have modified the map further so that it might better illustrate my story. (Note: The 1956 Brand Book is but one of a number of the Denver Westerners' Brand Books published over the years. They all contain fascinating articles and stories about Colorado history.)

Foote, Shelby. *Civil War: A Narrative.* Vol. 1, *Fort Sumter to Perryville.* New York: Random House, 1958.

Hafen, Le Roy R., ed. *Colorado and Its People.* New York: Lewis Historical Pub. Co., [1948].

Hall, Frank. *History of the State of Colorado.* Chicago: Blakely Printing Co., 1889.

Heynan, Max L., Jr. *Prudent Soldier: A Biography of Major General E. R. S. Canby, 1817 – 1873.* Glendale, CA: Arthur H. Clark Co., 1959.

Jessen, Kenneth. *Colorado Gunsmoke.* Boulder, CO: Pruett Publishing, 1986.

Keleher, William A. *Turmoil in New Mexico.* Albuquerque: University of New Mexico Press, 1952.

Perkins, Robert L. *The First Hundred Years.* Garden City, NY: Doubleday, 1959.

Simmons, Virginia McConnell. *Bayou Salado: The Story of South Park.* Rev. ed. Denver: Sage Books, 2002 edition. (The source of much of the information and many of the anecdotes about the Reynolds brothers, Buckskin Joe, Alma, Fairplay, Hamilton, and South Park.)

Smith, Duane. *The Birth of Colorado: A Civil War Perspective*. Norman: University of Oklahoma Press, 1989.

Stone, Wilbur Fiske. *History of Colorado*. Chicago: S. J. Clark Publishing Co., 1918.

Taylor, Ralph J. C. *Colorado, South of the Border*. Denver: Sage Books, 1963.

Ubbelohde, Carl; Maxine Benson; and Duane A. Smith. *A Colorado History*. Boulder, CO: Pruett Publishing, 1988.

Whitford, William C., *The Battle of Glorietta Pass; Colorado Volunteers in the Civil War; The New Mexico Campaign in 1862*. Glorietta, NM: Rio Grande Press, 1991.

Littleton, Colorado:

Hicks, Dave. *Littleton from the Beginning*. Denver: Egan Printing, 1975.

McQuarie, Robert J., and C. W. Buckholtz. *Littleton, Settlement to Centennial*. Littleton, CO: Littleton Historical Museum and Friends of the Littleton Library and Museum, 1990.

ABOUT THE AUTHOR

Dr. R. Reed Johnson is a third generation Coloradoan, born on December 25th, 1921, on Shadycroft Farm in Littleton, a small community south of Denver. He received his first twelve years of schooling in Littleton and Denver schools and his college education at the University of Colorado in Boulder. After earning his medical degree in July 1945 from the University of Colorado School of Medicine in Denver, he completed his internship at the United States Naval Hospital at Balboa Park in San Diego in July of 1946, and then spent the following two years on active overseas duty in the navy. Following his discharge, Dr. Johnson completed two years of residency training at Children's Hospital in Denver, and then worked for the next forty years practicing pediatrics in southeast Denver.

The author and his beloved 1954 Willy's Jeep. Together they have explored much of the Colorado High Country.
(Photograph taken by Keith Clerihue.)

In 1956, after his mother's premature death, Reed, his wife, Tee, and their three children moved back to Littleton in order to be near Reed's father, Julius Johnson Sr., who was living on a fifteen acre remnant of the old Shadycroft Farm. There, they raised their three children to maturity — primarily Tee's doing, however, for Dr. Johnson was kept busy with his practice until he retired in 1989. From that time on he has been happily engaged in landscaping and maintaining their five-acre farm, and, for the last eleven or twelve years, researching and writing *A Thread of Gold*.

ABOUT THE ILLUSTRATOR

Doctor Seymour Wheelock grew up, as did his friend Doctor Johnson, in Colorado before the state, with a Spanish name, became more than simply a healthy, pleasant place — "Out West" — to visit and perhaps to live. He passed through the doors of Denver's Children's Hospital at age five to have a tonsillectomy and sixty years later went out those doors, retiring as Director of the hospital's Ambulatory Pediatric Services and Clinical Professor Emeritus at the University of Colorado Health Sciences Center. Half of those active intervening years were spent in the private practice of pediatrics and the other half as a member of the hospital's full time staff.

"I always loved to draw and to paint in water colors for pleasure and for relaxation," Wheelock recalls. "It was also a fine way to entertain patients as well as our two children when they were small. Consequently, it was a pleasant preoccupation to capture visually the vigorous spirit of Doctor Johnson's wide ranging narrative of adventure in other times and in other places."

If you enjoyed *A Thread of Gold*, you may like reading these other titles from Western Reflections Publishing Co.:

Colorado Mining Stories: Hazards, Heroics, and Humor

Corpse on Boomerang Road: Telluride's War on Labor, 1899-1908

Early Days on the Western Slope of Colorado

Father Struck It Rich: Story of the Tom Walsh Family

Mountains of Silver: Life in Colorado's Red Mountain Mining District

Salone Italiano: The True Story of an Italian Immigrant Family's Struggles in Southwestern Colorado

San Juan Gold: A Mining Engineer's Adventures 1879-1891

Silver & Sawdust: Life in the San Juans

Silver Camp Called Creede: A Century of Mining

Wilderness Wanderers: The 1776 Expedition of Dominguez & Escalante

To find out more about these titles and others, visit our web site at www.westernreflectionspub.com or call for a free catalog at 1-800-993-4490.